THREE COMPLETE NOVELS

ROSAMUNDE
PILCHER

THREE COMPLETE NOVELS

ROSAMUNDE PILCHER

THE EMPTY HOUSE

~∞~

THE DAY OF THE STORM

~∞~

UNDER GEMINI

WINGS BOOKS®
NEW YORK

This 1999 edition is published by Wings Books®, an imprint of Random House Value Publishing, Inc., 201 East 50th Street, New York, NY 10022, by arrangement with St. Martin's Press, Inc.

Wings Books® and design are registered trademarks of Random House Value Publishing, Inc.

Random House
New York • Toronto • London • Sydney • Auckland
http://www.randomhouse.com/

Printed and bound in the United States of America

Library of Congress Cataloging–in–Publication Data
Pilcher, Rosamunde.
    [Novels. Selections]
    Three complete novels / Rosamunde Pilcher.
       p.   cm.
    Contents: The empty house — The day of the storm — Under Gemini.
    ISBN 0-517-20583-1
    1. Love stories, American.   I. Pilcher, Rosamunde. Empty house.
II. Pilcher, Rosamunde. Day of the storm.   III. Pilcher, Rosamunde.
Under Gemini.   IV. Title.   V. Title: Empty house.   VI. Title: Day of
the storm.   VII. Title: Under Gemini.
PR6066.I38A6   1999
823'.914—dc21   99-18818
                                           CIP

8 7 6 5 4 3 2 1

CONTENTS

THE EMPTY HOUSE

Chapter 1

IT WAS THREE O'CLOCK on a Monday afternoon in July, sunny and warm, the hay-scented air cooled by a sea breeze which blew in from the north. From the top of the hill, where the road wound up and over the shoulder of Carn Edvor, the land sloped down to distant cliffs; farmland, ribboned with yellow gorse, broken by outcrops of granite, and patchworked into dozens of small fields. Like a quilt, thought Virginia, and saw the pasture fields as scraps of green velvet, the greenish gold of new-cut hay as shining satin, the pinkish gold of standing corn as something soft and furry, to be stroked and touched.

It was very quiet. But when she closed her eyes the sounds of the summer afternoon obtruded, singling themselves out, one by one, for her attention. The humming of the wind, soft in her ears, stirred the bracken. A car climbed the long hill from Porthkerris, changed gear, came on up the road. From farther away came that pleasant summer-sound, the bee-murmur of combine harvesters. She opened her eyes and counted three, all minimized by distance to toy-size, scarlet and tiny as the models that Nicholas pushed around his nursery carpet.

The approaching car appeared over the crest of the hill, driven very slowly, its occupants, including the driver, staring from open windows at the marvellous view. Their faces were red with sunburn, spectacles glinted, arms bulged in sleeveless blouses, the car seemed packed with humanity. As it passed the lay-by where Virginia had left her own car, one of the women in the back looked up and saw her watching them from the hillside. For a startling second their eyes met, and then the car had gone, around the next corner and away to Land's End.

Virginia looked at her watch. A quarter past three. She sighed and stood up, dusted grass and bracken fronds from the seat of her white jeans, walked back down the hill to her car. The leather seat was griddle-hot with sunshine. She turned the car and started back towards Porthkerris, her mind filled with random images. Of Nicholas and Cara, incarcerated in the alien London nursery, taken to Kensington Gardens each day by Nanny; to the Zoo and the Costume Museum and suitable films by their grandmother. It would be hot in London, stuffy and airless. She wondered if they had cut Nicholas's hair. She wondered if she should buy him a model combine harvester and send it to him with some suitable, informative, maternal letter.

Today I saw three of these working in the fields at Lanyon, and I thought of you and thought you would like a model so that you could see how it worked.

A letter for Lady Keile to read approvingly aloud because Nicholas, every inch a male, saw no reason in puzzling out his mother's writing if his grandmother was ready and willing to read it aloud to him. She thought of the other letter, the one from her heart.

My darling child, without you and Cara I am without reason, aimless. I drive around in the car because I can think of nothing else to do, and the car takes me to places that I used to know, and I watch and wonder who it is who drives the monster combine, turning out the hay bales, square and strong as neatly tied parcels.

The old farmhouses with their great barns and outbuildings were strung along the five miles of coast like uncut stones on a rugged necklace, so that there was no telling where the fields of Penfolda finished and those of the next farm started. And so distant were the combines that it was impossible to guess at the identity of the men who drove them, or the tiny figures who walked behind, forking the bales into rough stooks to stand and dry in the midsummer sun.

She was not even sure that he still lived here, that he still farmed Penfolda, and yet could not imagine him existing anywhere else in the world. She let her mind's eye, like the lens of some great camera, zoom down on to the busy scene. The figures sprang into focus, huge and clear, and he was there, high at the wheel of the combine harvester, shirt sleeves rolled back from brown forearms, his hair tousled by the

2

wind. And because there was danger in moving in so close, Virginia swiftly presented him with a wife, pictured her walking across the fields with a basket, flasks of tea, and perhaps a fruit cake to eat, and she wore a pink cotton dress and a blue apron and her long bare legs were brown.

Mrs. Eustace Philips. Mr. and Mrs. Eustace Philips of Penfolda.

The car nosed over the crest of the hill, and the bay and the white beaches and the distant headlands spread out before her, and far below, spilling down to around the blue goblet of the harbour, were the clustered houses and the Norman church tower of Porthkerris.

Wheal House, where the Lingards lived, and with whom Virginia was staying, lay on the far side of Porthkerris. If she had been a stranger, new to the district and visiting it for the first time, she would have followed the main road which led right down into the town and out the other side, and consequently become hopelessly ensnared in crawling traffic and hordes of aimless sightseers who spilled off the narrow pavements, or stood about at strategic corners, sucking ice-creams, choosing postcards and gazing in shop windows filled with brass piskies and pottery mermaids and other horrors considered suitable as souvenirs.

But, because she was not a stranger, Virginia turned off the road long before the houses started and took the narrow, high-hedged lane that wound up and over the hill which stood at the back of the town. It was the long way home, by no means a short cut, but eventually emerged out on the main road again, through a tunnel of wild rhododendrons and not fifty yards from the main entrance to Wheal House.

There was a white-barred gate and a rough drive that ran up between hedges of pink-flowered escallonia. The house was neo-Georgian, pleasingly proportioned, with a pedimented porch over the front door. The drive swept up between shaven green lawns and flower-beds heavy with the scent of wallflowers, and as Virginia parked the car in the shade of the house, there was a sharp cacophony of barking, and Dora, Alice Lingard's old spaniel, emerged from the open front door where she had been lying, for coolness, on the polished floor of the hall.

Virginia stopped to pat her and speak to her and then went indoors, taking off her sunglasses because after the bright day outside, the house seemed pitch dark.

Across the hall the garden doors stood open to the patio, which, facing south and trapping all the sun, was a favourite spot of Alice's in all but really wintry weather. Today, because of the heat, she had unrolled the split cane awnings, and the bright canvas chairs and the low tables, already set out with tea things, were narrowly striped by the shadow patterns which they cast.

On the table in the middle of the hall lay the afternoon's mail. Two letters for Virginia, both with London postmarks. She laid down her handbag and her glasses and picked them up. One from Lady Keile and one from . . . Cara. The italic letters, which she learned at school, were painfully formed, dearly familiar.

Mrs. A. Keile,
   c/o Mrs. Lingard,
     Wheal House,
      Porthkerris,
       Cornwall.

No mistakes, no mis-spellings. Virginia wondered if she had managed by herself or whether Nanny had had to help. With the letters in her hand she went on across the hall and out to where her hostess sat, reclining gracefully on a long chair, with some sewing in her lap. She was making a cushion cover, stitching silk cord around the edge of the coral velvet square, and the colour lay in her lap like some huge fallen rose petal.

She looked up. "There you are! I was wondering what had happened to you. I thought perhaps you'd got stuck in a traffic jam."

Alice Lingard was a tall, dark woman in her late thirties, her firmly-built figure belied by long and slender arms and legs. She was what Virginia always thought of as a middle-aged friend, not middle-aged in the strictest sense of the word, but belonging to that generation which lay half-way between Virginia and Virginia's mother. She was, in fact, a lifelong family friend, and years ago had been a small bridesmaid at Virginia's mother's wedding.

She herself had married, eighteen years or so ago, Tom Lingard, then a young man on the verge of taking over the small family business of Lingard Sons which specialized in the manufacture of heavy engineering machinery in the nearby town of Fourbourne. Under Tom's chairmanship the firm had expanded and prospered, and after a series of successful take-over bids now controlled interests which spread from

Bristol to St. Just, and included mining rights, a small shipping business and the sale of agricultural machinery.

They had never had children, but Alice had diverted her natural domestic talents to her house and garden, and over the years had transformed what had once been a fairly unimaginative establishment into an enchanting house and a garden which was constantly being photographed and written about by the Garden Editors of the glossier magazines. Ten years ago, when Virginia and her mother had come to Cornwall to spend Easter with the Lingards, the work had only just started. This time, having not visited Wheal House during the intervening years, Virginia had scarcely recognized the place. Everything had been subtly altered, straight lines curved, outlines and boundaries magically removed. Trees had grown up, casting long shadows on smooth lawns which seemed to spread as far as the eye could see. The old orchard had been transformed to a wild garden tangled with all the sweetest of old-fashioned roses, and where once had drilled rows of runner beans and raspberry canes, now stood magnolias, creamy petalled, and heady-scented azaleas taller than a man could reach.

But, domestically, the patio was Alice's most successful project, neither house nor garden, but with the combined charm of both. Geraniums spilled from terrace pots, and up a trellised wall she had started to train a dark purple-flowered clematis. She had lately decided that she would also grow a vine, and was currently picking the brains of both friends and reference books, to decide on the best way to set about doing this. Her energies appeared to be endless.

Virginia pulled up a chair and dropped into it, surprised to find how hot and tired she felt. She shucked off her sandals and propped up her bare feet on to a handy stool. "I didn't go to Porthkerris."

"You didn't? But I thought you'd gone to the post office."

"I only wanted some stamps. I can buy them another time. There were so many people and so many buses and so much crushed and sweating humanity that I got claustrophobia and never stopped. Just went on driving."

"I can lend you stamps," said Alice. "Let me pour you some tea." She laid down her sewing and sat up to reach for the teapot. Steam rose from the delicate cup, fragrant, refreshing.

"Milk or lemon?"

"Lemon would be delicious."

"So much more refreshing, I think, on a hot day." She handed Virginia the cup and lay back again. "Where did you drive?"

"Um? . . . oh, the other way . . ."

"Land's End?"

"Not so far. I only got as far as Lanyon. I parked the car in a lay-by and climbed the hill for a bit and sat in the bracken and looked at the view."

"So beautiful," said Alice, threading her needle.

"They're cutting hay on the farms."

"Yes, they would be."

"It never changes, does it? Lanyon, I mean. No new houses, no new roads, no shops, no caravan parks." She took a mouthful of scalding hot lapsang suchong and then, with care, laid the cup and saucer down on the paved floor beside her chair. "Alice, does Eustace Philips still farm Penfolda?"

Alice stopped sewing, and put up a hand to take off her dark glasses and stare at Virginia. There was a puzzled frown between her dark brows.

"What do you know about Eustace Philips? How do you know him?"

"Alice, your memory is appalling. It was you yourself who took me out there, you and Tom, for an enormous barbecue on the cliffs at Penfolda. There must have been at least thirty people and I don't know who organized it, but we cooked sausages over a fire and drank beer out of a barrel. Oh, surely you remember, and then Mrs. Philips gave us tea in her kitchen!"

"Now you remind me, of course I do. It was bitterly cold but quite beautiful and we watched the moon rise from behind Boscovey Head. I do remember. Now, who was it who threw that party? It certainly wasn't Eustace, he was always too busy milking cows. It must have been the Barnets—he was a sculptor and had a studio for a couple of years in Porthkerris before he went back to London. His wife wove baskets or belts or something, terribly folksy, and they had a lot of children who never wore shoes. They were always thinking up the most original parties. It must have been the Barnets . . . How extraordinary! I hadn't thought about them in years. And we all went out to Penfolda." But here her memory let her down. She looked at Virginia blankly. "Or did we? Who went to that party?"

"Mother didn't come. She said it wasn't up her street . . ."

6

"How right she was."

"But you and I and Tom went."

"Of course. Bundled up in sweaters and socks. I'm not sure I didn't wear a fur coat. But we were talking about Eustace. How old were you, Virginia? Seventeen? Fancy your remembering Eustace Philips after all these years."

"You haven't answered my question. Is he still at Penfolda?"

"As the farm belonged to his father, and *his* father, and as far as I know *his* father before that, do you really think it likely that Eustace would up sticks and depart?"

"I suppose not. It's just that they were cutting hay this afternoon and I wondered if it was he who drove one of the combines. Do you ever see him, Alice?"

"Hardly ever. Not because we don't want to, understand me, but he's a hard-working farmer, and Tom's so busy being a tycoon, that their paths don't often cross. Except sometimes they meet at the hare shoot, or the Boxing Day meet . . . you know the sort of thing."

Virginia picked up her tea-cup and saucer, and observed, minutely, the rose painted upon its side.

"He's married," she said.

"You say that as though you were stating an irrefutable fact."

"Aren't I?"

"No, you're not. He never married. Heaven knows why. I always thought he was so attractive in a sun burned, D. H. Lawrence-ish sort of way. There must have been a number of languishing ladies in Lanyon, but he resisted the lot. He must like it that way."

Eustace's wife, so swiftly imagined, as swiftly died, a wraith blown to nothing by the cold wind of reality. Instead, Virginia saw the Penfolda kitchen, cheerless and untidy, with the remains of the last meal abandoned on the table, dishes in the sink, an ashtray filled with cigarette stubs.

"Who looks after him?"

"I don't know. His mother died a couple of years ago I believe . . . I don't know what he does. Perhaps he's got a sexy housekeeper, or a domesticated mistress? I really don't know."

And couldn't care less, her tone implied. She had finished sewing on the silk cord, now gave a couple of neat firm stitches and then broke the thread with a little tug. "There, that's done. Isn't it a divine colour? But it's really too hot to sew." She laid it aside. "Oh dear, I suppose I

7

must go and see what we'll have for dinner. What would you say to a delicious fresh lobster?"

"I'd say 'pleased to see you.' "

Alice stood up, unfolding her long height to tower over Virginia. "Did you see your letters?"

"Yes, they're here."

Alice stooped to pick up the tray. "I'll leave you," she said, "to read them in peace."

Keeping the best to the last, Virginia opened her mother-in-law's letter first. The envelope was dark blue, lined with navy blue tissue. The writing-paper was thick, the address blackly embossed at its head.

32 Welton Gardens, S.W.8.

My dear Virginia,

I hope you are enjoying this wonderful weather, quite a heatwave and into the nineties yesterday. I expect you are swimming in Alice's pool, such a joy not having to drive to the beach every time you want to swim.

The children are both well and send their love. Nanny takes them into the park every day and they take their tea with them and eat it there. I took Cara to Harrods this morning to buy some new dresses, she is getting so tall and was quite out of her old ones. One is blue with appliquéd flowers, the other pink with a little smocking. I think you would approve!

Tomorrow they are going to tea with the Manning-Prestons. Nanny is looking forward to a good gossip with their Nanny, and Susan is just the right age for Cara. It would be nice for them to be friends.

My regards to Alice, and let me know when you decide to come back to London, but we are managing beautifully, and don't want you to cut short your holiday at all for any reason. You really were due for one.

Affectionately,
Dorothea Keile

She read the letter twice, torn by conflicting emotions. Double meanings sprang at her from between the meticulously-penned, well-turned sentences. She saw her children in the park, the baked London grass turned yellow in the heat, trodden and tired, and fouled by dogs. She saw the white-hot morning sky high above the roof tops and the little girl being fitted into dresses that she would neither like nor want,

8

but would be too polite to reject. She saw the Manning-Prestons's tall, terraced house, with the paved garden at the back where Mrs. Manning-Preston held her famous cocktail parties, and where Cara and Susan would be sent to play while the Nannies talked about knitting patterns and what a terror Nanny Brigg's little charge was going to be. And she saw Cara standing silent, petrified with shyness, and Susan Manning-Preston treating her with contempt because Cara wore spectacles and Susan thought she was a ninny.

And "we are managing beautifully." The statement seemed to Virginia completely ambiguous. Who was "we"? Nanny and the grandmother? Or did it include the children, Virginia's children? Did they let Cara sleep with the old Teddy that Nanny swore was unhygienic? Did they remember always to leave the light on so that Nicholas could get himself to the bathroom in the middle of the night? And were they ever left alone, disorganized, dirty, untidy, to play secret, pointless games in small corners of the garden, with perhaps a nut or a leaf, and all the imaginings that were contained within their small, clever, bewildering brains?

She found that her hands were shaking. She was a fool to get into this state. Nanny had looked after the children since they were born, she knew all their idiosyncrasies and nobody could cope with Nicholas's sudden rages better than she.

(But should he have such rages? At six, shouldn't he have grown out of them? What frustration sparks them off?)

And Nanny was gentle with Cara. She made dolls' clothes and knitted scarves and sweaters for the teddies out of left-over bits of wool. And she let Cara wheel her doll's perambulator into the park; over the crossing by the Albert Memorial, they went. (But did she read to Cara, the books that Cara loved? *The Borrowers* and *The Railway Children* and every word of *The Secret Garden*.) Did she love the children, or simply possess them?

These were all familiar questions which, lately, had been raising themselves with ever-increasing frequency within the confines of Virginia's own head. But never answered. Knowing that she was evading a vital issue, she would shelve her own anxiety, always with some excuse to herself. I can't think about it now, I'm too tired. Perhaps in a couple of years when Nicholas goes away to Prep. school, perhaps then I'll tell my mother-in-law that I don't need Nanny any longer; I'll say to Nanny it's time to go, to find another new baby to look after. And perhaps just now I'm too emotional, I wouldn't be good for the children; they're better with Nanny: after all, she's been looking after children for forty years.

Like a familiar sedative the well-worn excuses came pat, blunting Virginia's uneasy conscience. She put the blue letter back into its expensive envelope and turned, in relief, to the second one. But the relief was short-lived. Cara had borrowed her grandmother's writing-paper, but the sentences this time were neither meticulously penned nor well-turned. The ink was blotched and the lines ran down the side of the paper as though the words were tumbling hopelessly downhill.

Darling Mother,

I hope you are having a good time. I hope it is nise wether. It is hot in London. I have to go and have tea with Susan Maning Preston. I dont no what we will play. Last night Nicholas screemed and Granny had to give him a pil. He went all red. One of my dolls eyes has come out and I cant find it. Please will you rite to me soon and tell me when we are going back to Kirkton.

With love from Cara.
P.S. Dont forget to rite.

She folded the letter and put it away. Across the garden, across the lawns, the blue of Alice's swimming-pool glimmered like a jewel. The cooling air was filled with bird-song and the scent of flowers. From inside the house she could hear Alice's voice talking to Mrs. Jilkes, the cook, doubtless about the lobster which they were going to eat for dinner.

She felt helpless, totally inadequate. She thought of asking Alice to have the children here, and in the next instant knew that it was impossible. Alice's house was not designed for children, her life did not cater for their inclusion. She would be irritated beyond words by Cara forgetting to change her gum-boots, or by Nicholas kicking his football into the treasured flower-borders, or drawing "pictures" on the wallpaper. For without Nanny, he would doubtless be impossible because he was always twice as naughty without her to keep an eye on him.

Without Nanny. Those were the operative words. On her own. She had to have them on her own.

And yet the very thought filled her with dread. What would she do with them? Where would they go? Like feelers her thoughts probed around, searching for ideas. A hotel? But hotels here would be filled to the brim with summer visitors and terribly expensive. Besides, Nicholas in a hotel would be as nerve-racking as Nicholas at Wheal House. She thought of hiring a caravan, or camping with them on the beach, like the summer migration of hippies, who lit fires of driftwood and slept curled up on the chilly sand.

Of course, there was always Kirkton. Some time, she would have to go back. But all her instincts shied away from the thought of returning to Scotland, to the house where she had lived with Anthony, the place where her children had been born, the only place they thought of as home. Thinking of Kirkton, she saw tree shadows flickering on pale walls, the cold northern light reflected on the white ceilings, the sound of her own feet going up the uncarpeted, polished stairway. She thought of clear autumn evenings when the first skeins of geese flew over, and the park, in front of the house, sweeping down to the banks of the deep, swift-flowing river . . .

No. Not yet. Cara would have to wait. Later, perhaps, they would go back to Kirkton. Not yet. Behind her a door slammed, and she was jerked back to reality by the arrival of Tom Lingard, back from work. She heard him call Alice, then drop his brief-case on the hall-table, and come out to the patio in search of his wife.

"Hallo, Virginia." He bent and dropped a kiss on the top of her head. "All alone? Where's Alice?"

"Interviewing a lobster in the kitchen."

"Letters from the children? All well? Well done, that's great . . ." One of Tom's idiosyncrasies was that he never bothered to wait for an answer to any of his questions. Virginia sometimes wondered if this was the secret of his outstanding success. "What have you been doing all day? Lying in the sun? That's the job. How about coming and having a swim with me now? The exercise'll do you good after all this lazing about. We'll get Alice to come too . . ." He went, spring-footed and bursting with energy, back into the house and down the passage towards the kitchen, bellowing for his wife. And Virginia, grateful for directions, stood up and collected her mail and went indoors, obediently, and upstairs to her bedroom to change into a bikini.

Chapter 2

The solicitors were called Smart, Chirgwin and Williams. At least, those were the names on the brass plate by the door, a plate which had been polished so long and so hard that the letters had lost their sharpness and were quite difficult to read. There was a brass knocker on the door, too, and a brass door knob, as smooth and shining as the plate, and when Virginia turned the knob and opened the door, she stepped into a narrow hall of polished brown linoleum and shining cream paint and it occurred to her that some hard-working woman was using up an awful lot of elbow grease.

There was a glass window, like an old-fashioned ticket-office with INQUIRIES written over it, and a bell to press. Virginia pressed the bell and the window flew up.

"Yes?"

Startled, Virginia told the face behind the window that she wanted to see Mr. Williams.

"Have you got an appointment?"

"Yes. It's Mrs. Keile."

"Just a moment, please."

The window slammed down and the face withdrew. Presently a door opened and the face reappeared, along with a well-upholstered body and a pair of legs that went straight down into sturdy lace-up shoes.

"If you'd like to come this way, Mrs. Keile."

The building which housed the solicitors' office stood at the top of the hill which led out of Porthkerris, but even so Virginia was taken unawares by the marvellous view which leapt at her as soon as she

12

walked into the room. Mr. Williams's desk stood in the middle of the carpet and Mr. Williams was, even now, getting to his feet behind it. But, beyond Mr. Williams, a great picture-window framed, like some lovely painting, the whole jumbled, charming panorama of the old part of the town. Roofs of houses, faded slate and whitewashed chimneys, tumbled without pattern or order down the hill. Here a blue door, there a yellow window; here a window-sill bright with geraniums, a line of washing gay as flags, or the leaves of some unsuspected and normally unseen tree. Beyond the roofs and far below them was the harbour, at full tide and sparkling with sunshine. Boats rocked at anchor and a white sail sped out beyond the shelter of the harbour wall, heading for the ruler line of the horizon where the two blues met. The air was clamorous with the sound of gulls, the sky patterned with their great gliding wings and as Virginia stood there, the church bells from the Norman tower struck up a simple carillon and clock chimes rang out eleven o'clock.

"Good morning," said Mr. Williams, and Virginia realized that he had already said this twice. She tore her attention from the view and tried to focus it on him.

"Oh, good morning. I'm Mrs. Keile, I . . ." But it was impossible. "How *can* you work in a room with a view like that?"

"That's why I sit with my back to it . . ."

"It's breathtaking."

"Yes, and quite unique. We're often asked by artists if they can paint the harbour from this window. You can see the whole structure of the town, and the colours are always different, always beautiful. Except, of course, on a rainy day. Now—" his manner changed abruptly as though anxious to get down to work and to waste no more time— "what can I do for you?" He drew a chair forward for her.

Trying to stop looking out of the window and to concentrate on the matter in hand, Virginia sat down. "Well I've maybe come to quite the wrong person, but you see I can't find an estate agent anywhere in the town. And I looked in the local paper for a house to rent, but there didn't seem to be one. And then I saw your name in the telephone book, and I thought perhaps you might be able to help me."

"Help you find a house?" Mr. Williams was young, very dark, his eyes frankly interested in the attractive woman who faced him across his desk.

"Just to rent . . ."

13

"For how long?"

"A month . . . my children go back to school the first week in September."

"I see. Well, we don't actually *deal* in this sort of thing, but I could ask Miss Leddra if there's anything that she could suggest. But of course this is the high season, and the town is already packed to the gunwales with visitors. Even if you do find something, I'm afraid you'll have to pay a fairly steep rent."

"I don't mind."

"Well, just a moment . . ."

He left her and went out, and Virginia heard him speaking to the woman who had let her in. She got up and went back to the window, and opened it wide and laughed as a furious gull flew crossly off the sill where he had been perching. The wind off the sea was cool and fresh. A pleasure boat packed with passengers started off across the harbour and suddenly Virginia longed to be on board, irresponsible, sunburned, wearing a hat with KISS ME written on it and screaming with laughter as the first waves sent the boat rocking.

Mr. Williams came back. "Can you wait a moment? Miss Leddra's making a few inquiries . . ."

"Yes, of course." She returned to her chair.

"Are you staying in Porthkerris?" Mr. Williams asked conversationally.

"Yes. I'm staying with friends. The Lingards up at Wheal House."

His previous manner had been neither off-hand nor familiar, but all at once he was almost deferential.

"Oh yes, of course. What a charming place that is."

"Yes. Alice has made it lovely."

"Have you been there before?"

"Yes. Ten years ago. But I haven't been since."

"Are your children with you?"

"No. They're in London, with their grandmother. But I want to get them down here with me, if I can."

"Is London your home?"

"No. It's just that my mother-in-law lives in London." Mr. Williams waited. "My home . . . that is, we live in Scotland."

He looked delighted . . . Virginia could not think why it should delight him that she lived in Scotland. "But how splendid! What part?"

"In Perthshire."

14

"The most beautiful. My wife and I spent a holiday there last summer. The peace of it all, and the empty roads and the quiet. How could you bear to come away?"

Virginia had opened her mouth to tell him when the discussion was mercifully interrupted by the arrival of Miss Leddra, bearing a sheaf of papers.

"Here it is, Mr. Williams. Bosithick. And the letter from Mr. Kernow saying that if we could find a tenant for August he'd be willing to rent. But only to a *suitable* tenant, Mr. Williams. He's very firm about that point."

Mr. Williams took the papers and smiled at Virginia over the top of them.

"Are you a suitable tenant, Mrs. Keile?"

"It depends. On what you're offering me, doesn't it?"

"Well, it's not actually in Porthkerris . . . thank you, Miss Leddra . . . but not too far away . . . out at Lanyon actually . . ."

"Lanyon!"

She must have sounded appalled, for Mr. Williams sprang at once to Lanyon's defence. "But it's a most charming spot, quite the most beautiful bit of coastline left anywhere."

"I didn't mean that I didn't like it. I was just surprised."

"Were you? Why?"

He was too sharp, like a beady-eyed bird. "No reason, really. Tell me about the house."

He told her. It was an old cottage, neither distinguished nor beautiful, but with a small claim to fame in that a famous writer had once lived and worked there during the nineteen-twenties.

Virginia said, "Which?"

"I beg your pardon?"

"Which famous writer?"

"Oh, I'm sorry. Aubrey Crane. Didn't you know that he spent some years in this part of the world?"

Virginia did not. But Aubrey Crane had been one of the many authors of whom Virginia's mother did not approve. She remembered her mother's chill expression, lips pursed, whenever his books were mentioned; remembered them being returned swiftly to the library before the young Virginia could get her eyes on them. For some reason this seemed to make the cottage called Bosithick even more desirable. "Go on," said Virginia.

Mr. Williams went on. Despite its age Bosithick had been modernized to a certain degree—there was now a bathroom and a lavatory and an electric cooker.

"Who does it belong to?" Virginia asked.

"Mr. Kernow is the nephew of the old lady who used to own the house. She left it to him, but he lives in Plymouth so he uses it just for holidays. He and his family intended coming down for the summer, but his wife fell ill and can't make the trip. As we are Mr. Kernow's solicitors, he put the matter in our hands, with the instructions that, if we did let the house, it must be to a tenant who can be trusted to take care of it."

"How big is it?"

Mr. Williams perused his papers. "Let's see, a kitchen, a sitting-room, a downstairs bathroom, and a hall, and three rooms upstairs."

"Is there a garden?"

"Not really."

"How far is it from the road?"

"About a hundred yards down a farm lane as far as I can remember."

"And could I have it right away?"

"I can see no objection. But you must see it first."

"Yes, of course . . . when can I see it?"

"Today? Tomorrow?"

"Tomorrow morning."

"I'll take you out myself."

"Thank you, Mr. Williams." Virginia stood up and made for the door, and he had to make a little rush to get there and open it before she did.

"There's just one thing, Mrs. Keile."

"What's that?"

"You haven't asked what the rent is."

She smiled. "No I haven't, have I? Goodbye, Mr. Williams."

Virginia said nothing to Alice and Tom. She did not want to have to put into words what was, at best, only a vague idea. She did not want to be drawn into an argument, to be persuaded either that the children were best left in London with their grandmother or that Alice could disregard the possible destruction that they might perpetrate at Wheal House and would insist on having them there. When Virginia had found somewhere for them all to live, she would present Alice with

16

what she had done as a *fait accompli*. And then Alice would maybe help her take the biggest hurdle of all, which was to persuade the grandmother to let the children come to Cornwall without Nanny. At the very prospect of this ordeal, Virginia's imagination turned and ran, but there were other and smaller obstacles to be overcome first, and these she was determined to do by herself.

Alice was a perfect hostess. When Virginia told her that she would be out for the morning it never occurred to Alice to quiz her as to what she intended doing. She only said, "Will you be in for lunch?"

"I don't think so . . . Better say not . . ."

"I'll see you at tea time, then. We'll have a swim together afterwards."

"Heaven," said Virginia. She kissed Alice and went out, got into her car and drove down the hill into Porthkerris. She parked the car near the station and walked to the solicitors' office to pick up Mr. Williams.

"Mrs. Keile, I couldn't be more sorry, but I'm not going to be able to come out with you this morning to Bosithick. An old client is coming down from Truro and I must be here to see her; I do hope you understand! But here are the keys of the house, and I've drawn a fairly detailed map of how to find it . . . I don't think you could go wrong. Do you mind going on your own, or would you like to take Miss Leddra with you?"

Virginia imagined the daunting presence of the formidable Miss Leddra and assured Mr. Williams that she'd manage perfectly on her own. She was given a ring of large keys, each with a wooden label. Front Door, Coal Shed, Tower Room. "You'll need to watch out for the lane," Mr. Williams told her, as they went together towards the door. "It's fairly bumpy and although there's no room to turn by the gate of Bosithick itself, you can manage easily if you carry on down the lane; you'll come to an old farmyard and you can turn the car there. Now, you're sure you'll be all right . . . I couldn't be more sorry about this, but I'll be here, of course, waiting to hear what you think of the place. Oh, and Mrs. Keile . . . it's been empty for some months. Try not to be influenced if it feels a little dingy. Just throw open a few windows and imagine it with a nice cheerful fire."

Slightly discouraged by these parting remarks, Virginia went back to her car. The keys of the unknown house weighed heavy as lead in her handbag. All at once, she longed for company, and even considered, for a mad moment, returning to Wheal House to make a true confession to Alice and persuade her to come out to Lanyon and lend a little moral support. But that was ridiculous. It was just a little cottage, to be viewed, and either rented or rejected. Any fool . . . even Virginia . . . could surely do that.

The weather was still beautiful and the traffic still appalling. She crawled, one of the long queue of cars, down into the depths of town and out the other side. At the top of the hill where the roads forked, the traffic thinned a little and she was able to put on some speed and pass a line of dawdling cars. As she went up and over the moor and the sea dropped and spread beneath her, her spirits rose. The road wound like a grey ribbon through the bracken-covered hillside; to her left towered the great outcrop of Carn Edvor stained purple with heather, and on her right the country swept away down to the sea, the familiar patchwork of fields and farms, that she had sat and watched only two days before.

She had been told by Mr. Williams to look out for a clump of wind-leaning hawthorns by the side of the road. Beyond this was a steep corner and then the narrow farm track which led down towards the sea. Virginia came upon it and turned the car down into it, no more than a stony lane high-hedged with brambles. She went into bottom gear and edged cautiously downhill, attempting to avoid bumps and pot-holes and trying not to think about the damage that the prickly gorse bushes were inflicting on the paintwork of her car.

There was no sign of any house, until she turned a steep corner and was instantly upon it. A stone wall, and beyond, a gable and a slated roof. She stopped the car in the lane, reached for her handbag and got out. There was a cool, salty wind blowing in from the sea, and the smell of gorse. She went to open the gate, but the hinges were broken and it had to be lifted before she could edge through. A path of sorts led down towards a flight of stone steps and so to the house, and Virginia saw that it was long and low with gables to the north and the south, and at the north end, looking out over the sea, had been added an extra room with a square tower above it. The tower imparted an oddly sanctified look to the house which Virginia found chilling. There was no garden to speak of, but at the south end a patch of unmown grass blew in the wind and two leaning poles supported what had once been a washing line.

She went down the steps and along a dank pathway that led along the side of the house towards the front door. This had once been painted dark red and was scarred with splitting sun blisters. Virginia took out the key and put it in the keyhole and turned the door knob and the key together and the door instantly, silently, swung inwards. She saw a tiny flight of stairs, a worn rung on bare boards, smelt damp and . . . mice? She swallowed nervously. She hated mice, but now that she had come so far there was nothing for it but to go up the two worn steps and tread gingerly over the threshold.

It did not take long to go over the old part of the house, to glance in at the tiny kitchen with its inadequate cooker and stained sink; the sitting-room cluttered with ill-matching chairs. An electric fire sat in the cavern of the huge old fireplace, like a savage animal at the mouth of its lair. There were curtains of flimsy cotton hanging at the windows, fly-blown and dejected, and a dresser packed with cups and plates and dishes in every sort of size and shape and state of dilapidation.

Without hope, Virginia went upstairs. The bedrooms were dim with tiny windows and unsuitable, looming pieces of furniture. She returned to the top of the stairs, and so up another pair of steps, to a closed door. She opened this, and after the gloom of the rest of the house, the blast of bright, northern light by which she was immediately assailed, was dazzling. Stunned by it, she stepped blindly into an astonishing room, small, completely square, windowed on three walls, it stood high above the sea like the bridge of a ship, with a view of the coastline that must have extended for fifteen miles.

A window-seat with a faded cover ran along the north side of this room. There was a scrubbed table, and an old braided rug and in the centre of the floor, like a decorative well-head, the wrought-iron banister of a spiral staircase which led directly down to the room beneath, the "Hall" of Mr. Williams's prospectus.

Cautiously Virginia descended, to a room dominated by an enormous *art nouveau* fireplace. Off this was the bathroom; and then another door, and she was back where she'd started, in the dark and depressing sitting-room.

It was an extraordinary, a terrible house. It sat around her, waiting for her to make some decision, contemptuous of her faintness of heart. To give herself time, she went back up to the tower room, sat on the window-seat and opened her bag to find a cigarette. Her last. She would have to buy some more. She lit it and looked at the bare scrubbed table, and the faded colours of the rug on the floor, and knew that this had been Aubrey Crane's study, the workroom where he had wrestled out the lusty love stories that Virginia had never been encouraged to read. She saw him, bearded and knickerbockered, his conventional appearance belying the passions of his rebellious heart. Perhaps in summertime, he would have flung wide these windows, to catch all the scents and sounds of the countryside, the roar of the sea, the whistle of the wind. But in winter it would be bitterly cold, and he would have to wrap himself in blankets, and write painfully with chilblained fingers mittened in knitted wool . . .

Somewhere in the room a fly droned, blundering against the window-pane. Virginia leaned her forehead on the cool glass of the window and stared sightless at the view and started one of the interminable ding-dong arguments she had been having with herself for years.

I can't come here.

Why not?

I hate it. It's spooky and frightening. It's got a horrible atmosphere.

That's just your imagination.

It's an impossible house. I could never bring the children here. They've never lived in such a place. Anyway, there's nowhere for them to play.

There's the whole world for them to play in. The fields and the cliffs and the sea.

But looking after them . . . the washing and the ironing, and the cooking. And there's no refrigerator, and how would I heat the water?

I thought that all that mattered was getting the children to yourself, away from London.

They're better in London, with Nanny, than living in a house like this.

That wasn't what you thought yesterday.

I can't bring them here. I wouldn't know where to begin. Not on my own like that.

Then what are you going to do?

I don't know. Talk to Alice, perhaps I should have talked to her before now. She hasn't children of her own, but she'll understand. Maybe she'll know about some other little house. She'll understand. She'll help. She has to help.

20

So much, said her own cool and scathing voice, *for all those strong resolutions.*

Angrily, Virginia stubbed out the half-smoked cigarette, ground it under her heel and got up and went downstairs and took out the keys and locked the door behind her. She went back up the path to the gate, stepped through and shut it. The house watched her the small bedroom windows like derisive eyes. She tore herself from their gaze and got back into the safety of her car. It was a quarter past twelve. She needed cigarettes and she was not expected back at Wheal House for lunch, so, when she had turned the car, and was driving back up on to the main road again, she took not the road to Porthkerris, but the other way, and she drove the short mile to Lanyon village, up the narrow main street, and finally came to a halt in the cobbled square that was flanked on one side by the porch of the square-towered church and on the other by a small whitewashed pub called The Mermaid's Arms.

Because of the fine weather, there were tables and chairs set up outside the pub, along with brightly coloured sun-umbrellas and tubs of orange nasturtiums. A man and a woman in holiday clothes sat and drank their beer, their little boy played with a puppy. As Virginia approached, they looked up to smile good morning, and she smiled back and went past them in through the door, instinctively ducking her head beneath the blackened lintel.

Inside it was dark-panelled, low-ceilinged, dimly illuminated by tiny windows veiled in lace curtains; there was a pleasant smell, cool and musty. A few figures, scarcely visible in the gloom, sat along the wall, or around small wobbly tables, and behind the bar, framed by rows of hanging beer-mugs, the barman, in shirtsleeves and a checkered pullover, was polishing glasses with a dishcloth.

". . . I don't know 'ow it is, William," he was saying to a customer who sat at the other end of the bar, perched disconsolately on a tall stool, with a long cigarette ash and half a pint of bitter, ". . . but you put the litter bins up and nobody puts nothing into them . . ."

"Ur . . ." said William, nodding in sad agreement and sprinkling cigarette ash into the beer.

"Stuff blows all over the road, and the County Council don't even come and empty them. Ugly old things they are, too, we'd be better without them. Managed all right without them before, we did . . ."

He finished polishing the glass, set it down with a thump and turned to attend to Virginia.

"Yes, madam?"

He was very Cornish, in voice, in looks, in colouring. A red and wind-burned face, blue eyes, black hair.

Virginia asked for cigarettes.

"Only got packets of twenty. That all right?" He turned to take them from the shelf and slit the wrapper with a practised thumb-nail. "Lovely day, isn't it? On holiday, are you?"

"Yes." It was years since she had been into a pub. In Scotland women were never taken into pubs. She had forgotten the atmosphere, the snug companionship. She said, "Do you have any Coke?"

He looked surprised. "Yes, I've got Coke. Keep it for the children. Want some, do you?"

"Please."

He reached for a bottle, opened it neatly, poured it into a glass and pushed it across the counter towards her.

"I was just saying to William, here, that road to Porthkerris is a disgrace . . ." Virginia pulled up a stool and settled down to listen. ". . . All that rubbish lying around. Visitors don't seem to know what to do with their litter. You'd think coming to a lovely part like this they'd have the sense they was born with and take all them old bits of paper home with them, in the car, not leave them lying around on the roadside. They talk about conservation and ecology, but, my God . . ."

He was off on what was obviously his favourite hobby-horse, judging by the well-timed grunts of assent that came from all corners of the room. Virginia lit a cigarette. Outside, in the sunny square, a car drew up, the engine stopped, a door slammed. She heard a man's voice say good morning, and then footsteps came through the doorway and into the bar behind her.

". . . I wrote to the MP about it, said who was going to get the place cleaned up, he said it was the responsibility of the County Council, but I said . . ." Over Virginia's head he caught sight of the new customer. " 'Allo, there! You're a stranger."

"Still at the litter bins, Joe?"

"You know me, boy, worry a subject to death, like a terrier killing a rat. What'll you have?"

"A pint of bitter."

Joe turned to draw the beer, and the newcomer moved in to stand between Virginia and lugubrious William, and she had recognized his voice at once, as soon as he spoke, just as she had known his footfall, stepping in over the flagged threshold of The Mermaid's Arms.

She took a mouthful of Coke, laid down the glass. All at once her cigarette tasted bitter; she stubbed it out and turned her head to look at him, and she saw the blue shirt, with the sleeves rolled back from his brown forearms, and the eyes very blue and the short, rough, brown hair cut like a pelt, close to the shape of his head. And because there was nothing else to be done she said, "Hallo, Eustace."

Startled, his head swung round and his expression was that of a man who had suddenly been hit in the stomach, bemused and incapable. She said, quickly, "It really is me," and his smile came, incredulous, rueful, as though he knew he had been made to look a fool.

"Virginia."

She said again, stupidly, "Hallo."

"What in the name of heaven are you doing here?"

She was aware that every ear in the place was waiting for her to reply. She made it very light and casual. "Buying cigarettes. Having a drink."

"I didn't mean that. I mean in Cornwall. Here, in Lanyon."

"I'm on holiday. Staying with the Lingards in Porthkerris."

"How long have you been here?"

"About a week . . ."

"And what are you doing out here?"

But before she had time to tell him, the barman had pushed Eustace's tankard of beer across the counter, and Eustace was diverted by trying to find the right money in his trouser pocket.

"Old friends, are you?" asked Joe, looking at Virginia with new interest, and she said, "Yes, I suppose you could say that."

"I haven't seen her for ten years," Eustace told him, pushing the coins across the counter. He looked at Virginia's glass. "What are you drinking?"

"Coke."

"Bring it outside, we may as well sit in the sun."

She followed him, aware of the unblinking stares which followed them; the insatiable curiosity. Outside in the sunshine he put their glasses down on to a wooden table and they settled, side by side on a bench, with the sun on their heads and their backs against the white-washed wall of the pub.

"You don't mind being brought out here, do you? Otherwise we couldn't say a word without it being received and transmitted all over the county within half an hour."

"I'd rather be outside."

Half turned towards her, he sat so close that Virginia could see the rough, weather-beaten texture of his skin, the network of tiny lines around his eyes, the first frosting of white in that thick brown hair. She thought, *I'm with him again.*

He said, "Tell me."

"Tell you what?"

"What happened to you." And then quickly: "I know you got married."

"Yes. Almost at once."

"Well, that would have put paid to the London Season you were dreading so much."

"Yes, it did."

"And the coming-out dance."

"I had a wedding instead."

"Mrs. Anthony Keile. I saw the announcement in the paper." Virginia said nothing. "Where do you live now?"

"In Scotland. There's a house in Scotland . . ."

"And children?"

"Yes. Two. A boy and a girl."

"How old are they?" He was really interested, and she remembered how the Cornish loved children, how Mrs. Jilkes was for ever going dewy-eyed over some lovely little great-nephew or niece.

"The girl's eight and the boy's six."

"Are they with you now?"

"No. They're in London. With their grandmother."

"And your husband? Is he down? What's he doing this morning? Playing golf?"

She stared at him, accepting for the first time the fact that personal tragedy is just that. Personal. Your own existence could fall to pieces but that did not mean that the rest of the world necessarily knew about it, or even bothered. There was no reason for Eustace to know.

She laid her hands on the edge of the table, aligning them as though their arrangement were of the utmost importance. She said,

"Anthony's dead." Her hands seemed all at once insubstantial, almost transparent, the wrists too thin, the long almond-shaped nails, painted coral pink, as fragile as petals. She wished suddenly, fervently, that they were not like that, but strong and brown and capable, with dirt engrained, and fingernails worn from gardening and peeling potatoes and scraping carrots. She could feel Eustace's eyes upon her. She could not bear him to be sorry for her.

He said, "What happened?"

"He was killed in a car accident. He was drowned."

"Drowned?"

"We have this river, you see, at Kirkton . . . that's where we live in Scotland. The river runs between the house and the road, you have to go over the bridge. And he was coming home and he skidded, or misjudged the turn, and the car went through the wooden railings and into the river. We'd had a lot of rain, a wet month, and the river was in spate and the car went to the bottom. A diver had to go down . . . with a cable. And the police eventually winched it out . . ." Her voice trailed off.

He said gently, "When?"

"Three months ago."

"Not long."

"No. But there was so much to do, so much to see to. I don't know what's happened to the time. And then I caught this bug—a sort of 'flu, and I couldn't throw it off, so my mother-in-law said that she'd have the children in London and I came down here to stay with Alice."

"When are you going away again?"

"I don't know."

He was silent. After a little he picked up his glass and drained his beer. As he set it down he said, "Have you got a car here?"

"Yes." She pointed. "The blue Triumph."

"Then finish that drink and we'll go back to Penfolda." Virginia turned her head and stared at him. "Well, what's so extraordinary about that? It's dinner time. There are pasties in the oven. Do you want to come back and eat one with me?"

". . . Yes."

"Then come. I've got my Land-Rover. You can follow me."

"All right."

He stood up. "Come along, then."

25

Chapter 3

SHE HAD BEEN to Penfolda once before, only once, and then in the cool half-light of a spring evening ten years before.

"We've been invited to a party," Alice had announced over lunch that day.

Virginia's mother was immediately intrigued. She was immensely social and with a seventeen-year-old daughter to launch into society one only had to mention a party to capture her attention.

"How very nice! Where? Who with?"

Alice laughed at her. Alice was one of the few people who could laugh at Rowena Parsons and get away with it, but then Alice had known her for years.

"Don't get too excited. It's not really your sort of thing."

"My dear Alice, I don't know what you mean. Explain!"

"Well, it's a couple called Barnet. Amos and Fenella Barnet. You may have heard of him. He's a sculptor, very modern, very *avant-garde*. They've taken one of the old studios in Porthkerris, and they have a great number of rather unconventional children."

Without waiting to hear more Virginia said. "Why don't we go?" They sounded exactly the sort of people she was always longing to meet.

Mrs. Parsons allowed a small frown to show between her beautifully aligned eyebrows. "Is the party in the studio?" she inquired, obviously suspecting doctored drinks and doped cigarettes.

"No, it's out at Lanyon at a farm called Penfolda, some sort of a barbecue on the cliffs. A camp fire and fried sausages . . ." Alice saw that Virginia was longing to go. ". . . I think it might be rather fun."

"I think it sounds terrible," said Mrs. Parsons.

"I didn't think you'd want to come. But Tom and I might go, and we'll take Virginia with us."

Mrs. Parsons turned her cool gaze upon her daughter. "Do you *want* to go to a barbecue?"

Virginia shrugged. "It might be fun." She had learned, long ago, that it never paid to be too enthusiastic about anything.

"Very well," said her mother, helping herself to lemon pudding. "If it's your idea of an amusing evening and Alice and Tom don't mind taking you along . . . but for heaven's sake wear something warm. It's bound to be freezing. Far too cold, one would have thought, for a picnic."

She was right. It was cold. A clear turquoise evening with the shoulder of Carn Edvor silhouetted black against the western sky and a chill inland wind to nip the air. Driving up the hill out of Porthkerris, Virginia looked back and saw the lights of the town twinkling far below, the ink-black waters of the harbour brimming with shimmering reflections. Across the bay, from the distant headland, the lighthouse sent its warning signal. A flash. A pause. A flash. A longer pause. Be careful. There's danger.

The evening ahead seemed full of possibilities. Suddenly excited, Virginia turned and leaned forward, resting her chin on crossed arms on the back of Alice's seat. The unpremeditated gesture was clumsy and spontaneous, a reflection of natural high spirits that were normally battened firmly down under the influence of a domineering mother.

"Alice, where is this place we're going?"

"Penfolda. It's a farm, just this side of Lanyon."

"Who lives there?"

"Mrs. Philips. She's a widow. And her son Eustace."

"What does he do?"

"He farms, silly. I told you it was a farm."

"Are they friends of the Barnets?"

"I suppose they must be. A lot of artists live out around this part of the world. Though I've no idea how they could ever have met."

Tom said, "Probably at The Mermaid's."

"What's The Mermaid's?" Virginia asked.

"The Mermaid's Arms, the pub in Lanyon. On a Saturday night all the world and his wife go there for a drink and a get-together."

"Who else will be at the party?"

"Our guess is probably as good as yours."

"Haven't you *any* idea?"

"Well . . ." Alice did her best. ". . . Artists and writers and poets and hippies and drop-outs and farmers and perhaps one or two rather boring and conventional people like us."

Virginia gave her a hug. "You're not boring or conventional. You're super."

"You may not think we're quite so super at the end of the evening. You may hate it, so grit your teeth and reserve your judgment."

Virginia sat back, in the darkness of the car, hugging herself. *I shan't hate it.*

There were headlights like fireflies, coming from all directions, converging on Penfolda. From the road the farmhouse could be seen to be blazing with light. They joined the queue of assorted vehicles which bumped and groaned their way down a narrow, broken land and eventually were directed into a farmyard which had been turned temporarily into a car park. The air was full of voices and laughter as friends greeted friends, and already a steady trickle of people were making their way over a stone wall and down over the pasture fields towards the cliffs. Some were wrapped in rugs, some carried old-fashioned lanterns, some—Virginia was glad all over again that her mother had not come—a clanking bottle or two.

Someone said, "Tom! What are you doing here?", and Tom and Alice dropped back to wait for their friends, and Virginia went on, loving the feeling of being alone. All about her the soft, dark air smelled of peat and sea-wrack and wood-smoke. The sky was not yet empty of light and the sea was of so dark a blue that it was almost black. She went through a gap in a wall and saw, below her, at the bottom of the field, the golden flames of the fire, already ringed with lanterns and the shapes and shadows of about thirty people. As she came closer, faces sprang suddenly into focus, illuminated in firelight, laughing and talking, everybody knowing everybody. There was a barrel of beer, propped on a wooden stand, from which brimming glasses were being continually filled, and there was the smell of potatoes cooking and burning fat, and somebody had brought a guitar and begun to play and gradually a few people gathered about him and raised uncertain voices in song.

There is a ship
And she sails the sea,
She's loaded deep
As deep can be.
But not as deep
As the love I'm in . . .

A young man, running to pass Virginia, stumbled in the dusk and bumped into her. "Sorry." He grabbed her arm, as much to steady himself as her. He held his lantern high, the light in her face. "Who are you?"

"Virginia."

"Virginia who?"

"Virginia Parsons."

He had long hair and a band around his forehead and looked like an Apache.

"I thought it was a new face. Are you on your own?"

"N . . . no. I've come with Alice and Tom . . . but . . ." She looked back. "I've lost them . . . they're coming . . . somewhere . . ."

"I'm Dominic Barnet . . ."

"Oh . . . it's your party . . ."

"No, my father's, really. At least he's paid for the barrel of beer which makes it his party and my mother bought the sausages. Come on . . . let's get something to drink," and he grabbed her arm with an even firmer grip and marched her down into the seething, noisy firelit circle of activity. "Hey, Dad . . . here's someone who hasn't got a drink . . ."

A huge bearded figure, medieval in the strange light, straightened up from the tap of the barrel. "Well, here's one for her," he said, and Virginia found herself holding an enormous mug of beer. "And here's a sausage." The young man whisked one nearly off a passing tray and handed it to her, impaled on a stick. Virginia took that too, and was just about to embark upon some polite social conversation when Dominic saw another familiar face across the circle of firelight, yelled "Mariana!" or some such name, and was away, leaving Virginia once more alone.

She searched in the darkness for the Lingards but could not find them. But everyone else was sitting, so she sat too, with the enormous

29

beer mug in one hand and the sausage, still too hot to eat, in the other. The firelight scorched her face and the wind was cold on her back and blew her hair all over her face. She took a mouthful of beer. She had never drunk beer before and immediately wanted to sneeze. She did so, enormously and from behind her an amused voice said, "Bless you."

Virginia recovered from the sneeze and said, "Thank you," and looked up to see who had blessed her, and saw a large young man in corduroys and rubber boots and a massive Norwegian sweater. He was grinning down at her and the firelight turned his brown face to the colour of copper.

She said, "It was the beer that made me sneeze."

He squatted beside her, took the mug gently from her hand and laid it on the ground between them. "You might sneeze again and then you'd spill it all and that would be a waste."

"Yes."

"You have to be a friend of the Barnets."

"Why do you say that?"

"I haven't seen you before."

"No, I'm not. I came with the Lingards."

"Alice and Tom? Are they here?"

"Yes, somewhere."

He sounded so pleased that the Lingards were here that Virginia fully expected him to go, then and there, in search of them, but instead he settled himself more comfortably on the grass beside her, and seemed quite happy to remain silent, simply watching in some amusement, the rest of the party. Virginia ate her sausage, and when she had finished and he still had said nothing, she decided that she would try again.

"Are you a friend of the Barnets?"

"Um . . ." His attention interrupted, he turned to look at her, his eyes a clear and unwinking blue. "Sorry?"

"I wondered if you were a friend of the Barnets, that's all."

He laughed. "I'd better be. These are my fields they're desecrating."

"Then you must be Eustace Philips."

He considered this. "Yes," he said at last. "I suppose I must be."

Soon after that he was called away . . . some of his Guernseys had wandered in from a neighbouring field and a batty girl who had drunk too much wine thought that she was being attacked by a bull and

30

had thrown a pretty fit of hysterics. So Eustace went to put the matter to rights, and Virginia was presently claimed by Alice and Tom, and although she spent the rest of the evening watching out for him, she did not see Eustace Philips again.

The party, however, was a wild and memorable success. Near midnight, with the beer finished, and the bottles going round, and the food all eaten and the fire piled with driftwood until the flames sprang twenty feet high or more, Alice suggested gently that perhaps it might be a good idea if they went home.

"Your mother will be sitting up thinking you've either been raped or fallen into the sea. And Tom's got to be at the office at nine in the morning and it really is getting bitterly cold. What do you say? Have you had enough? Have you had fun?"

"Such fun," said Virginia, reluctant to leave.

But it was time to go. They walked in silence, away from the firelight and the noise, up the slopes of the fields towards the farm-house.

Now, only one light burned from a downstairs window, but a full moon, white as a plate, sailed high in the sky, filling all the night with silver light. As they came over the wall into the farmyard, a door in the house opened, yellow light spilled out over the cobbles, and a voice called out across the darkness. "Tom! Alice! Come and have a cup of tea or coffee—something to warm you up before you go home."

"Hallo, Eustace." Tom went towards the house. "We thought you'd gone to bed."

"I'm not staying down on the cliffs till dawn, that's for certain. Would you like a drink?"

"I'd like a whisky," said Tom.

"And I'd like tea," said Alice. "What a good idea! We're frozen. Are you sure it's not too much trouble?"

"My mother's still up, she'd like to see you. She's got the kettle on . . ."

They all went into the house, into a low-ceilinged, panelled hall, with a flagged slate floor covered with bright rugs. The beams of the roof scarcely cleared the top of Eustace Philips's head.

Alice was unbuttoning her coat. "Eustace, have you met Virginia? She's staying with us at Wheal House."

"Yes, of course—we said hallo," but he scarcely looked at her. "Come into the kitchen, it's the warmest place in the house. Mother,

31

here are the Lingards. Alice wants a cup of tea. And Tom wants whisky and . . ." He looked down at Virginia. "What do you want?"

"I'd like tea."

Alice and Mrs. Philips at once busied themselves, Mrs. Philips with the teapot and the kettle, and Alice taking cups and saucers down from the shelves of the painted dresser. As they did this they discussed the Barnets's party, laughing about the girl who thought the cow was a bull, and the two men settled themselves at the scrubbed kitchen table with tumblers and a soda siphon and a bottle of Scotch.

Virginia sat too, wedged into the broad window-set at the head of the table, and listening to, without actually hearing, the pleasant blur of voices. She found that she was very sleepy, dazed by the warmth and comfort of the Penfolda kitchen after the bitter cold of the outdoors, and slightly fuzzy from the unaccustomed draught beer.

Sunk into the folds of her coat, hands deep in its pockets, she looked about her and decided that never had she been in a room so welcoming, so secure. There were beams in the ceiling, with old iron hooks for smoking hams, and deep window-sills crammed with flowering geraniums. There was a huge stove where the kettle simmered, and a cane chair with a cat curled in its seat, and there was a Grain Merchant's calendar and curtains of checked cotton and the warm smell of baking bread.

Mrs. Philips was small as her son was large, grey-haired, very neat. She looked as though she had never stopped working from the day she was born and would have it no other way, and as she and Alice moved about the kitchen, deft and quick, gossiping gently about the unconventional Barnets, Virginia watched her and wished that she could have had a mother just like that. Calm and good-humoured with a great comforting kitchen and a kettle always on the boil for a cup of tea.

The tea made, the two women finally joined the others around the table. Mrs. Philips poured a cup for Virginia and handed it to her, and Virginia sat up, pulling her hands out of her pockets and took it, remembering to say "Thank you."

Mrs. Philips laughed. "You're sleepy," she said.

"I know," said Virginia. They were all looking at her, but she stirred her tea and would not look up because she did not want to have to meet that blue and disconcerting gaze.

But eventually it was time to go. With their coats on again, they stood, crowded in the little hallway. The Lingards and Mrs. Philips were already at the open front door when Eustace spoke from behind Virginia.

"Goodbye," he said.

"Oh." Confused, she turned. "Goodbye." She began to put out her hand, but perhaps he did not see it, for he did not take it. "Thank you for letting me come."

He looked amused. "It was a pleasure. You'll have to come back again, another time."

And all the way home, she hugged his words close as though they were a marvellous present that he had given her. But she never came back to Penfolda.

Until today, ten years later, and a July afternoon of piercing beauty. Roadside ditches brimmed with ragged robin and bright yellow coltsfoot, the gorse was aflame and the bracken of the cliff-tops lay emerald against a summer sea the colour of hyacinths.

So engrossed had she been in her business of the day, collecting keys, and finding the cottage at Bosithick, and considering such practical questions as cookers and fridges and bedclothes and china, that all the heaven-sent morning had somehow gone unnoticed. But now it was part of what had suddenly happened and Virginia remembered long ago, how the lighthouse had flashed out over the dark sea, and she had been, for no apparent reason, suddenly excited and warm with a marvellous anticipation.

But you're not seventeen any longer. You're a woman, twenty-seven years old and independent, with two children and a car and a house in Scotland. Life doesn't hold those sort of surprises any longer. Everything is different. Nothing ever stays the same.

At the top of the lane which led down to Penfolda was a wooden platform for the milk churns, and the way sloped steep and winding between high stone walls. Hawthorns leaned distorted by the winter winds, and as Virginia followed the back of Eustace's Land-Rover around the corner of the house, two collies appeared, black and white, barking and raising a din that sent the brown Leghorn hens squawking and scuttling for shelter.

Eustace had parked his Land-Rover in the shade of the barn and was already out of it, toeing the dogs gently out of the way. Virginia put her car behind his and got out as well, and the collies instantly made for her, barking and leaping about and trying to put their front paws on her knees and stretching up to lick her face.

"Get down . . . get down, you devils!"

"I don't mind . . ." She fondled their slim heads, their thick coats. "What are their names?"

"Beaker and Ben. That's Beaker and this is Ben . . . shut up, you, boy! They do this every time . . ."

His manner was robust and cheerful as though during the course of the short drive he had decided that this was the best attitude to adopt if the rest of the day was not to become a sort of wake for Anthony Keile. And Virginia, who did not in the least want this to happen, gratefully took her cue from him. The dogs' noisy welcome helped to break the ice, and it was in an entirely natural and easy fashion that they all went up the cobbled path together, and into the house.

She saw the beams, the flagged floor, the rugs. Unchanged.

"I remember this."

There was a smell of hot pasties, mouth-watering. He went in through the kitchen door, leaving Virginia to follow behind, and across to the stove, whisking an oven cloth off a rack as he passed, and crouching to open the oven.

"They aren't burnt, are they?" she asked anxiously. Fragrant smoky smells issued out.

"No, just right."

He closed the oven door and stood up.

She said, "Did you make them?"

"Me? You must be joking."

"Who did?"

"Mrs. Thomas, my housekeeper . . . like a drink, would you?" He went to open a fridge, to take a can of beer from the inside of the door.

"No, thank you."

He smiled. "I haven't got any Coke."

"I don't want a drink."

As they spoke, Virginia looked about her, terrified that anything in this marvellous room should have been altered, that Eustace might have changed something, moved the furniture, painted the walls. But it was just she remembered. The scrubbed table pulled into the bay of the window, the geraniums on the window-sills, the dresser packed with bright china. After all these years it remained the epitome of everything a proper kitchen should be, the heart of the house.

When they had taken over Kirkton and were doing it up, cellar to attic, she had tried to get a kitchen like the Penfolda one. Somewhere comfortable and warm where the family would congregate, and drink tea and gossip round the scrubbed table.

"Who wants to go into a kitchen?" Anthony had asked, not understanding at all.

"Everybody. A farmhouse kitchen's like a living-room."

"Well, I'm not going to live in any kitchen, I'll tell you that."

And he ordered stainless steel fitments and bright Formica worktops and a black and white chequered floor that showed every mark and was the devil to keep clean.

Now Virginia leaned against the table and said with deep satisfaction, "I was afraid it would have changed, but it's just the same."

"Why should it have changed?"

"No reason. I was just afraid. Things do change. Eustace, Alice told me that your mother had died . . . I'm sorry."

"Yes. Two years ago. She had a fall. Got pneumonia." He chucked the empty can neatly into a trashbucket and turned to survey her, propping his length against the edge of the sink. "And how about your own mother?"

His voice held no expression; she could detect no undertones of sarcasm or dislike.

"She died, Eustace. She became very ill a couple of years after Anthony and I were married. It was dreadful, because she was ill for so long. And it was difficult, because she was in London and I was at Kirkton . . . I couldn't be with her all the time."

"And I suppose you were all the family she had?"

"Yes. That was part of the trouble. I used to visit her as often as I could, but in the end we had to bring her up to Scotland, and eventually she went into a nursing home in Relkirk, and she died there."

"That's bad."

"Yes. And she was so young. It's a funny thing when your mother dies. You never really grow up till that happens." She amended this. "At least, I suppose that's how some people feel. You were grown up long before then."

"I don't know about that," said Eustace. "But I know what you mean."

"Anyway, it was all over years ago. Don't let's talk about miserable things. Tell me about you, and Mrs. Thomas. Do you know, Alice

Lingard said you'd either have a domesticated mistress or a sexy house-keeper? I can't wait to meet her."

"Well, you'll have to. She's gone to Penzance to see her sister."

"Does she live at Penfolda?"

"She has the cottage at the other end of the house. This used to be three cottages, you know, in the old days, before my grandfather bought the place. Three families lived here and farmed a few acres. Probably had half a dozen cows for milking and sent their sons down the tin mines to keep the wolf from the door."

"Two days ago," said Virginia, "I drove out to Lanyon and sat on the hill, and there were combine harvesters out, and men haymaking. I thought one of them was probably you."

"Probably was."

She said, "I thought you'd be married."

"I'm not."

"I know. Alice Lingard said that you weren't."

After he had finished his beer, he took knives and forks from a drawer and began to lay the table but Virginia stopped him. "It's too nice indoors. Couldn't we eat the pasties in the garden?"

Eustace looked amazed, but said, "All right," and found her a basket for the knives and forks and plates and the salt and pepper and glasses, and he eased the piping hot pasties out of the oven on to a great flowered china dish, and they went out of a side door into the sunshine and the untidy little farmhouse garden. The grass needed cutting and the flower-beds were brimming with cheerful cottage flow-ers, and there was a washing line, flapping with bright white sheets and pillow-cases.

Eustace had no garden furniture so they sat on the grass, tall with daisies and plantains, with the dishes of their picnic spread about them.

The pasties were enormous, and Virginia had only eaten half of hers, and was defeated by the remainder, by the time that Eustace, propped on an elbow, had consumed the whole length of his.

She said. "I can't eat any more," and gave him the rest of hers, which he took and placidly demolished. He said, through a mouthful of pastry and potato: "If I weren't so hungry, I'd make you eat it, fatten you up a bit."

"I don't want to be fat."

"But you're much too thin. You were always small enough, but now you look as though a puff of wind would blow you away. And you've cut your hair. It used to be long, right down your back, flowing about in the wind." He put out a hand and circled her wrist with his thumb and forefinger. "There's nothing of you."

"Perhaps it was the 'flu."

"I thought you'd be enormous after all these years of eating porridge and herrings and haggis."

"You mean, that's what people eat in Scotland."

"It's what I've been told." He let go of her wrist and peacefully finished the pasty, and then began to collect the plates and the basket and carry everything indoors. Virginia made movements as though to help, but he told her to stay where she was, so she did this, lying back in the grass and staring at the straight grey roof on the barn, and the seagulls perched there, and the scudding shapes of small, white fine-weather clouds, blown from the sea across the incredibly blue sky.

Eustace returned, carrying cigarettes and green eating apples and a Thermos of tea. Virginia lay where she was, and he tossed her an apple and she caught it, and he sat beside her again, unscrewing the cap of the Thermos.

"Tell me about Scotland."

Virginia turned the apple, cool and smooth, in her hands.

"What shall I tell you?"

"What did your husband do?"

"How do you mean?"

"Didn't he have a job?"

"Not exactly. Not a nine-to-five job. But he'd been left this estate . . ."

"Kirkton?"

". . . Yes, Kirkton . . . by an uncle. A great big house and about a thousand acres of land, and after we'd got the house in order, that seemed to take up most of his time. He grew trees, and farmed in a rather gentlemanly way . . . I mean, he had a grieve—a bailiff you'd call him—who lived in the farmhouse. Mr. McGregor. It was he who really did most of the work, but Anthony was always occupied. I mean . . ." she finished feebly . . . "he seemed to be able to fill in his days."

Shooting five days a week in the season, fishing and playing golf. Driving north for the stalking, taking off for St. Moritz for a couple of months every winter. It was no good trying to explain a man like

37

Anthony Keile to a man like Eustace Philips. They belonged to different worlds.

"And what about Kirkton now?"

"I told you, the grieve looks after it."

"And the house?"

"It's empty. At least, the furniture's all there, but there's nobody living in it."

"Are you going back to this empty house?"

"I suppose so. Some time."

"What about the children?"

"They're in London, with Anthony's mother."

"Why aren't they with you?" asked Eustace, sounding not critical, merely curious, as though he simply wished to know.

"It just seemed a good idea, my coming away on my own. Alice Lingard wrote and asked me to come, and it seemed a good idea, that's all."

"Why didn't you bring the children too?"

"Oh, I don't know . . ." Even to herself her own voice sounded elaborately casual, unconvincing. "Alice doesn't have any children and her house isn't geared for them . . . I mean, everything's rather special and rare and breakable. You know how it is."

"In fact, I don't, but go on."

"Anyway, Lady Keile likes having them with her . . ."

"Lady Keile?"

"Anthony's mother. And Nanny likes going there because she used to work for Lady Keile. She was Anthony's own Nanny when he was a little boy."

"But I thought the children were quite big."

"Cara's eight and Nicholas is six."

"But why do they have to have a Nanny? Why can't you look after them?"

Over the years Virginia had asked herself that question time without number, and had come up with no sort of an answer, but for Eustace to voice it, unasked, out of the blue, filled her with a perverse resentment.

"What do you mean?"

"Just what I say."

"I do look after them. I mean, I see a lot of them . . ."

"If they've just lost their father, surely the one person they need

38

to be with is their mother, not a grandmother and an old inherited Nanny. They'll think everybody's deserting them."

"They won't think anything of the sort."

"If you're so sure, why are you getting so hot under the collar?"

"Because I don't like you interfering, airing your opinions about something you know nothing about."

"I know about you."

"What about me?"

"I know your infinite capacity for being pushed around."

"And who pushes me around?"

"I wouldn't know for sure." She realized with some astonishment that, in a cold way, he was becoming as angry as she. "But at a rough guess I would say your mother-in-law. Perhaps she took over where your own mother left off?"

"Don't you dare to speak about my mother like that."

"But it's true, isn't it?"

"No, it's not true."

"Then get your children down here. It's inhuman leaving them in London for the summer holidays, in weather like this, when they should be running wild by the sea and in the fields. Take your finger out, ring up your mother-in-law and tell her to put them on a train. And if Alice Lingard doesn't want them at Wheal House, because she's afraid of the ornaments getting broken, then take them to a pub, or rent a cottage . . ."

"That's exactly what I intend doing, and I didn't need you to tell me."

"Then you'd better start looking for one."

"I already have."

He was momentarily silenced, and she thought with satisfaction: That took the wind out of his sails.

But only momentarily. "Have you found anything?"

"I looked at one house this morning but it was impossible."

"Where?"

"Here. In Lanyon." He waited for her to tell him. "It was called Bosithick," she added ungraciously.

"Bosithick!" He appeared delighted. "But that's a marvellous house."

"It's a terrible house"

"Terrible?" He could not believe his ears. "You do mean the cot-

39

tage up the hill where Aubrey Crane used to live? The one that the Kernows inherited from his old aunt."

"That's the one, and it's creepy and quite impossible."

"What does creepy mean? Haunted?"

"I don't know. Just creepy."

"If it's haunted by the ghost of Aubrey Crane you might have quite an amusing time. My mother remembered him, said he was a dear man. And very fond of children," he added with what seemed to Virginia a classic example of a *non sequitur*.

"I don't care what sort of a man he was, I'm not going to take the house."

"Why not?"

"Because I'm not."

"Give me three good reasons . . ."

Virginia lost her patience. "Oh, for heaven's sake . . ." She made as if to get to her feet, but Eustace, with unexpected speed for such a large man, caught her wrist in his hand and pulled her back on to the grass. She looked angrily into his eyes and saw them cold as blue stones.

"Three good reasons," he said again.

She looked down at his hand on her arm. He made no effort to move it and she said, "There's no fridge."

"I'll lend you a meat-safe. Reason number two."

"I told you. It's got a spooky atmosphere. The children have never lived anywhere like that. They'd be frightened."

"Not unless they're as hen-brained as their mother. Now, number three."

Desperately she tried to think up some good, watertight reason, something that would convince Eustace of her nameless horror of the odd little house on the hill. But all she came out with was a string of petty excuses, each sounding more feeble than the last. "It's too small, and it's dirty, and where would I wash the children's things, and I don't even know it there's an iron for the ironing or a lawn-mower to cut the grass. And there's no garden, just a sort of washing green place, and inside all the furniture is so depressing and . . ."

He interrupted her. "These aren't reasons, Virginia, and you know they're not. They're just a lot of bloody excuses."

"Bloody excuses for *what*?"

"For not having a show-down with your mother-in-law or the old

Nanny or possibly both. For making a scene and asserting yourself and bringing your own children up the way you want them to go."

Fury at him caught in her throat, a great lump that rendered her speechless. She felt the blood surge to her cheeks, she began to tremble, but although he must have seen all this, he went calmly on, saying all the terrible things that the voice in the back of her head had been saying for years, but to which she had never had the moral courage to pay any attention.

"I don't think you can give a damn for your children. You don't want to be bothered with them. Someone else has always done the washing and the ironing and you're not going to start now. You're too bloody idle to take them for picnics and read them books and put them to bed. It's really nothing to do with Bosithick. Whatever house you found, you'd be sure to find something wrong with it. Any excuse would do provided you never have to admit to yourself that you can't be bloody bothered to take care of your own children."

Before the last word was out of his mouth, she was on her feet, tearing her arm free of his grip.

"It's not true! It's none of it true! I do want them! I've been wanting them ever since I got here . . . !"

"Then get them here, you little fool . . ." He was on his feet too, and they were shouting at each other across three feet of grass as though it were a desert.

"That's what I'm going to do. That's just exactly what I'm going to do."

"I'll believe that when you do it!"

She turned and fled and was into her car before she remembered her handbag, still lying on the kitchen table. By now in floods of tears, she was out of the car and running into the house to retrieve it before Eustace reached her again. Then back to the car and turning it furiously, dangerously in the narrow confines of the farmyard, then back up the lane, with a roar of the engine and a great spattering of loose gravel from the back wheels.

"Virginia!"

Through tears, through the driving-mirror she saw him standing far behind her. She jammed her foot on the accelerator and swung out on to the main road without bothering to wait and see if anything was coming. By good chance it wasn't, but she didn't slow down all the way back to Porthkerris, down into the town and up the other side, parking the car on the double yellow lines outside the solicitors' office and leaving it there while she ran inside.

This time she did not ring the bell, nor wait for Miss Leddra, but went, like the wind, through the outer office to fling open wide the door of Mr. Williams's room, where Mr. Williams was rudely interrupted in the course of interviewing an autocratic old lady from Truro about the seventh set of alterations to her will.

Both Mr. Williams and the old lady, silenced by astonishment, stared, open-mouthed. Mr. Williams, recovering first, began to scramble to his feet. "Mrs. Keile!" But before he could say another word Virginia had flung the keys of Bosithick on to his desk and said, "I'll take it. I'll take it right away. And as soon's I've got my children, I'm moving in!"

Chapter 4

ALICE SAID, "I'm sorry Virginia, but I think you're making the most terrible mistake. What's more, it's a classic mistake and one so many people make when they suddenly find themselves alone in the world. You're acting on impulse, you haven't really thought about this at all . . ."

"I have thought about it."

"But the children are fine, you know they are, settled and happy with Nanny and your mother-in-law. The life they're leading is simply an extension of life at Kirkton, all the things they know and that helps them to feel secure. Their father's dead, and nothing's ever going to be the same for them again. But if there have to be changes, at least let them happen slowly, gradually; let Cara and Nicholas have time to get used to them."

"They're my children."

"But you've never looked after them. You've never had them on your own, except the odd times when Nanny could be persuaded to take a holiday. They'll exhaust you, and honestly, Virginia, at the moment I don't think you're physically capable of doing it. After all, that's why you came here, to recuperate from that loathsome 'flu, and generally have a little peace and quiet, give yourself time to get over the bad things that have been happening. Don't deprive yourself of that. You're going to need all your resources when you do eventually go back to Kirkton and start picking up the threads and learning to live without Anthony."

"I'm not going to Kirkton. I'm going to Bosithick. I've already paid the first week's rent."

Alice's expression stopped being patient and became exasperated.

"But it's so ridiculous! Look, if you feel so strongly about having the children down here, then have them by all means, they can stay here, but for heaven's sake let Nanny come too."

Only yesterday the idea could have been tempting. But now Virginia never even let herself consider it.

"I've made up my mind."

"But why didn't you *tell* me? Why didn't you discuss it with me?"

"I don't know. It was just something I had to do on my own."

"And where *is* Bosithick?"

"It's on the Lanyon road . . . You can't see it from the road, but it's got a sort of tower . . ."

"The place where Aubrey Crane lived? But, Virginia, it's ghastly. There's nothing there but moor and wind and cliffs. You'll be totally isolated!"

Virginia tried to turn it into a joke. "You'll have to come and see me. Make sure the children and I aren't driving each other slowly insane."

But Alice did not laugh, and Virginia, seeing her frown and the disapproving set of her mouth, was suddenly, astonishingly reminded of her own mother. It was as though Alice was no longer Virginia's contemporary, her friend, but had swung back a generation and from that lofty height was telling the young Virginia that she was being a fool. But perhaps, after all, this was not so strange. She had known Rowena Parsons long before Virginia was born, and the fact that she had no children of her own to contend with meant that her attitudes and opinions remained rigidly unchanged.

She said at last, "It isn't that I want to interfere, you know that. But I've known you all your life, and I can't stand to one side and watch you do this insane thing."

"What's so insane about having your children on holiday with you?"

"It's not just that, Virginia, and you know it. If you take them away from Lady Keile and Nanny without their approval, which I doubt very much you'll get, there's going to be one devil of a row."

Virginia felt sick at the thought of it. "Yes, I know."

"Nanny will probably take the most terrible umbrage and give in her notice."

"I know . . ."

"Your mother-in-law will do everything she can to stop you."

"I know that too."

Alice stared at her, as though she were staring at a stranger. Then suddenly, she shrugged and laughed, in a hopeless sort of way. "I don't understand. What made you suddenly so determined?"

Virginia had said nothing about her encounter with Eustace Philips and had no intention of doing so.

"Nothing. Nothing in particular."

"It must be the sea air," said Alice. "Extraordinary what it does for people." She picked a fallen newspaper off the floor, began folding it meticulously. "When are you going to London?"

"Tomorrow."

"And Lady Keile?"

"I'll phone her tonight. And Alice, I am sorry. And thank you for being so kind."

"I haven't been kind, I've been critical and disapproving. But somehow, I always think of you as someone young and helpless. I feel responsible for you."

"I'm twenty-seven. And I'm not helpless. And I'm responsible for myself."

Nanny answered the telephone. "Yes?"

"Nanny?"

"Yes."

"It's Mrs. Keile."

"Oh, hallo! Do you want to speak to Lady Keile?"

"Is she there? . . ."

"Just a moment and I'll get her."

"Nanny."

"Yes."

"How are the children?"

"Oh, they're very well. Having a lovely time. Just gone to bed." (This was slipped in quickly in case Virginia should ask to speak to them.)

"Is it hot?"

Oh, yes. Lovely. Perfect weather. Hold on and I'll tell Lady Keile you're there."

There were the sounds of Nanny putting down the receiver, her footsteps going across the hall, her distant voice. "Lady Keile!"

Virginia waited. *If I was a woman who was taking to drink I would have one in my hand, right now. A great tall tumbler of dark-coloured whisky.* But she wasn't and her stomach lay heavy with impending doom.

More footsteps, sharp neat, unmistakable. The receiver was lifted once more.

"Virginia."

"Yes, it's me."

The situation was hideously complicated by the fact that Virginia had never known what to call her mother-in-law. "Call me Mother," she had said kindly, as soon as Virginia and Anthony were married, but somehow this was impossible. And "Lady Keile" was worse. Virginia had compromised by only corresponding by postcard or telegram, and always calling her "you."

"How nice to hear you, dear. How are you feeling?"

"I'm very well . . ."

"And the weather? I believe you're having a heatwave."

"Yes, it's unbelievable. Look . . ."

"How is Alice?"

"She's very well, too . . ."

"And the darling children, they've been swimming today—the Turners have got a delicious pool in their garden, and invited Cara and Nicholas over for the afternoon. What a pity they're in bed; why didn't you call earlier?"

Virginia said, "I've got something to tell you."

"Yes?"

She closed her hand around the receiver until her knuckles ached. "I've been able to find a little cottage, quite near here. It's near the sea, and I thought it would be nice for the children if they came down and we spent the rest of the holidays together."

She paused, waiting for comment but there was only silence.

"The thing is, the weather is so beautiful and I feel so guilty enjoying it all on my own . . . and it would be good for them to have some sea air before we all have to go back to Scotland and they have to go back to school."

Lady Keile said, "A cottage? But I thought you were staying with Alice Lingard?"

"Yes, I am. I have been. I'm calling from Wheal House now. But I've taken this cottage."

"I don't understand."

"I want the children to come down and spend the rest of the holidays with me. I'll come up tomorrow in the train to fetch them."

"But what sort of a cottage?"

"Just a cottage. A holiday cottage . . ."

"Well, if that's what you want . . ." Virginia began to breathe a sigh of relief. ". . . But it seems hard luck on Nanny. It's not often she gets the chance of being in London and seeing all her own friends." The relief swiftly died. Virginia went back into the attack again.

"Nanny doesn't have to come."

Lady Keile was confused. "I'm sorry, the line's not very clear. I thought you said Nanny didn't have to come."

"She doesn't. I can look after the children. There's not room for her anyway. I mean there isn't a bedroom for her, or a nursery . . . and it's terribly isolated, and she'd hate it."

"You mean you intend taking the children *away* from Nanny?"

"Yes."

"But she'll be most terribly upset."

"Yes, I'm afraid she will, but . . ."

"Virginia . . ." Lady Keile's voice was upset, distressed. "Virginia, we can't talk about this over the telephone."

Virginia imagined Nanny on the upstairs landing, listening to the one-sided conversation.

"We don't need to. I'm coming up to London tomorrow. I'll be with you about five o'clock. We can talk about it then."

"I think," said Lady Keile, "that that would be best."

And she rang off.

The next morning Virginia drove to Penzance, left her car in the station park and caught the train to London. It was another hot, cloudless morning and she had not had time to reserve a seat, and, despite the fact that she managed to get hold of a porter and tip him handsomely, he could only find her an empty corner in a carriage that was already uncomfortably full. Her fellow passengers were going home at the end of their annual holidays, grumpy and disconsolate at the thought of returning to work, and resentful at leaving the sea and the beaches on such a perfect day.

There was a family, a father and mother and two children. The baby slept damply in its mother's arms, but as the sun climbed higher into the unwinking sky and the train rattled northwards through the shimmering heat of a midsummer noon, the elder child became more and more fractious, whining, grizzling, never still, and grinding his dirty sandalled feet on to Virginia's every time he wanted to look out the window. At one point, in order to keep the child quiet, his father bought him an orangeade, but no sooner was the bottle opened than the train lurched and the entire contents went all over the front of Virginia's dress.

The child was promptly slapped by his distracted mother and roared. The baby woke up and added his wails to his brother's. The father said, "Now look what you've done," and gave the child a shake for good measure, and Virginia, trying to mop herself up with face tissues, protested that it didn't matter, it couldn't be helped, it didn't matter at all.

After a good deal of screaming the child subsided into hiccuping sobs. A bottle was produced from somewhere and stuffed into the baby's mouth. It sucked for a bit, and then stopped sucking, struggled into a sitting position and was sick.

And Virginia lit a cigarette and looked firmly out of the window and prayed, "Don't let Cara and Nicholas ever be like that. Don't let them ever be like that on a railway journey, otherwise I shall go stark, staring mad."

London was airless and stuffy, the great cavern of Paddington Station hideous with noise and aimless, hurrying crowds. As soon as she was off the train Virginia, carrying her suitcase, and filthy and crumpled in her stained, sticky dress, walked the length of the platform to the booking-office and, like a secret agent making sure of his escape route, bought tickets and reserved three seats on the Riviera for the following morning. Only then did she return to the taxi rank, wait in the long queue, and finally capture a cab to take her home.

"Thirty-two Melton Gardens, please. Kensington."

"OK. 'op in."

They went down by Sussex Gardens, across the park. The brown grass was littered with picnicking families, children in scanty clothes, couples entwined beneath the shade of trees. In Brompton Road there were window boxes bright with flowers, shop windows filled with clothes "For Cruising," the first of the rush hour crowds was being sucked, a steady stream of humanity, down Knightsbridge Underground.

The cab turned into the network of quiet squares that lay behind

Kensington High Street, edged down narrow roads lined with parked cars, and finally turned the corner into Melton Gardens.

"It's the house by the pillar box."

The taxi stopped. Virginia got out, put her case on the pavement, opened her bag for the fare. The driver said, "Thanks very much," and snapped up his flag, and Virginia picked up her case and turned towards the house and, as she did so, the black-painted door opened and her mother-in-law waited to let her in.

She was tall, slim, immensely good-looking. Even on this breathless day she looked cool and uncrushed, not a wrinkle in her linen dress, not a hair out of place.

Virginia went up the steps towards her.

"How clever of you to know I was here."

"I was looking out of the drawing-room window. I saw the taxi."

Her expression was friendly, smiling, but quite implacable, like the matron of a lunatic asylum come to admit a new patient. They kissed, touching cheeks.

"Did you have a terrible journey?" She closed the door behind them. The cool, pale-coloured hall smelt of beeswax and roses. At the far end steps led down to the glass side door, and beyond it could be seen the garden, the chestnut tree, the children's swing.

"Yes, it was ghastly. I feel filthy and a revolting child spilt orange juice all over me." The house was silent. "Where are the children?"

Lady Keile began to lead the way upstairs to the drawing-room. "They're out with Nanny. I thought perhaps it would be better. They won't be long, not more than half an hour. That should give us time to get this all thrashed out."

Treading behind her, Virginia said nothing. Lady Keile reached the top of the stairs, crossed the small landing and went in through the drawing-room door and Virginia followed her, and, despite her anxiety of mind, was struck, as always, by the timeless beauty of the room, the perfect proportions of the long windows which faced out over the street, open today, the fine net curtains stirring. There were long mirrors, filling the room with reflected light and these gave back images of highly polished antique furniture, tall cabinets of blue and white Meissen plates, and the flowers with which Lady Keile had always surrounded herself.

They faced each other across the pale, fitted carpet. Lady Keile said, "We may as well be comfortable," and lowered herself, straight as a ramrod, into a formal, wide-lapped French chair.

Virginia sat too, on the very edge of the sofa, and tried not to feel like a domestic servant being interviewed for a job. She said, "There really isn't anything to thrash out, you know."

"I thought I must have misunderstood you on the telephone last night."

"No, you didn't misunderstand me. I decided two days ago that I wanted the children with me. I decided it was ridiculous, me being in Cornwall and them in London, specially during the summer holidays. So I went to a solicitor and I found this little house. And I've paid the rent and I've got the keys. I can move in right away."

"Does Alice Lingard know about this?"

"Of course. And she offered to have the children at Wheal House, but by then I'd committed myself and couldn't go back."

"But Virginia, you *surely* can't mean that you want them without Nanny?"

"Yes, I do."

"But you'll never manage."

"I shall have to try."

"What you mean is that you want the children to yourself."

"Yes."

"Are you sure you aren't being a little . . . selfish?"

"*Selfish?*"

"Yes, selfish. You're not thinking of the children, are you? Only yourself."

"Perhaps I am thinking of myself, but I'm thinking of the children too."

"You can't be if you intend taking them away from Nanny."

"Have you spoken to her?"

"I had to, of course. She had to have some idea of what I understood you wanted to do. But I hoped I would be able to change your mind."

"What did she say?"

"She didn't say very much. But I could tell that she was very upset."

"Yes, I'm sure."

"You must think of Nanny, Virginia. Those children are her life. You must consider her."

"With the best will in the world I don't see that she comes into this."

"Of course she comes into it. She comes into everything that we do. Why, she's family, she's been part of the family for years, ever since Anthony was a tiny boy . . . and the way she's looked after those babies of yours, she's devoted herself, given her life to them. And you say she doesn't come into this."

"She wasn't my Nanny," said Virginia. "She didn't look after me when I was a little girl. You can't expect me to feel quite the same about her as you do."

"You really mean to say you feel no sort of loyalty towards her? After letting her bring up your children? After virtually living with her for eight years at Kirkton? I must say you fooled me. I always thought there was a very happy atmosphere between you."

"If there was a happy atmosphere it was because of me. It was because I gave in to Nanny over every little thing, just to keep the peace. Because if she didn't get her own way, she would go into a sulk that would last for days, and I simply couldn't bear it."

"I always imagined you were the mistress of your own home."

"Well, you were wrong. I wasn't. And even if I'd plucked up the courage to have a row with Nanny, and asked her to leave, Anthony would never have heard of it. He thought the sun rose and fell on her head."

At the mention of her son's name Lady Keile had gone a little pale. Her shoulders were consciously straight, her clasped hands tightened in her lap. She said, icily, "And I suppose now that no longer has to be considered."

Virginia was instantly repentant. "I didn't mean that. You know I didn't mean that. But I'm left now. I'm on my own. The children are all I have. Perhaps I'm being selfish, but I need them. I need them so badly with me. I've missed them so much since I've been away."

Outside, across the street, a car drew up, a man began to argue, a woman answered him in anger, her voice shrill with annoyance. As though the noise were more than she could stand, Lady Keile stood up and went over to close the window.

She said, "I shall miss them too."

If we had ever been close, thought Virginia, I could go now and put my arms around her and give her the comfort she is longing for.

But it was not possible. Affection had existed between them, and respect. But never love, never familiarity.

"Yes, I'm sure you will. You've been so wonderfully good to them, and to me. And I'm sorry."

Her mother-in-law turned from the window, brisk again, emotion controlled. "I think," she said, making for the bell-pull which hung at the side of the fireplace, "that it would be a good idea if we were to have a cup of tea."

The children returned at half past five. the front door opened and shut and their voices rose from the hall. Virginia laid down her tea-cup and sat quite still. Lady Keile waited until the footsteps had passed the landing outside the drawing-room door and were on their way upstairs to the nursery. Then she got up and went across the drawing-room and opened the door.

"Cara. Nicholas."

"Hallo, Granny."

"There is someone here to see you."

"Who?"

"A lovely surprise. Come and see."

Much later, after the children had gone upstairs for their bath and supper, after Virginia herself had bathed and changed into a clean cool silk dress, and before the gong rang for dinner, she went upstairs to the nursery to see Nanny.

She found her alone, tidying away the children's supper things and straightening the room before she settled to her nightly session with the television.

Not that the room needed straightening, but Nanny could not relax until every cushion was plump and straight on the sofa, every toy put away, and the children's dirty clothes discarded, and clean ones set out for the following morning. She had always been like this, revelling in the orderly pattern of her own rigid routine. And she had always looked the same, a neat spare woman, over sixty now, but with scarcely a trace of grey in her dark hair which she wore drawn back and fastened in a bun. She appeared to be ageless, the type that would continue, unchanging, until she was an old woman when she would suddenly become senile and die.

She looked up as Virginia came into the room, and then hastily away again.

"Hallo, Nanny."

"Good evening."

Her manner was frigid. Virginia shut the door and went to sit on the arm of the sofa. There was only one way to deal with Nanny in a mood and that was to jump right in off the deep end. "I'm sorry about this, Nanny."

"I don't know what you mean, I'm sure."

"I mean about my taking the children away. We're going back to Cornwall tomorrow morning. I've got seats on the train." Nanny folded the checked tablecloth, corner to corner into perfect squares. "Lady Keile said she'd spoken to you."

"She certainly mentioned something about some hare-brained scheme . . . but it was hard to believe that my ears weren't playing me tricks."

"Are you cross because I'm taking them, or because you're not coming too?"

"Who's cross? Nobody's cross, I'm sure . . ."

"Then you think it's a good idea?"

"No, that I do not. But what I think doesn't seem to matter any more, one way or the other."

She opened a drawer in the table and laid the cloth away, and shut the drawer with a little slam which instantly betrayed her scarcely-banked rage. But her face remained cool, her mouth primly set.

"You know that what you think matters. You've done so much for the children. You mustn't think I'm not grateful. But they're not babies any longer."

"And what is that meant to convey, if I might ask?"

"Just that I can look after them now."

Nanny turned from the table. For the first time, her eyes met Virginia's. And as they watched each other, Virginia saw the slow, angry flush spread up Nanny's neck, up her face, up to her hair line.

She said, "Are you giving me my notice?"

"No, that's not what I intended at all. But perhaps, now we've started to discuss it, it would be the best thing. For your sake as much as anyone else's. Perhaps it would be better for you."

"And why would it be better for me? All my life I've given to this family, why, I had Anthony to look after from the beginning, and there was no reason why I should come up to Scotland and take care of your babies, I never wanted to go, to leave London, but Lady Keile asked me, and because it was the family, I went, a real sacrifice I made, and this is all the thanks I get . . ."

"Nanny . . ." Virginia interrupted gently when Nanny paused for a breath ". . . It would be better for you because of this. For that very reason. Wouldn't it be better to make a clean break, and maybe have a new baby to take care of, a new little family? You know how you always said a nursery wasn't a nursery without a little baby, and Nicholas is six now . . ."

"I never thought I'd live to see the day . . ."

"And if you don't want to do that, then why not speak to Lady Keile? You could maybe make some arrangement with her. You get on so well together, and you like being in London, with all your friends . . ."

"I don't need you to give me any suggestions, thank you very much . . . given up the best years of my life . . . bringing up your children . . . never expected any thanks . . . never would have happened if poor Anthony . . . if Anthony had been alive . . ."

It went on and on, and Virginia sat and listened, letting the invective pour over her. She told herself that this was the least she could do. It was over, it was done, and she was free. Nothing else mattered. To wait, politely, for Nanny to finish was no more than a salute of respect, a tribute paid by the victor to the vanquished after a bloodthirsty but honourable battle.

Afterwards, she went to say good night to the children. Nicholas was already asleep, but Cara was still deep in her book. When her mother came into the room, she looked up slowly, dragging her eyes away from the printed page. Virginia sat on the edge of her bed.

"What are you reading now?"

Cara showed her. "It's *The Treasure Seekers.*"

"Oh, I remember that. Where did you find it?"

"In the nursery bookcase."

Carefully, she marked the place in her book with a cross-stitched marker she had made herself, closed it and put it down on her bedside table. "Have you been talking to Nanny?"

"Yes."

"She's been funny all day."

"Has she, Cara?"

"Is something wrong?"

It was hard to be so perceptive, so sensitive to atmosphere when you were only eight years old. Especially when you were shy and not very pretty and had to wear round steel spectacles that made you look like a little owl.

"No, nothing's wrong. Just different. And new."

"What do you mean?"

"Well, I'm going back to Cornwall tomorrow morning in the train, and I'm going to take you and Nicholas with me. Will you like that?"

"You mean . . ." Cara's face lit up. "We're going to stay with Aunt Alice?"

"No, we're going to stay in a house on our own. A funny little house called Bosithick. And we're going to have to do all the house-keeping ourselves and the cooking . . ."

"Isn't Nanny coming?"

"No. Nanny's staying here."

There was a long silence. Virginia said, "Do . . . you mind?"

"No, I don't mind. But I expect she will. That's why she's been so funny."

"It's not easy for Nanny. You and Nicholas have been her babies ever since you were born. But somehow I think you're growing out of Nanny now, like you grow out of coats and dresses . . . You're both old enough to look after yourselves."

"You mean, Nanny's not going to live with us any more?"

"No, she's not."

"Where will she live?"

"She'll maybe go and find another little new baby to take care of. Or she may stay here with Granny."

"She likes being in London," said Cara. "She told me so. She likes it much better than Scotland."

"Well, there you are!"

Cara considered this for a moment. Then she said, "When are we going to Cornwall?"

"I told you. Tomorrow on the train."

"When will we leave?" She liked everything cut and dried.

"About half past nine. We'll get a taxi to the station."

"And when are we going back to Kirkton?"

"I expect when the holidays are over. When you have to go back to school." Cara remained silent. It was impossible to tell what she was thinking. Virginia said, "It's time to go to sleep now . . . we've got a long day tomorrow," and she leaned forward and gently unhooked Cara's spectacles and kissed her good night.

But as she went towards the door, Cara spoke again.

"Mummy."

Virginia turned. "Yes."

"You came."

Virginia frowned, not understanding.

"You came," said Cara again. "I said to write to me, but you came instead."

Virginia remembered the letter from Cara, the catalyst that had started everything off. She smiled. "Yes," she said. "I came. It seemed better." And she went out of the room, and downstairs to endure the ordeal of a silent dinner in the company of Lady Keile.

Chapter 5

VIRGINIA AWOKE SLOWLY, to a quite unaccustomed mood of achievement. She felt purposeful and strong, two such alien sensations that it was worth lying for a little, quietly, to savour them. Pillowed in Lady Keile's incomparably comfortable spare bed, lapped in hem-stitched linen and cloudy blankets, she watched the early sunshine of another perfect summer morning seep in long strands of gold through the leafy branches of the chestnut tree. The bad things were over, the dreaded hurdles somehow cleared, and in a couple of hours she and the children would be on their way. She told herself that after last night she would never be afraid to tackle anything, no problem was insur-mountable, no problem too knotty. She let her imagination move cau-tiously forward to the weeks ahead, to the pitfalls of coping with Cara and Nicholas single-handed, the discomfort and inconvenience of the little house she had so recklessly rented for them, and still her good spirits remained undismayed. She had turned a corner. From now on everything was going to be different.

It was half past seven. She got up, revelling in the fine weather, the sound of bird-song, the pleasant, distant hum of traffic. She bathed and dressed and packed and stripped her bed and went downstairs.

Nanny and the children always had breakfast in the nursery and Lady Keile hers on a tray in her bedroom, but this was a perfectly ordered household and Virginia found that coffee had been set out for her on the dining-room hot-plate, and a single place laid at the head of the polished table.

She drank two cups of scalding black coffee and ate toast and marmalade. Then she took the key from the table to the hall and let herself out of the front door into the quiet morning streets and walked down to the small old-fashioned grocer's patronized by Lady Keile. There she laid in sufficient provisions to start them off when they eventually got back to Bosithick. Bread and butter and bacon and eggs and coffee and cocoa, and baked beans (which she knew Nicholas adored, but Nanny had never approved of) and tomato soup and chocolate biscuits. Milk and vegetables they would have to find when they got down there, meat and fish could come later. She paid for all this, and the grocer packed it for her in a stout cardboard carton and she walked back to Melton Gardens with her weighty load carried before her in both arms.

She found the children and Lady Keile downstairs; no sign of Nanny. But the small suitcases, doubtless perfectly packed, were lined up in the hall, and Virginia dumped the carton of groceries down beside them.

"Hallo, Mummy!"

"Hallo." She kissed them both. They were clean and tidy, ready for their journey, Cara in a blue cotton dress and Nicholas in shorts and a striped shirt, his dark hair lately flattened by a hairbrush. "What have you been doing?" he wanted to know.

"I've been buying some groceries. We probably won't have time to go shopping when we get to Penzance; it would be terrible if we didn't have anything to eat."

"I didn't know till this morning when Cara told me. I didn't know till I woke up that we were going in the train."

"I'm sorry. You were asleep last night when I came in to tell you and I didn't want to disturb you."

"I wish you had. I didn't know until *breakfast*." He was very resentful.

Smiling at him, Virginia looked up at her mother-in-law. Lady Keile was drawn and pale. Otherwise she looked, as always, perfectly groomed, quite in charge of the situation. Virginia wondered if she had slept at all.

"You should telephone for a taxi," said Lady Keile. "You don't want to risk missing the train. It's always best to be on the early side. There's a number by the telephone."

Wishing that she had thought of this herself Virginia went to do as she was told. The clock in the hall struck a quarter past nine. In ten minutes' time the taxi was there and they were ready to leave.

"But we have to say goodbye to Nanny!" said Cara.

Virginia said, "Yes, of course. Where is Nanny?"

"She's in the nursery." Cara started for the stairs, but Virginia said, "No."

Cara turned and stared, shocked by the unaccustomed tone of her mother's voice.

"But we *have* to say goodbye."

"Of course. Nanny will come down and see you off. I'll go up now and tell her we're just on our way. You get everything together."

She found Nanny determinedly occupied in some entirely unnecessary task.

"Nanny, we're just going."

"Oh, yes."

"The children want to say goodbye."

Silence.

Last night Virginia had been sorry for her, had, in a funny way, respected her. But now all she wanted to do was take Nanny by her shoulders and shake her till her stupid head fell off. "Nanny, this is ridiculous. You can't let it end this way. Come downstairs and say goodbye to them."

It was the first direct order she had ever given to Nanny. The first, she thought, and the last. Like Cara, Nanny was obviously shaken. For a moment she stalled, her mouth worked, she seemed to be trying to think up some excuse. Virginia caught her eye and held it. Nanny tried to stare her out, but was defeated, her eyes slid away. It was the final triumph.

"Very well, madam," said Nanny and followed Virginia back down to the hall, where the children rushed at her in the most gratifying way, hugged her and kissed her as though she were the only person in the world they loved, and then, with this demonstration of affection safely over, ran down the steps and across the pavement and into the waiting taxi.

"Goodbye," said Virginia to her mother-in-law. There was nothing more to be said. They kissed once more, leaning cheeks, kissing the air. "And goodbye, Nanny." But Nanny was already on her way up to the nursery again, fumbling for her handkerchief and blowing her nose. Only her legs were visible, treading upstairs, and the next moment she had reached the turn of the landing and disappeared.

She need have had no fear about her children's behaviour. The novelty of the train journey did not excite, but silenced them. They had not often been taken on holiday, and never to the seaside, and when they travelled to London to stay with their grandmother had been bundled into the night train already dressed in their pyjamas and had slept the journey away.

Now, they stared from the window at the racing countryside as though they had neither of them ever seen fields or farms or cows or towns before. After a little, when the charm of this wore off, Nicholas opened the present Virginia had bought for him at Paddington and smiled with satisfaction when he saw the little red tractor.

He said, "It's like the Kirkton one. Mr. McGregor had a Massey Fergusson just like this." He spun the wheels and made tractor noises in the back of his throat, running the toy up and down the prickly British Railway upholstery.

But Cara did not even open her comic. It lay folded on her lap, and she continued to stare out of the window, her bulging forehead leaning against the glass, her eyes intent behind her spectacles, missing nothing.

At half past twelve they went for lunch and this was another adventure, lurching down the corridor, rushing through the scary connections before the carriages came apart. The dining-car they found enthralling, the tables and the little lights, the indulgent waiter and the grown-upness of being handed a menu.

"And what would madam like?" the waiter asked, and Cara went pink with embarrassed giggles when she realized that he was speaking to her, and had to be helped to order tomato soup and fried fish, and to decide the world-shaking problem of whether she would eat a white ice-cream or a pink.

Watching their faces Virginia thought: Because it's new and exciting to them, it's new and exciting for me. The most trivial, ordinary occurrences will become special because I shall see them through Cara's eyes. And if Nicholas asks me questions that I can't answer, I shall have to go and look them up and I shall become informed and knowledgeable and a brilliant conversationalist.

The idea was funny. She laughed suddenly, and Cara stared and then laughed back, not knowing what the joke was, but delighted to be sharing it with her mother.

* * *

"When did you first come on this train down to Cornwall?" Cara asked.

"When I was seventeen. Ten years ago."

"Didn't you come when you were a little girl my age?"

"No, I didn't. I used to go to an aunt in Sussex."

Now, it was afternoon and they had the compartment to themselves. Nicholas, charmed by the adventure of the corridor, had elected to stay out there, and could be seen straddle-legged, trying to adjust his small weight to the rocking of the train.

"Tell me."

"What? About Sussex?"

"No. About coming to Cornwall."

"Well, we just came. My mother and I, to stay with Alice and Tom Lingard. I'd just left school, and Alice wrote to invite us, and my mother thought it would be nice to have a holiday."

"Was it a summer holiday?"

"No. It was Easter. Spring time. All the daffodils were out and the railway cuttings were thick with primroses."

"Was it hot?"

"Not really. But sunny, and much warmer than Scotland. In Scotland we never really have a proper spring, do we? One day it's winter and the next day all the leaves are out on the trees and it's summer time. At least that's the way it's always seemed to me. In Cornwall the spring is quite a long season . . . that's why they're able to grow all the lovely flowers and send them to Covent Garden to be sold."

"Did you swim?"

"No. The sea would have been icy."

"But in Aunt Alice's pool?"

"She didn't have a pool in those days."

"Will we swim in Aunt Alice's pool?"

"Sure to."

"Will we swim in the sea?"

"Yes, we'll find a lovely beach and swim there."

"I . . . I'm not very good at swimming."

"It's easier in the sea than in ordinary water. The salt helps you to float."

"But don't the waves splash into your face?"

"A little. But that's part of the fun."

61

Cara considered this. She did not like getting her face wet. Without her spectacles things became blurred and she couldn't swim with her spectacles on.

"What else did you do?"

"Oh, we used to go out in the car, and go shopping. And if it was warm we used to sit in the garden, and Alice used to have friends to tea, and people for dinner. And sometimes I used to go for walks. There are lovely walks there. Up to the hill behind the house, or down into Porthkerris. The streets are all steep and narrow, so narrow you could scarcely get a car down them. And there were lots of little stray cats, and the harbour, with fishing boats and old men sitting around enjoying the sunshine. And sometimes the tide was in and all the boats were bobbing about in the deep blue water, and sometimes it was out, and there'd be nothing but gold sand, and all the boats would be leaning on their sides."

"Didn't they fall over?"

"I don't think so."

"Why?"

"I haven't any idea," said Virginia.

There had been a special day, an April day of wind and sunshine. On that day the tide was high, Virginia could remember the salt smell of it, mixed with the evocative sea-going smells of tar and fresh paint.

Within the shelter of the quay the water swelled smooth and glassy, clear and deep. But beyond the harbour it was rough, the dark ocean flecked with white horses and, out across the bay, the great seas creamed against the rocks at the foot of the lighthouse, sending up spouts of white spray almost as high as the lighthouse itself.

It was a week since the night of the barbecue at Lanyon, and for once Virginia was on her own. Alice had driven to Penzance to attend some committee meeting, Tom Lingard was in Plymouth, Mrs. Jilkes, the cook, had her afternoon off and had departed, in a considerable hat to visit her cousin's wife, and Mrs. Parsons was keeping her weekly appointment with the hairdresser.

"You'll have to amuse yourself," she told Virginia over lunch.

"I'll be all right."

"What will you do?"

"I don't know. Something."

In the empty house, with the empty afternoon lying, like a gift, before her, she had considered a number of possibilities. But the marvellous day was too beautiful to be wasted, and she had gone out and started walking, and her feet had taken her down the narrow path that led to the cliffs, and then along the cliff path, and down to the white sickle of the beach. In the summer this would be crowded with coloured tents and ice-cream stalls and noisy holiday-makers with beach balls and umbrellas, but in April the visitors had not started to arrive, and the sand lay clean, washed by the winter storms, and her footsteps left a line of prints, neat and precise as little stitches.

At the far end, a lane leaned uphill and she was soon lost in a maze of narrow streets that wound between ancient, sun-bleached houses. She came upon flights of stone steps and unsuspected alleys and followed them down until all at once she turned a corner out at the very edge of the harbour. In a dazzle of sunshine she saw the bright-painted boats, the peacock-green water. Gulls screamed and wheeled overhead, their great wings like white sails against the blue, and everywhere there was activity and bustle, a regular spring-cleaning going on. Shop fronts were being white-washed, windows polished, ropes coiled, decks scrubbed, nets mended.

At the edge of the quay a hopeful vendor had set up his ice-cream barrow, shiny white, and lettered seductively "Fred Hoskings, Cornish Ice-cream, The Best Home-made" and Virginia suddenly longed for one, and wished she had brought some money. To sit in the sunshine on such a day and lick an ice-cream seemed, all at once, the height of luxury. The more she thought about it the more desirable it seemed, and she even went through all her pockets in the hope of finding some forgotten coin, but there was nothing there. Not so much as a half-penny.

She sat on a bollard and gazed disconsolately down on to the deck of a fishing boat where a young boy in a salt-stained smock was brewing up tea on a spirit lamp. She was trying not to think about the ice-cream when, like the answer to a prayer, a voice spoke from behind her.

"Hallo."

Virginia looked around over her shoulder, pushing her long dark hair out of her face, and saw him standing there, braced against the wind, with a package under his arm, and wearing a blue polo-necked sweater that made him look like a sailor.

She stood up. "Hallo."

"I thought it was you," said Eustace Philips, "but I couldn't be sure. What are you doing here?"

"Nothing. I mean, I just came for a walk, and I stopped to look at the boats."

"It's a lovely day."

"Yes."

His blue eyes gleamed, amused. "Where's Alice Lingard?"

"She's gone to Penzance . . . she's on a committee . . ."

"So you're all alone?"

"Yes." She was wearing worn blue sneakers, blue jeans and a white cable-stitch sweater, and felt miserably convinced that her naïvete was painfully obvious not only in her clothes but her lack of small-talk as well.

She looked at his package. "What are *you* doing here?"

"I came in to pick up a new rick cover. The wind last night blew the old one to ribbons."

"I expect you're going back now."

"Not immediately. How about you?"

"I'm not doing anything. Just exploring, I suppose."

"Don't you know the town?"

"I've never got this far before."

"Come along then, I'll show you the rest of it."

They began to walk back along the quay, in no hurry, their slow paces matched. He caught sight of the ice-cream barrow and stopped to talk.

"Hallo, Fred."

The ice-cream man, resplendent in a white starched coat like a cricket umpire, turned and saw him. A smile spread across features browned and wizened as a walnut.

" 'Allo, Eustace. 'Ow are you?"

"Fine. How's yourself?"

"Oh, keeping not too bad. Don't often see you down 'ere. 'Ow are things out at Lanyon?"

"All right. Working hard." Eustace ducked his head at the barrow. "You're early out. There's nobody here yet to buy ice-creams."

"Oh well, early bird catches the worm I always say."

Eustace looked at Virginia. "Do you want an ice-cream?"

She could not think of any person who had offered her, so instantly, exactly what she wanted most.

"I'd love one, but I haven't any money."

Eustace grinned. "The biggest you've got," he said to Fred, and reached his hand into the back pocket of his trousers.

He took her the length of the wharf, up cobbled streets at whose existence she had never even guessed, through small, surprising squares, where the houses had yellow doors and window-boxes, past little courtyards filled with washing-lines and flights of stone steps where the cats lay and sunned themselves and attended to their ablutions. They came out at last on to a northern beach which lay with its face to the wind, and the long combers rolled in jade green with the sun behind them, and the air was misted with blown spume.

"When I was a boy." Eustace told her, raising his voice above the wind, "I used to come here with a surf-board. A little wooden one my uncle made me, with a face painted on the curve. But now they have these Malibu surf-boards, made of fibreglass they are and they surf all year round, winter and summer."

"Isn't it cold?"

"They wear wet suits."

They came to a sea wall, curved against the wind with a wooden bench built into its angle and here Eustace, apparently deciding that they had walked far enough, settled himself, his back to the wall and his face to the sun and his long legs stretched in front of him.

Virginia, consuming the last of the mammoth ice-cream, sat beside him. He watched her, and when she had demolished the final mouthful and was wiping her fingers on the knees of her jeans he said, "Did you enjoy it?"

His face was serious but his eyes laughed at her. She didn't mind. "It was delicious. The best. You should have had one too."

"I'm too big and too old to go walking round the streets licking an ice-cream."

"I shall never be too big or too old."

"How old are you?"

"Seventeen, nearly eighteen."

"Have you left school?"

"Yes, last summer."

"What are you doing now?"

"Nothing."

"Are you going to University?"

She was flattered that he should imagine she was so clever. "Goodness, no."

"What are you going to do, then?"

Virginia wished that he had not asked.

"Well, eventually, I suppose, next winter I'll learn how to cook or do shorthand and typing or something gruesome like that. But you see my mother has this bee in her bonnet about being in London for the summer and going to all the parties and meeting all the right people and generally having a social whirl."

"I believe," said Eustace, "it's called 'Doing the Season.'"

His tone of voice made it very clear that he thought as little of the idea as she did.

"Oh, don't. It gives me the shivers."

"It's hard to believe, in this day and age, that anybody bothers any more."

"I know, it's fantastic. But they do. And my mother's one of them. She's already met some of the other mothers and had ghastly tea parties with them. She's even booked a date for a dance, but I'm going to try my hardest to talk her out of that one. Can you think of anything worse than having a coming-out dance?"

"No, I can't, but then I'm not a sweet seventeen-year-old." Virginia made a face at him. "If you feel so strongly about it why don't you dig in your toes, tell your mother you'd rather have the price of a return ticket to Australia or something?"

"I already have. At least I've tried. But you don't know my mother. She never listens to anything I say, she just says that it's so *important* to meet all the right people, and be asked to all the right parties and be seen at all the right places."

"You could try getting your father on your side."

"I haven't got a father. At least I never see him; they were divorced when I was a baby."

"I see." He added, without much heart: "Well, cheer up—who knows—you might enjoy it."

"I shall hate every moment of it."

"How do you know?"

"Because I'm useless at parties, and I get tongue-tied with strangers, and I can never think of anything to say to young men."

"You're thinking of plenty to say to me," Eustace pointed out.

"But you're different."

"How am I different?"

"Well, you're older. I mean you're not young." Eustace began to laugh and Virginia was embarrassed. "I mean you're not really young, like twenty-one or twenty-two." He was still laughing. She frowned. "How old *are* you?"

"Twenty-eight," he told her. "Twenty-nine next birthday."

"You are lucky. I wish I was twenty-eight."

"If you were," said Eustace, "you probably wouldn't be here now."

All at once it turned dark and cold. Virginia shivered, and looked up and saw that the sun had disappeared behind a large grey cloud, the vanguard of a bank of dirty weather which was blowing in from the west.

"That's it," said Eustace. "We've had the best of the day. It'll be raining by this evening." He looked at his watch. "It's nearly four o'clock, time I made for home. How are you getting back?"

"Walking, I suppose."

"Do you want a ride?"

"Have you got a car?"

"I've got a Land-Rover, parked round by the church."

"Won't I be taking you out of your way?"

"No. I can go back to Lanyon over the moor."

"Well, if you're certain . . ."

Driving back to Wheal House, Virginia fell silent. But it was a natural, companionable silence, comfortable as an old shoe, and had nothing to do with being shy or unable to think of anything to say. She could not remember when she had felt so at ease with a person—and certainly never with a man whom she had known such a short time. The Land-Rover was an old one, the seats worn and dusty and there were stray scraps of straw lying about the floor and a faint smell of farmyard manure. Virginia did not find this in the least offensive— rather, she liked it because it was part of Penfolda.

She realized that she wanted, above all things, to go back there. To see the farm and the fields in daylight, to inspect the stock and be shown around, perhaps to be allowed to see the rest of the farmhouse and be asked to tea in that enviable kitchen. To be accepted.

They came up the hill out of the town, where the houses of the old residential area had all been turned into hotels, with gardens bull-dozed into car parks, and glassed-in porches. There were sun-rooms and palm trees, dismal against the grey sky, and municipal flower-beds planted with straight rows of daffodils.

High above the sea, the road levelled out. Eustace changed into top gear and said, "When are you going back to London?"

"I don't know. In about a week."

"Do you want to come out to Penfolda again?"

This was the second time that day that he had offered her what she craved most. She wondered if he were psychic.

"Yes, I'd love to."

"My mother was very taken with you. Not often she sees a new face. It would be nice for her if you'd come and have a cup of tea with her."

"I'd like to come."

"How would you get out to Lanyon?" asked Eustace, his eyes on the road ahead.

"I could borrow Alice's car. I'm sure if I asked her she'd let me borrow it. I'd be very careful."

"Can you drive?"

"Of course. Otherwise I wouldn't borrow the car." She smiled at him. Not because it was meant to be a joke, but because all at once she felt so good.

"Well, I'll tell you," said Eustace in his deliberate way. "I'll have a word with my mother, find out which day suits her best, give you a ring on the telephone. How would that be?"

She imagined waiting for the call, having it come, hearing his voice over the wire. She almost hugged herself with pleasure.

"It would be all right."

"What's the number?"

"Porthkerris three two five."

"I'll remember that."

They had reached home. He turned into the white gates of Wheal House and roared up the drive between the hedges of escallonia.

"There you are!" He stopped with a great jerk of brakes and a splattering of gravel. "Home safely, just in time for tea."

"Thank you so much."

He leaned on the wheel, smiling at her. "That's all right."

"I mean, for everything. The ice-cream and everything."

"You're welcome." He reached across and opened the door for her. Virginia jumped down on to the gravel, and as she did so, the front door opened and Mrs. Parsons emerged, wearing a little suit of rasp-berry-red wool, and a white silk shirt, tied like a stock at the neck.

"Virginia!"

Virginia swung around. Her mother came across the gravel to-wards them, immaculate as always, but her hair, short and dark, blew casually in the wind and had obviously not been attended to that after-noon.

"Mother!"

"Where have you been?" The smile was friendly and interested.

"I thought you were at the hairdresser."

"The girl who usually does me is in bed with a cold. They offered me another girl of course, but, as she's the one who usually spends her days sweeping hair off the floor, I declined with thanks." Still smiling, she looked beyond Virginia to where Eustace waited. "And who is your friend?"

"Oh. It's Eustace Philips . . ."

But now Eustace had decided to get out of the car. He jumped down on to the gravel and came around the front of the Land-Rover to be introduced. And, hating herself, Virginia saw him through her mother's eyes; the wide powerful shoulders beneath the sailor's sweater, the sun-burned face, the strong, calloused hands.

Mrs. Parsons came forward graciously. "How do you do."

"Hallo," said Eustace, meeting her eye with an unblinking blue gaze. Her hand was half-way out to shake his, but Eustace either didn't see this or chose to ignore it. Mrs. Parsons's hand dropped back to her side. Her manner became, subtly, a fraction more cool.

"Where did Virginia meet *you*?" The question was harmless, even playful.

Eustace leaned against the Land-Rover and crossed his arms. "I live out at Lanyon; farm Penfolda . . ."

"Oh, of course, the barbecue. Yes, I heard all about it. And how nice that you met up again today."

"By chance," said Eustace, firmly.

"But that makes it even nicer!" She smiled. "We're just going to have tea, Mr. Philips. Won't you join us?"

Eustace shook his head. His eyes never left her face. "I've got seventy cows waiting to be milked. I'd better be getting back . . ."

"Oh, of course. I wouldn't want to keep you from your work."

Her tone was that of the lady of the house dismissing the gardener, but she continued to smile.

"I wouldn't let you," said Eustace, and went to get back into the car.

"Goodbye, Virginia."

"Oh. Goodbye," said Virginia faintly. "And thank you for bringing me home."

"I'll ring you up some time."

"Yes, do that."

He gave a final salute with his head, then started the engine, put the Land-Rover into gear, and without a backward glance, shot away, down the drive and out of sight, leaving Virginia and her mother standing, staring after him, in a cloud of dust.

"Well!" said Mrs. Parsons, laughing, but obviously nettled.

Virginia said nothing. There did not seem to be anything to say.

"What a very basic young man! I must say, staying down here, one does meet all types. What's he going to ring you up about?"

The tone of her voice implied that Eustace Philips was something of a joke, a joke that she and Virginia shared.

"He thought perhaps I might go out to Lanyon and have tea with his mother."

"Isn't that marvellous? Pure Cold Comfort Farm." It began, very lightly, to rain. Mrs. Parsons glanced at the lowering sky and shivered. "What are we doing, standing out here in the wind? Come along, tea's waiting . . ."

Virginia thought nothing of the shiver, but the next morning her mother complained of feeling unwell, she had a cold, she said, an upset stomach, she would stay indoors. As the weather was horrible nobody questioned this, and Alice laid and lit a cheerful fire in the drawing-room, and by this Mrs. Parsons reclined on the sofa, a light mohair rug over her knees.

"I shall be perfectly all right," she told Virginia, "and you and Alice must just go off and not bother about me at all."

"What do you mean, we must just go off? Where is there to go off to?"

"To Falmouth. To lunch at Pendrane." Virginia stared blankly. "Oh, darling, don't look so gormless, Mrs. Menheniot asked us ages ago. She wanted to show us the garden."

"Nobody ever told me," said Virginia, who did not want to go. It

70

would take all day to get to Falmouth and back again and have lunch and see the boring garden. She wanted to stay here and sit by the telephone and wait for Eustace to ring.

"Well, I'm telling you now. You'll have to change. You can't go out for lunch dressed in jeans. Why not wear that pretty blue shirt I bought for you? Or the tartan kilt? I'm sure Mrs. Menheniot would be amused by your kilt."

If she had been any other sort of a mother Virginia would have asked her to listen for the telephone, to take a message. But her mother did not like Eustace. She thought him ill-mannered and uncouth, and her smiling reference to Cold Comfort Farm had put the official stamp of disapproval upon him. Since his departure his name had not been mentioned, and although, during dinner last night, Virginia had tried more than once to tell Alice and Tom about her chance encounter, her mother had always firmly overridden the conversation, interrupting if necessary, and steering it into more suitable channels. While she changed, Virginia debated what to do.

Eventually, dressed in the kilt and a canary yellow sweater, with her dark hair brushed clean and shining, she went along to the kitchen to find Mrs. Jilkes. Mrs. Jilkes was a new friend. One wet afternoon she had taught Virginia to make scones, at the same time regaling her with a great deal of gratuitous information concerning the health and longevity of Mrs. Jilkes's numerous relations.

" 'Allo, Virginia."

She was rolling pastry. Virginia took a scrap and began, absently, to eat it.

"Now, don't go eating that! You'll fill yourself up, won't have no room for your lunch."

"I wish I didn't have to go. Mrs. Jilkes, if a phone call comes through for me, would you take a message?"

Mrs. Jilkes looked coy, rolling her eyes. "Expecting a phone call are you? Some young man, is it?"

Virginia blushed. "Well, all right, yes. But you will listen, won't you?"

"Don't you worry, my love. Now, there's Mrs. Lingard calling . . . time you was off. And I'll keep an eye on your mother, and give her a little lunch on a tray."

They did not return home until half past five. Alice went at once to the drawing-room, to inquire for Rowena Parsons's health, and to tell her all that they had done and seen. Virginia had made for the stairs, but the instant the drawing-room door was safely closed, turned and sprinted down the kitchen passage.

"Mrs. Jilkes!"

"Back again, are you?"

"Was there a phone call?"

"Yes, two or three, but your mother answered them."

"Mother?"

"Yes, she had the phone switched through to the drawing-room. You'll have to ask her if there are any messages."

Virginia went out of the kitchen, and back down the passage, across the hall and into the drawing-room. Across Alice Lingard's head, her eyes met and held her mother's cool gaze. Then Mrs. Parsons smiled.

"Darling! I've been hearing all about it. Was it fun?"

"It was all right." She waited, giving her mother the chance to tell her that the telephone call had come through.

"All right? No more? I believe Mrs. Menheniot's nephew was there?"

". . . Yes."

Already the image of the chinless young man was so blurred that she could scarcely remember his face. Perhaps Eustace would ring tomorrow. He couldn't have phoned today. Virginia knew her mother. Knew that, however much she disapproved, Mrs. Parsons would be meticulous about such social obligations as passing on telephone messages. Mothers were like that. They had to be. Because if they didn't live by the code of behaviour which they preached, then they lost all right to their children's trust. And without trust there could be no affection. And without affection, nothing.

The next day it rained. All morning, Virginia sat by the fire in the hall, pretending to read a book, and flying to answer the telephone each time it rang. It was never for her; it was never Eustace.

After lunch her mother asked her to go down to the chemist in Porthkerris to pick up a prescription. Virginia said she didn't want to go.

". . . It's pouring with rain."

"A little rain won't hurt you. Besides, the exercise will do you good. You've been sitting indoors all day, reading that silly book."

"It's not a silly book . . ."

"Well, anyway, reading. Put on some wellingtons and a raincoat and you won't even notice the rain . . ."

It was no good arguing. Virginia made a resigned face and went to find her raincoat. Trudging down the road towards the town, the pavements dark and grey between the dripping trees, she tried to face up to the unthinkable possibility that Eustace was never going to ring her.

He had said that he would, certainly, but it all seemed to depend on what his mother said, when she would be free, when Virginia would be able to borrow the car and drive herself out to Lanyon.

Perhaps Mrs. Philips had changed her mind. Perhaps she had said, "Oh Eustace, I haven't got time for tea parties . . . what were you thinking of, saying she could come out here?"

Perhaps, having met Virginia's mother, Eustace had changed his own mind about Virginia. They said that if you wanted to know what sort of a wife a girl was going to turn into, you looked at her mother. Perhaps Eustace had looked and decided that he did not like what he saw. She remembered the challenge in his unblinking blue eyes, and that final bitter exchange.

"I wouldn't want to keep you from your work."

"I wouldn't let you."

Perhaps he had forgotten to telephone. Perhaps he had had second thoughts. Or perhaps—and this was chilling—Virginia had misconstrued his friendliness, unburdened all her problems, and so aroused his sympathy. Perhaps that was all it was. That he was sorry for her.

But he said he would telephone. He said he would.

She collected the prescription and started home once more. It was still raining. Across the street from the chemist stood a call-box. It was empty. It would all be so simple. It wouldn't take a moment to look up his number, to dial. She had her purse in her pocket, with coins to pay for the call. *It's Virginia*, she would say, and make a joke of it, teasing him. *I thought you were going to ring me up!*

She almost crossed the road. At the edge of the pavement she hesitated, trying to pluck up the courage to take the initiative in a situation which was beyond her.

She imagined the conversation.

"Eustace?"

"Yes."

"This is Virginia."

73

"Virginia?"

"Virginia Parsons."

"Oh, yes. Virginia Parsons. What do you want?"

But at this point her courage turned on its heels and fled, and Virginia never crossed the road to the telephone box, but carried on up the hill with the rain in her face and her mother's pills deep in the pocket of her waterproof coat.

As she came in through the front door of Wheal House she heard the telephone ringing, but by the time she had got her wellingtons off the ringing had stopped, and by the time she burst into the drawing-room, her mother was just putting down the receiver.

She raised her eyebrows at her breathless daughter.

"Whatever's wrong?"

"I . . . I thought it might be for me."

"No. A wrong number. Did you get my pills, darling?"

"Yes," said Virginia dully.

"Sweet of you. And the walk has done you good. I can tell. Your cheeks are quite pink again."

The next day Mrs. Parsons announced out of the blue that they must return to London. Alice was astonished. "But, Rowena, I thought you were going to stay at least another week."

"Darling, we'd love to, but you know, we do have a very busy summer to put in, and a lot of arrangements and organization to be seen to. I don't think we can sit here enjoying ourselves for another week. Much as I would adore to."

"Well, anyway, stay over the week-end."

Yes, stay over the week-end, Virginia prayed. *Please, please, please stay over the week-end.*

But it wasn't any use. "Oh, adore to, but we must go . . . Friday at the latest I'm afraid. I'll have to see about booking seats on the train."

"Well, it seems a shame, but if you really mean it . . ."

"Yes, darling, I really do mean it."

Let him remember. Let him phone. There wouldn't be time to go out to Penfolda but at least I could say goodbye, I'd know that he'd meant it . . . perhaps I could say I'd write to him, perhaps I could give him my address.

"Darling, I wish you'd get on with your packing. Don't leave anything behind, it would be such a bore for poor Alice to have to parcel it up. Have you put your raincoat in?"

This evening. He'll ring this evening. He'll say, I am sorry but I've been away; I've been so busy I haven't had a moment; I've been ill.

"Virginia! Come and write your name in the visitors' book! There, under mine. Oh, Alice, my dear, what a wonderful holiday you've given us. Sheer delight. We've both adored it, haven't we, Virginia? Can't bear to go."

They went. Alice drove them to the station, saw them into their first-class carriage, the corner seats reserved, the porter being deferential because of Mrs. Parsons's expensive luggage.

"You'll come again soon," said Alice as Virginia leaned out of the window to kiss her.

"Yes."

"We've loved having you . . ."

It was the last chance. *Tell Eustace I had to go. Tell him goodbye for me.* The whistle shrilled, the train began to move. *Ring him up when you get back.*

"Goodbye, Virginia."

Send him my love. Tell him I love him.

By Truro her misery had become so obvious with sniffs and sobs and brimming tears that her mother could ignore them no longer.

"Oh, darling." She put down her newspaper. "Whatever is the matter?"

"Nothing . . ." Virginia stood at the window swollen-faced, unseeing.

"But it has to be something." She put out a hand and put it, gently, on Virginia's knee. "Was it that young man?"

"Which young man?"

"The young man in the Land-Rover, Eustace Philips? Did you break your heart over him?" Virginia, weeping, could make no reply. Her mother went on, reassuring, gentle. "I wouldn't be too unhappy. It's probably the first time you've been hurt by a man, but I assure you it won't be the last. They're selfish creatures, you know."

"Eustace wasn't like that."

"Wasn't he?"

"He was kind. He was the only man I've ever really liked." She blew her nose lustily and gazed at her mother. "You didn't like him, did you?"

Mrs. Parsons was momentarily taken aback by such unusual directness. "Well . . . let's say I've never been very fond of his type."

"You mean, you didn't like him being a farmer?"

"I never said that."

"No, but that's what you mean. You only like chinless weeds like Mrs. Menheniot's nephew."

"I never met Mrs. Menheniot's nephew."

"No. But you would have liked him."

Mrs. Parsons did not reply to this at once. But after a little she said, "Forget him, Virginia. Every girl has to have one unhappy love affair before she finally meets the right man and settles down and gets married. And this summer's going to be such fun for us both. It would be a pity to spoil it, yearning for something that probably never even existed."

"Yes," said Virginia and wiped her eyes and put her sodden handkerchief away in her pocket.

"That's a good girl. Now, no more tears." And, satisfied that she had poured oil on troubled waters, Mrs. Parsons sat back in her seat and picked up the newspaper again. But presently, disquieted, disturbed by something, she lowered the paper and saw that Virginia was watching her, unblinking, an expression in her dark eyes that her mother had never seen before.

"What is it?"

Virginia said, "He said he'd phone. He promised he'd telephone me."

"Well?"

"Did he? You didn't like him, I know. Did you take the call and never tell me?"

Her mother never hesitated. "Darling! What an accusation. Of course not. You surely didn't think . . . ?"

"No," said Virginia dully as the last flicker of hope died. "No, I never thought." And she turned to lean her forehead against the smeared glass of the train window, and the rocketing countryside, together with everything else that had happened, streamed away, for ever, into the past.

That was April. In May Virginia met up again with an old schoolfriend, who invited her down to the country for the week-end.

"It's my birthday, darling, too super, Mummy says I can ask anyone I like, you'll probably have to sleep in the attic, but you won't mind, will you? We're such a madly disorganized family."

Virginia, taking all this with a pinch of salt, accepted the invitation. "How do I get there?"

"Well, you *could* catch a train, and someone *could* meet you, but that's so dreadfully boring. I tell you what, my cousin's probably coming, he's got a car, he'll maybe give me a lift. I'll speak to him and see if he's got room for you. You'll probably have to squeeze in with the luggage or sit on the gear lever, but anything's better than fighting the crowds at Waterloo . . ."

Rather surprisingly, she duly arranged this. The car was a dark blue Mercedes coupé, and once Virginia's luggage had been crammed into the over-loaded boot, she was invited to squash herself into the front seat, between the girl-friend and the cousin. The cousin was tall and fair, with long legs and a grey suit and hair that curled in ducks' tails from beneath the brim of his forward-tilted brown trilby hat.

His name was Anthony Keile.

Chapter 6

TRAVEL-WORN AND TIRED, and with all the problems of Bosithick still to be faced, Virginia got out of the train at Penzance, took a lungful of cool sea air, and was thankful to be back. The tide was low, the air strong with the smell of seaweed. Across the bay, St. Michael's Mount stood gold in the evening sun, and the wet sands were streaked with blue, where small streams and shallow pools of sea-water gave back the colour of the sky.

Miraculously, here was a porter. As they followed him and his barrow out of the station Nicholas said, "Is this where we're going to stay?"

"No, we've got to drive over to Lanyon."

"How are we going to drive?"

"I told you, I left my car here."

"How do you know it hasn't been stolen?"

"Because I can see it, waiting for us."

It took some time to pack all their belongings into the boot of the Triumph. But in the end it was all piled in, crowned by the cardboard crate of groceries, and Virginia tipped the porter and they got in, all three of them in the front seat, with Cara in the middle, and the door on Nicholas's side firmly locked.

She had put down the hood and then tied a scarf around her head, but the wind blew Cara's hair forward all over her face.

"How long will it take us to get there?"

"Not long, about half an hour."

"What does the house look like?"

"Why don't you wait and see?"

At the top of the hill she stopped the car, and they looked back to see the view, the lovely curve of Mount's Bay, still and blue, enclosed in the warmth of the day that was over. And all about them were little fields, and ditches blue with wild scabious, and they went on and dropped into a miniature valley filled with ancient oak trees, and a stream ran beneath a bridge, and there was an old mill and a village, and then the road twined up on to the moor again, and all at once the straight bright horizon of the Atlantic lay before them, glittering to the westward in a dazzle of sun.

"I thought the sea was behind us," said Nicholas. "Is that another sea?"

"I suppose it is."

"Is that our sea? Is that the one we're going to use?"

"I expect so."

"Is there a beach?"

"I haven't had time to look. There are certainly a lot of steep cliffs."

"I want a beach. With sand. I want you to buy me a bucket and spade."

"All in good time," said Virginia. "How about taking things one at a time?"

"I want to buy a bucket and spade *tomorrow*."

They joined the main road and turned east, running parallel to the coast. They left Lanyon village behind them and the road which led to Penfolda, and they climbed the hill and came to the clump of leaning hawthorns which marked the turning to Bosithick.

"Here we are!"

"But there's no house."

"You'll see."

Bumped and jarred, the car and its occupants lurched down the lane. From beneath them came sinister banging sounds, the great gorse bushes closed in at either side, and Cara, anxious for their provisions, reached back a hand to hang on to the grocery carton. They swung around the last corner with a final lurch, ran up on to the grass bank at a frightening angle, and stopped with a jerk. Virginia put on the hand-brake, turned off the engine. And the children sat in the car and stared at the house.

In Penzance there had been no wind, the air was milky and breathlessly warm. Here, there was a faint whining, a coolness. The broken washing line stirred in the breeze and the long grass at the top of the stone hedge lay flattened like a fur coat, stroked by a hand.

And there was something else. Something was wrong. For a moment Virginia stared, trying to think what it was. And then Cara told her. "There's smoke in the chimney," said Cara.

Virginia shivered, a frisson of unease, like a trickle of cold water ran down her spine. It was as though they had caught the house unawares, they had not been expected by the nameless, unimagined beings who normally occupied it.

Cara felt her disquiet. "Is anything wrong?"

"No, of course not." She sounded more robust than she felt. "I was just surprised. Let's go and investigate."

They got out of the car, leaving the cases and groceries behind. Virginia manhandled the gate open and stood aside for the children to go through while she felt in her bag for the ring of keys.

They went ahead of her, Nicholas running, to investigate what lay around the far corner of the house, but Cara trod cautiously as though trespassing, avoiding an old rag, a broken flower-pot, her hands held fastidiously, anxious not to be asked to touch anything.

Together, they opened the front door. As it swung inwards Cara said, "Do you suppose it's Gipsies?"

"What's Gipsies?"

"Who've lit the fire."

"Let's look . . ." The smell of mice and damp had gone. Instead the house felt fresh and warm, and when they stepped into the living-room they found it bright with firelight. The whole aspect of the house was changed by this, it was sullen and depressing no longer . . . on the contrary, quite cheerful. The hideous electric fire had somehow been disposed of, and a tall rush basket stood by the hearth, piled with a good supply of logs.

What with the fire and the last of the afternoon sun filtering in through the west window, the room was very warm. Virginia went to open a window, and saw, through the open kitchen door, the bowl set on the table, piled with brown eggs, the white enamel milk pan. She went into the kitchen and stood in the middle of the floor and stared. Someone had been in and cleaned the place up, the sink was shining and the curtains laundered.

Cara stole in behind her, still cautious. "It's like fairies," she said.

"It's not fairies," said Virginia, smiling. "It's Alice."

"Aunt Alice Lingard?"

"Yes, isn't she a dear? She pretended to be so disapproving about us coming to Bosithick and then she goes and does a thing like this. But that's just like Alice. She's very kind. We'll have to go tomorrow and thank her. I'd ring up, only we haven't got a telephone."

"I hate the telephone anyway. And I want to go and see her. I want to see the swimming pool."

"If you take your bathing-suit you can have a swim."

Cara stood staring up at her mother. Virginia thought she was still thinking about swimming and was surprised when she said, "How did she get in?"

"Who?"

"Aunt Alice. We've got the keys."

"Oh. Well. I expect she got a spare key from Mr. Williams. Something like that. Now what are we going to do first?"

Nicholas appeared at the door. "I'm going to look all over the house and then I want some tea. I'm starving!"

"Take Cara with you."

"I want to stay with *you*."

"No." Virginia gave her a gentle push. "You go and tell me what you think of the rest of the house. Tell me if you don't think it the funniest house you've ever seen in your life. And I'll put the kettle on and we'll boil some eggs, and after that we'll bring all the stuff in from the car and see about unpacking and making the beds."

"Aren't the beds even made?"

"No, we've got to do it all. We're really on our own now."

Somehow, by the end of the evening they had managed to attain a semblance of order, but finding the switch for the hot-water tank and the cupboard where the sheets were kept, and trying to decide who was going to sleep in which bed, all took a very long time. For supper Nicholas wanted baked beans on toast, but they couldn't find a toaster and the grill on the cooker was fiercely temperamental, so he had baked beans on bread instead.

"We need washing-up stuff and a mop, and tea and coffee . . ." Virginia searched for a piece of paper and a pencil and started, frantically, to make a list.

Cara chimed in, ". . . And soap for the bathroom and stuff to clean the bath with, because it's got a *horrid* dirty mark."

"And a bucket and spade," said Nicholas.

"And we'll have to get a fridge," said Cara. "We haven't got anywhere to keep our food and it'll all grow a blue beard if we let it just lie about."

Virginia said, "Perhaps we could borrow a meat-safe," and then remembered who had offered to lend her one, and frowned down at her shopping list and hastily changed the subject.

When the little water tank finally heated up, they had baths in the gimcrack bathroom, Nicholas and Cara going in together, and then Virginia swiftly before the water went cold. In dressing-gowns, by fire-light, they made cocoa . . .

"There isn't even a television."

"Or a wireless."

"Or a clock," said Nicholas cheerfully.

Virginia smiled and looked at her watch. "If you really want to know, it's ten past nine."

"Ten past nine! We should be in bed ages ago."

"It doesn't matter," she told them.

"Doesn't *matter*? Nanny would be furious!"

Virginia leaned back in her chair, stretched out her legs and wriggled her bare toes at the heat of the fire.

"I know," she said.

After they were in bed, after she had kissed them, and left the door open on the landing and showed them how the light worked, she left them, and went down the narrow passage and up the two steps that led to the Tower Room.

It was cold. She sat by the window and looked out across the still, shadowed fields, and saw that the peaceful sea had turned pearly in the dusk, and the sky in the afterglow of sunset was streaked in long scarves of coral. Clouds were gathered in the west. They lay, piled beyond the horizon, threaded with shafts of gold and pink light, but gradually even these last shreds of light filtered away, and the clouds turned black, and in the east a little new moon, like an eyelash, floated up into the sky.

One by one lights started to twinkle out across the soft darkness, along the whole length of the coast, from farm-houses, and cottages and barns. Here, a window burned square and yellow. There a light bobbed across a rick yard. A pair of headlights tunnelled up a lane, and headed out on to the main road towards Lanyon, and Virginia wondered if it was Eustace Philips, making for Lanyon and The Mermaid's

Arms, and she wondered if he would come and see how they were getting along, or whether he would be taciturn and sulky and wait for Virginia to produce some sort of an olive branch. She told herself that it would be worth doing even this, if it were only for the satisfaction of seeing his face when he realized how well she and Cara and Nicholas were managing for themselves.

But next day it was different.

In the night the wind had got up, and the dark clouds which last evening had lain banked on the horizon, were blown inland, bringing with them a dark and drenching rain. The sound of gutters trickling and dripping, the rattle of raindrops against the glass of the window-pane were the sounds which woke Virginia up. Her bedroom was so gloomy that she had to turn on the lamp before she could read her watch. Eight o'clock.

She got of bed and went and shut the window. The floor-boards beneath her feet were quite wet. The rain curtained everything, and she could see no more than a few yards. It was like being in a ship, marooned in a sea of rain. She hoped the children would not wake up for hours.

She dressed in trousers and her thickest jersey and went downstairs and found that the rain had come down the chimney and effectively put out the fire, and the room felt damp and chilly. There were matches, but no firelighters; wood, but no kindling. She pulled on a raincoat and went out into the rain and across to the sagging garden shed, and found a hatchet, blunt with age and misuse. On the stone front doorstep, and at considerable personal danger to herself, she chopped a log into kindling, then took some paper which had been wrapped in with their groceries, and kindled a little fire. The sticks snapped and crackled, the smoke, after one or two surly billows into the room, ran sweetly up the chimney. She piled on logs and left the fire to burn.

Cara appeared when she was cooking breakfast.

"Mummy!"

"Hallo, my love." She bent to kiss her. Cara wore sky blue shorts, a yellow tee shirt, an inadequate little cardigan. "Are you warm enough?"

"No," said Cara. Her fine, straight hair was bunched into a slide, her spectacles were crooked. Virginia straightened them. "Go and put on some more clothes, then. Breakfast isn't ready yet."

"But there isn't anything else. In my suitcase, I mean. Nanny didn't pack anything else."

"I don't believe it!" They gazed at each other. "You mean no jeans or raincoats or gum-boots."

Cara shook her head. "I suppose she thought it was going to be hot."

"Yes, I suppose she did," said Virginia mildly, mentally cursing Nanny. "But you'd have thought she knew enough about packing to put a raincoat in."

"Well, we've sort of got raincoats, but not proper ones."

She looked so worried that Virginia smiled. "Don't worry."

"What shall we do?"

"We'll have to go and buy you both some clothes."

"Today?"

"Why not? We can't do anything else in weather like this."

"How about seeing Aunt Alice and swimming in her pool?"

"We'll keep that for a finer day. She won't mind. She'll understand."

They drove through the downpour to Penzance. At the top of the hill the mist was thick and grey, swirling in the wind, parting momentarily to allow a glimpse of the road ahead, and then closing in once more so that Virginia could scarcely see the end of the bonnet.

Penzance was awash with rain, traffic and disconsolate holiday-makers, prevented by the weather from their usual daily ploy of sitting on the promenade or the beach. They clogged the pavements, stood in shop doorways, aimlessly surged round the counters of shops, looking for something to buy. Behind the steamy windows of cafés and ice-cream shops they could be seen, packed in at little tables, slowly sipping, licking, munching; spinning it out, making it last, so that as to postpone the inevitable moment when they had to go out into the rain again.

Virginia drove around for ten minutes before she found a place to leave the car. In the rain they searched the choked streets until they came to a shop where fishermen's oilskins were for sale, and huge thigh-length rubber boots and lanterns and rope, and they went in and she bought jeans for Cara and Nicholas, and dark blue Guernseys, and black oilskins and sou'westers which obliterated the children like candle-snuffers. The children put on the new oilskins and the sou'westers, then and there, but the rest of the clothes were tied up in a brown paper parcel. Virginia took the parcel and paid the bill, and with the children, stiff as robots in their new coats, blinded by the brims of the hats, she went out into the street again.

It still poured. "Let's go home now," said Cara.

"Well, while we're here, we may as well get some fish or some meat or a chicken. And we haven't any potatoes or carrots or peas. There may be a supermarket."

"I want a bucket and spade," said Nicholas.

Virginia pretended not to hear. They found the supermarket, and joined the herd-like crowds, queuing and choosing, waiting and paying, packing the parcels into carriers, lugging them out of the shop.

The gutters gurgled, water streamed from drainpipes.

"Cara, can you really carry that?"

"Yes . . ." said Cara, dragged down to one side by the weight of the carrier.

"Give half of it to Nicholas."

"I want a bucket and spade," said Nicholas.

But Virginia had run out of money. She was about to tell him that he would have to wait until the next shopping expedition, but he turned up his face under the brim of the sou'wester, and his mouth was mutinous, but his eyes huge and beginning to brim with tears. "I want a bucket and spade."

"Well, we'll buy you one. But first I'll have to find a bank and cash a cheque and get more money."

The tears, as if by magic, vanished. "I saw a bank!"

They found the bank, filled with queuing customers.

The children made their way to a leather bench and sat, exhausted, like two little old people, their chins sunk into their chests, and their legs stuck out in front of them, regardless of whom they might trip up. Virginia waited in a queue, then produced her bank card and wrote her cheque.

"On holiday?" asked the young cashier. Virginia wondered how he could still be good-tempered at the end of such a morning.

"Yes."

"It'll clear up by tomorrow, you'll see."

"I hope so."

The red bucket and the blue spade was their final purchase. Laden, they walked the long way back to the car, and for some reason it was all uphill. Nicholas, banging the bucket with the spade as though it were a drum, trailed behind. More than once Virginia had to turn and wait for him, exhort him to get a move on. Finally, she lost her patience. "Oh, Nicholas, *do* hurry," and a passing woman heard the suppressed irritation in her voice, and glanced back, her face full of disapproval at such a disagreeable and short-tempered mother.

And that was after only one morning.

It still rained. They came at last to the car, and loaded the boot with parcels, and pulled off their dripping raincoats and stuffed them into the boot, and then scrambled into the car and slammed the door, thankful beyond words to be at last sitting down and out of the rain.

"Now," said Nicholas, still banging the bucket with the spade, "do you know what I want?"

Virginia looked at her watch. It was nearly one o'clock. "Something to eat?" she guessed.

What I would like would be to go back to Wheal House and know that Mrs. Jilkes had lunch ready and waiting, and there would be a cheerful fire in the drawing-room, and lots of new magazines and newspapers and nothing to do for the rest of the afternoon except read them.

"Yes, that. But something else as well."

"I don't know."

"You've got to guess. I'll give you three guesses."

"Well." She thought. "You want to go to the loo?"

"No. At least not yet."

"You want . . . a drink of water?"

"No."

"Give in."

"I want to go to a beach this afternoon and dig. With my new bucket and spade."

The young man in the bank proved to be quite correct in his weather forecast. That evening, the wind swung around to the north, and the shredded clouds were sent bowling away, over the moors. At first small patches of sky appeared, and then these grew larger and brighter and at last the evening sun broke through, to set, triumphantly, in a welter of glorious pinks and reds.

"Red Sky At Night, Shepherd's Delight," said Cara as they went to bed. "That means it's going to be a lovely day tomorrow."

It was.

"I want to go to the beach today and dig with my bucket and spade," said Nicholas.

"You will," Virginia told him firmly. "But first we have to go and see Aunt Alice Lingard, otherwise she'll think we're the rudest, most ungrateful people she's ever known."

"Why?" said Nicholas.

"Because she got the house all ready for us and we haven't even said thank you . . . finish up your egg, Nicholas, it's getting all cold."

"I wish I could have cornflakes."

"We'll buy cornflakes," said Virginia, and Cara got the pencil and the shopping list and they wrote Cornflakes underneath Steel Wool, Peanut Butter and Caster Sugar, Splits, Jellies, Soap Powder and Cheese. Virginia had never done so much shopping in her life.

She sent them off to play while she did the breakfast dishes and went upstairs to make the beds. The children's room was awash with clothes. Virginia had always imagined they were neat and tidy, but realized now that it had simply been Nanny, who moved along behind them, picking up and putting away everything that they dropped. She gathered up the clothes, not knowing if they were dirty or clean, took a sock from the top of the chest of drawers, and carefully did not touch a crumpled paper bag with two sticky sweets in the corner.

There was also a big pigskin folder of photographs. This belonged to Cara, and had been packed by Nanny, with what intention Virginia could only guess. One side of the folder was taken up with a selection of small photographs, many of which had been taken by Cara herself, and arranged with more affection than artistry. The front of the house, rather crooked; the dogs, the farm men on the tractor; an aerial view of Kirkton, and a picture postcard or two. On the other side was an impressive studio portrait of Anthony, a head and shoulders, all lighting and angles, so that his hair looked white blond, and his jaw very square and determined. The photographer's impression was of a strong man, but Virginia knew the narrowed eyes, and the weak, handsome mouth. And she saw the striped collar of the Turnbull and Asher shirt, the discreetly patterned silk of the Italian tie, and she remembered how clothes had mattered to Anthony; just as his car was important, and the furnishings of his house and his manner of living. Virginia had always imagined that these were subsidiary considerations, and took their shape from the character of the individual. But with Anthony Keile it was the other way round, and he had invariably given the highest priority to the smallest details, as though realizing that they were the props behind his image, and without them his inadequate personality would crumble.

Carrying the armful of clothes, she went downstairs and washed them in the tiny sink. When she took these outside to peg them crookedly on to the knotted clothes-line, she found only Nicholas, alone, playing with his red tractor and a few pebbles and bits of grass. He wore his new navy-blue Guernsey and was already scarlet in the face with heat, but Virginia knew better than to suggest that it might be a good idea if he took the sweater off.

"What are you playing?"

"Nothing much . . ."

"Is the grass straw?"

"Sort of."

Virginia pegged out the last pair of pants. "Where's Cara?"

"She's inside."

"Reading, I expect," said Virginia and went in to find her. But Cara was not reading; she was in the Tower Room, sitting by the window staring sightlessly out across the fields to the sea. When Virginia appeared at the door, she turned her head slowly, bemused, unrecognizing.

"Cara . . ."

Her eyes behind the spectacles came into focus. She smiled. "Hallo. Is it time to go . . . ?"

"I'm ready when you are." She sat beside Cara. "What are you doing? Thinking, or looking at the view."

"Both, really."

"What were you thinking about?"

"I was really wondering how long we were going to stay here . . ."

"Oh—I suppose about a month. I've taken it for a month."

"But we'll have to go back to Scotland, won't we? We'll have to go back to Kirkton."

"Yes, we'll have to go back. There's your school for one thing." She waited. "Don't you want to go?"

"Isn't Nanny coming with us?"

"I shouldn't think so."

"It'll be funny, won't it, Kirkton, without Daddy or Nanny? It's so big for just the three of us. I think that's why I like this house. It's just the right size."

"I thought perhaps you wouldn't like it."

"I love it. And I love this room. I've never seen a room like it, with the stairs going down in the middle of the floor and all the windows and the sky." She was obviously not bothered by spooky sensations. "Why isn't there any furniture, though?"

"I think it was built as a study, a workroom. There was a man who lived here, about fifty years ago. He wrote books and he was very famous."

"What did he look like?"

"I don't know. I suppose he had a beard, and perhaps he was rather untidy and forgot to do up his sock suspenders, and buttoned his suit all wrong. Writers are often very absent-minded."

"What was his name?"

"Aubrey Crane."

"I'm sure he was nice," said Cara, "to have made such a pretty room. You can just sit and see everything that happens."

"Yes," said Virginia, and together they gazed out at the patchwork fields, where peaceful cows grazed, and the grass was emerald green after the rain, and stone walls and leaning gate posts were tangled with brambles which, in just a month or two, would be sweet and heavy with black fruit. Away to the west a tractor hummed. She turned her head, pressing her forehead against the window and saw the patch of scarlet, bright as a pillar-box, and the man sitting up behind the wheel, wearing a shirt as blue as the sky.

"Who's that?" asked Cara.

"That's Eustace Philips."

"Do you know him?"

"Yes. He farms Penfolda."

"Are these all his fields?"

"I expect so."

"When did you know him?"

"A long time ago."

"Does he know you're here?"

"Yes, I think so."

"I expect he'll come for a drink or something."

Virginia smiled. "Yes, perhaps he will. Now come and comb your hair and get ready. We're going to see Alice Lingard."

"Shall I put in my bathing things? Can we swim in her pool?"

"That's a good idea."

"I wish we had a swimming pool."

"What, here? There wouldn't be room in the garden."

"No, not here. At Kirkton."

"Well, we could," said Virginia, without thinking. "If you really wanted one. But do let's go, otherwise it'll be lunchtime, and we shall have done nothing but sit here and talk."

But when they got to Wheal House, they found only Mrs. Jilkes at home. Virginia had rung the bell but only as a formality, immediately opening the door and stepping into the hall with the children at her heels. She waited for the dog to start barking, for Alice's voice to say "Who is it" and Alice to appear through the drawing-room door. But she was met only by silence, broken by the slow ticking of the grandfather clock which stood by the fireplace.

"Alice?"

Somewhere a door opened and shut. And then Mrs. Jilkes came up the kitchen passage, like a ship in full sail with her starched white apron. "Who is it?" She sounded quite cross until she saw Virginia standing there with the children beside her.

Then she smiled. "Oh, Mrs. Keile, you did surprise me, I couldn't think who you were, standing there. And these are your children. My, aren't they lovely? Aren't you lovely?" she inquired conversationally of Cara, who had never been asked such a question before. She wondered if she would say "no" because she knew that she wasn't lovely, but she was too shy to say anything. She simply stared at Mrs. Jilkes.

"Cara, isn't it? And Nicholas. Brought your swimming things, too, I can see. Going to go and have a dip in the pond?" She turned back to Virginia. "Mrs. Lingard's not here."

"Oh dear."

"Been away she has, ever since you went. Mr. Lingard had to go to some big dinner in London, so Mrs. Lingard suddenly decided she'd go too. Said she hadn't been up for a bit. She'll be home this evening, though."

Virginia worked this out. "You mean, she's been away since Thursday?"

"Thursday afternoon she went."

"But . . . Bosithick . . . A fire had been lighted when we got there, and it was all clean and there were eggs and milk waiting for us . . . I thought it was Mrs. Lingard."

Mrs. Jilkes looked coy.

"No. But I'll tell you who it was, though."

"Who was it?"

"It was Eustace Philips."

"*Eustace?*"

"Well, don't sound so shocked, it's not as though he's done anything wrong."

"But how do you know it was Eustace?"

"Because he telephoned me," Mrs. Jilkes said, importantly. "Least, he telephoned Mrs. Lingard, but her being in London I spoke to him instead. And he said was anybody doing anything about you coming back to Bosithick with those children, and I said I didn't know, and told him Mrs. Lingard was away, and he said, 'Well, never mind, I'll look after it,' and that was it. Make a good job, did he?"

"You mean he came in and did all that *house-cleaning*?"

"Oh no. Eustace wouldn't know one end of a duster from the other. That would have been Mrs. Thomas. She'd scrub the flags off the floor if you'd give her half a chance."

Cara put her hand into Virginia's. "Is that the man on the tractor we saw this morning?"

"Yes," said Virginia, distracted.

"But won't he think we're terribly rude? We haven't said thank you."

"No, I know. We'll have to go this afternoon. When we get back, we'll go down to Penfolda and explain."

Nicholas was furious. "But you said I could dig on the beach with my bucket and spade!"

Mrs. Jilkes knew a rebellious voice when she heard one. She stooped towards Nicholas, hands on her knees, her face close to his, her voice seductive.

"Why don't you go and have a lovely swim? And when you come out you and your Mummy and your sister can come and eat shepherd's pie, in the kitchen with Mrs. Jilkes . . ."

"Oh, but Mrs. Jilkes . . ."

"*No.*" Mrs. Jilkes shook her head at Virginia's interruption. "It's no trouble. All waiting to be eaten it is. And I was just beginning to think that the house was somehow empty, and me rattling around in it like a pea in a drum." She beamed at Cara. "You'd like to do that, wouldn't you, my lovely?"

She was so kind that Cara's icy shyness thawed. She said, "Yes, please."

That warm Sunday afternoon they walked across the fields to Penfolda, across the stubble fields where, only a week ago, Virginia had watched the harvesters at work; across the grassy meadows, going from field to field by stiles made of granite steps laid across the open ditches. As they approached the farm, they saw the dutch barns, the gates, the concrete cattle court, the milking parlours. Cautiously opening and shutting the gates behind them they crossed the court and came out in the old cobbled farmyard. There was the sound of scrubbing, wet bristles on stone, and Virginia went to an open door of what looked like stables, with loose boxes, and found a man, who was not Eustace, cleaning the place out. He wore a faded navy-blue beret on the back of his curly grey head, and old-fashioned dungarees with braces.

He saw her and stopped sweeping. Virginia said, "I'm sorry, I'm looking for Mr. Philips . . ."

" 'E's around somewhere . . . up at the back of the house . . ."

"We'll see if we can find him."

They went through a gate, and along a path that led between the farmhouse and the tangled little garden where she and Eustace had shared the pasty. A tabby cat sat on the doorstep in a warm patch of sun. Cara squatted to pet it and Virginia knocked on the door. There were footsteps and the door opened, and a little round woman stood there, cosy as an arm-chair, upholstered in a black dress and loose-covered with a print apron. From behind her, from the kitchen, came a good smell, the memory of a hearty Sunday dinner.

"Yes?"

"I'm Virginia Keile . . . from Bosithick . . ."

"Oh *yes* . . ."

A smile creased the rosy face, pushing up her cheeks into two little bunches.

"You must be Mrs. Thomas."

"That's right . . . and these your children, are they?"

"Yes. Cara and Nicholas. We feel so bad because we never came down to thank you. For cleaning the house I mean, and leaving the eggs and the milk and the firewood and everything."

"Oh, that wasn't me. I just cleaned the place up a bit, opened a few windows. It was Eustace who got the logs there, took up a load on the back of the tractor . . . left the milk and the eggs at the same time. We thought you wouldn't have had time to do much before you went to London . . . dismal it is coming home to a dirty house; couldn't let you do that."

"We'd have come before, but we thought it was Mrs. Lingard . . ."

"Want to see Eustace, do you? He's up in the vegetable garden at the back, digging me a bucket of potatoes." She smiled down at Cara. "Do you like the little pussy cat?"

"Yes, she's sweet."

"She's got kittens in the barn. Do you want to go and see them?"

"Will she mind?"

"She won't mind. Come along, Mrs. Thomas will show you where to find them."

She made for the barn, with the children at her heels; not a backward glance did they spare for their mother, so intent were they on seeing the kittens. Left alone, Virginia went up on the garden path, through a wicket gate, arched in ivy. Eustace's blue shirt could be glimpsed beyond the pea-vines, and she made her way towards this and found him forking up a drill of potatoes. Round and white and smooth as sea pebbles, they were, caked in earth the same colour and consistency as rich, dark chocolate cake.

"Eustace."

He looked over his shoulder and saw her. She waited for him to smile, but he did not. She wondered if he had taken offence. He straightened up, leaning on the handle of the spade.

"Hallo," he said, as though it were a surprise to see her there.

"I've come to say thank you. And I'm sorry."

He shifted the spade from one hand to another. "What have you got to be sorry for?"

"I didn't realize it was you who'd brought the wood and lit the fire and everything. I thought it was Alice Lingard. That's why we haven't been down before."

"Oh, that," said Eustace and she wondered if there was something else she should be sorry about.

"It was terribly kind. The milk and the eggs and everything. It just made all the difference." She stopped, terrified of sounding insincere. "But how did you get into the house?"

Eustace drove the prongs of the fork into the ground, and started towards her. "There's a key here. When my mother was first married, she used to go over sometimes, do a bit of work for old Mr. Crane. His wife was ailing, my mother used to clean the place up. He gave her a key to hang on the dresser and it's been there ever since."

He reached her side, and stood, looking down at her, then he suddenly smiled, his blue eyes crinkled with amusement and she knew that her fears were unjustified, and that he bore no grudge. He said, "So you decided to take the house after all."

Ruefully, Virginia said, "Yes."

"I felt badly, saying those things, and you so upset about everything. I lost my temper, but I shouldn't have."

"You were right. It was all I needed to make me make up my own mind."

"That's why I brought up the logs and stuff . . . I thought it was the least I could do. You'll be wanting more milk . . ."

"Could you let us have it every day?"

"If someone comes and fetches it."

"I could, or one of the children. I hadn't realized, but over the fields and the stiles it's no distance at all."

They had begun to walk back towards the gate.

"Are your children here?"

"They've gone with Mrs. Thomas to see some kittens."

Eustace laughed. "They'll fall in love with them, so be warned. That little tabby got caught by a Siamese up the road, and you've never seen such pretty kittens." He opened the gate for Virginia to go through. "Blue eyes they've got and . . ."

He stopped, watching over her head as Cara and Nicholas came, slowly, carefully, out of the barn, their cupped hands held cradled to their chests, their heads bent in adoration. "What did I tell you?" said Eustace and shut the gate behind them.

The children came up the slope of the lawn, ankle deep, knee deep, in plantains and great white daisies. And all at once Virginia saw them with fresh eyes, with Eustace's eyes, as though she were seeing them for the first time. The fair head and the dark, the blue eyes and the brown. And the sun blinked on to Cara's spectacles so that they flashed like the headlights of a little car, and their new jeans, bought too big, slipped down over their hips and Nicholas's shirt-tail hung out over his firm, round little bottom.

A love-like pain caught at Virginia's throat, unshed tears prickled at the back of her eyes. They were so defenceless, so vulnerable, and for some reason it mattered so much that they should make a good impression on Eustace.

Nicholas caught sight of her. "Look what we've got, Mummy; Mrs. Thomas said that we could bring them out."

"Yes," said Cara, "and they're tiny and they've got their eyes . . ." She saw Eustace, behind her mother, and stopped dead, where she was standing, her face closed up, her eyes watching him from behind her glasses.

But Nicholas came on . . . "Look, Mummy you've got to look. It's all furry and it's got tiny claws. But I don't know if it's a boy or girl. Mrs. Thomas says she can't tell." He looked up and saw Eustace and smiled engagingly into his face. "They've stopped sucking their mother, Mrs. Thomas says, she was getting too thin, and she's put a little saucer of milk out for them, and they lap and their tongues are tiny," he told Eustace.

Eustace put out a long brown finger and scratched the top of the kitten's head. Virginia said, "Nicholas, this is Mr. Philips, you're meant to say how do you do."

"How do you do. Mrs. Thomas said that if we wanted one we could have one but we had to ask you, but you wouldn't mind, would you, Mummy? It's so little and it could sleep on my bed and I'd look after it."

Virginia found herself coming out with all the classic arguments produced by the parents of children, in the same situation as herself. *Too young to be taken from its mother yet. Still needs her to keep him warm. Only at Bosithick for the holidays, and think how he'd hate the train journey back to Scotland.*

Eustace had put down the bucket of potatoes and now went over to where Cara stood, clutching her kitten. Virginia, in agony for her, saw Eustace squat to Cara's height, loosen her fingers gently with his own. "You don't want to hold him too tight, otherwise he won't be able to breathe."

"I'm frightened of dropping him."

"You won't drop him. He wants to look out and see what's happening in the world. He's never seen sun as bright as that." He smiled at the kitten, at Cara. After a little, slowly, she smiled back, and you forgot the ugly spectacles and the bumpy forehead and the straight hair, and saw only the marvellous sweetness of her expression.

After a little he sent them to put the kittens back, and, telling

Virginia to stay outside in the sunshine, went into the house with the potatoes for Mrs. Thomas, only to emerge a moment or so later with a packet of cigarettes and a bar of chocolate. They lay where they had lain before, in the long grass, and were joined there by the children.

He gave them the chocolate but talked to them like adults. What have you been doing? What did you do yesterday in all that rain? Have you been swimming yet?

They told him, voices chiming against each other, Cara, her shyness over, as eager to impart information as Nicholas.

"We bought raincoats, and we got *drenched*. And Mummy had to go to the bank to get more money, and Nicholas got a bucket and spade."

"But I haven't been to the beach to dig yet!"

"And we swam this morning at Mrs. Lingard's. We swam in her pool. But we haven't swum in the sea yet."

Eustace raised his eyebrows. "You haven't swum in the sea and you haven't been to a beach? That's all wrong!"

"Mummy says there hasn't been time . . ."

"But she promised me," Nicholas reminded of his grievance, became indignant. "She said today I could dig with the spade, but I've not been near one grain of sand."

Virginia began to laugh at him, and he became, naturally, angrier than ever. "Well, it's true, and it's what I want more than anything."

"Well," said Eustace, "if you want it more than anything, what are we doing sitting around here talking our heads off?"

Nicholas stared at Eustace, his eyes narrowed suspiciously. "You mean go to the beach?"

"Why not?"

"Now?" Nicholas could not believe his ears.

"Is there anything else you'd rather do?"

"No. Nothing. Nothing else." He sprang to his feet. "Where shall we go? Shall we go to Porthkerris?"

"No, we don't want to go there—nasty crowded place. We'll go to our own private beach, the one that nobody knows about, that belongs to Penfolda and Bosithick."

Virginia was astonished. "I didn't know we had one. I thought there was nothing but cliffs."

By now Eustace was also on his feet. "I'll show you . . . come along, we'll take the Land-Rover."

"My bucket and spade's at our house."

"We'll pick them up on the way."

"And our swimming things," said Cara.

"Those too."

He went into the house to fetch his own things, shouted a message to Mrs. Thomas, led the way through the gate and back across the farmyard. He whistled and the dogs, barking, came rushing around the side of the barn, knowing that the whistle meant a walk, smells, rabbits, maybe a swim. Everybody, including the dogs, clambered into the Land-Rover, and Cara, her shyness now quite forgotten, screamed with delight, as they lurched out of the cobbled farmyard, and went bumping and bouncing up the lane towards the main road.

"Is it far?" she asked Eustace.

"No distance at all."

"What's the beach called?"

"Jack Carley's cove. And it's not a place for babies, only for big children who can look after themselves and climb down the cliff."

They assured him hastily that they came into this category and Virginia watched Nicholas's face, and saw the joyful satisfaction upon it at being indulged, at last, in the one thing he had been wanting to do for a whole day. And what was more, doing it instantly. Not told maybe, or tomorrow, or to wait or to be patient. And she knew exactly how he felt for long ago Eustace had done the very same, performed the same miracle for the young Virginia; had bought her the ice-cream she had been yearning for, and then, out of the blue, asked her to come back to Penfolda.

Chapter 7

THEY LEFT the Land-Rover in the deserted farmyard below Bosithick and started to walk down towards the sea. At first, crossing the fields, they went in a bunch, four abreast, Eustace taking Nicholas by the hand because he was inclined to lag. But then the fields gave way to brambles and bracken and they fell into single file with Eustace leading the way; over crumbling stone walls and across a stream, where rushes grew shoulder high to a small person. Then over another wall, and the path disappeared beneath a jungle of green bracken. Through this they pushed their way, gorse bushes pressing in at either side. The ground all at once slid steeply away from beneath their feet, and the path zig-zagged down through the undergrowth, down to the very lip of the curving cliff. And beyond, space. Blue air. Soaring, screaming gulls, and the distant creaming of the sea.

At this point the coast seemed to fling itself out into a jagged headland, composed of great granite outcrops. Between these the turf was smooth and very green, stained with patches of purple-belled heather, and the path wound down between these outcrops and as they followed its convolutions, a little cove, sheltered and enclosed, gradually revealed itself, far below. The sea was deep and still, purple over the rocks and jade green over the sand. The beach was tiny, and backed by the remains of an old sea wall. Beyond this the land sloped up to the green wedge of the cliff, down which trickled, in a series of small waterfalls, a fresh-water stream. And above the sea wall, tucked snug against the foot of the cliff, stood the remains of a cottage; derelict, windows broken, slates torn from the roof.

They stood in a row, the four of them, buffeted by the gentle wind, looking down. It was a disturbing sensation. Virginia wondered if the children might suffer from vertigo, but neither of them seemed in the least disturbed by the dizzy emptiness of the great height.

"There's a house," said Cara.

"That was where Jack Carley lived."

"Where does he live now?"

"With the angels, I reckon."

"Did you know him?"

"Yes, I knew him. He was an old man when I was a boy. Didn't like people coming down here. Not any old people. Had a great barking dog and he used to chase them away."

"But he let you come?"

"Oh, yes, he let me come." He grinned down at Nicholas. "Do you want me to carry you, or can you manage?"

Nicholas peered out and over. The path trickled down the face of the cliff and so out of sight. Nicholas remained undismayed.

"No. I don't want to be carried, thank you. But I'd like it better if you went first."

In fact, the dogs went first, unafraid, sure-footed as goats. The humans followed at a more prudent speed, but Virginia found that the path was not as dangerous as it appeared. After the dry spell the ground was hard and firm underfoot, and in steep places, steps had been cut, shored up with driftwood or fashioned roughly out of cement.

Much sooner than she had expected they were all safely down. Above them, the cliff loomed, dark and cold in the shadow, but when they jumped down on to the beach they came out of the shade and into the sunshine, and the sand was warm, and there was the smell of tar from the little house, and no sound but the gulls and the creaming sea, and the splash of the stream.

There was an air of unreality about the little cove, as though they had somehow strayed out of time and space. The air was still, the sun burning hot, the sand white and the green water clear as glass. The children stripped off their clothes, and took Nicholas's new bucket and spade and went at once to the water's edge, where they began to dig a sand castle, moated and turreted with bucket-shaped towers.

"If the tide comes in it'll wash the whole castle away," said Cara.

"No, it won't, because we're going to make a great huge moat and then the water will go into that."

"If the tide comes in higher than the castle, it's going to wash it away. Like King Canute."

Nicholas considered this. "Well, it won't for ages."

It was the sort of day that they would remember for the rest of their lives. Virginia imagined them, middle-aged, reminiscing, nostalgic.

There was a little cove and a ruined cottage and not another soul but us. And there were two dogs and we had to climb down a suicidal path.

Who took us?

Eustace Philips.

But who was he?

I can't remember . . . he must have been a farmer, some sort of a neighbour.

And they would argue over details.

There was a stream.

No, it was a waterfall.

There was a stream running down the middle of the beach. I can remember it quite clearly. And we dammed it with a sandbank.

But there was a waterfall too. And I had a new spade.

When the tide was high, they all swam, and the water was clear and salt and green and very cold. Virginia had forgotten her cap and her dark hair lay sleek to her head, and her shadow moved across the pebbled sea-bed like some strange new variety of fish. Holding Cara, she floated, drifting between the sea and the sky, with her eyes dazzled by water and sunshine; and the air was cleft with screaming gulls, and always the gentle murmur of breaking waves.

She became very cold. The children showed no signs of chill, however, so she left them with Eustace, and came out of the water, and went to sit on the dry sand, above the high water mark.

She sat on the sand because they had brought no rug, no supersized bath-towels. And no comb or lipstick, or biscuits or knitting, and no Thermos of tea, and no extra cardigan. And no plum cake or chocolate biscuits, and no money for the donkey rides or the man with the ice-cream.

She was joined at last by Cara, teeth chattering. Virginia wrapped her in a towel and began gently to dry her. "You'll soon be swimming at this rate."

Cara said, "What time is it?"

Her mother squinted up at the sun. "I suppose, nearly five . . . I don't know."

"We haven't had tea yet."

"No, nor we have. And I don't suppose we will either."

"Not have any *tea*?"

"It doesn't matter for once. We'll have supper later on."

Cara made a face, but raised no objections. Nicholas, however, was vociferous in his complaints when he realized that Virginia had brought nothing for him to eat.

"But I'm hungry."

"I'm sorry."

"Nanny always had shivery bites and you haven't got anything."

"I know. I forgot. We were in such a hurry and I never thought of biscuits."

"Well, what am I going to eat?"

Eustace caught the tail end of this conversation as he came, dripping, up the beach. "What's this?" He stopped to pick up a towel.

"I'm very hungry and Mummy hasn't brought anything to eat."

"Too bad," said Eustace unsympathetically.

Nicholas sent him a long, measured look, and turned away, headed in a sulky silence back to his digging, but Eustace caught him by an arm and pulled him gently back and held him against his knees, rubbing at him absently with the towel, rather as though he were fondling one of the dogs.

Virginia said, placatingly, "Anyway, we'll have to go soon, I expect."

"Why?" asked Eustace.

"I thought you had all those cows to milk."

"Bert's doing them."

"Bert?"

"He was at Penfolda today, cleaning out the loose boxes."

"Oh, yes."

"He used to work for my father, he's retired now, but he comes along every alternate Sunday, gives me a hand. He likes to do it, and Mrs. Thomas feeds him a good dinner, and it means I have a few hours to myself."

Nicholas became irritated by the pointless small-talk. He reared around in Eustace's hands, turned up a furious face towards him. "I am *hungry*."

"So am I," said Cara, wistful if not so vehement.

"Well, listen," said Eustace.

They listened. And heard, over the sound of the sea and the gulls, another sound. The soft drumming of an engine, putt-putt-putt, all the time coming closer.

"What is it?"

"You watch and see."

The sound grew louder. Presently around the point they saw approaching a small open boat, white with a blue stripe, riding the waves with a scud of white spray. A stocky figure stood at its stern. Putt-putt, it swung round into the shelter of the cove, and the engine idled down to a steady throb . . .

They all stared. "There you are!" said Eustace, smug as a conjuror who has brought off a difficult trick.

"Who is it?"asked Virginia.

"That's Tommy Bassett from Porthkerris. Come to pick up his lobster pots."

"But he won't have any biscuits," said Nicholas, who would never be diverted from the matter in hand.

"No. But he might have something else. Shall I go and see?"

"All right." But they sounded doubtful.

He put Nicholas aside and went back down the sand and into the sea, diving through the eye of a peacock-coloured wave, and swimming, with a strong and steady crawl, far out to where the boat bobbed. The lobster pots were already being hauled aboard. The fishermen emptied one and dropped it back, and then saw Eustace coming, and stood, watching.

"Hallo there, boy!" His voice carried across the water.

They saw Eustace catch the gunwales with his hands, hang there for a moment, and then with a heave pull himself clean out of the water and into the rocking boat.

"What a long way to swim," said Cara.

Nicholas said, "I hope he isn't going to bring back a lobster."

"Why not?"

"Lobsters have got claws."

In the boat, some discussion seemed to be taking place. But at last Eustace stood up, and they saw that he was carrying some sort of bundle. He let himself overboard and started back, swimming more slowly this time, hampered as he was by his mysterious burden. This proved to be, of all things, a string shopping-bag, but it contained, wet and dripping, a dozen gleaming mackerel.

Nicholas opened his mouth to say, "I don't like fish," but caught Eustace's eye, and closed his mouth and said nothing instead.

"I thought he might have a few," Eustace told them. "He usually puts a line out when he's coming out to the pots." He smiled down at Cara. "Ever eaten mackerel, have you?"

"I don't think so. But," said Cara, "fancy giving you the string bag." To her, this seemed far more amazing than the gift of the mackerel. "Doesn't he want it back again?"

"He didn't say he did."

"Shall we have to take them back to Bosithick."

"What would we do that for? . . . No, we cook them here . . . come on, you can come and help."

And he collected six or seven big stones, round and smooth, and built them into a ring, and he took matches, and a scrap of an old cigarette packet, and some chips of driftwood and straw, and he kindled a fire and sent the children off to find more wood and soon they had a regular bonfire going. And when the wood ash was deep and grey and burned red when you blew on it, he laid the fish there, in a row, and there was a sizzling and a spitting and presently a most delicious smell.

"But we haven't got knives and forks," said Cara.

"Fingers were made before forks."

"But it'll be hot."

She and Nicholas squatted by the fireside, hair on end, naked except for their bathing pants and a coating of sand. They looked like savages, and perfectly content.

Cara watched Eustace's clever hands. "Have you done this before?"

"What, whittled a stick?"

"No, had a fire, and cooked fish."

"Many times. This is the only way to cook mackerel, and eat it, fresh out of the sea."

"Did you use to do this when you were a boy?"

"Yes."

"Was the old man alive then? Jack Carley."

"Yes. He used to come out and sit on the beach and join in the party. Bring a bottle of rum with him and a smelly old pipe and sit there and tell us yarns so hair-raising we could never be quite sure if they were true."

"What sort of yarns?"

"Oh, adventures . . . he'd been all over the world, done everything. Been a cook in a tanker, a lumberjack, built roads and railways, worked in the mines. He was a tin miner, see. A tinner. Went off to Chile, worked there for five years or more, came home a rich man, but all his money was gone within the twelve months, and he was off again."

"But he came back."

"Yes, he came back. Back to Jack Carley's cove." Cara shivered. "You cold?"

"Nanny calls it a ghost going over your grave."

"Put on a sweater then, and that'll keep the ghosts away, and then it'll be time to eat our tea."

And seeing him with her children, Virginia thought of Anthony who had missed so much because he had never wanted to have anything to do with them. If Cara had been pretty, perhaps he would have paid attention to her . . . Cara who longed for attention and love and thought her father the most wonderful being in the world. But she was plain and shy and wore spectacles, and he never endeavoured to hide the fact that he was ashamed of her. And Nicholas . . . with Nicholas it might have been different. When he was old enough, Anthony would have taught him to shoot and play golf and fish, they would have become friends and gone about together. But now Anthony was dead, and none of this would happen and she felt sorry because they would never now remember swimming with him, they would never crouch with him round a camp fire, listening to his stories and watching his clever hands whittle wooden skewers to be used instead of forks.

The sun slipped down out of the sky, shone directly in upon them, and the sea was turned to a liquid dazzle. It would soon be evening and then it would be dark. And Jack Carley had lived here, just as Aubrey Crane had lived at Bosithick. You didn't see them. You didn't hear them. But you knew that they were still around.

It was disturbing, this awareness of the past, but somehow elemental, and so not really frightening. And it was not possible to live in this part of the world as a nervous or a timid person, for, beneath the beauty it was a savage land, and danger lurked everywhere. In the sea, deep and treacherous, with its undertows and unsuspected currents. In the cliffs and caves, so swiftly cut off and submerged by racing tides. Even the quiet fields down which they had walked this afternoon concealed unthought-of horrors; abandoned mine workings, deep pits and shafts, black as wells, lay hidden beneath the bracken. And scraps of fur and feather, and little bleached bones bore witness to the foxes who built their lairs in earthly hollows under the gorse.

And after nightfall the owl set up his predatory hooting, and the badger emerged to tunnel and scavenge. Not for him the thrill of the hunt. He was just as content to push the lid off a dustbin in the middle of the night, causing such a clatter as to waken the farmer's wife in a cold sweat of fright.

"Mummy. It's cooked." Cara's voice broke across her thoughts. She looked up and saw Cara holding a stick aloft, a fragment of fish impaled dangerously upon its point. "Come and get it *quickly* before it falls off!" Her voice was agonized, and Virginia got to her feet, dusting the sand off the seat of her bathing-suit, and went down to join in the picnic.

In the afterglow of the setting sun, with the offshore wind cool on their faces, they climbed slowly home. After the swim the children were sleepy and silent. Nicholas was not too proud to accept a piggy-back from Eustace, and Virginia carried the wet bathing things and towels in the string bag which had been used for the mackerel, and helped Cara along with the other hand. They were all sandy, salty, tousled, weary, and the path was steep and the climb, up through the bracken and the treacherous undergrowth, exhausting. But at last they reached the fields at the top, and after that the going was easy. Behind them the sea, luminous, in the half-light, reflected all the colours of the sky, and ahead was Bosithick, cradled in the curve of the hill, with the road behind it flickering, every now and then, with the searchlight glare of a passing car.

Some of Eustace's cows had strayed through a gap in the hedge into the top field. In the dusk they loomed, brown and white, and made pleasant munching sounds, raising their heads to watch as the small procession walked by.

Nicholas said, leaning forward to speak into Eustace's ear, "Are you going to come back with us?"

He smiled. "Time I was getting home."

"We would like you to stay for supper."

"You've had your supper," Eustace told him.

"I thought that was tea."

"Don't tell me you've got room for more food."

Nicholas yawned. "No, maybe not."

Virginia said, "I'll make you cocoa, and you can drink it in bed."

"Yes," said Nicholas. "But it would be nice if Eustace would come and talk to us while we had our baths . . ."

Cara chimed in. "Yes, and then Mummy could get our cocoa ready, and you could talk to us."

"I'll do more than that," said Eustace. "I'll scrub the sand off your backs."

They giggled in a high-pitched fashion as though this were very funny, and as soon as they were indoors raced for the bathroom to fight over the taps. Ominous splashing sounds came from beyond the door, and Eustace, rolling up his sleeves, moved in to break it up. Virginia heard him saying, "Quiet now, you'll sink the ship if you don't watch out."

Leaving him to it, she carried the fishy string bag out to the kitchen and emptied the bathing things and the sand-encrusted towels into the sink, and rinsed them out and wrung them, and carried them out into the dark garden, and, by feel, found the clothes-line and pegged them out, leaving them to billow and flap like ghosts in the darkness.

Back in the kitchen, she poured milk into a sauce-pan, put it on to heat, stood watching it, leaning against the cooker, yawning a little. She put up a hand to her eyes, and found that her face was rough with sand, so she took the little mirror out of her handbag, and a comb, and propped the mirror on one of the shelves of the dresser and tried to do something about her hair, but it was stiff and dry with salt, and full of sand. She thought that if there had been a shower, she would have washed it, but the idea of putting it under a tap was somehow all too difficult, too complicated. In the inadequate light her reflection gazed back at her from the round mirror, and there were freckles across the bridge of her nose, but her eyes were shadowed, dark as two holes in her face.

The milk rose in the pan. She made the two mugs of cocoa, put them on a tray, started upstairs with them. She saw that the bathroom was empty, a trail of damp towels and footprints led upstairs. She heard voices and came along the passage, and their bedroom door stood open.

They were inside and they did not see her. She stood and watched them. Eustace sat, with his back to her, on Cara's bed, and the children were perched on Nicholas's bed. All three heads together, Eustace was being given a guided tour of Cara's photographs.

"And this is Daddy. The big one here. He's terribly good-looking, don't you think? . . ." This was Cara, as chatty now as she could be with someone with whom she was completely at ease. "And this is our house in Scotland, that's my bedroom, and that's Nicholas's bedroom, and that's the nursery up at the top . . ."

"That's my bedroom!"

"I said it was that bedroom, silly. And this is Nanny's room, and that's Mummy's room, but you can't see the rooms at the back because they're round at the back. And this is an aerial view . . ."

"A man took it in an aeroplane . . ."

"And that's all the park and the river. And that's the walled garden."

"And that's Mr. McGregor on his tractor, and that's Bob and that's Fergie."

Eustace was beginning to lose the thread . . . "Hold on now, who are Bob and Fergie?"

"Well, Bob helps Mr. McGregor and Fergie helps the gardener. Fergie plays the bagpipes and do you know who taught him? His uncle. And do you know what his uncle is called? Muncle." Nicholas triumphantly produced the answer.

Eustace said, "Uncle Muncle."

"And this is Daddy skiing at St. Moritz, and that's all of us at a grouse shoot—at least, we went to the picnic bit, we didn't go up the hill. And that's the bit of the river where we sometimes swim, but it's not always very safe, and the stones hurt your feet. But Mummy says we can have a swimming pool, she says when we go back to Kirkton, we can have a swimming pool, just like Aunt Alice Lingard's . . ."

"And that's Daddy's car, it's a great big Jaguar. It's a . . ." Nicholas faltered. "It was a great big Jaguar." He finished bravely, "Green."

Virginia said, "Here's your cocoa."

"Oh Mummy, we were showing Eustace all the photographs of Kirkton . . ."

"Yes, I heard."

"That was very nice," said Eustace. "Now I know all about Scotland."

He stood up, as though to get out of Virginia's way, and went to put the photograph frame back on to the chest of drawers.

The children climbed into bed. "You'll have to come and see us. You'll have to come and stay. Won't he, Mummy? He can sleep in the spare room, can't he?"

"Maybe," said Virginia. "But Eustace is a busy man."

"That's it," said Eustace. "Busy. Always got plenty to do. Well . . ." He moved towards the open door. "I'll say good night."

"Oh, good night, Eustace. And thank you for taking us to that lovely place."

"Don't dream about Jack Carley."

"Even if I do I shan't be frightened."

"That's the way. Good night, Nicholas."

"Good night. I'll see you in the morning."

Virginia said to him, "Don't go. I'll be down in a moment."

He said, "I'll wait downstairs."

The cocoa was duly consumed, between yawns. Their eyes drooped. At last they lay down and Virginia kissed them good night. But when she kissed Nicholas he did a surprising thing. Most undemonstrative of children, he put his arms around her neck and held her cheek down against his own.

She said, gently, "What is it?"

"It was a nice place, wasn't it?"

"You mean the little beach?"

"No. The house where Eustace lives."

"Penfolda."

"Will we go back?"

"Sure to."

"I loved that little kitten."

"I know you did."

"Eustace is downstairs."

"Yes."

"I shall hear you talking." His voice was filled with satisfaction. "I shall hear you go talk, talk, talk."

"Will that be cosy?"

"I think so," said Nicholas.

They were near to sleep, but still she stayed with them, moving quickly about the room, picking up stray clothes and folding them and putting them, neat as Nanny, across the seats of the two rickety cane chairs. This done, she went to close the window a little, for the night air was growing chill, to draw the skimpy curtains. The room, by the meagre light of the bedside lamp was all at once enclosed, safe, soft with shadows, the only sound the ticking of Cara's clock and the breathing of the children.

She was filled, in that moment, with love. For her children; for this strange little house; for the man, downstairs, who waited for her. And aware, too, of a marvellous sense of completion, of rightness. It will be the first time, she thought, that Eustace and I have been alone, with all the time in the world. Just the two of us. She would light the fire for company and draw the curtains and make him a jug of coffee. If they wished, they could talk all night. They could be together.

Cara and Nicholas were sleeping. She turned off the light and went downstairs to unexpected and surprising darkness. For an incredulous moment she thought that Eustace had changed his mind and already gone, but then she saw that he stood by the window, smoking, watching the very last of the light fade from the sky. A little of this light was reflected upon his face, but when he heard her footstep he turned, and she could see no expression on his face, only shadows.

She said, "I thought you'd gone."

"No. I'm still here."

The darkness disturbed her. She reached for the lamp on the table and switched it on. Yellow light was thrown, like a pool, between them. She waited for him to speak, but when he said nothing, simply stood there, smoking, she began to fill the silence with words.

"I . . . I don't know about supper. Do you want something to eat? I don't even know what time it is."

"I'm all right."

"I could make you some coffee . . ."

"You haven't got a can of beer?"

She made a helpless gesture. "I haven't, Eustace. I'm sorry. I never bought any. I never drink it." That sounded priggish, as though she disapproved of beer. "I mean, I just don't like the taste." She smiled, trying to turn it into a joke.

"It doesn't matter."

The smile collapsed. Virginia swallowed. "Are you sure you wouldn't like coffee?"

"No, thank you." He began to look about for somewhere to stub out his cigarette. She found him a saucer and put it on the table, and he demolished the stub as through he had a personal, vicious grudge against it.

"I must go."

"But . . ."

He turned towards her, waiting for her to finish. She lost her nerve. "Yes. It's been a good day. It was kind of you to give up your day for us and show us the cove and . . . everything." Her voice sounded high-pitched and formal as though she were opening a sale of work. "The children loved it."

"They're good children."

"Yes. I . . ."

"When are you going back to Scotland?"

The abruptness of the question, the coldness of his voice, were shocking. She was suddenly cold, a shiver of apprehension trickling down her spine like a stream of icy water.

"I . . . I'm not sure." She took hold of the back of one of the wooden chairs, leaning against it as if for support. "Why do you ask?"

"You're going to go back."

It was a statement, not a question. Faced with it, Virginia's natural diffidence leapt to the worst conclusion. Eustace expected her to go, even wanted her to go. She heard herself telling him, with marvellous lightness, "Well, some time, of course. After all, it's my home. The children's home."

"I hadn't realized until this evening that it was such a considerable property . . ."

"Oh, you mean, Cara's photographs . . ."

"But then, you have plenty of people to help you run it."

"I don't run it, Eustace."

"Then you should. Learn something about farming. You'd be surprised how much there is to it. You should take an interest, start up something new. An Aberdeen Angus herd. Did your husband ever think of doing that? You can sell a good bull at the Perth sales for sixty, seventy thousand pounds?"

It was like a conversation in a nightmare, mad and pointless. She said, "Can you?" but her mouth was dry and the words scarcely made any sound at all.

"Of course. And who knows, one day you may have built up something really great to hand on to that boy of yours."

"Yes."

He said again, "I must go." The trace of a smile crossed his features. "It was a good day."

But Virginia remembered a better one, that other day she had spent with Eustace, the spring afternoon of sun and wind when he had brought her an ice-cream and finally driven her home. And he had promised to telephone her, and then forgotten, or perhaps he had changed his mind. She realized that she had been waiting, all afternoon, for him to tell her what really happened. She had been expecting him to bring up the subject, perhaps as a story for the children to share, or as a scrap of harmless nostalgia to be remembered, over the years, by two old friends. But he had said nothing. And now she would never know.

"Yes." She let go of the chair and straightened up, folding her arms across her chest as though she were trying to stay warm. "A special day. The kind that people never forget."

He moved towards her, around the edge of the table, and Virginia turned away from him and went to open the door. Cool air, smelling sweet and damp, flooded in from a night arched in a sapphire sky, bright with stars. Out of the darkness a curlew sent up its long mournful cry.

He was beside her. "Good night, Virginia."

"Good night, Eustace."

And then he was going down the steps, away from her, over the wall and down the fields towards the old farmyard where he had left his car. The dusk swallowed him. She closed the door and locked it and went back to the kitchen and took the children's cocoa mugs and washed them, slowly and carefully. She heard his Land-Rover go grinding up past the gate, up the lane towards the main road, heard the sound of the engine die away into the quiet night, but she never looked up from what she was doing. When the mugs were dry, the tea towel folded and there was nothing more to do, she found that she was exhausted. She turned off the lights and went slowly upstairs and undressed and climbed into bed. Her body lay slack, but the inside of her head behaved as though she had been living on black coffee for a week.

He doesn't love you.

I never thought he did.

But you were beginning to think so. After today.

Then I was wrong. We have no future together. He made that very clear.

What did you imagine was going to happen?

I imagined that he would be able to talk about what happened ten years ago.

Nothing happened. And why should he remember?

Because I did. Because Eustace was the most important person, the most important thing that ever happened to me.

You didn't remember. You married Anthony Keile.

They were married in London, in July; Virginia in a cream satin dress with a six foot train and a veil that had belonged to Lady Keile's grandmother, and Anthony in a grey frock-coat and an immaculately cut pair of sponge-bag trousers. They emerged from St. Michael's, Chester Square, with bells jangling, sun shining, and a small retinue of beribboned bridesmaids extorting *oohs* and *aahs* of admiration from the thin crowd of inquisitive women who had realized that there was a wedding going on, and hung about to see what turned up when the doors were opened.

The excitement, the champagne, the pleasures of being loved and congratulated and kissed kept Virginia going until it was time to go upstairs and change. Her mother was there, ubiquitous, efficient, to unzip the clinging satin and unpin the borrowed tiara and the filmy veil.

"Oh, my dear, it all went off so beautifully, and you really did look enchanting, even though perhaps I shouldn't say anything so conceited about my own child . . . Darling, you're shivering, you're surely not cold?"

"No. I'm not cold."

"Change your shoes, then, and I'll help you on with your dress."

It was rose pink, with a tiny petalled hat to match, a charming useless ensemble that she would never wear again. She imagined coming back from her honeymoon, still wearing paper silk and pink petals, a little crushed by now, and going brown at the edges. (But of course they couldn't go brown, they weren't real, they were pretence petals . . .)

"And your suitcase is in the boot of Anthony's car, such a good

112

idea taking a taxi round to the flat and picking the car up there, then you have none of this terrible horse-play with kippers and old shoes."

A roar, a galloping of feet, came from the passage outside the bedroom. Anthony's voice was raised in a comic sound like a hunting horn. "There! He sounds as though he's ready." She kissed Virginia briskly. "Have a good time, my darling."

The door burst open, and Anthony stood there, wearing the suit that he had chosen to go away in, and with a large sun hat on the top of his head. He was considerably drunk.

"Here she is! We're off to the South of France, my love, which is why I am wearing this hat."

Mrs. Parsons, laughing indulgently, removed it, smoothed his hair with her long fingers, straightened his tie. She might have been the bride, not Virginia, who stood and watched this little ceremony with a face that held no expression whatsoever. Anthony held out a hand to her. "Come on," he said. "Time we went."

The hired car, awash in confetti, took them back to the Parsons' flat, where Anthony's car was waiting for them. The plan had been that they should get straight into his car and drive to the airport, but Virginia had a latch-key in her purse, and instead, they let themselves in and went into the kitchen, and she tied an apron around the pink silk dress, and Anthony sat on the table and watched while she brewed him up a jug of black coffee.

For their honeymoon they had been lent a villa in Antibes. By their second day Anthony had met an old friend; by the end of the first week, he knew everyone in the place. Virginia told herself that this was what she had expected, was what she wanted. Anthony's gregarious instincts were part of his charm, and one of the things that had attracted her to him in the first place. Besides, after one day it became very obvious that they were going to find it hard to think of things to say to each other. Conversation at meals was inclined to be distinctly sticky. She realized then, that they had never been alone together before now.

There was a couple, called Janey and Hugh Rouse; he was a writer and they had rented a house at Cap Ferrat. Janey was older than Virginia and Virginia liked her, and found her easy to talk to. Once, sitting on the terrace at the Rouses's house, waiting for the men to come up from the rocks, Janey had said, "How long have you known Anthony, honey?" She had lived, as a child, in the States, and although she did not speak with an American accent, her speech was spattered with words and phrases which instantly gave her origins away.

"Not very long. I met him in May."

"Love at first sight, hm?"

"I don't know. I suppose so."

"How old are you?"

"Eighteen."

"That's awfully young to settle down. Not that I can see that Anthony settling down too much for a few years yet."

"He'll have to," Virginia told her. "You see, we're going to live in Scotland. Anthony's been left this estate, Kirkton . . . it used to belong to an uncle who was a bachelor. And we're going to go and live there."

"You mean, you think Anthony will spend all his time tramping around in a tweed suit with mud on his boots?"

"Not exactly. But I can't believe that living in Scotland is going to be quite the same as living in London."

"It won't," said Janey, who had been there. "But don't expect the simple life, or you'll be disappointed."

But Virginia did expect the simple life. She had never seen Kirkton, never been to Scotland for that matter, but she had once spent an Easter holiday with a schoolfriend who lived in Northumberland and somehow she imagined that Scotland would be rather like that, and that Kirkton would be a low-ceilinged, rambling, stone farmhouse, with flagged floors, and worn Turkey carpets, and a dining-room with a great log fire and hunting prints on the walls.

Instead, she was presented with a tall, square, elegantly proportioned Adam house, with sash windows full of reflected sunshine, and a flight of stone stairs which led, from the carriage sweep, up to the front door.

Beyond the gravel was grass, and then a ha-ha wall, and then the park, landscaped with giant beeches, sloping down to the distant silver curve of the river.

Overwhelmed, silent, Virginia had followed Anthony up the steps and through the door. The house was empty, old-fashioned and unfurnished. Between them they were going to do it up. To Virginia the task seemed daunting, but when she said as much Anthony overrode her.

"We'll get Philip Sayer on to it, he's this interior decorator my mother got to do the house in London for her. Otherwise we'll make the most ghastly mistakes and the place will be a mess."

Virginia privately thought she preferred her own glastly mistakes to somebody else's impeccable taste—it was more homely; but she said nothing.

"And this is the drawing-room, and then the library beyond. And the dining-room, and there are kitchens and stuff downstairs."

The room soared and echoed, the icy prisms of crystal chandeliers glinted, dependent from ornately decorated ceilings. There was panelling and marvelous cornices over the tall windows. There was dust and a distinct feeling of chill.

They mounted to the first floor up a curved stairway, airy and elegant, and their steps echoed on the polished treads and through the empty house. Upstairs, there were bedrooms, each with its own bathroom, dressing-rooms, linen rooms, housemaid's cupboards, even a boudoir.

"What would I do with a boudoir?" Virginia wanted to know.

"You can come and boud in it, and if you don't know what that means, it's French for sulk. Oh, come on, take that horrified expression off your face and look as though you're enjoying yourself."

"It's just so big."

"You talk as though it were Buckingham Palace."

"I've never been in such a big house. I certainly never thought I would live in one."

"Well, you're going to, so you'd better get used to it."

Eventually they were outside again, standing by the car, staring up at the elegant front elevation, regularly spaced with windows. Virginia put her hands deep in the pockets of her coat and said, "Where's the garden?"

"What do you mean?"

"I mean flower-beds and stuff. Flowers. You know. A garden."

But the garden was a half-mile away, enclosed in a wall. They drove there and went inside and found a gardener and rows of fruit and vegetables like soldiers, waiting to be picked off.

"This is the garden," said Anthony.

"Oh," said Virginia.

"What's that meant to mean?"

"Nothing. Just oh."

The interior decorator duly arrived. Hard on his heels came vans and lorries, builders, plasterers, painters, men with carpets, men with curtains, men in pan-technicons which spilled out furniture like cornucopias, endlessly, as though they would never run out.

Virginia let it all happen. "Yes," she would say, agreeing to whatever shade of velvet Philip Sayer was suggesting. Or "Yes" when he thought of Victorian brass bedsteads in the spare room, and thick white crochet bedcovers. "Terribly Osborne, my dear, you know, Victorian Country Life."

The only time that she had raised her voice with an independent idea was over the kitchen. She wanted it like the one she remembered, the marvellous room at Penfolda with its air of stability, the suggestion in the air of good things cooking, the cat in the chair and the geraniums crowded on the window-sill.

"A farmhouse kitchen! That's what I want. A farmhouse kitchen's like a living-room."

"Well, I'm not going to live in any kitchen, I'll tell you that."

And she had let Anthony have his way because, after all, it was not her house, and it was not her money which paid for the stainless steel sinks, and the black and white floor and the patent self-cleaning cooking unit with eye-level grill, and a spit for broiling chickens.

It was finished and Virginia was pregnant.

"How marvellous for Nanny!" said Lady Keile.

"Why?"

"Well, darling, she's in London, doing temporary work, but she's longing, but longing for a new baby. Of course she won't be all that keen on leaving London, but she's bound to make friends, you know what this Nanny's network's like, better than the English Speaking Union I always say. And that top floor is *meant* to be a nursery, you can tell by the gate at the top of the stairs, and the bars on the windows. Gorgeously sunny. I think pale blue, don't you? For carpets, I mean, and then French chintz curtains . . ."

Virginia tried to stand up for herself. To say, *No. I will look after my own baby.* But she was so sick carrying Cara, so weak and unwell, that by the time she once again felt strong enough to cope with the situation and stand on her own two feet, the nursery had been decorated and Nanny was there, established, rigid, immovable.

I'll let her stay. Just until the baby's born and I'm on my feet again. She can stay for a month or two, and then I'll tell her that she can go back to London because I want to look after my baby for myself.

But by then, there were further complications. Virginia's mother, in London, complained of pains and tiredness; she thought she was losing weight. Virginia at once went south to see her, and after that, her loyalties were torn between her baby in Scotland and her mother in London. Travelling up and down in the train it became very clear that it would be madness to get rid of Nanny until Mrs. Parsons had recovered. But of course, she didn't recover and, by the time the whole ghastly nightmare was over, Nicholas had arrived and, with two babies in the nursery, Nanny was dug in for good.

At Kirkton they were surrounded, within a radius of ten miles or so, by a number of entertaining neighbours. Young couples with time and money to spare, some with young children like the Keiles', all with interests which matched Anthony's.

For appearances' sake, he put in a certain amount of time on the farm, talking to McGregor, the grieve, finding out what McGregor thought should be done, and then telling McGregor to do it. The rest of the day was his own, and he used it to the full, doing exactly what he wanted. Scotland is a country geared to the pleasures of menfolk, and there was always shooting to be got, grouse in the summer, and partridges and pheasants in the autumn and winter. There were rivers to be fished and golf courses and a social life which was even gayer than the one he had left behind in London.

Virginia did not fish or play golf and Anthony would not have invited her to join him even if she had wanted to. He preferred the company of his men-friends, and she was expected to be present only when they had been invited specifically as a couple. To a dinner or a dance, or perhaps to lunch before a point-to-point, when she would go through agonies trying to decide what to put on, and inevitably turn up in what everybody had been wearing last year.

She was still shy. And she didn't drink so there seemed no artificial way of getting over this terrible defect. The men, Anthony's friends, obviously thought her a bore. And their wives, though kind and friendly, terrified her with their private jokes and their incomprehensible references to places and persons and events known only to them. They were like a lot of girls who had all been to the same school.

Once, driving home after a dinner party, they quarrelled. Virginia had not meant to quarrel but she was tired and unhappy, and Anthony was more than a little drunk. He always seemed to drink too much at

117

parties, almost as though it were a social grace that was expected of him. This evening it made him aggressive and bad-tempered.

"Well, did you enjoy yourself?"

"Not particularly."

"You certainly didn't look as though you did."

"I was tired."

"You're always tired. And yet you never seem to do a thing."

"Perhaps that's why I'm tired."

"And what does that mean?"

"Oh, nothing."

"It has to mean something."

"All right, it means that I get bored and lonely."

"That's not my fault."

"Isn't it? You're never there . . . sometimes you're not in the house all day. You have lunch in the club at Relkirk . . . I never see you."

"OK. Me and about a hundred other chaps. What do you suppose their wives do? Sit and mope?"

"I've wondered what they do with their time. You tell me."

"Well, they get around, that's what. They see each other, take the children to Pony Club meets, play bridge; I suppose, garden."

"I can't play bridge," said Virginia, "and the children don't want to ride ponies, and I would garden only there isn't a garden at Kirkton, just a four-walled prison for flowers, and a bad-tempered gardener who won't let me so much as cut a bunch of gladioli without asking him first."

"Oh, for heaven's sake . . ."

She said, "I watch other people. Ordinary couples, sometimes on Saturdays in Relkirk. Doing the shopping together in the rain or the sunshine, and children with them, sucking ice-creams, and they put all the parcels into shabby little cars and drive home, and they look so happy and cosy, all together."

"Oh, God. You can't want that."

"I want not to be lonely."

"Loneliness is a state of mind. Only you can do anything about that."

"Weren't you ever lonely, Anthony?"

"No."

"Then you didn't marry me for company. And you didn't marry me for my startling conversation."

"No." Coldly agreeing, his profile was stony.

"Then why?"

"You were pretty. You had a certain fawn-like charm. You were very charming. My mother thought you were very charming. She thought your mother was very charming. She thought the whole bloody arrangement was charming."

"But you didn't marry me because your mother told you to."

"No. But you see, I had to marry somebody, and you turned up at such a singularly opportune time."

"I don't understand."

He did not reply to this. For a little he drove in silence, perhaps prompted by some shred of decency not to tell her the truth, now or ever. But Virginia, having come so far, made the mistake of pressing him. "Anthony, I don't understand," and he lost his temper and told her.

"Because I was left Kirkton on condition that I was married when I took it over. Uncle Arthur thought I would never settle down, would break the place up if I moved in as a bachelor . . . I don't know what he thought, but he was determined that if I lived at Kirkton I'd do it as a family man."

"So that's why!"

Anthony frowned. "Are you hurt?"

"I don't think so. Should I be?"

He fumbled for her hand with his own . . . the car swerved slightly as his fingers closed over hers. He said, "It's all right. It may be no better, but it's certainly no worse than other marriages. Sometimes it's a good thing to be frank and clear the air. It's better to know where we both stand."

She said, "Do you ever regret it? Marrying me, I mean."

"No. I don't regret it. I'm just sorry that it had to happen when we were both so young."

One day she found herself in the house alone. Quite alone. It was Saturday, and afternoon. Mr. McGregor, the grieve, had gone to Relkirk, taking Mrs. McGregor with him. Anthony was playing golf, and Nanny and the children were out for a walk. An empty house and nothing to do. No washing to be done, no cake to be baked, no ironing, no garden to weed. Virginia walked through it, going from room to room, as though she were a stranger who had paid to see around, and her footsteps echoed on the polished staircase, and there was the tick of the clock, and everywhere order, neatness. This was what Anthony loved. This was what he had created. This was why he had married her. She ended up in the hall, opened the front door and went down the steps on to the gravel, thinking that she would maybe spy Nanny and the children in the distance; she would go to meet them, run and snatch Cara up in her arms, hug her and hold her, if only to prove that she really existed, that she was not a dream-child that Virginia had conceived, like some frustrated spinster, out of her own imagination.

But there was no sign of Nanny and, after a little, she went back up the steps and so indoors again, because there did not seem to be anywhere else to go.

There was a pretty girl, called Liz, married to a young lawyer who worked in Edinburgh. He worked in Edinburgh, but they lived only a mile or two from Kirkton, in an old, converted Presbyterian manse, with a wild garden, that was filled with daffodils in the spring, and a paddock for the ponies.

She had young children, dogs, a cat, and a parrot in a cage, but—perhaps because she missed her husband who was in Edinburgh all week, or perhaps because she was simply a girl who enjoyed people—her house was always full. Other mothers' children lolloped about on the ponies, crowded the dining-room table at tea-time, played rounders on the lawn. If she didn't have whole families staying with her, then she had whole families for the day, feeding them on huge roasts of beef, and steak and kidney pies, marvellous old-fashioned puddings, and home-made ice-creams. Her drink cupboard, which must have taken a frightening beating from the hordes who passed through her hospitable doorway, was always open, always at hand for any guest in need of a little liquid refreshment.

"Help yourself," she would call through the open door, while she knocked up a three-course dinner for ten unexpected guests. "There's ice in the fridge if the ice-bucket's empty."

Anthony, naturally enough, adored her, flirted cheerfully and openly with her, put on a great show of jealousy when the week-ends came around and her husband was home.

"Get that bloody man out of the house," he would tell Liz, and she would go into gales of delighted laughter, as would everybody else

120

who was listening. Virginia smiled, and over their heads met the eye of Liz's husband. He was a quiet young man, and though he stood there, with a glass in his hand, smiling, it was almost impossible to tell what he was thinking.

"You'll have to watch out for that husband of yours," one of the other wives said to Virginia. But she only said, "I have been, for years," and changed the subject, or turned to speak to somebody else.

One Tuesday, Anthony called her from the club in Relkirk. "Virginia. Look, I've got embroiled in a poker game, God knows when I'll be home. But don't wait, I'll get a bite to eat here. See you later."

"All right. Don't lose too much money."

"I shall win," he told her. "I shall buy you a mink coat."

"That's just what I need."

He arrived home, after midnight, stumbling up the stairs. She heard him moving about in his dressing-room, dropping things, opening and shutting drawers, swearing at some cuff-link or button.

After a little, she heard him getting into bed, and the light beyond the open door went out, and there was only darkness. And she wondered if he had chosen to sleep in his dressing-room out of consideration to Virginia, or whether there was some other, more sinister reason.

She soon knew. The society in which they moved, the narrow clique, was too small for secrets. "Virginia darling, I told you to watch out for that naughty man of yours."

"What's he done now?"

"You are marvellous, the way you never get ruffled. You obviously know all about it."

"All about what?"

"Darling, the intimate dinner party that he had with Liz."

". . . Oh, yes, of course. Last Tuesday."

"He is an old devil. I suppose he thought none of us would find out. But then Midge and Johnny Gray suddenly decided on the spur of the moment to go up to the Strathtorrie Arms for dinner, you know, there's a new manager now, and it's all frightfully dark and chic and you can get a very good dinner. Anyway, off they went, and of course there were Anthony and Liz, all snugged up in a corner. And you knew all the time!"

"Yes."

"Any you don't mind?"

"No."

That was the terrible thing. She didn't mind. She was apathetic, bored by Anthony and the outrageous schoolboy charm that had, as far as Virginia was concerned, long since worn itself to shreds. And this was not the first affair. It had happened before and it would doubtless happen again, but still, it was daunting to look down the years ahead and see herself tied for ever to this tedious Peter Pan. A man so unperceptive that he could gaily embark on a clandestine involvement, and yet conduct the whole affair on what was virtually his own front doorstep.

She thought about divorce, but knew that she would never divorce Anthony, not simply because of the children, but because she was Virginia, and she could no more embark, voluntarily, upon such a course, than she could have flown to the moon.

She was not happy, but what could be the good of broadcasting her failure, her disillusion, to the rest of the world? Anthony did not love her, had never loved her. But then she had never loved him. If he had married Virginia to get his hands on Kirkton, then she had married Anthony on the rebound, in an emotional state of extreme unhappiness, and in a desperate bid to avoid the London Season that her mother had planned for her, culminating in the final nightmare of a coming-out dance.

She was not happy, but, to all intents and purposes, she had everything. A lovely house, a handsome husband, and the children. The children were worth everything. For them she would shore up her crumbling marriage, and for them she would create a world of security that they would never know again.

Anthony had been with Liz that night he was killed. He had called in at the Old Manse for a drink on his way back from Relkirk and was invited to stay for supper.

He rang Virginia.

"Liz has got the Cannons staying. She wants me to eat here and make up a four for bridge. I'll be home some time. Don't wait up."

Liz's cupboard with the whisky bottle stood open, as always. And as always Anthony helped himself liberally and with a generous hand. It was two o'clock before he started home, a black and starless night of pouring rain. It had been raining for days and the river was in spate. Afterwards the police came with tape measures and bits of chalk, and they measured the skid marks, and hung over the broken rail of the bridge and stared down into the muddy, swirling waters. And Virginia stood with them, in the drenching rain, and watched the divers go down, and there was a kindly sergeant who kept urging her to go back to the house, but she wouldn't go because, for some reason, she had to be there, because he had been her husband and the father of her children.

And she remembered what he had said, that night he told her about Kirkton. *I'm just sorry that it had to happen when we were both so young.*

Chapter 8

THE QUIET NIGHT moved slowly past, the seconds, the minutes, the hours, measured by the ticking of Virginia's wrist-watch which she had put on the table by her bed. Now, she reached out for it and saw that it was nearly three o'clock in the morning. She got out of bed, wrapped herself in the quilt and went to sit on the floor by the open window. It was the hour before dawn, dark and very still. She could hear, a mile or more away, the gentle movement, like breathing, of the sea. She could hear the soft shufflings and munchings of the Guernseys, grazing two or three fields distant; she could hear rustlings and whisperings and creepings from hedgerow and burrow, and the hooting of a night owl.

She found that she was devilled by the memory of Liz. Liz had come to Anthony's funeral wearing a face of grief and guilt so naked that instinctively one had turned away from it, not wanting to witness such pain. Soon afterwards her husband had taken her to the South of France for a holiday and Virginia had not seen her again.

But now she knew that she must go back to Scotland and soon, if it was only to square things up with Liz. To convince Liz that no blame could ever be laid at her door, to make—as far as was humanly possible —friends with her again. She thought of returning to Kirkton and this time her imagination did not turn and run but took the journey quietly and without horror. Off the road it went, and down over the bridge and the river, and up the drive between the lush meadows of the park. It came to the curving sweep in front of the house, and went up the steps and in through the front door, and now there was no longer the old familiar sensation of loneliness, of being trapped. But simply a sadness that the lives of the people who had lived in this beautiful house had achieved no lasting cohesion, but had unravelled like a length of badly spun yarn, and finally shredded away.

She would sell the house. Somewhere, some time, her subconscious had made the decision and now presented it to her conscious mind as a *fait accompli*. How much this phenomenon had to do with Eustace, Virginia could not at the moment comprehend. Later on, no doubt, it would all work itself out. For now the relief was enormous, like the shedding of a load carried too long, and she felt grateful, as though another person had stepped in and made the decision for her.

She would sell Kirkton. Buy another house, a little house . . . somewhere. Again, later on, it would all work itself out. She would make a new home, new friends, create a garden, buy a puppy, a kitten, a canary in a cage. Find schools for the children, fill the holidays with pleasures she had previously been too diffident to attempt. She would learn to ski; they would go on ski-ing holidays together. She would build kites and mend bicycles, let Cara read all the books she ever wanted, and go to Nicholas's sports days wearing the right sort of hat, and achieve marvellous things like winning the egg-and-spoon race.

And it would happen because she would make it happen. There was no more Eustace, no more dreams, but other good things were constant. Like pride, and resolution, and the children. The children. And she smiled, knowing that, like the arrow on the compass for ever pointing north, whatever she did and however she behaved, she was always left, facing squarely in their direction.

She was beginning to be cold. The first lightening of dawn was beginning to creep up into the sky. She got up off the floor, took a sleeping-pill and a glass of water and climbed back into bed. When she opened her eyes again the sun, high in the sky, was shining full in her face, and from downstairs came a terrible racket, a banging at the front door and a voice calling her name.

"Virginia! It's me. Alice! Wake up, or are you all dead?"

Dazed with shock and sleep, Virginia stumbled out of bed, across the floor, and hung out of the window. "Alice! Stop making such a din. The children are asleep."

Alice, foreshortened, turned up an astonished face. Her voice dropped to an exaggerated stage-whisper. "I'd begun to think you'd all passed out. It's past ten. Come down and let me in!"

Yawning, incapable, Virginia groped for her dressing-gown, pushed her feet into slippers and went downstairs, pausing at the open door of the children's room on the way. To her surprise they were still asleep, undisturbed by Alice's shouting. She thought, we must have been late last night. We must have been much later than I realized.

She unlocked the door, to let in a flood of sunshine and Alice. Alice wore a crisp blue linen dress, a silk scarf over her head. As usual she was bright-skinned, clear-eyed, maddeningly awake.

"Do you usually wake up at this hour?"

"No, but . . ." Virginia swallowed a yawn. ". . . I couldn't get to sleep last night. Eventually I took a pill. It must have knocked me out."

"And the children?"

"I didn't give them a pill, but they're still asleep. We were late, we were out all day." She yawned again, forced her eyes open. "How about some coffee?"

Alice looked amused. "You certainly look as though you'll need some. I tell you what. I'll make it, you go and get yourself woken up, and put some clothes on. It's no good talking to you when you're in this state." She laid her handbag on the table in a purposeful way. "I must say, this really isn't too bad a little house, is it? And here's the kitchen. A little poky, perhaps, but perfectly adequate . . ."

Virginia ran a bath, got into it and washed her hair. Afterwards, she went upstairs, wrapped in a towel, and took clean clothes from the drawer, and a cotton dress, as yet unworn, from the wardrobe. She pushed her feet into sandals, combed her sleek wet hair into place, and feeling clean and strangely hungry, went back downstairs to Alice.

She found her thoroughly organized, the kettle on the gas, the jug ready with the coffee, mugs laid out on the table.

"Oh, there you are . . . we're just about ready . . . I thought we'd have proper coffee; I get so fed up with this wishy-washy stuff, don't you?"

Virginia sat on the edge of the table. "When did you get back from London?"

"Last night."

"How was it? Did you have fun?"

"Yes, but I didn't come here to talk about London."

"In that case, what brought you here at ten o'clock on a Monday morning?"

"Curiosity," said Alice. "Sheer, undiluted curiosity."

"About me?"

"About Eustace Philips!"

Virginia said, "I don't understand."

"Mrs. Jilkes told me. I was scarcely in through the front door when I was hearing all about it. She said that Eustace had telephoned her while I was away to ask if anybody was getting Bosithick ready for you and the children. And she said I was in London, and he said not to bother, he'd see to it."

"Yes, that's right . . . and he did too . . ."

"But Virginia . . . You talked about Eustace, but you never told me that you'd met him again."

"Didn't I?" Virginia frowned. "No, I didn't, did I?"

"But when did you meet him?"

"That day I came out to see the cottage. Do you remember? I said I wouldn't be back for lunch. And I went to the pub in Lanyon to buy cigarettes and I met him there."

"But why didn't you say anything about it? Was there any particular reason that you didn't want me to know?"

"No." She tried to remember. "But I suppose I just didn't want to talk about him." She smiled. "It wasn't as though it had been such a friendly reunion. In fact, we had the most terrible row . . ."

"But did you *mean* to meet him again?"

"No. It just happened."

"And he remembered you? After all this time? But he'd only ever seen you that once at the barbecue."

"No," said Virginia. "I did see him again."

"*When?*"

"About a week after the barbecue. I met him in Porthkerris. We spent the afternoon together and he drove me back to Wheal House. You didn't see him because you were out that day. But my mother was there. She knew about it."

"But why was it all kept such a secret?"

"It wasn't a secret, Alice. It was just that my mother didn't like Eustace. I must say, he didn't make much of an effort to impress her, and he was rude and the Land-Rover was covered with bits of straw and mud and manure . . . not my mother's cup of tea at all. She treated the whole incident as though it were a sort of joke, but I knew that he had made her angry, and that she didn't like him."

"But you could have talked to me about him. After all, it was I who introduced you to Eustace."

"I tried, but every time I started, my mother somehow broke into the conversation or changed the subject or interrupted in some way. And . . . you mustn't forget this, Alice . . . you were her friend, not mine. I was just the little girl, out of the nursery. I never imagined for a moment that you'd take my side against hers."

"Was it a question of taking sides?"

"It would have been. You know what a snob she was."

"Oh, yes, of course, but it was harmless."

"No, Alice, it wasn't harmless. It was terribly dangerous. It affected everything she did. It deformed her."

"Virginia!" Alice was shocked.

"That's why we suddenly went back to London. You see, she knew, she guessed right away, that I was in love with Eustace."

The kettle boiled. Alice lifted it, and filled the coffee jug, and the kitchen was suffused with a delicious fresh smell. Alice drew a spoon gently across the surface of the coffee.

"And were you?" she asked at last. "In love with Eustace?"

"Of course I was. Wouldn't you have been at seventeen?"

"But you married Anthony Keile."

"Yes."

"Did you love him?"

"I . . . I married him."

"Were you happy?"

"I was lonely . . ."

"But, Virginia, I always thought . . . I mean, your mother always said . . . I thought you were so happy," Alice finished, hopeless with confusion.

"No. But it wasn't all Anthony's fault. It was my fault, too."

"Did Lady Keile know this?"

"No." Nor did she know the circumstances of Anthony's death. Nor did she know about Liz. Nor was she ever going to. "Why should she know? She used to come and stay with us, but never for more than a week at a time. It wasn't difficult to foster the illusion of an idyllically happy marriage. It was the least we could do for her . . ."

"I'm surprised Nanny never said anything."

"Nanny never saw anything she didn't want to see. And to her, Anthony was perfection."

"It can't have been easy."

"No. but like I said, it wasn't all Anthony's fault."

"And Eustace?"

"Alice, I was seventeen; a little girl, waiting for someone to come and buy her a ice-cream."

"But not now . . ." said Alice.

"No. Now I'm twenty-seven and the mother of two children. And I'm not waiting for ice-creams any longer."

"You mean, he has nothing to give you."

"And he needs nothing from me. He's self-sufficient. He has his own life. He has Penfolda."

"Have you discussed this with him?"

"Oh, Alice . . ."

"You obviously haven't. So how can you be so certain?"

"Because all those years ago, he said he'd phone me. He said that he wanted me to come out to Penfolda for tea or something, to meet his mother again. And I was going to borrow your car and drive myself out here. But you see, he never telephoned. I waited, but he never telephoned. And before there was time to find out why, or do anything about it, I'd been whisked back to London by my mother."

Alice said, "And how do you *know* he never telephoned?" She was beginning to sound impatient.

"Because he never did."

"Perhaps your mother took the call."

"I asked her. And she said there'd never been any telephone call."

"But, Virginia, she was perfectly capable of taking a call and never telling you about it. Specially if she didn't like the young man. Surely you realized that."

Her voice was brisk and practical. Virginia stared, scarcely able to believe her ears. That Alice should say such things about Rowena Parsons—Alice of all people, her mother's oldest friend. Alice, coming out with a dark truth that Virginia had never had the courage to find out for herself. She remembered her mother's face, smiling across the railway carriage, the laughing protest. *"Darling! What an accusation. Of course not. You surely didn't think . . ."*

And Virginia had believed her. She said at last, helplessly, "I thought she was telling me the truth. I didn't think she was capable of lying."

"Let's say she was a determined person. And you were her only child. She always had great ambitions for you."

"You knew this. You knew this about her and yet she was still your friend."

"Friends aren't people you particularly like for any special reason. You just like people because they're your friends."

"But if she was lying, then Eustace must have thought that I didn't want to see him again. All these years he's been thinking I simply let him down."

"But he wrote you a letter," said Alice.

"A *letter*?"

"Oh, Virginia, don't be so dense. That letter that came for you. The day before you went back to London." Virginia continued to stare blankly. "I know there was a letter. It came by the afternoon post, and it was on the table in the hall and I thought 'How nice' because you didn't get many letters. And then I went off to do something or other and when I came back the letter had gone. I presumed you'd taken it."

A letter. Virginia saw the letter. Imagined the envelope as white, the writing very black, addressed to her. Miss Virginia Parsons. Lying unattended and vulnerable upon that round table that still stood in the centre of the hall at Wheal House. She saw her mother come out of the drawing-room, perhaps on her way upstairs, pause to inspect the afternoon's mail. She was wearing the raspberry-red suit with the white silk shirt, and when she put out her hand to pick up the letter, her nails were painted the same raspberry-red, and her heavy gold charm bracelet made a jingling sound, like bells.

She saw her frown at the writing, the black masculine writing, inspect the postmark, hesitate for perhaps a second, and then slip the envelope into the pocket of her jacket and carry on with what she was doing, unperturbed, as though nothing had happened.

She said, "Alice, I never got that letter."

"But it was there!"

"Don't you see? Mother must have taken it. Destroyed it. She would, you know. She would say, 'It's all for Virginia's sake. For Virginia's own good.'"

Illusions were gone for ever, the veil torn away. She could look back with a cool, objective regard and see her mother the way she had really been, not merely snobbish and determined, but devious too. In some odd way, this was a relief. It had taken some effort, all these years, to sustain the legend of an irreproachable parent, even though

130

Virginia had been deceiving nobody but herself. Now, remembered, she seemed much more human.

Alice was looking upset, as though already regretting any mention of the letter.

"Perhaps it wasn't from Eustace."

"It was."

"How do you know?"

"Because if it had been from anyone else, then she would have given it back to me, with some excuse or other about opening it by mistake."

"But we don't know what was in the letter."

Virginia got off the table. "No. But I'm going to find out. Now. Will you stay here till the children wake up? Will you tell them I shan't be long?"

"But where are you going?"

"To see Eustace, of course," said Virginia, from the door.

"But you haven't drunk your coffee. I made you coffee and you haven't even drunk it. And what are you going to say to him? And how are you going to explain?"

But Virginia had already gone. Alice was speaking to an empty room, an open, swinging door. With an exclamation of exasperation, she put down her coffee cup and went to the door as though to call Virginia back, but Virginia was already out of earshot, running like a child through the tall summer grass, across the fields in the direction of Penfolda.

She took the field path because it would have taken too long to get into the car and turn it and drive back along the main road. And time was too precious to be wasted. They had already lost ten years, and there was not another moment to spare.

She was running, through a joyous morning of honey-scents and white daisies and tall grass that whipped at her bare legs. The sea was a dark, purplish blue, striped with ribbons of turquoise, and the horizon was blurred in a haze that promised great heat. She was running, long-legged, taking the steps of the stiles two at a time, and the ditches of the stubble fields brimmed with red poppies and the air was filled with the petals of yellow gorse flowers, blown to confusion, like confetti, by the sea-wind.

She came across the last field, and Penfolda lay ahead of her, the house and the long barns, and the little garden, wall-enclosed from the wind. She went over the last stile that led into the vegetable garden, and down the path and through the gate, and she saw that the cat and her half-Siamese kittens lay in the sun on the doorstep, and the front door stood open and she went indoors and called Eustace, and the house was dark after the brightness of the day outside.

"Who's that?"

It was Mrs. Thomas, carrying a duster, peering over the banister.

"It's me. Virginia. Virginia Keile. I'm looking for Eustace."

"He's just coming in from milking . . ."

"Oh, thank you." Without bothering to wait and explain, she went back out of doors, and started across the lawn, making for the cattle court and the milking parlour. But at that moment he appeared, coming through the gate that opened into the far side of the garden. He was in shirt sleeves, aproned, wearing rubber boots and carrying a polished aluminum pail of milk. Virginia stopped dead. He closed the latch of the gate behind him and looked up and saw her.

She had meant to be very sensible. To say, calmly and quietly, "I want to ask you about the letter you wrote me." But it didn't happen like that at all. For everything was said in that long moment, while they stood and looked at each other, and then Eustace set down his bucket and started towards her, and she ran down the slope of the grass and into his arms, and she was laughing, her face pressed into the front of his shirt, and he was saying, "It's all right. It's all right," just as though she were crying, not laughing. And Virginia said, "I love you," and then she burst into tears.

He said, "Of course I telephoned. Three or four times. But you were never there. It was always your mother and each time I felt more of a fool and each time she said that she'd tell you I'd called and that you'd ring me back. And I thought maybe you'd changed your mind. I thought perhaps you'd decided you had better things to do than come and have tea with someone like me and my old mother. I thought maybe your mother had talked you round. She didn't lose any love on me, not from the first moment she set eyes on me. But you knew that, didn't you?"

"Yes, I knew. And I wondered. Once, I nearly rang you up. I thought perhaps you'd forgotten . . . and then I lost my nerve. And then, out of the blue, my mother said we had to go back to London and after that, there wasn't any time. And in the train, I asked her,

132

straight out, if you'd ever called and she said never. And I believed her. That was the terrible thing, I always believed her. I should have known. It was my fault, I should have known. Oh, Eustace, why was I such a ninny?"

They had come indoors, ostensibly to find a clean handkerchief for Virginia, and for no particular reason had stayed there, ending up, inevitably, in the kitchen, sitting at the scrubbed table, with the air filled with the smell of baking saffron bread, and the only sound to disturb them the slow ticking of the old-fashioned pendulum clock.

"You weren't a ninny," said Eustace. "You were seventeen. That was another of the things that bothered me. It would have been easy to persuade you, push you around, before you'd even had time to grow up and make up your own mind about things. That's what I said in the letter. When you never rang me back, I thought maybe you'd got cold feet. So I said that if you wanted to wait a couple of years, I'd be ready to wait too, see how we felt about things then." He grinned, ruefully. "It took some writing, I can tell you. I'd never said such things to a girl before, nor have since."

"And you thought I'd never even bothered to reply?"

"I didn't know what to think . . . And then, the next thing, I saw in the paper that you were getting married."

"Eustace, if I'd got the letter, I wouldn't have gone back to London. I'd have refused."

"You couldn't refuse, you were under age."

"I'd have had hysterics, then. A nervous breakdown. Made the most ghastly scenes. Made myself ill."

"You'd still have gone."

She knew that he was right. "But I'd have known you were there, waiting. And I would never have married Anthony. I would never have gone to Scotland. I would never have wasted all these years."

Eustace raised his eyebrows. "Wasted? They weren't wasted. What about Cara and Nicholas?"

Virginia's eyes stung with sudden tears. She said, "Now it's all too complicated."

He put his arms around her, kissed the tears away, pushed her hair back off her face. He said, "Things happen the way they're meant to. There's a pattern and a shape to everything. You look back and see it all. Nothing happens without a reason. Nothing is impossible, like

133

meeting again, walking into The Mermaid's Arms and seeing you sitting there, just as though you'd never been away. Like a miracle."

"You didn't behave as though it were a miracle. In no time at all you were bawling at me."

"I was scared of getting hurt a second time. I was scared that I'd been mistaken about you, that all the things that were so important to your mother had become important to you, too."

"I told you. They were never important."

He took her hand in his. "After the picnic yesterday, I thought it was going to be all right. After being with you and Cara and Nicholas, and swimming and cooking the fish, and you all seeming to enjoy it so much, I thought then, coming up the cliff, that it was like being back where we started. And I thought I would be able to talk about that time, when you went back to London and I was left not knowing what had happened, and we never saw each other again. I thought we could have talked about it, perhaps made a new beginning."

"But I was thinking the same, you stupid man, and all you did was to tell me to go back to Scotland and learn how to be a farmer. I want to be farmer's wife, but I don't want to be a farmer. And I wouldn't know one end of an Aberdeen Angus herd from the other."

Eustace grinned again, faintly sheepish. "I told you, it was those photographs of Cara's. We'd seemed so close all day, and all at once I realized that we weren't close, we belonged to different worlds. We always have done, Virginia. A place like Kirkton and a little farm like Penfolda, well, you just don't talk about them in the same breath. And suddenly it seemed insane to imagine that I could ask you to leave all that, give it all up, just for the sake of being with me. Because that's all I've got to offer."

"And that's what I want. That's all I've ever wanted. Kirkton was Anthony's house. Without him to keep it going, it has no life at all. Anyway, I'm going to sell it. I decided last night. I shall have to go back, of course, break the news to everybody, put the whole thing in the lawyer's hands . . ."

"Have you thought about the children?"

"I never stop thinking about them. And they'll understand."

"It's their home."

"Penfolda's going to be their home." She smiled at the thought, and Eustace took her shoulders between his big hands and leaned forward to kiss her open, smiling mouth. "A new home and a new father," she finished when she had got her breath back.

But Eustace did not seem to be listening to her. "Talk of the devil," he said.

And Virginia heard the children, coming across the garden, talking, their voices high-pitched.

"Look, there are the kittens. Look, they're in the sun, and they haven't drunk their milk."

"Oh, leave them, Nicholas. They're having a sleep."

"This one isn't sleeping. It's got its eyes open. Look. Its eyes are open."

"I wonder where Mummy is? Mummy!"

"In here," called Eustace.

"Mummy, Aunt Alice Lingard wants to know if you're ever coming home again." Cara appeared at the kitchen door, her spectacles crooked, her hair hanging out of its slide. "She gave us some bacon and eggs, but we've been waiting and waiting and she says Mrs. Jilkes will think that she's been in a car accident, and died . . ."

"Yes," said Nicholas, appearing, hard on her heels, with a kitten spread-eagled by pin-like claws across the front of his sweater. "And we didn't wake up till ten past ten when Aunt Alice came up to see us, and we very nearly didn't have any breakfast at all, we very nearly just waited until lunch-time . . . but I was . . . so hungry . . ."

His voice trailed away. He had realized that nobody was talking but him. His mother and Eustace were simply sitting, watching him, and Cara was staring at her mother as though she had never seen her before. Nicholas was disconcerted. "Well, what's wrong? Why isn't anybody talking?"

"We're waiting for you to stop," said Virginia.

"Why?"

Virginia looked at Eustace. Eustace leaned forward to draw Cara towards him. Very gently, seriously, he set her spectacles straight. Then Nicholas saw that he was smiling.

"We've got something to tell you," said Eustace.

THE DAY OF THE STORM

1

IT ALL STARTED on a Monday at the end of January. A dull day at a dull time of the year. Christmas and the New Year were over and forgotten and yet the new season had not started to show its face. London was cold and raw, the shops filled with empty hope and clothes "for cruising". The trees in the park stood lacy and bare against low skies, the trodden grass beneath them dull and dead, so that it was impossible to believe that it could ever again be carpeted with drifts of purple and yellow crocus.

It was a day like any other day. The alarm woke me to darkness, but a darkness made paler by the wide expanse of the uncurtained windows, and through them I could see the top of the plane tree, illuminated by the orange glow of distant street lights.

My room was unfurnished, except for the sofa bed on which I lay, and a kitchen table which I was going to strip of paint when I had the time, and polish with a coat of beeswax. Even the floor was bare, boards stretching to the wainscotting. An orange box did duty as a bedside table, and a second one filled in for a chair.

I put out a hand and turned on the light and surveyed the desolate scene with the utmost satisfaction. It was mine. My first home. I had moved in only three weeks ago but it belonged entirely to me. With it, I could do as I pleased. Cover the white walls with posters or paint them orange. Sand the bare floor or stripe it in colour. Already I had started to acquire a proprietary interest in junk and antique shops, and could not pass one without scanning the window for some treasure that I might be able to afford. This was how the table had come into my possession, and I already had my eye on an antique gilt mirror, but had not yet plucked up the courage to go into the shop and find out how much it was going to cost. Perhaps I would hang it in the centre of the chimney breast, or on the wall opposite the window, so that the reflections of the sky and the tree would be caught, like a picture, within its ornate frame.

These pleasant imaginings took some time. I looked again at the clock, saw that it was growing late, and climbed out of bed to pad, barefooted, across the floor and into the tiny kitchen, where I lit the gas and put the kettle on to boil. The day had begun.

143

The flat was in Fulham, the top floor of a small terrace house which belonged to Maggie and John Trent. I had met them only at Christmas, which I had spent with Stephen Forbes and his wife Mary and their large family of untidy children, in their large and untidy house in Putney. Stephen Forbes was my boss, the owner of the Walton Street bookshop where I had been working for the past year. He had always been enormously kind and helpful towards me and when he found out, from one of the other girls, that I would be on my own for Christmas, he and Mary had immediately issued a firm invitation— more an order, really—that I should spend the three days with them. There was plenty of space, he insisted vaguely, a room in the attic, a bed in Samantha's room, somewhere, but I wouldn't mind, would I? And I could always help Mary baste the turkey and pick all those torn bits of tissue paper off the floor.

Considering it from this angle, I finally accepted, and had a wonderful time. There's nothing like a family Christmas when there are children everywhere and noise and paper and presents, and a pine-smelling Christmas tree, glittering with baubles and crooked home-made decorations.

On Boxing Night, with the children safely in bed, the Forbeses threw a grown-up party, although we still seemed to continue playing childish games, and Maggie and John Trent came to this. The Trents were young marrieds, she the daughter of an Oxford don, whom Stephen had known well in his undergraduate days. She was one of those laughing, cheerful out-going people, and after she had arrived the party went with a swing. We were introduced but we didn't manage to talk until a game of charades, when we found ourselves side by side on a sofa, trying to guess, from the most incoherent gestures, that Mary was trying to act to us, in dumb show, the title of a film. *"Rose Marie!"* somebody yelled, for no apparent reason.

"Clockwork Orange!"

Maggie lit a cigarette and sank back on the sofa, defeated. "It's beyond me," she said. She turned her dark head to look at me. "You work in Stephen's shop, don't you?"

"Yes."

"I'll come in next week and spend all my Christmas book tokens. I've been given dozens."

"Lucky girl."

"We've just moved into our first house, so I want lots of coffee table stuff so that all our friends think I'm wildly intelligent . . ." Then somebody shouted, "Maggie, it's your turn," and she said "Cripes," and shot to her feet, and went stalking off to find out what she was going to have to act. I can't remember what it was, but watching her make a cheerful fool of herself, my heart warmed to her, and I hoped that I would see her again.

I did, of course. True to her word, she came into the shop a couple of days after the holiday wearing a sheepskin coat and a long purple skirt, and carrying a bulging handbag stuffed with book tokens. I wasn't serving anybody at that particular moment and I came out from behind a neat stack of shiny-jacketed novels and said, "Hallo."

"Oh, good, there you are. I was hoping I'd find you. Can you help me?"

"Yes, of course."

Together, we chose a cookery book, a new autobiography which everybody was talking about, and a marvellously expensive volume of Impressionist paintings for the legendary coffee table. All this came to a little more than the book tokens did, so she groped around in that handbag and took out a cheque book in order to pay for the balance of the amount.

"John'll be furious," she told me happily, writing out the amount with a red felt pen. The cheque was yellow and the effect quite gay. "He says we're spending far too much money as it is. There." She turned it over to write her address. "Fourteen Bracken Road, SW6." She said it aloud in case I couldn't read her writing. "I haven't got used to writing it yet. We've only just moved in. Terribly exciting, we've bought it freehold, believe it or not. At least our parents chipped in with the deposit and John managed to con some building society or other into giving us a loan for the rest. But of course because of this, we've got to let the top floor to help pay the mortgage, but still, I suppose it'll all work out." She smiled. "You'll have to come and see it."

"I'd like to." I was wrapping her parcel, being meticulous about matching the paper and folding the corners.

She watched me. "You know, it's terribly rude, but I don't know your name. I know it's Rebecca, but Rebecca what?"

"Rebecca Bayliss."

"I suppose you don't know of a nice peaceful individual who wants an unfurnished flat?"

I looked at her. Our thoughts were so close I scarcely had to speak.

145

I tied the knot on the parcel and snapped the string. I said, "How about me?"

"You? But are you looking for somewhere to live?"

"I wasn't until a moment ago. But I am now."

"It's only a room and a kitchen. And we have to share the bath."

"I don't mind if you don't. And if I can afford the rent. I don't know what you're asking."

Maggie told me. I swallowed and did a few mental calculations and said, "I could manage that."

"Have you got any furniture?"

"No. I've been living in a furnished flat with a couple of other girls. But I can get some."

"You sound as though you're desperate to get out."

"No, I'm not desperate, but I'd like to be on my own."

"Well, before you decide you'd better come and see it. Some evening, because John and I both work."

"*This* evening?" It was impossible to keep my impatience and excitement out of my voice and Maggie laughed.

"All right," she said. "This evening," and she picked up the beautifully wrapped parcel of books and prepared to depart.

I suddenly panicked . . . "I . . . I don't know the address . . ."

"Yes you do, silly, it's on the back of the cheque. Get a twenty-two bus. I'll expect you about seven."

"I'll be there," I promised.

Jolting slowly down the Kings Road in the bus I had to consciously damp down my enthusiasm. I was out to buy a pig in a poke. The flat might be totally impossible, too big, too small or inconvenient in some unimagined way. Anything was better than being disappointed. And indeed, from the outside, the little house was entirely unremarkable, one of a row of red brick villas, with fancy pointing around the doors and a depressing tendency towards stained glass. But inside Number 14 was bright with fresh paint and new carpets and Maggie herself in old jeans and a blue sweater.

"Sorry I look such a mess but I've got to do all the housework, so I usually change when I get back from the office. Come on, let's go up and see it . . . put your coat on the banisters, John's not home yet, but I told him you were coming and he thought it was a frightfully good idea . . ."

Talking all the time, she led the way upstairs and into the empty room which stood at the back of the house. She turned on the light.

"It faces south, out over a little park. The people who had the house before us built an extension on underneath, so you've got a sort of balcony on its roof." She opened a glass door and we stepped together out into the cold dark night, and I smelt the leaf-smell of the park, and damp earth, and saw, ringed by lamplight from the streets all around, the stretch of empty darkness. A cold wind blew suddenly, gustily, and the black shape of the plane tree rustled and then the sound was lost in the jet roar of an aeroplane going overhead.

I said, "It's like being in the country."

"Well, next best thing perhaps." She shivered. "Let's go in before we freeze." We stepped back through the glass door, and Maggie showed me the tiny kitchen which had been fashioned out of a deep cupboard, and then, halfway down the stairs, the bathroom, which we would all share. Finally, we ended up downstairs again in Maggie's warm, untidy sitting-room, and she found a bottle of sherry and some potato crisps which she swore were stale, but tasted all right to me. "Do you still want to come?" she asked.

"More than ever."

"When do you want to move in?"

"As soon as possible. Next week if I could."

"What about the girls you're sharing with just now?"

"They'll find someone else. One of them has a sister who's coming to London. I expect she'll move into my room."

"And what about furniture?"

"Oh . . . I'll manage."

"I expect," said Maggie comfortably, "your parents will come up trumps, they usually do. When I first came to London, my mother produced the most wonderful treasures out of the attic and the linen cupboard and so . . ." Her voice died away. I watched her in rueful silence, and she finally laughed at herself. "There I go again, opening my mouth and putting my foot in it. I'm sorry. I've obviously said something idiotically tactless."

"I haven't got a father, and my mother's abroad. She's living in Ibiza. That's really why I want somewhere of my own."

"I am sorry. I should have known, you spending Christmas with the Forbeses . . . I mean, I should have guessed."

"There's no reason why you should guess."

"Is your father dead?"

She was obviously curious, but in such an open and friendly way that all at once it seemed ridiculous to close up and shut up the way I usually did when people began asking me questions about my family.

"I don't think so," I said, trying to sound as though it didn't matter. "I think he lives in Los Angeles. He was an actor. My mother eloped with him when she was eighteen. But he soon got bored with domesticity, or perhaps he decided that his career was more important than raising a family. Anyway, the marriage lasted only a few months before he upped and left her, and then my mother had me."

"What a terrible thing to do."

"I suppose it was. I've never thought very much about it. My mother never talked about him. Not because she was particularly bitter or anything, just that when something was over and in the past, she usually forgot it. She's always been like that. She only looks forward, and always with the utmost optimism."

"But what happened after you were born? Did she go back to her parents?"

"No. Never."

"You mean, nobody sent a telegram saying 'Come back all is forgiven'?"

"I don't know. I honestly don't know."

"There must have been the most resounding row when your mother ran off, but even so . . ." Her voice trailed away. She was obviously unable to understand a situation which I had accepted with equanimity all my life. ". . . what sort of people would do a thing like that to their daughter?"

"I don't know."

"You must be joking!"

"No. I honestly don't know."

"You mean you don't know your own grandparents?"

"I don't even know who they are. Or perhaps who they were. I don't even know if they're still alive."

"Don't you know anything? Didn't your mother ever say anything?"

"Oh, of course . . . little scraps of the past used to come into her conversation but none of it added up to anything. You know how mothers talk to their children, remembering things that happened and things they used to do when they were little."

"But—Bayliss." She frowned. "That's not a very usual name. And it rings a bell somehow but I can't think why. Haven't you got a single clue?"

I laughed at her intensity. "You talk as though I really wanted to know. But you see, I don't. If you've never known grandparents, then you don't miss them."

"But don't you wonder . . ." she groped for words . . . "where they *lived?*"

"I know where they lived. They lived in Cornwall. In a stone house with fields that sloped down to the sea. And my mother had a brother called Roger but he was killed during the war."

"But what did she do after you were born? I suppose she had to go out and get a job."

"No, she had a little money of her own. A legacy from some old aunt or other. Of course, we never had a car or anything, but we seemed to manage all right. She had a flat in Kensington, in the basement of a house that belonged to some friends. And we stayed there till I was about eight, and then I went to boarding school, and after that we sort of . . . moved around . . ."

"Boarding schools cost money . . ."

"It wasn't a very grand boarding school."

"Did your mother marry again?"

I looked at Maggie. Her expression was lively and avidly curious, but she was kind. I decided that, having gone so far, I may as well tell her the rest.

"She . . . wasn't exactly the marrying type . . . But she was always very, very attractive, and I don't remember a time when there wasn't some adoring male in attendance . . . And once I was away at school, I suppose there wasn't much reason to go on being circumspect. I never knew where I was going to spend the next set of holidays. Once it was in France, in Provence. Sometimes in this country. Another time it was Christmas in New York."

Maggie took this in, and made a face. "Not much fun for you."

"But educational." I had long ago learned to make a joke of it. "And just think of all the places I've seen, and all the extraordinary places I've lived in. The Ritz in Paris once, and another time a gruesomely cold house in Denbighshire. That was a poet who thought he'd try sheep farming. I've never been so glad in my life when that association came to an end."

"She must be very beautiful."

"No, but men think she is. And she's very gay and improvident and vague, and I suppose you'd say utterly amoral. Maddening. Everything is 'jokey'. It's her big word. Unpaid bills are 'jokey' and lost handbags and unanswered letters, they're all 'jokey'. She has no idea of money and no sense of obligation. An embarrassing sort of person to live with."

"What's she doing in Ibiza?"

"She's living with some Swedish man she met out there. She went out to stay with a couple she knew, and she met this guy and the next thing I knew I had a letter saying that she was going to move in with him. She said he was terribly Nordic and dour but he had a beautiful house."

"How long is it since you've seen her?"

"About two years. I eased out of her life when I was seventeen. I did a secretarial course and took temporary jobs, and finally I ended up working for Stephen Forbes."

"Do you like it?"

"Yes. I do."

"How old are you?"

"Twenty-one."

Maggie smiled again, shaking her long hair in wonderment. "What a lot you've done," she said, and she did not sound in the least bit sorry for me but even slightly envious. "At twenty-one I was a blushing bride in a beastly busty white wedding dress and an old veil that smelt of mothballs. I'm not really a trad. person, but I've got a mother who is, and I'm very fond of her so I usually used to do what she wanted."

I could imagine Maggie's mother. I said, resorting to the comfort of clichés, because I couldn't think of anything else to say, "Oh, well, it takes all sorts," and at that moment we heard John's key in the lock and after that we did not bring up the subject of mothers and families again.

It was a day like any other day, but it had a bonus attached to it. Last Thursday I had worked late with Stephen, trying to complete the last of the January stocktaking, and in return he had given me this morning off so that I had until lunchtime to my own devices. I filled it in cleaning the flat (which took, at most, no more than half an hour), doing some shopping and taking a bundle of clothes to the launderette. By eleven thirty all this domesticity was completed so I put on my coat and set off, in a leisurely way, for work, intending to walk some of the way, and maybe stand myself an early lunch before getting to the shop.

It was one of those cold, dark, damp days when it never really gets light. I walked, through this gloom, up into the New Kings Road, and headed west. Here, every other shop seems to sell either antiques or second-hand beds or picture frames, and I thought I knew them all, but all at once I found myself outside a shop which I had not noticed

150

before. The outside was painted white, the windows framed in black, and there was a red and white awning pulled out as protection against the imminent drizzle.

I looked up to see what the shop was called and read the name TRISTRAM NOLAN picked out in neat black Roman capitals over the door. This door was flanked by windows filled with delectable odds and ends and I paused to inspect their contents, standing on the pavement bathed in brightness from the many lights which burned within. Most of the furniture was Victorian, re-upholstered and restored and polished. A buttoned sofa with a wide lap and curly legs, a sewing box, a small picture of lap dogs on a velvet cushion.

I looked beyond the windows and into the shop itself, and it was then that I saw the cherrywood chairs. They were a pair, balloon backed, with curved legs and seats embroidered with roses.

I craved them. Just like that. I could picture them in my flat, and I wanted them desperately. For a moment I hesitated. This was no junk shop and the price might well be more than I could afford. But after all, no harm could be done by asking. Before I could lose my nerve, I opened the door and went in.

The shop was empty, but the door opening and closing had rung a bell, and presently there was the sound of someone coming down the stairs, the woollen curtain that hung over the door at the back of the shop was drawn aside and a man came into view.

I suppose I had expected someone elderly and formally attired, in keeping with the ambience of the shop and its contents, but this man's appearance rocked all my vague, preconceived notions. For he was young, tall and long-legged, dressed in jeans—faded to a soft blue and clinging like a second skin—and a blue denim jacket, equally old and faded, with the sleeves turned back in a businesslike way to reveal the checked cuffs of the shirt he wore beneath it. A cotton handkerchief was knotted at his neck and on his feet he wore soft moccasins, much decorated and fringed.

That winter the most unlikely people were drifting around London dressed as cowboys, but somehow this one looked real, and his worn clothes appeared as genuine as he was. We stood and looked at each other, and then he smiled and for some reason this took me unawares. I don't like being taken unawares, and I said "Good morning" with a certain coolness.

He dropped the curtain behind him and came forward, soft footed. "Can I help you?"

He may have looked like a genuine, dyed-in-the-wool American, but the moment he opened his mouth it was clear that he was no such thing. For some reason this annoyed me. The life I had led with my mother had left me with a thick streak of cynicism about men in general, and phoneys in particular, and this young man, I decided then and there, was a phoney.

"I . . . I was going to ask about these little chairs. The balloon-back ones."

"Oh, yes." He came forward to lay his hand on the back of one. The hand was long and shapely, with spade-tipped fingers, the skin very brown. "There's just the pair of them."

I stared at the chairs, trying to ignore his presence.

"I wondered how much they were."

He squatted beside me to search for a price ticket and I saw his hair fell thick and straight to his collar, very dark and lustrous.

"You're in luck," he told me. "They're going very cheap because the leg of one has been broken and then not very professionally re-paired." He straightened up suddenly, surprising me by his height. His eyes were slightly tip-tilted, and a very dark brown, with an expression in them that I found disconcerting. He made me uncomfortable and my antipathy for him began to turn to dislike. "Fifteen pounds for the pair," he said. "But if you'd like to wait and pay a little more, I can get the leg reinforced, and perhaps a small veneer put over the joint. That would make it stronger and it would look better too."

"Isn't it all right now?"

"It would be all right for you," said the young man, ". . . but if you had a large fat man for dinner, he'd probably end up on his backside."

There was a pause while I regarded him—I hoped coldly. His eyes were brimming, with a malicious amusement which I had no intention of sharing. I did not appreciate the suggestion that the only men who would ever come and have dinner with me would necessarily be large and fat.

I said at last, "How much would it cost me to have the leg re-paired?"

"Say five pounds. That means you get the chairs for a tenner each."

I worked this out, and decided that I could just afford them.

"I'll take them."

"Good," said the young man and put his fists on his hips and smiled amiably, as though this were the end of the transaction.

I decided he was utterly inefficient. "Do you want me to pay for them now, or to leave a deposit . . . ?"

"No, that doesn't matter. You can pay for them when you collect them."

"Well, when will they be ready?"

"In about a week."

"Don't you want my name?"

"Not unless you want to give it to me."

"What happens if I never come back?"

"Then I expect they'll be sold to someone else."

"I don't want to lose them."

"You won't," said the young man.

I frowned, angry with him, but he only smiled and went to the door to open it for me. Cold air poured in, and outside the drizzle had started and the street looked dark as night.

He said, "Goodbye," and I managed a frosty smile of thanks and went past him, out into the gloom, and as I did so I heard the bell ring as he shut the door behind me.

The day was, all at once, unspeakable. My pleasure in buying the chairs had been wrecked by the irritation which the young man had generated. I did not usually take instant dislikes to people and I was annoyed not only with him, but with myself, for being so vulnerable. I was still brooding on this when I walked down Walton Street and let myself into Stephen Forbes's bookshop. Even the comfort of being indoors and the pleasant smell of new paper and printers' ink did nothing to dispel my wretched mood.

The shop was on three levels, with new books on the ground floor, second-hand books and old prints upstairs, and Stephen's office in the basement. I saw that Jennifer, the second girl, was busy with a customer, and the only other person visible was an old lady in a tweed cape engrossed in the Gardening section, so I headed for the little cloakroom, unbuttoning my coat as I went, but then I heard Stephen's heavy, unmistakeable footsteps coming up from downstairs, and for some reason I stopped to wait for him. The next moment he appeared, tall, stooping and spectacled, with his usual expression of vague benevolence. He wore dark suits that always managed to appear as though in need of a good press, and already, at this early hour, the knot of his tie had begun to slip down, revealing the top button of his shirt.

"Rebecca," he said.

"Yes, I'm here . . ."

"I'm glad I've caught you." He came to my side speaking low-voiced, so as not to disturb the customers. "There's a letter for you downstairs; it's been forwarded on from your old flat. You'd better nip down and collect it."

I frowned. "A letter?"

"Yes. Airmail. Lots of foreign stamps. It has, for some reason, an air of urgency about it."

My irritation, along with all thoughts of new chairs, was lost in a sudden apprehension.

"Is it from my mother?"

"I don't know. Why don't you go and find out?"

So I went down the steep, uncarpeted stairs to the basement, lit, on this dark day, by long strip-lights let into the ceiling. The office was marvellously untidy—as usual—littered with letters and parcels and files, piles of old books, and cardboard boxes and ashtrays which nobody ever remembered to empty. But the letter was on the middle of Stephen's blotter and instantly visible.

I picked it up. An airmail envelope, Spanish stamps, an Ibizan postmark. But the writing was unfamiliar, pointed and spiky, as though a very fine pen had been used. It had been sent to the old flat, but this address had been crossed out and the address of the bookshop substituted in large, girlish, handwriting. I wondered how long the letter had lain on the table by the front door, before one of the girls realized that it was there and had taken the trouble to forward it on to me.

I sat down in Stephen's chair and slit the envelope. Inside, two pages of fine airmail paper, and the date at the head was the third of January. Very nearly a month ago. My mind sounded a note of alarm and, suddenly frightened, I began to read.

Dear Rebecca,

I hope you do not mind me calling you by your Christian name, but your mother has spoken to me of you a great deal. I am writing because your mother is very ill. She has been unwell for some time and I wished to write to you before but she would not let me.

Now, however, I am taking matters into my own hands, and with the doctor's approval I am letting you know that I think you should come out to see her.

If you can do this, perhaps you will cable me the number of your aeroplane flight so that I can be at the airport to meet you.

I know that you are working and it may not be easy to make this trip, but I would advise you to waste no time. I am afraid that you will find your mother very changed, but her spirit is still high.

> With good wishes.
> Sincerely,
> Otto Pedersen.

I sat in unbelief, and stared at the letter. The formal words told me nothing and everything. My mother was very ill, perhaps dying. A month ago I had been asked to waste no time but to go to her. Now it was a month later, and I had only just got the letter and perhaps she was already dead—and I had never gone. What would he think of me, this Otto Pedersen whom I had never seen, whose name, even, I had not known until this moment?

2

I READ the letter again, and then again, the flimsy pages rustling in my hands. I was still there, sitting at his desk, when Stephen finally came downstairs to find me.

I turned to look up at him over my shoulder. He saw my face and said, "What is it?"

I tried to tell him, but could not. Instead I thrust the letter at him, and while he took it, and read it, I sat with my elbows on his desk, biting my thumbnails, bitter and angry, and fighting a terrible anxiety.

He was soon finished reading. He tossed the letter down on the desk between us, and said, "Did you know she was ill?"

I shook my head.

"When did you last hear from her?"

"Four, five months ago. She never wrote letters." I looked up at him and said, furiously, choked by the great lump in my throat, "That was nearly a *month* ago. That letter's been lying in the flat, and nobody bothered to send it to me. She may be dead by now and I never went, and she'll think I simply didn't care!"

"If she had died," said Stephen, "then we'd have surely heard. Now, don't cry, there isn't time for that. What we have to do is get

155

you out to Ibiza with all convenient speed, and let—" he glanced down at the letter again—"Mr Pedersen know you're arriving. Nothing else matters."

I said, "I can't go," and my mouth began to grow square and my lower lip tremble as though I were a ten-year-old.

"Why can't you go?"

"Because I haven't got enough money for the fare."

"Oh, my dear child, let me worry about that . . ."

"But I can't let you . . ."

"Yes, you can, and if you get all stiff-necked about it then you can pay me back over the next five years and I'll charge you interest, if it'll make you feel happier, and now for God's sake don't let's mention it again . . ." He was already reaching for the directory, behaving in an altogether efficient and un-Stephen-like fashion. "Have you got a passport? And nobody's going to clamp down on you for small-pox injections or anything tiresome like that. Hallo? British Airways? I want to make a reservation on the first plane to Ibiza." He smiled down at me, still fighting tears and temper, but already feeling a little better. There is nothing like having a large and kindly man to take over in times of emotional stress. He picked up a pencil and drew a sheet of paper towards him and began to make notes. "Yes. When? Fine. Can we have a reservation, please? Miss Rebecca Bayliss. And what time does it get to Ibiza? And the flight number? Thank you so much. Thank you. Yes, I'll get her to the airport myself."

He put down the receiver and surveyed, with some satisfaction, the illegible squiggles his pencil had made.

"That's it, then. You fly tomorrow morning, change planes at Palma, get to Ibiza about half-past-seven. I'll drive you to the airport. No, don't start arguing again, I wouldn't feel happy unless I saw you actually walk on to the aeroplane. And now we'll cable Mr Otto Pedersen—" he picked up the letter again—"at the Villa Margareta, Santa Catarina, and let him know that you're coming." He smiled down at me with such cheerful reassurance that I was suddenly filled with hope.

I said, "I can't ever thank you . . ."

"I don't ever want you to," said Stephen. "It's the least I can do."

I flew the next day, in a plane half-filled with hopeful winter holiday tourists. They even carried straw hats against an improbably blazing sun, and their faces, as we stepped out into a steady drizzle at Palma,

156

were disappointed but resolutely cheerful, as though, for certain, to-morrow would be better.

The rain never ceased, all the four hours I waited in the transit lounge, and the flight out of Palma was bumpy with thick, wet clouds. But as we rose above them and headed out across the sea, the weather brightened. The clouds thinned and broke, disclosing an evening sky of robin's egg blue, and far below the crumpled sea was streaked with the pink light of the setting sun.

It was dark when we landed. Dark and damp. Coming down the gangway beneath a sky full of bright southern stars, there was only the smell of petrol, but as I walked across the puddled tarmac towards the lights of the terminal building I felt the soft wind in my face. It was warm and smelt of pines, and was evocative of every summer holiday I had ever spent abroad.

At this quiet time of the year the plane had not been full. It did not take long to get through Customs and Immigration, and—my passport stamped—I picked up my suitcase and walked into the Arrivals Lounge.

There were the usual small groups of waiting people standing about or sitting hunched apathetically on the long plastic banquettes. I stopped and looked about me, waiting to be identified, but could see nobody who looked in the least like a Swedish writer come to meet me. And then a man turned from buying a newspaper at the bookstall. Across the room our eyes met, and he folded the newspaper and began to walk towards me, pushing his paper into his jacket pocket as though it were no longer of any use to him. He was tall and thin, with hair that was either blond or white—it was impossible to tell in the bright, impersonal electric light. Before he was half way across the polished floor I smiled tentatively, and as he approached he said my name, "Rebecca?" with a question mark at the end of it, still not entirely certain that it was I.

"Yes."

"I'm Otto Pedersen." We shook hands and he gave a formal little bow as he did so. His hair, I saw then, was pale blond, turning grey, and his face was deeply tanned, thin and bony, the skin dry and finely wrinkled from long exposure to the sun. His eyes were very pale, and more grey than blue. He wore a black polo-necked sweater and a light oatmeal-coloured suit with pleated pockets, like a safari shirt, and a belt which hung loose, the buckle swinging. He smelt of aftershave and looked as clean as if he had been bleached.

Having found each other, it was suddenly difficult to find anything to say. All at once we were both overwhelmed by the circumstances of our meeting and I realized that he was as unsure of himself as I. But he was also urbane and polite, and dealt with this by taking my suitcase from me and asking if this was all my luggage.

"Yes, that's all."

"Then let us go to the car. If you like to wait at the door, I will fetch it and save you the walk . . ."

"I'll come with you."

"It's only across the road, in the car park."

So we went out together, into the darkness again. He led me to the half empty car park. Here, he stopped by a big black Mercedes, unlocked it, and tossed my case on to the back seat. Then he held the door open so that I could get in before coming around to the front of the car to settle himself beside me.

"I hope you had a good journey," he said, politely, as we left the terminal behind us and headed out into the road.

"It was a little bumpy in Palma. I had to wait four hours."

"Yes. There are no direct flights at this time of the year."

I swallowed. "I must explain about not answering your letter. I've moved flats, and I didn't get it till yesterday morning. It wasn't forwarded to me, you see. It was so good of you to write, and you must have wondered why I never replied."

"I thought something like that must have happened."

His English was perfect, only the precise Swedish vowel sounds betraying his origins, and a certain formality in the manner in which he expressed himself.

"When I got your letter I was so frightened . . . that it would be too late."

"No," said Otto. "It is not too late."

Something in his voice made me look at him. His profile was knife sharp against the yellow glow of passing street lights, his expression unsmiling and grave.

I said, "Is she dying?"

"Yes," said Otto. "Yes, she is dying."

"What is wrong with her?"

"Cancer of the blood. You call it leukaemia."

"How long has she been ill?"

"About a year. But it was only just before Christmas time that she became so ill. The doctor thought that we should try blood transfusions, and I took her to the hospital for this. But it was no good, because as soon as I got her home again, she started this very bad nose

158

bleed, and so the ambulance had to come and take her back to hospital again. She was there over Christmas and only then allowed home again. It was after that I wrote to you."

"I wish I'd got the letter in time. Does she know I'm coming?"

"No, I didn't tell her. You well know how she loves surprises, and equally how she hates to be disappointed. I thought there was a chance that something would go wrong and you wouldn't be on the plane." He smiled frostily, "But of course you were."

We stopped at a cross-roads to wait for a country cart to pass in front of us, the feet of the mule making a pleasant sound on the dusty road, and a lantern swinging from the back of the cart. Otto took advantage of the pause to take a cheroot from the breast pocket of his jacket and light it from the lighter on the dashboard. The cart passed, we moved on.

"How long is it since you have seen your mother?"

"Two years."

"You must expect a great change. I am afraid you will be shocked, but you must try not to let her see. She is still very vain."

"You know her so well."

"But of course."

I longed to ask him if he loved her. The question was on the tip of my tongue, but I realized that at this stage of our acquaintance it would be nothing but impertinence to ask such an intimate and personal thing. Besides, what difference did it make? He had met her and wanted to be with her, had given her a home, and now, when she was so ill, was cherishing her in his own apparently unemotional manner. If that wasn't love, then what was?

After a little, we began to talk of other things. I asked him how long he had lived on the island, and he said five years. He had come first in a yacht and had liked the place so well that he had returned the next year to buy his house and settle here.

"You're a writer . . ."

"Yes, but I am also a Professor of History."

"Do you write books on history?"

"I have done so. At the moment I am working on a thesis concerned with the Moorish occupation of these islands and southern Spain."

I was impressed. As far as I could remember, none of my mother's previous lovers had been even remotely intellectual.

"How far away is your house?"

"About five miles now. The village of Santa Catarina was quite unspoiled when I first came here. Now, however, large hotel developments are planned and I fear it will become spoiled like the rest of the island. No, that is wrong. Like some parts of the island. It is still possible to be entirely remote if you know where to go and have a car or perhaps a motor boat."

It was warm in the car and I rolled down the window. The soft night air blew in on my face and I saw that we were in country now, passing through groves of olives, with every now and then the glimmering light of a farmhouse window shining beyond the bulbous, spiked shapes of prickly pear.

I said, "I'm glad she was here. I mean, if she has to be ill and die, I'm glad it's somewhere like this, in the south, with the sun warm and the smell of pines."

"Yes," said Otto. And then, precisely as ever, "I think that she has been very happy."

We drove on in silence, the road empty, telegraph poles rushing to meet the headlights of the car. I saw that now we were running parallel to the sea, which spread to an invisible, dark horizon and was dotted here and there with the lights of fishing boats. Presently there appeared ahead of us the neon-lighted shape of a village. We passed a sign reading "Santa Catarina" and then were driving down the main street; the air was filled with the smell of onions and oil and grilling meat. Flamenco music flung itself at us from open doorways, and dark faces, filled with absent curiosity, turned to watch us pass. In a moment we had left the village behind us, and had plunged forward into the darkness which lay beyond, only to slow down almost immediately to negotiate a steep corner which led up a narrow lane between orchards of almond trees. The headlights bored into the darkness, and ahead I saw the villa, white and square, pierced by small, secretive windows and with a lighted lantern swinging over the great, nailed front door.

Otto braked the car and switched off the engine. We got out, Otto taking my suitcase from the back seat and leading the way across the gravel. He opened the door and stood aside and I walked in ahead of him.

We were in a hallway, lit by a wrought-iron chandelier and furnished with a long couch covered in a bright blanket. A tall blue and white jar stood by the door containing a selection of ivory-handled walking sticks and sun umbrellas. As Otto closed the front door, another opened ahead of us and a small, dark-haired woman appeared, wearing a pink overall and flat, worn slippers.

160

"Señor."

"Maria."

She smiled, showing a number of gold teeth. He spoke to her in Spanish, asking a question to which she replied and then, turning, introduced me to her.

"This is Maria, who takes care of us. I have told her who you are . . ."

I held out my hand and Maria took it: we made friends by smiling and nodding. Then she turned back to Otto and spoke some more. Presently he handed her my suitcase, and she withdrew.

Otto said, "Your mother has been asleep but she is awake now. Let me take your coat."

I unbuttoned it, and he helped me off with it and laid it across the end of the couch. Then he went across the floor towards yet another door, motioning me to follow. I did, and was suddenly nervous, afraid of what I was going to find.

It was the salon of the house into which he led me. A long low-ceilinged room, white-washed like the rest of the house, and furnished with a pleasing mixture of modern Scandinavian and antique Spanish. The tile floor was scattered with rugs, there were a great many books and pictures, and in the centre of the room a round table was laid out, seductively, with neatly ordered magazines and newspapers.

A wood fire burned in a great stone fireplace, and in front of this was a bed, with a low table alongside, holding a glass of water and a jug, a few pink geraniums in a mug, some books and a lighted lamp.

This lamp and the flicker of flames provided the only light in the room, but from the door I could see the narrow shape which humped the pink blankets and the attenuated hand and arm which was extended as Otto came forward to stand on the hearth rug.

"Darling," she said.

"Lisa." He took the hand and kissed it.

"You haven't been long after all."

"Maria says you have slept. Do you feel ready for a visitor?"

"A visitor?" Her voice was a thread. "Who?"

Otto glanced up at me, and I moved forward to stand beside him. I said, "It's me. Rebecca."

"Rebecca. Darling child. Oh, how blissfully jokey." She held out both arms to me, and I knelt down beside the bed to kiss her; her body gave me no resistance or support at all, so thin was she, and when I touched her cheek it felt papery beneath my lips. It was like

161

kissing a leaf that has long since been wrenched by the wind from its parent tree.

"But what are you doing *here?*" She looked over my shoulder at Otto, and then back at me again. She put on the pretence of a frown. "You didn't *tell* her to come?"

"I thought you would like to see her," said Otto. "I thought it would cheer you up."

"But darling, why didn't you tell me?"

I smiled. "We wanted it to be a surprise."

"But I wish I'd known, then I could have looked forward to seeing you. That's what we always used to think, before Christmas. Half the fun was anticipation." She let me go and I sat back on my heels. "Are you going to stay?"

"For a day or so."

"Oh, how utterly perfect. We can have the most gorgeous gossips. Otto, does Maria know she's staying?"

"Of course."

"And what about dinner tonight?"

"It's all arranged . . . we'll have it together, in here, just the three of us."

"Well, let's have something now. A little drinkey. Is there any champagne?"

Otto smiled. "I think I can find a bottle. In fact, I think I remembered to put one on ice for just such an occasion."

"Oh, you clever man."

"Shall I get it now?"

"Please, darling."

She slid her hand in mine and it was like holding chicken bones. "And we'll drink to being together."

He went away to fetch the champagne and we were alone. I found a little stool and pulled it up so that I could sit close to her. We looked at each other, and she could not stop smiling. The dazzling smile and the bright dark eyes were still the same, so was the dark hair that spread like a stain over the snowy pillowcase. Otherwise her appearance was horrifying. I had never known anyone could be so thin and still be alive. And to make it more unreal, she was not pale and colourless but quite brown, as though she still spent most of the day lying in the sun. But she was excited. It seemed she could not stop talking.

"So sweet of the darling man to know how much I would love to see you. The only thing is, I'm so boring just now, I don't feel like

162

doing anything, he should have waited until I'm better and then we could have had some fun together, and gone swimming and out in the boat and had picnics and things."

I said, "I can come again."

"Yes, of course you can." She touched my face with her hand as though needing this contact to reassure her that I was really there. "You're looking gorgeous, do you know that? You've got your father's colouring, with those big grey eyes, and that corn-coloured hair. Is it corn, or is it gold? And I love the way you're doing it." Her hand travelled to the single plait which fell forward, like a rope over my right shoulder. "It makes you look like something out of a fairy story; you know, those old-fashioned books with the magical pictures. You're very pretty."

I shook my head. "No. I'm not."

"Well, you look it, and that's the next best thing. Darling, what are you doing with yourself? It's such ages since I wrote or heard from you. Whose fault was that. Mine, I suppose, I'm hopeless at writing letters."

I told her about the book shop and the new flat. She was amused by this. "What a funny person you are, building a little nest for yourself without anybody to share it with. Haven't you met anybody yet you want to marry?"

"No. Nor anyone who wants to marry me."

She looked malicious. "What about the man you work for?"

"He's married, he's got a charming wife and a brood of children."

She giggled. "That never bothered me. Oh, darling, what a dreadful mother I was to you, trailing you round in that reprehensible fashion. It's a wonder you haven't collected the most ghastly selection of neuroses or hang-ups or whatever they call them these days! But you don't look as though you have, so perhaps it was all right after all."

"Of course it was all right. I just grew up with my eyes open and that was no bad thing." I added, "I like Otto."

"Isn't he divine? So correct and punctilious and *northern*. And so blazingly intelligent . . . So lucky he doesn't want me to be intelligent too! He just likes having me make him laugh."

Somewhere, in the middle of the house, a clock struck seven, and as the last note chimed Otto came back into the room carrying a tray with the champagne bottle in a bucket of ice, and three wine glasses. We watched as he expertly loosened the cork and the golden foaming wine spilled into the three glasses, and we each took one and raised them, all of us smiling because it was suddenly a party. My mother said, "Here's to the three of us and happy times. Oh, so divinely jokey."

Later, I was shown to my bedroom, which was either simply luxurious or luxuriously simple, I couldn't decide which. A fitted bathroom led off it, so I showered, and changed into trousers and a silk shirt, and brushed my hair and replaited it, and returned to the salon. I found Otto and my mother waiting for me, Otto also changed for the evening, and Mother wearing a fresh bedjacket of powder blue with a silk shawl embroidered with pink roses flung across her knees, its long fringe brushing the floor. We had another drink and then Maria served dinner on a low table by the fire. My mother never stopped talking—it was all about the old days when I was growing up, and I kept thinking that Otto would be shocked, but he wasn't shocked at all, he was curious and much amused and kept asking questions and prompting my mother to tell us more.

". . . and that dreadful farm in Denbighshire . . . Rebecca, do you remember that terrible house? We nearly died of cold and the fire smoked whenever we lit it. That was Sebastian," she explained for Otto's benefit. "We all thought he was going to be a famous poet, but he wasn't any better at writing poetry than he was at sheep farming. In fact, if anything, worse. And I couldn't think how on earth I could leave him without hurting his feelings and then luckily Rebecca got bronchitis so I had the most perfect excuse."

"Not so lucky for Rebecca," suggested Otto.

"It certainly was. She hated it just as much as I did; anyway he had a horrible dog that was always threatening to bite her. Darling, is there any more champagne?"

She ate hardly anything, but sipped glass after glass of the icy wine while Otto and I worked our way steadily through Maria's delicious, four-course dinner. When it was finished, and the dishes cleared away, my mother asked for some music, and Otto put a Brahms concerto on the record player, turned very low. Mother just went on talking, like a toy that has been overwound and will only stop whirring senselessly around the floor when it finally breaks.

Presently, saying that he had work to do, Otto excused himself and left us, first building up the fire with fresh logs and making sure that we had everything we needed.

"Does he work every evening?" I asked, when he had gone.

"Nearly always. And in the mornings. He's very punctilious. I think that's why we've got on so well because we're so different."

I said, "He adores you."

"Yes," said my mother, accepting this. "And the best bit is that he never tried to turn me into someone else; he just accepted me, with my wicked ways and my lurid past." She touched my plait again. "You're growing more like your father . . . I always thought you looked like me, but you don't, you look like him now. He was very handsome."

"You know, I don't even know what his name was."

"Sam Bellamy. But Bayliss is a much better name, don't you think? Besides, having you all on my own like that, I always felt you were my child and nobody else's."

"I wish you'd tell me about him. You never have."

"There's so little to tell. He was an actor, and too good-looking for words."

"But where did you meet him?"

"He came down to Cornwall with a Summer Stock company doing open-air Shakespeare. It was all terribly romantic, dark blue summer nights and the damp, dewy smell of the grass, and that divine Mendelssohn music and Sam being Oberon.

> Through the house give glimmering light,
> By the dead and drowsy fire;
> Every elf and fairy sprite;
> Hop as light as bird from brier.

It was magical. And falling in love with him was part of the magic."

"Was he in love with you?"

"We both thought he was."

"But you ran away with him, and married him . . ."

"Yes. But only because my parents left me with no alternative."

"I don't understand."

"They disliked him. They disapproved. They said I was too young. My mother said why didn't I marry some nice young man who lived locally, why didn't I settle down and stop making an exhibition of myself? And if I married an actor, what would people say? I sometimes thought that was all she cared about, what people would say. As if it could possibly matter what anybody said."

It was, unbelievably, the first time I had ever heard her mention her mother. I said, cautiously prompting, "Didn't you like her?"

"Oh, darling, it's so long ago. It's so difficult to remember. But she stifled and repressed me. I sometimes felt she was trying to choke me with conventions. And Roger had been killed and I missed him so dreadfully. Everything would have been different if Roger had been there." She smiled. "He was so nice. Almost too nice. A real BV right from the very start."

"What's a BV?"

"Bitches' Victim. He always fell in love with the most impossible girls. And finally he married one. A little blonde doll, with dolly hair and dolly china blue eyes. My mother thought she was sweet. I couldn't stand her."

"What was she called?"

"Mollie." She made a face as though the very word tasted bad.

I laughed. "She can't have been as bad as all that."

"I thought she was. So maddeningly tidy. Always cleaning out her handbag or putting her shoes into trees, or sterilizing the baby's toys."

"She had a baby then?"

"Yes, a little boy. Poor child, she insisted on calling him Eliot."

"I think that's a nice name."

"Oh, Rebecca, it's sickening." It was obvious that nothing Mollie had done could find favour in my mother's eyes. "I always felt sorry for the child, being saddled with such a dreadful name. And somehow he lived up to it, you know how people do, and after Roger was killed the poor scrap was worse than ever, always hanging round his mother's neck and having to have a light on in his room at night."

"I think you're being very unkind."

She laughed. "Yes, I know, and it wasn't his fault. He probably turned into quite a personable young man if his mother gave him half a chance."

"I wonder what happened to Mollie?"

"I don't know. I don't particularly care, either." My mother could always be cruelly off-hand. "It's like a dream. Like remembering dream people. Or perhaps—" her voice trailed away—"perhaps they were real and I was the dream."

I felt uncomfortable, because this was too near the truth that I was trying to keep at bay. I said quickly, "Are your parents still alive?"

"My mother died that Christmas we spent in New York. Do you remember that Christmas? The cold and the snow and all the shops full of the sound of 'Jingle Bells'? By the end of that Christmas I felt I never wanted to hear that damned tune again. My father wrote to me, but of course the letter didn't reach me until months later by which time it had followed me half round the world. And then it was really

166

too late to write and say anything. Besides, I'm so useless about writing letters. He probably thought I simply didn't care."

"Didn't you ever write?"

"No."

"Didn't you like him either?" It seemed a sorry state of affairs.

"Oh, I adored him. He was wonderful. Terribly good looking, attractive to women, frightfully fierce and frightening. He was a painter. Did I ever tell you that?"

A painter. I had imagined everything, but never a painter. "No, you never said."

"Well, if you'd had any sort of education at all you'd probably have guessed. Grenville Bayliss. Doesn't that mean anything to you at all?"

I shook my head sadly. It was terrible never to have heard of a famous grandfather.

"Well, why should it? I was never any good at trailing you round art galleries or museums. come to think of it, I was never much good at anything. It's a wonder you've turned out so well on a solid diet of maternal neglect."

"What did he look like?"

"Who?"

"Your father."

"How do you imagine him?"

I considered the question and came up with Augustus John. "Bohemian, and bearded and rather leonine . . ."

"Wrong," said my mother. "He wasn't like that at all. He started off his life in the Navy and the Navy left an indelible stamp on him. You see, he didn't decide to be a painter until he was nearly thirty, when he threw up a promising career and enrolled at the Slade. It nearly broke my mother's heart. And moving to Cornwall and setting up house at Porthkerris simply added insult to injury. I don't think she ever forgave him for being so selfish. She'd adored queening it in Malta, and probably fancied herself as wife to the Commander-in-Chief. I must say, he was tailor-made for the part, very blue-eyed and imposing and terrifying. He never lost what was known in those days as a quarter-deck manner."

"But you weren't terrified of him?"

"No. I loved him."

"Then why didn't you go home?"

Her face closed up. "I couldn't. I wouldn't. Terrible things had been said, by all of us. Old resentments and old truths had all come boiling up, and threats were made and ultimatums handed out. And the more they opposed me, the more determined I became, and the more impossible it was, when the time came, to admit that they'd been right, and I'd been wrong, and I'd made a hideous mistake. And if I had gone home, I would never have got away again. I knew that. And you wouldn't have belonged to me any more, you'd have belonged to your grandmother. I couldn't have borne that. You were such a precious little thing." She smiled and added rather wistfully, "And we did have fun, didn't we?"

"Yes, of course we did."

"I would have liked to go back. Sometimes I very nearly did. It was such a lovely house. Boscarva it was called, and it was rather like this villa, standing square on a hill above the sea. When Otto first brought me here, it reminded me of Boscarva. But here it's warm and the winds are gentle; there, it was wild and stormy, and the garden was honeycombed with tall hedges to shelter the flower beds from the sea winds. I think the wind was the thing that my mother most hated. She used to seal all the windows and shut herself indoors, playing bridge with her friends or doing needlepoint."

"Didn't she ever do things with you?"

"Not really."

"But who looked after you?"

"Pettifer. And Mrs Pettifer."

"Who were they?"

"Pettifer had been in the Navy, too; he looked after my father and cleaned the silver and sometimes drove the car. And Mrs Pettifer did the cooking. I can't tell you how cosy they were. Sitting by the kitchen fire with them making toast and listening to the wind battering at the windows, knowing that it couldn't get in . . . it made you feel so safe. And we used to read fortunes from the teacups . . ." Her voice trailed off, memories uncertain now. And then, "No, that was Sophia."

"Who was Sophia?"

She did not reply. She was staring at the fire, her expression far away. Perhaps she had not heard me. She said at last, "After my mother died I should have gone back. It was naughty of me to stay away, but I was never over-endowed with what is known as moral fibre. But, you know, there are things at Boscarva that belong to me."

"What sort of things?"

"A desk, I remember. A little one, with drawers down the side, and a lid that opened up. I think it's called a davenport. And some jade that my father brought home from China and a Venetian looking-glass. They were all mine. On the other hand, I moved around so much that they would just have been a nuisance." She looked at me, frowning a little. "But perhaps you don't think they are a nuisance. Have you got any furniture in this flat of yours?"

"No. Practically none."

"Then perhaps I'll see if I can get hold of them for you. They must still be at Boscarva, provided the house hasn't been sold or burned down or something. Would you like me to try and get hold of them?"

"More than anything. Not just because I need furniture, but because they belonged to you."

"Oh, darling, how sweet, too jokey the way you long for roots, and I could never bear to have any. I always felt they would just tie me down in one place."

"And I always feel that they would make me belong."

She said, "You belong to me."

We stayed talking until the early hours of the morning. About midnight, she asked me to refill her waterjug, and I found my way into the deserted kitchen and did this for her, and realized then that Otto, with gentle tact, had probably taken himself quietly off to bed, so that we could be together. And when at last her voice grew tired and her words began to trail off in a blur of exhaustion, I said that I was sleepy too, which I was, and I stood up, cramped from sitting, stretched, and put more logs on the fire. Then I took away her second pillow so that she lay, ready for sleep. The silken shawl had slipped to the floor, so I picked this up and folded it and laid it on a chair. It remained only to stoop and kiss her, turn off the lamp, and leave her there in the firelight. As I went through the door, she said, as she always used to say when I was a little girl, "Good night, my love. Goodbye until tomorrow."

The next morning I was awake early, aware of sunshine streaming through the gaps in the shutters. I got up and went to open them, and saw the brilliant Mediterranean morning. I stepped out through the open windows on to the stone terrace which ran the length of the house and saw the hill sloping down to the sea, maybe a mile distant. The sand-coloured land was veiled in pink, the first tender blossoms of the almond trees. I went back into my room, dressed, and went out again—across the terrace, down a flight of steps, and through the ordered, formal garden. I vaulted a low stone wall, and walked on in the direction of the sea. Presently, I found myself in an orchard, surrounded by almond trees. I stopped and looked up at a froth of pink blossom and beyond it a pale and cloudless blue sky.

I knew that each flower would bear a precious fruit which, when the time came, would be frugally cropped, but even so I could not resist picking a single spray, and I was still carrying this when an hour or so later, having walked to the sea and back, I retraced my steps up the hill towards the villa.

It was steeper than I had realized. Pausing for breath, I looked up at the house, and saw Otto Pedersen standing on the terrace watching my progress. For an instant we both stood still; then he moved and started down the steps, and came down the garden to meet me.

I went on more slowly, still holding the spray of blossom. I knew then. I knew before he came close enough for me to see the expression on his face, but I went on, up through the orchard, and we met at last by the little drystone wall.

He said my name. That was all.

I said, "I know. You don't have to tell me."

"She died during the night. When Maria went in this morning to wake her . . . it was all over. It was so peaceful."

It occurred to me that we were not doing much to comfort each other. Or maybe there was no need. He put out a hand to help me over the wall, and kept my hand in his as we walked together up through the garden to the house.

She was buried, according to Spanish law, that very day, and in the little churchyard in the village. There was only the priest present, and Otto and Maria and myself. When it was all over, I put the spray of almond blossom on to her grave.

I flew back to London the next morning, and Otto drove me to the airport in his car. For most of the time we travelled in silence, but as we approached the terminal he suddenly said, "Rebecca, I don't know whether this has any significance, but I would have married Lisa. I would have married her, but I already have a wife in Sweden. We do not live together, and have not done so for a number of years, but she will not divorce me because her religion will not allow it."

"You didn't need to tell me, Otto."

"I wanted you to know."

"You made her so happy. You took such care of her."

"I am glad that you came. I am glad that you saw her."

"Yes." There was, all at once, a terrible lump in my throat, and my eyes filled and brimmed with painful tears. "Yes, I am glad too."

In the terminal, my ticket and my luggage checked, we stood and faced each other.

"Don't wait," I said. "Go now. I hate goodbyes."

"All right . . . but first . . ." He felt in his jacket pocket and took out three fine, worn silver bracelets. My mother had worn them always. She had been wearing them that last night. "You must have these." He took my hand and slipped them on to my wrist. "And this." Out of another pocket came a folded wad of British notes. He pressed it into my palm and closed my fingers over it. "They were in her handbag . . . so you must have them."

I knew they hadn't been in her handbag. She had never any money in her handbag except a few coppers for the next telephone call, and some dog-eared bills, long overdue. But there was something in Otto's face that I couldn't refuse, so I took the money and kissed him, and he turned on his heel, without a word.

I flew back to London in a state of miserable indecision. Emotionally I was empty, drained even of grief. Physically I found that I was exhausted but I could neither sleep nor face the meal that the stewardess offered me. She brought me tea and I tried to drink that, but it tasted bitter and I left it to grow cold.

It was as though a long-locked door had been opened, but only a crack, and it was up to me to open it wide, although what lay behind it was dark and fraught with uncertainty.

Perhaps I should go to Cornwall and seek out my mother's family, but the glimpses I had been given of the set-up at Porthkerris were not encouraging. My grandfather would be very old, lonely and probably bitter. I realized that I had made no arrangement with Otto Pedersen about letting him know that my mother was dead, and so there was the hideous possibility that if I went to see him, I should be the one who would have to break the news. As well, I blamed him a little for having let his daughter make such a mess of her life. I knew that she was impulsive and thoughtless, and stubborn too, but surely he could have been a little more positive in his dealings with her. He could have sought her out, offered to help, inspected me, his grandchild. But he had done none of these things, and surely this would always stand like a high wall between us.

And yet, I longed for roots. I did not necessarily want to live with them, but I wanted them to be there. There were things at Boscarva that had belonged to my mother, and so now belonged to me. She had wanted me to have them, had said as much, so perhaps I was under an obligation to go to Cornwall and claim them as my own, but to go only for this reason seemed both soulless and greedy.

I leaned back and dozed and heard again my mother's voice.

I was never frightened of him. I loved him. I should have gone back.

And she had said a name—Sophia—but I had never found out who Sophia was.

I slept at last and dreamed that I was there. But the house in my dream had no shape or form and the only real thing about it was the sound of the wind, battering its way inland, fresh and cold from the open sea.

I was in London by the early afternoon, but the dark day had lost its shape and meaning, and I could not think what I was meant to do with what remained of it. In the end I got a taxi and went to Walton Street to seek out Stephen Forbes.

I found him upstairs, going through a box of books out of an old house which had just been sold up. There was no one else with him, and as I appeared at the top of the stairs he stood up and came towards me, thinking that I was a potential customer. When he saw that I was not, his manner changed.

"Rebecca! You're back."

I stood there, with my hands in my coat pockets.

"Yes. I got in about two." He watched me, his face a question. I said, "My mother died, early yesterday morning. I was just in time. I had an evening with her, and we talked and talked."

"I see," said Stephen. "I'm glad you saw her." He cleared some books from the edge of a table, and leaned against it, folding his arms and eyeing me through his spectacles. He said, "What are you going to do now?"

"I don't know."

"You look exhausted. Why not take a few days off?"

I said again, "I don't know."

He frowned. "What don't you know?"

"I don't know what to do."

"What's the problem?"

"Stephen, have you ever heard of an artist called Grenville Bayliss?"

"Heavens, yes. Why?"

"He's my grandfather."

Stephen's face was a study. "Good Lord. When did you find that out?"

"My mother told me. I'd never heard of him," I had to admit.

"You should have."

"Is he well known?"

"He was, twenty years ago when I was a boy. There was a Grenville Bayliss over the dining-room fireplace in my father's old house in Oxford. Part of my growing up, one might say. A grey stormy sea and a fishing boat with a brown sail. Used to make me feel seasick to look at it. He specialized in sea-scapes."

"He was a sailor. I mean, he'd been in the Royal Navy."

"That follows."

I waited for him to go on, but he was silent. I said at last, "What am I to do, Stephen?"

"What do you want to do, Rebecca?"

"I never had a family."

"Is it so important?"

"Suddenly it is."

"Then go and see him. Is there any reason not to?"

"I'm frightened."

"Of what?"

"I don't know. Of being snubbed, I suppose. Or ignored."

"Were there dreadful family rows?"

"Yes. And cuttings off. And never darken my door again. You know the sort of thing."

"Did your mother suggest that you went?"

"No. Not in so many words. But she said there were some things that belonged to her. She thought I should have them."

"What sort of things?"

I told him. "I know it's nothing very much. Perhaps not even worth making the journey for. But I'd like to have something that belonged to her. Besides—" I tried to turn it into a joke—"they might help to fill up some of the blank spaces in the new flat."

"I think collecting your possessions should be a secondary reason for going to Cornwall. Your first should be making friends with Grenville Bayliss."

"Supposing he doesn't want to make friends?"

"Then no harm has been done. Except possibly a little bruising to your pride, but that won't kill you."

"You're rail-roading me into this," I told him.

"If you didn't want my advice, then why did you come to see me?"

He had a point. "I don't know," I admitted.

He laughed. "You don't know much, do you?" and when at last I smiled back, he said, "Look. Today's Thursday. Go home and get some sleep. And if tomorrow's too soon, then go down to Cornwall on Sunday or Monday. Just go. See how the land lies, see how the old boy is. It may take a few days, but that doesn't matter. Don't come back to London until you've done all you can. And if you can get hold of your own bits and pieces, well and good, but remember that they're of secondary importance."

"Yes. I'll remember."

He stood up. "Then push off," he said. "I've got enough to do without wasting my time running a private Tell Auntie column on your account."

"Can I come back to work when all this is over?"

"You better had. I can't manage without you."

"Goodbye then," I said.

"Au revoir," said Stephen, and as if on an afterthought, leaned forward to give me a clumsy kiss. "And Good Luck!"

I had already spent enough money on taxis, so, still carrying my case, I walked up to the bus stop and waited until one came, and lurched my way back to Fulham. Gazing, unseeing, out of the window at the grey, crowded streets, I tried to make some plans. I would go to Cornwall, as Stephen suggested, on Monday. At this time of year it shouldn't be difficult to get a seat on the train or find somewhere to stay when I finally got to Porthkerris. And Maggie would keep an eye on my flat.

Thinking of the flat made me remember the chairs I had bought before I had gone to Ibiza. That day seemed a lifetime ago. But if I did not claim them then they would be sold as the disagreeable young man had threatened. With this in mind, I got off the bus a few stops before my own so that I could call into the shop and pay for the chairs and thus be certain that they would be waiting for me when I returned.

I had steeled myself to do business once more with the young man in the blue denims, but as I let myself in and the bell rang with the opening and the closing of the door, I saw with some relief that it was not he who stood up from behind the desk at the back of the shop, but another man, older, with grey hair and a dark beard.

He came forward, taking off a pair of horn-rimmed spectacles, as I thankfully put down my suitcase.

"Good afternoon."

"Oh, good afternoon. I came about some chairs I bought last Monday. Cherrywood, balloon-back ones."

"Oh, yes, I know."

"One of them had to be repaired."

"It's been done. Do you want to take them with you?"

"No. I've got a suitcase. I can't carry them. And I'm going away for a few days. But I thought if I paid for them now, perhaps you'd keep them until I got back."

"Yes, of course." He had a charming, deep voice, and when he smiled his rather saturnine face lit up.

I began to open my bag. "Will it be all right if I write you a cheque? I've got a Bankers Card."

"That's all right . . . would you like to use my desk? And here's a pen."

I began to write. "Who shall I make it out to?"

"To me. Tristram Nolan."

I was gratified to know that it was he who owned this pleasant shop and not my mannerless, cowboy friend. I wrote the cheque and crossed it, and handed it to him. He stood, head down, reading it, and took so long that I thought I must have forgotten something.

"Have I put the date?"

"Yes, that's perfect." He looked up. "It's just your name. Bayliss. It's not very common."

"No. No it's not."

"Are you any relation to Grenville Bayliss?"

Having his name flung at me, just now, was extraordinary and yet not extraordinary at all, in the same way that a name, or a relevant item of news, will spring at you, unbidden, from a page of close print.

I said, "Yes, I am." And then because there was no reason why he shouldn't know, "He's my grandfather."

"Extraordinary," he said.

I was puzzled. "Why?"

"I'll show you." He laid my cheque down on his desk and went to pull out from behind a drop-leafed sofa table a large, sturdy oil painting in a gilt frame. He held it up, balancing one corner on his desk, and I saw that it was by my grandfather. His signature was in the corner, and the date below it, 1932.

"I've only just bought it. It needs cleaning, of course, but I think it's very charming."

I stepped closer to inspect it, and saw sand dunes in an evening light, and two young boys, naked, bent over a collection of shells. The work was perhaps old-fashioned, but the composition charming—the colouring delicate and yet somehow robust—as though the boys, vulnerable in their nakedness, were still tough, and creatures to be reckoned with.

"He was good, wasn't he?" I said, and could not hide the note of pride in my voice.

"Yes. A marvellous colourist." He put the picture back. "Do you know him well?"

"I don't know him at all. I've never met him."

He said nothing, simply stood, waiting for me to enlarge on this odd statement. To fill the silence I went on. "But I've decided that perhaps it's time I did. In fact, I'm going to Cornwall on Monday."

"But that's splendid. The roads will be empty at this time of the year, and it's a lovely drive."

"I'm going by train. I haven't got a car."

"It will still be a pleasant journey. I hope the sun shines for you."

"Thank you very much."

We moved back to the door. He opened it, I picked up my suitcase. "You'll look after my chairs for me?"

"Of course. Goodbye. And have a good time in Cornwall."

3

BUT THE SUN did not shine for me. Monday dawned grey and depressing as ever and my faint hopes that the weather would improve as the train rocketed westwards soon died, for the sky darkened with every mile and the wind got up and the day finally dissolved into pouring rain. There was nothing to be seen from the streaming windows; only the blurred shapes of hills and farmsteads, and every now and then the clustered roofs of a village flashed by, or we raced through the half-empty station of some small anonymous town.

By Plymouth, I comforted myself, it would be different. We would cross the Saltash Bridge and find ourselves in another country, another climate, where there would be pink-washed cottages and palm trees and thin winter sunshine. But of course all that happened was that the rain fell even more relentlessly; as I stared out at flooded fields and leafless wind-torn trees, my hopes finally died and I began to be discouraged.

It was nearly a quarter to five by the time we reached the junction which was the end of my journey, and the dark afternoon had sunk, already, into twilight. As the train slowed down alongside the platform, I saw an incongruous palm tree, silhouetted like a broken umbrella against the streaming sky, and the falling rain shimmered and danced in front of the lighted sign which said "St Abbotts, change for Porthkerris." The train finally stopped. I shouldered my rucksack and opened the heavy door which was instantly torn out of my grasp by the wind. The sudden impact of strong cold air, driven inland, over the dark sea, made me gasp, and with some idea of making haste I picked up my bag and jumped out on to the platform. I followed the general exodus of travellers up and over the wooden bridge to the station building on the far side. Most of the other passengers seemed to have friends to meet them, or else walked through the ticket office in a purposeful fashion, as though knowing that a car was waiting for them on the far side. Blindly, I followed them, feeling very new and strange but hoping that they would lead me to a taxi. But when I came out into the station yard, there were no taxis. I stood about, hopeful of being offered a lift, but too shy to ask for one, until the tail light of the last car, inevitably, disappeared up the hill in the direction of the main road and I was forced to return to the ticket office for help and advice.

I found a porter, stacking hen coops in a smelly parcels office.

"I'm sorry, but I have to get to Porthkerris. Would there be a taxi?"

He shook his head slowly, without hope, and then said, brightening slightly, "There's a bus. Runs every hour." He glanced up at the slow-ticking clock high on the wall. "But you've just missed one, so you'll 'ave to wait some time."

"Can't I ring up for a taxi?"

"Isn't much call for taxis at this time of the year."

I let my heavy rucksack slip to the floor and we gazed at each other, both defeated by the enormity of the problem. My wet feet were slowly congealing. As we stood there, there came, above the noise of the storm, the sound of a car, driven very fast down the hill from the road.

I said, raising my voice slightly in order to make my point, "I must get a taxi. Where could I telephone?"

"There's a box just out there . . ."

I turned to go in search of it, trailing my rucksack behind me, and

177

as I did so I heard the car stop outside in the yard; a door slammed, footsteps ran, and the next moment a man appeared, banging the door open and shut against the icy wind. He shook himself like a dog before crossing the floor and disappearing through the open door of the Parcels Office.

I heard him say, "Hallo, Ernie. I think there's a parcel here for me. From London."

" 'Ullo, Mr Gardner. That's a dirty night."

"Filthy. The road's awash. That looks like it . . . that one over there. Yes, that's it. Want me to sign for it?"

"Oh, yes, you'll 'ave to sign. 'Ere we are . . ."

I imagined the slip of paper, smoothed on a table top, the stub of a pencil taken from behind Ernie's ear. And for the life of me I could not remember where I had heard that voice before, nor why I knew it so well.

"That's great. Thanks very much."

"You're welcome."

The telephone, the taxi, forgotten for the moment, I watched the door, waiting for him to reappear. When he did, carrying a large box stuck with red GLASS labels, I saw the long legs, the blue denims drenched in mud to the knee, and a black oilskin, beaded and running with rivulets of water. He was bare-headed, his black hair plastered to his skull, and he saw me for the first time and stopped dead, holding the parcel in front of him like an offering. In his dark eyes was first a flicker of puzzlement, and then recognition. He began to smile. He said, "Good God!"

It was the young man who had sold me the two little cherrywood chairs.

I stood open-mouthed, feeling obscurely that someone had played me a mean and unfair trick. If ever I was in need of a friend it was at this moment, and yet fate had chosen to send me, possibly, the last person on earth I ever wanted to see again. And that he should see me thus, drenched and desperate, was somehow the last straw.

His smile widened. "What a fantastic coincidence. What are you doing here?"

"I've just got off the train."

"Where are you going?"

I had to tell him. "To Porthkerris."

"Is someone coming for you?"

I very nearly lied and told him "yes." Anything to get rid of him. But I was always a useless fibber, and he would be bound to guess the

178

truth. I said, "No," and then I went on, trying to sound competent, as though I could take good care of myself, "I'm just going to phone for a taxi."

"It'll take hours. I'm going to Porthkerris, I'll give you a ride."

"Oh, you don't need to bother . . ."

"No bother, I'm going anyway. Is that all your luggage?"

"Yes, but . . ."

"Come on then."

I still hesitated, but he seemed to consider the matter already settled, going over to the door to open it, and holding it open with his shoulder, waiting for me to follow. So eventually I did so, edging past him, and out into the fury of the dark evening.

In the dim light I saw the Mini pick-up, parked, with the sidelights burning. Letting the door slam behind him, he crossed over to this, and gently loaded his parcel into the back, and then took my rucksack from me, and heaved this in too, covering the two bundles in a cursory fashion with an old piece of tarpaulin. I stood watching him, but he said, "Go on, get in, there's no point us both getting wet through," so I did as I was told, settling myself in the passenger seat with my bag jammed between my legs. Almost at once he had joined me, shutting his door with an almighty slam, and switching on the engine as though there were not a moment to be lost. We roared up the hill away from the station, and the next moment had turned on to the main road and were heading for Porthkerris.

He said, "Tell me more, now. I thought you lived in London."

"Yes, I do."

"Have you come down for a holiday?"

"Sort of."

"That sounds good and vague. Are you staying with friends?"

"Yes. No. I don't know."

"What does that mean?"

"Just that. It means I don't know." This sounded rude but it couldn't be helped. I felt as though I had no control over what I was saying.

"Well, you'd better make up your mind before you get to Porthkerris, otherwise you'll be spending the night on the beach."

"I . . . I'm going to stay in a hotel. Just for tonight."

"Well, that's great. Which one?"

I sent him an exasperated look and he said, reasonably enough, "Well, if I don't know which one, I can't take you there, can I?"

179

He seemed to have me cornered. I said, "I haven't booked in to any hotel. I mean, I thought I could do that when I arrived. There *are* hotels, aren't there?"

"Porthkerris is running with them. Every other house is a hotel. But at this time of the year most of them are closed."

"Do you know some that are open?"

"Yes. But it depends what you want to pay."

He glanced at me sideways, taking in my patched jeans, scuffed shoes, and an old fur-lined leather coat that I had worn for warmth and comfort. At the moment this garment looked and smelt like a wet dog.

"We go from one extreme to the other. The Castle, up on the Hill, where you change for dinner, and dance the foxtrot to a three-piece orchestra, right down to Mrs Kernow who does Bed and Breakfast at Number Two, Fish Lane. Mrs Kernow I can recommend. She looked after me for three months or more before I got into my own place, and her prices are very reasonable."

I was diverted. "Your own place? You mean you live here?"

"I do now. Have done for the last six months."

"But . . . the shop in the New Kings Road . . . where I bought the chairs?"

"I was just helping out for a day or so."

We came to a crossroads, and, slowing down, he turned to look at me. "Have you got the chairs yet?"

"No. But I've paid for them. They'll still be there when I get back."

"Good," said the young man.

We drove for a little in silence. Through a village, and up over a wild bit of country high above the sea; then the road leaned down again, and there were trees on either side of us. Through these, through twisted trunks and branches tortured by the wind, there presently appeared, far below us, the twinkling lights of a little town.

"Is that Porthkerris?"

"It is. And in a moment you're going to have to tell me if it's to be The Castle or Fish Lane."

I swallowed. The Castle was out of the question, obviously, but if I went to Fish Lane I would necessarily place myself under an obligation to this managing person. I had not come to Porthkerris for any other reason than to see Grenville Bayliss, and I had an uncomfortable feeling that if I once got involved with this man he would stick like a burr.

I said, "No, not The Castle . . ." meaning to suggest some other, more modest establishment, but he cut me short.

"That's great," he said, with a grin. "Mrs Kernow of Fish Lane it is, and you won't regret it."

My first impression of Porthkerris, in the dark and the gusty rain, was confused to say the least of it. The town was, on this unsalubrious evening, nearly empty of people; the deserted streets gleamed wetly with reflected light, and the gutters ran with water.

At a great speed, we plunged down into a warren of baffling lanes and alleys, at one time emerging out on to the road which circled the harbour, only to turn back once more into the maze of cobbled roads and uneven, haphazard houses.

We turned at last into a narrow street of grey terrace houses, with front doors opening flush on to the pavement.

All was seemly and respectable. Lace curtains veiled windows, and there could be glimpsed statuettes of girls with dogs, or large green pots containing aspidistras.

The car slowed at last and stopped.

"We're here." He switched off the engine, and I could hear the wind and, above its whine, the nearby sound of the sea. Great breakers thundered up on to the sand, and there was the long hiss of the retreating waves.

He said, "You know, I don't know your name."

"It's Rebecca Bayliss. And I don't know yours."

"Joss Gardner . . . it's short for Jocelyn, not Joseph." With this useful bit of information he got out of the car and rang a bell in a door and, while waiting for an answer, went to retrieve my rucksack from underneath the tarpaulin. As he heaved it out, the door opened and he turned and was illuminated in a shaft of warm light which streamed from inside the house.

"Joss!"

"Hallo, Mrs Kernow."

"What are you doing here?"

"I've brought you a visitor. I said you were the best hotel in Porthkerris."

"Oh, my soul, I don't belong to take visitors at this time of the year. But come along in now, out of the rain, what weather isn't it? Tom's down at the Coastguard lodge, been some sort of a warning up from the Trevose way, but I don't know, I haven't heard no rockets . . ."

Somehow we were all inside and the door shut and there was scarcely room for the three of us to stand in the narrow hall.

"Come along in by the fire . . . it's nice and warm, I'll get you a cup of tea if you like . . ." We followed her into a tiny, cluttered, cosy parlour. She knelt to poke the fire to life and add more coal, and for the first time I was able to take a good look at her. I saw a small, bespectacled lady, quite elderly, wearing bedroom slippers and a pinafore over her good brown dress.

"We don't really want tea," he told her. "We just want to know if you can give Rebecca a bed—for a night or so."

She stood up from the fireplace. "Well, I don't know . . ." She looked at me doubtfully, and what with my appearance and the dog-smelling coat I didn't blame her for being doubtful.

I started to open my mouth, but Joss sailed in before I could say a word. "She's highly respectable and she won't run away with the spoons. I'll vouch for her."

"Well . . ." Mrs Kernow smiled. Her eyes were pretty, a very pale blue. "The room's empty, so she may as well have it. But I can't give her supper tonight, not expecting anybody, I haven't anything in the house but a couple of little pasties."

"That's all right," said Joss. "I'll feed her."

I started to protest, but once again I was overborne. "I'll leave her here to get settled in and unpacked, and then I'll be back about—" he glanced at his watch—"seven thirty, to pick her up. That all right?" he flung casually in my direction. "You're an angel, Mrs Kernow, and I love you like a mother." He put an arm around her and kissed her. She looked delighted; then he gave me a final, cheerful grin, said, "See you," and so departed. We heard his car roaring away down the street.

"He's a lovely boy," Mrs Kernow informed me. "I had him living here three months or more . . . now come along, pick up your little bag and I'll show you your room. 'Course it'll be cold, but I've got an electric fire you can have, and the water in the tank's nice and hot if you want a bath . . . I always say you feel so mucky coming off those dirty trains . . ."

The room was as tiny as all the other rooms in this little house, furnished with an enormous double bed which took up nearly all the space. But it was clean and, presently, warm, and after Mrs Kernow had shown me where to find the bathroom she went back downstairs and left me to myself.

I went to kneel by the low window and draw back the curtains. The old frames had been jammed tight shut against the wind by rubber wedges, and the dark glass streamed with rain. There was

182

nothing to be seen, but I stayed there anyway, wondering what I was doing in this little house, and trying to work out why Joss Gardner's sudden re-appearance in my life had left me with this unexplained feeling of unease.

4

I NEEDED DEFENCES. I needed to build up my confidence and my self-esteem, disliking the role of rescued waif in which I had suddenly found myself. A hot bath and a change of clothes went a long way towards restoring my composure. I did my hair, made up my eyes, splashed on the last of a bottle of expensive scent and was halfway towards being in charge again. I had already unpacked a dress from the ubiquitous rucksack and hung it hopefully to shed its wrinkles; now I put it on, a dark cotton with long sleeves, and dark stockings, very fine, and shoes with heels and old-fashioned buckles which I had found, long back, on a stall in the Portobello Road . . . As I fastened my pearl ear-rings I heard, over the rattle and bang of the gusty wind, the sound of Joss Gardner's little van, tyres drumming on the cobbles, coming up the street. It screeched to a noisy halt outside the door, and the next moment I heard his voice downstairs, calling first for Mrs Kernow and then for me.

I continued, slowly, to screw the fastening of the last ear-ring. I picked up my bag, and then my leather coat. This I had draped near the electric fire in the hope that it would dry off, but it hadn't. The heat had merely emphasized the smell of a spaniel come in from a wet walk, and it still weighed heavy as lead. Lugging it over my arm, I went down the stairs.

"Hallo, there." Joss, in the hall, looked up at me. "Well, what a transformation. Feel better now?"

"Yes."

"Give me your coat . . ."

He took it from me intending to help me on with it, and instantly became a comic weightlifter, sagging at the knees with the sheer bulk of it.

"You can't wear this, it'll drive you into the ground. Anyway it's still wet."

"I haven't got another." Still toting the coat, he started to laugh. My self-esteem began to drain away and some of this must have showed on my face, because he suddenly stopped laughing and shouted for Mrs Kernow. When she appeared, with an expression both exasperated and loving on her face, he bundled my coat into her arms, told her to dry it for me, unbuttoned and removed his own black oilskin and laid it, with a certain grace, around my shoulders.

Beneath it he wore a soft grey sweater, a cotton scarf knotted at the neck. "Now," he said, "we are ready to go." He opened the door, on to a curtain of rain.

I protested, "But you'll get wet," but he only said "Scuttle" so I scuttled, and he scuttled too, and the next instant we were back in the van, scarcely wet at all, with the doors banged tight and shut against the storm, although small puddles of rain on my seat and at my feet gave rise to the suspicion that this staunch vehicle was no longer as watertight as it had once been. But he started the noisy engine and we were away, and with the volume of water both outside and inside the car it was a little like being taken for a fast ride in a leaky motor boat.

I said, "Where are we going?"

"The Anchor. It's just round the corner. Not very smart. Do you mind?"

"Why should I mind?"

"You might mind. You might have wanted to be taken to The Castle."

"You mean to foxtrot to a three-piece orchestra?"

He grinned. He said, "I can't foxtrot. Nobody ever learned me."

We flashed down Fish Lane, around a right angled corner or two, beneath a stone archway and so out into a small square. One side of this was formed by the low, uneven shape of an old inn. Warm light shone from behind small windows spilled from a crooked doorway and the Inn sign over the door swung and creaked in the wind. There were four or five cars already parked outside, and Joss inserted the van neatly into a tidy space between two of them, turned off the engine, said, "One, two, three, run," and we both got out and sprinted the short distance between the car and the shelter of the porch.

There Joss shook himself slightly, brushed the rain from the soft surface of his sweater, took the oilskin off my shoulders and opened the door for me to go ahead of him.

It was warm inside, and low-ceilinged and smelt the way old pubs have always smelt. Of beer and pipe smoke and musty wood. There was a bar, with high stools, and tables around the edge of the room. Two old men were playing darts in a corner.

The barman looked up and said, "Hi, Joss." Joss put the oilskin up on a coat hook, and led me across the room to be introduced.

"Tommy, this is Rebecca. Rebecca, this is Tommy Williams. He's been here man and boy; anything you want to know about Porthkerris, or the people who live here, you come and ask Tommy."

We said, "How do you do." Tommy had grey hair and a lot of wrinkles. He looked as though he might be a fisherman in his spare time. We sat ourselves on two stools, and Joss ordered a scotch and soda for me and a scotch and water for himself, and while Tommy fixed these the two men began to talk, falling comfortably into conversation the way men in pubs always seem to.

"How are things going with you?" That was Tommy.

"Not too bad."

"When are you opening up?"

"Easter, maybe, with a bit of luck."

"Place finished is it?"

"More or less."

"Who's doing the carpentry?"

"Doing it myself."

"That'll save you something."

My attention wandered. I lit a cigarette and looked around me, liking what I saw. The two old men playing darts; a young couple, jeaned and long-haired, crouched over a table and a couple of pints of bitter, discussing, with avid and intense concentration—existentialism? Concrete painting? How they were going to pay the rent? Something. But it mattered, intensely, to both of them.

And then a party of four, older, expensively dressed, the men self-consciously casual, the women unwittingly formal. I guessed they were staying at The Castle, and out of boredom with the weather, perhaps, had come down the town for a spot of slumming. They seemed uncomfortable, as though they knew they looked out of place, and could scarcely wait to get back to the padded velvet comfort of the big hotel on the hill.

My eyes moved on around the room, and it was then that I caught sight of the dog. He was a beautiful dog, a great red setter, his coat handsome and shining, his tail a silken plume of copper fur against the grey flags of the floor. He sat very still, close to his master, and every now and then the tail would move slightly in a thump of approval, a private applause.

Intrigued, I inspected the man who appeared to own this enviable creature, and found him almost as interesting as the dog. Sitting, with an elbow on the table top, and his chin resting on his fist, he presented to me a clear and unblurred profile, almost as though he were posing for my inspection. His head was well shaped, and his hair had that thick silver-fox look of a person who has started to go grey early in life. The single eye which his profile allowed me was deep set, and darkly shadowed, the nose was long and aquiline, the mouth pleasant, the chin strongly formed. And, from the length of his wrist, emerging from a checked shirt cuff and the sleeve of a grey tweed jacket, and the way he disposed of his legs beneath the little table, I guessed that he was tall, probably over six feet.

As I watched him, he laughed suddenly at something his companion had said. This drew my attention to the other man, and I felt a shock of surprise, because, for some reason, they did not match. Where the one was slender and elegant, the other was short, fat, red of face, and dressed in a tight-fitting navy blue blazer and a shirt collar that looked as though it were about to strangle him. It was not overly warm in the pub, but there was a shine of sweat on the ruddy brow, and I saw that the dark hair had been barbered with some ingenuity, so that a long oiled lock was combed up and over, concealing what would otherwise have been a totally bald head.

The man with the dog was not smoking, but the fat man suddenly crushed out his own cigarette in the brimming ashtray on the table, as though emphasizing some point that he was making, and almost instantly reached into his pocket for a silver case and another cigarette.

But the man with the dog had decided that it was time to go. He took his hand from his chin, pushed back his shirt cuff to consult his watch, and then finished his drink. The fat man, apparently anxious to comply with the other's arrangements, hastily lit the cigarette and then tossed back his whisky. They began to get up, pushing back their chairs with a hideous scraping sound. The dog stood up, his tail swooping in exultant circles.

Standing, one so short and fat and the other so tall and slim, the two men looked more ill-assorted than ever. The thin one reached for a raincoat which had been lying across the back of his chair and slung it over his shoulders like a cloak, and then turned towards us, heading for the door. For an instant I was disappointed, because full face, his finely drawn good looks did not live up to the promise of that intriguing profile. And then I forgot about being disappointed, because he suddenly saw Joss. And Joss, perhaps sensing his presence, stopped talking to Tommy Williams and turned to see who was standing behind him. For an instant they both looked disconcerted, and then the tall man smiled, and the smile etched lines down his thin brown cheeks and creased up his eyes, and it was impossible not to be warmed by such charm.

He said, "Joss. Long time no see." His voice was pleasant and friendly.

"Hi," said Joss, not getting off his stool.

"I thought you were in London."

"No. Back again."

The creaking swing of the door caught my attention. The other man, the fat man, had quietly left. I decided that he had an urgent appointment and thought no more about it.

"I'll tell the old boy I've seen you."

"Yes. Do that."

The deep set eyes moved in my direction, and then away again. I waited to be introduced, but nothing happened. For some reason this lack of manners on Joss's part was like a slap in the face.

At last, "Well, see you around," said the tall man, and moved off.

"Sure," said Joss.

"Night, Tommy," he called to the barman as he pushed the door open and let the dog out ahead of him.

"Good night, Mr Bayliss," said the barman.

I felt my head jerk around as though someone had pulled a string. He had already disappeared, leaving the door swinging behind him. Without thinking, I slipped off the stool to go after him, but a hand caught my arm and restrained me, and I turned to find Joss holding me back. For a surprising second our eyes clashed, and then I shook myself free. Outside I heard a car start up. Now it was too late.

I said, "Who is he?"

"Eliot Bayliss."

Eliot. Roger's boy. Mollie's child. Grenville Bayliss's grandson. My cousin. My family.

"He's my cousin."

"I didn't know that."

"You know my name. Why didn't you tell him? Why did you stop me going after him?"

"You'll meet him soon enough. Tonight it's too late and too wet and too dark for family reunions."

"Grenville Bayliss is my grandfather, too."

"I thought there was probably some connection," said Joss coolly. "Have another drink."

By now I was really angry. "I don't want another drink."

"In that case, let's go and eat."

"I don't want to eat either."

I thought that I truly didn't want to. I didn't want to spend another moment with this boorish and overbearing young man. I watched him finish his drink and get down off his stool, and for an instant I thought that he was actually going to take me at my word; was going to drive me back to Fish Lane and there dump me, un-nourished. But, luckily, he did not call my bluff, simply paid for the drinks, and without a word led the way through a door at the far end of the bar, which gave on to a flight of stairs and a small restaurant. I followed him because there didn't seem to be anything else to do. Besides, I was hungry.

Most of the tables were already occupied, but a waitress saw Joss and recognized him and came over to say good evening, and led us to what was obviously the best table in the room, set in the narrow alcove of a jutting bay window. Beyond the window could be seen the shapes of rain-washed roofs, and beyond them again the liquid darkness of the harbour, a-shimmer with reflections from the street lamps on the quay and the riding lights of fishing boats.

We faced each other. I was still deeply angry and would not look at him. I sat, drawing patterns with my finger on the table mat, and listened to him ordering what I was to eat. Apparently I was not even to be allowed the right of making my own choice. I heard the waitress say, "For the young lady, too?" as though even she were surprised by his cursory behaviour, and Joss said, "Yes, for the young lady, too," and the waitress went off, and we were alone.

After a little I looked up. His dark gaze met mine, unblinking. The silence grew, and I had the ridiculous feeling that he was waiting for me to apologize to him.

I heard myself say, "If you won't let me talk to Eliot Bayliss, perhaps you'll talk about him."

"What do you want to know?"

"Is he married?" It was the first question that came into my head. "No."

"He's attractive." Joss acknowledged this. "Does he live alone?"

188

"No, with his mother. They have a house up at High Cross, six miles or so from here, but about a year ago they moved into Boscarva, to be with the old man."

"Is my grandfather ill?"

"You don't know very much about your family, do you?"

"No." I sounded defiant.

"About ten years ago Grenville Bayliss had a heart attack. That's when he stopped painting. But he always appears to have had the constitution of an ox, and he made a miraculous recovery. He didn't want to leave Boscarva, and he had this couple to take care of him . . ."

"The Pettifers?"

Joss frowned. "How do you know about the Pettifers?"

"My mother told me." I thought of the long-ago tea parties by the kitchen fire. "I never imagined they'd still be there."

"Mrs Pettifer died last year, so Pettifer and your grandfather were left on their own. Grenville Bayliss is eighty now, and Pettifer can't be far behind him. Mollie Bayliss wanted them to move up to High Cross and sell Boscarva, but the old man was adamant, so in the end she and Eliot moved in with him. Without noticeable enthusiasm, I may add." He leaned back in his chair, his long clever hands resting on the edge of the table. "Your mother . . . was she called Lisa?" I nodded.

"I knew Grenville had a daughter who'd had a daughter, but the fact that you call yourself Bayliss threw me slightly."

"My father left my mother before I was born. She never used his name."

"Where's your mother now?"

"She died—just a few days ago. In Ibiza." I repeated, "Just a few days ago," because all at once it seemed like a lifetime.

"I'm sorry." I made some sort of vague gesture, because there weren't any words. "Does your grandfather know?"

"I don't know."

"Have you come to tell him?"

"I suppose I may have to." The idea of doing so was daunting.

"Does he know you're here? In Porthkerris?"

I shook my head. "He doesn't even know me. I mean we've never met. I've never been here before." I made the final admission. "I don't even know how to find his house."

"One way and another," said Joss, "you're going to give him something of a shock."

I felt anxious. "Is he very frail?"

"No, he's not frail. He's fantastically tough. But he's getting old."

"My mother says he was frightening. Is he still frightening?"

Joss made a gruesome face, doing nothing to comfort me. "Terrifying," he said.

The waitress brought our soup. It was oxtail, thick and brown and very hot. I was so hungry that I ate it right down to the bottom of the bowl without saying another word. As I finally laid down my spoon, I looked up and saw that Joss was laughing at me.

"For a girl who didn't want to eat, you haven't done so badly."

But this time I did not rise. I pushed the empty bowl away, and leaned my elbows on the table.

"How is it that you know so much about the Bayliss family?" I asked him.

Joss had not bolted his soup as I had. Now, he was taking his time, buttering a roll, being maddeningly slow.

"It's easy," he said. "I do a certain amount of work up at Boscarva."

"What sort of work?"

"Well, I restore antique furniture. And don't gape in that unattractive fashion, it does nothing for you."

"*Restore antique furniture?* You must be joking."

"I'm not. And Grenville Bayliss has a houseful of old and very valuable stuff. In his day he made a lot of money, and he invested most of it in antiques. Now, some of the things are in a shocking state of repair, not that they haven't been polished to within an inch of their lives, but ten years ago he put in central heating and that wrecks old furniture. Drawers shrink and veneers curl and crack, and legs fall off chairs. Incidentally—" he added, diverted by the memory—"it was I who mended your cherrywood chair."

"But how long have you been doing this?"

"Let's see, I left school when I was seventeen, and I'm twenty-four now, so that makes it about seven years."

"But you had to *learn* . . ."

"Oh, sure. I did joinery and carpentry first, four years of it at a trade school in London, and then when I'd got that under my belt, I apprenticed myself for another couple of years to an old cabinetmaker down in Sussex. I lived with him and his wife, did all the dirty jobs in the workshop, learned everything I know."

I did a few sums. "That's only six years. You said seven."

He laughed. "I took a year off in the middle to travel. My parents said I was becoming parochial. My father has a cousin who runs a

190

cattle ranch up in the Rockies, south-west Colorado. I worked as a ranch hand nine months or more." He frowned. "What are you grinning about?"

I told him. "That first time I saw you, in the shop . . . you looked like a ranch hand . . . you looked real. And somehow it annoyed me that you weren't."

He smiled. "And you know what you looked like?"

I cooled off. "No."

"The head girl of a nicely run orphanage. And that annoyed *me*."

A small clash of swords, and once more we were on opposite sides of the fence.

I eyed him with dislike as he cheerfully finished his soup; the waitress came to take away the empty plates, and to set down a carafe of red wine. I had not heard Joss ordering the wine, but now I watched him pour two full glasses and I saw the long spade-tipped fingers; I liked the idea of them working with wood and old and beautiful things, shaping and measuring and oiling and coaxing into shape. I picked up the glass of wine and against the light it glowed red as a ruby. I said, "Is that all you're doing in Porthkerris? Restoring Grenville Bayliss's furniture?"

"Good God, no. I'm opening a shop. I managed to rent these premises down on the harbour six months or so ago. I've been here, off and on, ever since. Now, I'm trying to get it into some sort of order before Easter, or Whitsun, or whenever the summer business really starts."

"Is it an antique shop?"

"No, modern, furniture, glass, textiles. But antique restoring goes on in the background. I mean I have a workroom. I also have a small pad on the top floor which is where I now live, which is why you were able to take over my room at Mrs Kernow's. One day when you've decided that I'm trustworthy you can climb the rickety stairs and I'll show it to you."

I ignored this fresh little sally.

"If you work down here, what were you doing in that shop in London?"

"Tristram's? I told you, he's a friend; I drop in and see him whenever I'm up in town."

I frowned. There were so many coincidences. Our lives seemed to be tied up in them, like a parcel well-knotted with ends of string. I watched him finish his wine and once more was visited with the unease which I had known earlier in the evening. I knew I should ask him a thousand questions, but before I could think of one the waitress arrived at our table once more, bearing steaks and vegetables and fried potatoes and dishes of salad. I drank some wine and watched Joss, and when the waitress had gone I said, "What does Eliot Bayliss do?"

"Eliot? He runs a garage up at High Cross, specializes in highly-powered second-hand cars, Mercedes, Alfa Romeos. If you've got the right sort of cheque book he can supply you with practically anything."

"You don't like him, do you?"

"I never said I didn't like him."

"But you don't."

"Perhaps it would be nearer the mark to say he doesn't like me."

"Why?"

He looked up, his eyes dancing with amusement. "I haven't any idea. Now why don't you eat up your steak before it gets cold."

He drove me home. It was still raining and I was, all at once, deathly tired. Outside Mrs Kernow's door Joss stopped the car, but left the engine running. I thanked him and said good night and began to open the door, but before I could do so he had reached across and stopped me. I turned to look at him.

He said, "Tomorrow. Are you going to Boscarva?"

"Yes."

"I'll take you."

"I can go alone."

"You don't know where the house is, and it's a long climb up the hill. I'll pick you up in the car. About eleven?"

Arguing with him was like arguing with a steamroller. And I was exhausted. I said, "All right."

He opened the door for me and pushed it open.

"Good night, Rebecca."

"Good night."

"I'll see you in the morning."

5

THE WIND did not drop during that night. But when I woke, the little window of my room at Mrs Kernow's gave me sight of a square of pale blue traversed by ballooning white clouds travelling at some speed. It was very cold, but bravely I got up and dressed and went downstairs in search of Mrs Kernow. I found her outside in the little yard at the back of the house, pegging out her washing on a line. At first, battling with flailing sheets and towels, she didn't see me, but when I appeared between a shirt and a modest lock-knit petticoat she gave a great start of surprise. Her own astonishment amused her, and she shook with shrill laughter, as though the two of us were a double act on the halls.

"You gave me some shock. I thought you were still asleep! Comfortable were you? That dratted wind's still around the place, but the rain's stopped, thank heaven. Want your breakfast do you?"

"A cup of tea, perhaps."

I helped her peg out the rest of the washing and then she picked up her empty basket and led the way back indoors. I sat at the kitchen table and she boiled a kettle and began to fry bacon.

"Have a good supper last night did you? Go to The Anchor? Tommy Williams keeps a good place there, always packed, winter and summer. I heard Joss bring you home. He's a lovely boy. I missed him when he moved out. Still, I go down sometimes to his new place, clean it up a bit for him, bring his washing home and do it here. Sad, a young man like that on his own. All wrong somehow, not having someone to take care of him."

"I should think Joss could take care of himself."

"It's not right a man doing woman's work." Mrs Kernow obviously did not believe in Women's Lib. "Besides, he's busy enough working for Mr Bayliss."

"Do you know Mr Bayliss?"

"Everyone knows he. Lived here nearly fifty years now. One of the old ones, he is. And some lovely painter he was before he took ill. Used to have an exhibition every year, and all sorts used to come down from London, famous people, everybody. 'Course, lately we don't see so much of him. He can't walk up and down the hill like he used to, and it's a bit of a business Pettifer getting that great car down these narrow lanes. Besides, in the summer, you can't move for traffic and visitors. The place is teeming with them. Sometimes you'd think half the population of the country is jammed into this little town."

She flipped the bacon on to a warm plate and set it in front of me. "There now, eat that up before it gets cold."

I said, "Mrs Kernow, Mr Bayliss is my grandfather."

She stared at me, frowning. "Your grandfather?" Then, "Whose child are you?"

"Lisa's."

"Lisa's child." She reached for a chair and slowly sat down upon it. I saw that I had shocked her. "Does Joss know?"

It seemed irrelevant. "Yes, I told him last night."

"She was a lovely little girl." She stared into my face. "I can see her in you . . . except that she was so dark and you're fair. We missed her when she went, and never came back. Where is she now?"

I told her. When I had finished she said, "And Mr Bayliss doesn't know you're here?"

"No."

"You must go now. Right away. Oh, I wish I could be there to see the old man's face. He worshipped your mother . . ."

A tear gleamed. Quickly, before we were both awash with sentiment, I said, "I don't know how to get there."

Trying to tell me, she confused the two of us so much that finally she found an old envelope and the stub of a pencil and drew a rough map. Watching her I remembered Joss's promise to come at eleven o'clock and take me to Boscarva in his ramshackle van, but all at once it seemed a much better idea to go at once, on my own. Besides, last night I had been altogether too meek and compliant. It would do Joss's boundless ego no harm to arrive here and find me already gone. The thought of this happening cheered me considerably and I went upstairs to fetch my coat.

Outside I was instantly buffeted by the wind which tunnelled down the narrow street like the draught in a chimney. It was a cold wind, smelling of the sea, but when the sun burst out from behind the racing clouds the brightness was dazzling, full of glare, and overhead gulls screamed and floated, their wings white sails against the blue of the sky.

I walked and soon I was climbing. Up narrow, cobbled streets,

194

between haphazard lines of houses. Up flights of steps, and leaning alleys. The higher I went the stronger became the wind. As I climbed the town dropped below me, and the ocean revealed itself, dark blue, streaked with jade and purple and flecked with white horses. It spread to the horizon where the sky took over, and below me the town and the harbour shrank to toy-size, to insignificance.

I stood looking at it, catching my breath, and all at once a funny thing happened. For this new place was not new to me at all, but totally familiar. I felt at home, as though I had returned to somewhere I had known all my life. And though I had scarcely thought of my mother since making the decision to come to Porthkerris, she was suddenly beside me, climbing the steep streets, long-legged, breathless, and warm with exertion as I was.

I was comforted by this sense of *déjà-vu*. It made me feel less lonely and much more brave. I went on and was glad I had not waited for Joss. His presence was disturbing, but I could not for the life of me decide why. He had, after all, been quite open with me, answering questions, giving perfectly believable reasons for his every action.

It was obvious that there was no love lost between himself and Eliot Bayliss, but I could easily understand this. The two young men would have nothing in common. Eliot, albeit unwillingly, was living at Boscarva. He was a Bayliss and the house was, for the time being, his home. On the other hand Joss's occupation in the house would give him the freedom to come and go in his own time. Be found, unexpectedly, at odd hours of the day, perhaps when his presence was neither convenient nor welcome. I imagined him on easy terms with everybody, sometimes getting in the way, and worst of all, blithely unaware of the trouble he was causing. A man like Eliot would resent this and Joss, in return, would react to his resentment.

Busy with these thoughts and the exertion of climbing, I did not observe my surroundings, but now the road levelled off beneath my feet, and I stopped to look around and take my bearings. I was on top of the hill, that was for sure. Behind and below me lay the town; ahead stretched the rugged coastline, curving away into the distance. It bordered a green country, patchworked with small farms and miniature fields, traversed by deep valleys, thick with hawthorn and stunted elm, where narrow streams channelled their way down to the sea.

I looked about me. This too was country. Or a year ago it had been. But since then a farm, perhaps, had been bought out, the bulldozers brought in, old hedges demolished, the rich earth torn up and flat-

195

tened, and a new housing estate was in the process of being erected. All was raw, stark and hideous. Cement mixers churned, a lorry ground through a sea of mud, there were piles of brick and concrete, and in front of it all, like a proud banner, a hoarding which announced the man responsible for this carnage.

ERNEST PADLOW
DESIRABLE DETACHED HOUSES
FOR SALE
Apply Sea Lane, Porthkerris
Telephone Porthkerris 873

The houses were certainly detached, but only just. Scarcely three feet lay between them, and one window stared straight into another.

My heart mourned for the lost fields and the lost opportunities. As I stood there, mentally re-designing the entire project, a car came up the hill behind me, and drew to a halt in front of the hoarding. It was an old Jaguar, navy blue, and the man who stepped out of it, shutting the door behind him with a resounding thump, wore a workman's donkey jacket and carried a clip board and a lot of papers which fluttered in the wind. He turned and saw me, hesitated for only a second and then walked towards me, trying to flatten his hair down over his bald head.

"Morning." His smile was familiar as though we were old friends.

"Good morning."

I had seen him before. Last night. At The Anchor. Talking to Eliot Bayliss.

He glanced up at the hoarding.

"Thinking of buying a house for yourself?"

"No."

"You should. Get a good view up here."

I frowned. "I don't want a house."

"Be a good investment."

"Are you the foreman?"

"No." He glanced, with some pride, up at the hoarding which reared above us. "I'm Ernest Padlow."

"I see."

"Lovely site this . . ." He looked around at the devastation with some satisfaction. "Lot of people after this site, but the old girl who owned the land was a widow, and I managed to charm her into letting me have it."

196

I was surprised. As he spoke he reached for and lit himself a cigarette; he did not offer me one, his fingers were stained with nicotine and he seemed to me the most uncharming man I had ever met.

He turned his attention back to me. "Haven't seen you around, have I?"

"No."

"Visiting?"

"Yes, perhaps."

"It's better out of season. Not so crowded."

I said, "I'm looking for Boscarva."

Caught unawares, the bonhomie slid from his manner. His eyes were sharp as pebbles in his florid face. "Boscarva? You mean old Bayliss's place?"

"Yes."

His expression became wily. "Looking for Eliot?"

"No."

He waited for me to enlarge on this. When I didn't he tried to make a joke of it. "Well, I always say, least said, soonest mended. You want Boscarva, you go down that little lane. About half a mile. You'll see the house down towards the sea. It's got a slate roof, a big garden round it. You can't miss it."

"Thank you." I smiled politely. "Goodbye."

I turned and began to walk, feeling his eyes on my back. Then he spoke once more and I turned back. He was smiling, all friends again.

"You want a house, make up your mind quickly. They're selling like hot cakes."

"Yes, I'm sure. But I don't want one. Thank you."

The lane led downhill towards the great blue bowl of the sea, and now I was truly in the country, in a farmland of fields grazed by sweet-faced Guernseys. Wild violets and primroses grew in the grassy hedges, and the sun came out and turned the rich grass to emerald. Presently, I came around a corner and saw the white gates, set between low drystone walls; a driveway curved down, out of sight, and there were high hedges of escallonia and elm trees, tortured to unnatural shapes by the relentless winds.

I could not see the house. I stood at the open gates and looked down the drive, my courage seeping away like bathwater after the plug has been pulled out. I could not think what I was meant to do, nor what I was going to say once I had done it.

My mind was, unexpectedly and mercifully, made up for me. Down by the house, out of sight, I heard a car start up and come at some speed up the drive towards me. As it approached, a low-slung open sports car of some age and style, I stood aside to let it flash past between the gate posts and up the hill in the direction from which I had come, but still there was time to see the driver and the great red setter sitting up on the back seat, with the deliriously joyful expression of any dog being taken for a ride in an open car.

I thought that I had not been noticed but I was wrong. A moment later the car stopped with a screech of brakes and a shower of small stones flung from the back wheels. Then it went into reverse, and returned, with scarcely less speed back to the spot where I stood. It stopped, the engine was killed, and Eliot Bayliss, leaning an arm on the driving wheel, surveyed me across the empty passenger seat. He was bare-headed and wore a sheepskin car coat, and his expression was one of amusement, perhaps intrigue.

"Hallo," he said.

"Good morning." I felt a fool, bundled in my old coat, with the wind blowing stray strands of hair over my face. I tried to push them away.

"You look lost."

"No. I'm not."

He continued to regard me, frowning slightly. "I saw you last night, didn't I? At The Anchor? With Joss."

"Yes."

"Are you looking for Joss? As far as I know he's not arrived yet. That is, if he's decided to come today."

"No. I mean I'm not looking for him."

"Then who—" asked Eliot Bayliss gently—"are you looking for?"

"I . . . I wanted to see old Mr Bayliss."

"It's a little early for that. He doesn't usually appear 'til mid-day."

"Oh." I had not thought of this. Some of my disappointment must have shown in my face, for he went on, in the same gentle and friendly voice, "Perhaps I could help. I'm Eliot Bayliss."

"I know. I mean . . . Joss told me last night."

A small frown appeared between his eyebrows. He was obviously and naturally puzzled by my relationship with Joss.

"Why did you want to see my grandfather?" And when I did not reply, he suddenly leaned across to open the door of the car and said, with cool authority, "Get in."

I got in, closing the door behind me. I could feel his eyes on me, the shapeless coat, the patched jeans. The dog leaned forward to nuzzle my ear; his nose was cold and I reached over my shoulder to stroke the long, silky ear.

I said, "What's he called?"

"Rufus. Rufus the Red. But that doesn't answer my question, does it?"

I was saved by another interruption. Another car. But this time it was the Post Office van, rattling scarlet and cheerful, down the lane towards us. It stopped, and the postman rolled down the window to say to Eliot, good naturedly, "How can I get down the drive and deliver the letters if you park your car in the gateway?"

"Sorry," said Eliot, unperturbed, and he got out from behind the driving wheel and went to take a handful of mail and a newspaper from the postman. "I'll take it—it'll save you the trip."

"Lovely," said the postman. "Be nice if everyone did my job for me," and with a grin and a wave he went on his way, presumably to some outlying farmstead.

Eliot got back into the car.

"Well," he said, smiling at me. "What am I going to do with you?"

But I scarcely heard him. The pile of mail lay loosely in his lap, and on the top was an airmail envelope, postmarked Ibiza, and addressed to Mr Grenville Bayliss. The spiky handwriting was unmistakable.

A car is a good place for confidences. There is no telephone and you can't be unexpectedly interrupted. I said, "That letter. The one on the top. It's from a man called Otto Pedersen. He lives in Ibiza."

Eliot, frowning, took up the envelope. He turned it over and read Otto's name on the back. He looked at me. "How did you know?"

"I know his writing. I know him. He's writing to . . . to your grandfather to tell him that Lisa is dead. She died about a week ago. She was living with Otto in Ibiza."

"Lisa. You mean Lisa Bayliss?"

"Yes. Roger's sister. Your aunt. My mother."

"You're Lisa's child?"

"Yes." I turned to look directly at him. "I'm your cousin. Grenville Bayliss is my grandfather, too."

His eyes were a strange colour, greyish-green, like pebbles washed by some fast-moving stream. They showed neither shock nor pleasure, simply regarded me levelly without expression. He said at last, "Well I'll be damned."

It was hardly what I expected. We sat in silence because I could think of nothing to say, and then, as though coming to a sudden decision, he tossed the pile of mail into my lap, started the car up once

199

more, and swung the wheel around so that once more we were facing the drive.

"What are you doing?" I asked.

"What do you think? Taking you home of course."

Home. Boscarva. We came around the curve of the drive and it was there, waiting for me. Not small, but not large either. Grey stone, smothered in creeper, grey slate roof, a semicircular stone porch with the door open to the sunshine, and inside a glimpse of red tiles, a clutter of flowerpots, the pinks and scarlets of geranium and fuchsia. A curtain fluttered at an open upstairs window and smoke plumed from a chimney. As we got out of the car the sun came out from behind a cloud and, caught in the spread arms of the house, sheltered from the north wind, it was suddenly very warm.

"Come along," said Eliot and led the way, the dog at his heels. We went through the porch and into a dark, panelled hallway illuminated by the big window on the turn of the stairs. I had imagined Boscarva as being a house of the past, sad and nostalgic, filled with the chill of old memories. But it wasn't like that at all. It was vital, humming with a sense of activity. There were papers lying on the table, a pair of gardening gloves, a dog's lead. From beyond a doorway came the kitchen sounds of voices and the clatter of crockery. From upstairs a vacuum-cleaner hummed. And there was a smell compounded of scrubbed stone and old polished floors, and years of woodfires.

Eliot stood at the foot of the staircase and called, "Mamma." But when there was no answer, only the continued hum of the vacuum-cleaner, he said, "You'd better come this way." We went down the hall and through a door which led into a long, low drawing room, palely panelled and sensuous with the brightness and scent of spring flowers. At one end, in a fireplace of carved pine and Dutch tiles, a newly lit fire flickered cheerfully, and three tall windows, curtained in faded yellow silk, faced out over a flagged terrace, and beyond the balustrade of this I could see the blue line of the sea.

I stood in the middle of this charming room as Eliot Bayliss closed the door and said, "Well, you're here. Why don't you take your coat off?"

I did so. It was very warm. I laid it over a chair where it looked like some great, dead creature.

He said, "When did you get here?"

"Last night. I caught the train from London."

"You live in London?"

"Yes."

"And you've never been here before?"

"No. I didn't know about Boscarva. I didn't know about Grenville Bayliss being my grandfather. My mother never told me till the night before she died."

"How does Joss come into it?"

"I . . ." It was too complicated to explain. "I'd met him in London. He happened to be at the junction when my train got in. It was a coincidence."

"Where are you staying?"

"With Mrs Kernow in Fish Lane."

"Grenville's an old man. He's ill. You know that, don't you?"

"Yes."

"I think . . . this letter from Otto Pedersen . . . we'd better be careful. Perhaps my mother would be the best person . . ."

"Yes, of course."

"It was lucky you saw the letter."

"Yes. I thought he would probably write. But I was afraid that I would have to break the news to you all."

"And now it's been done for you." He smiled, and all at once he looked much younger . . . belying those strange coloured eyes and the thick silver-fox hair. "Why don't you wait here and I'll go and find my mother and try to put her in the picture. Would you like a cup of coffee or something?"

"Only if it's not a nuisance."

"No nuisance. I'll tell Pettifer." He opened the door behind him. "Make yourself at home."

The door closed softly, and he was gone. Pettifer. *Pettifer had been in the Navy too, he looked after my father and sometimes drove the car and Mrs Pettifer did the cooking.* So my mother had told me. And Joss had told me that Mrs Pettifer had died. But in the old days she had taken Lisa and her brother into the kitchen and made hot buttered toast. She had drawn the curtains against the dark and the rain, and made the children feel safe and loved.

Alone, I inspected the room where I had been left to wait. I saw a glass-doored cabinet filled with Oriental treasures, including some small pieces of jade, and wondered if these were the ones that my mother had mentioned to me. I glanced around, thinking that perhaps I might find the Venetian mirror and the davenport desk as well, but then my attention was caught by the picture over the mantelpiece, and I went to look at it, all else forgotten.

It was a portrait of a girl, dressed in the fashion of the early 1930s, slender, flat-chested, her white dress hanging straight to her hips, her dark, bobbed hair revealing with enchanting innocence the long, slender neck. She sat, in the picture, on a tall stool, holding a single long-stemmed rose, but you could not see her face, for she was looking away from the artist, out of some unseen window, into the sunshine. The effect was all pink and gold, with sunlight filtering through the thin stuff of her white dress. It was enchanting.

Behind me the door opened suddenly and I turned, startled, as an old man came into the room, stately, bald-headed, a little stooped, perhaps; treading cautiously. He wore rimless spectacles and a striped shirt with an old-fashioned hard collar, and over it all a blue and white butcher's apron.

"Are you the young lady wanting a cup of coffee?" He had a deep, lugubrious voice, and this, with his sombre appearance, made me think of a reliable undertaker.

"Yes, if it's not too much trouble."

"Milk and sugar?"

"No sugar. Just a little milk. I was looking at the portrait."

"Yes. It's very pleasing. It's called 'Lady Holding a Rose'."

"You can't see her face."

"No."

"Did my . . . Did Mr Bayliss paint it?"

"Oh yes. That was hung in the Academy, could have been sold a hundred times over, but the Commander would never part with it." As he said this, he carefully took off his spectacles, and was now staring at me intently. His old eyes were pale. He said, "For a moment, when you spoke, you reminded me of someone else. But you're young and she'd be middle-aged by now. And her hair was dark as a blackbird. That's what Mrs Pettifer used to say. Dark as a blackbird's wing."

I said, "Eliot didn't tell you?"

"What didn't Mr Eliot tell me?"

"You're talking about Lisa, aren't you? I'm Rebecca. I'm her daughter."

"Well." Fumbling a little he put his spectacles back on again. A faint gleam of pleasure showed on his gloomy features. "I was right then. I'm not often wrong about things like that." And he came forward, holding out a horny hand. "It's a real pleasure to meet you . . . A pleasure that I never thought I should have. I thought you'd never come. Is your mother with you?"

I wished that Eliot had made it a little easier for me.

202

"My mother's dead. She died last week. In Ibiza. That's why I'm here."

"She died." His eyes clouded. "I'm sorry. I'm really sorry. She should have come back. She should have come home. We all wanted to see her again." He took out a copious handkerchief and blew his nose. "And who—" he asked— "is going to tell the Commander?"

"I think . . . Eliot's gone to fetch his mother. You see, there's a letter for my grandfather in the post, it came this morning. It's from Ibiza, from the man who was . . . taking care of my mother. But if you think that wouldn't be a very good idea . . ."

"What I think won't make no difference," said Pettifer. "And whoever tells the Commander, it's not going to lessen his sorrow. But I'll tell you one thing. You being here will help a lot."

"Thank you."

He blew his nose again and put away his handkerchief.

"Mr Eliot and his mother . . . well, this isn't their home. But it was either the old Commander and me moving up to High Cross or them coming here. And they wouldn't be here if the doctor hadn't insisted. I told them we could manage all right, the Commander and me. We've been together all these years . . . but there, we're neither of us as young as we used to be, and the Commander, he had this heart attack . . ."

"Yes, I know . . ."

"And after Mrs Pettifer passed on, there wasn't anyone to do the cooking. Mind, I can cook all right, but it takes me a good part of my time taking care of the Commander, and I wouldn't want to see him going about the place looking shabby."

"No, of course not . . ."

I was interrupted by the slam of a door.

A hearty male voice called, "Pettifer!" and Pettifer said, "Excuse me a moment, miss," and went out to investigate, leaving the door open behind him.

"Pettifer!"

I heard Pettifer say, with what sounded like the greatest satisfaction, "Hallo, Joss."

"Is she there?"

"Who, here?"

"Rebecca."

"Yes, she's right here, in the sitting-room . . . I was just going to get her a cup of coffee."

"Make it two would you, there's a good chap. And black and strong for me."

His footsteps came down the hall, and the next moment he was there, framed in the doorway, long-legged, black-haired, and—it was obvious—angry.

"What the hell do you think you're doing?" he demanded.

I could feel my hackles rising, like a suspicious dog. Home, Eliot had said. This was Boscarva, my home, and whether I was here or not was nothing to do with Joss.

"I don't know what you're talking about."

"I went to pick you up and Mrs Kernow told me you'd already left."

"So?"

"I told you to wait for me."

"I decided not to wait."

He was silent, fuming, but finally appeared to accept this inescapable fact.

"Does anyone know you've arrived?"

"I met Eliot at the gate. He brought me here."

"Where's he gone?"

"To find his mother."

"Have you seen anyone else? Have you seen Grenville?"

"No."

"Has anyone told Grenville about your mother?"

"A letter came by this morning's post, from Otto Pedersen. But I don't think he's seen it yet."

"Pettifer must take it to him. Pettifer must be there when he reads it."

"Pettifer didn't seem to think that."

"I think it," said Joss.

His apparently outrageous interference left me without words, but as we stood glaring at each other across the pretty patterned carpet and a great bowl of scented narcissus, there came the sound of voices and footsteps down the uncarpeted staircase and along the hall towards us.

I heard a woman's voice say, "In the sitting-room, Eliot?"

Joss muttered something that sounded unprintable, and marched over to the fireplace where he stood with his back to me, staring down into the flames. The next instant, Mollie appeared in the doorway, hesitated for a moment and then came towards me, hands outstretched.

"Rebecca." (So it was to be a warm welcome.) Eliot, following behind her, closed the door. Joss did not even turn round.

I worked it out that by now Mollie must be over fifty, but this was hard to believe. She was plump and pretty, her fading blonde hair charmingly coiffed, her eyes blue, her skin fresh and lightly scattered with freckles which helped to create this astonishing illusion of youth. She wore a blue skirt and cardigan and a creamy silk blouse; her legs were slim and shapely and her hands beautifully manicured, decorated with pale pink fingernails, and many rings and fine gold bracelets. Scented, immaculately preserved, she made me think of a charming little tabby cat, curled precisely in the centre of her own satin cushion.

I said, "I'm afraid this is something of a shock."

"No, not a shock, but a surprise. And your mother . . . I'm so dreadfully sorry. Eliot's told me about the letter . . ."

At this Joss swung around from the fireplace.

"Where is the letter?"

Mollie turned her gaze upon him, and it was impossible to guess whether this was the first time she had realized he was there, or whether she had seen him and simply decided to ignore him.

"Joss. I didn't think you were coming this morning."

"Yes. I just got here."

"You know Rebecca, I believe."

"Yes, we've met." He hesitated, seeming to be making an effort to pull himself together. Then he smiled, ruefully, turned to lean his broad shoulders against the mantelpiece and apologized. "I'm sorry. And I know it's none of my business, but that letter that came this morning . . . where is it?"

"In my pocket," said Eliot, speaking for the first time. "Why?"

"It's just that I think Pettifer should be the one to break the news to the old man. I think Pettifer is the only person to do it."

This was greeted by silence. Then Mollie let go of my hands and turned to her son.

"He's right," she said. "Grenville's closest to Pettifer."

"That's all right by me," said Eliot, but his eyes, on Joss, were cold with antagonism. I did not blame him. I felt the same way myself—I was on Eliot's side.

Joss said again, "I'm sorry."

Mollie was polite. "Not at all. It's very thoughtful of you to be so concerned."

"None of my business, really," said Joss. Eliot and his mother

205

waited with pointed patience. At last he took the hint, heaved his shoulders away from the mantelpiece, and said, "Well, if you'll excuse me, I'll go and get on with some work."

"Will you be here for lunch?"

"No, I can only stay a couple of hours. I'll have to get back to the shop. I'll pick up a sandwich at the pub." He smiled benignly at us all, not a trace of his former temper showing. "Thanks all the same."

And so he left us, modest, apologetic, apparently cut down to size. Once more the young workman, an employee, with a job to do.

6

Mollie said, "You must forgive him. He's not always the most tactful of men."

Eliot laughed shortly. "That's the understatement of the year."

She turned to me, explaining, "He's restoring some of the furniture for us. It's old and it had got into bad repair. He's a marvellous craftsman, but we never know when he's going to arrive or when he's going to go!"

"One day," said her son, "I shall lose my temper with him and punch his nose into the back of his neck." He smiled at me charmingly, his eyes crinkling, belying the ferocity of his words. "And I'm going to have to go too. I was late as it was, now I'm bloody late. Rebecca, will you excuse me?"

"Of course. I'm sorry, I'm afraid it was my fault. And thank you for being so kind . . ."

"I'm glad I stopped. I must have known how important it was. I'll see you . . ."

"Yes, of course you will," said Mollie quickly. "She can't go away now that she's found us."

"Well I'll leave the two of you to fix everything up . . . ." He made for the door, but his mother interrupted gently.

"Eliot." He turned. "The letter."

"Oh, yes, of course." He took it from his pocket, the fateful letter, a little crumpled now, and handed it to Mollie. "Don't let Pettifer make too big a meal of it. He's a sentimental old chap."

"I won't."

He smiled again, saying goodbye to both of us. "See you at dinner." And he was gone, whistling up his dog as he went down the hall. We heard the front door open and shut, his car start up. Mollie turned to me.

"Now," she said, "come and sit by the fire and tell me all about it."

I did so, as I had already told Joss and Mrs Kernow, only this time I found myself stumbling a little when I got to the bit about Otto and Lisa living together, as though I were ashamed of it, which was a thing which I had never been. As I talked and Mollie listened, I tried to work this out, and to understand why my mother had disliked her so much. Perhaps it was simply a natural antipathy. It was obvious that they would never have had anything in common. And my mother had never had much tolerance for women who bored her. Men, now, were different. Men were always amusing. But women had to be very special for my mother to be able to tolerate their company. No, it could not all have been Mollie's fault. Sitting across the fireside from her, I resolved that I would be friends with her, and perhaps compensate, in a small way, for the short shrift she had received from Lisa.

"And how long are you going to be able to stay in Porthkerris? Your job . . . do you have to get back?"

"No. I seem to have been given a sort of indefinite leave."

"You'll stay here, with us?"

"Well, I've got this room with Mrs Kernow."

"Yes, but you'd be much better here. There's not a lot of space, that's the only thing; you'll have to sleep up in the attic, but it's a dear little room if you don't mind the sloping ceilings and you manage not to bump your head. You see, Eliot and I seem to have filled up the guest rooms, and as well I've got my niece staying for a few days. Perhaps you'll make friends with her. It'll be nice for her to have someone young about the place."

I wondered where the niece was. "How old is she?"

"Only seventeen. It's a difficult age, and I think that her mother felt it would be a good thing if she was out of London for a little. They live there, you see, and of course she has so many friends, and there is so much going on . . ." She was obviously finding it difficult to find the right words . . . "Anyway, Andrea's down here for a week or two to have a little change, but I'm afraid she's rather bored."

I imagined myself at seventeen, in the unseen Andrea's shoes, staying in this warm and charming house, cared for by Mollie and Pettifer, with the sea and the cliffs on my doorstep, the countryside inviting long walks, and all the secret crooked streets of Porthkerris waiting to be explored. To me it would have been heaven, and impossible to be bored. I wondered if I would have very much in common with Mollie's niece.

"Of course," she went on, "as you've probably gathered, Eliot and I are only here because Mrs Pettifer died and really the two old men couldn't manage on their own. We've got Mrs Thomas, she comes in each morning to help do the housework, but I do all the cooking, and keep the place as bright and pretty as I can."

"The flowers are so lovely."

"I can't bear a house without flowers."

"What about your own house?"

"My dear, it's empty. I shall have to take you up to High Cross one day to show it to you. I bought a pair of old cottages just after the war and converted them. Even though I shouldn't say so, it is very charming. And, of course, it's so handy for Eliot's garage; as it is, living here, he seems to be perpetually on the road."

"Yes, I suppose so."

I could hear footsteps coming down the hall again; in a moment the door opened, and Pettifer edged around it, cautiously, carrying a tray laden with all the accoutrements of mid-morning coffee, including a large silver pot with steam drifting from its spout.

"Oh, Pettifer, thank you . . ."

He came forward, stooped with the weight of the tray, and Mollie got up to fetch a stool and place it swiftly beneath the tray so that the old man could put it down before it tilted so sharply that everything on it went hurtling to the floor.

"That's splendid, Pettifer."

"One of the cups was for Joss."

"He's upstairs working. He must have forgotten about the coffee. Never mind, I'll drink it for him. And, Pettifer . . ." He straightened, slowly, as though all his old joints were aching. Mollie took the letter from Ibiza off the mantelpiece where she had placed it for safety. "We thought, all of us, that perhaps it would be the best if you told the Commander about his daughter and then gave him this letter. It would be best, we thought, coming from you. Would you mind?"

Pettifer took the thin blue envelope.

"No, Madam. I'll do it. I'm just on my way up now to get the Commander up and dressed."

"It would be a kindness, Pettifer."

208

"That's all right, Madam."

"And tell him that Rebecca is here. And that she's staying. We'll have to make up the bed in the attic but I think she'll be quite comfortable."

Again a gleam came into Pettifer's face. I wondered if he ever really smiled, or whether his face had dropped permanently into those lugubrious lines and a cheerful expression had become physically impossible.

"I'm glad you're staying," he said. "The Commander will like that."

When he'd gone, I said, "You'll have a lot to do. Shouldn't I go, and get out from under your feet?"

"You'll have to collect your things from Mrs Kernow anyway. I wonder how we could manage that? Pettifer could take you, but now he'll be occupied with Grenville and I must speak to Mrs Thomas about your room and then start thinking about lunch. Now what are we going to do?" I could not imagine. I was certainly not going to be able to carry all my belongings up the hill from the town. But luckily Mollie answered her own question. "I know. Joss. He can take you and bring you back up the hill in his van."

"But isn't Joss working?"

"Oh, for once we'll interrupt him. It's not often he's asked to put himself out—I'm sure he won't mind. Come along, we'll go and find him."

I had thought that she would take me to some forgotten outhouse or shed where we would find Joss, surrounded by wood shavings and the smell of hot glue, but to my surprise, she led me upstairs, and I forgot about Joss, because these were my first impressions of Boscarva, where my mother had been brought up, and I didn't want to miss a thing. The stairs were uncarpeted, the walls half panelled and then darkly papered above and hung with heavy oil paintings. All was at variance with the pretty, feminine sitting-room which we had left downstairs. On the first-floor landing passages led to left and right, there was a tallboy of polished walnut, and bookcases heavy with books, and then we went on again, up the stairs. Here was red drugget, white paint, again the passages led away to either side, and Mollie took the right-hand one. At the end of this passage was an open door, and from behind it the sound of voices, a man's and a girl's.

She seemed to hesitate and then her footsteps quickened, determined. Her back view became, all at once, formidable. With me following she went down the passage and through the door, and we were in an attic which had been converted, by means of a skylight, to a studio, or perhaps a billiard room, for against one wall was a massive, leather-seated sofa with oaken arms and legs. Now, however, this cold and airy room was being used as a workshop, with Joss in the middle of it, surrounded by chairs, broken picture frames, a table with a crooked leg, some scraps of leather, tools and nails, and a gimcrack gas ring on which reposed an unsavoury-looking glue pot. Wrapped in a worn blue apron, he was carefully fitting beautiful scarlet hide over the seat of one of the chairs, and as he did this, was being entertained by a young and female companion, who turned, disinterested, to see who had come into the room, and was so breaking up this cosy *tête-à-tête*.

Mollie said, "Andrea!" And then, less sharply, "Andrea, I didn't realize you were up."

"Oh, I've been up for hours."

"Did you have any breakfast?"

"I didn't want any."

"Andrea, this is Rebecca. Rebecca Bayliss."

"Oh, yes," she turned her eyes on to me. "Joss has been telling me all about you."

I said, "How do you do." She was very young and very thin, with long seaweedy hair that hung on either side of her face, which was pretty, except for her eyes which were pale and slightly protuberant, and not improved by a great deal of clumsy mascara. She wore, inevitably, jeans, and a cotton tee-shirt which did not look entirely clean and which revealed, with no shadow of a doubt, the fact that she wore nothing beneath it. On her feet were sandals which looked like surgical boots that had been striped in green and purple. There was a leather bootlace around her neck upon which hung a heavy silver cross of vaguely Celtic design. Andrea, I thought. So bored with Boscarva. And it made me uncomfortable to think that she and Joss had been discussing me. I wondered what he had said.

Now, she did not move, but stayed where she was, legs straddled, leaning against a heavy old mahogany table.

"Hi," she said.

"Rebecca's going to stay here," Mollie told them. Joss looked up, his mouth full of tacks, his eyes bright with interest, a lock of black hair falling over his forehead.

"Where's she going to sleep?" asked Andrea. "I thought we were a full house."

210

"In the bedroom along the passage," her aunt told her crisply. "Joss, would you do a favour for me?" He spat the tacks neatly into his palm and stood up, pushing his hair back with his wrist. "Would you take her, now, down to Mrs Kernow, and tell Mrs Kernow that she's coming here, and then help her with her suitcases and bring her back up to Boscarva again? Would that be very inconvenient?"

"Not at all," said Joss, but Andrea's face assumed an expression of bored resignation.

"It's a nuisance, I know, when you're busy, but it would be such a help . . ."

"It's no trouble." He laid down his little hammer and began to untie the knot of his apron. He grinned at me. "I'm getting quite used to carting Rebecca about."

And Andrea gave a snort, whether of disgust or impatience it was impossible to tell, sprang to her feet and marched out of the room, leaving the impression that we had been lucky to escape without a monumentally slammed door.

And so I was back where I started, with Joss, crammed into the ramshackle little van. We drove in silence away from Boscarva, through Mr Padlow's building estate, and on to the slope of the hill that led down to the town.

It was Joss who broke the silence.

"So, it all worked out."

"Yes."

"How do you like your family?"

"I haven't met them all yet. I haven't met Grenville."

He said, "You'll like him," but the way he said it, he made it sound. "You'll like *him*."

"I like them all."

"That's good."

I looked at him. He wore his blue denim jacket, a navy polo-necked sweater. His profile was impassive. I felt it would be easy to be maddened by him.

"Tell me about Andrea," I said.

"What do you want to know about Andrea?"

"I don't know. I just want you to tell me."

"She's seventeen, and she thinks she's in love with some guy she met at Art School, and her parents don't approve so she's been rusticated with Auntie Mollie. And she's bored stiff."

"She seems to have taken you into her confidence."

211

"There's no one else to talk to."

"Why doesn't she go back to London?"

"Because she's only seventeen. She hasn't got the money. And I think she hasn't quite got the courage to stand up to her parents."

"What does she do with herself all day?"

"I don't know. I'm not there all day. She doesn't seem to get up until lunchtime, and then she sits around watching television. Boscarva's a house of old people. You can't blame her for being bored."

I said, without thinking, "Only the boring are bored." This had once been drummed into me by a wise and well-meaning headmistress.

"That," said Joss, "sounds uncomfortably sanctimonious."

"I didn't mean it to."

He smiled. "Were you never bored?"

"Nobody who lived with my mother was ever bored."

He sang, "You may have been a headache, but you never were a bore."

"Exactly."

"She sounds great. Exactly my sort of female."

"That's what most men thought about her."

When we got to Fish Lane Mrs Kernow was out, but Joss seemed to have a key. We let ourselves in and I went upstairs to pack my suitcase and my rucksack while Joss wrote Mrs Kernow a note to explain the new arrangements.

"How about paying her?" I asked as I came downstairs, bumping the rucksack behind me.

"I'll fix that when I next see her. I've told her so in the note."

"But I can pay for myself."

"Of course you can, but let me do it for you." He took my suitcase and went to open the door, and there did not seem to be opportunity for further argument.

Once more my belongings were heaved into the back of the little truck, once more we headed for Boscarva, only this time Joss took me round by the harbour road.

"I want to show you my shop . . . I mean, I just want to show you where it is. Then if you want to get hold of me for any reason, you'll know where to find me."

"Why should I want to get hold of you?"

"I don't know. You might need wise counselling; or money; or just a good laugh. There it is, you can't miss it."

It was a tall narrow house, boxed in between two short fat houses. Three storeys high with a window on each floor, and the ground floor still in a state of reconstruction, with new wood unpainted and great circles of whitewash splashed over the plate glass of the shop window.

As we flashed past it, tyres rattling on the cobbles, I said, "That's a good position, you'll get all the visitors coming in to spend their money."

"That's what I hope."

"When can I see it?"

"Come next week. We'll be more or less straight then."

"All right. Next week."

"It's a date," said Joss, and turned the corner by the church. He put the little truck into second gear and we roared up the hill with a noise like a badly tuned motor bicycle.

Back at Boscarva, it was Pettifer who, hearing our arrival, emerged from the front door as Joss lifted my suitcase from the back of the truck.

"Joss, the Commander's downstairs and in his study. He said to bring Rebecca in to see him just as soon as you arrived."

Joss looked at him. "How is he?"

Pettifer ducked his head. "Not too bad."

"Was he very upset?"

"He's all right . . . now you leave that case, and I'll carry it upstairs."

"You'll do no such thing," said Joss, and for once I was glad that he was being his usual bossy self. "I'll take it up. Where's she sleeping?"

"In the attic . . . the other end from the billiard room, but the Commander did say, right away."

"I know," Joss grinned, "and Naval time is five minutes beforehand. But there's still time to take the girl up to her room, so stop fussing, there's a good man."

Leaving Pettifer still mildly protesting, I followed him up the two flights of stairs that I had already climbed this morning. The sound of the vacuum had stopped, but there was the smell of roasting lamb. I realized then that I was very hungry and my mouth watered. Joss's long legs sped ahead of me, and by the time I reached the slope-ceilinged bedroom which was to be mine, he had set down the suitcase and the rucksack and gone to fling wide the dormer window, so that I was met by a blast of cold, salty air.

"Come and look at the view."

I went to stand beside him. I saw the sea, the cliffs, the gold of bracken and the first yellow candles of gorse. And below was the Boscarva garden which, because of the stone balustrade of the terrace, I had not been able to see from the drawing-room window. It had been built in a series of terraces, dropping down the slope of the hill, and at the bottom, tucked into a corner of the garden wall, was a stone cottage with a slate roof. No, not a cottage, perhaps a stable, with a commodious loft above it.

I said, "What's that building?"

"That's the studio," Joss told me. "That's where your grandfather used to paint."

"It doesn't look like a studio."

"From the other side it does. The entire north wall is made of glass. He designed it himself, had it built by a local stonemason."

"It looks shut up."

"It is. Locked and shuttered. It hasn't been opened since he had his heart attack and stopped painting."

I shivered suddenly.

"Cold?" asked Joss.

"I don't know." I moved away from the window, undoing my coat, dropping it over the end of the bed. The room was white, the carpet dark red. There was a built-in wardrobe, shelves full of books, a wash-basin. I went over to wash my hands, turning the soap beneath the warm water. Over the basin was a mirror which gave me back a reflection both dishevelled and anxious. I realized then how nervous I was of meeting Grenville for the first time, and how important it was that he should get a good impression of me.

I dried my hands, went to unbuckle my rucksack, and found a brush and comb. "Was he a good painter, Joss? Do you think he was a good artist?"

"Yes. The old school, of course, but magnificent. And a marvellous colourist."

I pulled the rubber band from the end of my plait, shook the coils free, and went back to the mirror to start brushing. Over my reflected shoulder I could see Joss watching me. He did not speak while I brushed and combed and finally re-plaited my hair. As I fastened the ends, he said, "It's a wonderful colour. Like corn."

I laid down the brush and comb. "Joss, we mustn't keep him waiting."

"Do you want me to come with you?"

"Please."

214

I realized then that this was the first time I had ever had to ask him to help me.

I followed him downstairs, down the hall and past the sitting-room, to a door which stood at the end of the passage. Joss opened it and put his head around.

He said, "Good morning."

"Who's that? Joss? Come along in . . ." The voice was higher pitched than I had imagined, more like the voice of a much younger man.

"I've brought someone to see you . . ."

He opened the door wide, and put his arms behind me to propel me gently forward into the room. It was a small room, with french windows leading out on to a paved terrace and a secret garden, warm with trapped sunshine, and enclosed by dense hedges and escallonia.

I saw the fire flickering in the grate; the panelled walls covered either with pictures or books; the model, on the mantelpiece, of an old-fashioned naval cruiser. There were photographs in silver frames, a table littered with papers and magazines, and a blue and white Chinese bowl filled with daffodils.

As I entered, he was already heaving himself—with the aid of a stick—out of a red leather arm-chair, which stood half turned towards the warmth of the fire. I was amazed that Joss did nothing to help him, and I began to say, "Oh, please don't bother . . ." but by then he was on his feet and erect, and a pair of blue eyes surveyed me calmly from beneath jutting brows and bristling white eyebrows.

I realized then that I had steeled myself to finding him pathetic in some way, old, infirm, perhaps a little shaky. But Grenville Bayliss, at eighty, was formidable. Very tall, very upright, starched and barbered, smelling faintly of Bay Rum, he was a credit to his servant Pettifer. He wore a dark blue blazer, of Naval cut, neatly creased grey flannels, and velvet slippers with his initials embroidered in gold. He was also very tanned, his bald head brown as a chestnut beneath the thinning strands of white hair, and I imagined him spending much time in that little sunny secret garden, reading his morning paper, enjoying a pipe, watching the gulls and the white clouds scudding across the sky.

We looked at each other. I wished that he would say something but he simply looked. I hoped that he liked what he saw, and was glad I had taken the time to brush my hair. And then he said, "I've never been in this situation before. I'm not quite sure how we're meant to greet each other."

I said, "I could give you a kiss."

"Why don't you do that?"

So I did, stepping forward and raising my face, and he stooped slightly and my lips touched the smooth clean skin of his cheek.

"Now," he said, "why don't we sit down? Joss, come and sit down."

But Joss excused himself, said that if he didn't start work soon then he would have done nothing all day. But he stayed long enough to help the old man back into his chair, and pour us both a glass of sherry from the decanter on the side table, and then he said, "I'll leave you. You'll have a lot to talk about," and with a cheerful wave of his hand, slipped away. The door closed quietly behind him.

Grenville said, "I believe you know him quite well."

I pulled up a stool so that I could sit and face him. "Not really. But he's been very kind, and . . ." I tried to think of the right word. "Convenient. I mean, he always seems to be there when people need him."

"And never when they don't?" I was not sure if I could entirely agree with this. "He's a clever boy, too. Doing up all my furniture."

"Yes, I know."

"Good craftsman. Lovely hands." He laid down his sherry glass, and once more I was subjected to that piercing blue stare. "Your mother died."

"Yes."

"Had a letter from this Pedersen fellow. He said it was leukaemia."

"Yes."

"Did you meet him?"

I told him about going to Ibiza and the night I had spent with Otto and my mother.

"He was a decent chap, then? Good to her?"

"Yes. He was immensely kind. And he adored her."

"Glad she ended up with somebody decent. Most of the chaps she picked on were just a lot of bounders."

I smiled at the old-fashioned word. I thought of the sheep-farmer, and the American in his Brooks Brothers shirts, and wondered how they would have liked being called bounders. They probably wouldn't even have known what it meant.

I said, "I think she sometimes got a little carried away."

A gleam of humour showed in his eyes. "You seem to have adopted a fairly worldly attitude?"

"Yes. I did. Long ago."

"She was a maddening woman. But she'd been the most enchanting little girl it was possible to imagine. I painted her often. I've still got one or two canvases of Lisa as a child. I'll have to get Pettifer to look them out, show them to you. And then she grew up and everything changed. Roger, my son, was killed in the war, and Lisa was always at loggerheads with her mother, rushing off in her little car, never coming home at night. Finally she fell in love with this actor fellow, and that was it."

"She really *was* in love with him."

"In love." He sounded disgusted. "That's an overrated expression. There's a lot more to life than just being in love."

"Yes, but you have to find that out for yourself."

He looked amused. "Have you found it out?"

"No."

"How old are you?"

"Twenty-one."

"You're mature for twenty-one. And I like your hair. You don't look like Lisa. You don't look like your father either. You look like yourself." He reached for his sherry glass, raised it carefully to his mouth, took a sip, and then replaced the glass on the table by his chair. In such cautious actions did he betray his age and his infirmity.

He said, "She should have come back to Boscarva. At any time we would have welcomed her. Come to that, why didn't *you* come?"

"I didn't know about Boscarva. I didn't know about you until the night before she died."

"It was as though she'd put the past out of her life. And when her mother died and I wrote to tell her, she never even replied."

"We were in New York that Christmas. She didn't get your letter till months later. And then it seemed too late to write. And she was so bad at writing letters."

"You're standing up for her. You don't resent the fact that she kept you from this place? You could have been brought up here. This could have been your home."

"She was my mother. That was the important thing."

"You seem to be arguing with me. Nobody argues with me nowadays. Not even Pettifer. It gets very dull." Once more I was fixed with that blue stare. "Have you met Pettifer? He and I were in the Navy together about a century ago. And Mollie and Eliot? Have you met them?"

"Yes."

217

"They shouldn't be living here at all, of course, but the doctor insisted. Doesn't make that much difference to me, but it's hard luck on poor Pettifer. And Mollie's got a niece here as well, dreadful child with sagging breasts. Have you seen her?"

I managed not to giggle. "Yes, for a moment."

"A moment would be too long. And Boscarva. What do you think of Boscarva?"

"I love it. What I've seen of it, I love."

"The town's creeping out over the hill. There was a farm at the top, belonged to an old lady called Mrs Gregory. But this builder fellow talked her into selling up to him and now they've bulldozed the fields flat as a pancake and they're putting up houses nineteen to the dozen."

"I know. I saw them."

"Well, they can't come any further, because the farm at the back of this place and the fields on either side of the lane belong to me. Bought them when I bought Boscarva, back in 1922. Wouldn't like to tell you how little it cost me. But a bit of land around you gives you a feeling of security. Remember that."

"I will."

He frowned. "What's your name again? I've forgotten it already."

"Rebecca."

"Rebecca. And what are you going to call me?"

"I don't know. What do you want me to call you?"

"Eliot calls me Grenville. You call me Grenville too. It sounds more friendly."

"All right."

We drank our sherry, smiling, content with each other. Then, from the back of the house, came the sound of a gong being rung. Grenville put down his glass and got painfully to his feet, and I went to open the door for him. Together, we went down the passage towards the dining room and family lunch.

7

EXHAUSTION HIT ME at the end of that long, eventful day, and unfortunately in the middle of dinner. Luncheon had been a sustaining, homely meal, eaten at a round table set in the bay window of the big dining room. This had been laid with a simple checked cloth, and everyday china and glass, but dinner was a different affair altogether.

The long, polished table in the middle of the room was set for the five of us, with fine linen mats, and old silver and glass sparkling in the candlelight.

Everybody, it seemed, was expected to change in honour of this apparently nightly ritual. Mollie came downstairs in a brocade house-coat the colour of sapphires, which emphasized the brightness of her eyes. Grenville wore a faded velvet dinnerjacket and Eliot a pale flannel suit in which he looked as elegant as a greyhound. Even Andrea, probably under much protest, had put on a different pair of trousers and a blouse of broderie anglaise which looked as though it could have done with a press, or a wash, or maybe both. Her lank hair was tied back with a scrap of velvet ribbon, the expression on her face continued to be one of resentful boredom.

Not in the habit of attending formal dinner parties, I had neverthe-less packed a garment which would obviously have to appear every evening as long as I stayed in this house, for I had no other. It was a caftan of soft brown jersey wool, with silver embroidery at the neck and the wrists of the flowing sleeves. With it, I wore my silver brace-lets and a pair of hoop ear-rings which my mother had given me for my twenty-first birthday. Their weight, on this occasion, gave me odd comfort and confidence, two things which I badly needed.

I did not want to have dinner with my newly acquired family. I did not want to have to make conversation, to listen, to be intelligent and charming. I wanted to go to bed and be brought something unde-manding, like Bovril or a boiled egg. I wanted to be alone.

But there was soup and duckling, and red wine, dispensed by Eliot. The duckling was rich and the room very warm. As the meal slowly

219

progressed I felt more and more strange, disembodied, light-headed. I tried to concentrate on the flames of the candles in front of me, but as I stared at them they separated and repeated themselves, and the voices around me became blurred and unintelligible, like the hum of conversation heard from a distant room. Instinctively, I pushed my plate away from me, knocked over the wineglass, and watched, in hopeless horror, as the red wine spread amongst the shattered splinters of glass.

In a way the accident was a blessing, for they all stopped talking and looked at me. I must have gone quite pale, for Eliot was on his feet in an instant and at my side . . .

"Are you all right?"

I said, "No, I don't think I am. I'm sorry . . ."

"Oh, my dear." Mollie flung aside her napkin and pushed back her chair. From across the table Andrea eyed me with chill interest.

"The glass . . . I'm so sorry . . ."

From the head of the table Grenville spoke. "It doesn't matter about the glass. Leave the glass. The girl's exhausted. Mollie, take her up and put her to bed."

I tried to protest, but not very hard. Eliot drew back my chair and helped me to my feet, his hands firm beneath my elbows. Mollie had gone to open the door, and cooler air moved in from the hall—already I felt better, as though, perhaps, after all I was not going to faint.

As I passed Grenville, I said, "I'm sorry," for the third time; "forgive me. Good night." I bent and kissed him, and left them all. Mollie closed the door behind us and came upstairs with me. She helped me undress and get into bed, and I was asleep before she had even turned off the light.

I slept for fourteen hours, waking at ten o'clock. I had not slept so late for years, and beyond my window the sky was blue and the cold bright northern light reflected from the sloping white-painted walls of my room. I got up, pulled on a dressing-gown and went and had a bath. Dressed, I felt wonderful, apart from the sinking sensation of shame at my behaviour the night before. I hoped they had not all thought that I was drunk.

Downstairs, I finally ran Mollie to earth in a little pantry, arranging a great mass of purple and pink polyanthus in a flowered bowl.

"How did you sleep?" she asked at once.

"Like the dead. I'm sorry about last night . . ."

"My dear, you were tired out. I'm sorry I didn't realize before. You'll want some breakfast."

"Just coffee."

She took me into the kitchen and heated coffee while I made some toast. "Where is everybody?" I asked.

"Eliot's at the garage, of course, and Pettifer's taken the car to Fourbourne to do some shopping for Grenville."

"What can I do? There must be something I can do to help."

"Well . . ." she debated. I looked at her. This morning she wore a cashmere sweater the colour of caramel and a slender tweed skirt. Immaculately made up, with every strand of hair in place, she seemed almost inhumanly neat. "You could go and fetch the fish for me in Porthkerris. The fishmonger rang up to say he'd got some halibut and I thought we'd have it for dinner. I could lend you my little car. Do you drive?"

"Yes, but couldn't I walk down? I like walking and it's such a lovely morning."

"Of course, if you want to. You could take the short cut over the fields and along the cliff. I know—" she appeared to be suddenly struck by inspiration—"take Andrea with you, and then she can show you the way, and show you where the fish shop is. Besides, she never takes any exercise if she can possibly help it and a walk would do her good." She made Andrea sound like a lazy dog. I did not particularly relish the idea of Andrea's company for the entire morning but I was sympathetic to Mollie, being encumbered by this unengaging girl, so I said that I would do as she suggested, and when I had finished my breakfast went in search of Andrea whom Mollie had last seen out on the terrace.

I found her bundled in a rug, lying on a long cane chair in a patch of sunshine, and peevishly regarding the view, like a seasick passenger on a liner.

"Will you walk down to Porthkerris with me?" I asked her.

She fixed me with her protuberant stare. "Why?"

"Because Mollie's asked me to go and pick up some fish and I don't know where the shop is. Besides, it's a lovely morning, and she thought we might go down to the cliffs."

She considered my suggestion, said, "All right," uncoiled herself from the rug and stood up. She wore the same dirty jeans as yesterday and a vast black and white sweater which reached below her narrow hips. We went back to the kitchen to fetch a basket and then set out, by way of the terrace and the sloping garden, down in the direction of the sea.

At the bottom of the garden, stone steps led up and over the wall, and Andrea went ahead of me, but I paused because I wanted to inspect the studio from this new angle. It was, as Joss had said, locked and shuttered, and somehow desolate, and the great window on the north wall had been closed off by tightly-drawn curtains so that not a chink presented itself to any inquisitive passer-by.

Andrea stood on the top of the wall, her gaze following mine.

"He never paints now," she told me.

"I know."

"I can't think why. There's nothing wrong with him." She jumped, hair flying, down off the wall, and totally disappeared. I took a last look at the studio and then followed her and we took a trodden path that led down through small, irregular fields, and came out at last, through the hazard of some waist-high gorse bushes, to a stile, and so on to the cliff path.

This was obviously a favourite walk with visitors to Porthkerris, for there were seats set in sheltered view points, and litter bins for rubbish, and notices warning people not to go too near the edge of the cliff which was likely to collapse.

Andrea instantly went to the very edge and peered over. Gulls wheeled and screamed all around her, the wind tore at her hair and the baggy sweater, and from far below came the distant thunder of surf on rocks. She flung her arms wide and teetered slightly as though about to fall over the edge, but when she saw that I didn't care whether she committed suicide or not, she returned to the path, and in single file we walked on, Andrea in front.

The cliff curved and the town came into view in front of us, the low grey houses nestled around the sweep of the bay and climbing the steep hill to the moor behind. We went through a gate, and were now on to a proper road, and so able to walk side by side.

Andrea became conversational.

"Your mother's just died, hasn't she?"

"Yes."

"Aunt Mollie was telling me about her. She said she was a tart."

Painfully, I remained serene. It would have been instant victory for Andrea if I had been anything else.

"She didn't really know her. They hadn't seen each other for years."

"Was she a tart?"

222

"No."

"Mollie said she lived with men."

I realized then that Andrea was not merely trying to needle me, she was genuinely curious, and there was envy there as well.

I said, "She was very gay and very loving and very beautiful."

She accepted this. "Where do you live?"

"In London. I've got a little flat."

"Do you live alone, or with somebody?"

"No, I live alone."

"Do you go to parties and things?"

"Yes, if someone asks me and I want to go."

"Do you work? Do you have a job?"

"Yes. In a bookshop."

"God, how grim."

"I like it."

"Where did you meet Joss?"

Now, I thought, we're getting down to business, but her face was empty of expression.

"I met him in London . . . he mended a chair for me."

"Do you like him?"

"I don't know him well enough to dislike him."

"Eliot hates him. So does Aunt Mollie."

"Why?"

"Because they don't like having him around the place all the time. And they treat him as though he should call them Sir and Madam, and of course he doesn't. And he talks to Grenville and makes him laugh. I've heard them talking."

I imagined her creeping up to closed doors, listening at keyholes.

"That's nice, if he makes the old man laugh."

"He and Eliot had a terrible row once. It was about some car that Eliot had sold to a friend of Joss's and Joss said it wasn't roadworthy and Eliot called him an insolent, interfering bastard."

"Did you listen in to that one as well?"

"I couldn't help hearing. I was in the loo and the window was open and they were out on the gravel by the front door."

"How long have you been staying at Boscarva?" I asked, curious to know how long it had taken her to dig all these skeletons out of the family cupboards.

"Two weeks. It seems like six months."

"I should have thought you'd have loved coming down."

223

"For heaven's sake, I'm not a child. What am I meant to do with myself. Go bucket and spading on the beach?"

"What do you do in London?"

She kicked a pebble, viciously, hating Cornwall. "I was at an art school, but my parents *didn't approve*—" she put on a mealy voice— "of my friends. So they took me away and sent me here."

"But you can't stay here for ever. What are you going to do when you go back?"

"That's up to them, isn't it?"

I felt a twinge of pity for her parents, even parents who had somehow raised such an obnoxious child.

"I mean, isn't there anything you *want* to do?"

"Yes, just get away, be on my own, do my own thing. Danus, this fabulous chap I went around with, he had a friend who was running a pottery on the Isle of Skye, and he wanted me to go and help . . . It sounded super, you know, living in a sort of commune, and right away from everybody . . . but my grotty mother shoved her great oar in and spoiled it all."

"Where's Danus now?"

"Oh, he went to Skye."

"Has he written to tell you about it?"

She tossed her head, fiddled with her hair, would not meet my eye. "Yes, actually, long letters. Reams of them. He still wants me to go there, and I'm going to, just as soon as I'm eighteen and they can't stop me any more."

"Why don't you go back to Art School first, and get some sort of a qualification . . . that'd give you time . . ."

She turned on me. "You know something? You talk like all the rest of them? How old are you anyway? You sound like someone with one foot in the grave."

"It's crazy to wreck your life before it's even started."

"It's my life. Not yours."

"No, it's not my life."

Having thus stupendously quarrelled, we continued our walk into the town in silence, and when Andrea did speak again, it was to say, "That's the fish shop," and wave a hand in its direction.

"Thank you." I went in to collect the halibut but she stayed, pointedly, outside on the cobbled pavement. When I emerged again, she had gone, only to appear the next moment from a papershop next door, where she had been buying a lurid magazine called *True Sex*.

"Shall we go back now?" I asked her. "Or do you want to do more shopping?"

"I can't shop, I haven't any money. Only a few pence."

I was suddenly, irrationally, sorry for her. "I'll stand you a cup of coffee if you'd like one."

She looked at me with sudden delight and I thought she was going to gleefully accept my modest offer, but instead she said, "Let's go and see Joss."

I was taken unawares. "Why do you want to go and see Joss?"

"I just do. I often go and see him when I come down to the town. He's always pleased to see me. He made me promise always to go and see him if I'm down here."

"How do you know he'll be there?"

"Well, he's not at Boscarva today, so he must be at the shop. Have you been there? It's super, he's got a sort of pad on the top floor, just like something out of a magazine, with a bed that's a sort of sofa and masses of cushions and things, and a log fire. And at night—" her voice became dreamy—"it's all closed-in and secret, and there's noth ing but firelight."

I tried not to gape. "You mean . . . you and Joss . . ."

She shrugged, tossing her hair. "Once or twice, but nobody knows. I don't know why I told you. You won't tell the others, will you?"

"But don't they . . . doesn't Mollie . . . ask questions?"

"Oh, I tell her I'm going to the cinema. She doesn't seem to mind me going to the cinema. Come on, let's go and see Joss . . ."

But after this revelation, nothing would have induced me to go near Joss's shop. I said, "Joss will be working, he won't want to be interrupted. And anyway there isn't time. And I don't want to go."

"You said there was time for coffee, why isn't there time for Joss?"

"Andrea, I told you, I don't want to go."

She began to smile. "I thought you liked Joss."

"That's not the point. He doesn't want us under his feet every time he turns round."

"Do you mean me?"

"I mean *us*." I was beginning to be desperate.

"He always wants to see me. I know he does."

"Yes, I'm sure," I said gently. "But let's go back to Boscarva."

I reminded myself that from the very start I had not liked Joss. Despite his concern and apparent friendliness he had always left me with that strange sensation of disquiet, as though someone were creeping up behind my back. Yesterday I had begun to forget this

225

initial antipathy, even to like him, but after Andrea's confidences it was not hard to whip back to life my first distrust of the man. He was too good-looking, too charming. Andrea could be a liar, but she was no fool; she had pigeon-holed the rest of the family with disconcerting accuracy, and even if there was only a grain of truth in what she said about Joss, I wanted to have no part of it.

If I had known him and liked him better, I would have taken him aside and taxed him with what she had said. As it was, he held no importance for me. Besides, I had other things to think about.

Grenville did not come down for lunch that day.

"He's tired," Mollie told us. "He's having a day in bed. Perhaps he'll join us for dinner. Pettifer's going to take him up a tray."

So the three of us ate lunch together. Mollie had changed into a neat woollen dress and a double string of pearls. She was going, she said, to play bridge with friends in Fourbourne. She hoped that I would be able to occupy myself.

I said that of course I would be perfectly all right. Across the table, we smiled at each other and I wondered if she had really told Andrea that my mother was a tart, or if this was simply Andrea's interpretation of some vague euphemistic explanation that Mollie had given her. I hoped it was the latter, but still I wished that Mollie had not found it necessary to discuss Lisa with Andrea. She was dead now, but once she had been funny and enchanting and full of laughter. Why couldn't she be remembered that way?

As we sat around the table, the day outside changed its face. A wind got up from the west, and with great speed a bank of grey cloud sped over the blue sky, obliterating the sunshine, and presently it started to rain. It was in this rain that Mollie set off for her bridge party, driving her little car, and saying that she would be home about six. Andrea, perhaps exhausted by her morning's exercise, but more likely bored to death with my company, disappeared up to her bedroom with her new magazine. Alone, I stood at the foot of the stairs, wondering how to amuse myself. The silence of the gloomy afternoon was broken only by the ticking of the grandfather clock and small, occupied sounds which came from the direction of the kitchens, and which, investigated, proved to be Pettifer, seated at a wooden table in his pantry and cleaning silver.

He looked up as I put my head around the door.

"Hallo. I didn't hear you."

"How's my grandfather?"

"Oh, he's all right. Just a bit weary after all the excitement of yesterday. We thought it would be better if he had a day with his toes up. Has Mrs Roger gone?"

"Yes." I pulled up a chair and sat opposite him.

"Thought I heard the car."

"Do you want me to help you?"

"That'd be very kind . . . those spoons there need a good rub up with the shammy. Don't know how they get so marked and stained. But, there, I do know. It's this damp sea air. One thing silver really hates it's damp sea air." I began to rub at the thin worn bowl of the spoon. Pettifer looked at me over the top of his glasses. "Funny to have you sitting there after all these years. Your mother used to spend half her life in the kitchen . . . When Roger went off to boarding school there wasn't anyone else for her to talk to. So she used to come and spend her time with Mrs Pettifer and me. Taught her to make Fairy Cakes, Mrs Pettifer did, and how to play two-handed whist. We had great times. And on a day like this, she used to make toast at the old range . . . mind, that's gone now, we've got a new one and good thing too . . . but that old range was cosy, with the fire burning behind the bars, and all the brass knobs polished up lovely."

"How long have you been at Boscarva, Pettifer?"

"Ever since the Commander bought it, back in 1922. That was the year he left the Navy, decided to be a painter. Old Mrs Bayliss didn't like that. For three months or more she wouldn't even talk to him."

"Why did she mind so much?"

"She'd been with the Navy all her life. Her father was the Captain of the *Imperious* when the Commander was First Lieutenant. That was how they met. They were married in Malta. A lovely wedding with an arch of swords and all. Being with the Navy meant a lot to Mrs Bayliss. When the Commander said he was going to leave they parted brass rags good and proper, but she couldn't make him change his mind. So we left Malta, for good and all, and the Commander found this house, and then we all moved down here."

"And you've been here ever since?"

"More or less. The Commander enrolled at the Slade, and that meant working in London, so he had this little *pied-à-terre*, just off St James's it was, and when he went up to London I went too, to keep an eye on him, and Mrs Pettifer stayed here with Mrs Bayliss and Roger. Your mother wasn't born then."

"But, when he'd finished at the Slade . . . ?"

"Well, then he came back for good. And built the studio. That was when he was painting at his best. Lovely stuff he did then, great seascapes, so cold and bright you could smell the wind, feel the salt on your lips."

"Are there many of his pictures in this house?"

"No, not many. There's the fishing boat over the dining-room fireplace, and one or two little black and white drawings along the upstairs passage. He's got three or four in his study, and then there's a couple in the room where Mrs Roger sleeps."

"And the one in the drawing room . . ."

"Oh, yes, that one of course. 'Lady Holding a Rose.' "

"Who was she?"

He did not reply; was, perhaps, preoccupied with his silver, rubbing away at a fork as though determined to flatten the pattern.

"Who was she? The girl in the picture?"

"Oh," said Pettifer. "That was Sophia."

Sophia. Ever since my mother had fleetingly mentioned her I had wanted to know about Sophia, and now here was Pettifer bringing up her name as though it were the most natural thing in the world.

"She was a girl who used to model for the Commander. I think she first worked for him in London when he was a student, and then she used to come down here sometimes during the summer months, take lodgings in Porthkerris and work for any artist who was ready and able to pay her."

"Was she very beautiful?"

"Not my idea of a beauty. But lively, and what a talker! She was Irish, she'd come from County Cork."

"What did my grandmother think of Sophia?"

"Their paths never crossed, any more than your grandmother would have had social dealings with the butcher or the girl who did her hair."

"So Sophia never came to Boscarva?"

"Oh, yes, she used to come and go. She'd be down at the studio with the Commander, and then he'd get tired, or lose his patience with her, and call it a day, and she'd come up the garden and through the back door calling out, 'Any chance of a cup of tea?' and because it was Sophia, Mrs Pettifer always had the kettle on."

"She used to tell fortunes from teacups."

"Who told you that?"

"My mother."

"That's right, she did. And wonderful things she told us were going to happen to us all. 'Course, they didn't, but it was fun listening to her, just the same. She and your mother were great friends. Sophia used to take her down to the beach and Mrs Pettifer would pack a picnic. And if it was stormy weather they'd go long walks up on the moor."

"But what was my grandmother doing all this time?"

"Oh, playing bridge or mah-jongg most afternoons. She had a very select circle of friends. She was a nice enough lady, but not really interested in children. Perhaps if she'd been more interested in Lisa when she was a child, they'd have had more in common when Lisa grew up, and maybe your mother wouldn't have run off like that, breaking all our hearts."

"What happened to Sophia?"

"Oh, she went back to London, she got married and she had a baby, I think. Then, in 1942, she was killed in the Blitz. The baby was down in the country and her husband was overseas, but Sophia stayed in London because she was working in a hospital there. We didn't hear about it for a long time, till long after it happened. Mrs Pettifer and I felt as though a light had gone out of our lives."

"And my grandfather?"

"He was sorry, of course. But he hadn't seen her for years. She was just a girl who'd once worked for him."

"Are there any more pictures of her?"

"There's pictures of Sophia in provincial art galleries up and down the country. There's one in the gallery in Porthkerris if you want to go and look at that. And there's a couple upstairs in Mrs Roger's bedroom."

"Could we go and look at them now?" I sounded eager and Pettifer looked surprised, as though I were suggesting something faintly indecent. "I mean Mrs Bayliss wouldn't mind, would she?"

"Oh, she wouldn't mind. I don't see why not . . . come on."

He got laboriously to his feet, and I followed him upstairs and along the first-floor passage to the bedroom over the drawing room, which was large and furnished in a very feminine fashion with old-fashioned Victorian furniture and a faded pink and cream carpet. Mollie had left it painfully neat. The two little oil paintings hung side by side between the windows, one of a chestnut tree with a girl lying in its shade, the other of the same girl hanging out a line of washing on a breezy day. They were scarcely more than sketches, and I was disappointed.

"I still don't know what Sophia looks like."

Pettifer was about to reply when, from the depths of the house, came the ringing of a bell. He cocked his head, like a dog listening. "That's the Commander, he's heard us talking through the wall. Excuse me a moment."

I followed him out of Mollie's room and closed the door behind me. He went on down the passage a little way and opened a door, and I heard Grenville's voice.

"What are you two muttering about in there?"

"I was just showing Rebecca the two pictures in Mrs Roger's room . . ."

"Is Rebecca there? Tell her to come in . . ."

I went in, past Pettifer. Grenville was not in bed, but sitting in a deep arm-chair with his feet propped up on a stool. He was dressed, but there was a rug over his knees and the room was cheered by the flicker of a fire. Everything was very neat and shipshape and smelt of the Bay Rum he put on his hair.

I said, "I thought you were in bed."

"Pettifer got me up after lunch. I get bored stiff lying in bed all day. What have you been talking about?"

"Pettifer was showing me some of your pictures."

"I expect you think they're very old-fashioned. They're going back to realism now, you know, these young artists. I knew it would come. You'll have to have one of my pictures. There are racks of them in the studio that have never been sorted out. I closed the place up ten years ago, and I haven't been there since. Pettifer, where's the key?"

"Put safely away, sir."

"You'll have to get the key off Pettifer, go down and nose around, see if there's anything you'd like. Got anywhere to hang it?"

"I've got a flat in London. It needs a picture."

"I thought of something else sitting here. That jade in the cabinet downstairs. I brought it back from China years ago, gave it to Lisa. Now, it belongs to you. And a mirror that her grandmother left her—where's that, Pettifer?"

"That's in the morning room, sir."

"Well, we'll have to get it down, give it a clean. You'd like that, wouldn't you?"

"Yes, I would." I felt greatly relieved. I had been wondering how to bring up the subject of my mother's possessions, and now, without any prompting, Grenville had done it for me. I hesitated and then, striking while the iron was hot, mentioned the third thing. ". . . and there was a davenport desk."

"Hm?" He fixed me with his ferocious stare. "How do you know?"

230

"My mother told me about the jade and the mirror, and she said there was a davenport desk." He continued to glare at me. I wished all at once that I had said nothing. "I mean, it doesn't matter, it's just that if nobody did want it . . . if it wasn't being used . . ."

"Pettifer, do you remember that desk?"

"Yes, I do, sir, now you come to mention it. It was up in the other attic bedroom, but I can't remember having seen it lately."

"Well, look for it some time, there's a good fellow. And put another bit of wood on the fire . . ." Pettifer did so. Grenville, watching him, said suddenly, "Where is everybody? The house is quiet. Only the sound of the rain."

"Mrs Roger's out to a bridge party. I think Miss Andrea's in her room . . ."

"How about a cup of tea?" Grenville cocked an eye at me. "You'd like a cup of tea, wouldn't you? We haven't had the chance of getting to know each other. Either you're keeling over in the middle of dinner, or I'm too old and infirm to get out of bed. We make a fine pair, don't we?"

"I'd like to have tea with you."

"Pettifer will bring up a tray."

"No," I said. "I will. Pettifer's legs have been up and down these stairs all day. Let's give him a rest."

Grenville looked amused. "All right. You bring it up, and let's have a good big plateful of hot buttered toast."

I was to wish, many times over, that I had never brought up the subject of the davenport desk. Because it could not be found. While Grenville and I ate our tea, Pettifer began to look for it. By the time he came to take the tray away, he had combed the house from top to bottom, and the desk was nowhere.

Grenville scarcely believed him. "You've just missed it. Your eyes are getting as old as mine."

"I could scarcely miss seeing a desk." Pettifer sounded aggrieved.

"Perhaps," I said, trying to be helpful, "it was sent away to be mended or something . . ." They both looked at me as though I were a fool, and I hastily shut up.

"Would it be in the studio?" Pettifer ventured.

"What would I do with a desk in the studio? I painted there, I didn't write letters. Didn't want a desk cluttering the place up . . ." Grenville was getting quite agitated. I stood up, "Oh, it'll turn up," I said in my best, soothing voice, and picked up the tea tray to carry it downstairs. In the kitchen I was joined by Pettifer, upset by what had happened.

"It's not good for the Commander to get worked up about anything . . . and he's going to go after this like a terrier after a rat. I can tell."

"It's all my fault. I don't know why I even mentioned it."

"But I remember it. I just can't remember having seen it lately." I began to wash the cups and saucers and Pettifer picked up a tea towel in order to dry them. "And there's another thing. There was a Chippendale chair that used to go with it . . . mind, they didn't match, but the chair always sat in front of that desk. It had a tapestry seat, rather worn, birds and flowers and things. Well, that's gone, too . . . but I'm not going to tell the Commander that and neither are you."

I promised that I wouldn't. "Anyway," I said, "it doesn't matter to me one way or the other."

"No, but it matters to the Commander. Artistic he may have been, but he had a memory like an elephant and that's one thing he hasn't lost." He added gloomily, "I sometimes wish he had."

That evening when I went downstairs, changed once more into the brown and silver caftan, I found Eliot in the drawing room, alone except for that inevitable companion, his dog. Eliot sat by the fire with a drink and the evening paper, and Rufus was stretched, like some glorious fur, on the hearthrug. They looked companionable, caught in the light of the lamp, but my appearance disturbed the peaceful scene, and Eliot stood up, dropping the paper behind him on the seat of the chair.

"Rebecca. How are you?"

"I'm all right."

"I was afraid last night that you were going to be ill."

"No. I was just tired. I slept till ten o'clock."

"My mother told me. Would you like a drink?"

I said that I would and he poured me some sherry and I went to crouch by the fire and fondle the dog's silky ears.

As Eliot brought me my drink I asked, "Does he go everywhere with you?"

"Yes, everywhere. To the garage, to the office, out to lunch, into the pubs, anywhere I happen to be going. He's a very well-known dog in this part of the world."

I sat on the hearthrug, and Eliot subsided once more into his chair and picked up his drink. He said, "Tomorrow I have to go over to Falmouth, see a man about a car. I wondered if you'd like to come with me, see a bit of the country. Does that appeal to you?"

I was surprised by my own pleasure at this invitation. "I'd love it."

"It won't be very exciting. But perhaps you can amuse yourself for an hour or two while I'm doing business, and then we'll stop at a little pub I know on the way home. They serve delicious sea food. Do you like oysters?"

"Yes."

"Good. So do I. And then we'll come home by High Cross, and you can see where we normally live, my mother and I."

"Your mother told me about it. It sounds charming."

"Better than this mausoleum . . ."

"Oh, Eliot, it's not a mausoleum . . ."

"I was never much of a one for Victorian relics . . ."

Before I could protest further, we were joined by Grenville. At least, we heard him coming, step by step downstairs; heard him talking to Pettifer, the high-pitched voice and the low growl; heard them coming down the hall, the tap of Grenville's stick on the polished wood.

Eliot made a small face at me and went to open the door, and Grenville moved in, like the prow of some great, indestructible ship . . .

"That's all right, Pettifer, I can manage now." I had got up from the hearthrug, wanting to help push forward the chair which he had used the night before, but this seemed to madden him. He was obviously not in a good mood.

"For God's sake, girl, stop fussing around. Do you think I want to sit *in* the fire, I'll burn to death sitting there . . ."

I edged the chair back to its original position and finally Grenville reached it and sank into it.

"How about a drink?" Eliot asked him.

"I'll have a whisky . . ."

Eliot looked surprised . . . "Whisky?"

"Yes, a whisky. I know what that fool of a doctor said but tonight I'm having a whisky."

Eliot said nothing, just nodded his head in patient acquiescence and went to pour the drink. As he did so Grenville leaned round the edge of the chair and said, "Eliot, have you seen that davenport desk around the place?" and my heart sank into my shoes.

"Oh, Grenville, don't start that again . . ."

"What do you mean, start that again? We've got to find the damned thing. I told Pettifer just now, got to go on looking till we've found it."

233

Eliot came back with the glass of whisky. He drew up a table and set the glass within Grenville's reach.

"What davenport desk?" he asked patiently.

"Little davenport desk, used to be in one of the bedrooms. Belonged to Lisa, and now it belongs to Rebecca. She wants it. She's got a flat in London, wants to put it there. And Pettifer can't find it, says he's been through the house with a toothcomb, can't find it. You haven't seen it, have you?"

"I've never set eyes on it. I don't even know what a davenport desk is."

"It's a little desk. Got drawers down the side. Bit of tooled leather on the top. They're rare now, I believe. Worth a lot of money."

"Pettifer's probably put it somewhere and forgotten."

"Pettifer doesn't forget things."

"Well, perhaps Mrs Pettifer did something with it and forgot to tell him."

"I've already *said*; he doesn't forget things."

We were joined at this moment by Mollie, who appeared, smiling determinedly, as though she had heard the angry voice raised beyond the closed door, and was about to spread oil on troubled waters.

"Hallo, everybody, I'm afraid I'm a little late. I had to go and do some very exciting things to that delicious piece of halibut Rebecca bought for me this morning. Eliot, dear . . ." she kissed him, apparently seeing him for the first time that evening. "And Grenville—" she stooped to kiss him too—"you're looking more rested." Then, before he could contradict her, she smiled across the top of his head at me. "Did you have a good afternoon?"

"Yes, thank you. How was the bridge?"

"Not too bad. I won twenty pence. Eliot darling, I'd love a drink. Andrea's just coming. She won't be a moment . . ." But she finally ran out of defensive small talk, and Grenville instantly opened fire. "We've lost something," he told her.

"What have you lost? Your cuff-links again?"

"We have lost a davenport desk."

It was becoming ludicrous.

"You've *lost* a davenport desk?"

For her benefit, Grenville went through the whole rigmarole. On being told that it was I who had precipitated this crisis, Mollie looked at me with some reproach, as though she thought this a poor way to return her hospitality and kindness. I was inclined to agree with her.

"But it must be somewhere." She took her glass from Eliot, drew

234

up a stool and sat, all ready to work the whole thing out. "It must have been put somewhere for safety."

"Pettifer has looked for it."

"Perhaps he hasn't seen it. I'm sure he should get his glasses changed. Perhaps it's been put somewhere and he's forgotten."

Grenville thumped the arm of his chair with a balled fist. "Pettifer does not forget things."

"In fact—" said Eliot coolly—"he forgets things all the time."

Grenville glared at him. "And what does that mean?"

"Nothing personal. Just that he's getting older."

"I suppose you're blaming Pettifer . . ."

"I'm not blaming anybody . . ."

"You just said he's too old to know what he's doing. If he's too old what the hell do you think I am?"

"I never said that . . ."

"You blamed *him* . . ."

Eliot lost his patience. "If I was going to blame anybody," he said, raising his voice almost to the pitch of Grenville's, "I'd ask a few questions of young Joss Gardner." There was a pause after he'd come out with this. And then, in a more controlled, reasonable voice, he went on. "All right, so nobody wants to accuse another man of stealing. But Joss is in and out of this house all the time, in and out of all the rooms. He knows what's in this place better than anybody. And he's an expert, he knows what it's worth."

"But why should Joss take a desk?" asked Mollie.

"A valuable desk. Don't forget that. It's rare and it's valuable, Grenville just said so. Perhaps he needed the money. To look at him he could do with a bit of extra cash. And he's an expert. He's up and down to London all the time. He'd know where to sell it."

He stopped, abruptly, as though realizing that already he had said too much. He finished his whisky, and went, without speaking, to pour himself a second glass.

The silence became uncomfortable. To break it, Mollie said, briefly, "I don't think that Joss . . ."

"Just a lot of poppycock," Grenville interrupted her savagely.

Eliot set down the whisky bottle with a thump. "How do you know? How do you know anything about Joss Gardner? He turns up, like a hippy, out of nowhere, says he's going to open a shop, and the next thing you've opened up the house to him and given him the job of patching up all the furniture. What do you know about Joss? What do any of us know about him?"

"I know that I can trust him. I was trained to judge a man's character . . ."

"You could be wrong . . ."

Grenville raised his voice and rode over Eliot's, ". . . and it would be no bad thing if you were to take a few lessons in choosing your companions."

Eliot's eyes narrowed. "What does that mean?"

"It means that if you want to be made a fool of, try doing business with that little shyster Ernest Padlow."

If I could have escaped at that moment, I would. But I was caught, jammed into the corner behind Grenville's chair.

"What do you know about Ernest Padlow?"

"I know you've been seen around with him . . . drinking in bars . . ."

Eliot shot a glance at me, and then said, under his breath, "That bastard Joss Gardner."

"It wasn't Joss who told me, it was Hargreaves, at the bank. He came up for a glass of sherry the other day. And Mrs Thomas came in to do my fire this morning, she'd seen you with Padlow, up at that gimcrack nightmare he calls a housing estate."

"Back-stairs gossip."

"You hear the truth from truthful people. It doesn't matter in which direction they live. And if you think I'm selling up my land to that jumped-up little beachsweeper, you're wrong . . ."

"It won't always be your land."

"And if you're so sure it will be yours, all I can say is, don't count your chickens before they're hatched. Because you, dear boy, are not my only grandchild."

And at this dramatic moment, like a nicely stage-managed play, the door opened and Andrea appeared to tell us that Pettifer had told her to tell us that dinner was ready.

8

It was hard to sleep that night. I tossed and turned, fetched a glass of water, paced the floor, looked out of the window, climbed back into bed and tried once more to compose myself, but always, when I closed my eyes, the evening came back to me like a film played over and over, voices drummed in my ears, and would not be stilled.

All right, so nobody wants to accuse another man of stealing. What do any of us know about Joss?

If you want to be made a fool of, try doing business with that little shyster Ernest Padlow. And if you think I'm selling my land to that jumped-up little beachsweeper, you're wrong . . .

It won't always be your land . . .

. . . you, dear boy, are not my only grandchild.

Dinner had been a gruesome meal. Eliot and Grenville had scarcely spoken a word from beginning to end. Mollie, to make up for their silence, had kept up a patter of meaningless conversation to which I had tried to respond. And Andrea had watched us all, a gleam of triumph in her round, seeking eyes, while Pettifer trod heavily to and fro, removing dishes, handing round a lemon soufflé rich with whipped cream, which nobody seemed to want.

When at last it was over, they had all dispersed. Grenville to his bedroom, Andrea to the morning room from whence we presently heard the blare of the television set. Eliot, with no explanations, put on a coat, whistled up his dog and banged out of the front door. I guessed he had gone to get drunk and didn't entirely blame him. Mollie and I ended up in the drawing room, one on either side of the fire. She had some tapestry and seemed quite prepared to sit and sew in silence, but this would have been unbearable. I said, plunging straight in with the apology which I felt I owed her, "I am sorry about this evening. I wish I'd never mentioned that desk."

She did not look at me. "Oh, it can't be helped."

"It was just that my mother had mentioned it to me, and when

237

Grenville spoke about the jade and the mirror, well, it never occurred to me that I'd start such a storm in a tea-cup."

"Grenville's a strange old man. He's always been stubborn about people, he'll never see that there can be two sides to every situation."

"You mean about Joss . . ."

"I don't know why he's so taken with Joss. It's frightening. It's as though Joss were able to exert some hold over him. Eliot and I never wanted him in and out of the house this way. If Grenville's furniture needed to be repaired, surely he could have come and fetched it in his van and taken it down to his workshop, like any other tradesman would do. We tried to talk Grenville out of it, but he was adamant, and, after all, this is his house. It isn't ours."

"But it will be Eliot's one day."

She sent me a cold look.

"After this evening, one wonders."

"Oh, Mollie, I don't want Boscarva, Grenville would never leave a place like this to me. He just said that to win a point; perhaps it was the first thing that came into his head. He didn't mean it."

"He hurt Eliot."

"Eliot will understand. You have to make allowances for old people."

"I'm tired of making allowances for Grenville," said Mollie, viciously snapping at a strand of wool with her silver scissors. "My life has been disrupted by Grenville. He and Pettifer could have come and lived at High Cross; that's what we wanted. The house is smaller and more convenient and it would have been better for everybody. And Boscarva should have been made over to Eliot years ago. As it is, death duties are going to be exorbitant. Eliot is never going to be able to afford to keep it going. The whole situation is *so* unrealistic."

"I suppose it's hard to be realistic when you're eighty and you've lived in a place most of your life."

She ignored this. "And all that land, and the farm. Eliot is simply trying to make the best of it all, but Grenville won't see that. He's never shown any interest, never encouraged Eliot in any way. Even the garage at High Cross, Eliot got that going entirely on his own. At the beginning, he asked his grandfather to help, but Grenville said he wasn't going to have anything to do with second-hand cars, and there was a row, and finally Eliot borrowed the money from someone else, and he's never asked his grandfather for a shilling since that day. You'd think he'd deserve some credit for that."

She was pale with anger on Eliot's account—a little tigress, I thought, fighting for her cub, and I remembered my mother's low opinion of the way in which she had possessed and molly-coddled the young Eliot. Perhaps neither of them had ever grown out of the habit.

To change the subject I told her about Eliot's invitation for the next day. "He said he'd take me into High Cross on the way home."

But Mollie was only momentarily diverted. "You must go in and see the house, Eliot's got the key. I go up most weeks to make sure everything's all right, but really I get so depressed having to leave my darling little house and come back to this gloomy place . . ." and then she laughed at herself wryly. "It's getting me down, isn't it? I must try to pull myself together. But really I'll be glad when it's all over."

When it's all over. That meant when Grenville finally died. I didn't want to think about him dying any more than I wanted to think about Joss coupled with the unsavoury Andrea; any more than I wanted to think about Joss helping himself to a davenport desk and a Chippendale chair, heaving them into the back of his little truck, and selling them to the first dealer who made him a good offer.

What do you know about Joss? What do any of us know about him?

For my part I wished I knew nothing. I turned in bed, thumped at the pillows, and waited, without much hope, for sleep.

It rained in the night, but the next morning it was still and clear, the sky a pale, washed blue, everything wet and shining, translucent in the cool spring light. I leaned out of the window and smelt the dampness, mossy and sweet. The sea was flat and blue as a sheet of silk, gulls drifted lazily over the rim of the cliff, a boat moved out from the harbour, heading for distant fishing-grounds, and so still was the air that I could hear the distant chug of its engine.

My spirits rose. Yesterday was over, today would be better. I was glad to be getting out of the house, away from Mollie's reproach and Andrea's unsettling presence. I bathed and dressed and went downstairs and found Eliot in the dining room, eating bacon and eggs, and looking—I was thankful to see—cheerful.

He looked up from the morning paper. "I wondered," he said, "if I was going to have to come and wake you up. I thought perhaps you'd forgotten."

"No, I didn't forget."

"We're the first down. With any luck we'll be out of the house before anyone else appears." He grinned, ruefully, like a repentant

239

boy. "The last thing I want on a beautiful morning like this is recrim-
inations."

"It was all my fault, mentioning that stupid desk. I said I was sorry
last night to your mother."

"It'll all blow over," said Eliot. "These little differences of opinion
always do." I poured myself a cup of coffee. "I'm just sorry that you
were involved."

We left straight after breakfast, and there was a marvellous feeling
of relief to be in his car, with Rufus perched on the back seat, and to
be escaping. The car roared up the hill away from Boscarva; the wet
road was blue with reflected sky, and the air smelt of primroses. As
we climbed up and over the moor, the view spread and dipped before
us—there were hills topped by ancient cairns and standing stones,
and tiny forgotten villages, tucked into the folds of unexpected valleys where little rivers ran, and ancient clumps of oak and elm stood
clustered by narrow, hump-backed bridges.

But I knew that we could not enjoy our day together, that we could
not be entirely at ease, until I had made my peace with him.

I said, "I know that it'll blow over, and that perhaps it *wasn't* important, but we have to talk about last night."

He smiled at me, glancing sideways. "What do we have to say?"

"Just that, what Grenville said about having another grandchild.
He didn't mean it. I know he didn't mean it."

"No, perhaps he didn't. Perhaps he was just trying to set us against
each other, like a pair of dogs."

"He'd never leave me Boscarva. Never in a thousand years. He
doesn't even know me, I've only just come into his life."

"Rebecca, don't give it another thought. I'm not going to."

"And, after all, if it is going to be yours one day, I don't see why
you shouldn't start thinking about what you're going to do with it."

"You mean Ernest Padlow? What a lot of gossips those old people
are, carrying tales and making mischief. If it isn't the bank manager
it's Mrs Thomas, and if it isn't Mrs Thomas it's Pettifer."

I made myself sound casual. "Would you sell the land?"

"If I did, I could probably afford to live at Boscarva. It's time I set
up on my own."

"But—" I chose my words tactfully—"but wouldn't it be rather
. . . spoiled . . . I mean, living there with rows of Mr Padlow's little houses all round you?"

Eliot laughed. "You've got entirely the wrong end of the stick. This
wouldn't be a building estate like the one at the top of the hill. This

would be high-class stuff, two acre lots, very high specifications as to the style and the price of the houses built on them. No cutting down of trees, no despoiling of the amenities. They'd be expensive houses for expensive people, and there wouldn't be a lot of them. How does that sound to you?"

"Have you told Grenville this?"

"He won't let me. He won't listen. He's not interested and that's it."

"But surely if you explained . . ."

"I've been trying to explain things to him all my life and I've never got anywhere. And now, is there anything else you want to discuss?"

I considered. I certainly didn't want to discuss Joss. I said, "No."

"In that case shall we forget about last night and enjoy ourselves?"

It seemed a good idea. We smiled at each other. "All right," I said at last. We crossed a bridge and came to a steep hill, and Eliot changed down, expertly, with the old-fashioned gear stick. The car poured up the savage slope, its long, elegant bonnet seeming to point straight to the sky.

We got to Falmouth about ten o'clock. While Eliot attended to his business I was turned loose to explore the little town. Facing south, sheltered from the north wind, with gardens already filled with camellias and scented daphne bushes, it made me think of some Mediterranean port, and this illusion was strengthened by the blue of the sea on that first warm spring day, and the tall masts of the yachts which lay at anchor in the basin.

I felt, for some reason, impelled to shop. I bought freesias for Mollie, tightly in bud with their stalks wrapped in damp moss so that they would not wither before I got home, a box of cigars for Grenville, a bottle of fruity sherry for Pettifer, a record for Andrea. The sleeve portrayed a transvestite group with sequined eyelids. It seemed to me to be right up her street. And for Eliot . . . I had noticed that his watch strap was wearing thin. I found a narrow strap in dark crocodile, very expensive, exactly right for Eliot. Then I bought a tube of toothpaste for myself, because I needed one. And for Joss . . . ? Nothing for Joss.

Eliot picked me up, as we had arranged, in the lounge of the big hotel in the middle of town. We drove very fast out of the town and through Truro, and down into the little maze of lanes and wooded creeks that lay beyond until we came to a village called St Endon, where there were white cottages, palm trees and gardens full of flowers. The road wound down towards the creek, and at the very bottom was a little pub, right on the water's edge, with the high tide lapping at the wall below the terrace. Kittiwakes perched along the top of it, their eyes bright and friendly, unlike the greedy, wild gulls of Boscarva.

We sat out in the sunshine, drinking sherry, and I gave Eliot his present, then and there; he seemed inordinately delighted, ripping off the old watch strap right away and fitting on the new, shining leather one, adjusting the little clips with the blade of his penknife.

"What made you think of giving me that?"

"I noticed your old one was worn. I thought perhaps that you might lose your watch."

He leaned back in his chair, watching me across the table. It was so warm that I had pulled off my sweater and rolled up the sleeves of my cotton shirt. He said, "Did you buy presents for everybody?"

I was embarrassed. "Yes."

"I thought you had a lot of parcels. Do you always buy presents for people?"

"It's nice to have people to buy presents for."

"Isn't there anyone in London?"

"Not really."

"No one special?"

"There's never been anyone special."

"I can't believe it."

"It's true." I could not think why I was confiding in him this way. Perhaps it had something to do with the warmth of the day, surprising me by its beneficence, lowering all my guards. Perhaps it was the sherry. Perhaps it was simply the intimacy of two people who had weathered such a storm as the row that had taken place last night. Whatever the reason, it was easy that day to talk to Eliot.

"Why is that?" he asked.

"I don't know. It may have something to do with the way I was brought up . . . my mother lived with one man after another, so I lived with them too. And there's nothing like living at close quarters with people to destroy that marvellous illusion of romance."

We laughed. "That could be a good thing," said Eliot. "But it could be a bad thing, too. You mustn't close up altogether. Otherwise nobody's ever going to get near you."

"I'm all right."

"Are you going back to London?"

"Yes."

"Soon?"

"Probably."

"Why not stay for a bit?"

"I don't want to wear out my welcome."

"You won't do that. And I've hardly spoken to you. Anyway, how can you go back to London and leave all this behind you . . . ?" His gesture included the sky, the sun, the quiet, the lap of water, the promise of the coming spring.

"I can, because I have to. I've a job to get back to and a flat that needs painting, and a life to pick up and start all over again."

"Can't that wait?"

"Not indefinitely."

"There's no reason to go." I did not reply. "Unless," he went on, "you were put off by what happened last night." I smiled and shook my head, because we had promised not to mention that again. He leaned on the table, his chin on his fist. "If you really wanted a job you could get one here. If you wanted a flat of your own you could rent that too."

"Why should I stay?" But I was flattered at being so persuaded.

"Because it would be good for Grenville, and for Mollie, and for me. Because I think we all want you to stay. Particularly me."

"Oh, Eliot . . ."

"It's true. There's something very serene about you. Did you know that? I noticed it that first evening I saw you before I even knew who you were. And I like the shape of your nose, and the sound of your laugh, and the way you can look marvellously ragamuffin one minute, in jeans and with your hair coming all unravelled, and then, the next minute, like a princess in a fairy story, with your plait over your shoulder and that stately gown you wear in the evenings. I feel as though I'm finding out new things about you every day. And this is why I don't want you to go. Not just yet."

I found that I could think of no rejoinder to this long speech. I was touched by it, and embarrassed too. But still, it was gratifying to be liked and admired, and even more gratifying to be told so.

Across the table, he began to laugh at me. "Your face is a picture. You don't know where to look and you're blushing. Come along, finish your drink and we'll go and eat oysters—I promise I'll not pay you any more compliments!"

We lingered over lunch in the small, low-ceilinged dining room, eating at a table which wobbled so much on the uneven floor that Eliot was forced to prop up one of the legs with a scrap of folded paper. We ate oysters and steak and a fresh green salad and drank our

243

way through a bottle of wine. We took our coffee back into the sun-shine, and sat on the edge of the terrace wall, watching two boys, sunburned and barelegged, rig up a dinghy and take her sailing out on to the blue waters of the creek. We saw the striped sail fill with some mysterious, unfelt breeze, as the dinghy heeled and went away from us, around the tip of a wooded promontory. And Eliot said that if I stayed in Cornwall, he would borrow a boat and teach me to sail; we would go mackerel fishing from Porthkerris—in the summer he would show me all the tiny coves and secret places which the tourists never found.

At last it was time to go, and the afternoon wound itself in like a long, shining ribbon. Sleepy and replete he drove me slowly back to High Cross, taking the long road that led through forgotten villages and the heart of the country.

When we got to High Cross, I realized that it stood at the very summit of the peninsula, so that the village had two aspects, one north to the Atlantic, the other south to the Channel; it was like being on an island, swept with clean winds and ringed by the sea. Eliot's garage stood in the middle of the village street, a little back from the road, with a cobbled forecourt set about with tubs of flowers, and inside the glass-fronted showroom stood the gleaming, racy cars. Everything was very new and expensive looking and immaculately kept. I wondered, as we crossed the forecourt towards the showrooms, how much Eliot had had to sink into such a venture, and why he had decided that it was a viable proposition to open such a specialized garage in this out-of-the-way spot.

He pulled one of the sliding glass doors aside and I went in, my feet making no sound on the highly polished rubber floors.

"Why did you decide to start your garage here, Eliot? Wouldn't it have been better in Fourbourne or Falmouth or Penzance?"

"Psychological selling, my dear. Get a good name for yourself and people will come from the ends of the earth to buy what you've got to sell." And he added with disarming candour, "Besides, I already owned the land, or at least my mother did, which was an excellent incentive to build the garage here."

"Are all these cars for sale?"

"Yes. As you can see we concentrate on continental and sports cars. We had a Ferrari in last week, but that was sold a couple of days ago. It had been crashed, but I've got this young mechanic working for me, and by the time he'd finished with it it was as good as new . . ."

I laid my hand on the gleaming yellow bonnet. "What's this?"

244

"A Lancia Zagato. And this is an Alfa Romeo Spyder, only two years old. Beautiful car."

"And a Jensen Interceptor . . ." That was one that I recognized.

"Come and see the workshop." I followed him through another sliding door at the back of the showroom and decided that this was more like my idea of a garage. Here was the usual clutter of dismantled engines, oil cans, long flexes trailing from the ceiling, naked bulbs, tool benches, old tyres and trolleys.

In the middle of all this a figure was stooped over the stripped-down engine of a skeletal car. He wore a welding mask which made him appear monstrous, and worked with the roaring blue flame of a welding gun. The noise of the gun was overlaid by non-stop blaring music from a surprisingly small transistor radio perched on a beam above him.

Whether or not he saw us coming was anybody's guess, but it was only when Eliot switched off the radio that he shut off his gun and straightened up, pushing the welding mask up and back off his face. I saw a thin, dark young man, oil-stained and in need of a shave, his hair long, his eyes sharp and bright.

"Hallo, Morris," said Eliot.

"Hallo."

"This is Rebecca Bayliss, she's staying at Boscarva."

Reaching for a cigarette, Morris looked my way and gave me a nod. I said, "Hallo," just to be friendly, but got no more response. He lit his cigarette, then slipped the fancy lighter back into the pocket of his oily overalls.

"Thought you'd be coming in this morning," he told Eliot.

"I told you I was going over to Falmouth."

"Any luck?"

"A 1933 Bentley."

"What sort of condition?"

"Looked OK. A bit of rust."

"Get the old paint spray out. There was a chap in the other day, wanting one of them."

"I know, that's why I bought it. Thought we'd take the transporter over, tomorrow or the next day, pick her up."

They fell silent. Morris went to his transistor and turned it on again, if anything louder than before. I looked down at the confusion of engineering on which he had been working and finally asked Eliot what sort of a car it had originally been.

"A 1971 Jaguar XJ6 4.2 litre, if you really want to know. And it will be again when Morris has finished with it. This is another that was in a crash."

Morris came back to stand between us.

"What exactly are you doing to it?" I asked him.

"Straightening out the chassis, fixing the wheel alignment."

"What about the brake shoes?" said Eliot.

"It could have done with new brake shoes, but I fixed the old ones to cover us for the guarantee . . . and Mr Kemback rang up from Birmingham . . ."

They began to talk shop. I drifted away, deafened by the sound of rock, went back through the showroom and out into the forecourt where Rufus waited, with dignity and patience, behind the driving wheel of Eliot's car. Together we sat there until we were rejoined by Eliot. "Sorry about that, Rebecca; I wanted to check on another job. Morris is a good mechanic, but he gets shirty if he's expected to answer the telephone as well."

"Who's Mr Kemback? Another customer?"

"No, not exactly. He was down here last summer on holiday. He runs a motel, a garage, just off the M6. He's got quite a selection of old cars. Wants to start a museum, you know, a sort of sideline to the bacon-and-egg trade. He seems to want me to run it for him."

"You mean go and live in Birmingham?"

"Doesn't sound very tempting, does it? Anyway, that's it. Let's go and look at my mother's house."

We walked there, just a little way down the street, then up a short lane and through a double white gate, and the path sloped up to a long, low white house, which had been converted from two ancient thick-walled stone cottages. Eliot took a key out of his pocket and opened the door and inside it was cold, but not musty or damp. It was furnished like an expensive London flat, with pale, thick, fitted carpets and pale walls and sofas upholstered in mushroom-coloured brocade. There were a great many mirrors and little crystal bag chandeliers hanging from the low-beamed ceilings.

It was all charming, and just what I had imagined, and somehow wrong. A kitchen like an advertisement, a dining room furnished with gleaming mahogany, upstairs there were four bedrooms and three bathrooms, a sewing room and a linen cupboard of mammoth proportions, richly smelling of soap.

At the back of the house was a little patio, and then a long garden sloped up to a distant hedge. I looked at the patio and could see Mollie out there, entertaining her friends, with cane furniture set out on the flagstones, and martinis to drink, served from an expensive glass trolley.

I said, "It's a perfect house," and meant it. But I did not love it as I loved Boscarva. Perhaps because it was too perfect.

We stood in the elegant out-of-place drawing room and eyed each other. Our day together seemed to have come to an end. Perhaps Eliot felt this too and wanted to postpone it, for he said, "I could put on a kettle and make you a cup of tea, only I know that there's no milk in the fridge."

"I think we should go home." I was surprised by an enormous yawn, and Eliot laughed at me. He took my shoulders between his hands. "You're sleepy."

"Too much fresh air," I answered. "Too much wine."

I tipped my head back to look up into his face, and we were very close. I could feel his fingers tighten over my shoulders. He wasn't laughing any more, but his deep-set eyes held an expression as gentle as anything I had ever seen.

I said, "It's been a wonderful day . . ." but that was as far as I got, because he kissed me then, and for some time I was not able to say anything at all. When at last he drew away I was so shaken that all I could do was lean limply against him, wanting to cry, feeling a fool, knowing that the situation was fast slipping out of my control. My cheek was against his coat, and his arms around me held me so close that I could feel, like the throb of a drum, the solid beating of his heart.

Over the top of my head, I heard him say, "You mustn't go back to London. You mustn't ever go away again."

9

THE SHOPPING which I had done in Falmouth proved to be an unexpected blessing. I must have been inspired, for, without thinking, I provided exactly the small talking point we all needed to smooth over the embarrassment of the previous uncomfortable evening. Mollie was charmed with her freesias; she couldn't grow them at Boscarva, she explained, the winds were too cold, the garden too exposed. She paid me the compliment of arranging them with more artistry than one would have thought possible, and finally giving them the place of honour in the middle of the mantelpiece in the drawing room. They filled the room with their rich romantic scent, and the cream and the violet and the deep pink drew one's eye, quite naturally, up to the portrait of Sophia. The flowers seemed to complement the glowing skin tones and the fragile shimmer of the white dress.

"Beautiful," said Mollie, standing back, but I could not be sure whether she was referring to the flowers or the portrait. "It was sweet of you to bring them. And did Eliot take you to see my house? So now you can understand how I feel about having to live in this great place." She regarded me thoughtfully, her eyes narrowed. "You know, I believe the day has done you good. I could even imagine you've caught the sun. You've got quite a good colour. The air must agree with you."

Pettifer accepted his sherry with dignity, but I could tell that he was pleased. And Grenville was wickedly delighted with his cigars, for the doctor had warned him against smoking and Pettifer had hidden his usual supply. I understood that he was parsimonious about doling them out. Grenville took and lit one instantly, puffing away with immense satisfaction and leaning back in his big chair like a man without a care in the world. Even with Andrea I had for once done the right thing. *"The Creepers!* How did you know they're my favourite group? Oh, I wish there was a record player here, but there isn't and I left mine in London. Gosh, aren't they fabulous, groovy . . . ?" And then she came down to earth again, searching for the price tag. "That must have cost you something."

It was as though, with peace offerings, we had all formed an unspoken pact. Last night was never discussed. There was no mention of the davenport desk, of Ernest Padlow, of the possible sale of Boscarva Farm. There was no mention of Joss. After dinner Eliot set up a table, and Mollie got out the rosewood box containing the mah-jongg set, and we played until bed time, Andrea sitting with Mollie in order to learn the rules.

I caught myself thinking that, if a stranger were to come, unexpectedly, upon us, how he would be charmed by the picture we made, caught, like flies in amber, in the pool of light from the standard lamp, absorbed by our timeless occupation. The distinguished painter, mellow in the twilight of his years, surrounded by his family; the pretty daughter-in-law and the handsome grandson—and even

Andrea, for once alert and interested, absorbed by the intricacies of
the game.

I had played as a child with my mother, sometimes making up a
foursome with two of her friends, and found myself comforted by the
remembered touch of the ivory and bamboo tiles, by their beauty, and
the satisfying sound they made, like sea pebbles disturbed by the tide,
as we stirred them around in the middle of the table.

At the start of each round we built the four walls, two tiles high,
and closed them together into a tight square, "to keep the evil spirits
out," we were told by Grenville, who had learned to play as a young
Sub-Lieutenant in Hong Kong and knew all the traditional supersti-
tions of the ancient game. I thought how easy it would be, how safe, if
ghosts and doubts and skeletons-in-the-cupboard could be thus shut
out and kept at bay.

The travel brochures and holiday posters of Porthkerris inevitably
portrayed a place where the sea and the sky were always a bright and
unsullied blue, the houses white with sunshine, the odd palm tree in
the foreground lending that suggestion of Mediterranean glamour.
The imagination was led, naturally, to visions of fresh lobster, eaten
out of doors; artists with beards and paint-stained smocks; and
weather-beaten fishermen, picturesque as pirates, sitting on bollards,
smoking their pipes and discussing last week's catch.

But Porthkerris, in February, in a north-east gale, had no shred of
connection with this nebulous paradise.

The sea, the sky, the very town were grey, the maze of baffling,
narrow streets subjected to onslaughts of bitter wind. The tide was
high; the waves broke against the sea-wall and splashed across the
road, misting the windows of the houses opposite with salt, and filling the gutters with yellow foam, like dirty soapsuds.

It was as though the place were under some sort of a siege. Shop-
pers were wrapped, buttoned, scarved in every sort of protective
clothing, their faces half hidden by hoods or deep coat collars, their
bodies bundled into ambiguity, so that men and women all looked
alike, gumbooted and shapeless.

The sky was the colour of the wind, the air filled with flying flot-
sam, old leaves, twigs, scraps of paper, even tiles torn from roofs. In
the shops, people forgot what they had come to buy, the talk was all
of the weather, the wind, the damage the storm was going to do.

I had come, once more, to shop for Mollie, fighting my way down
the hill in borrowed raincoat and rubber boots, because I felt safer on

my feet than I would have driving Mollie's insubstantial car. Now that I was more familiar with the town I no longer needed Andrea to show me the way . . . anyway Andrea was still in bed when I left Boscarva, and for once I did not blame her. The day was not inviting and it was hard to believe that only yesterday I had been sitting out, in my shirtsleeves, basking in a sun as warm as May.

The last of the shopping completed, I emerged from the baker's as the clock in the tower of the Norman church struck eleven. Normally, under such conditions, I would have headed straight back up the hill to Boscarva, but I had other plans. With my head down, the heavy basket over one arm, I made for the harbour.

The Art Gallery, I knew, was housed in an old Baptist Chapel, somewhere in the maze of streets which lay to the north of the town. I had thought that I would simply go and look for it, but as I braved the harbour road, battling with alternate assaults of wind and spray, I saw the old fisherman's lodge which had been converted to a Tourist Information Bureau and decided that I would save myself both time and effort if I made a few inquiries.

Inside, I found an unenthusiastic girl huddled over a paraffin stove; booted and shivering, she looked like the sole survivor of some Arctic expedition. When I appeared she did not move from her chair but said, "Yes?" and stared at me through a pair of unbecoming spectacles.

I tried to feel sorry for her. "I'm looking for the Art Gallery."

"Which one did you want?"

"I didn't know there was more than one."

Behind me the door opened and shut and we were joined by a third person. The girl looked over my shoulder and a faint interest gleamed behind her pebble glasses.

"There's the Town Gallery and the New Painters," she said, much more lively.

"I don't know which I want."

"Perhaps," said a voice behind me, "I can help."

I swung around and Joss stood there, in rubber boots and a streaming black oilskin, a fisherman's cap jammed down on to his head. His face was wet with rain, his hands jammed into the deep pockets of the coat, his dark eyes glinting with amusement. One half of me could see exactly why the sluggish girl behind the counter had suddenly come to life. The other half was maddened by his extraordinary ability to turn up just when I was least expecting him.

250

I remembered Andrea. I remembered the desk and the chair. I said, coolly, "Hallo, Joss."

"I saw you come in. What are you wanting to do?"

The girl chipped in. "She wants the Art Gallery."

Joss waited for me to enlarge on this and, thus cornered, I did so. "I thought perhaps there might be some pictures of Grenville's there . . ."

"You're quite right, there are three. I'll take you . . ."

"I don't need to be taken, I just want to be told how to get there."

"I'd like to take you . . . here—" he removed my heavy basket from my arm, smiled at the girl and went to open the door. A howl of wind and a blast of spume-laden air poured in from the outside and a pile of leaflets flew and scattered from the counter all over the floor. Before we could do any more damage, I hurried out, and the door swung shut behind us. As though it were the most natural thing in the world, Joss took my arm and we made our way down the middle of the cobbled road, Joss carrying on a cheerful conversation despite the fact that the wind tore the words from his mouth, and that, even with his arm in mine, it was taking all my efforts to progress at all.

"What on earth brings you down to the town on a day like this?"

"You're carrying it. Mollie's shopping."

"Couldn't you have brought the car?"

"I thought I might get blown off the road."

"I love it," he told me. "I love a day like this." He looked as though he loved it too, wind-whipped and wet and bursting with vitality. "Did you have a good day yesterday?"

"What do you know about yesterday?"

"I was up at Boscarva and Andrea told me you'd gone to Falmouth with Eliot. Don't imagine you can keep any secrets in this place. If Andrea hadn't told me, Pettifer would, or Mrs Thomas, or Mrs Kernow, or Miss Bright-Eyes in the Information Bureau. It's part of the fun of living in Porthkerris, everybody knows exactly what everybody else is up to."

"I'm beginning to realize that."

We turned away from the harbour and began to climb a steep cobbled hill. Houses closed in on either side of us, a cat flashed across the street and disappeared through a crack in a window. A woman in a pot hat and a blue apron was scrubbing her steps. She looked up and saw us, and said, " 'Ullo my lover," to Joss; her fingers were like a bunch of pink sausages, made so by the hot water and the cold wind.

At the end of the street, we found ourselves in a little square which

I had not seen before. One side of this was taken up by a large barn-like structure, with arched windows set high along the wall. By the door was a sign, PORTHKERRIS ART GALLERY, and Joss let go of my arm, pushed open the door with his shoulder and stood aside to let me go ahead of him. Inside it was bitterly cold, draughty, totally empty. The white walls were hung with paintings, of all sorts and shapes and sizes, and two great abstract sculptures were marooned in the middle of the floor, like rocks exposed by an ebb tide. There was a table by the door, with neat stacks of catalogues and folders and copies of *The Studio,* but despite this window-dressing the gallery stayed thick with the atmosphere of joyless bygone Sundays.

"Now," Joss put down my basket and took off his cap, shaking it free of rain as a dog shakes its coat, "what do you want to see?"

"I want to see Sophia."

He glanced at me sharply with a sudden turn of his head, but in the same instant smiled and put his hat on his head again, pulling the peak down over his eyes, like a guardsman.

"Who told you about Sophia?"

I smiled sweetly. "Perhaps it was Mrs Thomas. Perhaps it was Mrs Kernow. Perhaps it was Miss Bright-Eyes in the Information Bureau."

"Insolence will get you nowhere."

"There *is* a portrait of Sophia here. Pettifer told me."

"Yes. It's over this way."

I followed him down the length of the floor, our rubber-booted footsteps sounding loud in the emptiness.

"There," he said. I stopped beside him and looked up, and she was there, sitting in a beam of lamplight with some sewing in her hands.

I stared at it for a long time and finally let out a long sigh of disappointment. Joss looked down at me from under the ridiculous peak of his cap.

"What's that sigh for?"

"You still can't see her face. I still don't know what she looks like. Why didn't he ever paint her face?"

"He did. Often."

"Well, I still haven't seen it. It's always the back of her head, or her hands, or else she's so small a part of the picture she doesn't have a face at all, just a blob."

"Does it matter what she looked like?"

"No, it doesn't matter. It's just that I want to know."

"How did you know about Sophia in the first place?"

"My mother told me about her. And then Pettifer, and the picture of her—the one at Boscarva in the drawing room—is so charming and feminine, one feels she must have been beautiful. But Pettifer says that she wasn't beautiful at all. Just very charming and attractive." We looked again at the picture. I saw the hands, and the shine of lamplight on her dark hair. "Pettifer says that art galleries up and down the country have portraits of Sophia hanging on their walls. I shall just have to go on from Manchester to Birmingham, to Nottingham, to Glasgow, until I find one that isn't of the back of her head."

"What will you do then?"

"Nothing. Just know what she looks like."

I turned from my disappointment and began to walk back to the door where my laden basket waited for me, but Joss was there first, stooping to swing it up and out of my reach.

I said, "I must go back."

"It's only—" he consulted his watch—"half past eleven. And you've never seen my shop. Come back with me and let me show it off, and I'll make you a cup of coffee and drive you home. You can't possibly walk up the hill with this great weight on your arm."

"Of course I can."

"I won't let you." He opened the door. "Come along."

I couldn't go without the basket and he obviously wasn't going to give it up, so, resigned and reluctant, I went with him, pushing my hands into my pockets so that he could not take my arm. He seemed in no way put out by my ungraciousness, which in itself was disconcerting, but when we got back to the harbour and were once more in the teeth of the wind, I nearly lost my balance with the unexpectedness of it, and he laughed and pulled my hand out of my pocket, taking it in his own. It was hard not to be disarmed by this protective and forgiving gesture.

As soon as the shop came in view, the tall narrow house shouldering up between the two short fat ones, I saw that indeed changes had taken place. The window frames were now painted, the plate glass had been cleaned, and a sign put up over the door. JOSS GARDNER.

"How does that look?" He was full of pride.

"Impressive," I had to admit.

He took a key out of his pocket and unlocked the door and we went into the shop. Packing cases stood about on the flagged floor, and around the walls, shelving was being erected in varying widths, up to the ceiling. In the centre of the room was another structure, rather like a child's climbing frame, and this had already been set out with modern Danish glass and china, cooking pots in bright colours, and brightly striped Indian rugs. The walls were white, the woodwork had been left in its natural state, and this and the grey floor provided a simple and effective background to the bright wares which he had to sell. At the back of the shop an open staircase rose to the upper floors, and beneath this was another door, ajar, leading down into what appeared to be a dark cellar. "Come upstairs . . ." He led the way.

I followed him. "What's that door there?"

"That's my workshop. It's in a dreadful mess, I'll show you that another time. Now this—" we emerged on to the first floor, and could scarcely move for baskets and wickerwork—"I haven't exactly got this straight but, as you can see, this is where you buy baskets for logs, clothes pegs, shopping, babies, laundry, anything you care to put in them."

None of it was very spacious. The narrow house was just a glorified staircase with a landing on each floor.

"Up again. How are your legs? Now we come to the *pièce de résistance,* the owner's palatial living quarters." I passed a tiny bathroom squeezed into the turn of the stairs. And lagging behind Joss's long legs found myself remembering Andrea's yearning descriptions of his flat, and hoping it would not be the way she had described it to me, but entirely different, so that I would know that her imagination had taken control, and that she had made the whole thing up.

Just like something out of a magazine. With a bed that's a sort of sofa and masses of cushions and things and a log fire.

But it was just the way she had said. As I came up the last stairs, my fleeting hope swiftly died. And there *was* something closed-in and secret about it, with the ceiling sloping down to the floor and a dormer window set into the gable with a seat below it. I saw the little galley, enclosed behind a counter, like a bar, and the old Turkish carpet on the floor, and the divan, red-blanketed, pushed against the wall. As she had said, it was scattered with cushions.

Joss had put down my basket and was already divesting himself of his wet clothes and hanging them on an old-fashioned cane hat-stand.

"Take your things off before you die of cold," he told me. "I'll light a fire . . ."

"I can't stay, Joss . . ."

"No reason not to light the fire. And please, take off that coat."

I did, unbuttoning it with frozen fingers, pulling off my damp woollen hat and shaking my plait down over my shoulder. While I hung these up beside Joss's things, he was busy at the fireplace, snapping twigs, balling paper, scraping together the ashes from some previous fire, lighting it all with a long taper. When it was crackling he took some pieces of driftwood, tar-soaked, from a basket by the fireplace, and stacked them round the flames. They spat, and spluttered, and swiftly caught. And the room, by firelight, sprang to life. He stood up and turned to face me.

"Now, what do you want? Coffee? Tea? Chocolate? Brandy and soda?"

"Coffee?"

"Two coffees coming up." He retired behind his counter, filled a kettle and lit the gas. As he collected a tray and cups, I went over to the window, knelt on the seat and looked down through the fury of the storm to the street below, washed by spray as the waves broke over the sea wall. The boats in the harbour bobbed about like demented corks, and huge herring gulls floated over their swinging mastheads, screaming at the wind. Absorbed in the task of making our coffee, Joss moved with economy from one side of the galley to the other, neat-fingered and self-sufficient as a single-minded yachtsman. So occupied, he appeared harmless enough, but the disconcerting point about Andrea's revelations was that they all seemed to contain an element of truth.

I had known Joss for only a few days, but already I had seen him in every sort of mood. I knew he could be charming, stubborn, angry, and downright rude. It was not difficult to imagine him as a ruthless and passionate lover, but it was distasteful to imagine him with Andrea.

He looked up suddenly and caught my eye. I was embarrassed, caught with my thoughts. I said, quickly, to divert us both, "In good weather you must have a lovely view."

"Clear out to the lighthouse."

"In the summer it must be like being abroad."

"In the summer it's like Piccadilly Underground at rush hour. But that only lasts for two months." He came out from behind his counter, carrying a tray with the steaming cups, the sugar bowl and the milk jug. The coffee smelt delicious. He pulled forward a long stool with his foot, set the tray at one end of it and himself at the other. Thus, we faced each other.

"I want to hear more about yesterday," said Joss. "Where did you go besides Falmouth?"

255

I told him about St Endon and the little pub by the water's edge.

"Yes, I've heard about it, but I've never been there. Did you get a good lunch?"

"Yes. And it was so warm that we sat out in the sunshine."

"That's the south coast for you. And what happened then?"

"Nothing happened then. We came home."

He handed me my cup and saucer. "Did Eliot take you to High Cross?"

"Yes."

"Did you see the garage?"

"Yes. And Mollie's house."

"What did you think of all those elegant, sexy cars?"

"I thought just that. That they were elegant and sexy."

"Did you meet any of the guys who work for him?"

His voice was so casual that I became wary.

"Who, for instance?"

"Morris Tatcombe?"

"Joss, you didn't ask me here for coffee at all, did you? You're pumping me."

"I'm not. I promise I'm not. It's just that I wondered if Morris was working for Eliot."

"What do you know about Morris?"

"Just that he's rotten."

"He's a good mechanic."

"Yes, he is. Everybody knows that, and it's the only good thing about him. But he's also totally dishonest and vicious to boot."

"If he's totally dishonest, why isn't he in jail?"

"He's already been. He's just come out."

This took the wind out of my sails, but I soldiered bravely on, sounding more sure of myself than I felt.

"And how do you know he's vicious . . . ?"

"Because he picked a quarrel with me one night in a pub. We went outside and I punched him in the nose, and it was lucky for me I hit him first, because he was carrying a knife."

"Why are you telling me this?"

"Because you asked. If you don't want to be told things, you shouldn't ask questions."

"And what am I meant to do about it?"

"Nothing. Absolutely nothing. I'm sorry I brought it up. It was just that I'd heard Eliot had given him a job and I hoped it wasn't true."

"You don't like Eliot, do you?"

"I don't like him, I don't dislike him. He's nothing to do with me. But I'll tell you something. He picks bad friends."

"You mean Ernest Padlow?"

Joss sent me a glance that was full of reluctant admiration.

"You don't waste much time, I'll say that for you. You seem to know it all."

"I know about Ernest Padlow because I saw him with Eliot that first night when you gave me dinner at The Anchor."

"So you did. That's another rotten egg. If Ernest had his way the whole of Porthkerris would be bulldozed into car parks. There wouldn't be a house left standing. And we would all have to go up the hill and live in his fancy little semis which in ten years' time will be leaking, leaning, cracking up and generally bagging at the knees."

I did not reply to this outburst. I drank my coffee and thought how pleasant it would be to have a conversation without being instantly drawn into longstanding vendettas which had nothing to do with me. I was tired of listening to everybody I wanted to like running down the reputations of everybody else.

I finished my coffee, set down the cup and said, "I must get back."

Joss, with an obvious effort, apologized. "I'm sorry."

"Why?"

"For losing my temper."

"Eliot's my cousin, Joss."

"I know." He looked down, turning his cup in his hands. "But, without meaning to, I've become involved with Boscarva, too."

"Just don't take your prejudices out on me."

His eyes met mine. "I wasn't angry with you."

"I know." I stood up. "I must go," I said again.

"I'll drive you back."

"You don't have to . . ." But he paid no attention to my protest, just took my coat from its hook and helped me on with it. I pulled the wet woollen hat over my ears and picked up the heavy basket.

The telephone rang.

Joss, in his oilskin, went to answer it, and I started downstairs. I heard him call, just before he took the receiver off the hook, "Rebecca, wait for me. I won't be a moment . . ." and then, into the telephone, "Yes? Yes, Joss Gardner here . . ."

I went down to the ground floor and the shop. It was still raining. Upstairs I could hear Joss deep in conversation.

Bored with waiting for him, perhaps a little curious, I pushed open the door of the workshop, turned on the light, and went down four stone steps. There was the usual confusion, benches, woodshavings, scraps, tools, vises; over all hung the smell of glue, of new wood, of polish. There was also a clutter of old furniture, so dusty and ramshackle it was impossible to tell whether it was of any value or not. A chest of drawers missing all its handles, a bedside cupboard without a leg.

And then, at the very back of the room, in the shadows, I saw them. A davenport desk, in apparently perfect repair, and alongside it a chair in the Chinese Chippendale style, with a tapestry seat, embroidered in flowers.

I felt sick, as though I had been kicked in the stomach. I turned and went up the steps, turning off the light and closing the door, going through the shop and out into the bitter windblast of that wicked February day.

My workshop's in a dreadful mess, I'll show you that another time.

I walked and then found that I was running up towards the church, into a warren of little lanes where he would never find me. I was running, always uphill, encumbered by the shopping basket, heavy as lead, and my heart pounded in my chest and there was the taste of blood in my mouth.

Eliot had been right. It was too easy for Joss and he had simply taken his chance. It was my desk; it was *my* desk that he had taken, but he had taken it from Grenville's house, flinging the old man's trust and kindness back in his face.

I could imagine killing Joss, and it was easy. I told myself that I could never speak to him, could never bear to be near him again. I had never been so angry in my life. With him; but worse with myself, for having been taken in by his empty charm, for having been proved so totally wrong. I had never been so angry.

I stumbled on up the hill.

But if I was so angry, then why was I crying?

10

It was a long and exhausting climb back to Boscarva, and I have never found it possible to sustain extreme emotion for more than ten minutes. Gradually, fighting my way up the hill against the weather, I calmed down, wiped my tears away with my gloved hand, pulled myself together. In an apparently intolerable situation, there is nearly always something one can do, and long before I reached Boscarva I had decided what it was. I would go back to London.

I left the shopping basket on the kitchen table and went upstairs to my room, took off all my drenched clothes, changed my shoes, washed my hands, carefully re-plaited my hair; thus calmed I went in search of Grenville and found him in his study, sitting by the fire and reading the morning paper.

He lowered this and looked over the top of it as I came in.

"Rebecca."

"Hallo. How are you this wild morning?" I sounded determinedly cheerful, like a maddening nurse.

"Full of aches and pains. The wind's a killer even if you never go out in it. Where've you been?"

"Down in Porthkerris. I had to do some shopping for Mollie."

"What time is it?"

"Half past twelve."

"Then let's have a glass of sherry."

"Is that allowed?"

"I don't give a damn if it's allowed or not. You know where the decanter is."

I poured two glasses, carried his over and set it carefully down on the table by his chair. I pulled up a stool and sat facing him. I said, "Grenville, I have to go back to London."

"What?"

"I have to go back to London." The blue eyes narrowed, the great jaw thrust out; I hastily made Stephen Forbes my scapegoat. "I can't stay away for ever. I've already been away from work nearly two weeks, and Stephen Forbes, the man I work for, he's been so good about it, I can't just go on taking advantage of his kindness and generosity. I've just realized that it's Friday already. I must go back to London this weekend. I must be back at work on Monday morning."

"But you've only just come." He was obviously thoroughly disgusted with me.

"I've been here three days. After three days fish and guests stink."

"You're not a guest. You're Lisa's child."

"But I still have commitments. And I like my job and I don't want to stop working." I smiled, trying to divert him. "And now I've found the way to Boscarva, perhaps I can come again, when I've got more time to spare, to spend with you."

He did not reply but sat, looking old and grumpy, staring into the fire.

He said dismally, "I may not be here then."

"Oh, of course you will be."

He sighed, took a slow, shaky mouthful of sherry, set down his glass, and turned to me, apparently resigned.

"When do you want to go?"

I was surprised, but relieved, that he had given in so easily.

"Perhaps tomorrow night. I'll get a sleeper. And then I can have Sunday to get myself settled into my flat."

"You shouldn't be living in a flat in London on your own. You weren't made for living alone. You were made for a man, and a home, and children. If I were twenty years younger and could still paint, that's how I'd show you to the world, in a field or a garden, knee-deep in buttercups and children."

"Perhaps it'll happen one day. And then I shall send for you."

His face was suddenly full of pain. He turned away from me and said, "I wish you'd stay."

I longed to say that I would, but there were a thousand reasons why I couldn't. "I'll come back," I promised.

He made a great and touching effort to pull himself together, clearing his throat, re-settling himself in his chair. "That jade of yours. We'll have to get Pettifer to pack it in a box, then you can take it with you. And the mirror . . . could you manage that on the train, or is it too big? You ought to have a car, then there would be no problems. Have you got a car?"

"No, but it doesn't matter . . ."

"And I suppose that desk hasn't . . ."

"It doesn't matter about the desk!" I interrupted, so loudly and so suddenly that Grenville looked at me in some surprise, as though he had not expected such bad manners.

"I'm sorry," I said quickly. "It's just that it really doesn't matter. I couldn't bear everybody to start quarrelling about it again. Please, for my sake, don't talk about it, don't think about it any more."

He regarded me thoughtfully, a long unblinking stare that made me drop my eyes.

He said, "You think I'm unfair to Eliot?"

"I just think that perhaps you never talk to each other, you never tell each other anything."

"He'd have been different if Roger hadn't been killed. He was a boy who needed a father."

"Couldn't you have done as a father?"

"Could never get near him for Mollie. He was never made to stick to anything. Always chopping and changing jobs and then he started that garage up three years ago."

"That seems to be a success."

"Second-hand cars!" His voice was full of unjustified contempt. "He should have gone into the Navy."

"Suppose he didn't want to go into the Navy?"

"He might have, if his mother hadn't talked him out of it. She wanted to keep him at home, tied to her apron strings."

"Oh, Grenville, I think you're being thoroughly old-fashioned and very unfair."

"Did I ask you for your opinion?" But already he was cheering up. A good argument was, to Grenville, like a shot in the arm.

"I don't care whether you asked for it or not, you've got it."

He laughed then, and reached forward to gently pinch my cheek. He said, "How I wish I could still paint. Do you still want one of my pictures to take back to London with you?"

I was afraid that he had forgotten. "More than anything."

"You can get the key of the studio from Pettifer. Tell him I said you could have it. Go and nose around, see what you can find."

"You won't come with me?"

Again the pain came into his face. "No," he said gruffly, and turned away to take up his sherry. He sat, looking down at the amber wine, turning the glass in his hand. "No, I won't come with you."

At lunch he broke the news to the others. Andrea, livid that I was going back to London while she had to stay in horrible, boring Cornwall, went into a sullen sulk. But the others were gratifyingly dismayed.

"But do you have to go?" That was Mollie.

"Yes, I really must. I've got a job to do and I can't stay away for ever."

"We really love having you here." She could be charming when she wasn't aggressive and possessive about Eliot, resentful of Grenville and Boscarva. I saw her again as a pretty little cat, but now I was aware of long claws hidden in the soft velvet paws, and I knew that she had no compunction about using them.

"I've loved it too . . ."

Pettifer was more outspoken. After lunch I went out to the kitchen to help him with the dishes, and he minced no words.

"What you want to go away for now, just when you're settling down and the Commander's getting to know you—well, it's beyond me. I didn't think you were that sort of a person . . ."

"I'll come back. I've said I'll come back."

"He's eighty now. He's not going to last for ever. How are you going to feel, coming back and him not here, but six feet under the ground and pushing up the daisies?"

"Oh, Pettifer, *don't.*"

"It's all very well saying 'Oh, Pettifer, *don't.*' There's nothing I can do about it."

"I've got a job. I must go back."

"Sounds like selfishness to me."

"That's not fair."

"All these years he's not seen his daughter, and then you turn up and stay three days. What sort of a grandchild are you?"

I didn't reply because there was nothing to say. And I hated feeling guilty and being put in the wrong. We finished the dishes in silence, but when they were done and he was wiping down the draining board with a damp cloth, I tried to make my peace with him.

"I'm sorry. I really am. It's bad enough having to go without you making me feel a brute. And I will come back. I've said I will. Perhaps in the summer . . . he'll still be here in the summer, and the weather will be warm and we can do things together. Perhaps you could take us out in the car . . ."

My voice trailed away. Pettifer hung his cloth neatly over the edge of the sink. He said, gruffly, "The Commander said you were to have the key of the studio. Don't know what you'll find down there. A lot of dust and spiders, I should think."

"He said I could have a picture. He said I could go and choose one."

He slowly dried his worn, gnarled hands. "I'll have to find the key. It's put away for safe keeping. Didn't want it lying around where anyone could get their hands on it. There's a lot of good stuff down in the studio."

"Any time will do." I could not bear his disapproval. "Oh, Pettifer, don't be angry with me."

He melted then. "Oh, I'm not angry. Perhaps it's me who's being selfish. Perhaps it's me who doesn't want you to go."

I saw him suddenly, not as the ubiquitous Pettifer around whom this household revolved, but as an old man, nearly as old as my grandfather and probably as lonely. A stupid lump came into my throat and for a terrible moment I thought I was going to burst into tears, which would have made it the second time that day, but then Pettifer said, "And don't go choosing one of them nudes, they wouldn't be suitable," and the dangerous moment was behind me and we were smiling, friends again.

That afternoon Mollie lent me her car, and I drove the five miles to the railway junction and there bought myself a ticket back to London and reserved a sleeper for the night train on Saturday. The violence of the wind had dropped a little, but it was still wild and stormy, with trees down and devastation everywhere, smashed greenhouses, broken branches, and fields of early spring bulbs flattened by the gales.

I got home to find Mollie in the garden at Boscarva, bundled up against the weather (even Mollie could not look elegant on such a day) and trying to tie up and rescue some of the more fragile shrubs that grew around the house. When she saw the car, she decided to call it a day, for as I put it away and walked back towards the house I met her coming towards me, stripping off her gloves and tucking a strand of hair into her head-scarf.

"I can't bear it a moment longer," she told me. "I hate wind, it exhausts me. But that darling little daphne was being snapped to ribbons, and all the camellias have been burnt by this wind. It turns them quite brown. Let's go in and have a cup of tea."

While she changed I put the kettle on, and set out cups on a tray. "Where is everybody?" I asked her when she reappeared, miraculously neat once more, down to her pearls and her matching earrings.

"Grenville's having a nap and Andrea's up in her room . . ." she sighed. ". . . I must say, she really isn't the easiest of girls. If only she'd do something to amuse herself instead of skulking around in this tiresome manner. I'm afraid it's not doing her any good being down here, I didn't think it would, to be quite honest, but my poor sister was quite desperate." She looked around the comfortable kitchen. "This is cosy. Let's have our tea in here. The drawing room's so draughty when the wind's from the sea, and we can scarcely draw the curtains at half past four in the afternoon . . ."

She was right, it was cosy in the kitchen. She found a cloth and laid the tea, setting out cakes and biscuits, sugar bowl and silver milk jug. Even for kitchen tea, it appeared, her standards were meticulous. She pulled up two wheel-back chairs, and was in the act of reaching for the teapot when the door opened and Andrea appeared.

"Oh, Andrea, dear, just in time. We're having kitchen tea today. Do you want a cup?"

"I'm sorry, I haven't got time."

This unexpectedly mannerly reply made Mollie look up sharply. "Are you going out?"

"Yes," said Andrea, "I'm going to the cinema."

We both stared at her like fools. For the impossible had happened— Andrea had suddenly decided to take much trouble with her appearance. She had washed her hair and tied it back off her face, found a clean polo-necked tee-shirt, and even, I was delighted to see, a bra to wear beneath it. Her Celtic cross hung around her neck on its thread of leather, her black jeans were neatly pressed, her clumpy shoes polished. Over her arm was a raincoat and a fringed leather handbag. I had never seen her look so presentable. And, best of all, the expression on her face was neither sulky nor malevolent, but . . . demure? Could one possibly describe Andrea as looking demure?

"I mean," she went on, "if that's all right by you, Auntie Mollie."

"Well, of course. What are you going to see?"

Mary of Scotland. It's on at the Plaza."

"Are you going by yourself?"

"No, I'm going with Joss. He rang me while you were out gardening. He's going to give me supper afterwards."

"Oh," said Mollie, faintly. And then, feeling that further comment was expected of her, ". . . how are you going to get down there?"

"I'll walk down, and I expect Joss will drive me home . . ."

"Have you got some money?"

"I've got 50p. I'll be all right."

"Well . . ." But Mollie was defeated. "Have a good time."

"I will," she flashed us both a smile. "Goodbye."

The door swung to behind her.

"Goodbye," said Mollie. She looked at me. "Extraordinary," she said.

I was concentrating on my cup of tea. "Why so extraordinary?" I said casually.

"Andrea and . . . Joss. I mean he's always been quite polite to her, but . . . to ask her out . . . ?"

"You shouldn't sound so surprised. She's attractive when she cleans herself up and bothers to smile. Probably she smiles at Joss all the time."

"You think it's all right, letting her go? I mean I do have responsibilities . . . ?"

"Honestly, I don't see how you could have stopped her going. Anyway she's seventeen, she's not a child. She can surely look after herself by now . . ."

"That's just the trouble," said Mollie . . . "That's always been the trouble with Andrea."

"She'll be all right."

She would not be all right, and I knew this, but I could not disillusion Mollie. Besides, what did it matter? It was no business of mine if Joss chose to spend his evenings making firelit love to an adolescent nymphomaniac. They were two of a kind. They deserved each other. They were welcome to each other.

When we had finished tea, Mollie tied a neat apron around her waist and started preparing dinner. I cleared away the cups and saucers and washed them up. As I was drying the last plate, and putting it away, Pettifer appeared, bearing in his hand a large key which looked as though it might unlock a dungeon.

"I knew I'd put it somewhere safely, found it in the back of a drawer in the Commander's bureau . . ."

"What's that, Pettifer?" Mollie asked.

"The key to the studio, Madam . . ."

"Heavens, who wants that?"

"I do," I said. "Grenville said I could go down and choose a picture to take back to London."

"My dear child, what a task you'll have. The place must be in the most terrible mess, it hasn't seen the light of day for ten years."

"I don't mind." I took the key which weighed heavy as lead in my hand.

"Are you going now? It's getting dark."

"Aren't there any lights?"

265

"Oh, yes, of course, but it's very cheerless. Wait till tomorrow morning."

But I wanted to go now. "I'll be all right. I'll put on a coat."

"There's a torch on the hall table, you'd better take that as well, the path down the garden is quite steep and slippery."

And so, buttoned into my leather coat, and armed with the torch and the key, I set off, letting myself out of the house by the garden door. The wind from the sea was still violent, carrying with it squalls of thin, cold rain, and I had to struggle to get the door closed behind me. The dismal afternoon was turning early to darkness, but still there was enough light to pick my way cautiously down the sloping garden, and I did not turn on the torch until I reached the studio when I needed its beam to find the keyhole.

I fitted the key and it turned reluctantly, needing oil; the door swung inwards, creakingly. There was a damp and musty smell, a suggestion of cobwebs and mould, and I quickly put my hand inside and felt for the light switch. At once a single naked bulb, high in the roof, sprang to a chill and insubstantial life, and I was surrounded by leaping shadows, for the draught caused the long flex to swing to and fro like the pendulum of a clock.

I went in and shut the door behind me and the shadows, slowly, were stilled. Around me, dust-covered shapes loomed in the half-light, but across the room was a standard lamp, with a crooked, broken shade. I picked my way over to this, found the switch and turned that on, and at once everything looked a little less forlorn.

I saw that the studio had been designed on two levels with a sleeping gallery at the south end, reached by a stair like a ship's ladder.

I went half-way up the ladder and saw the divan and the striped blanket. Over the bed was a window tightly shuttered, and a pillow had shed feathers, perhaps the work of some marauding mouse. The remains of a small dead bird lay, twig-like and dehydrated, in the corner of the floor. I shuddered slightly at the desolation, and descended again to the studio.

The wind banged and rattled at the huge north window. A complicated contraption of strings and pulleys worked the long curtains, and I struggled with these for a moment, but was finally defeated by their mechanics and left the curtains closed.

In the middle of the floor was a model's throne, with a sheeted shape in the middle which proved to be an ornate gilt chair. The mice had been at the seat of this, too—scraps of red velvet and horsehair were scattered about, along with mouse-droppings and a great deal of dust.

Under another sheet I found Grenville's work-bench; his brushes, his trays of paint-tubes, palettes, knives, bottles of linseed oil, piles of unused canvases, grimy with age. There was also a little collection of *objets trouvés*, small things which, perhaps, had taken his fancy. A sea-polished stone, half a dozen shells, a bunch of gulls' feathers, probably collected for the practical purpose of cleaning his pipe. There were curling, faded snapshots, of nobody I recognized, a blue and white Chinese ginger jar filled with pencils, some bottles of fossilized Indian ink, a scrap of sealing wax.

It was like prying, as though I were reading another person's diary. I put back the sheet and went on to the true purpose of my visit, which was the stack of unframed canvases standing around the wall, each with its face turned inwards. These had been dust-covered too, but the sheets had slipped, draping themselves about the floor, and as I dislodged the first pile my fingers touched cobwebs, and a huge, disgusting spider went scuttling across the floor and lost itself in the shadows.

It was a slow business. Five or six at a time, I lifted out the pictures, dusted them off, leaned them in rows against the model's throne, shifting the rickety standard lamp so that the light should shine on them. Some were dated, but they were stacked away in no sort of chronological order, and for the most part I could tell neither when nor where they had been painted. I only knew that they compassed the whole of Grenville's professional life and all his interests.

There were landscapes, seascapes—the ocean in all its moods— charming interiors, some sketches of Paris, some that looked like Italy. There were boats and fishermen, street scenes of Porthkerris, a number of rough charcoal sketches of two children, whom I knew were Roger and Lisa. There were no portraits.

I began to make my selection, setting aside the pictures which I found particularly engaging. By the time I had reached the final pile, there were half a dozen of them propped against the seat of a sagging couch, and I was dirty and cold, with grimy hands and cobwebs clinging to my clothes. With the good feeling of a task nearly completed I went to sort out the last pile of canvases. There were three pen and ink drawings, and a view of a harbour with yachts at anchor. And then . . .

It was the last canvas and the biggest of all. It needed two hands and all my efforts to lift it out of its dark corner and turn it around to face the light. I held it upright with one hand and stood back, and the face of the girl leapt out to meet me, the dark, tip-tilted eyes smiling with a vitality undimmed by the dust of the years that passed. I saw the dark hair and the bumpy cheekbones and the sensuous mouth, not smiling, but seeming to tremble on the brink of laughter. And she wore the same fragile white dress, the dress that she had worn for the portrait that hung over the fireplace in the drawing room at Boscarva.

Sophia.

Ever since my mother had mentioned her name I had been fascinated by her. The frustrations of never knowing what she looked like had only increased my obsession. But now that I had found her and we were face to face at last, I felt like Pandora. I had opened the box and the secrets were out, and there was no way in the world of packing them back and locking the lid once more.

I knew that face. I had talked to it, argued with it; seen it scowl and smile; seen the dark eyes narrowed in anger and glint with amusement.

It was Joss Gardner.

11

ALL AT ONCE I was bitterly cold. It was dark now and the studio was icy, but as well I could feel the blood drain from my face like water out of a basin; I could hear the laboured thumping of my own heart, and I started, violently, to shiver. My first instinct was to put the portrait back where I had found it, pile some other canvases on top of it and hide it, like a criminal trying to conceal a body, or something worse.

But in the end I reached for a chair and arranged it carefully, so that it supported Sophia's portrait like an easel, and then I backed away on shaking legs and carefully lowered myself on to the sagging seat of the aged sofa.

Sophia and Joss.

Sophia the enchanting, and the baffling Joss, whom I had finally learned was not to be trusted.

268

She went to London, she got married, she had a baby, I think, Pettifer had told me. Then in 1942 she was killed in the Blitz.

But he had not mentioned Joss. And yet Joss and Sophia were so obviously, inextricably linked.

And I thought of my desk, my mother's desk that she meant me to have, hidden away at the back of Joss's workshop.

And I heard Mollie's voice. *I don't know why Grenville's so taken with Joss. It's frightening. It's as though Joss were able to exert some hold over him.*

Sophia and Joss.

It was dark now. I had no watch and I had lost all track of time. The wind drowned all other sound, so that I did not hear Eliot coming down the garden from the house, picking his way through the darkness because I had taken the torch. I did not hear anything until the door burst open, as though on a gust of wind, causing the light to start up its demented swinging, and frightening me nearly out of my wits. The next instant Rufus bounded in and flung himself up on the sofa beside me, and I realized that I had company.

My cousin Eliot stood in the open doorway framed in darkness. He wore a suede jacket and a pale blue polo-necked sweater and he had slung a raincoat around his shoulders like a cloak. The cruel light drained all the colour from his thin face, and turned his deep-set eyes into two black holes.

"My mother told me you were down here. I came to . . ."

He stopped, and I knew that he had seen the portrait. I couldn't move, I was too petrified with cold, and anyway, now it was too late to do anything about it.

He came into the studio and closed the door. The leaping shadows, once more, were slowly stilled.

We neither of us said anything. I held Rufus's head, instinctively seeking comfort in his soft, warm fur, and watched while Eliot shrugged off his raincoat, dropped it across a chair, and came slowly to sit beside me. His eyes never left the portrait.

At last he spoke. "Good God," he said.

I said nothing.

"Where did you find that?"

"In a corner . . ." My voice came out as a croak. I cleared my throat and tried again. "In a corner, behind a lot of other canvases."

"It's Sophia."

"Yes."

"It's Joss Gardner."

269

There was no denying it. "Yes."

"Sophia's grandson, do you suppose?"

"Yes. I think he must be."

"Well, I'll be damned." He leaned back, and crossed his long, elegant legs, suddenly relaxed, like a knowledgeable art critic at a private view.

His obvious satisfaction puzzled me, and I did not want him to think that I shared it.

I said, "I wasn't looking for it. I've been wanting to know what Sophia looked like, but I had no idea there was a portrait of her down here. I just came to look for a picture because Grenville said I could have one to take back to London."

"I know. My mother told me."

"Eliot, we mustn't say anything."

He ignored this. "You know, there was always something funny about Joss, something unexplained. The way he turned up in Porthkerris, out of the blue. And the way Grenville knew that he was there; the way he gave him a job, and the run of Boscarva. I never trusted Joss farther than I could see him. And the desk disappearing —the desk that should have come to you. It was all fishy beyond words."

I knew that I should tell Eliot then that I had found the desk. I opened my mouth with the intention of doing just this thing, and closed it again because somehow the words would not be spoken. Besides, Eliot was still talking and had not noticed my incipient interruption.

"My mother swore he had some sort of a hold over Grenville."

"You make it sound like blackmail."

"Perhaps, in a modified form, it was. You know, 'Here I am Sophia's grandson, what are you going to do for me?' And Pettifer must have known as well. Pettifer and Grenville have no secrets from each other."

"Eliot, we mustn't say that we found the picture."

He turned his head to look at me.

"You sound anxious, Rebecca. On Joss Gardner's behalf?"

"No. On Grenville's."

"But you like Joss."

"No."

He pretended to be amazed. "But everybody likes Joss! Everybody, it seems, has fallen under his spell of boyish charm. Grenville and Pettifer; Andrea is besotted by him, she never leaves him alone, but I think there may be something just a little physical in that attraction. I thought that you were bound to have joined the club." He frowned. "You *did* like Joss."

"Not now, Eliot."

He began to be intrigued. He shifted his position slightly, so that we half-faced each other on the sofa, his arm along its carved back, behind my shoulder.

"What happened?" he asked.

What had happened? Nothing. But I had never felt quite easy about Joss, and all the coincidences that seemed to tie our lives together. And he had stolen my mother's desk. And he was now, at this moment, carrying on his clandestine affair with the unsavoury Andrea. At the very idea of this, my imagination was apt to turn and run.

Eliot was waiting for my reply. But I only shrugged and shook my head hopelessly and said, "I changed my mind."

"Could yesterday have had anything to do with it?"

"Yesterday?" I thought of sitting with Eliot on the sunbaked terrace of the little pub; of the two boys sailing their dinghy down the blue waters of the creek; and finally Eliot's arms, encircling and holding me, the feel of his kisses, and the sensation of losing control, of sliding over a cliff.

I shivered again. My hands, cold and grimy, lay in my lap. Eliot put his own over them and said, in some surprise, "You're freezing."

"I know, I've been here for hours."

"My mother told me you want to go back to London." We seemed to have dropped the subject of Joss and I was thankful for this.

"Yes, I have to go."

"When?"

"Tomorrow night."

"You never told me."

"I didn't decide until this morning."

"You seem to have changed your mind, and made a lot of decisions all in one day."

"I hadn't realized how the time had flown. I've been away from work for nearly two weeks."

"Yesterday, I asked you to stay."

"I have to go."

"What would make you stay?"

"Nothing. I mean . . . I can't . . ." I was stammering like a fool, but I was too cold, too dirty and too tired for such a conversation. Later, perhaps, I would be able to cope . . .

271

"Would you stay if I asked you to marry me?"

My head shot up. Something like horror must have shown on my face, for he put back his head and laughed.

"Don't look so shocked. There's nothing shocking about getting married."

"But we're cousins."

"That doesn't matter."

"But we don't . . . I mean . . . You don't love me."

It was an appalling thing to say, but Eliot took it in his stride.

"Rebecca, you are stammering and stuttering like a shy schoolgirl. Perhaps I do love you. Perhaps I would have loved you for a long time before asking you to marry me, but you've precipitated this situation by suddenly announcing out of the blue that you're going to go back to London. So if I'm going to say it at all, I'd better say it now. I want you to marry me. I think it would work very well."

Despite myself, I was touched. No one had ever asked me to marry them before, and I found it flattering. But even as I listened to Eliot with one part of my mind, the other part ran round in circles like a squirrel in a cage.

Because there was still Boscarva, and the land that Eliot needed to sell to Ernest Padlow.

You are not my only grandchild.

". . . it seems ridiculous to say goodbye and walk out of each other's lives when we've only just met each other, and there are so many good things going for us."

I said quietly, "Like Boscarva."

His smile froze slightly around the edges. He raised an eyebrow. "Boscarva?"

"Let's be honest and truthful, Eliot. For some reason you need Boscarva. And you think that Grenville might leave it to me."

He took a deep breath as though to deny this, hesitated, and then let it all out in a long sigh. His smile was rueful. He ran a hand over the top of his head.

"How cool you are. The Ice Princess all of a sudden."

"You need Boscarva so that you can sell the farm to Ernest Padlow to build his houses."

He said, carefully, "Yes." I waited. "I needed money to build the garage. Grenville wasn't interested so I approached Padlow. He agreed and the security was the Boscarva farm. Gentleman's agreement."

"But it wasn't yours."

272

"I was sure it would be. There was no reason why it shouldn't be. And Grenville was old and ill. The end could have come any day." He spread his hands. "Who would have imagined that three years later he'd still be with us?"

"You sound as though you want him dead."

"Old age is a terrible thing. Lonely and sad. He's had a good life. What is there for him to cling on for?"

I knew that I could not agree with Eliot. Old age, in Grenville's case, meant dignity and purpose. I had only just got to know him, but already I loved him and he was part of me; I could not bear to think of him dying.

I said, trying to stay practical, "Isn't there some other way you could pay off Mr Padlow?"

"I could sell the garage. The way things are going I might have to do that anyway."

"I thought you were doing so well."

"That's what everybody's meant to think."

"But if you sold the garage, what would you do then?"

"What do you suggest I should do?" He sounded amused as though I were a child with whims to be indulged. I said, "How about Mr Kemback, and the car museum in Birmingham?"

"What an uncomfortably good memory you've got."

"Would working for Mr Kemback be such a bad thing?"

"And leave Cornwall?"

"I think that's what you should do. Make a new start. Get away from Boscarva and . . ." I stopped, and then thought, *in for a penny, in for a pound*, ". . . and your mother." I finished in a rush.

"My mother?" Still that amusement, as though I were a beguiling fool.

"You know what I mean, Eliot."

There was a long pause. Then, "I think," said Eliot, "you have been talking to Grenville."

"I'm sorry."

"One thing's for certain, either Joss or I will have to go. As they say in Westerns, 'This town ain't big enough for the two of us.' But I'd rather Joss went."

"Joss is unimportant. He's not worth taking a stand over."

"If I sold the garage and went to work in Birmingham, would you come with me?"

"Oh, Eliot . . ."

I turned away from him and came face to face once more with

273

Sophia's portrait. Her eyes met mine and it was as though Joss sat there, listening to every word we were saying, laughing at us. Then Eliot put his hand beneath my chin and jerked my head around so that once more I was forced to meet his eye.

"Listen to what I'm saying!"

"I am listening."

"We don't have to be in love with each other. You know that, don't you?"

"I always imagined it was important."

"It doesn't happen to everyone. Perhaps it won't ever happen to you."

It was a chill prospect. "Perhaps not."

"In that case," his voice was very gentle and reasonable, "would a compromise be such a bad thing? Wouldn't a compromise be better than a nine to five job for the rest of your life and an empty flat in London?"

He had touched me on the raw. I had been alone for too long, and the prospect of staying alone for the rest of my life was frightening. Grenville had said, *You were made for a man and a home and children.* And now they were all there, waiting for me. I had only to reach out my hand, to accept what Eliot was offering me.

I said his name, and he put his arms around me, and drew me very close, kissing my eyes, my cheeks, my mouth. Sophia watched us and I did not care. I told myself that she was dead, and Joss I had already put out of my life. Why should I care what either of them thought of me?

Eliot said at last, "We must go." He held me away from him. "You must have a bath and wash all those dirty marks off your face, and I must get the ice out of the fridge, and be all ready and dutiful to pour drinks for Grenville and my mother."

"Yes." I drew away from his arms, and pushed a lock of hair out of my face. I felt deathly tired. "What time is it?"

He looked at his watch, the strap that I had given him still shining and new. "Nearly half past seven. We could stay here all night, but unfortunately life has to go on."

I got wearily to my feet. Without looking at the portrait I took it up and put it back in its hidden, dusty corner, along with the cobwebs and the spiders, its face to the wall. Then I picked up other pictures, at random, and piled them around and against it. Everything, I told myself, was just as it had been before. We tidied up in a cursory fashion and covered the canvases with the fallen dust-sheet. Eliot switched off the standard lamp, and I picked up the torch. We went out of the studio, turning off the light and closing and locking the door. Eliot took the torch from me, and together, following the bobbing circle of light, we went up the garden, stumbling a little over hidden verges and tussocks of grass, mounting the shining wet steps of the terrace. Above us the house loomed, lighted rooms glowing behind drawn curtains, and all around us was the wind and the silhouettes of leafless, tormented trees.

"I've never known a storm to last so long," said Eliot, as he opened the side door and we went inside. The hall felt warm and safe, and there was the good smell of the chicken casserole that we were to have for dinner.

We parted, Eliot heading for the kitchen, and I upstairs to shed my filthy clothes, draw a bath and wallow in warm, scented steam. Relaxed at last I thought about nothing. I was too tired to think. I would fall asleep, I decided, and probably drown. For some reason the idea of this did not alarm me.

But I did not fall asleep, because as I lay there, I heard, above the noise of the wind, the sound of an approaching car. The bathroom faced over the back of the house, the drive and the front door. I had not bothered to draw the curtains and the headlights of the car flashed for a second against the dark glass. A door banged, there were voices. Thus disturbed, I climbed out of the bath, dried myself and started across the passage to my room, but stopped dead when I heard the raised voices carrying up the stairwell from the hall.

". . . found her half way up the hill . . ." a man's voice, unrecognized.

And then Mollie, ". . . but my dear child . . ." This was interrupted by a wild cacophony of sobbing. I heard Eliot say, "For heaven's sake, girl . . ." And then Mollie again. "Come in by the fire . . . come along now, you're all right. You're safe now . . ."

I went into my room, pulled on my clothes, buttoned the neck of the brown caftan, brushed and plaited my hair, all in the space of moments. I painted on a layer of lipstick—there was no time for more —thrust my bare feet into sandals and ran downstairs, screwing on my ear-rings as I did so.

As I reached the bottom of the stairs Pettifer appeared through the kitchen door with a face like a thundercloud and bearing in his hand a glass of brandy. It was indicative of the gravity of the situation that he had omitted to put it on a silver salver.

"Pettifer, what's happened?"

"I don't know what's happened, exactly, but it sounds as though that girl's having hysterics."

"I heard a car coming. Who brought her home?"

"Morris Tatcombe. Says he was driving home from Porthkerris when he found her on the road."

I was horrified. "You mean *lying* on the road? Had she been hit by a car, or something?"

"I don't know. Probably just had a tumble."

At the far end of the hall the drawing room door burst open and Mollie came towards us, half running.

"Oh, Pettifer, don't stand talking, hurry with the brandy." She saw me standing, quite at a loss. "Oh, my dear Rebecca, what a terrible thing, quite terrible. I'm going to ring the doctor." She was at the telephone, thumbing through the book, unable to see because she had somewhere mislaid her glasses. "Look it up for me, there's a dear. It's Doctor Trevaskis . . . we ought to have it written down somewhere, but I can't find . . ."

Pettifer had gone. I took the telephone book and started to look for the number. "What's happened to Andrea?" I asked.

"It's the most ghastly story. I can hardly believe it's true. What a mercy Morris found her. She could have been there all night. She could have died . . ."

"Here it is. Lionel Trevaskis. Porthkerris 873."

She put a hand to her cheek. "Oh, of course, I should know it off by heart." She lifted the receiver and dialled. While she waited she spoke to me, swiftly. "Go and sit by her, the men are so useless, they never know what to do."

Mystified and oddly reluctant to know the details of Andrea's unhappy experience, I nevertheless did as she asked me. I found the drawing room in something approaching a shambles. Grenville, apparently nonplussed, stood in front of the fireplace with his hands behind his back and said nothing. The rest of them were grouped around the sofa; Eliot had given Morris a drink, and they watched while Pettifer, with commendable patience, was trying to trickle some brandy down Andrea's throat.

And Andrea . . . despite myself I was shocked and frightened by her appearance. The neat sweater and the pressed jeans in which she had set out so gaily were soaking wet and smeared with mud. Through the tear in the jeans I could see her knee, cut and bleeding, vulnerably childlike. She had lost, it seemed, a shoe. Her hair clung, like seaweed, to her skull, her face was blotched with crying, and when I said her name she turned her head to look at me from pathetic, streaming eyes; I saw with horror the great bruise on her temple, as though she had been savagely struck. The Celtic cross on its leather thong was also lost; torn off, perhaps, in some unthinkable struggle.

"Andrea!"

She gave a great wail and heaved herself over to press her face into the back of the sofa, spilling the brandy as she did so, and knocking the tumbler clean out of Pettifer's hand.

"I don't want to talk about it. I don't want to talk about it . . . !"

"But you must!"

Pettifer, exasperated, collected the glass and went from the room. I told myself that he had never liked the girl. I took his place beside her, sitting on the edge of the sofa, trying to turn her shoulders toward me.

"Did somebody do this to you?"

Andrea flung herself back at me, her body convulsed. "Yes!" She screamed at my face as though I were deaf. "Joss!" And with that she dissolved once more in a welter of sobs.

I looked up at Grenville and was subjected to a stony, unblinking glare. His features might have been carved from wood. I decided there was no help to be expected from that quarter. I turned to Morris Tatcombe.

"Where did you find her?"

He shifted, one foot to another. I saw that he was dressed as though for a night on the town. A leather jacket, decorated with a rash of embroidered emblems, and spotted with rain, skin-tight jeans and boots with high heels. Even with high heels the top of his head scarcely reached to Eliot's shoulder, and his long hair hung damp and lank.

He tossed this back, a gesture both aggressive and self-conscious.

"Half way up Porthkerris Hill. You know, where the road narrows and there isn't a pavement. She was half way up the bank, half in the ditch. Lucky I saw her, really. Thought she'd been hit by a car, but it wasn't that. Seems she had this row with Joss Gardner."

I said, "He asked her to go to the cinema with him."

"I don't know how it all started," said Morris.

"But this, it seems—" said Eliot gravely— "is how it ends."

"But . . ." There had to be some other explanation. I was about to tell them this when Andrea let out another wail, like some aged sibyl keening at a wake, and I lost my temper.

"Oh, for goodness sake, girl, shut up!" I took her by her shoulders and gave her a little shake so that her head bobbed on the silk cushion like a badly stuffed rag-doll. "Stop making that dementing noise and tell us what happened."

Words began to spill out of her mouth, made ugly with weeping. (I thought briskly, *at least she isn't missing any teeth*, and hated myself for my own hard heart.)

"I . . . we . . . went to the cinema . . . and wh . . . when we came out, we went to a pub, and . . ."

"Which pub?"

"I don't know . . ."

"You must know which pub . . ."

My voice rose in impatience. Behind me, Mollie, whom I had not heard come into the room, said, "Oh, don't shout at her. Don't be unkind."

I made an effort and tried again, more gently.

"Can't you remember where you went?"

"No. It was d . . . dark . . . and I . . . couldn't see. And then . . . and then . . ."

I held her firmly, trying to calm her "Yes. And then?"

"And Joss had a lot of whisky to drink. And he wouldn't bring me home. He wanted me to g . . . go back to his flat with him . . . and . . ."

Her mouth went square, her features dissolved into uncontrollable weeping. I let her go and stood up, backing away from her. At once Mollie took my place.

"There," she said. "There, there." She was more gentle than I, her voice as soothing as a mother's. "Now there's nothing more to worry about. The doctor's on his way, and Pettifer's putting a nice hot bottle in your bed. You don't need to tell us any more. You don't need to talk about it any more."

But, perhaps calmed by Mollie's manner, Andrea seemed anxious to make a clean breast of it, and, through interminable sobs and gasps, we were to hear the rest of the story.

"And I didn't want to go. I . . . I wanted to come home. And I . . . left him. And he came after me. And . . . I tried to run, and I tripped on the p . . . pavement, and my shoe . . . c . . . came off. And then he c . . . caught me, and he be . . . began shouting at me . . . and I screamed and he *hit* me . . ."

I looked at the faces around me, and the same horror and consternation, in varying degrees, was mirrored upon them. Only Grenville appeared coldly, deeply angry, but still he did not move, he did not say a word.

"It's all right," Mollie said again, her voice shaking only a little. "Now, everything's all right. Come along, upstairs."

Somehow Andrea, wilted and bedraggled, was eased off the sofa, but her legs would not hold her weight, and she started to collapse. It was Morris who, standing nearest to her, stepped forward and caught her before she fell, swinging her up, with surprising strength, into his puny arms.

"There," said Mollie, "Morris will carry you upstairs. You'll be all right . . ." She moved towards the door. "If you'll come this way, Morris."

"OK," said Morris, who did not appear to have much option in the matter.

I watched Andrea's face. As Morris moved, her eyes opened and looked straight into mine, and our glances clashed and held. And I knew that she was lying. And she knew that I knew she was lying.

Leaning her head against Morris's chest, she began to cry again. Swiftly, she was borne from the room.

We listened as Morris's burdened footsteps went down the hall, started up the staircase. Then Eliot said, with masterly understatement, "An unsavoury business." He glanced at Grenville. "Shall I ring the police now or later?"

Grenville spoke at last. "Who said anything about ringing the police?"

"You surely don't intend to let him get away with it?"

I said, "She was lying."

Both men looked at me in some surprise. Grenville's eyes narrowed and he was at his most formidable. Eliot frowned. "What did you say?"

"Some of her story may be true. Most of it probably is. But still, she was lying."

"How was she lying?"

"Because as you said yourself, she was besotted with Joss. She wouldn't leave him alone. She told me that she'd been often to his flat, and she must have been, because she described it to me and every detail was right. I don't know what happened this evening. But I do know that if Joss wanted her to go back with him, she'd have gone like a shot. No arguments."

"Then how," asked Eliot smoothly, "do you account for the bruise on her face?"

"I don't know. I said I don't know about the rest of her story. But that bit, for sure, she made up."

Grenville moved. He had been standing for a long time. Slowly, he went to his chair and lowered himself carefully into it.

"We can find out what really happened," he said at last.

"How?" Eliot's question came out like the shot of a gun.

Grenville swung his head around and fixed his gaze on Eliot.

"We can ask Joss."

Eliot let out a sound, which in old-fashioned novels would have been written as "Pshaw."

"We shall ask him. And we will be given the truth."

"He doesn't know what the truth means."

"You have no justification for making such a statement."

Eliot lost his temper. "Oh, for God's sake, does the truth have to be thrown in your face before you recognize it?"

"Don't raise your voice to me."

Eliot was silent, staring in disbelief and disgust at the old man. When at last he spoke, it was in scarcely more than a whisper. "I've had enough of Joss Gardner. I've never trusted him nor liked him. I believe he's a phoney, a thief and a liar, and I know that I'm right. And one day you too will know that I'm right. This is your house. I accept that. But what I will not accept is his right to take it over, and us with it, just because he happens to be . . ."

I had to stop him. "Eliot!" He turned to look at me. It was as though he had forgotten I was there. "Eliot, please. Don't say any more."

He looked down at his glass, finished the drink in a single mouthful. "All right," he said at last. "For the moment, I won't say any more."

And he went to pour himself another whisky. As he did this, with Grenville and I watching him in silence, Morris Tatcombe came back into the room.

"I'll be off then," he said to the back of Eliot's head.

Eliot turned and saw him. "Is she all right?"

"Well, she's upstairs. Your mother's with her."

"Have another drink before you go."

"No, I'd better be off."

"We really can't thank you enough. What would have happened if you hadn't seen her . . ." He stopped, the unfinished sentence con-

280

juring up visions of Andrea dying of exposure, exhaustion, loss of blood.

"Just lucky I did." He backed away, obviously anxious to be off, but not quite sure how to get there. Eliot put the stopper into the decanter, left his freshly filled glass on the table and came to his rescue.

"I'll see you to the door."

Morris ducked his head in the general direction of Grenville and myself.

"Night, all."

But Grenville had hauled himself to his feet with massive dignity. "You've handled things very sensibly, Mr Tatcombe. We're grateful to you. And we would be grateful, too, if you would keep the girl's version of what happened to yourself. At least until it has been authenticated."

Morris looked sceptical. "These things get around."

"But not, I am sure, through you."

Morris shrugged. "It's your affair."

"Exactly. Our affair. Good night, Mr Tatcombe."

Eliot led him away.

Grenville laboriously settled himself once more in his chair. He passed a hand over his eyes, and it occurred to me that such scenes could not be good for him.

"Are you all right?"

"Yes. I'm all right."

I wished that I could confide in him, tell him that I knew about Sophia, and Joss being her grandson. But I knew that if there were any telling to be done, it had to come from him.

"Would you like a drink?"

"No."

So I left him alone, busying myself in tidying the cushions on the flattened sofa.

It was some time before Eliot re-appeared, but when he did he seemed quite cheerful again, the sudden row which had flared between him and Grenville now quite forgotten. He went to pick up his drink. "Good health," he said, raising his glass to his grandfather.

"I suppose we're in debt to that young man," said Grenville. "I hope one day we'll be able to settle it."

"I shouldn't worry too much about Morris," Eliot replied lightly. "I should think he's quite capable of settling it for himself. And Pettifer has asked me to tell you both that dinner is ready."

We ate alone, the three of us. Mollie stayed with Andrea, and in the middle of dinner the doctor arrived and was taken upstairs by Pettifer. Later, we heard him talking to Mollie in the hall, then she showed him out and came into the dining room to tell us what he had said.

"Shock, of course. He's given her a sedative, and she has to stay in bed for a day or two."

Eliot had gone to pull out a chair for her, and she sank into this looking exhausted and shaken. "Imagine such a thing happening. How I'm going to tell her mother, I can't think."

"Don't think about it," said Eliot, "till tomorrow."

"But it was such an appalling story. She's only a child. She's only seventeen. What could Joss have been thinking of? He must have gone out of his mind."

"He was probably drunk," said Eliot.

"Yes, perhaps he was. Drunk and violent."

Neither Grenville nor I said anything. It was as though we had entered into some sort of an unspoken conspiracy, but this did not mean that I had forgiven Joss, nor condoned anything that he had done. Later, probably, when he had been interrogated by Grenville, the whole truth would come out. By then I would probably be back in London.

And if I was still here . . . Slowly, I ate a little bunch of grapes. This could be my last dinner at Boscarva, but I truly did not know whether I wanted it to be or not. I had reached a cross-roads, and had no idea which was the way I should take. But soon I was going to have to make up my mind.

A compromise, Eliot had said, and it had sounded tepid. But after the histrionics of this evening, the very words had a solid ring to them, sensible and matter-of-fact, with their feet planted squarely on the ground.

You were made for a man and a home and children.

I reached for my wine glass and, glancing up, saw that Eliot watched me across the polished table. He smiled, as though we were conspirators. The expression on his face was both confident and triumphant. Perhaps, while I was thinking that I would probably end up by marrying him, he already knew that I would.

We were back in the drawing room, sitting around the fire and finishing our coffee, when the telephone started to ring. I thought that Eliot would go to answer it, but he was deep in a chair with the paper and a drink, and managed to linger so long that it was Pettifer who finally took the call. We heard the kitchen door open and his old feet go so slowly across the hall. The ringing stopped. For some reason I glanced up at the clock on the mantelpiece. It was nearly a quarter to ten.

We waited. Presently the door opened and Pettifer's head came around the edge of it, his spectacles glinting in the lamplight.

"Who is it, Pettifer?" asked Mollie.

"It's for Rebecca," said Pettifer.

I was surprised. "For me?"

Eliot said, "Who's ringing you at this hour of the day?"

"I've no idea."

I got up and went out of the room. Perhaps it was Maggie, wanting to tell me something about the flat. Perhaps it was Stephen Forbes, wondering when I was going to return to work. I felt guilty, because I should have been in touch with him, letting him know what I was doing and when I planned to go back to London.

I sat on the hall chest and picked up the receiver.

"Hallo?"

A small, mouse-like voice began speaking, sounding very far away.

"Oh, Miss Bayliss, we were passing, and he was lying there . . . my husband said . . . so we got him up the stairs and into the flat . . . don't know what happened. Covered in blood and he could hardly talk. Wanted to call the doctor . . . but he wouldn't let us . . . frightened leaving him there on his own . . . there ought to be somebody there . . . said he'd be all right . . ."

I must have been exceptionally slow and stupid, but it took me a little time to realize that this was Mrs Kernow, calling me from the phone box at the end of Fish Lane, to tell me that something had happened to Joss.

12

I WAS AMAZED and gratified to find myself in a state of almost total calm. It was as though I had already been prepared for this crisis, been given my orders and told what to do. There were no doubts and so no indecision. I must go to Joss. It was as simple as that.

I went up to my bedroom and got my coat, put it on, did up the buttons, came downstairs again. The key of Mollie's car lay where I had left it, on the brass tray in the middle of the table in the hall.

I picked it up, and as I did so the drawing room door opened and Eliot came up the passage towards me. It never occurred to me that he would try to stop me going. It never occurred to me that anyone or anything could stop me going.

He saw me, bundled into my old leather coat. "Where are you off to?"

"Out."

"Who was that on the telephone?"

"Mrs. Kernow."

"What does she want?"

"Joss has been hurt. She and Mr Kernow were walking home along the harbour road, they'd been visiting her sister. They found him."

"So?" His voice was cold and very quiet. I expected to be intimidated, but I was not.

"I'm going to borrow your mother's car. I'm going to him."

His thin face hardened, the skin drawn tight over the jutting bones.

"Have you gone out of your mind?"

"I don't think so."

He said nothing. I slipped the key into my pocket and made for the door, but Eliot was faster than I, and in two strides was in front of me, standing with his back to the door and with his hand on the latch.

"You're not going," he said pleasantly. "You don't really think I'd let you go?"

"He's been hurt, Eliot."

"So what? You saw what he did to Andrea. He's rotten, Rebecca. You know he's rotten. His grandmother was an Irish whore, God knows who his father was, and he's a womanizing bastard."

The ugly words, which were meant to shock me, slid off my back like water from a duck. Eliot saw this and my unconcern infuriated him.

"Why do you want to go to him? What good could you do? He won't thank you for interfering, if it's thanks you're looking for. Leave him alone, he has no part of your life, he's none of your concern."

I stood watching him, hearing him, without making sense of anything he said. But I knew, all at once, that it was over, the uncertainty and the indecision, and I felt light with relief, as though a great weight had been lifted from my shoulders. I still stood at the cross-roads. My life was still a confusion. But one thing had made itself abundantly clear. I could never marry Eliot.

A compromise, he had said. But, for me, it would have been a poor bargain. All right, he was weak, and probably not the most successful of businessmen. I had recognized these flaws in his character and had been prepared to accept them. But the welcome he had shown me, the hospitality, and the charm which he could turn on and off like a tap, had blinded me to his vindictiveness and the frightening strength of his jealousy.

I said, "Let me go, Eliot."

"Supposing I say that I won't let you go? Supposing I keep you here?" He put his hands on either side of my head, pressing so tightly that it felt as though my skull would crack open, like a nut. "Supposing, now, that I said I loved you?"

I was sickened by him. "You don't love anyone. Only Eliot Bayliss. There's no room for anyone else in your life."

"I thought we decided that it was you who didn't know how to love."

His grip tightened. My head began to pound and I closed my eyes, enduring the pain.

"When I do—" I told him through clenched teeth—"it won't be you."

"All right then, go . . ." He let me loose so suddenly that I nearly lost my balance. Savagely he turned the handle and flung the door open, and instantly the wind poured in, like some monstrous creature that had been waiting all evening to invade the house. Outside was the dark and the rain. Without another word, not stopping to look at Eliot, I ran past him and out into it, as though to some sanctuary.

I had still to get to the garage, to struggle with doors in the darkness, to find Mollie's little car. I was convinced that Eliot was just behind me, as frightening as an imagined bogy man, waiting to jump, to catch me, to stop me from getting away. I slammed the car door shut, and my hand shook so much I could scarcely get the ignition key fitted. The first time I turned it, the engine did not start. I heard myself whimpering as I pulled out the choke and tried again. This time the engine caught. I put the car into gear and shot forward, through the darkness and the rain, up the puddled driveway with a great spattering of gravel, and so at last out and on to the road.

Driving, I regained some of my previous calm. I had eluded Eliot, I was going to Joss. I must drive with care and good sense, not allow myself to panic, not risk a skid or a possible collision. I slowed down to a cautious thirty miles per hour. I deliberately loosened my death-like clutch on the driving wheel. The road ran downhill, black and wet with rain. The lights of Porthkerris came up towards me. I was going to Joss.

Now, the tide was at full ebb. As I came out on to the harbour road, I saw the lights reflected in wet sand, the boats drawn up out of the reach of the storm. Overhead tattered scraps of cloud still poured across the sky. There were people about, but not very many.

The shop was in darkness. Only a single light glowed from the top window. I parked the car by the pavement and got out and went to the door and it opened. I smelt the new wood, my feet brushed through the shavings which still lay about the place. From the light of the street lamp outside I could see the staircase. I went up it, cautiously, to the first floor.

I called up, "Joss!"

There was no reply. I went on, up into the soft light. There was no fire and it was very cold. A squall of rain swept the roof above me.

"Joss."

He was lying on his bed, roughly covered by a blanket. His forearm lay across his eyes, as though to shut out some unbearable light. When I spoke he lowered this, and raised his head slightly to see who it was. Then he dropped back on to the pillow.

"Good God," I heard him say. "Rebecca."

I went to his side. "Yes, it's me."

"I thought I heard your voice. I thought I was dreaming."

"I called up, but you didn't reply."

His face was in a terrible mess, the left side bruised and swollen, the eye half-closed. Blood had trickled and dried from a cut in his lip, and there did not seem to be any skin on the knuckles of his right hand.

"What are you doing here?" He spoke muzzily, perhaps because of the lip.

"Mrs Kernow rang me."

"I told her not to say anything."

"She was worried about you. Joss, what happened?"

"I fell amongst thieves."

"Are you hurt anywhere else?"

"Yes, everywhere else."

"Let me see . . ."

"The Kernows bandaged me up."

But I stooped over him, gently drawing back the blanket. As far as

286

his rib-cage he was naked and below this tenderly swathed in what looked like strips torn from an old sheet. But the ugly bruising had spread up and on to his chest, and on his right side the red stain of blood had started to seep through the white cotton.

"Joss, who did this?"

But Joss did not answer me. Instead, with a strength surprising in one so hurt, he put up an arm and pulled me down so that I was sitting on the edge of his bed. My long, blonde plait of hair hung forward over my shoulder, and while he held me with his right arm, his left hand was occupied in slipping off the rubber band which held the ends together, and then, using his fingers like a comb, he loosened the strands, unravelling them, so that my hair hung like a silken tassel, brushing on to his naked chest.

He said, "I always wanted to do that. Ever since I first saw you looking like the head girl of . . . what was it I said?"

"The head girl of a nicely run orphanage."

"That's it. Fancy you remembering."

"What can I do? There must be something I can do?"

"Just stay. Just stay, my darling girl."

The tenderness in his voice . . . Joss, who had always been so tough . . . dissolved me. Tears sprang into my eyes and he saw these and pulled me down, so that I lay against him, and I felt his hand slip up beneath my hair and close around the back of my neck.

"Joss, I'll hurt you . . ."

"Don't talk," he said, as his seeking mouth found mine. And then, "I've always wanted to do this, too."

It was evident that none of his infirmities, his bruises, his bleeding, his cut lip, were to deter him in any way from getting exactly what he wanted.

And I, who had always imagined that loving was something to do with fireworks and explosions of emotion, discovered that it was not like that at all. It was warm, like sudden sunshine. It had nothing to do with my mother and the endless procession of men who had invaded her life. It was cynicism and preconceived ideas flying out of an open window. It was the last of my defences gone. It was Joss.

He said my name and he made it sound beautiful.

Much later, I lit a fire, piling on the driftwood so that the room was bright with flickering firelight. I would not let Joss move, so that he lay with his dark head propped on his arms, and I felt his eyes following every move I made.

I stood up, away from the fire. My hair fell loose on either side of my face, and my cheeks were warm from the fire. I felt soft with content.

Joss said, "We have to talk, don't we?"

"Yes."

"Get me a drink."

"What do you want?"

"Some whisky. It's in the galley, in the cupboard over the sink."

I went to find it, and two glasses. "Soda or water?"

"Soda. There's a bottle-opener hanging on a hook."

I found the opener and took the cap off the bottle. I did this clumsily and it fell to the floor, rolling in the maddening manner of such things into a dark corner. I went to retrieve it and my eye was caught by another small and shining object, lying half under the kickboard beneath the sink. I picked it up and it was Andrea's Celtic cross, the one that she had worn on a leather thong around her neck.

I kept it in my hand. I poured the drinks and took them back to Joss. I handed him one, and knelt on the floor beside him.

I said, "This was under the sink," and showed him the cross.

His swollen eye made it difficult for him to focus. He squinted at it painfully.

"What the hell's that?"

"It's Andrea's."

He said, "Oh, to hell." And then, "Get me some more pillows, there's a good girl. I could never drink whisky lying down."

I gathered up a couple of cushions off the floor, and propped him against them. The action of sitting up was agony for him and he let out an involuntary groan.

"Are you all right?"

"Yes, of course I'm all right. Where did you find that thing?"

"I told you. On the floor."

"She came here this evening. She said she'd been to the cinema. I was working downstairs, trying to get the shelving finished. I told her I was busy, but she just came up here, as though I'd never said a word. I followed her up and told her to go home. But she wouldn't go. She said she wanted a drink, she wanted to talk . . . you know the sort of drivel."

"She's been here before."

"Yes, once. One morning. I was sorry for her and I gave her a cup of coffee. But this evening I was busy; I had no time for her and I wasn't sorry for her. I said I didn't want a drink. I told her to go home. And then she said that she didn't want to go home, everybody hated her, nobody would talk to her, I was the only person she could talk to, I was the only person who understood."

"Perhaps you were."

"OK, so I was sorry for her. I used to let her come and get in my way when I was working at Boscarva, because there wasn't much else I could do about it, short of bodily throwing her out of the room."

"Did you do that this evening? Throw her out?"

"Not in so many words. But finally I'd had enough of her batty conversation and her totally unfounded belief that I was ready, willing and eager to jump into bed with her, and I lost my temper and told her so."

"What happened then?"

"What didn't happen? Screams, tears, accusations, routine hysteria. I was subjected to every sort of vilification. Face slapping, the lot. That was when I finally resorted to force, and I bundled her down the stairs and threw her raincoat and her beastly handbag after her."

"You didn't hurt her?"

"No, I didn't hurt her. But I think I frightened her, because she went then, like the hammers of hell. I heard her clattering down the stairs on those ghastly clogs she wears, and then I think she must have slipped because there was the most frightful thumping and bumping as she went down the last few stairs. I shouted down to make sure she was all right, but then I heard her running out of the shop and slamming the door behind her, so that I imagined she was."

"Could she have hit herself on anything? Bruised her face when she fell?"

"Yes, I suppose she could. There was a packing case full of china standing at the bottom of the stairs. She could have collided with that . . . Why do you ask anyway?"

I told him. When I had finished he let out a long, incredulous whistle. But he was angry too.

"The little bitch. I think she's a nymphomaniac, do you know that?"

"I've always thought so."

"She was always talking about some guy called Danus, going into the most gruesome of intimate details. And the bloody cheek of telling everyone that I had asked her to go to the cinema with me. I wouldn't ask her to empty a dustbin with me . . . What's happened to her now?"

"She's been put to bed. Mollie got the doctor."

"If he's worth his salt he'll have diagnosed self-induced hysteria. And he'll prescribe a good walloping and send her back to London. And that'll get her out of everybody's way."

"Poor Andrea. She's very unhappy."

As though he could not keep his hands off it, he reached out to touch my hair. I turned my head and kissed the back of his hand, the lacerated knuckles.

He said, "You didn't believe her, did you?"

"Not really."

"Did anyone else?"

"Mollie and Eliot did. Eliot wanted to call the police but Grenville wouldn't let him."

"That's interesting."

"Why?"

"Who was it who brought Andrea home?"

"I thought I'd told you. Morris Tatcombe . . . you know, the boy who works for Eliot . . ."

"Morris? Well I'll be . . ." He stopped in mid-sentence, and then said again, "Morris Tatcombe."

"What about him?"

"Oh, Rebecca, come along. Pull yourself together. Use your wits. Who do you think gave me this beating?"

"Not Morris." I did not want to believe it.

"Morris and three others. I went along to The Anchor for a glass of beer and a pie for my supper, and when I was walking home, they jumped me."

"You knew it was Morris?"

"Who else would it be? He's always had this grudge going for me ever since we last crossed swords and he ended up on his backside in the gutter. I thought his putting the boot in this time was just a continuation of our running feud. But it seems that it wasn't."

Without thinking I began to say, "Eliot . . ." and then stopped, but it was too late. Joss said quietly, "What about Eliot?"

"I don't want to talk about Eliot."

"Did he tell Morris to come after me?"

"I don't know."

"He could, you know. He hates my guts. It fits."

"I . . . I think he's jealous of you. He doesn't like your being so close to Grenville. He doesn't like Grenville being so fond of you. And . . ." I looked down at my drink, turning the glass in my hand, feeling suddenly nervous. "There's something else."

290

"From your expression one would think you'd murdered some-body. What is it?"

"It's . . . the desk. The desk downstairs in your workroom. I saw it this morning, when you were telephoning."

"I wondered why you'd suddenly gone cantering out into the rain. What about it?"

"The desk and the Chippendale chair. They come from Boscarva."

"Yes, I know."

His calmness shocked me. "You didn't *take* them, Joss?"

"*Take them?* No, I didn't take them. I bought them."

"Who from?"

"A man who runs an antique shop up beyond Fourbourne. I'd been to a sale about a month ago, and I dropped in to see him on the way back, and I saw the chair and the desk in his shop. By then I knew all Grenville's furniture and I knew they'd come from Boscarva."

"But who took them?"

"I regret to have to shatter your innocence, but it was your cousin Eliot."

"But Eliot knew nothing about them."

"Eliot most certainly did. They were in one of the attics, as far as I remember, and he probably imagined they'd never be missed."

"But why . . . ?"

"This is like playing the truth game. Because Eliot, my love, my darling child, is head over heels in debt. That garage was financed by Ernest Padlow in the first place, it cost a bomb and it's been losing money steadily for the past twelve months. God knows what use fifty pounds would have been to Eliot, a mere drop in the ocean one would have thought, but perhaps he needed a little ready cash to pay a bill or put on a horse or something . . . I don't know. Between you and me, I don't think he should be running his own business. He'd be better working for some other guy, being paid a regular salary. Perhaps, one evening, when you're sitting over drinks at Boscarva, you could try and persuade him."

"Sarcasm doesn't suit you."

"I know, but Eliot makes me edgy. Always has done."

I felt, obscurely, that I must stand up for Eliot, make excuses for him.

"In a way, he thinks that Boscarva and everything in it already belong to him. Perhaps he didn't feel it was . . . stealing . . . ?"

"When did they realize the things were missing?"

291

"A couple of days ago. You see, the desk belonged to my mother. Now it belongs to me. That's why we started to look for it."

"Unfortunate for Eliot."

"Yes."

"I suppose Eliot said I'd taken them."

"Yes," I admitted miserably.

"What did Grenville say?"

"He said that you'd never do a thing like that."

"And so there was another monumental row."

"Yes."

Joss sighed deeply. We fell silent. The room was growing cold again, the fire beginning to die down. I got up and went to put another log on it, but Joss stopped me.

"Leave it," he said.

I looked at him, surprised. He finished his drink and put the empty glass down on the floor beside him, and then pushed back the blanket and began, carefully, to get out of bed.

"Joss, you mustn't . . ."

I flew to his side, but he pushed me away, and slowly, with infinite caution, got to his feet. Once there, he grinned triumphantly down at me, a bizarre sight, bruised and battered, and dressed in bandages and a crumpled pair of jeans.

"Into battle," he said.

"Joss, what are you going to do?"

"If you'll find me a shirt and a pair of shoes, I'll get dressed. And then we're going to go downstairs, and get into the truck and drive back to Boscarva."

"But you can't drive like that."

"I can do anything I want," he told me, and I believed him. "Now find my clothes and stop arguing."

He would not even let me take Mollie's car. "We'll leave it there, it'll be all right. Someone can fetch it in the morning." His own little truck was parked around the corner, up a narrow alley. We got in, and he started the engine and backed out on to the road, with me giving directions because he was too stiff to turn around in the seat. We headed up through the town, along streets that had become familiar to me, over the cross-roads and up the hill.

I sat, staring ahead, with my hands clasped tightly in my lap. I knew that there was still something else we had to talk about. And it had to be now, before we reached Boscarva.

For some reason, as though he were immensely pleased with life in general, Joss has started to sing.

> *"The first time ever I saw your face*
> *I thought the sun rose in your eyes*
> *And the moon and stars . . ."*

"Joss."

"What is it now?"

"There's something else."

He sounded shocked. "Not another skeleton in the cupboard?"

"Don't joke."

"I'm sorry. What is it?"

I swallowed a strange obstruction in the back of my throat.

"It's Sophia."

"What about Sophia?"

"Grenville gave me the key of the studio so that I could go and choose a picture to take back to London. I found a portrait of Sophia. A proper one, with a face. And Eliot came to find me, and he saw it too."

There was a long silence. I looked at Joss but his profile was stony, intent on the road ahead. "I see," he said at last.

"She looks just like you; or you look just like her."

"Naturally enough. She was my grandmother."

"Yes, I thought that was probably it."

"So the portrait was in the studio?"

"Is . . . is that why you came to live in Porthkerris?"

"Yes. Grenville and my father fixed it between them. Grenville put up half the capital for my shop."

"Your father . . . ?"

"You've met him. Tristram Nolan Gardner. He runs an antique shop, in the New Kings Road. You bought a pair of balloon-back chairs from him. Do you remember?"

"And he found from my cheque that I was called Rebecca Bayliss."

"Right. And he found out, by cunning question and answer, that you were Grenville Bayliss's granddaughter. Right. And he found out that you were catching the train to Cornwall last Monday. Right."

"So he rang you up and told you to meet the train."

"Right."

"But why?"

293

"Because he felt involved. Because he thought you seemed lost and vulnerable. Because he wanted me to keep an eye on you."

"I still don't understand."

"You know something?" said Joss. "I love you very much."

"Because I'm being stupid?"

"No, because you're being marvellously innocent. Sophia wasn't only Grenville's model, she was his mistress as well. My father was born at the beginning of their relationship, long before your mother arrived. Sophia married, eventually, an old friend she'd known from childhood days, but she never had any more children."

"So Tristram . . . ?"

"Tristram is Grenville's son. And Grenville is my grandfather. And I am going to marry my half-cousin."

"Pettifer told me that Sophia meant nothing to Grenville. That she was just a girl who'd worked for him."

"If it meant protecting Grenville, Pettifer would swear that black is white."

"Yes, I suppose he would." But Grenville, in anger, had been less discreet. " 'You are not my only grandchild!' "

"Did Grenville say that?"

"Yes, to Eliot. And Eliot thought he meant me."

We had reached the top of the hill. The lights of the town were far behind us. Ahead, beyond the huddled shapes of Ernest Padlow's housing estate, lay the dark coastline, pricked with the tiny lights of random farms, and beyond it the black immensity of the sea.

I said, "I don't seem to remember you asking me to marry you."

The little van bumped and lurched down the lane towards Boscarva. "I'm not very good at asking things," said Joss. He took his hand off the wheel and put it over mine. "I usually just tell people."

As once before, it was Pettifer who came out to meet us. As soon as Joss switched off the engine of the van, the light in the hall went on, and Pettifer opened the door, as though he had known instinctively we were on our way.

He saw Joss open the car door and ease himself out, in obvious discomfort and pain. He saw Joss's face . . .

"For heaven's sake, what happened to you?"

"I had a difference of opinion with our old friend Morris Tatcombe. I probably wouldn't look like this except that he had three of his chums with him."

"Are you all right?"

"Yes, I'm fine. No bones broken. Come on, let's go in."

We went indoors and Pettifer closed the door.

"I'm glad to see you, Joss, and that's the truth. We've had a proper how-do-you-do here and no mistake."

"Is Grenville all right?"

"Yes, he's all right. He's still up, in the drawing room, waiting for Rebecca to come home."

"And Eliot?"

Pettifer looked from Joss's face to mine.

"He's gone."

Joss said, "You'd better tell us about it."

We ended up in the kitchen, around the table.

"After Rebecca had gone, Eliot went down to the studio and came back with that portrait of Sophia. The one we looked for, Joss. The one we never found."

I said, "I don't understand."

Joss explained. "Pettifer knew Sophia was my grandmother, but no one else did. No one else remembered her. It was all too long ago. Grenville wanted it to stay that way."

"But why was there only one picture of Sophia with a face? There must have been dozens Grenville painted of her. What happened to all of them?"

There was a pause while Joss and Pettifer looked at each other. Then it was Pettifer's turn to explain, which he did with much tact.

"It was old Mrs Bayliss. She was jealous of Sophia . . . not because she had any notion of the truth . . . but because Sophia was part of the Commander's other life, the life Mrs Bayliss didn't have no time for."

"You mean his painting."

"She would never have anything to do with Sophia, more than a frosty good morning if she happened to meet her in the town. And the Commander knew this, and he didn't want to upset her, so he let all the pictures of Sophia go . . . all except for the one you found. We knew it was somewhere around. Joss and I spent a day looking for it, but we never turned it up."

"What were you going to do with it if you found it?"

"Nothing. We just didn't want anyone else to find it."

"I don't see why it was so important."

Joss said, "Grenville didn't want anyone to know about what happened between him and Sophia. It wasn't that he was ashamed of it, because he'd loved her very much. And after he's dead, it won't matter any longer, he doesn't give a damn who knows then. But he's proud, and he's lived his life according to a certain set of standards. We probably think they're old-fashioned, but they're still his own. Does that make sense to you?"

"I suppose so."

"Young people now," said Pettifer heavily, "talk about a permissive society as though it were something they'd invented. But it's not new. It's been going on since the beginning of time, only in the Commander's day it was handled with a little more discretion."

We accepted this meekly. Then Joss said, "We seem to have gone off at a tangent. Pettifer was telling us about Eliot."

Pettifer collected himself. "Yes, well. So down to the drawing room Eliot went, and stormed in, with me behind him, went straight to the mantelpiece, and dumped it up there, alongside the other picture. The Commander never said a word, just watched him. And Eliot said, 'What's that got to do with Joss Gardner?' Then the Commander told him. Told him everything. Very quiet and very dignified. And Mrs Roger was there too, and she just about threw a fit. She said all these years the Commander had deceived them, letting Eliot believe that he was his only grandson, and he'd get Boscarva when the Commander died. The Commander said he'd never said anything of the sort, that it was all surmise, that they'd simply been counting their chickens before they were hatched. Then Eliot said, very cold, 'Perhaps now we can know what your plans are?' but the Commander said that his plans were his own business, and *quite right* he was too."

This little bit of championship was accompanied by Pettifer's fist coming down with a thump on the kitchen table.

"So what did Eliot do?"

"Eliot said in that case he was going to wash his hands of the whole lot of us . . . meaning the family, of course . . . and that he had plans of his own and he was thankful to be shed of us. And with that he collected a few papers and a brief-case and put on his coat and whistled up his dog and walked out of the house. Heard his car go up the lane and that was the end of him."

"Where's he gone?"

"To High Cross, I suppose."

"And Mollie?"

"She was in tears . . . trying to stop him doing anything stupid, she said. Begging him to stay. Turning on the Commander, saying it was all his fault. But of course, there wasn't anything she could do to stop Eliot. There's nothing you can do to stop a grown man walking out of the house, not even if you do happen to be his mother."

I was torn with sorrow and sympathy for Mollie.

"Where is she now?"

"Up in her room." He added gruffly, "I made her a little tea tray, took it up to her, found her sitting at her dressing-table like something carved out of stone."

I was glad I had not been here. It all sounded very dramatic. I stood up. Poor Mollie. "I'll go up and talk to her."

"And I—" said Joss—"will go and see Grenville."

"Tell him I'll be there in a moment or two."

Joss smiled. "We'll wait," he promised.

I found Mollie, white-faced and tear-stained, still sitting in front of her frilled dressing-table. (This was in character. Even the deepest excesses of grief would not cause Mollie to fling herself across any bed. It might crease the covers.) As I came into the room, she looked up, and her reflection was caught three times over in her triple mirror; for the first time ever, I thought that she looked her age.

I said, "Are you all right?"

She looked down, balling a sodden handkerchief in her fingers. I went to her side. "Pettifer told me. I'm so very sorry."

"It's all so desperately unfair. Grenville's always disliked Eliot, resented him in some extraordinary way. And of course, now we know why. He was always trying to run Eliot's life, come between Eliot and me. Whatever I did for Eliot was always wrong."

I knelt beside her, and put my arm around her, "I really believe he meant it for the best. Can't you try to believe that too?"

"I don't even know where he's gone. He wouldn't tell me. He never said goodbye."

I realized that she was a great deal more worried about Eliot's abrupt departure than she was about the evening's revelations concerning Joss. This was just as well. I could comfort her about Eliot. There was not a mortal thing I could do about Joss.

"I think," I said, "that Eliot may have gone to Birmingham."

She looked at me in horror. *"Birmingham?"*

"There was a man there who wanted to give him a job. Eliot told me. It was to do with second-hand cars. He seemed to think that it might be quite interesting."

"But I can't go and live in *Birmingham.*"

"Oh, Mollie, you don't have to. Eliot can live on his own. Let him go. Give him the chance of making something of his life."

"But we've always been together."

"Then perhaps it's time to start living apart. You've got your house at High Cross, your garden up there, your friends . . ."

"I can't leave Boscarva. I can't leave Andrea. I can't leave Grenville."

"Yes, you can. And I think Andrea should go back to London, to her own parents. You've done all you can for her, and she's miserable here. That's why all this happened, because she was unhappy and lonely. And as for Grenville, I'll stay with him."

I came downstairs at last, carrying the tea tray. I took it into the kitchen and put it on the table. Pettifer, sitting there, looked up at me over the edge of his evening paper.

"How is she?" he asked.

"All right now. She's agreed that Andrea should go home, back to London. And then she's going back to High Cross."

"That's what she's always wanted. And you?"

"I'm staying here. If that's all right with you."

A chill gleam of satisfaction crossed Pettifer's face, the nearest he could get to a look of delight. There was no need for me to say more. We understood each other.

Pettifer turned his paper. "They're in the drawing room—" he told me—"waiting for you," and he settled down to the racing page.

I went and found them, backed by the two portraits of Sophia in her white dress, Joss standing by the fire, and Grenville deep in his chair. They both looked up as I came in, the long-legged young man with his villainous black eye, and the old one, too tired to pull himself to his feet. I went towards them, the two people I loved most.

Under Gemini

I

ISOBEL

He stood at the window, with his back to her, framed by the faded curtains which she had chosen forty years before. The sun had bleached their bright roses to a faded pink, and the linings were so threadbare that they could no longer be sent to the cleaners for fear of total disintegration. But she loved their familiarity like that of old friends. For years her daughter Isobel had been trying to persuade her to buy new ones, but "They'll see me out," Tuppy had said, without thinking very much about it. "They'll see me out."

And now it seemed that they were going to do just that. She was seventy-seven and, after a lifetime of unblemished health, had gardened too late and too long, and had caught a chill which turned into pneumonia. She didn't remember very much about the pneumonia—only that when she emerged from what felt like a long dark tunnel of sheer discomfort, the doctor was calling three times a day and there was a nurse installed to take care of Tuppy. The nurse, a widow from Fort William, was

307

called Mrs. McLeod. She was tall and thin, with a face like a reliable horse, and wore navy blue uniforms with a starched bib to her apron that made her flat chest look like a slab, and shoes that went on forever. Her unprepossessing appearance notwithstanding, she was very kind.

So now the business of dying was no longer a remote and unconsidered possibility, but a cold and immediate fact.

It did not frighten her in the very least, but it was inconvenient. Her thoughts slid, as they so easily did these days, back into the past, and she remembered herself as a young wife, twenty years old, realizing that for the first time she was pregnant. And she had been annoyed and frustrated because it meant that by December she would be round and large as the Albert Hall and unable to go to any of the Christmas dances, and her mother-in-law had comforted her briskly by saying, "There is never a convenient time to have a baby." Perhaps dying was like that, too. You just had to take it when it came.

It had been a brilliant morning, but now the sun had gone in and a cold light filled the window beyond the doctor's bulk. "Is it going to rain?" Tuppy asked.

"More like a sea mist," he told her. "You can't see the Islands. Eigg disappeared about half an hour ago."

She looked at him, a big man, solid as a rock, comforting in his well-worn tweeds, standing there with his hands in his pockets as though he had nothing more urgent to do. He was a good doctor, as good as his father had been, though at first it was disconcerting to be taken care of and ordered about by someone you had known as a small sturdy boy in shorts, with his knees covered with grazes and sand in his hair.

Now, as he stood in the light she noticed with a pang that that hair was beginning to gray, just at the temples. This made her feel older than anything, even the thought of dying.

"You're going gray," she told him with some asperity, as though he had no right to take such liberties.

He turned, smiling ruefully, putting up a hand to his head.

"I know. The barber pointed it out the other day."

"How old are you?"

"Thirty-six."

"Just a boy. You shouldn't be going gray."

"Perhaps it's the wear and tear of looking after you."

He wore, beneath the tweed jacket of his suit, a knitted pullover. It was becoming unraveled at the neck, and there was a hole in the front in need of mending. Tuppy's heart bled for him. He was uncared-for, unloved. And he shouldn't be here at all, buried in the West Highlands, tending to the day-to-day ailments of a community of herring fishers and a handful of scattered crofters. He should be in London or Edinburgh, with a tall important house and a Bentley at the pavement, and a specialist's plate on the door. He should be teaching or doing research—writing papers and making medical history.

He had been a brilliant student, marvelously enthusiastic and ambitious, and they had all known that ahead of him lay a glittering career. But then he had met that silly girl in London; Tuppy could scarcely remember her name. Diana. He had brought her back to Tarbole and nobody could stand her, but all the objections his father had raised merely stiffened his determination to marry her. (That was in character. Hugh had always been stubborn as a mule and opposition only made him more so. His parent should have recognized this. He handled it all wrong, thought Tuppy, and if old Dr. Kyle had been alive now and available, she would have told him so, mincing no words.)

The misalliance had finally culminated in tragedy, and when it was all over, he had picked up the pieces of his shattered life and come home to Tarbole to take over from his father.

Now he lived alone, like any cheerless, aging bachelor. He was working too hard, and Tuppy knew that he took a good deal less care of himself than he did of his patients, and that more often than not, his supper was a glass of whisky and a pie from the local pub.

She said, "Why doesn't Jessie MacKenzie mend that jersey for you?"

"I don't know. Perhaps I forgot to ask her."

"You should get married again."

As though deliberately changing the subject, he came back to her bedside. At once the small curled-up ball of fur at the end of Tuppy's bed resolved itself into an elderly Yorkshire terrier, rearing up from the eiderdown like a cobra and growling ferociously with a great show of teeth sadly depleted by age.

"Sukey!" Tuppy reproved, but the doctor was undismayed.

"It wouldn't be Sukey if she didn't threaten to tear my throat out every time I came near you." He put out a friendly hand, and the growls rose in a tremendous crescendo. He stooped to pick up his bag. "I must go."

"Who are you going to see now?"

"Mrs. Cooper. And then Anna Stoddart."

"Anna? What's wrong with Anna?"

"Nothing's wrong with Anna. In fact, all is right with Anna. To break a professional confidence, she's going to have a baby."

"*Anna* is? After all this time?" Tuppy was delighted.

"I thought that would cheer you up. But don't say anything about it. She wants to keep it a secret, for the time being at any rate."

"I won't breathe a word. How is she?"

"Fine so far. Not even sick in the mornings."

"I'll keep my fingers crossed for her. Oh, she must keep this child. You'll take good care of her, won't you? What a silly question, of course you will. Oh, I *am* pleased."

"Now. Is there anything else you want?"

She eyed him and the hole in his sweater, and her thoughts moved naturally from babies to weddings, and so, inevitably, to her grandson Antony. She said, "I'll tell you what I want. I want Antony to bring Rose to see me."

". . . Is there any reason why he shouldn't?"

His hesitation in replying was so slight that Tuppy told herself she had imagined it. She sent him a sharp glance, but he did not meet it, being occupied with the balky fastening of his bag.

"It's a month now since they got engaged," she went on.

310

"And I want to see her again. It's five years since she and her mother stayed at the Beach House, and you know, I can scarcely remember what she looks like."

"I thought she was in America."

"Oh, she was. She went out after they got engaged. But Antony led me to believe that she'd be back in this country by now. He said he'd bring her up to Scotland, but that's about as far as it's got. And I want to know when they intend getting married, and where. There's such a lot to discuss and settle, and every time I ring Antony up he just sits there in Edinburgh and makes soothing noises. I hate being soothed. I find it very irritating."

He smiled. "I'll speak to Isobel about it," he promised.

"Get her to give you a glass of sherry."

"I told you, I have to go and see Mrs. Cooper." Mrs. Cooper was the Tarbole postmistress and a strict teetotaler. "She's got a low enough opinion of me anyway, without my breathing alcoholic fumes all over her."

"Stupid woman," said Tuppy. They smiled, in complete accord, and he went away and left her, closing the door behind him. Sukey crept up the bed and curled herself into the curve of Tuppy's arm. The window sash rattled slightly as, outside, a wind got up. She looked at the window and saw the misting of rain on the pane. It would soon be lunchtime. She slipped down on the pillows and drifted, as she so easily did these days, back into the past.

Seventy-seven. What had happened to the years? Old age seemed to have taken her unaware and totally unprepared. Tuppy Armstrong was not old. Other people were old, like one's own grandmother, or characters in books. She thought of Lucilla Eliot, in *The Herb of Grace*. The epitome, one would have thought, of a perfect matriarch.

But Tuppy had never liked Lucilla. She thought her possessive and domineering. And she abhorred the snobbery of Lucilla's beautifully cut black frocks. Tuppy had not owned a beautifully cut black frock in the whole of her life. A lot of pretty dresses, certainly, but never a beautifully cut black frock.

311

Most of the time she existed contentedly in antique tweed skirts and cardigans with darns in the elbows: sturdy, indestructible clothes which did not object to a spot of rose pruning or a sudden shower of rain.

And yet, on the appropriate occasion there was nothing like the old blue velvet dinner dress for making one feel rich and feminine. Especially if you splashed some eau de cologne around and jammed the old-fashioned diamond rings over the arthriticky joints of your fingers. Perhaps when Antony brought Rose they would have a dinner party. Nothing elaborate. Just a few friends. She imagined the white Irish linen mats and the silver candlesticks and a centerpiece of creamy Peace roses.

An enthusiastic hostess, she began to plan. And if Antony and Rose were to be formally married, then a list must be made of guests to be asked on the Armstrong side of the family. Perhaps Tuppy should do that now and give it to Isobel, so that Isobel should know who to ask. Just in case . . .

Suddenly, it didn't bear thinking about. She drew Sukey's little body tightly to hers and kissed the top of the bedraggled, slightly smelly head. Sukey aimed a cursory lick in her direction and went back to sleep. Tuppy closed her eyes.

Descending, Dr. Hugh Kyle reached the turn of the stairs and there stopped, his hand on the banister. He was troubled. Not solely for Tuppy, but also on account of the conversation he had just had with her. As he stood there, a preoccupied, solitary figure neither upstairs nor down, his anxieties and responsibilities were mirrored on his frowning face.

Below him the big hall stood empty. At the far side, glass doors gave onto the terrace, the sloping garden, and the sea, all drowned now in mist. He saw the polished floors, the worn rugs, the old chest with its copper bowl of dahlias, the slowly ticking grandfather clock. There were as well other, less picturesque bits of evidence of Armstrong family life: Jason's battered tricycle, pulled in out of the rain; the dogs' baskets and their drinking bowls; a pair of muddy gumboots, abandoned until

312

such time as their owner remembered to put them away in the cloakroom. To Hugh, it was all familiar from the beginning of time, for he had known Fernrigg all his life. But now it seemed as though the very house was waiting and watching for news of Tuppy.

There did not seem to be anybody about, although this was not surprising. Jason was at school; Mrs. Watty would be in the kitchen, busy with lunch. Isobel—he wondered where he would find Isobel.

Just as the question entered his mind, he heard her footsteps coming across the drawing room floor, and the scratch of Plummer's paws on the patches of parquet between the rugs. The next moment she appeared through the open door, with the fat old spaniel hard on her heels.

She saw Hugh at once, and stopped dead, tilting back her head to look up at him. They stared at each other and then, recognizing his own anxieties reflected in her eyes, he hastily pulled himself together, rearranging his features into an expression of robust cheerfulness.

"Isobel, I was wondering where I'd find you."

She said, in no more than a whisper, "Tuppy?"

"Not too bad." Swinging his bag, his other hand in his trouser packet, he came downstairs.

"I thought . . . When I saw you standing there . . . I thought . . ."

"I'm sorry, I was thinking about something else. I didn't mean to give you a fright. . . ."

She was unconvinced, but she tried to smile. She was fifty-four, the gawky stay-at-home daughter who had never married, instead spilling the intensity of her affection onto her mother, the house, the garden, her friends, her dog, her nephews, and now Jason, the little great-nephew who had come to live at Fernrigg House while his parents were abroad. Her hair, which had been flaming red when she was a girl, was now sandy and streaked with white, but the style had not changed as long as Hugh could remember. Nor had the expression on her face, still child-like and innocent, perhaps on account of the sheltered life

313

she had led. Her eyes were blue as a child's and sensitive as the sky on a squally day, reflecting every emotion like a mirror: shining with pleasure, or brimming with the tears over which she had never had any control.

Now, looking up at him, they were filled with anguish, and it was obvious that Hugh's hearty manner had done nothing to reassure her.

"Is she . . . is she going to . . . ?" Her lips could not, would not, frame the dreaded word. He put a hand beneath her elbow and ushered her firmly back into the drawing room and shut the door behind them.

"She may die, yes," he told her. "She's not a young woman and she's taken a battering. But she's tough. Like an old heather root. She has a good chance of pulling through."

"I can't bear the thought of her being an invalid—not being able to get about and do all the things she wants to do. She would hate it so much."

"Yes, I know. I do know."

"What can we do?"

"Well . . ." He cleared his throat, running a hand down the back of his neck. "There is one thing which I think would cheer her up, and that would be for Antony to come over and perhaps bring that girl he's engaged to . . ."

Isobel rounded on him. She, too, could remember him as a little boy, and sometimes a very tiresome one. "Hugh, don't call her 'that girl' in that horrid way. She's Rose Schuster and you know her as well as we all do. Not that that's very well, I admit, but at least you do know her."

"I'm sorry." Isobel was always fiercely protective of any person even remotely connected with the family. "Rose, then. I think Tuppy's longing to see her again."

"We all are, but she's been with her mother in America. The trip was all planned before she and Antony got engaged."

"Yes, I know, but she may be back by now. And Tuppy's fretting about it. Perhaps Antony could be nudged a little, persuaded to get Rose north and bring her over, even if it's only for a weekend."

314

"He always seems to be so *busy*."

"I'm sure if you explained the situation. . . . Tell him that perhaps it would be better not to put it off too long."

As he feared, Isobel's eyes became instantly bright with tears. "You *do* think she's going to die." Already she was fumbling up her sleeve for a handkerchief.

"Isobel, I didn't say that. But you know how Tuppy is about Antony. He's more of a son than a grandchild. You can see how much it means to her."

"Yes. Yes, I do see." Bravely Isobel blew her nose and stowed away her handkerchief. Searching for some diversion, her eyes alighted on the sherry decanter. "Have a drink."

He laughed, easing the tension. "No, I won't, thank you. I'm going to see Mrs. Cooper. She's got palpitations again, and they'll worsen if she thinks I've been drinking."

Isobel smiled, too, despite herself. Mrs. Cooper had always been something of a family joke. Together they went out of the room and across the hall. Isobel opened the front door onto the chill of the damp, mist-shrouded morning. The doctor's car, parked at the foot of the steps, was wet with rain.

He said, "And promise to ring me if you're the least bit worried."

"I will. But with Nurse here, I know I won't worry so much."

It was Hugh who had insisted that they get a nurse. Otherwise, he said, Tuppy must go into a hospital. On being faced with the daunting prospect of a resident nurse, Isobel's mind had shot off at panicky tangents. Tuppy must be very ill; and where would they find a nurse? And would Mrs. Watty raise objections? And would there be umbrage taken and bad feeling in the kitchen?

But Hugh had seen to it all. Mrs. Watty and Nurse had made friends, and Isobel was able to sleep at nights. He was, in truth, a tower of strength. Seeing him off Isobel asked herself, perhaps for the hundredth time, what they would all do without him. She watched him get into his car and drive away, down the short drive between the sodden rhododendrons, past

315

the lodge where the Wattys lived, and through the white gates which were never closed. She waited until he had gone. The tide was at the flood, and she could hear the gray waves breaking against the rocks below the garden.

She shivered, and returned indoors to phone Antony.

The telephone in the old-fashioned house stood in the hall. Isobel sat on the chest, and looked up the number of Antony's office in Edinburgh. She could never remember telephone numbers and had to look up even the most day-to-day people, like the grocer, and the man at the railway station. With one eye on the book, she dialed carefully and sat waiting for someone to reply. Her thoughts, anxious, darted in all directions: the dahlias would be dead tomorrow; she must pick some more; would Antony have already gone out for lunch? She mustn't be selfish about Tuppy. There was a time for everybody to die. If she could no longer work in her precious garden nor take Sukey for little walks, then she would not want to live. But what an unbearable void she would leave in all their lives! Despite herself, Isobel prayed wildly. *Don't let her die. Don't let us lose her just yet. Oh, God, be merciful unto us . . .*

"McKinnon, Carstairs, and Robb. Can I help you?"

She was jerked back to reality by the bright young voice. Feeling for her handkerchief again, she wiped her eyes and composed herself. "Oh, I am sorry, I wondered if it would be possible to speak to Mr. Armstrong. Mr. Antony Armstrong."

"Who's speaking, please?"

"Miss Armstrong. His aunt."

"Just a moment."

There came a couple of clicks, a pause, and then, wonderfully, Antony's voice. "Aunt Isobel."

"Oh, Antony . . ."

He was immediately alert. "Is anything wrong?"

"No. No, not wrong." She mustn't give a false impression. She must pull herself together. "Hugh Kyle's been. He's just left."

"Is Tuppy worse?" Antony asked bluntly.

"He . . . he says she's holding her own wonderfully. He

316

says she's as strong as an old heather root." She tried to make it light-hearted, but her voice let her down woefully. She could not get out of her mind that deeply grave expression that she had caught on Hugh's face. Had he really been telling her the truth? Had he been trying to spare her in some way? "He . . . he had a few words with Tuppy, though, and it seems that all she wants is to see you, and for you to bring Rose over. And I wondered if you'd heard from Rose—if she was back from America?"

There was only silence from the other end of the line, and trying to fill it, Isobel rattled on.

"I know how busy you always are, and I don't want to worry you. . . ."

"That's all right." Antony spoke at last. "Yes. Yes, she is back in London. I had a letter from her this morning."

"It means so much to Tuppy."

Another pause, and then steadily, Antony asked, "Is she going to die?"

Isobel couldn't help it. She dissolved into tears, furious with herself, but unable to check them. "I . . . I don't know. Hugh tried to reassure me, but I've never seen him look so concerned. And it would be so dreadful, unthinkable really, if anything should happen to Tuppy and she had never seen you and Rose together. It meant so much to her, your getting engaged. If you could bring Rose, perhaps it would make all the difference. It would give her a reason . . ."

She couldn't go on. She hadn't meant to say so much, and she could see nothing through the tears. She felt defeated, at the end of her tether, and as though she had been alone for too long. She blew her nose again and finished helplessly. "Do try, Antony."

It was a cry from the heart. He said, sounding almost as shaken as she did, "I didn't realize . . ."

"I think I've only just realized myself."

"I'll get hold of Rose. Somehow, I'll fix it. We'll be over next weekend. I promise."

"Oh, Antony." Relief washed over her. They would come.

317

If Antony said he would do something, he always kept his word, come hell or high water.

"And don't be too worried about Tuppy. If Hugh says she's as tough as a heather root, she probably is. She'll run rings round the lot of us, and most likely outlive us all."

Immensely comforted, Isobel raised a little laugh. "Well, it's not beyond the bounds of possibility."

"Nothing is," said Antony. "Anything can happen. See you next weekend."

"Bless you."

"Think nothing of it. And my love to Tuppy."

2

MARCIA

Ronald Waring said, perhaps for the fifth time, "We should go home."

His daughter Flora, bemused with sun and sleepy from swimming, said, "I know," also for the fifth time, and neither of them moved. She sat perched on a sloping face of granite, staring down into the jewel-blue depths of the immense rock pool in which they had had their evening swim. The sun, sliding down out of the sky, poured the last of its warmth onto her face. Her cheeks were still salty from the sea; wet hair clung to her neck. She sat with her arms wrapped around her legs, her chin on her knees, her eyes narrowed against the dazzle of the sea.

It was a Wednesday, and the last of a perfect summer's day. Or was September officially autumn? Flora couldn't remember. She only knew that in Cornwall, the summer had a charming way of spinning itself out beyond the end of the season. Down here, sheltered by the cliffs, there was no breath of

319

wind, and the rocks, soaked by a day's sunshine, were still warm to the touch.

The tide was coming in. The first trickle of water had slid between two limpet-encrusted rocks and emptied itself into the pool. Soon the trickle would swell to a flood, and the mirror surface of the water be shattered by the vanguard of the long Atlantic rollers. Finally, the rocks would become engulfed, and the pool submerged and lost until the next low tide should set it free again.

She could not remember how many times they had sat together, just as they sat now, mesmerized by the fascination of a flooding September tide. But this evening it was even more difficult to drag themselves away, because it was the last time. They would go up the cliff path, pausing from time to time as they always did, to look back at the ocean. They would take the path that led across the fields to Seal Cottage, where Marcia was waiting for them, with supper in the oven and flowers on the table. And after supper Flora would wash her hair and finish her packing, because tomorrow she was going back to London.

It had all been planned, and it was something that Flora had to do, but at this moment she could scarcely bear to contemplate the idea. For one thing, she always hated leaving her father. She looked at him where he sat on the rock a little below her. She saw his leanness, the deep tan of his skin, his long bare legs. He wore a disreputable pair of shorts and an ancient shirt, much darned, with the sleeves rolled back off his forearms. She saw his thinning hair, tousled from the swim, and the jutting jawline as he turned his head to watch a cormorant skimming by just above the surface of the sea.

She said, "I don't want to go tomorrow."

He turned to smile up at her. He said. "Then don't."

"I have to. You know that. I have to go out into the world and start being independent again. I've been home too long."

"I'd like you to stay for always."

She ignored the sudden lump in her throat. "You're not meant to say things like that. You're meant to be brisk and

320

unsentimental. You're meant to push your chick out of the nest."

"You promise me you're not going because of Marcia?"

Flora was truthful. "Yes, of course in a way I am, but that's not the point. Anyway, I adore her, you know that." When her father did not smile, she tried turning it into a joke. "All right then, she's a typical wicked stepmother, how's that for a reason? And I'm escaping before I find myself locked in a cellar with the rats."

"You can always come back. Promise me you'll come back if you can't find a job, or if things don't work out."

"I shall find a job with no difficulty whatsoever, and everything's going to work out."

"I still want the promise."

"You have it. But you'll probably regret it when I turn up on your doorstep again in a week's time. And now"—she picked up her bathing towel and a pair of threadbare espadrilles —"we should go home."

To begin with, Marcia had refused to marry Flora's father. "You can't marry me. You're the senior classics master of a reputable grammar school. You ought to marry some quiet, respectable female with a felt hat and a way with boys."

"I don't like quiet, responsible females," he had told her, slightly irritated. "If I did, I'd have married Matron years ago."

"It's just that I don't see myself as Mrs. Ronald Waring. It doesn't fit, somehow. 'And here, boys, is Mrs. Waring, to present the silver cup for the High Jump.' And there is me, falling over my feet, and forgetting what I'm meant to say, and probably dropping the cup or giving it to the wrong boy."

But Ronald Waring had always been a man who knew his own mind, and he persisted, courting and finally persuading her. They were married at the beginning of the summer, in the tiny stone church which was older than time and smelled musty, like a cave. Marcia had worn a very fetching emerald green dress and a huge straw hat with a drooping brim, like

321

Scarlett O'Hara's. And for once Ronald Waring was coordinated and all of a piece, with matching socks and his necktie firmly knotted, not slipping down to reveal the top button of his shirt. They made, thought Flora, a wonderful couple. She had taken snapshots of them as they came beaming out of the church, the brisk sea-breeze playing havoc with the brim of the bride's hat, while causing the bridegroom's thinning hair to stand up on end like the crest of a cockatoo.

Marcia was a Londoner born and bred who had somehow reached the age of forty-two without ever having been married —most likely, decided Flora, because she had never found the time. She had started her career as a drama student, graduated to wardrobe mistress with a provincial repertory company, and from that inauspicious beginning had cheerfully barged on through life, apparently ricocheting from one unexpected occupation to another, and her final job had been sales manager in a shop in Brighton which specialized in what Marcia called Arabian Tat.

Although Flora had taken to Marcia from the very first and encouraged like mad the alliance with her father, there had been certain inevitable reservations about Marcia's housewifely capabilities. After all, no girl wants to condemn her parent to a lifetime of bought pies, frozen pizza, and soup out of cans.

But even on that score Marcia succeeded in surprising them. She proved to be an excellent cook and an enthusiastic housekeeper, and was already developing all sorts of unlikely talents in the garden. Vegetables were already coming up in neat, soldierly rows; flowers bloomed if Marcia looked at them, and the deep windowsill over the kitchen sink stood two rows deep in the earthenware pots of geranium and Busy Lizzies which she had grown herself.

That evening, as they made their way up the cliffs and across the cool, long-shadowed fields, Marcia, who had been watching from the kitchen window, came to meet them. She wore green trousers and a cotton smock, heavily embroidered by some gnarled peasant hand, and the last rays of the sun lit her bright hair to a flame.

322

Ronald Waring, catching sight of her, lifted his head with pleasure and his footsteps quickened. Lagging behind, Flora decided that there was something special about two middle-aged people who shared a bond, not only of affection, but passion as well, so that when they met in the middle of the field, embracing without restraint or embarrassment, it was as though they were coming together after a separation of many months. Perhaps that was how they felt. Heaven knew, they had waited long enough for each other.

It was Marcia who drove Flora to the junction the next morning to catch the London train. The fact that she was actually able to do this was a source of great pride and satisfaction to Marcia. Because in attaining her great age, she had not only missed out on matrimony, but, as well, had never learned to drive.

When quizzed about this, she had a number of reasons to explain the omission. She was unmechanically minded, she had never owned a car, and there was usually someone around who was willing to drive her. But after she married Ronald Waring and found herself marooned in a small Cornish cottage at the end of nowhere, it was obvious that the time had come.

Now or never, said Marcia, and took lessons. Then tests. Three of them. She failed the first time because she ran the front wheels of the car over the booted toes of a constable. And the second time because, while backing the car into a tricky parking place, she inadvertently knocked over a perambulator which, fortunately, did not contain a baby at the time. Neither Flora nor her father imagined that she would have the nerve to try again, but they underestimated Marcia. She did, and finally passed. So when her husband regretted that he could not drive his daughter to catch the London train, owing to some educational conference which he was bound to attend, Marcia was able to say, with casual pride, "That's no trouble. I'll take her."

In a way, Flora was relieved. She hated goodbyes, inevitably becoming emotional at the sound of a train whistle. She knew that if her father were there, she would probably weep all

323

over him, which would make the parting all the worse for everybody.

It was another warm and cloudless day, the sky as blue as it had been all year, and the bracken gold. As well, there was a sparkle to the air which made the most mundane objects as clear-cut as crystal. Marcia, whose thought processes were comfortingly simple to follow, began to carol in her fruity contralto, "Oh, what a beautiful morning, oh, what a beautiful day . . ." and then abandoned her song and stooped down to feel for her handbag, which meant that she wanted a cigarette. The car, accordingly, weaved dangerously across the white line and over onto the wrong side of the road, so Flora said quickly, "I'll get it," and found the bag and the cigarette while Marcia got the car back on course again. Flora stuck the cigarette into Marcia's mouth, and then held the lighter so that Marcia wouldn't have to take her hands off the wheel.

The cigarette going, Marcia went on with her song.

"I've got a beautiful feeling, everything's going . . ." She stopped again, frowning. "Darling, you do promise me you're not going back to horrible London just because of me?"

This question had been asked every night at regular intervals for the last seven days. Flora took a deep breath. "No. I've told you, no. I'm simply picking up the threads of my life and carrying on where I left off a year ago."

"I can't get rid of this feeling that I'm turning you out of your own home."

"Well, you're not. And anyway, you can look at the situation from my point of view. Knowing my father has found a good woman to take care of him, I can go off and leave him with a clear conscience."

"I'd feel happier if I knew what sort of a life it was going to be. I've got a horrible preconceived pictures of you in a bedsitter, eating cold beans out of a tin."

"I've told you," said Flora robustly, "I'll find somewhere to live, and while I'm looking I'm going to stay with my friend Jane Porter. It's all been fixed. The girl who lives with her is on holiday with her boyfriend, so I can have her bed. And by the

324

time she comes back from her holiday, I shall have found myself a flat of my own and a fabulous job and I'll be home and dry." But Marcia continued to look gloomy. "Look, I'm twenty-two, not twelve. And a terribly, terribly efficient shorthand typist. There's not a thing to worry about."

"Well, if things don't work out, *promise* to call me and I'll come and mother you."

"I've never been mothered in my life and I can manage without it." Flora added, "I'm sorry. That wasn't meant to sound quite so brusque."

"Not brusque at all, darling, just plain fact. But you know, the more I think about it, the more fantastic it becomes."

"I'm not sure what you are talking about."

"Your mother. Abandoning you and your father, and you just an infant. I mean, I can imagine a woman abandoning a *husband*. At least, I can't imagine *anybody* abandoning darling Ronald—but a *baby*! It seems so completely inhuman. You'd have thought that having gone through all the business of actually *having* a child, you'd want to keep it."

"I'm glad she didn't keep me. I wouldn't have had anything different. How Pa managed, I shall never know, but I couldn't have had a more wonderful childhood."

"You know what we are, don't you? The Founding Members of the Ronald Waring Fan Club. I wonder why she went? Your mother, I mean. Was there another man? I've never liked to ask."

"No I don't think so. They were simply incompatible. That's what Pa always told me. She didn't like him being an unambitious schoolmaster, and he wasn't interested in cocktail parties and the merry life. And she didn't like his being vague and immersed in his job, and always looking as though he'd been thrown together out of a rag bag. And he obviously was never going to earn enough money to keep her in the style she fancied. I found a photograph of her once, in the back of a drawer. Very chic and elegant, and expensive-looking. Not Pa's scene at all."

325

"She must have been as hard as nails. I wonder why they got married in the first place."

"I think they met on a skiing holiday in Switzerland. Pa's a super skier—perhaps you didn't know that. I imagine they were both blinded by sun and snow, and intoxicated by heady Alpine air. Or maybe she was knocked flat by the manly figure he cut as he swooped down the mountainside. All I know is that it happened, and I was born, and then it was over."

They were on the main road now, approaching the little station where Flora was to catch the London train. "I do hope," said Marcia, "that he doesn't ask me to go skiing with him."

"Why ever not?"

"I can't," said Marcia.

"That wouldn't make any difference to Pa. He adores you, just the way you are. You know that, don't you?"

"Yes," said Marcia, "and aren't I the luckiest woman alive? But you're going to be lucky, too. You were born under Gemini, and I looked you up this morning and all the planets are moving in the right direction and you've got to Take Advantage of Opportunities." Marcia was a great one for horoscopes. "That means that within a week you're going to find a super job and a super flat, and probably a super tall dark man with a Maserati. A sort of job lot."

"Within a week? That doesn't give me much time."

"Well, it's all got to happen in a week, because next Friday you get a new horoscope."

"I'll see what I can do."

It was not a prolonged goodbye. The express stopped at the junction for no more than a moment, and no sooner were Flora and her considerable luggage on board than the stationmaster was walking down the platform, slamming doors and preparing to blow his whistle. Flora leaned out of the open window to kiss Marcia's upturned face. Marcia had tears in her eyes and her mascara had run.

"Telephone; let us know what happens."

"I will. I promise."

"And write!"

There was no time for more. The train began to move, gathering speed; the platform curved away. Flora waved, and the little station and Marcia's blue-trousered form grew smaller and then slid out of sight, and Flora, with her hair all over her face, shut the window and sat with a thump in the corner seat of the empty compartment.

She looked out of the window. That was a tradition, watching everything slip away, just as it was a tradition, when traveling in the opposite direction, to start leaning out of the window at Fourbourne in order to catch the very first glimpse of one familiar landmark after another.

Now the tide was low, the sand of the estuary a sort of pearly brown, patterned in blue where pools of slack water reflected the sky. On the far side was a village with white houses gleaming through trees, and then the dunes, and for an instant one could see the ocean out beyond the distant white breakers of the bar.

The railway curved inland, and a grassy headland swung into view while the ocean was lost behind a rash of seaside bungalows. The train rattled over a viaduct and through the next town, and then there were small green valleys and white cottages, and gardens where lines of washing bellied and flapped in the brisk morning breeze. The train thundered over a level crossing and a man waited at the closed gate with a red tractor and a trailer filled with bales of straw.

They had lived in Cornwall since Flora was five years old. Before that her father had taught Latin and French at an exclusive and expensive Sussex preparatory school, but the job, though comfortable, was not much of a challenge, and he had begun to run out of the sort of conversation acceptable to the mink-coated mothers of his well-heeled charges.

He had always had a hankering to live by the sea, having spent Easter and summer holidays in Cornwall as a boy. Thus, when the post of senior classic master at the Fourbourne Grammar School came up he promptly applied for it, much to the concern of the preparatory school headmaster, who felt that the

327

bright young man was destined for better things than pumping classics into the heads of the sons of farmers, shopkeepers, and mining engineers.

But Ronald Waring was adamant. At first he and Flora had lived in digs in Fourbourne, and her first memory of Cornwall was that small industrial town, surrounded by a bleak country of shallow hills spiked with old mine workings which stood out on the horizon like so many broken teeth.

But once they had settled down and her father had found his feet in his new job, he bought an ancient car, and on weekends father and daughter cast about for somewhere else to live.

Finally, following the directions of the estate agent's office in Penzance, they had taken the road from St. Ives out toward Lands End, and after one or two wrong turns found themselves bumping down a steep, brambly lane which led in the direction of the sea. They rounded a last corner, over a stream which ran permanently across the road, and came to Seal Cottage.

It was a bitter winter's day. The house was derelict, had no running water or sanitation and, when they finally forced the swollen old door open, appeared to have been overrun by mice. But Flora was not afraid of mice, and Ronald Waring fell in love not only with the house but also with its view. He bought it that very day, and it had been their home ever since.

At first their existence had been desperately primitive. It had been a struggle to simply keep warm and clean and fed. But Ronald Waring, besides being a classical scholar, was a gregarious man of great charm. If he went into a pub knowing nobody, he would become fast friends with at least half a dozen people by the time he left.

Thus, he found the stonemason who repaired the garden walls and rebuilt the sagging chimney. Thus, he met Mr. Pincher the carpenter, and Tom Roberts, whose nephew was a plumber with weekends to spare. Thus, he made the acquaintance of Arthur Pyper, and so of Mrs. Pyper, who bicycled in a stately fashion from the local village each day to wash the dishes, make the beds, and keep a motherly eye on Flora.

At ten years old, much to her disgust, Flora was dispatched to a boarding school in Kent where she stayed till she was sixteen. That was followed by a session learning how to be a shorthand typist, and another one learning how to be a Cordon Bleu cook.

As a cook, she took jobs in Switzerland (in the winter) and Greece (in the summer). Returning to London, she reverted to being a secretary, shared a flat with a girlfriend, waited in bus queues, shopped in her lunch hour; she went out with impoverished young men who were learning how to be chartered accountants, or slightly less impoverished young men who were opening boutiques. And in between times, she took the train up and down to Cornwall for holidays, to help with the spring cleaning, to roast the Christmas turkey.

But, at the end of last year, after a dose of flu and an unsatisfactory love affair, she had become disenchanted with the big city, homed to Cornwall for Christmas, and had needed little encouragement to stay there. It had been a wonderful, relaxed year, knowing, as the winter gave way to a particularly beautiful and early spring, and spring turned to summer, that she could stay and watch it all happening; there was no deadline; no day on the calendar when she would have to pack a suitcase and get back to the grindstone.

She did, in fact—to pass the time and earn a little money —take jobs, but they were all temporary, undemanding, and usually amusing: picking daffodils for a local market gardener; working as waitress in a coffee bar; selling caftans to summer tourists mad to spend their money.

It was in the caftan shop that she had first met Marcia and had taken her back to Seal Cottage for a drink. She had watched in delighted disbelief the instant rapport which sprang up between Marcia and her father. The rapport, it soon became obvious, was not simply a passing fancy.

Love made Marcia bloom like a rose, and Flora's father became so appearance-conscious that he actually went out and bought himself a new pair of trousers without anybody suggesting that he do so. As the relationship steadily deepened and strengthened, Flora tactfully tried to withdraw, making excuses

329

not to accompany them on their jaunts to the pub down the road and finding reasons for going out in the evening so that they could have Seal Cottage to themselves.

When they were married, she started making noises almost at once about returning to London and to work, but Marcia had persuaded her to stay on at Seal Cottage, at least for the summer. That she had done, but time was running out. It was no longer Flora's life, just as Seal Cottage was no longer her home. In September, she promised herself, she would go back to London. In September, she told Marcia, I'm leaving you two old lovebirds to yourselves.

Now, it was all over. Already it was in the past. And the future? *You're going to be lucky,* Marcia had said. *You were born under Gemini and all the planets are moving in the right direction.*

But Flora was not so sure. She took out of her coat pocket the letter which had come that morning, which she had opened and read, and then swiftly stowed away before Marcia should ask about it. It was from Jane Porter.

> 8 Mansfield Mews
> S.W.10

Darling Flora,
   The most ghastly thing has happened and I just hope this reaches you before you start out for London. Betsy, the girl I share with, has had the most ghastly row with her boyfriend, and after two days in Spain has *come home.* She's here now in the flat, weeping all over everything, and obviously waiting for the phone to ring, which it never does. So the bed I promised you isn't available, and though you'd be more than welcome to a sleeping bag on my bedroom floor, the whole atmosphere is so fraught and Betsy is so utterly impossible that I wouldn't ask my darkest enemy to share it. I do hope you can fix something just till you find a pad of your own. Terribly sorry to let you down like this, and hope you'll understand. Be sure to ring me so

330

that we can get down to a proper gossip. Longing to see
you again and I'm sorry, I'm sorry, but it wasn't my fault.
Masses of love,
Jane

Flora sighed, folded the letter, and pushed it back into her
pocket. She hadn't said anything to Marcia, because Marcia in
her new role of wife and mother had developed an alarming
tendency to fuss. Had she known that Flora was going back to
London without anywhere to lay her head, she would probably
have refused to let her go. And having made up her mind,
Flora felt that she could not bear to postpone her departure for
one more day.

Now, she applied herself to the problem of what she was
going to do. There were friends of course, but after a year, she
wasn't sure what they were doing, where they were living, nor
even who with. Her previous flatmate was now married and
living in Northumberland, and there was nobody else Flora felt
she could telephone out of the blue, to plead for temporary
accommodation.

It was a vicious circle. She didn't want to take a flat until
she'd found a job, but it would be difficult to do the rounds of
the agents without some sort of a base in which to park her
belongings.

In the end she hit upon the idea of the Shelbourne, the
small, old-fashioned hotel where her father used to take her en
route to one of their rare holidays abroad (perhaps to ski in
Austria, or spend a couple of weeks with one of Ronald Waring's esoteric friends, who owned a ramshackle mill in Provence). The Shelbourne was not smart and, if her father had
stayed there, would certainly not be expensive. She would
check in there for the night, and tomorrow start jobhunting.

It wasn't a great solution, but rather a compromise. And
life, as Marcia was wont to say, tearing the brim from one hat
and stitching it to the crown of another, was made up of com-
promises.

The Shelbourne was a relic like an old barge beached in a

331

backwater while the river of progress flowed by. Situated at the back of Knightsbridge in a narrow street which had once been elegant, it was slowly being dwarfed by plush new hotels, offices, and blocks of flats. Yet it clung grimly on, like an aging actress who refuses to retire.

Outside was present-day London: traffic jams, car horns, the roar of planes flying overhead, the vendor selling newspapers on the corner, the young girls with their black-rimmed eyes and their tottering clogs.

But entering through the slowly revolving doors of the Shelbourne was like stepping into yesterday. Nothing had changed—not the potted palms; not the face of the hall porter; not even the smell, a mixture of disinfectant and floor polish and hothouse flowers, rather like that of a hospital.

Behind the reception desk sat the same sad woman in her drooping black dress. Could it be the *same* dress? She looked up at Flora.

"Good evening, madam."

"Would it be possible to have a single room, just for tonight?"

"I'll just look . . ."

A clock ticked. Flora waited, her spirits sinking by the moment; she half-hoped that the answer would be no.

". . . Yes, I can let you have a room, but it's at the back of the hotel, and I'm afraid . . ."

"All right, I'll take it."

"If you could sign the register, and I'll ask a porter to take you up."

But the thought of long, stuffy hallways and a gloomy single bedroom at the end of it was too much for Flora.

"Not just now. I have to go out. Out to dinner," she improvised wildly. "I'll be back about half past nine. It doesn't matter about my luggage. Just leave it here in the hall till I get back. I'll take it up then."

"Just as you wish, madam. But don't you want to see your room?"

"No. It doesn't matter. I'm sure it's very nice. . . ." She

332

felt as if she were suffocating. Everything looked so dreadfully old. She picked up her bag and backed away, still mumbling excuses. She nearly knocked over a potted palm, rescued it in the nick of time, and finally fled out into the fresh air.

After two or three reviving gulps, she felt better. It was a lovely evening, chilly but clear, with a pellucid blue sky arched over the rooftops and one or two pink-tinged clouds aimlessly blowing along like balloons. Flora dug her hands into her pockets and began to walk.

An hour later, she found herself deep into Chelsea, heading south towards the King's Road. The little street lined with charming houses interspersed with small shops was familiar. Unfamiliar, however, was the small Italian restaurant which now stood where before Flora remembered a cobbler's with dusty windows filled with dog leads and luggage straps and unlikely plastic handbags.

The restaurant was called Seppi's. There were bay trees in tubs out on the cobbled pavement, a cheerful red-and-white striped awning, and a great deal of fresh white paint.

Just as Flora approached the door opened and a man came out carrying a small table which he set up on the pavement and covered with a checked red-and-white cloth. He went back into the shop and returned with two small wrought iron chairs and a Chianti bottle in a straw jacket, all of which were duly set out.

The breeze caught at the tablecloth and sent it flapping. The man looked up and saw Flora. His dark eyes flashed her a Mediterranean smile.

"Ciao, signorina."

Italians were wonderful, Flora decided. The smile, the greeting, made her feel like some old friend he was enchanted to be meeting again. No wonder they made such successful restaurateurs.

She smiled. "Hello, there. How are you?"

"Fantastic. After such a day, who could feel anything else? It is like being back in Rome. And you look like an Italian girl who has been to the sea for the summer. The tan." He made an

333

appreciative gesture which involved a kissing sound and an airy spread of finger tips. "Marvelous."

"Thank you." Disarmed, she stopped to talk, not unwilling to continue this delightful conversation. Through the open door of the restaurant drifted mouth-watering smells—suggestions of garlic and great red tomatoes and olive oil. Flora realised that she was ravenous. She had had no lunch on the train and since leaving the Shelbourne had walked, it seemed, for miles. Her feet ached and she was thirsty.

She looked at her watch. It was just past seven. "Are you open?"

"For you we are always open."

She said, accepting the compliment, "I only want an omelet or something."

"You, signorina, can have anything you want . . ." He stood aside, a welcoming arm outflung, and thus, so charmingly invited, Flora entered. Inside there was a little bar, and beyond this the long narrow restaurant reached back. Banquettes upholstered in knobbly orange material ran down the length of each wall, and there were scrubbed pine tables and fresh flowers and brightly checked napkins. The walls were mirrored, the floor scattered with straw matting. At the far end, judging from the clatter, smells, and raised Italian voices which emanated from that direction, was the kitchen. Everything felt cool and fresh, and after an exhausting day, Flora was left with the pleasant sensation of being welcomed home. She ordered a lager and then went in search of the ladies', where she washed the train grime from her hands and face and combed her hair. Back in the restaurant, the young Italian was waiting for her, a table pulled away from the wall, so that she could take her place, the tall frosted glass of lager neatly poured, some dishes of olives and nuts set out for her pleasure.

"You are sure you want only an omelet, signorina?" he inquired, as Flora sat down and the table was pushed in again, over her knees. "We have very good veal this evening. My sister Francesca will cook it for you like a dream."

"No, just an omelet. But you could put some ham in it. And perhaps a green salad."

"I will make the special dressing."

Up to now the place had been totally empty, but at this moment the door from the street opened and a few more customers drifted in, settling themselves around the bar. The young waiter excused himself to Flora and went to serve them, and she was left alone. She took an icy mouthful of lager and looked about her, wondering if any stray female who happened to wander into this delightful place was accorded the same welcome. Everybody said how grim London was becoming, how offhand were the people, how unhelpful. It was heartwarming, for once, to have everybody proved wrong.

She set down her glass, looked up, and caught sight of herself reflected in the long plate glass mirror which lined the opposite wall. The faded blue of her denim jacket and the orange of the seat behind her were the colors of Van Gogh. As for herself . . . she saw a thin girl, with strong features, dark brown eyes, and a mouth that was too big for the rest of her face. She was still tanned from the Cornwall summer, her skin shining and clean, and her hair the color of gleaming mahogany, casual, chin-length, looking like the hair of a young boy in need of a good cut. With her faded jeans and jacket she wore a white turtleneck sweater, a gold chain knotted at the neck. Her hands and wrists, emerging from the folded back cuffs, were long-boned and tanned as her face.

She thought, *I've been away from London too long. This casual image isn't going to get me any sort of a job. I ought to get my hair cut. I ought to buy . . .*

The door onto the street opened and shut again. A girl's voice called, "Hi, Pietro!" and the next instant the newcomer came right through the bar and into the restaurant, at home as a cat in familiar surroundings. Without looking in Flora's direction, she stopped at the table next to hers, pulled it out to make space for herself, and flopped down onto the banquette with her eyes shut and her legs stuck out in front of her.

So casual, almost insolent, were all these movements that

Flora decided she must be some relation to the Italian family who owned the restaurant. A cousin from Milan, perhaps, working in London . . .

Hi Pietro. No, of course not, not an Italian, an American. From the New York branch of the family . . .

Diverted by that intriguing possibility, but not wanting to stare, Flora shifted her gaze slightly and observed the other girl's reflection in the mirror opposite. She looked away. And then back again, so swiftly that she felt her hair swinging against her cheek. The perfect double take, she thought. The classic double take.

It was herself.

But it wasn't herself because there were two reflections in the mirror.

The newcomer, unaware of Flora's mesmerized gaze, pulled a bright silk scarf off her head, shook back her hair, and then reached into a black crocodile bag and took out a cigarette and lit it from a book of matches that lay in the ashtray on the table. At once the air was filled with the smell of strong French tobacco. She stuck out a booted foot, hooked it around the leg of the table, and yanked the table toward her. She leaned forward, twisting her head away from Flora, and called again, "Hi, Pietro!"

Flora could not drag her eyes from the mirror. The girl's hair was longer than her own, but shining and the same dark mahogany brown. She was carefully and elaborately made up, but that only served to emphasize the strong features and the mouth that was too big for her face. Her eyes were dark brown, the bristly lashes sooty with mascara. She reached out to pull the ashtray toward her, and Flora saw the dazzling, chunky ring and the scarlet nails, but the hands were slender and long-boned, their shape identical to Flora's own.

They were even dressed alike, in jeans and turtleneck sweaters. But the other girl's sweater was cashmere, and her jacket, which had been slung around her shoulders and was now shrugged aside, was a dark, gleaming mink.

The young waiter, having dealt with the customers at the

336

bar, answered her summons, suddenly appearing almost at a
run.

"Signorina, I am so sorry, I thought that . . ."

Slowly, he came to a standstill, his movements, his words,
his very voice seemed to run down to a halt, like an old-fashioned gramophone that nobody's remembered to wind.

After a little, "O.K., so what did you think?" said the girl
who sat beside Flora. "You must surely realize I'm needing a
drink."

"But I thought . . . I mean, I have already . . ." He had
gone quite pale. His dark eyes traveled cautiously to Flora's
face. So obviously shaken was he that Flora would not have
been surprised if he had crossed himself, or made that sinister
Mediterranean gesture which is meant to ward off the evil eye.

"Oh, Pietro, for heaven's sake . . ."

But in the middle of that small burst of exasperation, she
looked up and saw Flora watching her through the mirror.

The silence seemed to go on forever. Pietro broke it at last.
"It is amazing," he said, his voice scarcely audible and full of
wonder. "It is amazing."

They looked away from each other and into each other's
eyes and it was still like looking into the mirror.

The other girl recovered herself first. She said, "I'll say it's
amazing," and she did not sound nearly as sure of herself as she
had before.

But Flora could think of nothing to say.

Pietro broke in once more. "But Signorina Schuster, when
the other signorina came in, I thought it was yourself." He
turned to Flora. "I am sorry. You must have thought that I was
very familiar, but I naturally mistook you for Signorina
Schuster, she comes often, but I have not seen her for some
time, and . . ."

"I didn't think you were being familiar. I just thought you
were being very kind."

The girl with long hair was still staring at Flora, her dark
eyes moving over Flora's face, like an expert assessing a portrait. She said now, "You look just like me," and she even

337

sounded a little annoyed, as though this were some sort of an affront.

Flora felt moved to defend herself. "Well, you look like me," she told her mildly. "We look like each other." Still unnerved, she swallowed. "I think we probably even sound like each other."

This was instantly confirmed by Pietro, who still stood rooted to the ground, his head going from one face to the other, like a spectator at a tennis match.

"That is so. You have the same voice, the same eyes. Even the same clothes. I would not have believed it unless I had seen it for myself. Mamma mia, you could be twins. You are . . ." He made finger-snapping motions, searching for the right word. "The same. You know?"

"Identical," said Flora, flatly.

"That's it! Identical! It's fantastic!"

"Identical twins?" said the other girl, cautiously.

Their astonishment, the way that they couldn't take their eyes off each other, finally got through to Pietro.

"You mean that you have never seen each other before?"

"Never."

"But you must be sisters."

He put his hand over his heart. Suddenly, it seemed, he could take no more. Flora wondered if he was going to faint, and hoped that he wasn't. Instead, he took more practical action. He said, "I am going to open a bottle of champagne. It is a present . . . on the house. And I am going to drink a glass, too, because a miracle like this has never happened to me before. Just wait there . . ." he added, unnecessarily straightening the tables before them, as though afraid they might escape. "Don't move. Just wait there," and he bolted back to the bar, his starched white jacket alert with importance.

They scarcely heard him, scarcely noticed his going. Sisters. A strange obstruction had suddenly manifested itself in Flora's throat. She made herself say it. "Sisters?"

"Twin sisters," the other girl amended. "What's your name?"

338

UNDER GEMINI

"Flora Waring."

The other girl closed her eyes and opened them again, so slowly that it couldn't be called a blink. She said, with studied calm, "That's my name, too. Only I'm Rose."

3

ROSE

"Rose Waring?"

"Well, not strictly speaking. Rose Schuster, really. But Waring's my middle name, because my father was called Waring, but my stepfather's called Harry Schuster. And he's been my stepfather for years and years, so I've always been called Schuster, but Waring's my middle name." She stopped, having apparently run out of breath. They continued to gaze at each other, still astonished, but with a growing sense of recognition, of realization.

"Do you know who your real father was?" Flora asked at last.

"I never knew him. He and my mother separated when I was a baby. I think he was a schoolmaster."

Flora thought of her father. Vague, loping about, maddening, but always totally honest and truthful. She thought, *He couldn't have. He couldn't have done such a thing and never told me.*

340

The silence between the two girls lengthened. Rose seemed to have nothing more to say. With an effort, Flora searched for words.

"Your mother. Was she called . . ." The name, scarcely ever mentioned, swam up out of her subconscious. "Pamela?"

"That's right."

"How old are you?"

"Twenty-two."

"When is your birthday?"

"The seventeenth of June."

Now, it was final. "Mine, too."

"I was born under Gemini," said Rose, and it was disconcerting to hear Marcia's words of that very morning repeated so naturally. "The sign of the twins." She smiled. "That's appropriate enough, if you like."

My twin. My sister. "But what happened?" asked Flora.

"Simple. They decided to separate, and they took one each."

"But did you ever have the slightest idea?"

"Not the slightest. Did you?"

"No. That's what shakes me."

"Why should it shake you? It's perfectly normal human behavior. Very tidy, very fair."

"I think we should have been told."

"What good would that have done? What difference would it have made?"

It was obvious that Rose was more amused than shattered by the situation. "I think it's hysterical," she went on. "And the most hysterical part of the business is that our mother and father have been found out. And what a fantastic coincidence that we should meet up like this. Out of the blue. Have you ever been to this restaurant before?"

"Never."

"You mean, you just walked in?"

"I only arrived in London this evening. I've been in Cornwall for the past year."

"That makes it more unbelievable than ever. In the whole

of this immense city . . ." She spread her hands, leaving the sentence to finish itself.

"They always say," said Flora, "that London is made up of a lot of villages. I suppose if you stick to your own village, you're bound to meet someone you know."

"That's true enough. Walk into Harrod's and you bump into acquaintances all the way through. But it still doesn't stop it being the most extraordinary thing that's even happened to me." She pushed her hair back from her forehead with her fingers, a gesture that Flora recognized, with some shock, as one of her own. "What were you doing in Cornwall?" Rose asked, as if it could make any difference.

"My father and I went to live there. He still does. He teaches there."

"You mean he's still a schoolteacher?"

"Yes, he's still a schoolmaster." It was ridiculous to continue to feel as shaken as she did. She decided to be as matter of fact about the uncanny coincidence as Rose was. "And what happened to you?" she asked, sounding unreal, like a person at a formal cocktail party.

"Mother married again when I was about two. He's called Harry Schuster and he's an American, but he's spent most of his life in Europe as representative for his firm."

"So you were brought up in Europe?"

"You could say that. If it wasn't Paris it was Rome, and if it wasn't Rome, it was Frankfurt. You know how it is. . . ."

"Is he nice? Mr. Schuster, I mean."

"Yes. Sweet."

And terribly rich, thought Flora, eyeing the mink and the cashmere and the crocodile bag. Pamela, ditching the penniless schoolmaster, had done a good deal better for herself the second time around.

She thought of something else. "Do you have any brothers or sisters?"

"No. Just me. How about you?"

"I'm an only, and likely to stay that way. Pa's just married again. She's called Marcia and she's super, but she's not exactly a chicken."

"What does your father look like?"

"Tall. Scholarly, I suppose. Very kind. He wears horn-rimmed spectacles and he forgets things. He's very . . ." She searched for some brilliant word that would describe her father, but only came up with "charming." And she added, "And very truthful. That's why I find this all so extraordinary."

"You mean, he's never palmed you off with a fib?"

Flora was a little shocked. "I never imagined he was capable of suppressing a truth, let alone telling a lie."

"He must be something." Rose stubbed out her cigarette, thoughtfully grinding it to pieces in the middle of the ashtray. "My mother is perfectly capable of suppressing the truth, or even telling a wing-ding of a lie. But she also is charming. When she wants to be!"

Despite herself, Flora smiled, because Rose's description matched so exactly what she had always imagined for herself.

"Is she pretty?" she asked.

"Very slim and young-looking. Not beautiful, but everybody thinks she is. It's a sort of confidence trick."

"Is . . . is she in London now?" Flora made herself ask, thinking, *If she is and I have to meet her, what will I say to her? What will I do?*

"No, she's in New York. Actually, she and Harry and I have been on a trip; I only flew in to Heathrow last week. She wanted me to stay, but I had to come back, because . . ." She did not finish the sentence. Her eyes slid away as she reached for another cigarette and burrowed in her bag for her lighter. ". . . Oh, various reasons," she finished unsatisfactorily.

Flora waited hopefully to be told the reasons, but they were interrupted once more by Pietro returning with the champagne bottle and three glasses. With some ceremony he drew the cork and poured the wine, passing the neck of the bottle from glass to glass without spilling a drop. He wiped the bottle clean with a starched napkin, picked up his own glass, and raised it to them.

343

"To the reunion. To sisters finding each other. It is, I think, an act of God."

"Thank you," said Flora. "Happy days," said Rose. Pietro departed once more, by now quite moist at the eyes, and they were left with the bottle to finish between them. "We'll probably get plastered," said Rose, "but never mind about that. Where had we got to?"

"You were saying you had to come back to London from the States."

"Oh, sure. But now, I think I am going to Greece. Perhaps tomorrow or the next day. I haven't exactly decided."

It sounded a marvelously jet-set, spur-of-the-moment existence.

"Where are you staying?" Flora asked, expecting to be told the Connaught or the Ritz. But it appeared that Harry Schuster's job carried with it a flat in London as well as the apartments in Paris, Frankfurt, and Rome. The London flat was in Cadogan Gardens. "Just round the corner," said Rose, casually. "I always walk round here when I want something to eat. How about you?"

"You mean, where do I live? Nowhere at the moment. I told you, I only came up from Cornwall today. I was going to stay with a girlfirend, only it didn't work out, so I've got to find a flat. I've got to find a job, too, only that's beside the point."

"Where are you spending tonight?"

Flora told her about the Shelbourne, the luggage dumped in the hall, the potted palms, and the suffocating atmosphere. "I'd forgotten how depressing it was. But never mind, it's only for one night."

She became aware that Rose was watching her with a cool and thoughtful expression in her dark eyes. (Do I ever look like that? thought Flora. The word *calculating* sprang to mind and had to be hastily slapped down.)

Then Rose said, "Don't go back." Flora stared. "I mean it. We'll have something to eat here, and then we'll find a taxi and go and collect your luggage, and we'll go back to Harry's flat, and you can stay there. It's vast, and there are loads of beds.

344

Besides, if I go to Greece tomorrow I shan't see you again, and we've got so much to talk about, we shall need an entire night to ourselves. And anyway, it's super, because you can stay in the flat after I've gone. You can stay there until you've found somewhere else to live."

"But . . ." For some reason Flora found she was searching for objections to this apparently delightful plan. "But won't anybody mind?" was all she could come up with.

"Who should mind? I'll fix it with the hall porter. Harry never minds what I do. And as for Mother . . ." Something amused her. She left the sentence unfinished and began to laugh. "What would she say if she could see us now? Getting together, making friends. What do you think your father would say?"

Flora shied from the idea. "I can't imagine."

"Will you tell him that we've found each other?"

"I don't know. Perhaps. One day."

"Was it a cruel thing to do?" asked Rose, suddenly thoughtful. "Separating identical twins. Identical twins are meant to be two halves of the same person. Separating us was perhaps like cutting that person in half."

"In that case, they may have done us a kindness."

Rose's eyes narrowed. "I wonder," she said. "why my mother chose me, and your father chose you."

"Perhaps they tossed a coin." Flora spoke lightly, because for some reason, it didn't bear thinking about.

"Would everything have been upside down if the coin had fallen the other way?"

"It would certainly have been different."

Different. She thought of her father, of Seal Cottage by winter firelight, and the tarry smell of burning driftwood. She thought of tender, early springs and summer seas dancing with sun pennies. She thought of red wine in a carafe set in the middle of the scrubbed table and the comforting sound of Beethoven's *Pastoral* thundering from the record player. And now, she remembered the warm and loving presence of Marcia.

"Would you have wanted it to be different?" asked Rose.

Flora smiled. "No."

Rose reached out for the ashtray and stubbed out her cigarette. She said, "Nor me. I wouldn't have changed a thing."

Now it was Friday.

In Edinburgh, after a morning of cloud and rain, the sun had finally struggled through the murk, the sky was clearing, and the city glittered in a brilliant autumn light. To the north, beyond the deep indigo of the Firth of Forth, the hills of Fife lay serene against a sky of palest blue. Across Princes Street the municipal flower beds of the Waverly Gardens were ablaze with fiery dahlias, and on the far side of the railway line the cliffs swept up to the theatrical bulk of the castle with its distant, fluttering flag.

Antony Armstrong, emerging from his office into Charlotte Square, was taken unaware by the beauty of the afternoon. Because he was taking a long weekend, it had been an exceptionally busy morning. He had not bothered about lunch. He had not even raised his eyes to glance out of the window, imagining that the day was continuing much as it had started.

Preoccupied and anxious, he hurried to get to his car and drive to the airport. He was to catch the London plane and go in search of Rose. In spite of all that he was brought to a standstill by the unexpectedness of the sunshine reflected in still-damp pavements, by the glittering, coppery leaves of the trees in the square, and by the smell. It was a country smell, of autumn—a suggestion of peat and heather and wild uplands. It blew in with a freshening breeze from hills not after all so very far away. Antony, standing on the pavement with his raincoat slung over his shoulder and an overnight bag in his hand, took a few deep sniffs and was reminded of Fernrigg and of Tuppy. That he found comforting. It helped him to unwind and stop feeling so anxious.

Still, there was no time to waste, so he went and retrieved his car, drove out to Turnhouse, parked the car again, and checked in at the departure desk. Then, because there was half

346

an hour to wait before his flight, he went upstairs for a sandwich and a glass of beer.

The barman was an old acquaintance, familiar after many business trips to London.

"Haven't seen you for a while, sir."

"No. I guess it's been a month or more."

"Do you favor ham, or egg?"

"Better give me one of each."

"Going down to London?"

"That's right."

The barman assumed a knowing expression. "Nothing like a weekend off."

"It may not be a weekend. I may be back tomorrow. I don't know. It depends."

"You might as well take the weekend, and enjoy yourself." He slid the tankard of Export across the counter. "It's lovely warm weather down in London."

"It's not so bad here."

"No, it looks like a good afternoon. You'll have a pleasant flight."

He wiped down the top of the counter and went to serve another customer. Antony took his beer and his plate of sandwiches over to a table by the window, shed his raincoat and his bag, and lit a cigarette.

Beyond the window, beyond the parapet of the terrace, he saw the hills, the shredding clouds, the flying windsock. He was hungry. The beer and sandwiches waited. Sitting there, watching the cloud shadows run across the puddled runways, he forgot about being hungry and let his mind return to the problem of Rose.

That required no conscious effort at all on Antony's part. As far as Rose was concerned his thoughts seemed to have taken on a will of their own, worrying away like an old dog digging up a bone, fretting around in circles and never getting anywhere.

As though the action were in itself some answer to his dilemma, he reached into his jacket pocket and took out her letter, although he had already read it so many times that he knew it by heart. It was not in an envelope for the simple reason that it had not arrived in an envelope, but rather in an untidy parcel around a small box containing the sapphire and diamond ring that Antony had bought her.

He had given it to her four months ago in the restaurant of the Connaught Hotel. They had finished dinner, the waiter had brought their coffee to the table, and somehow, quite suddenly, the moment had arrived: the time, the place, and the woman. Antony, like a conjurer, had produced the little box from his pocket, flipped it open, and let the light sparkle on the jewels within.

Rose had said, instantly, "What a pretty thing."

"It's for you," said Antony.

She looked up into his eyes, incredulous, flattered, but something else as well. He had not been able to make up his mind what that something else was.

"It's an engagement ring," he went on. "I bought it this morning." For some reason, it had been important that the ring should be in his hand when he asked her to marry him, as though he knew that she needed this extra leverage, this material persuasion. "I think—and I'm hoping that you think so, too—I think that we ought to get married."

"Antony."

"Don't sound so reproachful."

"I'm not sounding reproachful. I'm sounding surprised."

"You can't say, 'this is so sudden,' because we've known each other for five years."

"But not really *known* each other."

"I feel as though we have."

And indeed, at that moment, that was just how Antony did feel. But their relationship was unusual, and the most unusual thing about it was the way that Rose kept recurring in his life—turning up when he least expected to meet her, as though the whole relationship had been preordained.

And yet, the first time he had met her, she had made no impression on him at all. But then he had been twenty-five and

348

in the throes of a love affair with a young actress doing a season in Edinburgh. And Rose was only seventeen. Her mother, Pamela Schuster, had taken the Beach House at Fernrigg for a summer holiday. Antony, home for a weekend, and escorting Tuppy to the beach for a picnic, had been introduced and eventually invited back to the Beach House for a drink. The mother was charming and very attractive, but for some reason Rose had been in a bad mood that afternoon. Antony had simply dismissed her leggy gawkiness along with her sulky expression and the monosyllabic replies she gave him each time he tried to talk to her. By the time he made his next weekend visit to Fernrigg, both she and her mother had gone, and he never gave the Schusters another thought.

But then, a year ago in London on business, he had come upon Rose having a drink in the Savoy bar with an earnest young American in rimless spectacles. Rose now was something quite different. Seeing her, recognizing her, Antony could scarcely believe it was the same girl. Slender, sensational-looking, she held the attention, open or otherwise, of every man in the place.

Antony moved in and introduced himself, and Rose, perhaps bored by her monumentally sincere companion, responded with flattering delight. Her parents, she told him, were on holiday in the south of France. She was flying to join them tomorrow afternoon. That had created a pleasant sense of urgency, and without much urging Rose abandoned the American and went out to dinner with Antony.

"When are you coming back from the south of France?" he wanted to know, already hating the thought of having to say goodbye to her.

"Oh, I don't know. I haven't thought."

"Don't you have a job, or anything?"

"Oh, darling, I'd be useless in a job. I'm never on time for anything and I can't type, so I'd just be the most dreadful nuisance. Besides, there's no need. And I'd just be taking bread from some deserving mouth."

Antony's Scottish conscience made him say, "You're a

drone. A disgrace to society." But he said it with a smile, because she amused him, and Rose took no sort of umbrage.

"I know." She checked her elaborate eye makeup in the little mirror she had fished out of her handbag. "Isn't it ghastly?"

"Let me know when you come back from the south of France."

"Of course." She flipped the compact shut. "Of course, darling."

But she hadn't let him know. Antony had no idea where she lived, and no address in London, so it was impossible for him to get in touch with her. He tried looking up Schuster in the telephone directory, but no number was listed. Discreetly, he made inquiries of Tuppy, but Tuppy only remembered the Schusters at the Beach House, and had no idea of their permanent address.

"Why do you want to know?" Her voice over the telephone was clearly curious.

"I met Rose again in London. I want to get in touch with her."

"Rose? That pretty child? How intriguing."

By the time Antony found her again, it was the beginning of the summer. London gardens were fragrant with lilac, and the parks veiled in the young green of newly opened leaves.

Once more Antony was south, interviewing a client for his firm. Lunching at Scott's in the Strand, he met an old school friend who asked him to a party that evening. The friend lived in Chelsea, and as Antony walked through the front door of the top-floor flat the first person he saw was Rose.

Rose. He knew after the way that she had behaved that he should be furious with her, but instead, his heart missed a beat. She wore a blue linen pantsuit and high-heeled boots, with her dark hair loose to her shoulders. She was talking to some man whom Antony did not even bother to inspect. She was here. He had found her. Fate had stepped in. Fate did not intend that they should be kept apart. Antony, brought up in a Highland household, was a great believer in fate.

He took a drink from a passing tray and went to claim her.

This time, it was perfect. He had three days in London, and she wasn't going to the south of France. As far as he could find out, she wasn't going anywhere. Her mother and father were in New York, where Rose planned to join them—sometime. Not just now. She was living in her father's flat in Cadogan Court. Antony checked out of his club and moved in too.

Everything went right. Even the weather smiled upon them. During the day the sun shone, spikes of lilac bobbed against the blue sky, windowboxes were filled with flowers, and there always seemed to be taxis and the best tables in restaurants waiting for them. At night a round, silver moon sailed up into the sky and bathed the city in its romantic light. Antony spent money like water—as though he were made of it—and the uncharacteristic orgy of extravagance culminated the morning he walked into a Regent Street jeweler's and bought the diamond and sapphire ring.

They were engaged. He could scarcely believe it. To make it true, they sent cables to New York, made telephone calls to Fernrigg. Tuppy was amazed, but delighted. She had been longing for Antony to get married and settle down.

"You must bring her up to see us. It's so long since she was here. I can scarcely remember what she looks like."

Antony, gazing at Rose, said, "She's beautiful. The most beautiful thing in the world."

"I can't wait to see her again."

He said to Rose, "She says she can't wait."

"Well, darling, I'm afraid she'll have to. I have to go to America for a moment. I promised my mother and Harry. He's made such plans, and he always gets into such a state if he has to change them. I must go. Explain to Tuppy."

Antony explained. "Later, we'll come," he promised. "Later, when Rose is back again. I'll bring her up to Fernrigg and you can get to know her all over again."

So Rose went to New York, and Antony, bemused with love and good fortune, returned to Edinburgh. "I'll write," she

351

had promised, but she didn't write. Antony penned long, loving screeds which she never answered. He began to fret. He sent cables, but there was no reply to them, either. In the end he put through a wildly expensive telephone call to her home in Westchester County, but Rose was away. A servant answered the telephone in an accent so strong as to be practically incomprehensible. He could only gather that Rose was out of town, her address unknown, and her return date uncertain.

He was beginning to feel desperate when the first postcard arrived. It was a picture of the Grand Canyon with a scrawled and affectionate message that told him nothing. A week later came the second. Rose stayed in America the entire summer and during that time he received five postcards from her, each more unsatisfactory than the one before.

Plaintive queries from Fernrigg did nothing to help the situation. Antony managed to fend them off with the same excuses that he had started making to himself. Rose was simply not a good correspondent.

But, despite these excuses, doubts loomed and grew like monstrous balloons, like clouds darkening his horizon. He began to lose confidence in his own solid, Scottish common sense. Had he made a fool of himself? Had those magical days in London with Rose simply been a blinding illusion of love and happiness?

And then something happened to drive all thoughts of Rose from his head. Isobel telephoned from Fernrigg to tell him that Tuppy was ill: she had caught a chill, it had turned to pneumonia, a nurse had been engaged to take care of her. Trying to sound calm, Isobel did her best to reassure Antony. "You mustn't worry. I'm sure it will be all right. It's just that I had to tell you. I hate worrying you, but I knew you'd want to know."

"I'll come home," he said instantly.

"No. Don't do that. It'll make her suspicious, make her think something's really wrong. Perhaps later, when Rose gets back from America. Unless . . ." Isobel hesitated hopefully. ". . . perhaps she's back already?"

"No," Antony had to tell her. "No. Not yet. But any day now, I'm sure."

"Yes," said Isobel. "I'm sure." She sounded as if she were comforting him, as she had comforted him through all the anxieties of his childhood, and Antony knew that he should be comforting her. That made him feel more miserable than ever.

It was like worrying about a grumbling appendix and suffering from acute toothache at one and the same time. Antony did not know what to do, and in the end, with a lack of decision that was quite foreign to his nature, he did nothing.

The nonaction lasted for a week, and then, simultaneously, all his problems came to a ghastly head. The morning post brought the parcel from Rose, untidily wrapped and sealed, postmarked London and containing his engagement ring along with the only letter she had ever written him. And while he was still reeling from the shock, the second telephone call came, from Isobel. That time Isobel had not been able to be brave. Her tears and her very real anguish broke through, and her shaking voice betrayed the shattering truth. Hugh Kyle was obviously worried about Tuppy. She was, Isobel suspected, much worse than any of them had guessed. She would perhaps die.

All Tuppy wanted was to see Antony and Rose. She was yearning for them, worrying, wanting to make wedding plans. And it would be so dreadful, said Isobel, if something should happen, and Tuppy was never to see Antony and Rose together.

The implication was obvious. Antony had not the heart to tell Isobel the truth, and even as he heard himself making that impossible promise, he wondered how the hell he was going to keep it. Yet he knew that he had to.

With a calmness born of desperation, he made arrangements. He spoke with his boss, and with as few explanations as possible, asked for and was granted a long weekend. In a mood of dogged hopelessness, he put through a telephone call to the Schuster flat in London; when there was no reply, he drafted a wordy telegram and sent that instead. He booked a seat on the London plane. Now, at the airport waiting for that plane to be called, he reached into the pocket of his jacket, and took out the letter. The writing paper was deep blue and opulent, the address thickly embossed at the head of the page.

Eighty Two Cadogan Court
London, S.W.1

But Rose's writing, unfortunately, did not live up to the address. Sprawling, unformed as a child's, it meandered cross the page, with the lines trailing downward, and the punctuation nonexistent.

Darling Antony.

I'm terribly sorry but I'm sending your ring back because I really don't think that after all I can bear to marry you, it's all been a horrible mistake. At least, not horrible, because you were sweet and the days we had together were fun, but it all seems so different now, and I realize that I'm not ready to settle down and be a wife, especially not in Scotland, I mean I don't have anything against Scotland, I think it's very pretty, but it isn't really my scene. I mean, not for ever. I flew into London last week, am here for a day or two, not sure what happens next. My mother sent her love, but she doesn't think I should get married yet and when I do she doesn't think I should live in Scotland. She doesn't think it's my scene either. So terribly sorry, but better now than later. Divorces are such messy things and take so long and cost such a lot of money.

Love (still)
Rose

Antony folded the sheet of paper and put it back into his pocket, and felt the smooth leather of the box with the diamond and sapphire ring inside. Then he started in on his beer and sandwiches. There was scarcely time to finish them before his flight was called.

He was at Heathrow at half past three, caught the bus to

the terminal, and then took a taxi. London was noticeably warmer than Edinburgh and bright with autumn sunshine. The trees had scarcely started to turn and the grass in the park was worn and brown after the long summer. Sloane Street seemed to be filled with light-hearted children going home from school hand in hand with smartly dressed young mothers. *If Rose isn't there,* he thought, *I shall sit down and bloody well wait for her.*

The taxi rounded the corner of the square, stopping in front of the familiar red-brick building. It was a new block, very plush, with bay trees at the head of the wide flight of stone steps, and a great deal of plate glass.

Antony paid off the taxi and went up the steps and through the glass door. Inside there was dark brown wall-to-wall carpeting and palm trees in tubs and an expensive smell, mostly compounded of leather and cigars.

The porter was not behind his desk, nor anywhere to be seen. Perhaps, thought Antony, pressing the bell for the lift, he's nipped out for an evening paper. The lift silently descended. Silently the doors slid open for him. As Antony went in they slid silently shut. He pressed the button for the fourth floor and recalled standing in that very lift with Rose in his arms, kissing her every time they passed another floor. It was a poignant memory.

The lift stopped and the doors opened. Carrying his bag, he stepped out, went down the long passage, stopped at the door of number Eighty-two and without giving himself time to think about it pressed the bell. From inside came the deep note of the buzzer. Setting down his bag and putting up a hand to lean against the edge of the door, he waited, without hope. She would not be there. Already he felt exhausted by what must follow.

And then from within he heard a sound. He stiffened, becoming suddenly alert, like a dog. A door shut. Another door opened. Footsteps came down the short passage from the kitchen, and the next moment the door was flung open. There stood Rose.

Staring at her like a fool, a number of thoughts flew

through Antony's mind. She was here, he had found her. She didn't look too furious. She had cut her hair.

She said, "Yes?" which was a funny thing for her to say, but then this was a funny situation.

Antony said "Hello, Rose."

"I'm not Rose," said Rose.

4

ANTONY

That Friday was, for Flora, fogged in a curious unreality, a carryover from the events of the previous incredible day. She had intended to do so much and had ended up by achieving nothing.

Physically, she went through the motions of jobhunting and visiting various estate gents, but her mind refused to concentrate on the matters in hand.

"Do you want permanent or temporary work?" the girl at the agency had asked, but Flora simply stared at her and did not reply, obsessed as she was by images that had nothing to do with shorthand and typing. It was as if a well-ordered house had suddenly been invaded and taken over by strangers. They had caught Flora's attention to the point where she could think of nothing else.

"There's a ground-floor flat going in Fulham. It's very small, of course, but if it was just for yourself . . . ?"

"Yes." She should go and see it. It sounded perfect. "Yes.

357

I'll think about it." And she stepped out into the street and continued on her way, aimless and preoccupied.

Part of the trouble, of course, was that she was short of sleep and physically exhausted by the traumas of yesterday. It had been a hysterical evening. Flora and Rose had dined together at Seppi's, finished the champagne, been presented with a second bottle, and sat over coffee until Seppi, with a queue of customers waiting for tables, had reluctantly had to let them leave. Rose had settled the bill with a credit card. The dinner cost more than Flora could believe possible, but Rose dismissed it airily. She said not to worry because Harry Schuster would settle the account. He always did.

They then found a taxi and drove to the Shelbourne Hotel, where Rose made derogatory remarks about the decor and the staff and the inhabitants, while Flora, embarrassed and trying not to laugh, explained the inexplicable situation to the sad lady behind the reception desk. A porter was finally persuaded to haul all the suitcases back out into the waiting cab, and they headed for Cadogan Court.

The flat was on the fourth floor. Flora had never dreamed of such luxury—so much carpeting, concealed lighting, and space-age plumbing. Plate-glass windows slid aside to allow access to a little balcony crammed with pot plants; a button could be pressed to draw the filmy linen curtains; in the bedrooms the carpets were white and about two inches deep (maddening if you dropped a ring or a bobby pin, Rose said), and the bathrooms all smelt of the most expensive soaps and oil.

Flora was carelessly assigned a bedroom (pale blue curtains made of Thai silk and mirrors everywhere) and told to unpack, which she did, to the extent of taking out her nightgown while Rose sat on the bed.

An idea suddenly struck Flora. "Do you want to know what your father looks like?"

"Photographs!" Rose sounded as though she had only just heard of such a thing.

Flora pulled out a big leather folder and handed it over to Rose, and they sat together on the big bed, dark head against dark head, their twin reflections caught in mirrors all about the room.

There was Seal Cottage, and the garden, and the wedding shot Flora had taken of her father and Marcia coming out of the church. There was the big one of him sitting on the rocks below the cottage, with a backdrop of sea and gulls, his face very brown and the breeze blowing his hair.

Rose's reaction was gratifying. "Oh, he's great! Like some smashing film star with spectacles. I can quite see why my mother married him. And yet I can't either. I mean, I can only imagine her married to a man like Harry."

"You mean a rich man."

"Yes, I suppose I do." She peered at the photograph again. "I wonder why they got married in the first place? Do you suppose they had anything in common?"

"Perhaps a mutual infatuation. They met on a ski holiday. Did you know that?"

"No kidding."

"Ski holidays are a bit like ocean voyages, or so I've been told. Wine-like air and tanned bodies and nothing to do except physically exhaust yourself and fall in love."

"I'll remember that," promised Rose. She was suddenly bored with the photographs. She tossed them down on the silk bedcover and looked long at her sister. Without any change in the tone of her voice, she asked, "Would you like a bath?"

So they both had baths, and Rose piled records onto the recordplayer while Flora made a pot of coffee. In their dressing gowns (Flora's, her old school one, and Rose's, a miracle of drifting flower-splashed silk) they sat on the king-size velvet sofa and talked.

And talked. There were many years to cover. Rose told Flora about the house in Paris and the finishing school at Chateau d'Oex, and the winters in Kitzbühel. And Flora filled Rose in on her own history (which didn't sound nearly so exciting), making the most of the finding and buying Seal Cottage, the arrival of Marcia into their lives, the jobs she had taken in Switzerland and Greece. That reminded her of something.

359

"Rose, did you say *you* were going to Greece?"

"I may be. But after this summer of flying around the United States, I'm beginning to feel I never want to get into another plane. Ever."

"You mean you spent the whole summer out there?"

"Most of it. Harry's been planning this trip for years, and we did everything from shooting the rapids on the Salmon River to riding down the Grand Canyon on muleback, hung about with cameras. Typical tourists." She frowned. "When did your father get married again?"

It was hard to keep track of her thought processes. "In May."

"Do you like Marcia?"

"Yes, I told you. She's great." Flora grinned, remembering Marcia's swelling hips and straining blouse buttons. "In more ways than one."

"He's so attractive, isn't he? I wonder how he managed to stay single for so long?"

"I've no idea."

Rose tipped her head to one side and regarded Flora from beneath long, bristling black lashes. "How about you? Are you in love, engaged, thinking of getting married?"

"Not at the moment."

"Have you ever thought about getting married?"

Flora shrugged. "You know how it is. At first, you think every new man you meet is going to end up standing next to you at some altar. And then it stops being important." She looked at Rose curiously. "How about you?"

"Same with me." Rose got up and went in search of a cigarette. Lighting it, her dark hair swung forward, hiding her face. "Anyway, who wants to settle down to boring old housework and yelling kids?"

"Perhaps it's not that bad."

"You'd probably like it. You'd probably like living in the depths of the country, in the back of beyond."

For some reason Flora felt compelled to stand up for such

360

an existence. "I like the country. And I'd live anywhere provided I was living with the man I wanted to live with."

"Married to him, though?"

"I'd prefer it that way."

Rose took her cigarette and turned her back on Flora. She went over to the window, drew back the curtain, and stood looking down into the lamp-lit square. After a little she said, "Talking about Greece—if I went tomorrow, and left you here alone, would you mind very much?"

It was hard not to sound taken aback. *"Tomorrow?"*

"I mean Friday. Well, that's today I suppose."

"Today?" Despite herself Flora's voice came out in a squeak of surprise.

Rose turned back. "You would mind," she told Flora. "Your feelings would be hurt."

"Don't be ridiculous. It's just that you took me by surprise. I mean, I didn't think you were serious about going to Greece. I thought you were just talking about it."

"Oh, yes. I've even got a seat booked on the plane, but I wasn't sure whether I wanted to go. But suddenly I think I will. You don't think it would be mean of me to go?"

"Of *course* not," said Flora, robustly.

Rose began to smile. She said, "You know, we're not as alike as I thought we were. You're so much more honest, transparently so. And I know what you're thinking."

"What am I thinking?"

"You're thinking I'm a bitch to leave you. You're wondering why I suddenly have to go to Greece."

"Are you going to tell me?"

"I think you've probably guessed. It's a man. You had guessed, hadn't you?"

"Perhaps."

"I met him at a party in New York, just before I flew back to London. He lives in Athens, but I got a cable from him yesterday morning, and he's in Spetsai, he's been lent a house by some friends. He wants me to join him."

"Then you must go."

361

"You really mean that, don't you?"

"Of course. I'm no reason for you to stay in London. Besides, I've got to get down to finding a job and somewhere to live."

"You'll stay in this flat till you do?"

"Well . . ."

"I'll fix it with the porter. Please." The tone of Rose's voice was anxious, almost pleading. "Say you will. Just for a day or two. For the weekend, anyway. It would mean so much to me if you would."

Flora was puzzled, but there was no obvious objection, nor reason to argue with such a pleasant invitation. "Well, all right. Till Monday. But only if you're sure it's all right."

"Of course it's all right." Rose's wide smile, the image of Flora's own, split her face. She came across the room to hug Flora in a great gesture of affection, only to revert almost at once to her usual disconcerting manner. "And now come and help me pack."

"But it's three o'clock in the morning!"

"That doesn't matter. You can make some more coffee."

"But . . ." Flora had been on the point of saying, "I'm exhausted," but for some reason she didn't. Rose was like that. She went so fast that you went too, caught up in the slipstream of her speed, whirled along behind her, without any clear idea of where you were headed.

Rose finally set out at eleven o'clock Friday morning on the first stage of her long journey to Spetsai. She left Flora standing on the pavement outside the block of flats.

"I'll see you," she said, hugging Flora goodbye. "Leave the key with the porter when you finally go."

"Send me a postcard."

"Of course. It's been great. I'll be in touch."

"Have fun, Rose."

Rose leapt into a waiting taxi, slammed the door, and leaned out of the open window. "Take care!" she called, and the taxi moved off with Rose still waving a mink-furred arm.

362

Flora stood there waving until the taxi rounded the corner of the square and disappeared into Sloane Street.

So that was it. It was over. Slowly Flora turned and went back indoors, up in the lift, and into the empty flat. She felt alien. Without Rose, everything seemed very quiet.

She went into the sitting room and began, in a desultory fashion, to plump up flattened cushions, draw back curtains, and empty ashtrays. Her attention was soon diverted, however, by Harry Schuster's bookshelves. Browsing, she forgot about housework and found that he read Hemingway and Robert Frost and Norman Mailer and Simenon (in French). There were albums of Aaron Copland in the stacks by the record player, and the Frederick Remington which hung over the fireplace bore witness to his pride in his own country and the best of its achievements.

Harry Schuster was taking shape. Flora decided that she would like him. But it was hard to feel so kindly toward a mother who had gaily abandoned you at birth and swanned off to a life of married ease, taking your twin sister with her.

From last night's session with Rose, plus photographs, Flora had built up a picture of Pamela Schuster so real that it seemed as if she had actually met her: beautiful and worldly, smelling of Patou's Joy, dressed by Dior, or slender as a boy in faded Levi's; Pamela at St. Tropez, skiing at St. Moritz, lunching at La Grenouille in New York; dark eyes bright with amusement, dark hair cut short, her smile a flash of white. She had all the charm and assurance in the world—but love, tenderness? Flora was doubtful.

The clock on the mantelpiece struck noon with silvery strokes. The morning had gone. Flora pulled herself together, made a sandwich, drank a glass of milk, picked up her handbag, and left the flat.

Without enthusiasm, she set out to look for a job. She returned to the flat at the end of the afternoon having achieved nothing except a sort of furious annoyance at her own indecision and procrastination. She was worn out from walking and climbing stairs. She went into the kitchen to put on the kettle

363

and make herself a cup of tea. This evening she would have a bath, watch television, and go to bed early. Rose had insisted she stay over the weekend. Perhaps by Monday she would feel more energetic and businesslike. Just as the kettle boiled, the front doorbell rang.

For some reason that was the last straw. Flora said, "Damn," switched off the kettle, and went out of the kitchen and down the passage to the front door.

Passing a mirror she caught a glimpse of herself looking both tired and untidy, her face shining and the sleeves of her white shirt rolled carelessly back from her wrists. She looked as though she had been scrubbing a floor and didn't care. She opened the door.

A man—tall, thin, quite young—was standing outside. He wore a smoothly cut brown herringbone suit, and his hair was a dark copper red, the color of an Irish setter. His face was fine drawn, with pale and freckled skin—the sort that would burn before it tanned. His eyes were light and clear, a sort of greenish gray. They stared down at Flora, as though waiting for her to make the first move. Finally Flora said, "Yes?"

He said "Hello, Rose."

"I'm not Rose," said Flora.

There was a short pause during which the young man's expression scarcely altered. Then he said, "Sorry?" as if he had not heard her properly.

"I'm not Rose," Flora repeated, raising her voice slightly, as if he were deaf, or stupid, or possibly both. "I'm Flora."

"Who's Flora?"

"Me," said Flora unhelpfully, and then instantly regretted it. "I mean, I'm staying here for the weekend."

"You have to be joking."

"No, I'm not."

"But you're identical . . ." His voice trailed away, lost in total confusion.

"Yes, I know."

He swallowed, and said in a voice that cracked slightly, "Twins?"

364

"Yes."

He tried again. "Sisters?"

"Yes."

"But Rose doesn't have a sister."

"No, she didn't, but she does now. I mean, she has since yesterday evening."

There was another long pause, and then the young man said, "Do you think you could explain?"

"Yes, of course. You see . . ."

"Do you think, before you start explaining, that I could come in?"

Flora hesitated, her thoughts racing. Harry Schuster's flat, full of precious things; her responsibility; unknown young man, possibly with criminal intentions. . . .It was her turn to swallow the slight obstruction in her throat.

"I don't know who you are."

"I'm Antony Armstrong. I'm a friend of Rose's. I've just flown down from Edinburgh." But Flora still hesitated. With some justification, perhaps, the young man became impatient. "Look, ask Rose. If she isn't there, go and ring her up. I'll wait."

"I can't ring her up."

"Why not?"

"She's gone to Greece."

"Greece?"

The incredulous horror in his voice and the way that the color drained from his face finally convinced Flora. No man, however evil his intentions, could feign such shock. She stood aside and said, "You'd better come in."

To her relief he seemed instantly at home in the flat, dropping his overnight bag and the raincoat he carried onto the chair in the hall as though he had done so many times before. Reassured by that, Flora suggested that he might like a cup of tea. He accepted her offer in a bemused sort of way. They went into the kitchen, and Flora switched on the kettle again. She began to get cups and saucers out of the cupboard, all the time

365

conscious of his unwinking stare as he watched her every movement.

"Do you want Indian or Chinese?" she asked him.

"Indian. Very strong." He found himself a tall kitchen stool and lankily hitched himself up onto it. "Now come along," he said, "tell."

"What do you want to know?"

"Are you really Rose's sister?"

"Yes. I really am."

"But what happened?"

In as few words as possible Flora told him: the broken marriage of Ronald and Pamela Waring; the splitting up of the twin babies; and the two sisters, each growing up in total ignorance of the other's existence until the meeting last night at Seppi's.

"You mean, this didn't happen till yesterday evening?"

"I told you that."

"I can scarcely believe it."

"We could scarcely believe it either, but it happened. Do you take milk and sugar?"

"Yes, both. So what happened then?"

"Well, we had dinner together, and then Rose invited me back here and we talked all night."

"And then this morning she went to Greece?"

"Yes."

"And what are you doing here?"

"Well, you see, I only came up from Cornwall yesterday on the train. I've been away from London for a year, living down there with my father and my stepmother. And actually, I haven't a job in London yet, nor a place to live. I meant to find something today but somehow I didn't. Anyway, Rose asked me to stay here over the weekend. She said it wouldn't matter. Nobody would mind." She turned to hand Antony his cup and was taken off guard by the expression on his face. She added, as though he needed placating, "She made it all right with the porter."

366

"Tell me, did she particularly ask you to stay here over the weekend?"

"Yes. Why? Shouldn't she?"

He took the cup and saucer from her and began to stir it, still not taking his pale eyes from Flora's face.

"Did she by any chance tell you that I was arriving?"

"She knew you were coming?"

"She didn't mention a telegram I sent her?"

"No." Flora, mystified, shook her head. "Nothing. She didn't say anything."

Antony Armstrong took a large mouthful of scalding tea, then laid down the cup and saucer, got off his stool, and went out of the room. A moment later he was back, a telegram in his hand.

"Where did you find that?" asked Flora.

"Where people invariably put telegrams and invitations and letters they mean to answer when they've got a moment to spare—behind the Rockingham sugar bowl at the end of the mantelpiece. Only in this flat, it happens to be a large, polished lump of alabaster." He held out the telegram to Flora. "You'd better read it."

Reluctantly, Flora took the telegram, while Antony perched himself once more on the stool and continued to drink his tea as if nothing extraordinary was happening.

"Go on, read it."

She did so.

PARCEL AND LETTER RECEIVED. VITALLY IMPORTANT I SEE YOU. TUPPY SERIOUSLY ILL. FLYING LONDON FRIDAY WILL BE WITH YOU LATE AFTERNOON. SIGNED ANTONY.

Flora's worst fears were confirmed. That was a telegraphic *cri de coeur* if ever there was one. And Rose had ignored it, never mentioning it to Flora. She had indeed run away from it.

It was hard to think of any intelligent comment to make. In the end, she said, "Who's Tuppy?"

367

"My grandmother. Did Rose say why she was going to Greece?"

"Yes, she . . ." Flora looked up. Antony's eyes narrowed, alert. All at once she did not want to tell him. She made an elaborately unconcerned face and tried to think up some elaborately unconcerned lie, but it wasn't any use. Like it or not, she was involved in it right up to the top of her head, and there seemed no way of getting out of it.

"Yes?" he prompted.

Flora gave in. "She's gone to see some man she met in New York. She met him at a party just before she came back to London. He's been lent a villa in Spetsai and he's invited Rose out to join him." This information was received in stony silence. "She had a seat booked on the plane. She went this morning."

After a little Antony said, "I see."

Flora held out the telegram. "I don't know what this— your grandmother—has to do with Rose."

"Rose and I were engaged to be married. But this week, she sent my ring back and broke it off. But Tuppy doesn't know that. She still thinks it's all going to happen."

"And you don't want her to know?"

"No, I don't. I'm thirty and she thinks it's high time I got married. She wants to see us both, make plans, think about the future."

"And what did you want Rose to do?"

"To come home with me. Ride along with the engagement story. Make Tuppy happy."

"Lie to her, in fact."

"Just for a single weekend." He added, his face very serious, "Tuppy's very ill. She's seventy-seven. She may be dying."

The word, final, despairing, hung in the silence between them. Flora could think of nothing to say. Awkwardly, she pulled out a chair and sat at the kitchen table, resting her elbows on its gleaming white surface. It became necessary to be very matter-of-fact. She asked, briskly, "Where's home?"

"The west of Scotland. Arisaig."

368

"I wouldn't know. I've never been to Scotland."

"Argyll, then."

"Do your parents live there?"

"I haven't any parents. My father's ship was lost during the war, and my mother died just after I was born. Tuppy brought me up. It's her house." He added, "It's called Fernrigg."

"Does Rose know Tuppy?"

"Yes, but not very well. Five years ago Rose and her mother took the Beach House at Fernrigg for two weeks in the summer, and we all got to know them then. Then they went away, and I never thought about them again, until about a year ago when I met up with Rose in London. But Tuppy hasn't seen her since that time."

Fernrigg. Argyll. Scotland. Rose hadn't mentioned Scotland. She had talked about Kitzbühel, St. Tropez, and the Grand Canyon, but she had not mentioned Scotland. It was all very confusing. But one thing was painfully clear. Confronted by crisis, Rose had decided to clear out.

"You . . . you said you came from Edinburgh."

"I work in Edinburgh."

"Will you go back there?"

"I don't know."

"What will you do?"

Antony shrugged and laid down his empty cup. "God knows. Go back to Fernrigg on my own, I suppose. Unless . . ." He looked at Flora, and went on, as though it were the most natural suggestion in the world. ". . . unless you'd like to come with me."

"Me?"

"Yes, You."

"What good could I do?"

"You could pretend to be Rose."

What really offended Flora was the calm way he came out with this outrageous suggestion: sitting there, cool and composed, and wearing on his face an expression of marvelous innocence. His original idea of conning Rose into pretending that

369

she was still engaged to him, had shocked Flora to the core. But this . . .

She found that she was so dismayed that it was difficult to find anything to say. "Thank you *very* much," was all she came up with, and very feeble it sounded, too.

"Why not?"

"Why not? Because it would be the most terrible, ghastly lie. And because it would mean deceiving someone I imagine you're very fond of."

"It's because I'm so fond of her that I'm prepared to deceive her."

"Well, I'm not deceiving anybody, so you'd better start thinking of something else. Like picking up your bag and your raincoat, and getting out of this flat and leaving me alone."

"You'd like Tuppy."

"I wouldn't like anybody I was lying to. You never lie to people who make you feel guilty."

"She'd like you, too."

"I'm not coming."

"If I said please, would it help?"

"No."

"Just for the weekend. That's all. Just the weekend. I've promised. I've never broken a promise to Tuppy in all my life."

Flora found that her indignation was fading, and this was frightening. Outrage was by far her best defense against this disarming young man. It wasn't any use being touched by his sincerity. It wasn't any use allowing herself to be sorry for him.

She said, "I won't do it. I'm sorry. I can't."

"But you can. You've already told me that you haven't got a job, that you haven't even got anywhere to live, except here. And your father's in Cornwall, so he presumably won't be worrying about you." He stopped. "Unless, of course, there's someone else to worry about you."

"You mean, have I got some man who's crazy about me and telephones every five minutes? Well, I haven't."

Antony did not reply to this outburst, but she saw a gleam

370

of humor in his eyes. "I don't know what's so funny about that," she said.

"It's not funny, it's ludicrous. I always thought Rose was the most gorgeous thing on two legs, and you're her identical twin. Nothing personal, I promise you, just an artistic appreciation. So what's wrong with all the men down here in this mealy-mouthed country south of the border? Have they lost their sight?"

Now he was laughing, and it was the first time that Flora had seen him smile. Before, she had thought him an ordinary-looking young man, even ugly in an attractive sort of way. But when he smiled he became, all at once, quite devastating. She began to see why Rose had succumbed to his charm. She began to wonder why Rose had thrown him over.

Reluctantly, despite herself, Flora smiled too. She said, "For a man who's just been jilted by the woman he loves, you don't seem to be too broken up."

His smile died. "No," he admitted. "But then at heart I'm a pawky, hard-headed Scottish businessman and I had seen the writing on the wall. Anyway, a man who never made a mistake never made anything. And it was good while it lasted."

"I wish she hadn't run out on you. She knew you needed her."

Antony crossed his arms. "I need you too," he told Flora.

"I couldn't do it."

"You just told me you'd never been to Scotland. And here I am, handing you a free trip on a plate, and you're turning it down. You'll never get such an offer again."

"I hope I don't."

"You'd like Fernrigg. And you'd like Tuppy. In fact, the two are so bound up together that it's impossible to imagine one without the other."

"Does she live alone?"

"Heavens, no. There's a family of us. Aunt Isobel and Watty the gardener, and Mrs. Watty who does the cooking. And I've got an older brother called Torquil with a wife called Teresa. I've even got a nephew called Jason. All Armstrongs."

371

"Does your brother live at Fernrigg?"

"No, he and Teresa are in the Persian Gulf. He's an oil man. But Jason was left at home with Tuppy, which is why he's at Fernrigg right now. It's a sort of dream place for small boys. The house is on the shore, with the sea all around and sands to walk on, and there's a little mooring where Torquil and I used to keep our dinghy. And inland there are streams full of trout and lochs covered with water-lilies, and now, in September, all the heather will be out and the rowan berries scarlet. Like beads. You really ought to come."

It was the most invidious sort of coaxing. Flora, with her elbows on the table and her chin in her hands, eyed Antony Armstrong thoughtfully. She said, "I once read a book about a man called Brat Farrar. And he pretended to be someone else— an impostor, you'd call him—and he had to spend months learning all about himself—about the person he was going to pretend to be. The very thought of it always gave me the shivers."

"But—" Antony got off his stool and came to sit across the table from Flora, so that they faced each other like a pair of conspirators. "But you see, you wouldn't need to do that. Because nobody knows Rose. Nobody's seen her for five years. Nobody known what she's been doing, except getting engaged to me. That's all they're interested in."

"Well, I don't know anything about *you.*"

"That's easy. I'm male, single, thirty years old, and Presbyterian. Educated at Fettes, did my training in London, went back to Edinburgh to join the firm I work for now. I've been with them ever since. What else do you want to know?"

"I'd like to know what makes you think I'd do this dreadful thing."

"It's not a dreadful thing. It's a kindness. Call it a kindness."

"Call it anything you like. I still couldn't do it."

"If I ask you again. If I say please, again, would you think about it? And remember that it isn't for myself I'm asking, it's

372

for Tuppy. And for Isobel too. For promises kept and not broken. Please, Flora."

She longed to be tough—not to be touched or sentimental. She longed for the strength to stick to her own convictions. Because she was right. She knew she was right.

She said cautiously, "If I said I'd come, when would we go?"

Antony's features took on an expression of wary excitement. "Tonight. Now, in fact. There's a plane just after seven; we ought to be able to catch it if we get our skates on. My car's at the airport in Edinburgh. We can drive to Fernrigg. We'll be there first thing in the morning."

"And when would I come back?"

"I have to be at work on Monday morning. You could catch the London plane from Edinburgh that day."

She knew instinctively that she could trust him. Antony would not break his word. "I couldn't be Rose," she warned him. "I could only be myself."

"That's all I want you to be."

She wanted to help him. She liked him, but it had, as well, obscurely, something to do with Rose. *I am my brother's keeper.*

"Rose is very naughty. She shouldn't have run out on you and left you in such a mess."

"The mess is as much my fault as hers. Rose owes me nothing. For that matter, neither do you."

The final decision, Flora knew, was hers. But it was hard not to be impressed by the lengths to which Antony Armstrong was prepared to go in order to keep his promise. Perhaps, she told herself, if a wrong thing were done for a right reason, then that made it right—at least not wholly bad.

A lie was a dangerous thing. Flora's finer instincts, painstakingly cultivated over the years by her father, reacted violently against the insane scheme. And yet, in some way, it was her father's fault. He was responsible for the dilemma in which she now found herself simply because he had never told her of the existence of Rose.

At the same time other, unsuspected reactions were manifesting themselves. They had to do with Rose, and on inspection proved to be part curiosity and part—Flora felt ashamed—envy. Rose seemed to have so much. The temptation offered by this young man to become Rose, just for a couple of days, was growing harder to resist by the minute.

He was waiting. She finally met his eyes across the table and discovered to her shame that when it came to the crunch, words were not going to be necessary. He sensed that she had fallen. A sudden smile lit up his face, and with it, the last of her defenses crumbled about her ears.

"You'll come!" It was a shout of triumph.

"I must be mad."

"You'll come. And you're not mad, you're marvelous. You're a super girl."

He remembered something, and from the pocket of his jacket took out a jeweler's box. Out of it he produced a sapphire and diamond ring. He took Flora's left hand, and pushed it on. She looked down at it, glittering on her finger and thought it looked very pretty. He closed her fingers into a fist and held it within his own two hands.

He said, "Thank you."

5

ANNA

Jason Armstrong, seven years old, sat up in the big double bed alongside his great-grandmother and listened while she read him *The Tale Of Two Bad Mice.* He was really too old for *Two Bad Mice.* He knew it, and Tuppy knew it, but her being in bed and unwell made him nostalgic for babyhood pleasures. When she sent him for a bedtime book, therefore, he had chosen *Two Bad Mice,* and she, being tactful, had not commented, but had put on her spectacles, opened the book at the front page, and started to read.

"Once upon a time there was a very beautiful doll's house."

He thought she read books very well. She read aloud to him every evening after he had had his bath and his supper, usually in the drawing room by the fire. But lately she hadn't been able to read to him at all, since she was too ill. "Now don't you go worrying your great-granny," Mrs. Watty had told him.

"I'll read to you," Aunt Isobel had promised, and had kept

her promise too, but somehow it wasn't the same as Tuppy's reading. Aunt Isobel didn't have the same voice. And she didn't smell of lavender the way Tuppy did.

But, as Mrs. Watty was apt to say, "Every cloud has its silver lining," and there was no denying that there was something pretty special about being in Tuppy's bed. It was unlike anybody else's bed. It was brass decorated with knobs; the pillows were enormous with great white monogrammed covers; and the linen sheets were hemstitched and very old and full of interesting patches and darns.

Even the furniture in Tuppy's room seemed magic and mysterious, made of carved mahogany and faded buttoned silk. The dressing-table was crowded with silver-topped jars and strange things like button hooks and hair nets which Tuppy had told him ladies used to use in the olden days, but now no longer had any need of.

"There were two red lobsters, and a ham, a fish, a pudding, and some pears and oranges."

The curtains were drawn, but outside a wind was getting up and a draft edged its way through the ill-fitting sash windows. The curtains ballooned slightly as though there were someone hidden behind them. Jason drew closer to Tuppy and was glad that she was there. These days he did not like being too far away from her in case something nameless happened and she would not be here when he got back again.

There was a nurse, a proper hospital nurse, who had come to Fernrigg to take care of Tuppy until she was better. Her name was Mrs. McLeod, and she had come all the way from Fort William to Tarbole on the train, and Watty had taken the car to Tarbole to fetch her. She and Mrs. Watty had made friends, and talked importantly in half whispers at the kitchen table over endless cups of tea. Nurse McLeod was thin and starched. She had varicose veins, too, which was perhaps one of the reasons that she and Mrs. Watty had made friends. They were always comparing their varicose veins.

"One morning Lucinda and Jane had gone out for a drive in the doll's perambulator."

Downstairs, in the cavern of the hall, the telephone started to ring. Tuppy stopped reading and looked up, taking off her spectacles.

After a little Jason said, "Go on."

"There's the telephone."

"Aunt Isobel will answer it. Go on."

Tuppy went on, but Jason could tell her mind wasn't on Lucinda and Jane. Then the ringing stopped and once more she stopped reading. Jason gave up. "Who do you think it is?" he asked.

"I don't know. But I've no doubt that in a moment or two Isobel will come upstairs and tell us."

They sat together in the big bed, the old lady and the small boy, expectant. The sound of Isobel's voice floated dimly up the staircase, but they could not hear what she said. At last there came the single ring as she put down the reciever, and then they heard her coming up the stairs and along the passage toward Tuppy's room.

The door opened and Isobel put her face around the edge of it. She was smiling, radiating suppressed excitement. Her soft grayish hair formed an untidy aureole about her beaming face. On such occasions she looked very young, not at all like a great-aunt.

"Do you two want to hear some nice happy news?" she asked, coming in and shutting the door behind her. Sukey, almost lost in the folds of the silk eiderdown, raised her head to give a cursory growl, but Isobel took no notice. She leaned on the rail at the end of Tuppy's bed and said, "That was Antony, calling from London. He's coming home for the weekend and he's bringing Rose."

"He's *coming.*" Tuppy loved Antony more than anyone else in the world, but now she sounded as though she were about to cry. Jason glanced at her anxiously but was relieved to see no sign of tears.

"Yes, they're coming. Just for a couple of days. They both have to go back on Monday. They're catching the evening flight

377

to Edinburgh and then driving over. They'll be here first thing in the morning."

"Well, isn't that splendid?" Two patches of color glowed on Tuppy's wrinkled cheeks. "They're really coming." She smiled down at Jason. "What do you think of that?"

Jason knew all about Rose. He knew that one day Antony was going to marry her. But, "I've never met Rose," he said.

"No, of course you haven't. You weren't living here when she and her mother stayed at the Beach House."

Jason knew about the Beach House, too. It had once been a fisherman's croft, tucked into the curve of the beach which lay to the north of Fernrigg. Tuppy had converted it into a little cottage and let it out in the summer to holiday people. But now the summer was over and the Beach House was closed and shuttered. Jason sometimes thought it would be a nice place to live. It would be pleasant to step out of the front door, straight onto the sand.

"What's she like?"

"Rose? Well, she was very pretty. I can't really remember very much else about her. Where is she going to sleep?" she asked Isobel.

"I thought the little single room, since it's warmer than the great big double one, and the bed's made up. I'll do some flowers."

"And Antony's room?"

"Mrs. Watty and I will do that this evening."

Tuppy laid down *The Tale Of Two Bad Mice.* "We must ask one or two people in . . ."

"Now, mother . . ." Isobel started in a warning sort of voice, but Tuppy took no notice of her. Perhaps because she was so happy, Isobel did not seem to have the heart to persist in her objections.

". . . Just a little supper party. When do you think we should have it? Sunday night? No, that wouldn't be any use because Antony will have to start back to Edinburgh. It'll have to be tomorrow night. Tell Mrs. Watty, will you, Isobel? Perhaps Watty can lay his hands on some pigeon, or better still,

378

some grouse. Or Mr. Reekie might be able to let us have some scampi."

"I'll see to it," promised Isobel, "on one condition—that you don't start trying to organize anything yourself."

"No, of course I won't, don't be so silly. And you must ring up Mr. and Mrs. Crowther, and we'll ask Anna and Brian Stoddart over from Ardmore; they knew Rose when she was out here before, and it'll be nice for Anna to have an evening out. You don't think it's too short notice, do you, Isobel? You'll have to explain, or they'll think we're very rude . . ."

"They'll understand. They won't think it's rude at all."

Mr. Crowther was the Presbyterian minister from Tarbole, and Mrs. Crowther taught Jason at Sunday School. He did not think it sounded a very gay party.

"Do I have to come?" he asked.

Tuppy laughed. "Not if you don't want to."

Jason sighed. "I wish you'd finish the story."

Tuppy began to read again, and Isobel went away to do her telephoning and confer with Mrs. Watty. Just as Tuppy reached the last page, with the picture of Hunca Munca with her dustpan and broom, Nurse McLeod came in. With her starchy rustle and her big red hands, she whisked Jason out of the bed and bundled him good-naturedly out of the way, scarcely giving him time to kiss his great-grandmother good-night.

"You don't want to make your great-granny tired," she told him. "And what Dr. Kyle would say to me if he were to come in the morning and find her all peely-wally, well, I wouldn't like to imagine."

Jason, who had sometimes overheard Dr. Kyle letting fly at something that had annoyed him, could imagine well, but decided to keep it to himself.

He went slowly through the door, not disliking Nurse, because it was nice that she was going to make Tuppy better, but wishing that she didn't always have to be in such a hurry. Feeling ill-used, he trailed along to the bathroom to clean his teeth. In the middle of this, he remembered that tomorrow was

Saturday, which meant that he did not have to go to school. And Antony was coming. Perhaps he would make Jason a bow and arrow. In good spirits, Jason finally retired to bed.

When the telephone rang at Ardmore House, Anna Stoddart was out in the garden. At that hour between daylight and darkness, the outdoors had a special magic for her and even more so at this time of the year, when the evenings were drawing in and the twilight was thick with nostalgia for the blue and gold evenings of the summer that was over.

It was easy to come indoors at tea time and draw the curtains and sit by the fire, forgetting about the scents and the sounds of outside. But then there would be a ruffle of wind against the windowpane or the scream of a gull or, at high tide, the whisper of the sea, and Anna would make some excuse, put on her jacket and gumboots, pick up her secateurs, and whistle up the dogs and go outdoors again.

From Ardmore the views of the coastline and the Islands were spectacular. This was why Anna's father, Archie Carstairs, had chosen the site for his pretentious granite mansion. Indeed, if one did not mind being a mile from Ardmore Village (where there was a general store cum post office, and the yacht club, and little else) and six miles from the shops of Tarbole, it was a marvelous place to live.

One of the reasons Anna usually liked this time of the evening was the lights. Just before dark they came on, shining out at sea, along the coast road, from the great mountains which shouldered up inland; the riding lights of fishing boats, and the warm yellow windows of distant crofts and farms. The street lights of Tarbole stained the night sky with a reddish-gold reflection, and beyond that again Fernrigg stretched like a long finger into the sea, with at its tip, half-hidden by trees, Fernrigg House.

But this evening there was nothing to be seen. The half-light swirled in mist, a fog horn sounded out at sea, and Ardmore was isolated by the weather like a house forgotten at the end of the world.

380

Anna shivered. Being able to see Fernrigg across the sound had always been a comfort to her. Fernrigg meant Tuppy Armstrong. Tuppy was Anna's touchstone, living proof that a person could live contentedly and usefully, surrounded by family and friends, never confused or lacking confidence, apparently totally happy. Tuppy, it always seemed to Anna, had lived her considerable life—and in many ways it had been a tragic one—in a straight line; never diverging, never faltering, never defeated.

Anna had been a shy little girl when she first remembered Tuppy, the only child of an elderly father more interested in his thriving business and his yachting ventures than his small silent daughter. Anna's mother had died soon after Anna was born, so that Anna had been cared for by a series of nannies and insulated from children her own age by her shyness and her father's considerable wealth.

But Tuppy never made Anna feel that she was either plain or stupid. She had always had time for Anna—time to talk and time to listen. "I'm just going out to plant bulbs," she would say. "Come and help me, and while we're working we can talk."

The memory made Anna want to cry. She pushed it to the back of her mind because she could not bear to think of Tuppy ill, much less imagine Tuppy dying. Tuppy Armstrong and Hugh Kyle were Anna's best friends. Brian was her husband and she loved him so much that it hurt, but he wasn't her friend and he never had been. She sometimes wondered if other married couples were friends, but she never got to know the women well enough to be able to ask them and find out.

She was picking the last of the roses, pale shapes in the gloom. She had meant to pick them that morning but had forgotten, and now was gathering a bunch before the first frost could nip them. The stems felt cold in her bare hands, and fumbling a little in the half light she pricked her thumb on a thorn. The smell of the roses was faint and somehow old as though already they had died, and all that remained of their summer glory was their scent.

381

She thought, *When they come again—the new buds and then the flowers—the baby will be here.*

That should have filled her with happy anticipation, but instead was more of a talisman, like touching wood. She would not think of this baby dying, of it never being born. It had taken so long to become pregnant again. After five years, she had almost given up hope. But now the living seed lay within her, growing every day. She was planning for it: knitting a tiny sweater, getting the old wicker cot down from the attic, putting her feet up in the afternoons the way Hugh had told her to do.

Next week she was going to Glasgow to buy a lot of expensive maternity clothes, and to have her hair done. A woman was at her most beautiful when she was pregnant—so the magazines proclaimed—and all at once Anna had visions of herself as a new person—someone romantic and feminine, loved and cherished.

The old-fashioned words started her. *Loved and cherished.* They seemed to reach her consciousness from some remote past. But now with the new baby coming, there was perhaps real reason to feel hopeful.

Brian had always wanted a child. Every man wanted a son. The fact that she had lost the last one had been Anna's own fault. She had worried too much and become upset too easily. But this time it was going to be different. She was older, less anxious to please, more mature. She would not lose this child.

It was nearly dark and, now, quite cold. She shivered again. Inside the house, she heard the telephone begin to ring. She thought that Brian would probably answer it, but turned toward the house anyway and began to walk up the garden, across the damp grass, up the slippery stone steps, across the crunching gravel, and through the garden door.

The telephone continued to ring. Brian had not appeared. She laid down the roses and, without bothering to remove her rubber boots, went across the hall to the corner under the stairs which, when he had built the house years ago, her father deemed a suitable place for the tiresome instrument. There

382

were other telephones at Ardmore now—in the drawing room, the kitchen, and by Anna and Brian's bed—but this one remained in its stuffy little nook.

She picked it up. "Ardmore House."

"Anna, it's Isobel Armstrong."

Fear caught at Anna. "Tuppy's all right?"

"Yes, she really is. She's looking better and she's eating quite well. Hugh got a nurse for us, a Mrs. McLeod from Fort William, and she's settled down splendidly. I think Tuppy quite likes her."

"What a relief."

"Anna, would you both be able to come over for supper tomorrow evening? It's rather short notice, but Antony is coming home for the weekend and bringing Rose, and of course the first thing Tuppy thought of was a party."

"I think we'd love to come. But isn't it too much for Tuppy?"

"Tuppy won't be there, but she's planning the whole thing. You know what she's like. And she specially wanted you and Brian to come."

"We'd love to. What time?"

"About seven thirty. And don't dress up or anything, it's just family, and maybe the Crowthers . . ."

"That'll be fun."

They chatted for a little longer, and then rang off. Isobel had not said anything about the baby because she didn't know. Nobody knew except Brian and Hugh. Anna didn't want anybody to know. If people knew perhaps she would never have it.

She came out of the little cubbyhole and began to take off her gumboots and her coat. She remembered Rose Schuster and her mother. She remembered the summer they had taken the Beach House, because that was the summer Anna had lost her baby. Pamela Schuster and her daughter were thus part of the nightmare, though that was not their fault, but Anna's own.

She remembered now that where Mrs. Schuster had been frighteningly sophisticated, her daughter was almost indecently youthful. Their glamour had rendered the shy Anna inarticulate. Because of that they had had nothing to say to Anna. Indeed after a few cursory remarks, they had taken no notice of her at all.

But Brian they had enjoyed. In the warmth of their appreciation he had been at his best, amusing and charming, his wit a match for anything they could offer. Anna, proud of her attractive young husband, had taken a back seat and been glad to do so. She wondered when her Rose had changed, whether being engaged to someone as nice as Antony had taken some of the sharp edge from her personality.

Now she stood listening, wondering where she would find Brian. The house was silent. She went across to the drawing-room door, opened it, and found the room full of light and firelight, and Brian stretched out in the armchair reading the *Scotsman*. A tumbler of whisky stood close by his hand.

He lowered the paper as she appeared and eyed her over the top of it. The telephone stood on the table by his side.

She said, "Didn't you hear the telephone ring?"

"Yes. But I guessed it would be for you."

She did not comment on this. She came over to the fire, stretching her cold hands to the blaze, warming herself. She said, "That was Isobel Armstrong."

"How's Tuppy?"

"She seems to be all right. They've got a nurse for her. They want us to go over and have supper at Fernrigg tomorrow. I said that we would."

"That's all right by me."

He began to go back to his newspaper and Anna said quickly, to keep the conversation going, "Antony's coming home for the weekend."

"So that's the reason for the celebration."

"He's bringing Rose with him."

There was a long silence. Then Brian lowered his paper, folded it, and laid it on his lap. He said, "Rose?"

"Rose Schuster. You remember. He's engaged to her."

"I thought someone said she was in America."

"Apparently not."

384

"You mean, she's coming to Fernrigg for the weekend?"

"That's what Isobel told me."

"Well, I never did," said Brian. He sat up, dropping the paper onto the hearth rug, and reached out for his drink. He tipped it back, finished it, got slowly up out of his chair and went over to the drink table to replenish his glass.

Anna said, "I've been out picking roses." The siphon swished into Brian's tumbler. "It's raining. The mist's coming in."

"It felt like that earlier on."

"I was afraid of frost."

With the glass in his hand, Brian came back to the fireside and stood looking down into the flames.

Anna straightened up. There was a mirror over the mantelpiece and their reflections stared back at them, only slightly distorted: the man, slim and dark, his eyebrows sharp-drawn as though some artist had brushed them on in India ink; and the woman, short, reaching only to his shoulder, dumpy and plain. Her eyes were close-set, her nose too big, her hair, neither brown nor fair, frizzed from the damp of the mist.

So convinced had she been by her own visions of an Anna made romantic by incipient motherhood, that her reflection came as a shock. Who was this person who stared back at her from the faded glass? Who was this person, this stranger, standing next to her handsome husband?

The answer, came, as it always came. Anna. Plain Anna. Anna Carstairs that was, Anna Stoddart that is. And nothing was ever going to change her.

Following the urgency of Antony's trip to London, the drama of their confrontation, and her eventual decision to accompany him, Flora imagined that once in Edinburgh they would get into his car and drive hotfoot or post-chaise, or whatever you wanted to call it, to Fernrigg.

But now that they were actually there, Antony's whole personality seemed to change. Like a man coming home and shrugging on an old jacket and a pair of comfortable slippers, he relaxed, slowed down, and appeared to be in no hurry to get to Fernrigg.

"We'd better get something to eat," he decided, after they had located the car, loaded Flora's suitcase into the trunk, and settled themselves in.

She looked at him in surprise. "Something to eat?"

"Yes. Aren't you hungry? I am."

"But we had a meal on the plane."

"That wasn't a meal. That was a plastic snack. And I have a horror of cold asparagus."

"But don't you want to get home as soon as possible?"

"If we start now, we'll arrive at four in the morning. The house will be locked, and we'll either have to sit outside for three hours, or wake somebody up and doubtless disrupt the entire household." He started up the engine. "We'll go into Edinburgh."

"But it's late. Will we find anything open at this hour?"

"Of course we will."

They drove to Edinburgh and Antony took her to a small club of which he was a member, where they had a drink and an excellent dinner, and then coffee. It was all very leisurely and pleasant and completely incongruous. It was nearly midnight when they finally emerged once more into the outdoors. The wind of the morning had died, and the streets of Edinburgh shone black with a thin, cold rain.

"How long will it take us?" Flora asked, as they got back into the car, fastened their seat belts and generally settled down to the long drive.

"About seven hours with this rain. The best thing you can do is go to sleep."

"I'm not very good at sleeping in cars."

"You can always try."

But Flora did not sleep. She was too excited, too apprehensive, and already suffering from a severe case of cold feet. The knowledge that she had burnt her boats, that she was on her way and there was not a mortal thing she could do now to change anything, left her feeling quite sick. If it had been a fine

386

bright night she might have tried to still her nerves by observing the passing countryside, or even reading their route on the map. But the rain was incessant, and there was nothing to be seen but the black, wet, winding road, pierced by the headlights of Antony's car, racing up to meet them in a succession of endless curves and bends, and falling away behind into the darkness to the hiss of tires on wet tarmac.

And yet, as they drove, the countryside made itself felt, even through the darkness and the deadening murk. It became more deserted, more desolate, the small country towns fewer and farther apart. They passed the long glimmer of an inland loch, and as they left it behind them the road began to climb, winding against the slope of the incline.

Through the half-open window came the smell of peat and heather. More than once Antony, with a murmured oath, was forced to brake the car to a standstill while a stray sheep or two, caught in the headlights, made its untroubled way off the crest of the road.

Flora was aware of mountains—not the little hills of home, the familiar cairns of Cornwall, but real mountains, sheer, rearing their way up at right angles and forming deep caverns and lonely glens down which the road ribboned ahead of them. There was bracken in the ditches, shining with rain, and always, even about the sound of the car's engine, the suggestion of running water which every now and then became a torrent as a waterfall leapt from some distant unseen ledge down onto the rocks of a roadside stream.

The dawn on that wet, gray morning came so gradually that Flora scarcely noticed it. It was simply a paling of the gloom, imperceptible, so that slowly it became possible to pick up the white glimmer of a hillside croft and to see the damp shapes of flocks of sheep before one was actually in danger of hitting them.

There had been little traffic on the road all night but now they began to meet great lorries coming in the opposite direction, passing them with roaring Diesel engines and waves of muddy water washing across the windscreen.

387

"Where have they suddenly appeared from?" asked Flora.

"They've come from where we're going," Antony told her.

"Fernrigg?"

"No, Tarbole. Tarbole used to be an unimportant fishing village, but it's a great herring port now."

"Where are the lorries going?"

"Edinburgh, Aberdeen, Fraserburgh—anywhere they can sell the herrings. The lobsters get taken to Prestwick and flown straight to New York. The scampi goes to London. Salted herrings go to Scandinavia."

"Hasn't Scandinavia got its own herrings?"

"The North Sea's been fished out. That's why Tarbole came into its own. Very prosperous we are these days. All the fishermen have new cars and color televisions. Jason goes to school with their children, and they have a low opinion of him because we don't have color television at Fernrigg. It cramps his style a bit, poor chap."

"How far is Tarbole from Fernrigg?"

"About six miles."

"How does he get to school each day?"

"He gets taken by Watty, the gardener. He'd like to bicycle, but Tuppy won't let him. She's quite right. He's only seven, and she lives in fear that some terrible accident will befall him."

"How long has he lived with Tuppy?"

"So far, a year. I don't know how much longer he'll stay. I suppose it depends on Torquil's job."

"Does he miss his parents?"

"Yes, of course he does. But the Persian Gulf is really no place for a child his age. And Tuppy wanted him to stay. She doesn't like the house without a little boy messing the place up. There have always been little boys at Fernrigg. I think that's one of the reasons Tuppy always seems ageless. She's never had time to grow old."

"And Isobel?"

"Isobel's a saint. Isobel was the person who looked after you when you were ill, and coped when you'd been sick, and woke up in the middle of the night to get you a drink of water."

388

"She never married?"

"No, she never married. I think the war had something to do with that. She was too young at the beginning of the war, and by the end all she wanted was to come back to Fernrigg to live. And the West Highlands aren't exactly teeming with eligible bachelors. There was a suitor once, but he was a farmer with every intention of buying a property on the Isle of Eigg. He made the mistake of taking Isobel to see it, and she was seasick on the way over, and when she got there it rained incessantly for the entire day. The farmhouse was intensely primitive, the loo was down at the end of the garden, she was seasick all the way home again, and after that the romance died an entirely natural death. We were all delighted. We didn't like the chap at all. He had a bright red face and was always talking about going back to the simple life. A terrible bore."

"Did Tuppy like him?"

"Tuppy liked everybody."

"Will she like me?"

Antony turned his head slightly and sent Flora a smile that was both rueful and conspiratorial, and not really a smile at all.

"She'll like Rose," he said.

Flora fell silent once more.

Now it was light, and the rain had turned to a soft blowing mist which was beginning to smell of the sea. The road ran downhill through cuttings of pinkish granite along sloping hills planted with stands of larch and fir. They came through small villages slowly starting to stir for the new day and by inland lochs where the dark water shivered under the touch of the west wind. With each turn of the road a new and marvelous prospect presented itself, and when at last they came to the sea, Flora realized it only when she saw the salty waves breaking onto weeded rocks at the head of yet another loch.

For a few miles they drove by the shore. Flora saw a ruined castle, the grass about its walls cropped by sheep; a coppice of silver birches, the leaves turned the color of bright new pennies; a farm with sheep pens and a dog barking. It was all remote and very beautiful.

She said, "It's romantic. Such a corny word to use, but the only one I can think of. It's romantic country."

"That's because it's Bonnie Prince Charlie country. Steeped in tradition and nostalgia. The birthplace of a thousand lost causes, the start of long years of exile and depopulation, and all those sterling Scottish women coming into their own."

"Wouldn't you like to live here? I mean, all the time."

"I have to earn a living."

"Couldn't you earn a living here?"

"Not as a chartered accountant. I could be a fisherman. Or a doctor, like Hugh Kyle. He looks after Tuppy and he's lived here, on and off, all his life."

"He must be a happy man."

"No," said Antony. "I don't really think he is."

They were in Tarbole by half past six, driving down the steep hill to the little harbor, empty now of the huge fish lorries and enjoying a quiet soon to be shattered by the boats coming in with the night's haul.

Because they were still too early, Antony drove down to the harbor road and parked the car in front of a wooden shack which faced out over the wharves and piers and the cranes and the smokehouses.

As they got out of the car the cold struck at them, rich with the smell of sea, tarred ropes, and fish. The shack had "Sandy Soutar. Teas, Coffees, Snacks" written over the door, and a warm yellow light shone from the steamy windows.

They went in, stepping up by means of an old herring box. Inside it was very warm, and smelt of new bread and bacon frying, and from behind the counter a fat woman in a flowered overall looked up from her urn, saw Antony, and broke at once into a welcoming smile.

"Antony Armstrong. For heaven's sake! What are you doing here, turned up like a bad penny?"

390

"Hello, Ina. I'm home for the weekend. Could you give us some breakfast?"

"Well, of course. Sit down. Make yourselves at home." She looked past him at Flora, her eyes bright with interest. "And is this your young lady you've brought with you? We heard you were going to be married."

"Yes," said Antony, and he took Flora's hand and pulled her forward. "This is Rose."

It was the first time. The first lie. The first hurdle.

"Hello," said Flora, and somehow, as easily as that, the hurdle was behind her.

6

JASON

Tuppy had been awake since five o'clock, expecting Antony and Rose since six.

If she had been well, she would have gotten up and dressed, gone downstairs into the silent sleeping house, and engaged herself in all the familiar routine jobs which she found so comforting. She would have opened the front door and let out the dogs and then gone into the kitchen to put on the kettle, all ready for a cup of tea. Back upstairs, she would have switched on the electric fires in the two prepared bedrooms and checked that all was ready and welcoming, with the bedcovers crisp and fresh, hangers in the wardrobes, and the drawers of the dressing tables lined with clean white paper.

Then down again to let in the dogs and give them biscuits and a little petting, to draw curtains, thus letting in the morning light, to stir the embers of the hall fire and lay on some more peat. All would have been warm and welcoming.

But she was old and now ill, and had to stay in bed while

others performed those pleasurable tasks. Frustration and boredom gnawed at her. For two pins, she thought, she would get up and get dressed, and Isobel and Nurse McLeod and Hugh Kyle could all go to the devil. But behind her resentment there was a very real fear. A miserable homecoming it would be for Antony to find his grandmother prone at the foot of the stairs because she hadn't the sense to do what she was told.

She sighed, accepting the inevitable. She ate a biscuit out of the tin by her bed and drank a little tea, which Nurse left each night in a thermos. She would contain herself in patience. But being ill, she decided, was a thorough bore. She was thankful she had never tried it before.

At seven o'clock the house began to stir. She heard Isobel come out of her room and go downstairs; she heard the sounds of dogs and the opening of the big front door, the dungeon-like iron bolts being shot back, and the great key being turned.

Presently Mrs. Watty's voice joined Isobel's and before very long the faint smell of breakfast cooking drifted up from below. Next she heard Jason go to the bathroom, and then his raised voice as he called over the banister, "Aunt Isobel!"

"Yes?"

"Have Rose and Antony come?"

"Not yet. Any moment now."

Tuppy watched her door. The handle turned, and it slowly opened. "I'm awake," she said, as Jason's blond head came around the edge of it.

"They haven't got here yet," he told her.

"By the time you get dressed, they'll probably be here."

"Did you sleep well?"

"Like a top," lied Tuppy. "Did you?"

"Yes. At least, I think I did. You don't know where my Rangers T-shirt is, do you?"

"Probably in the airing cupboard."

"Oh, all right. I'll go and look."

He disappeared, leaving the door open. The next event was the arrival of Sukey who, having been let in from her morning visit to the garden, had headed straight upstairs. She pattered

393

across the floor and leapt by means of a chair onto Tuppy's bed. With no more ado she settled herself in her usual place at the foot of the eiderdown.

"Sukey!" Tuppy reproached her, but Sukey was without conscience. She stared coldly at Tuppy for a moment, and then settled down to sleep.

Nurse was the next visitor, drawing curtains, shutting windows, turning on the fire, and making all Tuppy's ornaments rattle as she trod heavily about the room.

"We'll need to get you tidied up before your grandson and his young lady arrive," Nurse said, with a gleam in her eye. She pulled at sheets and pillows, reached into the depths of Tuppy's bed for her hot water bottle, asked her what she wanted for breakfast. "Mrs. Watty's frying bacon . . . she says Antony always looks forward to fried bacon his first morning home. Would you fancy a little yourself?"

And then, just as Tuppy was telling herself that she couldn't wait another moment, she heard the sound of Antony's car roaring up the road, through the open gates, and up the potholed driveway. The morning's calm was shattered by the double flourish of his horn, the screech of brakes, and the spatter of flying gravel. (In Tuppy's opinion, he always drove too fast.) Downstairs minor pandemonium broke out. Plummer began to bark, footsteps came up the back passage and across the hall, the door opened with a bang, and happy voices filled the house.

Here you are. Oh, how are you? How lovely to see you.

Jason said, "Hello, Antony. Did you have a good journey? Will you make me a bow and arrow?"

Tuppy heard Antony's voice. "How's Tuppy?" (Her heart melted with love for him.)

"She's *awake,*" she heard Jason telling him, his voice squeaky with excitement. "She's waiting for you."

Tuppy hugged herself in anticipation and sat watching her door and waiting for him to come, which he did almost immediately, taking the stairs two at a time as usual.

"Tuppy!"

394

"I'm here!"

Long strides took him down the landing and through the door. He burst into her room and stood beaming at her with a grin on his face like a Cheshire Cat.

"Tuppy." He wore Bedford cords and a thick sweater and a leather car coat, and when he came over to her bedside to give her a kiss she could feel the night's stubble on his chin scraping her cheeks. He was cold and his hair was too long and she could scarcely believe that he was really here.

They hugged enormously. He drew away from her. "But you're looking marvelous. What an old fraud you are."

"There's nothing wrong with me. You're later than usual. Did you have a horrid drive over?"

"No, a very good one. So good that we stopped for breakfast with Sandy in Tarbole. We're stuffed with sausages and strong tea."

"Is Rose with you?"

"Yes. Downstairs. Do you want to see her?"

"Of course I want to see her. Fetch her up at once."

He went out of the room, and she heard him calling down the stairs. "Rose!" There was no response. Then, louder this time, *"Rose!* Come along up. Tuppy's waiting to see you."

Tuppy watched the door. When he came back into the room, he was leading Rose by the hand.

She thought they both seemed shy, almost ill-at-ease, and she found this endearing, as though being in love had peeled away a little of Antony's bright veneer of sophistication.

She looked at Rose and remembered her, and thought that the five years between seventeen and twenty-two had transformed a pretty but sometimes sulky girl into something very special. She saw the tanned skin, clear with health and sheer cleanliness; the shining fall of brown hair; the eyes—such dark brown eyes. Tuppy had forgotten they were so dark. She wore the regular uniform of the young these days: washed-out jeans and a turtleneck sweater, and over it a navy blue coat with a tartan lining.

Rose said, shyly, "I'm afraid I don't look very tidy."

395

"Oh, my dear! How could you look tidy when you've been traveling all night? Anyway, I think you look charming. Now come and give me a kiss."

Rose came across and stooped to kiss Tuppy. The dark hair fell forward and touched Tuppy's cheek. Rose's own cheek was smooth and cool, reminding Tuppy of crisp, newly picked apples.

"I thought you were never coming to see me!"

Rose sat on the edge of the bed. "I'm sorry."

"You've been in America?"

"Yes."

"How's your mother?"

"Very well."

"And your father?"

"He's well too. We were on a trip." She caught sight of Sukey. "Oh, look, is this your dog?"

"You remember Sukey, Rose! She used to come on picnics on the beach with us."

"She . . . she must be getting quite old."

"She's ten. That's seventy in dog years. And even that's younger than I am. I've got more teeth than she has, but then Sukey hasn't been stupid and ill like me. Did you say you'd had breakfast?"

"Yes," said Antony. "We had it in Tarbole."

"Oh, what a shame, Mrs. Watty's frying bacon specially for you. You'll have to go and toy with it, or at least have a cup of coffee."

She smiled at Rose, feasting her eyes on the girl. She relished the thought of having her married to Antony and the pleasure of having her here, at Fernrigg.

She said, "Let me see your ring," and Rose showed it to her, the diamonds and sapphires glittering on the slender brown hand.

"What a pretty one! But then I knew it would be. Antony has very good taste."

Rose smiled. It was one of those all-embracing, lighting-up smiles that Tuppy loved . . . . the teeth very white with the two

396

front ones a little crooked, making her seem very young and vulnerable.

"How long can you stay?" asked Tuppy, not able to endure the idea that they would have to go away again, ever.

"Only till tomorrow night," said Antony. "We both have to get back."

"Two days. It's such a short time." She gave Rose's hand a little pat. "Never mind, long enough to enjoy ourselves. And we're going to have a little party tonight, just one or two people, as it's such a special occasion." She caught sight of Antony's expression. "Now, don't start fussing. I have that all the time from Isobel and Nurse. Did you know they engaged a nurse to look after me? Mrs. McLeod, and she comes from Fort William." She dropped her voice to a whisper. "She looks exactly like a horse." Rose gave a snort of laughter. "Such a lot of rubbish, but it does make things a little easier for Isobel. And of course I'm not coming to the party. I shall sit up here with a supper tray and listen to you all having a good time." She turned to Rose. "I asked Anna and Brian—you remember them, don't you? Yes, of course you do. I thought it would be fun for you to see them again."

Rose said, "I just wish you could be there too."

"How sweet you are. But if I stay in bed for just a little while longer, then I'll be on my feet for your wedding and that's the most important thing of all." She smiled again at them, her eyes moving from one face to the other. They watched her, the two pairs of eyes, one so pale and one so dark. Tuppy noticed that the dark eyes were shadowed with tiredness. She said, "Rose, have you slept at all?"

Rose shook her head. "I couldn't."

"Oh, my dear, you must be exhausted."

"I am, a little. Suddenly. Just sleepy."

"Would you like to go to bed? Sleep until lunchtime and then you'll feel better. And perhaps Antony . . ."

"I'm all right," Antony said quickly. "I'll maybe have a snooze later on in the day."

"But Rose must sleep. Mrs. Watty shall make you a hot-water bottle. And afterwards you can have a lovely bath. You'd like that, wouldn't you?"

"Yes, I would," Rose admitted.

"Then that's what you shall do. And now go down and placate Mrs. Watty by eating some bacon, and tell Nurse I'm ready for my breakfast, and," she added as they headed for the door, "thank you again, both of you, so much, for coming."

Waking was strange. The bed was strange, though marvelously soft and comfortable. The cornice of the ceiling was strange, the deep pink of the drawn curtains unfamiliar. Before she had even oriented herself, Flora drew her arm up out of the covers and looked at her watch. Eleven o'clock. She had been asleep for five hours. And here she was, at Fernrigg—Fernrigg House, in Arisaig, in Argyll, in Scotland. She was Flora, but now she was Rose, engaged to be married to Antony Armstrong.

She had met them all: Isobel; little Jason; Mrs. Watty, billowy and wholesome and floury as a newly baked scone; and Watty, her husband, tramping into the kitchen while they sat drinking coffee, with carefully doormatted boots and inquiries about vegetables. Everybody seemed delighted to see her, and it wasn't just because of Antony. Reminiscences had been the order of the day.

"And how's Mrs. Schuster?" Mrs. Watty had asked. "I remember that summer how she used to walk up to the garden every morning for fresh eggs, and Watty used to give her a head of lettuce, because she said she couldn't go a day without a fresh salad."

And Isobel remembered a certain picnic when it had been so warm that Tuppy had insisted on swimming, borrowing one of Pamela Schuster's elegant bathing suits for the purpose. "She wouldn't let any of us watch her going in. She looked indecent, she said, but actually she looked very nice, because she was always very slim."

And Antony had teased Isobel. "If Tuppy wouldn't let you

398

watch, how do you know she looked nice? You must have been peeping."

"Well, I just wanted to make sure she didn't get a cramp." Only Jason, much to his disgust, had nothing to remember. "I wish I'd been here when you were here," he told Flora, gazing at her in open and interested admiration. "But I wasn't. I was somewhere else."

"You were in Beirut," Isobel told him. "And even if you had been here you wouldn't remember very much, because you were only two."

"I can remember when I was two. I can remember lots of things."

"Like what?" asked Antony skeptically.

"Like . . . Christmas trees?" he tried hopefully.

Everybody smiled but nobody laughed at him, Flora noticed. Thus, although he knew that nobody quite believed him, his dignity remained unimpaired.

"Anyway," he added, "I would *certainly* have remembered Rose."

So their welcome was not just on account of the fact that Rose was meant to be marrying Antony. The Schusters had apparently made a certain impact on their own account five years ago which was still happily recalled, and that made things easier.

Flora looked at her watch again. Five past eleven now, and she was wide awake. She got out of bed, and went across to the windows and drew the curtains and looked straight out over the garden to the sea.

The rain had stopped and the mist was dissolving. Far away outlines of the distant islands were faintly beginning to take shape.

The tide was out, revealing a small jetty and a steep pebble beach, toward which the garden sloped in a series of grassy terraces. Away to one side she glimpsed the netting of a tennis court. Below her, the leaves of flowering shrubs were scarlet and gold, and a rowan tree hung heavy with the weight of its berries.

Flora withdrew from the window, closed it, and went in search of a bath. That she found to be a coffin-like Victorian structure enclosed in polished mahogany with sides so high that it took considerable effort to get into it at all. The water was boiling hot, very soft, and stained brown with peat. The rest of the bathroom and its accessories were all strictly period. The soap smelt faintly medicinal, the towels were vast and white and very fluffy, and there was a jar on the bathroom shelf labeled "bay rum." Altogether it was very old-fashioned and immensely luxurious.

Clean and dressed, having made her bed and hung up her clothes, Flora ventured out of her room. She walked to the end of the passage, to where the wide staircase led down to the big hall in a series of flights and landings. She stopped, listening for some sound of domestic activity, but heard nothing. She saw Tuppy's bedroom door, but was afraid of disturbing her in the middle of a nap, or in the midst of a session with her doctor or the brisk and businesslike nurse. She went downstairs and saw the smoldering fire in the huge hearth. She smelt the peat and thought it delicious.

Still there was no sound. Not really knowing her way around the house, Flora finally found the kitchen, where to her relief she saw Mrs. Watty standing at the table and plucking a bird. Mrs. Watty looked up through a drift of feathers.

"Hello, Rose. Have you had a nice wee rest?"

"Yes, thank you."

"Do you want a cup of coffee?"

"No, it's all right. I wondered, where is everybody?"

"Everybody's away on their own business. At least, as far as I know. Nurse is waiting for the doctor to come, and Miss Isobel's away to Tarbole for the errands for the party tonight, and Antony and Jason have gone over to Lochgarry to see if Willie Robertson can do something about patching up the potholes in the drive. Miss Isobel's been on at Antony each time he comes home to do something about those potholes, but you know how it is. There never seems to be enough time. But this morning he agreed and he and Jason went off about an hour ago. They'll be back for lunch." Mrs. Watty took up a murderous knife and severed the chicken's head from its body. "So it looks as though you've been left to your own devices."

Flora averted her eyes from the severed head. "Can't I do something to help you? I could lay a table or something. Or peel potatoes."

Mrs. Watty gave a peal of laughter. "Mercy, that's all done. There's nothing for you to worry your head about. Why don't you go out for a wee walk? The rain's stopped and a bit of fresh air won't do you any harm. You should go down to the Beach House. Have a look at it. See if it's changed after all these years."

"Yes," said Flora. It was a good idea. Then she would know about the Beach House and be able to talk about it the way Rose might. "But I can scarcely remember how to get there."

"Oh, you can't miss it. Just go away round the house and down the path to the sands. Mind, you should take a coat. I wouldn't trust the weather this morning, though the afternoon might be fine and bright."

Thus bidden, Flora fetched her coat from her room, came downstairs again and let herself out of the front door. The morning was cool and sweet and damp, smelling of dead leaves and peat smoke and, behind it all, the saltiness of the sea. She stood for a moment trying to get her bearings and then turned to the left, crossed the gravel in front of the house and so came to a path which led down between sloping lawns to a grove of rhododendrons.

When she finally emerged from the rhododendrons, she found herself in a newly planted stand of young firs. The path led on, however, through the saplings, until she came out at last by a gate in a drystone wall. Beyond and below this was heather, and then rocks, and then a beach of the whitest sand she had ever seen.

She realized that she had come out onto the southern shore of yet another sea loch. Now, at low tide, only a narrow channel of water split the two white beaches, and on the far

401

side the land sloped up to a pleasant prospect of shallow green hills patchworked in sheepfolds and small fields where the new-cut hay stood in hand-built stooks.

There was a small croft with blue smoke rising from the chimney and a dog at the door, and sheep (as always in this part of the world) dotted over the hillside.

Making her way down to the water's edge, Flora searched for the Beach House. She spotted it almost instantly, unmistakably tucked into the curve of the bay, and backed by a copse of gnarled oak trees.

As she started to walk towards it, she noticed the wooden steps which led up over the rocks from the beach, and the closed and shuttered face of the little house. The walls were painted white, the roof slate-blue, and the doors and shutters green. She went up the steps and saw the flagged terrace where a fiberglass dinghy had been pulled up, and a wooden tub stood filled with the dying remains of the summer's geraniums.

She turned and leaned her back against the door and looked at the view and, like an actress with a new part to play, tried to think herself into the person of Rose. Rose at seventeen. What had she done with herself that summer? How had she spent her time? Had it been fine and hot so that she could sunbathe on the terrace? Had she gone out on the loch at high tide in the little dinghy? Had she swum and collected shells and walked the shining sands?

Or had it bored her stiff? Had she sulked the days away, yearning for New York or Kitzbühel or any of her other hunting grounds? Flora wished she knew and could be more sure about Rose. She wished there had been time to get to know her sister better.

She turned and backed away from the house, gazing at it, trying to learn something from it. But its shuttered façade was like a secret face, telling her nothing. She abandoned it and went back to the beach right down to the edge of the sea, where the glass-clear water lapped the sand, and shells lay for the gathering, smooth and unbroken in the peaceful inlet.

She picked up one and then another, and became so absorbed in this aimless occupation that she lost all sense of time. There was therefore no way of knowing how long she had been there when, quite suddenly, Flora became aware that she was being watched. Looking up from the shells, she saw a car parked by the edge of the narrow road at the head of the loch. It had not been there before. And by it, motionless, his hands in his pockets, stood a man.

They were perhaps a hundred yards apart. But at once, realizing that Flora had seen him, he took his hands out of his pockets, made the short descent down onto the beach, and began to walk across the sands toward her.

Immediately Flora was self-conscious. She and the approaching man were the only two souls in sight (if you discounted a number of greedy sea-birds), and various fantasies flashed through her mind.

Perhaps he was lost and wanted to ask the way. Perhaps he was looking for somewhere to spend next summer's holiday with his wife and family, and Beach House had caught his eye. Perhaps he was a sex maniac out for a walk. Flora wished she had thought to bring a dog with her.

But then she told herself not to be a fool, for even at this distance, his solid respectability proclaimed itself: in his size, which was exceptional, for he was very tall and broad in proportion, wide-shouldered and long-legged; in his purposeful, unhurried stride which covered the distance between them with the easy lope of a man used to walking; in his conventional, country clothes. Perhaps he was a farmer or a neighboring landowner. She imagined a large, drafty house and shooting parties in August.

The time had come to make some sort of acknowledgment rather than just stand there with her hands full of shells, staring at him. Flora tried a faint smile, but got no response. He simply continued to approach, bearing down on her like a tank. He was perhaps between thirty and forty, with a face set in strong lines; his hair, his suit, even his shirt and tie were of no particular color and totally unobtrusive. Only his eyes broke the pattern, being so bright and deep a blue that Flora found herself

403

taken off guard. She had expected many things, but not this chill, this bright glare of antagonism.

He came at last to a halt, not a yard from where she stood, standing braced against the slope of the beach, with his weight on one foot. A wind stirred and blew a strand of hair across Flora's cheek. She pushed it away. He said, "Hello, Rose."

I'm not Rose.

"Hello," said Flora.

"Are you reviving happy memories?"

"Yes. I suppose I am."

"How does it feel to be back?" His voice held the soft cadence of the West Highlands. So he was a local man. And he knew Rose. But who was he?

"It feels nice," said Flora, wishing that her own voice would sound more sure of itself.

He slid his hands into his trouser pockets. "You know, I never believed that you'd actually come back."

"That's not a very kindly welcome. Or is it?"

"You were never a fool, Rose. Don't let's pretend that you ever expected anything else from me."

"Why shouldn't I come?"

He nearly smiled at that, but it did nothing to improve his expression.

"I don't think either you or I need to ask that question."

Somewhere, deep in the pit of Flora's stomach, small stirrings of annoyance began to make themselves felt. She did not like being so openly disliked.

"Did you walk all the way down the beach, just to tell me that?"

"No. I came to tell you one or two other things. To remind you that you are no longer an artless teenager. You're engaged to Antony. A grownup woman. I simply hope, for your own sake, you've learned to behave like one."

If she felt intimidated, she was determined not to show it.

"That sounds like a threat," said Flora as jauntily as she could.

404

"No. Not a threat. A warning. A friendly warning. And now, I'll bid you good day and leave you to your shells."

And with that he turned and left her, moving away from her as abruptly as he had come, apparently unhurried, but covering the ground with his long-legged stride and astonishing swiftness.

Flora, rooted to the ground, watched him go. In no time, it seemed, he had reached the rocks, mounted them easily, got into his car, turned it, and driven back onto the road which led to Tarbole.

Still she stood there like one punch-drunk, holding the shells, her mind seething with questions. But out of all this emerged only one possible answer. Rose, at seventeen, had had some sort of an ill-fated affair with that man. Nothing else she could think of could explain such resentment, such ill-concealed dislike.

She dropped the shells abruptly and began to walk, slowly at first and then more quickly, back towards the comfort of Fernrigg. She thought of finding Antony, of telling him, of taking him into her confidence; and then on second thought decided against it.

After all, she was not really involved. She was Flora, not Rose. She was only here at Fernrigg for two days. They would be leaving tomorrow night, and then she would never see any of them again. She would never see that man again. He had known Rose, but that did not mean he was a friend of the Armstrongs. Even if he were an acquaintance, it seemed highly unlikely that Tuppy Armstrong would ever ask such a disagreeable person to her house.

Having come to this conclusion, Flora vowed to put the entire incident out of her mind. But it was hard not to suspect that Rose had, perhaps, not behaved as well as she might.

After that it was something of a relief, as she emerged from the rhododendron grove, to see Antony and Jason walking across the grass toward her, coming to find her. They both wore disreputable jeans and large bulky sweaters. There were holes in the toes of Jason's canvas sneakers, and his shoe laces

405

were undone. When he saw Flora, he started to run to meet her, tripped on the lace, fell flat on his face, got up immediately, and continued running. Flora caught him as he reached her, picked him up, and swung him around.

"We've been looking for you," he told her. "It's nearly lunchtime, and it's shepherd's pie."

"I'm sorry. I didn't realize it was so late." She looked up over his head at Antony.

"Good morning," he said, and unexpectedly, stooped to kiss her. "How are you?"

"Very well."

"Mrs. Watty told us you'd come out for a walk. Did you find the Beach House?"

"Yes."

"Everything all right?"

He was not asking about the Beach House, but about Flora, about how she felt, how she was coping with the situation into which he had plunged her. His concern touched her, and because she did not want him to think that anything untoward might have happened, she smiled and told him firmly that everything was perfect.

"Did you go to the Beach House?" asked Jason.

"Yes." They began to walk back to the house, Jason holding Flora's hand. "But it's all shuttered up and I couldn't see inside."

"I know. Watty goes down at the end of every summer and does that, otherwise boys come out from Tarbole and break the windows. Once somebody broke a window and got in and stole a blanket." He made it sound as criminal as murder.

"And what have you been doing this morning?" Flora asked him.

"We went to Lochgarry to see Willie Robertson about the holes in the drive, and Willie's going to come with his tar machine and fill them all up. He said he'd come next week."

Antony was not so sure. "That probably means next year," he told Flora. "This is the west of Scotland and the passage of time is of no concern. *Mañana* means yesterday."

"And Mrs. Robertson gave me some toffee and then we went to the pier at Tarbole and there's a ship in from Denmark and they're packing herrings in barrels and I saw a gull and it ate a mackerel in *one gulp*."

"Herring gulls are always very greedy."

"And this afternoon, Antony's going to make me a bow and arrow."

"Perhaps," suggested Antony, "we should ask Rose what she wants to do."

Jason looked up at her in some anxiety. "You'd like to make a bow and arrow, wouldn't you?"

"Yes, I would. But I don't suppose it'll take very long. Perhaps there'd be time to do something else as well. Like go for a walk. Don't the dogs like being taken for walks?"

"Yes, Plummer loves it, but Sukey's lazy, she just likes sitting on Tuppy's bed," Jason answered.

"I must say, she looks very comfortable there."

"She's Tuppy's dog, you see. She's always belonged to Tuppy. Tuppy loves her. But I think Sukey's breath smells horrid."

As the dining-room table had already been laid for the supper party that evening, everyone had lunch in the kitchen, sitting around the big scrubbed table. It had been spread with a blue-and-white checked cloth and decorated with a jug of yellow chrysanthemums. Antony sat at one end of the table and Jason at the other, with Isobel, Nurse McLeod, Flora, and Mrs. Watty ranged down either side. There was the promised shepherd's pie, and then stewed apples and cream, all very simple and very hot and very delicious. When they had finished, Mrs. Watty made coffee, and they sat there discussing how they would spend the remainder of the day.

"I'm going to garden," said Isobel firmly. "It's going to be a beautiful afternoon and I've been wanting to get at that border for days."

"We thought we'd go for a walk," said Antony.

"In that case you can take Plummer with you."

Jason broke in. "But Antony, you said that . . ."

Antony interrupted him. "If you mention that bow and arrow once again, I shall make one and then shoot you with it, straight through the heart." He aimed an imaginary bow and arrow in the direction of Jason and fired it. "Twang."

With an air of righteousness, Jason said, "You mustn't ever fire things at people. Never never let your gun pointed be at anyone."

"It's a laudable stricture," said Antony, "but a useless piece of verse." He turned to Flora. "Shall we go up and see Tuppy for a moment?"

But Nurse McLeod invervened. "Mrs. Armstrong had a bad night and didn't sleep at all, so not just now, if you don't mind. I'm just away upstairs to settle her for a little nap. It doesn't do for her to get overexcited."

Antony, meekly, accepted this. "Just as you say, Nurse. You're the boss." Nurse pushed back her chair and stood up, towering over them all like some formidable nanny. "But when can we come and see her?"

"How about before dinner tonight? When you're all dressed up and ready for the party? It'll make a wee occasion for her, to see you all then."

"All right. Tell her we'll be along about seven o'clock, looking unbelievably dressy."

"I'll do that," said Nurse. "And now, if you'll all excuse me, I must see to my patient. And thank you for lunch, Mrs. Watty, it was just delicious."

"I'm glad you enjoyed it, Nurse," Mrs. Watty beamed, reaching out her huge arm to pour them all another cup of coffee.

When Nurse had left them, Antony leaned his elbows on the table and said, "She talks as though we were going to throw some great reception here, with all the men in boiled shirts and monocles, and Aunt Isobel sweeping about in the heirloom diamonds and a train. Who's actually coming?"

"Anna and Brian. And Mr. and Mrs. Crowther . . ."

"Gayer and gayer," murmured Antony. Isobel sent him a

408

fairly cool glance and went on, undeterred. "And, provided he isn't called out for a baby or an appendix, or some other emergency, Hugh Kyle."

"That's a bit better. Conversation will doubtless sparkle."

"Now don't try to be too clever," his aunt warned him.

"He'll not catch Mr. Crowther napping," Mrs. Watty observed. "Mr. Crowther is very quick at the repartee."

Flora asked, "Who's Mr. Crowther?"

"He's the Presbyterian meenister," Antony told her, in an accent more Highland than Mrs. Watty's own.

Jason chipped in. "And Mrs. Crowther teaches Sunday school, and she's got very big teeth."

Isobel said, "Jason!" but Antony said, "All the better to eat you with. Are you coming to the party, Jason?"

"No," said Jason. "I don't want to. I'm going to have supper here with Mrs. Watty, and Aunt Isobel's got me a bottle of Coke."

"If conversation gets too sticky in the dining room," said Antony, "I might well come and join you." Isobel said, "Antony!" again, but Flora could tell that she knew he was teasing. He had probably teased her all his life, which was one of the reasons she so missed him and looked forward to his coming home.

Making the bow and arrow took a little time. Antony's good penknife and a length of suitable string had to be found, and then the right sort and shape of branch for the bow. Antony was neat-fingered and had obviously done this thing many times before, but still indulged in a good deal of cursing and bad language before the new bow and a few arrows were finally done. Then with a piece of chalk he drew a target on the trunk of a tree, and Jason, straining every muscle of his puny arms, fired the arrows, missing with most but finally making some sort of contact with the target. The arrows, however, were not flying true.

"They need to be feathered," Antony told Jason.

"How do I feather them?"

"I'll show you tomorrow. It'll take too long now."

409

"I wish you'd show me now."

"No. We're going for a walk now. We're going to take Plummer. Do you want to come?"

"Yes."

"Well, put the bow and arrow away, and then we'll go."

Jason gathered up his new possessions and went back to the house to stow them inside the front door, along with a battered croquet set and a number of fraying deck chairs. Antony came over to where Flora and Plummer had been sitting patiently on the grass, waiting for the target practice to be over.

He said, "I'm sorry. It took a long time."

"That's all right. Do you know, it's like summer, sitting here. It's turned into a beautiful summer's day."

"I know. It happens in this part of the world. And tomorrow will probably be a drencher." Jason came running back up the grass toward them. Antony held out a hand to Flora. "Come along," he said.

They went down the drive, through the gate and across the road, and on up the hill that rose behind the house. They crossed fields of stubble and pastures full of sturdy cattle. They climbed a dike and jumped down into deep heather crisscrossed with sheep tracks. Plummer, nose down, tail going like a piston, startled a family of grouse which exploded out of the heather at their feet and sailed away ahead of them, calling, *Go back, go back, go back.*

The slope of the hill became steeper, sweeping on and up to the skyline. Ahead, the ruins of a croft appeared with a scarlet-berried rowan tree by the gaping doorway, and nearby a lonely Scots pine, twisted and deformed by the constant wind, stood guard.

In front of the croft was a stream, its water peat-brown, tumbling down the hill in a series of miniature waterfalls and deep pools where the dark foam gathered like lather beneath tufts of overhanging heather. Rushes grew in clumps as green as emerald. The ground was boggy and the white canna blew in the wind. They crossed the stream by means of some wobbling stepping stones and came into the shelter of the ruined walls.

410

They had now reached the crest of the hill. On all sides the land fell away, and suddenly unexpected breathtaking views revealed themselves. To the south, beyond the forested hills, lay the Sound of Arisaig; to the north the blue waters of an inland loch, imprisoned by massive flanks, reached deep into the hills. And to the west . . .

They sat with their shoulders against a crumbling dike and gazed at the incomparable view. The western sea, a brilliant blue now, was dancing with sun pennies. The sky was cloudless, and the visibility clear as crystal. Under those conditions, the islands lay on the water like mirages.

"Imagine living here," murmured Flora, "and looking at that every day of your life."

"Yes, except that you wouldn't see it. Most of the time you couldn't see the end of your nose for rain, and if it wasn't raining it would be blowing a force twelve gale."

"Don't spoil it."

He quoted, " 'A naked house, a naked moor, a shivering pool before the door.' Robert Louis Stevenson. Tuppy used to read him to Torquil and me when she thought we were in need of a little culture." He pointed. "The small island is Muck. And that is Eigg. The mountainous one is Rhum, and then away to your right is Sleat, and beyond Sleat the Cuillins."

The distant needle peaks glittered silver against the sky. "That looks like snow," said Flora.

"It is, too. We must be in for a hard winter."

"And the loch, the one in the mountains. What's that called?"

"That's Loch Fhada. You know the sea loch where the Beach House is? That's Fhada, too. The fresh-water loch runs out into the sea, right there, under the road bridge. There's a dam and a fish ladder for the salmon . . ."

His voice trailed away. Talking, they had forgotten about Jason. He stood beside them, listening, puzzlement in his eyes.

"Why?" he asked. "Why do you tell Rose all these things as though she'd never been here before? You make it sound as

411

though she'd never been to Fernrigg before. As though she'd never *been* here."

Antony said "Yes . . . well . . ."

But Flora spoke quickly. "It was so long ago, and when I was seventeen, I wasn't very interested in learning the names of places. But now I am."

"I suppose that's because you're coming to live here."

"No, I won't come and live here."

"But if you marry Antony?"

"Antony lives in Edinburgh."

"But you'll come and stay here, won't you? With Tuppy?"

"Yes," Flora finally had to agree, "yes, I expect I will."

The slightly strained silence which fell upon the party was tactfully broken by Plummer who, though old enough to know better, suddenly decided to chase a rabbit. Off he went, bouncing through the heather with his ears flying, while Jason, who knew that Plummer was quite capable of chasing the rabbit to the ends of the earth and losing himself in the process, went after him.

"Plummer! Plummer, you're very naughty. Come back!" His legs were spider-like, his high voice carried away by the wind. "Plummer, come back!"

"Ought we to help?" asked Flora.

"No, he'll catch him." Antony turned to her. "We nearly messed things up there, didn't we? Jason's a bright child. I never realized he was listening."

"I forgot, too."

"Are you going to be all right tonight? Conversation-wise, I mean?"

"If you stick near me, I'll be all right."

"I was teasing Aunt Isobel at lunchtime. They're nice people."

"Yes, I'm sure." She smiled, to reassure him.

He said, slowly, "You know, I can't get used to this idea that you look like Rose, but you aren't Rose. It keeps coming back and hitting me just as hard as it did the first time."

412

"Do you wish I were?"

"I didn't mean that. I meant that something—perhaps the chemistry—is different."

"You mean you're not in love with me like you were with Rose."

"But if I'm not in love with you, then why aren't I?"

"Because I'm Flora."

"You're nicer than Rose. You know that, don't you? Rose would never have had any time for Jason. Rose wouldn't have known how to talk to people like Mrs. Watty and Nurse."

"No, but she would have known what to say to you, and perhaps that's more important."

"She said goodbye to me," Antony pointed out with some bitterness. "And went off to Spetsai with some bloody Greek."

"And you told me you were so hard-headed."

He grinned, ruefully. "I know. But I do want to get married, that's the funny thing. After all, I'm thirty, I can't go on being a bachelor for the rest of my days. I don't know. I suppose I just haven't met the right girl."

"Edinburgh must be running with them. Fresh-faced lassies living on their own in Georgian flats."

He laughed. "Is that how you imagine life in Edinburgh?"

"Life in Edinburgh, to me, is dinner with Antony Armstrong, on a wet, black night." She looked at her watch. "You know, when Jason and Plummer finally return, I think we should go home. If Isobel's going to wear the family diamonds, I should at least wash my hair."

"Yes, of course. And Jason and I have promised to do the hens for Watty." He looked at her and gave a snort of laughter. "Family life. So glamorous." He stooped and kissed her, a proper kiss, on her mouth. When he drew away she asked, "Is that for Rose, or for Flora?"

"It's for you," Antony told her.

That evening the sun went down behind the sea in a welter of liquid golds and reds. Flora, having washed her hair and now trying to dry it with an old-fashioned device borrowed

413

from Isobel, left the curtains drawn back and watched the sunset with something like disbelief. Gradually, as the light altered, the colors changed, and the islands turned pink and then a dusky blue. The sea was a mirror for the sky and when the sun had finally gone, it darkéned to an inky indigo starred by the riding lights of fishing boats setting out from Tarbole for the night's work.

While all that was going on, the house rang with the pleasant sounds of the preparations for the evening's festivities. People went up and down stairs, called to each other, drew curtains, built up fires. There was the clatter of pots and china from the kitchen, and delicious smells of cooking presently began to drift upstairs.

What to wear was no problem for Flora, since she had brought only one possible outfit: a long skirt of turquoise wool, a silk shirt, and a wide belt to cinch the lot together. In fact, recalling the speed with which she had packed in London, she was amazed that she had brought even these. When she had done her hair and made up her eyes, she put them on, screwed on some earrings, and squirted herself with the Chamade that Marcia had given her for her birthday. The smell of it, in the way that smells are apt to do, brought back Marcia and her father and Seal Cottage so vividly that all at once Flora felt lost.

What was she doing here? The answer to the question was outrageous. The insanity of what she was doing hit her like a kick in the stomach, and she was overwhelmed with panic. Everything turned sour. She sat at the mirror staring at her own reflection and knew that the evening lay ahead of her like a nightmare of lies. She would make a fool of herself, give herself away, let Antony down. And they would all know that she was nothing but a lie on two legs, the worst sort of cheat.

Every instinct in her being told her to get out. Now. Before anybody could find out. Before anybody could be hurt. But how could she go? And where would she go? And hadn't she given Antony a sort of promise? Antony, who had embarked on the crazy deception with the best of intentions, and all for the sake of Tuppy.

She tried to pull herself together. After all, neither of them was going to get anything out of it. Neither of them stood to gain a mortal thing, except perhaps an uneasy conscience for the rest of their lives. It wasn't really going to affect anybody else.

Or was it? All afternoon Flora had resolutely not thought about the man on the beach. But now he came back again, that big antagonistic man, with his veiled threats that he had called a warning. While he existed there was no sense in pretending that the situation was simple. She could only hope that he had nothing to do with the Armstrongs. And, when one came down to basics, Tuppy was the only person who mattered. *Perhaps if a wrong thing were done for a good reason, that made it right.* And if ever there was a good reason, then it was Tuppy, the old lady in her room down the passage, waiting now for Flora to go and say goodnight to her.

Flora? No, not Flora. Rose.

She took a deep breath, turned away from the mirror, drew the curtains, turned off the lights, went out of her room and down the passage to Tuppy's door. She knocked and Tuppy called, "Come in."

Flora had expected to find Antony there, but Tuppy was alone. The room was half-dark, lit only be the bedside lamps which cast a warm circle of light over the great bed at the end of the room. In it, supported by many pillows sat Tuppy, wearing a fresh lawn nightdress with lace at the throat and a bedjacket of palest blue Shetland wool, tied with satin ribbons.

"Rose! I've been waiting for you. Come and let me look at you."

Flora obligingly stepped forward into the light and displayed herself.

"It's not very grand, but it's all I've got with me." She went to the bedside to give Tuppy a kiss.

"I love it. So young and pretty. And you look so tall and

415

slim with that tiny waist. There's nothing so pretty as a tiny waist."

"You look pretty too," Flora said, settling herself on the edge of the bed.

"Nurse dressed me up."

"I love the bedjacket."

"Isobel gave it to me last Christmas. It's the first time I've worn it."

"Has Antony been to see you yet?"

"He was in about half an hour ago."

"Did you sleep this afternoon?"

"A little. And what did you do?"

Flora began to tell her, and Tuppy lay back on her pillows and listened. The light fell on her face, and Flora was suddenly afraid for her, because all at once Tuppy looked frail and exhausted. There were dark smudges of fatigue beneath her eyes, and her hands, gnarled and brown as old tree roots, fidgeted restlessly with the hem of the sheet as Flora talked.

And yet it was a wonderful face. Probably as a girl she had not been beautiful, but in old age the bone structure, the vitality, came into their own, and Flora found her fascinating. Her skin, fine and dry, tanned by a lifetime of being outdoors, was fretted by wrinkles; to touch her cheek was like touching a withered leaf. Her white hair was short and curled disarmingly about her temples. The lobes of her ears had been pierced for earrings and had stretched, deformed by the weight of the old-fashioned jewelry she had worn all her life. Her mouth was the same shape as Antony's, and they shared the same warm, sudden smile. But it was Tuppy's eyes which held your attention, deep-set eyes, shining periwinkle blue, bright with interest in everything that was going on.

". . . And then we came home, and the boys went off to feed the hens and collect the eggs and I washed my hair."

"It looks lovely. Shiny. Like well-polished furniture. Hugh's just been in to see me, and I was telling him all about you. He's downstairs now, having a drink with Antony. So nice he could come. He's such a busy man, poor pet. In a way it's

416

his own fault, though. I'm always on at him to get a partner. The practice had grown too much for any single man over these last years. But he swears he can manage on his own. I think he prefers it that way. Then there isn't time for him to brood and be unhappy."

Flora remembered Antony talking about Hugh Kyle.

He's lived here on and off, all his life.

He must be a happy man.

No. I don't really think he is.

"Is he married?" she asked, without thinking.

Tuppy sent her a sharp look. "Don't you remember, Rose? Hugh's a widower. He was married, but his wife was killed in a car accident."

"Oh, Oh, yes, of course."

"It was all so sad. We've known Hugh all our lives. His father was the Tarbole doctor for years, and we watched Hugh growing up. He was always such a clever, bright little boy. He was working in London for his F.R.C.S., but when his wife died he threw the whole thing over and came back to Tarbole to take over from his father. He was still in his twenties then, and I could hardly bear it for him. Such a waste of all the promise, all that talent."

"Perhaps he should get married again."

"Of course he should, but he won't. He says he doesn't want to. He's got a housekeeper called Jessie McKenzie, but she's very slapdash and careless and between the two of them they manage to run a very cheerless establishment." Tuppy sighed. "But what can one do? We can't run other people's lives for them." She smiled, her eyes bright with amusement. "Even I can't run Hugh's life for him, hard though I try. You see, I've always been an impossibly bossy, interfering person. But my family and friends know this, and they've come to accept it quite graciously."

"I think they probably enjoy it."

"Yes." Tuppy became thoughtful. "You know, Rose, lying here this afternoon, I had such a good idea . . ." Her voice faltered a little, and she reached out and took Flora's hand in

417

her own, as though the physical contact would give her some of the younger person's strength. "Do you *have* to go back with Antony?" Flora stared at her. "I mean, Antony has to get back to Edinburgh because of his job, but I thought perhaps—do you have a job in London?"

"Well, no, not exactly, but . . ."

"But you have to get back?"

"Yes, I suppose I should. I mean . . ." It was Flora's turn to falter. She found herself, horrifyingly, without words.

"Because," Tuppy went on, more forcefully now, "if you didn't have to get back, you could stay here. We all love you so much, and two days is scarcely long enough to get to know you again. And there are so many things I want to do. I really ought to do. About the wedding . . ."

"But we don't know when we're getting married!"

"Yes, but there are lists to be made of people who ought to be invited. And then there are things here that belong to Antony, that he should have when he sets up an establishment of his own. Some silver that was his father's and pictures that belong to him. And furniture, and his grandfather's desk. All those things should be arranged. It isn't good to leave everything in the air."

"But Tuppy, you're not meant to be worrying about Antony and me. That isn't why we came back to see you. You're meant to be resting, getting strong again."

"But I may not get strong. I may never get better. Now, don't put on that prissy face, one must face facts. And if I don't, then it makes everything so much easier if all these tiresome little details have already been seen to."

There was a long pause. At last Flora, hating herself, said, "I really don't think I can stay. Please forgive me. But I must go tomorrow with Antony."

Disappointment clouded Tuppy's face, but only for an instant. "In that case," she said, smiling, and giving Flora's hand a little pat, "you'll just have to come back to Fernrigg again before too long, and we'll have a little session then."

"Yes, I'll try to do that. I . . . I'm truly sorry."

"My dear child, don't look so tragic. It's not the end of the world. Just a silly idea I had. And now, perhaps you should go downstairs. Our guests will be arriving and you must be there to greet them. Off you run."

"I'll see you tomorrow."

"Of course. Goodnight, my dear."

Flora leaned forward to kiss her goodnight. As she did so, the door behind them opened and Jason appeared in his dressing gown, with his bedtime book under his arm.

"I'm just going," Flora assured him, getting up off the edge of the bed.

He closed the door. "You look nice. Hello, Tuppy, did you have a good sleep this afternoon?"

"A splendid sleep."

"I didn't bring *Peter Rabbit,* I brought *Treasure Island,* because Antony says it's time I made myself brave enough to listen to it."

"Well, if it's too frightening," said Tuppy, "we can always stop and try something else."

He handed her the book and without more ado climbed into the large soft bed beside her, arranging the sheets and blankets over his knees, and generally making himself snug.

"Did you have a good supper?" asked Flora.

"Yes, delicious. I'm all burpy with Coke." Wanting her to go away so that he and Tuppy could get on with the story, he added, "Hugh's downstairs, but not anybody else yet."

"In that case," said Flora, "I'd better go down and say good evening."

She left them, closed the door behind her, and stood there, her hands pressed to her cheeks, trying to compose herself. She felt as though she had come through some dreadful ordeal, and hated herself for feeling this way. The disappointment she had seen in Tuppy's eyes would haunt her, she felt, for the rest of her life. But what else was there to say? What else could she have done, but refuse to stay?

Why couldn't life remain simple? Why did everything have to be complicated by people, emotions, and human rela-

419

tionship? What had started out as well-intended and innocent deception, was turning ugly, swelling out of all proportion. How could Flora have known what she was letting herself in for? Nothing Antony had said could have prepared her for the impact that Tuppy's warm and loving personality had made upon her.

She sighed deeply, bracing herself for the next hurdle. She started downstairs. The carpet felt thick beneath the soles of her gold slippers. There was a fresh arrangement of beech leaves and chrysanthemums on the windowsill. The hall had been tidied for the expected company, the curtains drawn across the french windows, the fire made up. The drawing-room door stood half-open and from beyond it came the sound of voices.

Antony was speaking. "What you're telling, us, Hugh, is that Tuppy's going to make some sort of a recovery. Is that it?"

"Certainly. I've said so all along."

The voice was deep, the intonation dismayingly familiar. Flora stopped dead, not meaning to eavesdrop but all at once unable to move.

"But Isobel thought . . ."

"What did Isobel think?"

Isobel replied, sounding both nervous and foolish, "I thought . . . I thought you were trying to protect me. To keep it from me."

"Isobel!" The voice was filled with reproach. "You've known me all my life. I would never keep anything from you. You must realize that. Most certainly if it was to do with Tuppy."

"It . . . it was the expression on your face."

"Unfortunately"—he sounded as if he were trying to make a joke of it—"I can do nothing about the expression on my face. I was probably born with it."

"No, I remember." Isobel was being very definite. "I came out of the drawing room, and you were standing halfway up the stairs. Just standing there. And there was a look on your face that frightened me. I knew it had to be about Tuppy . . ."

"But it wasn't about Tuppy. It was something else, something that was worrying me very much, but it wasn't about Tuppy. And I told you she was going to be all right. I told you, if I remember, that she was as strong as an old heather root, and she would probably outlive us all."

There was a pause and then, Isobel admitted, "I didn't believe you," sounding as if she were about to burst into tears.

Flora could bear it no longer. She walked in through the open door.

The drawing room at Fernrigg that evening had the aspect of a stage set, lit and furnished for the opening act of some Victorian piece. The illusion was heightened by the disposal of the three people who, as Flora suddenly appeared, stopped talking and turned to look at her.

She was aware of Antony, in a dark gray suit, occupied at a table on the far side of the room, and in the process of pouring a drink; and of Isobel in a long dress of heather-colored wool, standing at one side of the fireplace.

But she had eyes only for the other man. The doctor. Hugh Kyle. He faced Isobel across the hearthrug. He was so tall that his head and shoulders were reflected in the Venetian mirror that hung above the high, marble mantelpiece.

"Rose!" said Isobel. "Come close to the fire. You remember Hugh, don't you?"

"Yes," said Flora. As soon as she had heard his voice, she had known that it would be him. The man she had met on the beach that morning. "Yes, I remember."

421

7

TUPPY

"Of course," he said. "We remember each other. How are you, Rose?"

She frowned. "I couldn't help hearing. You were talking about Tuppy."

Antony, without asking what she wanted, brought her over a drink. "Yes," he said. "There seems to have been some sort of a misunderstanding."

She took the tumbler which was iced and very cold to her hand. "She's going to be all right?"

"Yes. Hugh says so."

Flora felt as if she might burst into tears.

"It was my fault," Isobel explained quickly. "My silly fault. But I was so upset. I thought Hugh was trying to tell me that Tuppy was going to . . ." She couldn't manage the word *die*. "That she wasn't going to get better. And that's what I told Antony."

"But it's not true?"

422

"No."

Flora looked at Antony and his steady eyes met hers. The two conspirators, she thought. Hoist with their own petard. They need never have come to Fernrigg. They need never have embarked on this maniacal charade. The whole carefully manufactured deception had been for nothing.

Antony had an expressive face. It was plain that he knew what Flora was thinking. They had made fools of themselves. He was sorry. And yet there was a sort of relief there, too, a lessening of the tension in his fine-drawn face. He was inexpressibly fond of his grandmother.

He said again, with the deepest satisfaction, "She's going to get better." Flora found his hand and pressed it. He turned back to the others and went on, "The thing is, that if Rose and I hadn't believed there was a certain urgency to the situation, we probably wouldn't have come at all this weekend."

"In that case," said Isobel, sounding recovered, "I'm very glad I was so silly and misunderstood Hugh. I'm sorry if I frightened you, but at least it got you here."

"Hear, hear," said Hugh. "I couldn't have prescribed a more effective medicine. You've both done Tuppy a world of good." He turned his back to the fire and settled his wide shoulders against the mantelpiece. Across the room, Flora felt his eyes on her. "And now that you're here, Rose, how does it feel to be back in Scotland?"

His manner was pleasant, but his blue eyes no warmer, and she remained wary of him.

"Very nice."

"Is this your first visit since you were last here?"

"Yes it is."

"She's been in the States all summer." That was Antony, the alert prompter in the wings.

Hugh raised his eyebrows. "Really? Whereabouts?"

Flora tried to remember where Rose had been. "Oh . . . New York. And the Grand Canyon. And places."

He inclined his head, acknowledging her traveled state. "How is your mother?"

"She's very well, thank you."

"Is she coming back to Fernrigg, too?" He sounded patient as he persevered with the sticky conversation.

"No. I . . . I think she's going to stay in New York for a bit."

"But she'll doubtless be coming over for the wedding. Unless you plan to be married in New York?"

"Oh, don't suggest such a thing," said Isobel. "How could we all get to New York?"

Antony said quickly, "Nothing's been decided, anyway. Not even a date, let alone where it's going to take place."

"In that case," said Hugh, "it sounds a little as though we're crossing bridges before we get to them."

"Yes. It does."

There was a small pause while they all sipped their drinks. Flora cast about for some fresh topic of conversation, but before she could think of one, there came the sounds of cars arriving, the slamming of doors, and Isobel said, "There are the others."

"It seems," said Antony, "that they've all come at once." And he laid down his drink and went out to greet the new arrivals.

After a moment Isobel said, "If you'll excuse me," and to Flora's horror, she, too, put down her glass and followed Antony, doubtless to take the ladies of the party upstairs, to divest themselves of coats and perhaps comb their hair.

Thus, Flora and Hugh Kyle were left alone. The silence that lay between them was pregnant with things unsaid. She toyed with the idea of going straight into the attack—of saying, *I can see that you want to keep the good opinion of the Armstrongs, but you're being a great deal more pleasant to me now than you were this morning.* But, she told herself, this was neither the time nor the place for a showdown. Besides, it was impossible to defend herself when she had no idea what it was she was supposed to have done.

The possibilities, however, were daunting. Rose, Flora was beginning to accept, was not a woman of the highest principles.

424

She had ditched Antony without a qualm of conscience, swanned off to Greece with some newly met swain, and deliberately left Flora to pick up the pieces of her broken engagement.

Who could guess at the horrors that Rose, at seventeen, would have been capable of committing? Flora had imagined her as young and frustrated and bored stiff. Was it so unlikely that in order to amuse herself, she had taken up with the first eligible man who came her way?

But Hugh Kyle did not look that sort of person. Not a man that any girl would consider playing fast and loose with. He was, in fact, formidable. Flora made herself look at him, standing as before with his back to the fire, his penetrating blue eyes watching her, unblinking, over the rim of his tumbler of whisky. This evening he wore a dark suit of some distinction, a silk shirt and some sort of a club tie with emblems on it. She wished that he were not so large. It was disconcerting having to stand there, looking up at him, and the expression she found on his face caused the very last of her courage to dribble away. She was confounded. She was without anything to say.

He seemed to be aware of her discomfiture and, surprisingly, to take pity on her, for it was he who broke the silence.

"Tuppy tells me that you and Antony have to leave tomorrow."

"Yes."

"Well, you've had one lovely afternoon."

"Yes, it was lovely."

"How did you spend it?"

"We went for a walk."

At that juncture they were mercifully interrupted by Antony, ushering in the two males among the newly arrived guests.

"Everyone came at the same time," he told them. "Rose, I don't believe you've met Mr. Crowther. He came to live in Tarbole after you'd been here."

Mr. Crowther was dressed in his minister's somber best, but with his red face, thick gray hair, and well-set-up figure he looked more like a successful bookie than a man of the church.

He took Flora's hand in a hefty grip and proceeded to pump it up and down, saying, "Well, this is a pleasure. I've been looking forward to meeting Antony's young lady. How do you do?"

He sounded like a bookie as well. The very timbre of his deep voice made the crystal baubles of the chandelier knock together with a fine chiming sound. Flora imagined him preaching hellfire and brimstone from his pulpit. She was sure he had a fine reputation for meaningful sermons.

"How do you do?"

"Mrs. Armstrong's been so looking forward to a visit from you, as indeed we all have." He caught sight of Hugh Kyle, let go her hand at last, and went toward the other man. "And it's yourself, Doctor. And how's life treating you?"

"Rose," said Antony.

She had been aware of the other man, waiting for all the effusion to run its course. Now she turned toward him.

"You remember Brian Stoddart?"

She saw the brown face, the dark eyebrows, the laughter lines around his eyes and mouth. His hair was dark, too, and his eyes a very pale, clear gray. Not as tall as Antony, and older, he nevertheless radiated a sort of animal vitality which Flora recognized as being immensely attractive. Unlike the other men of the party, he had put on semiformal evening clothes—dark trousers and a blue velvet smoking jacket—and with these he wore a white turtleneck sweater.

He said, warmly, "Rose, what a long time it's been." He held out his arms and without thinking Flora moved toward him, and they kissed each other, circumspectly, on both cheeks.

He held her off. "Let me see if you've changed."

"Everybody thinks she's got prettier," said Antony.

"Impossible. She couldn't get prettier. But she's looking wonderfully happy and well. You're a lucky man, Antony."

"Yes," said Antony, not sounding particularly certain. "Well, having decided that, and kissed the poor girl silly into the bargain, come over and tell me what you want to drink."

While they were thus occupied Isobel made her entrance escorting the two wives, and the whole scene was replayed, this

426

time with Isobel making the introductions. This was Mrs. Crowther, whom Rose had not met before. (Big teeth, as Jason had warned, but a pleasant-faced person, dressed, as if for a ceileidh, in a tartan dress pierced by a Cairngorm brooch.) Mrs. Crowther was as enthusiastic as her husband. "So lovely that you were able to come and see Mrs. Armstrong again. It's just a shame that she's not able to be with us tonight." She smiled over Flora's head. "Good evening, Dr. Kyle. Good evening, Mr. Stoddart."

". . . and Anna, Rose," said Isobel in her gentle voice. "Anna Stoddart of Ardmore."

Anna Stoddart smiled. She was obviously painfully shy and rather plain. It was hard to guess her age, and it was equally hard to guess how she had managed to collar such a devastating husband. She wore an expensive, if rather stodgy, dinner dress, but her jewelry was beautiful. Diamonds shone from her ears and her fingers, and trembled at the neck of the dull dress.

She put out her hand and then awkwardly withdrew it again, as though she had made a social gaffe. Flora, suffering for her shyness, quickly took hold of the hand before it disappeared altogether and held it firmly.

"Hello," she said, feeling for clues. "I do remember you, don't I?"

Anna gave a little laugh. "And I remember you," she said. "I certainly remember you. And your mother."

"And you've come from . . . ?"

"Ardmore. It's over the other side of Tarbole."

"It's a lovely place," Isobel told Flora. "Right out on the end of Ardmore point."

"Are you very isolated?" asked Flora.

"Yes, a little, but I've lived there all my life, so I'm quite used to it." There was a pause and then, as if encouraged by Flora's interest, she went on, in a rush of words. "You can see Ardmore from Fernrigg on a clear day. Right across the Sound."

427

"It was clear this afternoon, but I never thought of looking."

"Did you see the sunset?"

"Wasn't it fabulous? I watched it while I was dressing . . ."

Quite happy together, beginning to make friends, they were interrupted by Brian. "Anna, Antony wants to know what you're going to drink."

She seemed confused. ". . . I don't really want anything."

"Oh, come along," he said patiently, "you must have something."

"An orange juice, then . . ." He went away to fetch it for her.

Flora said, "Would you like a sherry?"

"No." Anna shook her head. "I don't really like it." With that the two of them were overwhelmed by Mr. Crowther's coming at them across the carpet like a ship in full sail, saying, "Now then, we can't let these two pretty girls spend their time talking together."

Somehow, the evening progressed. Flora talked and smiled until her face ached, sticking close to Antony (so devoted, everybody would be thinking), and avoiding Hugh Kyle. Anna Stoddart found a chair and sat down, and Mrs. Crowther drew up a stool and settled herself beside her. Brian Stoddart and Antony discussed some mutual friends in Edinburgh, and Mr. Crowther and Hugh Kyle gravitated back to the fireplace and appeared, from their gestures, to be swapping fishing experiences. Isobel, making sure that all her guests were happily occupied, slipped away to speak to Mrs. Watty.

Presently the gong sounded, and they all finished their drinks and trooped out of the room and across the hall to the dining room.

Even in her present state of nerves Flora could not help but notice how charming it all was: the dark walls, the old portraits, the brightly burning fire. White linen and shining silver were reflected in the gleam of the mahogany table. There

428

was a centerpiece of late roses, and pale pink candles filled the silver candelabra.

After some confusion on the part of Isobel, who had lost her plan and forgotten where everybody was meant to be, they were all finally seated in the right places: Hugh at one end of the table and Mr. Crowther at the other, while Brian and Antony faced each other across the middle. The women were placed in the four corners, Flora between Hugh and Brian, with Mrs. Crowther opposite her.

When at last they were all settled, unfolding enormous linen napkins and placing them across their laps, and before conversation could start in earnest, Isobel said quickly, "Mr. Crowther, would you say grace?"

Mr. Crowther rose ponderously to his feet. They all bowed their heads, and Mr. Crowther, in tones that would have filled a cathedral, gave thanks to the Lord for the food which they were about to eat, asked him to bless it and also all the people in this house, especially Mrs. Armstrong who could not be with them, but who held such a special place in all their hearts. Amen.

He sat down. Flora suddenly liked him very much. Mrs. Watty then emerged from the door at the other end of the dining room and, as conversation got going, began to serve the soup.

Flora, in agony in that she might be expected to make light conversation with Hugh Kyle, was thankful when Mrs. Crowther firmly took him over. Mrs. Crowther had had two sherries, and not only was her color high, but also her voice.

"I was visiting old Mr. Sinclair the other day, Doctor, and he was saying that you'd been to see him. He's not been keeping as well as he should . . ."

Beside Flora, Brian Stoddart said, "You're going to have to talk to me."

She turned to him, smiling. "That's all right by me."

"I can't tell you how wonderful it is to see you again. Like a breath of fresh air. That's the worst of living up here in the back of beyond. Without realizing it, we're getting older and

429

becoming very dull, and it's hard to know what to do about it. You're just in time to come and shake us all up."

"I can't believe you feel old or dull," Flora told him, partly because this was obviously what he wanted to be told, and partly because there was such a sparkle to his eyes that the temptation to flirt a little was hard to resist.

"I do hope that's a compliment."

"Not at all, it's a fact. You don't look old and you don't sound dull."

"It *is* a compliment!"

She began to eat her soup. "You've told me the worst of living up here. Now tell me the best."

"That's more difficult."

"I can't believe that. There must be a thousand advantages."

"All right. A comfortable house, good shooting, good fishing. A ketch moored in Ardmore Loch, and in the summer, time to sail her. And space on the roads to drive my car. How does that add up?"

She noticed, sadly, that he had not included his wife in this catalogue.

"Isn't it a little materialistic?"

"Now come, Rose. You didn't expect anything else."

"How about a few responsibilities?"

"You think I should have responsibilities?"

"Don't you?"

"Yes, of course I do."

"Such as . . . ?"

He seemed amused by her persistence, but remained obliging. "Running Ardmore uses up more of my time than you could possibly imagine. And then there's the 'Coonty Cooncil.' It takes many committee meetings to decide where they're going to widen the road for the fish lorries, or whether the Tarbole Primary School should have more lavatories. You know the sort of thing. Riveting stuff."

"And what else do you do?"

"What are you anyway, Rose? Because you sound like a

430

prospective employer." But he still looked amused, and she knew that he was enjoying himself.

"If that's all you do with your time, I'd say you were in real danger of becoming very dull indeed."

He laughed out loud. "Touché! O.K., does running the Yacht Club count as a job?"

"The Yacht Club?"

"Well, don't say, 'The Yacht Club?' in that blank voice as though you'd never heard of it before." He began to speak very clearly, as though she were both deaf and stupid. "The Ardmore Yacht Club. You Came There with Me Once."

"Oh. Did I?"

"Rose, if I didn't know you so well, I really would believe you'd forgotten. Those five years must stretch further back than I'd imagined."

"Yes, I suppose they do."

"You should renew your acquaintance with the Yacht Club. Except that it's closed for the winter right now, and there's not much going on. But you could come over to Ardmore House and see us. How long are you staying?"

"We're going tomorrow."

"Tomorrow? But you've only been here about five minutes."

"Antony has to get back to work."

"And you? Do you have to get back to work too?"

"No. But I have to get back to London."

"Why don't you stay on, for a week or so, anyway? Give us all a chance to get to know you again. Get to know you properly."

Something in his voice made Flora glance at him sharply, but his pale eyes were innocent.

"I can't stay."

"Don't you want to?"

"Yes, of course. I mean, I'd like to come over and visit you and Anna, but . . ."

Brian had taken up a roll and was crumbling it between his fingers. "Anna's going to Glasgow for a shopping spree at

431

the beginning of the week." His profile was dark and sharply cut against the glow of the candlelight. It seemed that the remark was significant, but Flora could not imagine why.

"Does she always go to Glasgow to shop?"

It was an innocent question, but now he laid down his spoon and turned to face her once more, smiling, his eyes dancing as though they were sharing some marvelous private joke.

"Almost always," he told her.

Their conversation was interrupted by Isobel's getting to her feet and going around the table to collect the empty soup plates. Antony, excusing himself, also rose, and went to the sideboard to deal with the wine. The door from the kitchen opened, and Mrs. Watty appeared once more with a tray laden with steaming dishes and a pile of plates. Mrs. Crowther, bereft of Antony, leaned across the table to tell Flora about the Christmas church sale, and the nativity play she planned to produce.

"Is Jason going to be in it?" Flora asked.

"Yes, of course."

"Not an angel, I hope," said Hugh.

"Now why shouldn't Jason be an angel?" Mrs. Crowther was playfully indignant.

"Somehow," said Hugh, "he doesn't quite have the countenance."

"It's amazing, Doctor, how angelic the most devilish child can become once you dress him in a white nightgown and a gold paper crown. You'll have to come and watch, Rose."

"Huh?" said Flora, caught unawares.

"Won't you be coming to Fernrigg for Christmas?"

"Well . . . I hadn't really thought." She looked for support from Antony across the table, but Antony's chair was empty. Casting about for some alternative assistance she found herself, to her annoyance, gazing blankly at Hugh.

He prompted gently, "Perhaps you'll be in New York?"

"Yes. Perhaps I will."

"Or London, or Paris?"

She thought, *How well he knows Rose!* "It depends," she said.

Brian leaned forward, chipping into the discussion. "I've already suggested that Rose not go back to London tomorrow but stay on here for a few days. But my idea was turned down flat. A blank refusal."

"But that's a shame!" Mrs. Crowther sounded quite indignant. "I think Brian's is a wonderful idea. Have a little holiday, Rose. Enjoy yourself. I think we can see to it that you have a good time. What do you say, Dr. Kyle?"

"I think," said Hugh, "that Rose would have a good time wherever she was. She certainly doesn't need any help from us." His voice was dry.

"Besides, just think how pleasant it would be for Mrs. Armstrong . . ."

But, if bemused by wine and company, Mrs. Crowther had not recognized Hugh's snub for what it was, Flora had. She felt herself blushing with angry embarrassment. Her glass was full, and she took it up and drank the wine as though she were suffering from some unquenchable thirst. She saw that her hand, as she set down the glass, was shaking.

Neatly, without fuss, the next course was served. Some sort of a casserole, then creamed spinach and mashed potatoes. Flora wondered how she was going to be able to eat it. At the sideboard Isobel, who had been helping Mrs. Watty with the serving, picked up a small tray and started for the door. Mr. Crowther, with his eagle eye, spied her from the far end of the table.

"And where are you off to, Miss Armstrong?"

Isobel paused, smiling. "I'm just going to take Tuppy's tray up to her. I promised I would, and tell her how the party's going."

Hugh got up to open the door for her.

"Send her our respects," said Mr. Crowther, eliciting a murmur of assent from around the table.

"Of course I will," Isobel promised as she went out of the room. Hugh closed the door behind her and came back to his chair. As he settled himself, Antony, having returned to his own place, leaned across Mrs. Crowther and asked Hugh if he had laid up his boat yet.

"Yes," Hugh told him. "Last week. Geordie Campbell's got her in the boatyard at Tarbole. I went to see him the other day. He was asking after you, Antony, and was very interested to hear that you'd got yourself engaged to be married."

"I should try and take Rose down to see him."

Fortified by the wine she had gulped, Flora had overcome her embarrassment, but Hugh Kyle's snub still rankled. Now, she broke into the conversation coolly, as though he had never made that remark. "What kind of a boat have you got?"

He told her, in a voice that seemed to suggest that she would have no idea of what he was talking about anyway.

"A gaff-rigged seven-tonner."

"Do you keep her at the Ardmore Yacht Club?"

"No, I've just said. She's in the boatyard at Tarbole."

"She must be getting pretty elderly now," said Brian.

Hugh sent a chilly glance in his direction. "She was built in nineteen twenty-eight."

"Like I said. Elderly."

"Does everyone have a boat?" Flora asked. "I mean, do you all sail?"

Hugh laid down his knife and fork, and, sounding as though he were trying to explain something to a particularly dim-witted child, said, "The west of Scotland has some of the best sailing in the world. Unless one was totally disinterested one would be a fool to live here and not take advantage of it. But you need to know what you're doing. You need experience and some knowledge to cope with, say, a Force Twelve gale when you find yourself out beyond the end of Ardnamurchan. It's not quite the same as sitting in Monte Carlo harbor with a gin-and-tonic in one hand and a blonde in a bikini in the other."

Mrs. Crowther laughed, but "I never thought it was," Flora told him coolly. He was not going to intimidate her. "Have you sailed a lot this summer?"

434

He picked up his knife and fork again. "Scarcely at all," he told her, sounding sour.

"Why not?"

"A sad lack of time."

"I suppose you're very busy?"

"Busy!" Mrs. Crowther could not listen in silence. "That's the understatement of the year. No man in Tarbole works harder or longer hours than Dr. Kyle."

"Tuppy thinks you should get a partner," Flora told him, meanly. "She told me so before, when I was saying goodnight to her."

Hugh was unimpressed. "Tuppy's been trying to run my life for me since I was six years old."

"If you'll excuse my saying so," said Brian, gently, "she seems to have made a melancholy failure of it."

There followed an icy silence. Even Mrs. Crowther was bereft of words. Flora looked for help from Antony, but he had turned to talk to Anna. She laid down her knife and fork, very gently, as though it were forbidden to make a noise, and reached again for her wineglass.

Across her, forever it seemed, the eyes of the two men met and clashed. Then Hugh took a mouthful of wine, laid down his glass and said, quietly, "The failures have all been my own."

"But of course, Tuppy is quite right," Brian went on in his light voice. "You should take a partner. Some energetic, ambitious, thrusting young medico. All work and no play makes Jack a dull boy."

"Better a dull Jack than an idle one," Hugh threw back at him.

It was time to intervene before they started striking each other. "Don't you . . . don't you have anyone to help you?" Flora asked.

"I have a nurse in the surgery." His voice was brusque. "She gives injections and eyedrops and makes up prescriptions and bandages cut knees. She's a tower of strength."

Flora imagined the nurse, aproned and buxom, perhaps

young and pretty in a fresh, country way. She wondered if she was in love with the doctor, like an old A. J. Cronin novel. It did not seem beyond the bounds of possibility. Discounting the fact that she heartily disliked him, he was a personable man, even handsome in his heavy-built and distinguished way. Perhaps this was what had attracted Rose. Perhaps Rose had made a pass at him, and he had taken it seriously, and remained bitterly resentful ever since.

She had forgotten about Isobel. Now the door opened and Isobel returned to the party, apologizing for having been so long. She helped herself from the sideboard and came back to her place beside Mr. Crowther, who got to his feet and held Isobel's chair for her.

"How is Tuppy?" everybody wanted to know.

"She's splendid. She sends you all her love." There was something special about Isobel this evening. "And she has a message for Rose."

They all turned to Flora, smiling, pleased because the message was for her; then they looked back at Isobel, waiting to hear what the message was.

"She thinks," said Isobel clearly, "that we should keep Rose for a little. She thinks that Rose should stay on at Fernrigg and let Antony go back to Edinburgh on his own." She beamed at Flora. "And I think it's a marvelous idea, and I do so hope, Rose, that you will."

Oh, Tuppy, you traitor.

Flora stared at Isobel, scarcely able to believe her ears. It was like being on stage, blinded by footlights, and with a thousand eyes looking at you. She had no notion of what she was meant to say. She looked at Antony and recognized her own appalled expression reflected in his face. Silently begging him to come to her aid, she heard herself saying in a voice scarcely recognizable as her own, "I . . . I don't think . . ."

Antony came, valiantly, to her rescue. "We told you, Isobel, Rose has to get back . . ."

But from all sides his excuses were shouted down.

"Oh, rubbish."

436

"Why does she have to go?"

"So lovely for us all to have her."

"So lovely for Tuppy."

"No reason why she should go . . ."

They were all smiling, beseeching her to stay. Beside her, Brian leaned back in his chair and said in a clear voice which silenced everybody else, "I've already made that suggestion. I think it's the best idea in the world."

Even Anna, from across the table, was trying to persuade her. "Do stay. Don't go back just yet."

Everybody had spoken except Hugh. Mrs. Crowther, from the other end of the table, noticed this. "How about you, Doctor? Don't you think that Rose should spend a few more days with us?"

They were all silent, looking expectantly toward Hugh, waiting for him to fall in with their suggestions, to agree with them.

But he didn't. "No, I don't think she should stay," he pronounced, and then added, too late to take the sting from his words, "Not unless she wants to." He looked at Flora, and his cold blue stare was a challenge.

Something happened to Flora: something to do with the wine she had drunk; something to do with that encounter on the beach this morning; something that was annoyance, and a good deal that was sheer contrariness.

From across the years, from a long time ago, she heard her father's cautionary voice. *You're cutting off your nose to spite your face.*

"If Tuppy wants me to stay," she told them all, "of course I'll stay."

After the ordeal of the evening was over—after everybody had gone, the dogs had been taken out, the coffee cups had been carried into the kitchen, and Isobel had kissed them both and gone upstairs to bed—Antony and Flora faced each other across the dying fire.

"Why?" asked Antony.

437

"I don't know."

"I thought you'd gone out of your mind."

"Perhaps I had. But it's too late now."

"Oh, Flora!"

"I can't go back on my word. You don't mind, do you?"

"I don't mind. If you can bear it, if you can cope and Tuppy wants it, then how can I mind? But . . ." He stopped.

"But what?"

"Believe it or not, it's you I'm thinking about. You made me promise it would only be for a weekend."

"I know. But it was different then."

"You mean, we thought Tuppy was going to die, and now we know she isn't?"

"Yes. That and other things."

He sighed heavily and turned to look down at the fire and poke a dying log with the toe of his shoe. He said, "What the hell is going to happen now?"

"It depends on you. You could tell Tuppy the truth."

"You mean, tell her that you're not Rose?"

"Would that be so impossible?"

"Yes. Impossible. I've never lied to Tuppy in my life."

"Till now."

"O.K. Till now."

"I think you underestimate her. I think she'd understand."

"I don't want to tell her." He sounded like a stubborn little boy.

"To be perfectly honest," Flora admitted, "neither do I."

They stared at each other, hopeless. Then Antony grinned, but there was not much mirth behind it. "What a couple of cowards we are."

"A couple of scheming conspirators."

"And not, I'm beginning to think very successful ones."

"Oh, I don't know." She tried to turn it into a joke. "For beginners, we're not doing too badly."

He said, in an aggrieved voice, "I wonder why the hell I can't fall in love with you."

"That would solve everything, wouldn't it? Especially if I

438

were to fall in love with you at the same time." It was getting chilly. Flora shivered and drew closer to what remained of the fire.

He said, "You look tired. And no wonder. It was a hell of an evening, and you sailed through it with flying colors."

"I don't think I did. Antony, Hugh, and Brian—they don't like each other, do they?"

"No, I don't suppose they do. But then they're so completely different, it's not surprising. Poor old Hugh. I often wonder if he ever sits through a complete meal without the telephone ringing and calling him away."

Hugh had gone before they had even finished the second course. Summoned by Antony, who had answered the telephone, he had gone out into the hall, and minutes later, wearing his overcoat, put his head around the door to make his apologies and say goodnight. His departure had left a very empty space at the head of the table.

"Antony . . . do you like Hugh?"

"Yes, I like him enormously. When I was growing up he was the person I most wanted to be like. He played rugger for Edinburgh University and I thought he was a sort of god."

"I don't think he likes me. I mean, for some reason, he doesn't like Rose."

"You're imagining things. He can be pretty dry, I know, but . . ."

"Could he and Rose ever have had . . . some sort of an affair?"

Antony was shocked into silence by genuine astonishment. "Hugh and Rose? Whatever gave you that idea?"

"Well, there's something."

"But not that. It could never have been that." He took her by the shoulders. "Shall I tell you something? You're tired, you're overwrought, and you're imagining things. And I'm tired, too. Do you realize that I haven't been to sleep for thirty-six hours? It's just beginning to hit me. I'm going to bed." He kissed her firmly. "Goodnight."

"Goodnight," said Flora. "Goodnight, Antony." And because by then there was nothing else to do and no more to be said, they put the guard on the fire, turned off the lights, and with their arms around each other, more for support than anything else, went slowly up the shadowed stairs.

Tuppy awoke early to the sound of a bird singing from the beech tree outside her window and to a warm sensation of happiness.

It was a long time since this had happened. In recent years, her awakenings had been deviled by forebodings—anxieties for her precious family, for her country, for the whole disastrous state of the world. She disciplined herself, each day, to read the papers, to watch the nine o'clock news on the television, but often, particularly in the early mornings, she wished that she didn't have to. Sometimes it seemed as if the cold light of dawn held no promise, no hope for any of them, and on such mornings it took a real effort on Tuppy's part to get up, put on her clothes, compose her features into their usual cheerful expression, and go downstairs to breakfast.

But this morning it was different. She seemed to be floating sweetly into consciousness from some particularly happy dream. For a second she was afraid to stir, even to open her eyes, for fear of the dream dissolving and cold reality taking its place.

But slowly it was borne upon her that it was true. It had really happened. Isobel had come upstairs at the end of dinner to say that Rose had finally been persuaded and had promised to stay on at Fernrigg after Antony had returned to Edinburgh.

She was not going away.

Tuppy opened her eyes. She saw the rail at the end of her bed, gleaming in the first place shine of light from the window. It was Sunday. Tuppy loved Sundays, which, once she had been to church, she liked to spend in celebrations of family, friends, and food. It had always been thus. At Fernrigg seldom did they sit down fewer than twelve to Sunday lunch. Afterward, according to the season, there might be tennis, or putting competitions on the bumpy lawn, or long blustery walks along Fhada

440

sands. Later, everyone would gather for tea, perhaps on the terrace, or by the drawing-room fire. There would be hot scones dripping with butter and blueberry jelly; chocolate cake and fruit cake; and a special sort of ginger biscuit which Tuppy had had sent from London. Then perhaps there would be a card game or reading the Sunday papers, and if there were any children present, reading aloud.

The Secret Garden, The Wind in the Willows, A Little Princess—all the old-fashioned books. How many thousands of times has she read them aloud! *Once upon a time there was a very beautiful doll's house.* The other evening it had been Jason. But with his small frame tucked into the curve of her arm, the crown of his head sweet-smelling from his bath, just under her chin, he could have been any of them. The little boys. So many little boys. Sometimes when she was tired, and time and memories became confused, she forgot when they had been born and when they had died.

James and Robbie, her baby brothers, playing with their lead soldiers on the hearth rug. And Bruce, her own child, wild as a gypsy, running barefoot, and everybody shaking their heads and saying it was because he didn't have a father. And then Torquil, and Antony, and now Jason.

They had perhaps looked different, but they had all kindled the same pleasures in Tuppy's heart, as well as clouding her life with the most appalling anxieties: broken arms and bleeding knees, measles and whooping cough. Say, Thank you. Say, Please can I get down? *Tuppy, don't get into a fuss or anything, But Antony's just fallen out of the fir tree.*

And the milestones. Learning to swim, learning to ride a bicycle, being given the first air gun. That was the worst of all. *Never never let your gun pointed be at anyone.* She had made them say it every night, aloud, before they said their prayers.

And there was going away to school, and the miserable counting of days, and the hideous tear-stained goodbyes at Tarbole station, with the new trunk packed, the tuck box, the faces already grimed with railway dust.

The little boys were part of a long golden thread stretching

441

back into the past. But the miracle was that the same thread reached steadfastly on into the future. There was Torquil—solid, capable Torquil, doing so well for himself, married to Teresa, living in Bahrein. Torquil had never caused Tuppy a mite of worry. But Antony now was a different kettle of fish. Restless, volatile, attractive, he had in his time brought dozens of girls back to Fernrigg, and yet never, it seemed, was it the right girl. Tuppy had begun to give up hope of his ever marrying and settling down. But now, out of the blue, he had met up with Rose Schuster again, and Tuppy's faith in miracles was restored once more.

Rose. Could he, she asked herself, in a thousand years, have found a more enchanting girl? As though Antony had presented Tuppy with some precious gift, her natural reaction was a desire to share her pleasure with the rest of the world. Not just the Crowthers and the Stoddarts, who were, after all, such close neighbors as to be almost family, but everybody.

The notion took seed and began to take shape in her active brain. The dinner party last night had, Isobel assured her, been a complete success. But Tuppy had had no part in it and had been frustrated beyond words by the distant hum which was all that she could glean of the dinner-table conversation. And Hugh, the overbearing brute, had forbidden visitors, so that Tuppy was denied even the pleasure of fresh faces and a little local gossip.

But by the end of the week. . . . She did a few calculations. Today was Sunday. Antony was going to leave Rose at Fernrigg and then return next weekend to spirit her away once more. They had a week. There was plenty of time.

They would have a party. A proper party. A dance. The very word conjured up the sound of music, and all at once her head was filled with the jig and beat of a Highland reel.

Diddle diddle dum dum, dum dum dum.

Her toes beneath the sheets began to beat time of their own accord. Excitement took hold of her, and as the seed of the idea exploded into inspiration, she forgot about being ill. The prospect of dying, which she had never taken seriously anyway, faded into insignificance. All at once there were a hundred more important things to think about.

It was nearly daylight. She reached out her hand to turn on her lamp and look at the time by the small gold clock which sat by her bed. Seven thirty. Cautiously, she drew herself up in her bed and pushed the pillows into shape with her elbows. She reached for her spectacles and then her bedjacket, which seemed to take rather a long time to put on. With clumsy fingers she tied the ribbon bow at the neck. Then she opened the drawer in her bedside table and found a pad of writing paper and a pencil. At the head of the clean sheet of paper she wrote:

Mrs. Clanwilliam

Her writing, which had once been so beautiful, seemed spidery, but what did that matter? She thought a little, her mind ranging round the neighborhood, and continued:

Charles and Christian Drummond

Harry and Frances McNeill

It would have to be on Friday. Friday was a good night for a dance, because Saturday was apt to slip into the small hours of the Sabbath, and that would offend people. Antony would have to get Friday afternoon off in order to be at Fernrigg in good time, but she had no doubt that he would be able to arrange this.

She wrote:

Hugh Kyle
Elizabeth McLeod
Johnny and Kirsten Grant

In the old days all the food, including the cold salmon, the great roast turkeys, the mouth-melting puddings, had all come out of the Fernrigg kitchen, but Mrs. Watty could scarcely be

443

expected to cope with that on her own now. Isobel must speak to Mr. Anderson at the Station Hotel in Tarbole. He had a perfectly adequate cellar and a capable chef. Mr. Anderson would see to the catering.

More names went on the list. The Crowthers and of course the Stoddarts, and that couple that had come to live in Tarbole —he had something to do with deep-freezing.

Tommy and Angela Cockburn
Robert and Susan Hamilton

Diddle diddle dum dum, dum dum dum.
The postmistress, Mrs. Cooper, had a husband who played the accordion and who could rustle up, if persuaded, a small band. Just a fiddle and some drums. Isobel must arrange that. And Jason would come to the party. Tuppy saw him dressed in the little kilt and velvet doublet that had belonged to his grandfather.

The page was nearly full, but still she wrote:

Sheamus Lochlan,
The Crichtons
The McDonalds

She turned to a fresh page. She had not been so happy in years.

It was Isobel who broke the news to the rest of the Fern-rigg household. Isobel, who had gone upstairs to say good morning to her mother and retrieve her breakfast tray, returned to the kitchen in what appeared to be a state of mild shock.

She laid down the tray on the table with something approaching a thump. Violence was so out of character with Isobel, that they all stopped what they were doing and looked at her. Even Jason, with a mouthful of bacon, ceased to chew. Something was obviously wrong. Isobel's wayward hair looked as though she had lately run distracted fingers through it, and

444

the expression on her gentle face held part exasperation and part a sort of grudging pride.

She did not speak at once, but simply stood there, lanky in her tweed skirt and her best Sunday sweater, defeated, and apparently lost for words. Her very silence claimed instant attention. Mrs. Watty, peeling potatoes for lunch, sat, waiting with knife poised. Nurse McLeod, taking last night's glasses from the dishwasher and giving them a final and unnecessary polish, was equally attentive. Flora laid down her coffee cup with a small chiming sound.

It was Mrs. Watty who broke the silence. "What is it?"

Isobel pulled out a kitchen chair and flopped into it, long legs stretched out before her. She said, "She wants to have another party."

Tuppy's household, with the debris of last night still very much in evidence, received this information in wordless disbelief. For a moment the only sound to break the silence was the slow ticking of the old-fashioned clock.

Isobel's eyes went from one blank face to the other. "It's true," she told them. "It's to be next Friday. It's to be a dance."

"A *dance*?" Nurse McLeod, with visions of her patient dancing reels, drew herself up with all the authority of her profession behind her. "Over my dead body," she declared.

"She has decided," Isobel went on, as though Nurse had said nothing, "that Mr. Anderson from the Station Hotel shall do the catering, and she is going to get Mrs. Cooper's husband to organize a band."

"For heaven's sakes," was all Mrs. Watty could come up with.

"And she has already drawn up a long list of people who are to receive invitations."

Jason, who could not think what all the drama was about, decided to finish his bacon. "Am I being invited?" he asked, but for once he was ignored.

"You told her no?" asked Nurse, coming forward and fixing Isobel with a steely eye.

"Of course I told her no."

"And what did she say?"

"She took absolutely no notice whatsoever."

"It's out of the question," said Nurse. "Think of the up-heaval, think of the noise. Mrs. Armstrong is not well. She is not up to such carryings on. And she's not by any chance imagining that she's going to come to the party?"

"No. On that score you can rest easy. At least," Isobel amended, knowing her mother, "I *think* you can."

"But why on earth?" demanded Mrs. Watty. "Why does she want another party? We haven't got the dining room straight after last night yet."

Isobel sighed. "It's for Rose. She wants everybody to meet Rose."

They all turned their eyes upon Flora. Flora, who had more reason than any of them to be completely horrorstruck by this latest bombshell, found herself blushing. "But I don't want a party. I mean, I said I'd stay on because Tuppy wanted me to, but I had no idea she had that up her sleeve."

Isobel patted her hand, comforting her. "She hadn't, last night. She thought it all up in the early hours of the morning. So it's none of it your fault. It's just Tuppy with her mania for entertaining."

Flora searched about for some practical objection. "But surely, there's not enough *time*. I mean, a dance. If you're go-ing to send out invitations, there's not even a week . . ."

But that, too, had been thought of. "The invitations are to be by telephone," Isobel told them, and added in a resigned voice, "with me doing the telephoning."

Nurse decided that this nonsense had gone on for long enough. She drew out a chair and sat down, the starched bib of her apron puffing out in front of her, so that all at once she looked like a pouter pigeon. "She'll have to be told no," she announced again.

Mrs. Watty and Isobel, in concert, sighed. "That's not go-ing to be so easy, Nurse," said Mrs. Watty, in the voice of a parent with a brilliant but maddening child. "You don't know Mrs. Armstrong the way Miss Isobel and I know her. Why,

446

once she sets her mind on something, then not *wild horses* will make her see differently."

Jason took some toast and buttered it. "I've never been to a dance," he observed, but again nobody took the slightest notice of him.

"How about Antony, could he not talk to her?" Nurse suggested hopefully.

But Mrs. Watty and Isobel shook their heads. Antony would be no use at all. Besides, Antony was still in bed, catching up on his sleep, and nobody was going to disturb him.

"Well, if none of her family can make her see reason," Nurse announced, her tones indicating that she thought them a very poor lot, "then Dr. Kyle will have to."

At the mention of Hugh's name, both Mrs. Watty and Isobel brightened visibly. For some reason, they had not thought of Hugh.

"Dr. Kyle," repeated Mrs. Watty thoughtfully. "Yes. Now, that is a good idea. She'll take no notice of anything we might have to say, but she'll take a telling from the doctor. Is he coming to see her this morning?"

"Yes," said Nurse. "He mentioned some time before lunch."

Mrs. Watty leaned her massive forearms on the table, and dropped her voice, like a conspirator. "Then why don't we just humor her till then? There's no point, and I'm sure you will agree, Nurse, in upsetting Mrs. Armstrong with a lot of argument and fuss. Let's just leave it to Dr. Kyle."

And so the problem was satisfactorily shelved for the time being, and Flora had it in her heart to be sorry for Hugh Kyle.

The morning wore on. Flora helped Mrs. Watty with the breakfast dishes, vacuumed the dining-room carpet, and laid the table for lunch. Isobel put on her hat and bore Jason off to church. Mrs. Watty started cooking, whereupon Flora, primed by Nurse, went upstairs to see Tuppy.

"And mind you're noncommittal about that dance," warned Nurse. "If she starts on about it, you just change the subject."

447

Flora said that she would. She was just on her way out of the kitchen when Mrs. Watty called her back, dried her hands, opened a drawer, and took out a large paper bag containing a number of hanks of gray with which she intended to knit a sweater for Jason.

"This'll be a nice little occupation for you," she told Flora. "You and Mrs. Armstrong can wind my wool for me. Why they can't sell it rolled in those neat wee balls is beyond my comprehension, but there it is, they don't seem to be able to."

Obediently bearing the bag of wool, Flora made her way upstairs to Tuppy's room. As soon as she went in she saw that Tuppy was looking better. Gone were the dark rings beneath her eyes, the air of restlessness. She sat up in bed and held out her arms as Flora appeared.

"I hoped it would be you. Come and give me a kiss. How pretty you're looking." Flora, in deference to Sunday, had put on a skirt and a Shetland sweater. "Do you know, this is the first time I've seen your legs. With legs like that I don't know why you have to cover them up with trousers all the time." They kissed. Flora began to draw away, but Tuppy held her. "Are you angry with me?"

"Angry?"

"About staying. It was very unfair of me to send you that message by Isobel last night, but I wanted you to change your mind, and I couldn't think of any other way of doing it."

Flora was disarmed. She smiled. "No, I'm not angry."

"It's not as though you had anything dreadfully important to get back to. And I wanted you to stay, so badly."

She let Flora go, and Flora settled herself on the edge of the bed. "But now you're in the doghouse," she told Tuppy, deliberately forgetting Nurse's instructions. "You know that, don't you?"

"I don't even know what a doghouse is."

"I mean you're in disgrace for planning another party."

"Oh, that." Tuppy chuckled, delighted with herself. "Poor Isobel nearly fainted when I told her."

"You're very naughty."

448

"But why? Why shouldn't I have another party? Stuck in this silly bed, I must have something to amuse myself."

"You're meant to be getting better, not planning wild parties."

"Oh, it won't be wild. And there have been so many parties in this house that it will practically run on its own momentum. Besides, nobody has to do anything. I've organized it all."

"Isobel's got to spend an entire day at the telephone, ringing people up."

"Yes, but she won't mind that. Anyway, it'll keep her off her feet."

"But what about the house, and the flowers that will have to be done, and the furniture moved and everything?"

"Watty can move the furniture. It won't take him a moment. And . . ." Tuppy cast about for inspiration. ". . . you can do the flowers."

"Perhaps I can't do flowers."

"Then we'll have pot plants. Or get Anna to help us. Rose, it's no good trying to put obstacles in my way, because I've already thought of everything."

"Nurse says it depends on what Hugh says."

"Nurse has had a face on like the back of a bus, all morning. And if it depends on Hugh, you can set your mind at rest. Hugh will think it's a splendid idea."

"I shouldn't count on that, if I were you."

"No, I'm not counting on it. I've known Hugh all my life, and he can be as pig-headed as the next man." Tuppy's expression changed to one of amused speculation. "But I'm surprised you've found that out so quickly."

"I sat next to him last night at dinner." Flora opened the paper bag and took out the first hank of gray wheeling. "Do you feel strong enough to wind wool for Mrs. Watty?"

"Yes, of course I do, I'll hold it and you can do the winding."

Once they had organized themselves and started in on this undemanding task, Tuppy went on, as though there had been

449

no pause in the conversation, "I want to hear about last night, all about it."

Flora told her, deliberately enthusiastic, making it all sound sheer fun from start to finish.

"And the Crowthers are so nice, aren't they?" said Tuppy, when Flora had finally run out of things to describe. "I really like him so much. He's rather overwhelming to meet for the first time, but such a really good man. And Hugh enjoyed himself?"

"Yes. At least, I think he did. But of course there was a telephone call for him halfway through the evening, and he had to go."

"The dear boy. If only he'd get someone to help him. But there it is . . ." Tuppy's hands dropped and Flora stopped winding wool and waited for her. ". . . I think that for Hugh being so busy is a sort of therapy. Isn't that what they call it nowadays? A therapy?"

"You mean, because of his wife's dying?"

"Yes. I think that's what I mean. You know, he was such a nice little boy. He used to come here quite a lot to play with Torquil. His father was our doctor—I told you that. Quite a humble man, from the Isle of Lewis, but he was a splendid doctor. And Hugh was clever, too. Hugh got a scholarship to Fettes, and then he went on to study medicine at Edinburgh University."

"He played rugger for the university, didn't he?"

"Antony must have told you that. Antony always thought the world of Hugh. Yes, he played rugger for the university, but what was more exciting was that he passed his finals with honors and he won the Cunningham Medal for Anatomy, and the whole wonderful world of medicine was open to him. Then Professor McClintock—he was professor of surgery at St. Thomas's in London—he asked Hugh to go down to London and study under him. We were all so proud. I couldn't have been more proud of Hugh if he'd been my own child."

Flora found it difficult to equate all this brilliance with the dour dinner companion of last night. "Why did it all go wrong?" she asked.

"Oh, it didn't go wrong exactly." Tuppy lifted her hands with the hank of wool looped around them, and Flora continued winding.

"He got married, though?"

"Yes. To Diana. He met her in London and they got engaged, and he brought her back to Tarbole."

"Did you meet her?"

"Yes."

"Did you like her?"

"She was very beautiful, very charming, very well turned out. I believe her father had a great deal of money. It couldn't have been easy for her, coming up here and knowing nobody. Tarbole was a very different world from the one she'd been used to, and she didn't really fit in. I think she thought we were all dreadfully dull. Poor Hugh. It must have been a desperate time for him. I didn't say anything to him, of course. It was nothing to do with me. But I believe that his old father was a little more outspoken. Too outspoken, perhaps. But by then Hugh was so besotted by her that it would have made no difference what any of us said. And although we didn't want to lose him, we *did* want him to be happy."

"And was he?"

"I don't know, Rose. We didn't see him again for two years, and when we did it was because Diana was dead—killed in a dreadful car accident—and Hugh had thrown everything up and come back to Tarbole to take over from his father. And he's been here ever since."

"How long is that?"

"Nearly eight years."

"You'd think he'd have got over it by now. Married again . . ."

"No. Not Hugh."

They fell silent, winding wool. The ball was getting quite big. Flora changed the subject. She said, "I liked Anna."

451

Tuppy's face lit up. "I am glad you liked Anna. I love her, but she's not easy to get to know. She's very shy."

"She told me that she's always lived here."

"Yes. Her father was a great friend of mine. He was called Archie Carstairs and he came from Glasgow. He'd made a great deal of money and everybody thought he was a very rough diamond—people were so silly and snobbish in those days—but I always liked him. He was a great sailing man—he used to cruise around in a very ostentatious ocean-going yacht. That's how he first came to Ardmore. He fell in love with the loch and the beautiful country, and indeed, who could blame him for that? There's nowhere like it in all the world. Anyway, just after the First World War, he built Ardmore House, and as the years went by he spent more and more time here, and eventually he retired to Ardmore. Anna was born there. Archie married late in life—I think he'd always been too busy making money to get married before—and so Anna was the child of quite elderly parents. In fact, her mother lived only for a few months after Anna was born. I often think, if her mother had survived, that Anna would have been a very different sort of person. But there it is, these things happen, and it's not for us to question why."

"And Brian?"

"What about Brian?"

"How did she meet Brian?"

Tuppy gave a little smile. "Brian sailed into Ardmore loch one summer, in a shabby little boat that he'd brought single-handed from the South of France. By then Archie had started the Ardmore Yacht Club. It was his toy, a hobby to keep him busy in retirement, and also to make sure that he kept in touch with all his old sailing friends. Brian tied up and came ashore for a drink, and Archie got talking to him, and he was so impressed by Brian's feat of seamanship that he asked him back to Ardmore House for dinner. For Anna it was like young Lochinvar, riding in on a white horse. She looked at Brian and lost her heart and she's been in love with him ever since."

"She married him."

"Of course."

"What did her father have to say about that?"

"He was fairly wary. He admired Brian and he even quite liked him, but he'd never intended him as his son-in-law."

"Did he try to talk Anna out of it?"

"To give him his due, yes, I think he did. But the most unexpected people can be very stubborn. Anna was a woman by then, no longer a child. She knew what she wanted and she intended having it."

"Was Brian in love with her?"

There was a long pause. Then Tuppy said, "No, I don't think so. But I do think that he was fond of her. And of course he was also fond of all the material things that being married to Anna represented."

"You're saying—in a very nice way—that he married her for her money."

"I don't want to say that, because I'm so fond of Anna."

"Does it matter anyway, provided they're happy?"

"That's what I asked myself at the time."

"Is she very rich?"

"Yes. When Archie died she inherited everything."

"And Brian?"

"Brian has nothing but the settlement Archie made on him. I happen to know it was very generous, but the capital, the bulk of the wealth, is Anna's."

"Supposing—the marriage broke up?"

"Then Brian's settlement would be dissolved. He would have nothing."

Flora thought of Anna with her diffidence and her beautiful diamonds. And she was sorry for her, all over again, because it must be a cheerless thing to have your husband tied to you by nothing but money.

"Brian's very attractive."

"Brian? Yes, of course he's attractive. Attractive and frustrated. He doesn't have nearly enough to do with himself."

"They've never had any children?"

"Anna lost a child, that summer you and your mother

453

were here. But I don't suppose you'd remember. You'd probably gone by then."

The ball of wool was nearly finished. The last few strands lay across Tuppy's thin wrists. "She's pregnant again," said Tuppy.

Flora stopped winding. "Anna? Is she? Oh, I am glad,"

Tuppy was instantly concerned. "I should never have said anything. It just slipped out. I wasn't meant to tell anyone. Hugh told me, just to cheer me up when I was feeling so ill. And I promised I'd keep it a secret."

"Your secret is safe with me," Flora vowed. "In fact, I've forgotten it already."

It was midday and they were onto the last hank of wool before Hugh appeared. They heard his footsteps up the stairs and along the passage. There came a cursory thump on the door, and the next moment he was in the room with them. He wore his workday suit. His bag swung from his hand and a stethoscope spilled from the pocket of his jacket.

"Good morning," he said.

Tuppy eyed him. "You don't look as though anybody had ever told you that Sunday is meant to be a day of rest."

"I forgot it was Sunday when I woke up this morning." He came to the foot of the bed and straight to the point. "What's all this I've been hearing?"

Tuppy made an exasperated face. "I knew they'd tell you before I had a chance to."

He set down his bag on the floor and leaned his arms on the brass rail at the end of her bed. "Then you tell me now."

The end of the wool slipped off Tuppy's wrists and onto the last fat ball.

"We're going to have a little party next Friday for Rose and Antony," Tuppy told him, as though it were the most natural thing in the world.

"How many people does a little party consist of?"

"About . . . sixty." She met his eye. "Seventy?" she amended hopefully.

454

"Seventy people bouncing about in the hall, drinking champagne and talking nineteen to the dozen. What do you think that's going to do to your state of health?"

"If anything, it will improve it."

"Who's going to organize all this?"

"It has already been organized. It took me exactly half an hour before breakfast. And now I shall wash my hands off the entire affair."

He looked, naturally, skeptical. "Tuppy, I find that hard to believe."

"Oh, don't be such an old stick-in-the-mud. Everybody's carrying on as though we were going to give a state ball."

Hugh looked at Flora. "And what does Rose think about it?"

"Me?" Flora had been gathering up the balls of wool, putting them back into the paper bag. "I . . . I think it's a lovely idea, but if you think it's going to be too much for Tuppy . . ."

"Don't be such a turncoat, Rose," Tuppy interrupted crossly. "You're just as bad as the rest of them." She turned back to Hugh. "I've told you, it's all planned. Mr. Anderson will do the catering, Rose will do the flowers, Watty will clear the hall of furniture, and Isobel will telephone everybody and ask them to come. And if you don't take that expression off your face, Hugh, *you* will not be asked."

"And what are you going to do?"

"Me? Not a thing. I shall simply sit here and stare into space."

Her blue gaze was innocent. Hugh cocked his head and watched her warily. "No visitors," he said.

"What do you mean, no visitors?"

"I mean, nobody nipping upstairs to see you and having little chats."

Tuppy looked bitterly disappointed. "Not even one or two?"

"Start with one or two, and by the end of the evening your bedroom would be like Piccadilly Underground at rush hour. No visitors. And I won't even take your word on it. I shall post

Nurse at the door as a sentry, armed with a pike or a bedpan or whatever weapon she chooses. And that, Mrs. Armstrong, is the deal." He straightened up and came around to the side of the bed. "And now, Rose, if you'd be so kind as to go and find Nurse, and tell her I'm here."

"Yes, of course." Thus dismissed, Flora kissed Tuppy quickly, got off the bed, and went out of the room. Nurse was already on her way upstairs, and they met on the landing.

Nurse's face was grim. "Is Dr. Kyle with Mrs. Armstrong?"

"Yes, he's waiting for you."

"I hope he's put an end to this scatter-brained idea of hers."

"I'm not sure. But I rather think the party is on."

"The Lord save us," said Nurse.

Mrs. Watty was more philosophical about it all. "Well, if it's a party she wants, why shouldn't she have it?" She added, "It's not as though we can't manage. Why, there've been so many parties given in this house that we could probably manage standing on our heads."

"I'm meant to be doing the flowers."

Mrs. Watty looked amused. "So you've been given your own wee job. Mrs. Armstrong's very good at giving people jobs to do."

"Yes, but I'm hopeless at flowers. I can't even put daffodils in a jug."

"Oh, you'll manage fine." She opened a cupboard and counted out a pile of plates. "Was the doctor easily persuaded?"

"Not easily, but he was persuaded. On condition that Tuppy doesn't have any visitors. Nurse is going to be put to stand guard at her door."

Mrs. Watty shook her head. "Poor Dr. Kyle, what a time he does have, to be sure. As if he didn't have enough to worry about without us unloading more trouble onto his shoulders. And, seemingly, he has no help at the moment. Jessie McKenzie—she's meant to be his housekeeper—well, two days ago I

456

hear she took the Skye Ferry over to Portree. Her mother lives there and seemingly the old lady's poorly."

"Oh, dear."

"It's not that easy to get help in Tarbole. Most of the women are working with the fish these days, packing herrings, or in the smokehouses." She glanced at the clock, remembered her roasting joint, and forgot about Dr. Kyle's woes. Cautiously she stooped to open her oven door, and they were assailed by fragrant steam and the sizzling of fat.

"Is Antony not up yet?" Mrs. Watty drove a skewer into the flank of the roast. "I think it's time you went and gave him a call. Otherwise he'll sleep through the day, and the next thing it'll be time for him to start for home."

Flora went to do this, but as she crossed the hall, she heard Hugh come out of Tuppy's room, and start down the upstairs landing. She had reached the foot of the stairs when he appeared. When he saw her, she stopped and, without really knowing why, waited for him to descend.

He was wearing horn-rimmed spectacles, which made him look distinguished. When he had reached her side he set down his bag, took off the spectacles, towing them in a case, and slipped the case into the pocket of his jacket. He looked at Flora. "Well?" he prompted, as though she should have something to say to him. To her surprise, Flora found that she had.

"Hugh, last night . . . You didn't want me to say I'd stay on, did you?"

He seemed unprepared for such forthrightness. "No. But I have a feeling that that is what made you change your mind."

"Why didn't you want me to stay?"

"Call it premonition."

"Of trouble?"

"If you like."

"Does Tuppy's party count as trouble?"

"We could have done without it."

"But it's on?"

"At the moment it is." She waited for him to enlarge on

457

this, and when he didn't, she became persistent. "But it will be all right? I mean, Tuppy will be all right?"

"Yes, provided she does as she's told. Nurse McLeod is rigidly disapproving. Her opinion of me has sunk to rock bottom. But, in fact, it may prove to be the small stimulus that Tuppy needs. And if it doesn't . . ." He stopped, letting the unsaid words speak for themselves.

He looked so worn down by all this that despite herself Flora was sorry for him. "Never mind," she said, trying to sound cheerful, "at least she's doing what she most loves doing. Like the old man of ninety, being asked how he wants to die, and choosing to be shot by a jealous husband."

Hugh's face broke into a smile, spontaneous as it was unexpected. She had never seen him smile properly before and was caught unaware by its sweetness, by the way it altered his whole face. For an instant she caught a glimpse of the young, light-hearted man that he had once been.

He said, "Exactly so."

The morning had been gray and gentle, very still. But now a breeze had got up, clouds were being blown aside, as they stood there at the foot of the stairs, the sun broke through and all at once everything was bathed in its liquid, golden light. It poured into the hall through the two tall windows which stood on either side of the front door. The beams became filled with floating dustmotes and previously unnoticed details sprang into vivid clarity and importance: the texture of his suit, shabby and, in places, growing threadbare; the pockets sagging with the weight of various articles which he had stuffed into them; his pullover, which had an inept darn, right in the middle; and his hand, which he had placed over the newel post as he talked. She saw the shape of it, the long fingers, the signet ring, the scrubbed and clean look.

She saw that he was tired. He was still smiling at the small joke she had made, but he looked bone-weary. She thought of him coming out to dinner last night, getting dressed in his best, searching the cheerless house for a clean shirt, because his

458

housekeeper had left him to go off to Portree to visit her mother.

She said, "Last night, the telephone call you had—I hope it wasn't anything serious."

"Serious enough. A very old man, getting older, and a daughter-in law at the end of her tether. He'd got out of bed to go to the lavatory and he'd fallen down the stairs."

"Did he hurt himself?"

"By a miracle, no bones were broken, but he's bruised and badly shocked. He should be in a hospital. There's a bed for him in Lochgarry Hospital, but he won't go. He was born in the house he lives in now, and that's where he wants to die."

"Where is the house?"

"Boturich."

"I don't know where Boturich is."

"Up at the far end of Loch Fhada."

"But that must be fifteen miles."

"Thereabouts."

"When did you get home?"

"About two o'clock this morning."

"And what time did you get up again?"

His eyes crinkled with amusement. "What is this? An inquisition?"

"You must be tired."

"I don't have time to be tired. And now"—he glanced at his watch and stooped to pick up his bag—"I must be on my way."

She went with him to the door to open it for him. The sunlight made a dazzle of damp grass and gravel and shining flame-colored leaves. He said, reverting to his usual manner, "I'll doubtless see you," and she watched him go down the steps, into his car, down between the rhododendrons past the lodge, and through the open gate.

In the sun, it should have been warm, but Flora shivered. She came indoors, closed the door, and started upstairs to wake Antony.

She found him already up and shaving, standing in front of

459

the basin dressed in a pair of scarlet leather slippers and two towels, one tied around his waist and the other slung like a muffler round his neck. As she put her head around the edge of the door he turned to look at her. His face was lopsided, one side soapy, the other clean.

She said, "I've been sent up to wake you. It's twelve thirty."

"I'm awake, and I know it is. Come on in."

He turned back to the mirror and continued his task. Flora shut the door and went to sit on the edge of the bed. She said, to his reflection, "How did you sleep?"

"Like the dead."

"How strong are you feeling?"

There was a pause and then, "For some reason," Antony told her, "that question fills me with nameless apprehensions."

"And so it should. There's going to be another party. Next Friday. A dance."

After a little, he said, "I see what you mean about feeling strong."

"Tuppy organized the whole thing before breakfast. And she seems to have steamrolled everyone, including Hugh Kyle, into letting her have her own way. The only person who's really opposed to it is Nurse, and she's going around with a face of doom."

"You mean, it's really on?"

"Yes. It's really on."

"I suppose it's for Antony and Rose."

Flora nodded.

"To celebrate the engagement."

"Right again."

He had finished shaving. Now he turned on the tap to wash his razor. "Oh, God," he said.

She was remorseful. "It's my fault. I shouldn't have said I would stay."

"How could you have known? How could any of us have guessed she'd think up something like this?"

"I don't suppose there's anything we can do about it."

460

He turned to face her, his copper-colored hair standing on end, and an expression of gloom on his usually cheerful face. He jerked the towel from round his neck and threw it across a chair.

"Not a bloody thing. It's like drowning in a quagmire. By the end of the week, all that will be left of us will be a couple of bubbles. And muddy ones at that."

"We could make a clean breast of it. Tell Tuppy the truth." The idea had been shadowing around at the back of Flora's mind all morning, but it was the first time she had brought it out into the open and acknowledged it, even to herself.

Antony said, "No."

"But . . ."

He turned on her. "I said no. O.K., so Tuppy's better. O.K., so Isobel got everything wrong and Tuppy's going to make a miraculous recovery. But she's old, and she's been very ill, and if anything happened just because you and I insisted on the luxury of a clean conscience, I'd never been able to forgive myself. You see that, don't you?"

Flora sighed. She said, miserably, "Yes, I suppose so."

"You are the most super girl." He stooped to give her a kiss. His cheek was smooth; he smelt clean and lemony.

"And now, if you'll excuse me, I must get some clothes on."

That afternoon, the tide was out. After lunch Flora and Antony, meanly evading Jason, who wanted to come with them, set out for a walk. They took the dogs—even Sukey, whom Antony had firmly scooped off Tuppy's eiderdown—and went down to Fhada sands, left clean and white by the ebb tide. They headed toward the distant breakers while the wind blew gusts of sunshine at them out of the west.

It was not a cheerful outing. Antony's departure for Edinburgh lay over them both like doom, and they talked scarcely at all. And yet the silence that lay between them was in its own way companionable, because Flora knew that Antony's thoughts were as troubled as her own.

461

At the water's edge they halted. Antony found a long rope of seaweed and flung it out into the waves for Plummer to retrieve, which he did with a great deal of splashy swimming. Moments later he was leaping back at them out of the sea with the seaweed trailing from the side of his mouth. Sukey, who did not like getting her feet wet, sat well back and observed him. Plummer laid down the seaweed, shook himself stupendously, and sat with his great wet ears pricked, waiting for Antony to throw it again. This he did, even farther out this time, and Plummer plunged once more into the breakers.

Standing in the wind, they watched him go. Flora said, "We'll have to tell them sometime, Antony. Sometime they'll have to know that I'm Flora, I'm not Rose. Perhaps a clean conscience is a luxury, but I can't live with this for the rest of my life." She looked at him. "I'm sorry, but I simply can't."

His profile was stony, his face ruddy from the wind. He dug his hands deep into his pockets and sighed.

"No, I know. I've been thinking that too." He turned his head to look down at her. "But it has to be me who does the telling. Not you."

She was a little hurt. "I'd never think of doing such a thing."

"No. But it isn't going to be easy for you these next few days. It's going to get worse, not better, and I'm not going to be here to support you. Next weekend, after the dance, if Tuppy's all right, then we'll make a clean breast of it. Confess, if you like." He looked quite drawn at the thought. "But meantime, you must promise not to say anything to any of them."

"Antony, I wouldn't."

"Promise."

She promised. The sun went behind a cloud, and it became suddenly chilly. They waited, shivering slightly, for Plummer to return to them, and then turned and started on the long trudge back to the house.

When they got home, Plummer was banished to Mrs. Watty's kitchen until he had dried off, and Sukey shot like an arrow back up the stairs to Tuppy's bedroom. Antony and Flora shed coats and gumboots and went into the drawing room, where they found Isobel and Jason by the fire eating tea, engrossed in some swashbuckling adventure on television. Conversation was obviously not expected so they joined them, in silence, eating buttered toast, and mindlessly watching some spirited sword-play and a great deal of running up and down flare-lit spiral staircases. It was finished at last, with the hero clapped into a dungeon until the following week's episode. Isobel switched off the television, and Jason turned his attention to Antony and Flora.

"I wanted to take a walk with you and when I looked for you, you'd *gone.*"

"Sorry," said Antony, sounding not sorry in the least.

"Will you play cards with me?"

"No." He laid down his empty teacup. "I've got to go and pack and then start back for Edinburgh."

"I'll come and help you."

"I don't want you to come and help me. Rose is going to come and help me."

"But why . . ." His voice rose to what sounded perilously like a whine. He was often in a bad humor on Sunday evenings because he knew tomorrow morning was Monday, which meant school again. Isobel tactfully intervened.

"Antony and Rose have got a lot of things they want to discuss without all of us listening. And if you get the cards out of the drawer, I'll play a game with you."

"It's not fair . . ."

"Do you want to play Beggar My Neighbor, or Pelmanism?"

They left Jason spreading the cards on the hearth rug for Pelmanism, and went up to Antony's room, which was painfully neat, almost as though he had already gone. The curtains had not been drawn; the center light was cheerless. He began collecting his shaving gear and putting it into his bag, while Flora stacked clean shirts and folded his dressing gown. It didn't take very long. He put his silver brushes on top of the

463

pile, closed the lid, and snapped the locks shut. The room, stripped of his possessions, became unfriendly.

He said, "You'll be all right?"

He looked so anxious that she made herself smile. "Of course."

He felt in his pocket and took out a scrap of paper. "I wrote my telephone numbers down for you in case you want to get in touch with me. That's the office, and that's my flat. If it's something you don't want anybody to hear, you could probably borrow one of the cars and get yourself to Tarbole. There's a call box down by the harbor."

"When will you be back?"

"As early on Friday afternoon as I can manage."

"I'll be here," she told him, unnecessarily.

"You'd better be."

Carrying his suitcase, he went along to say goodbye to Tuppy, while Flora went downstairs to tell Isobel and Jason that he was just about to leave. Jason was dispatched to fetch Mrs. Watty, who appeared from the kitchen with a box of buttered scones and a bag of apples. She could not bear the thought of one of the family setting out on any sort of a journey without being well-provisioned. Antony then came downstairs, kissed them all, and told them not to work too hard. They all said, "See you on Friday," and returned to their various occupations, while Antony and Flora let themselves out into the dusky evening. His car waited on the gravel outside the front door. He flung his case into the back seat, put his arms around Flora, and gave her a hug.

She said, feebly, "I wish you didn't have to go."

"So do I. Take care of yourself. And try not to get too involved."

"I'm involved already."

"Yes." He sounded hopeless. "Yes, I know."

She watched him drive away, the taillight of his car whisking out of sight beyond the gates. She went back into the house, closed the door, and stood in the hall feeling desolate. From

behind the drawing room door came the murmur of voices as
Isobel and Jason continued their game. Flora looked at her
watch. It was nearly a quarter to six. She thought she would go
upstairs and have a bath.

Her bedroom, which she had liked so much from the beginning, seemed, in the chill half-light, unfamiliar; the room of
a stranger staying in a strange house. She drew the curtains and
turned on the bedside lamp, thus improving things, but only
slightly. She turned on the electric fire and, longing to be warm,
knelt on the hearth rug as close to the reddening bars as she
could get.

It took a few moments to realize that she was suffering
from loss of identity. Antony had known that she was Flora,
but she hadn't realized that this was so important. Now, with
him gone, it was as though he had taken Flora with him, and
left only Rose behind. She knew that she had come to distrust
Rose, almost to dislike her. She thought of Rose in Greece,
trying to imagine the sort of things Rose would be doing, like
sunbathing, and dancing under the stars to soft guitar music or
whatever it was one danced to in Spetsai. But none of those
mental pictures had any depth. They were two-dimensional,
unconvincing, like overcolored postcards. Rose, it seemed, was
not in Greece. Rose was here, at Fernrigg.

Her hands were frozen. She spread them to the warmth.
I'm Flora. I'm Flora Waring.

The promise she had made to Antony hung on her conscience like a weight. Perhaps because she had made it, she
longed passionately to be able to tell the truth. To someone. To
anyone who would listen and understand.

But who?

The answer, when it came, was so obvious that she could
not think why it had not occurred to her right away. Promise
not to say anything to any of them, Antony had insisted. And
she had given him her word. But "any of them" surely only
meant the Armstrongs, the people who lived in this house.

There was a little bureau in the corner of her bedroom,
which she had not even thought to investigate. Now she got up

and went over to it, and lowered the flap. Inside, this being the well-ordered establishment that it was, she found embossed writing paper and envelopes, a blotting pad, and a pen in a silver tray. She pulled up a chair, took up the pen, drew a sheet of paper toward her, and wrote the date.

Thus she started what was to be a very long letter to her father.

BRIAN

Early the next morning, as Flora came down to breakfast the telephone rang. Crossing the hall, she hesitated. When nobody appeared to answer it, she answered it herself, going to sit on the edge of the chest and pick up the receiver.

"Hello."

A woman spoke. "Is that Fernrigg?"

"Yes."

"Is that Isobel?"

"No. Do you want Isobel?"

"Is . . . is that Rose?"

Flora hesitated. "Yes."

"Oh, Rose, it's Anna Stoddart."

"Good morning, Anna. Do you want to speak to Isobel?"

"No, it doesn't matter, you'll do just as well. I only wanted to say thank you for the dinner party on Saturday. I . . . I enjoyed it so much."

"I'm glad. I'll tell Isobel."

467

"I'm sorry about ringing so early, but I forgot to ring yesterday, and I'm just off to Glasgow. I mean, I'm leaving any moment now. And I didn't want to go without saying thank you."

"Well, I hope you have a good trip."

"Yes, I'm sure I will. I'm only going for a couple of days. Perhaps when I get back you'd like to come over to Ardmore and see me. We could have lunch, or tea or something . . ."

Her voice trailed away uncertainly as though she felt she had already said too much. Flora could not bear her being so diffident. She said quickly, making her voice enthusiastic, "I'd love it. How kind of you. I'd love to see your house."

"Really? That would be fun. I'll maybe give you a telephone call when I get back."

"You do that." She added, "Have you heard about the dance yet?"

"Dance?"

"I thought perhaps it might have got through to you via the grapevine. There's going to be a dance here next Friday night. Tuppy thought the whole thing up by herself yesterday morning."

"*This* Friday?" Anna sounded incredulous, as well she might.

"This very Friday. Poor Isobel's got to spend the morning on the telephone, ringing people up. I'll tell her I've told you; and that'll be one less call she'll have to make."

"But how exciting. I'm so glad you told me, because now I can get a new dress when I'm in Glasgow. I need a new dress anyway . . ."

Once more her voice faded uncertainly. Anna was obviously a person who found it difficult to round off a telephone call. Flora was just about to say, in a conclusive sort of way, well, have a good time, when Anna said, "Just a minute. Don't ring off."

"I wasn't going to."

There were a few murmurs from the other end of the line,

468

and then Anna said, "Brian wants to talk to you. I'll say good-bye."

Brian? "Goodbye, Anna. Have a good time." Then Brian Stoddart spoke in his light, clear voice.

"Rose!"

"Good morning," said Flora warily.

"What an unearthly hour for a telephone conversation. Have you had your breakfast yet?"

"I'm just going to have it."

"Has Antony gone?"

"Yes, he went yesterday after tea."

"So you're bereft. And Anna's just on the point of abandoning me. Why don't we keep each other company tonight? I'll take you out for dinner."

A number of thoughts chased themselves through Flora's mind, the most important being that Anna was obviously aware of the conversation, so there could be nothing underhand about his invitation. But what would Tuppy think about it? And Isobel? And was it wise to spend an evening with that devious and attractive man? And even if his suggestion was innocent and harmless, did she particularly want to?

"Rose?"

"Yes, I'm still here."

"I thought you'd gone. I couldn't even hear heavy breathing. What time shall I pick you up?"

"I haven't said that I'm coming yet."

"Of course you're coming, don't be so coy. We'll go to the Fishers' Arms down in Lochgarry and I'll stuff you with scampi. Look, I've got to go. Anna's just on the point of departure, she's waiting for me to go and see her off. I'll pick you up about seven thirty, eight o'clock. That be all right? If Isobel's feeling generous, she can give me a drink. Love to Tuppy, and thank Isobel for the party the other night. We both enjoyed it enormously. See you later."

He rang off, and Flora was left holding the dead receiver. An outrageous man. Slowly, she put the receiver down. She thought, well . . . and then she began to smile, because really

469

it was ridiculous. Brian's charm, which had come gusting down the telephone wires towards her, was too obvious to be dangerous, or even important. The whole incident was too trivial to merit a great session of soul-searching. Besides, she liked scampi.

She realized that she was hungry and went in search of breakfast.

Jason had gone, borne off to school by Mr. Watty. Isobel was still at the kitchen table, reading a letter and drinking a final cup of coffee with Nurse. Mrs. Watty, at the window, was slicing steak for a pie.

"Did I hear the telephone ring?" she asked. She liked keeping in touch with what was going on.

"Yes, I answered it." Flora sat down and filled a bowl with cornflakes. "It was Anna Stoddart, Isobel, saying thank you for the other night."

Isobel looked up from her mail. "Oh, how kind," she said vaguely.

"She's just off to Glasgow for a couple of days."

"Yes, she said something about that."

"And Brian's asked me to go out to dinner with him tonight."

She watched Isobel's face, waiting for the slightest shadow of disapproval. But Isobel only smiled. "What a nice idea. That is kind of him."

"He said as I was without Antony and he was without Anna we might as well keep each other company. And he's coming to pick me up at half past seven, and he says if you're feeling generous you can give him a drink."

Isobel laughed, but Mrs. Watty said, "He's a cheeky devil."

"Don't you like him, Mrs. Watty?"

"Oh, I like him well enough, but he's awful forward."

"What Mrs. Watty means," said Isobel, "is that he just doesn't happen to be a dour Scot. I think it's very nice of him to take pity on Rose."

"And I told them about the dance on Friday so you don't

need to ring them up. And Anna's going to buy herself a new dress."

"Oh, dear," said Isobel.

"What does that mean?"

"Anna's always buying new clothes. She spends the earth on them, and they all look exactly the same." She sighed. "I suppose we've all got to start thinking about what we're going to wear next Friday. I could bring out that blue lace thing again, but everybody must be getting very tired of it."

"You're bonny in your blue lace," Mrs. Watty assured her. "It's no matter if people have seen it before."

"And Rose. What are you going to wear, Rose?"

The question, for some reason, caught Flora quite unprepared. Perhaps because there had been so many other more important issues to worry about, the thought of what she would wear to Tuppy's party had not even entered her head. She looked around at their expectant faces. "I haven't the faintest idea," she told them.

Nurse stared at Flora in some disbelief. She still remained rigidly opposed to the very idea of Tuppy's party, but despite herself it was impossible not to be caught up in the general anticipation. She was also a great social snob, and now she could scarcely believe that a young lady would come away to stay in a house like Fernrigg without packing at least one ballgown and possibly a tiara to wear with it.

"Haven't you got anything in your suitcase?" she asked Flora.

"No. I only came for the weekend. I didn't think I'd need a dress for a dance."

There was a pregnant silence while they all digested this information.

"What about what you wore the other night?" suggested Isobel.

"That was just a woolen skirt, and a shirt."

"Oh, no," breathed Mrs. Watty. "The party's to be in your honor. You'll need something a little more dressy than that."

471

She felt that she was letting them all down. "Could I buy something?"

"Not in Tarbole," Isobel told her. "Not within a hundred miles could you buy something to wear."

"Perhaps I should have gone to Glasgow with Anna."

"Is there nothing in the house that we could alter?" asked Nurse. Flora had visions of herself in a dress made out of old slip-covers.

Isobel shook her head. "Even if there were, we're none of us what you'd call dressmakers."

Nurse cleared her throat. "I used to make all my own clothes when I was a girl. And perhaps I've got a little more time than the rest of you."

"You mean you'd make something for Rose?"

"If it would help . . ."

At this suggestion, Mrs. Watty turned from her meat slicing, her kindly face at variance with the murderous-looking knife in her hand. "What about the attic? Those trunks in the attic are just full of old things that once belonged to Mrs. Armstrong. And lovely materials . . ."

"Mothballs," said Isobel. "They all smell of mothballs."

"A good wash and a blow on the line would see to that." The idea took hold. Mrs. Watty laid down her knife, washed her hands, and said that she for one was going upstairs to look, and there was no time like the present. It seemed there wasn't. In no time, all four of them were trooping up to the attics.

These were huge, stretching from one end of the house to the other. They were also dimly lit, cobwebby, and smelling of camphor and old cricket boots. A number of fascinating objects which Flora would have loved to inspect stood about: a weighing machine of the old type with brass weights and a measuring stick attached to the side; a Victorian doll's pram; a dressmaker's dummy; some brass ewers once used for carrying hot water.

But Mrs. Watty snapped on a dingy light and made her way straight to the line of trunks which stood ranged along the wall. They were of immense size and weight, with rounded lids

472

and leather handles for carrying. Together Mrs. Watty and Isobel lifted the lid of the first. It was stuffed with clothes. The smell of mothballs was indeed distressingly strong, but out came the garments, each one more ornate and impossible than the one before: black silk with jet embroidery; tea-rose satin with a fringed skirt; a drooping bouclé jacket lined with shredded chiffon, which Isobel assured Flora used to be known as a bridge coat.

"Did Tuppy really wear all these things?"

"Oh, in her day, she could be quite dressy. And of course, being such a thrifty old Scot, she's never thrown a thing away."

"Whatever's that?"

"It's an evening cape." Isobel shook out the crumpled velvet and blew on the fur collar. Out of the fur flew an intrepid moth. "I can remember Tuppy wearing this . . ." Her voice grew dreamy as she recalled far-off days.

It became more and more hopeless. Flora was on the point of suggesting that she go now to Tarbole, catch the next train to Glasgow and buy herself something there, when Mrs. Watty pulled out something that had obviously once been white, in lawn and lace. Like an old handkerchief, Flora thought, but it was a dress with a high neckband and long sleeves.

Isobel recognized it in some excitement. "But that was Tuppy's tennis dress."

"Tennis dress?" Flora was incredulous. "She surely didn't play tennis in that?"

"Yes, she did when she was a girl." Isobel took it from Mrs. Watty and held it up by the shoulders. "What do you think, Nurse? Could we do anything with that?"

Nurse handled the cobweb cotton with experienced fingers, pursing up her lips. "There's nothing wrong with it . . . and there's lovely work there."

"But it's much too short for me," objected Flora.

Nurse held it against her. It was too short, but there was, Nurse opined, *a good hem.* "I could let it down and you'd never notice."

Secretly Flora thought it was awful. But at least it wasn't

473

old slip-covers, and anything was better than having to make the trip to Glasgow.

"It's completely transparent. I'd have to wear something underneath."

"I could line it," said Nurse. "In some pretty shade. Perhaps pink."

Pink. Flora's heart sank, but she said nothing. Mrs. Watty and Isobel looked at each other for inspiration. Then Mrs. Watty remembered that when Isobel's bedroom curtains had been replaced they had ordered too much lining cotton. A length of it, good as new, must still be lying around somewhere. Finally, after a certain amount of pondering and poking around, Mrs. Watty, with a cry of triumph, produced it from the top drawer of a yellow-varnished dressing table.

"I knew I'd put it somewhere. I just couldn't mind where."

It was a pale eggshell blue. She shook it out of its folds and held it behind the drooping garment of yellowed lawn that was to be Flora's ball dress.

"What do you think?" she asked Flora.

The blue at least was better than pink. Perhaps when washed the dress wouldn't be too bad. She looked up and saw that they were all watching her dubious face, anxious for her approval. Like three ill-assorted fairy godmothers, they waited to turn her into the belle of the ball. Flora felt ashamed of her own lack of enthusiasm. To make up for it, she now smiled as though delighted and told them that if she had searched for a week, she couldn't have found a more perfect dress.

By afternoon the bulky letter addressed to Ronald Waring had still not been posted. For one thing, Flora had no stamp. For another, she had no idea where to find a letter box. After lunch, when Isobel asked her what she would like to do, Flora remembered the letter.

"Would you mind if I went to Tarbole? I've got a letter I want to post."

"I wouldn't mind in the least. In fact, it would be splendid because I've run out of hand cream and you can buy me some."

474

She added, "And you can fetch Jason from school and that will save Watty a journey." A thought occurred to her. "I suppose you *can* drive a car?"

"Yes, if nobody minds my borrowing one."

"You can take the van," Isobel told her placidly. "Then it doesn't matter if you do hit something."

The word went round that a trip was being made to Tarbole, and at once Flora was inundated with errands to be performed. Nurse needed fine sewing needles and blue silk to match the lining of the new dress. Tuppy wanted face tissues and four ounces of extra strong peppermints. Flora, with her shopping list in her hand, went into the kitchen to search out Mrs. Watty.

"I'm going to Tarbole. And I'm going to fetch Jason from school. Do you want me to get anything for you?"

"Does Watty know that he doesn't have to go to Tarbole?"

"No, I'm going to tell him on my way out. Isobel said I could take the van."

"Well, if Watty isn't going," said Mrs. Watty, heading for her fridge, "then you can deliver this for me." And she withdrew, from the fridge, a large steak pie in an enamel dish.

"Where do you want me to take that?"

"This is for Dr. Kyle." She took grease-proof paper from a drawer, tore off a generous sheet, and wrapped the pie in it. "I was making one for the dinner tonight, and I said to Miss Isobel, I might just as well make one for that poor man without his housekeeper. At least, he'll have one square meal in the day."

"But I don't know where he lives. I don't know where his house is."

"In Tarbole, up at the top of the hill. You can't miss it," Mrs. Watty added, which made Flora certain that she would, "because you'll see the new surgery tacked onto the side. And there's a brass plate on the gate."

She handed Flora the parceled pie. It was extremely heavy and should nourish Dr. Kyle, she reckoned, for at least four days.

"What shall I do with it? Leave it on the front doormat?"

"No." Mrs. Watty obviously thought Flora was being dense. "Take it inside into the kitchen and put it in the refrigerator."

"What if the door's locked?"

"Then the key will be on the ledge, inside the porch, on the righthand side."

Flora gathered up the rest of her things. She said, "Well, I just hope I leave it in the right house," and made her way out through the back door, leaving Mrs. Watty in fits of laughter, as though she had made a joke.

Watty was found in the vegetable garden. Flora gave him the message about Jason and said that Miss Armstrong had said that she could take the van. Watty told her that it was in the garage, and the key in the ignition. He added that the van had no peculiarities.

It may have been easy to drive, but for all that it was a peculiar van:—Tuppy's pride, Mrs. Watty's shame, and the joke of Tarbole. Tuppy, having decided that the old Daimler used too much petrol and that another, smaller, car was needed for day-to-day runs, had bought it secondhand off Mr. Reekie, the Tarbole fishmonger. And although Watty, bidden by his wife, had given it a coat of paint, the lettering on the side was still clearly visible:

Archibald Reekie
Fish of Quality
Freshly Smoked Kippers Delivered Daily

Flora, seeing it for the first time, thought it had great class. She got in behind the wheel, turned on the engine and, with only a small amount of gear-crashing, sped toward Tarbole.

The little town was a seething mass of activity that afternoon. The harbor was full of boats and the quays were packed with lorries. The air was full of the sounds of engines running and the churning of cranes, shouted orders, the gush of high-pressure hoses, and the endless screaming of the hungry gulls.

476

There were people everywhere: fishermen in yellow oilskins, lorry drivers in overalls, harbor officials in their uniforms. There were women in rubber boots and striped aprons, and all of them were involved in the complicated business of unloading the fish from the boats, gutting it, packing it, loading it into the waiting lorries, and sending it on its way.

She remembered Antony telling her about Tarbole—how only a short time ago it had been simply a small fishing village, but lately it had become the center of a vast herring industry. Inevitably, all that prosperity had left its mark. As she came down the road from Fernrigg, Flora passed the new school which had been built to accommodate the growing population of Tarbole children. Council houses spread up the hill behind the town, and not only fish lorries, but cars as well, choked the narrow streets around the harbor.

After driving Mr. Reekie's van around in circles for five minutes, Flora finally parked it in front of the bank beside a sign which said, *Parking Strictly Forbidden.* She did her shopping—which did not take long, since most of the purchases were made in the same shop—and then without much difficulty found the post office. She bought a stamp which she stuck onto the envelope addressed to her father, and then hesitated only for a moment before dropping it into the box. She heard it land with a fat thud and stood for a moment, not sure whether she felt glad or sorry that it was actually gone, out of her hands, beyond control. She thought of her father receiving it, reading it first to himself, and then perhaps aloud to Marcia. Knowing Marcia would be with him made all the difference. Everything would seem less dramatic, and he would perhaps not think too badly of Flora. More important, Marcia would not let him think badly of himself.

She made her way back to the car, but as she came around the corner was horrified to see a young constable standing waiting beside it. She began to run, meaning to apologize, beg for mercy, get into the car, and race away, but when she reached him, he only said, "You'll be a friend of Mrs. Armstrong of Fernrigg?"

Flora was taken aback. "Yes, I am."

"I thought I recognized the wee car."

"I am sorry, I thought . . ."

"Have you more errands to do?"

"Yes. I've got to deliver a pie to Dr. Kyle. And then I've got to get Jason from school."

"If you're going to Dr. Kyle's house, you'd be better to walk up the hill and leave the van here. Don't be worrying, I'll keep an eye on it."

"Oh. Thank you."

He opened the door for her, in a most courteous fashion. She tipped the parcels onto the seat and extracted the pie. The young constable smiled down at her benevolently.

"You . . . you couldn't tell me where he lives?"

"Up the hill, out of the town. It's the last house on the left, just before you get to the hotel. It has a garden in the front, and Dr. Kyle's plate on the gate."

"Thank you so much."

The young constable smiled, bashful. "You're welcome," he said.

The hill out of the town was very steep, so steep that the pavement had been graded into steps. It was a little like climbing a long, shallow flight of stairs. At first there were small terraced cottages flush with the street, and then a pub, and then more cottages. The houses became larger, each set in its own little garden. Finally, near the top of the climb Flora came to the last house of all, which was bigger than any of them, solid and unadorned, set back from the road, with a tiled path that led up from the gate to the porch. It had a white concrete building attached to its side which looked rather like an enormous shoebox. Though she did not need that last assurance, Flora inspected the wrought iron gate, and there was the brass plate with Hugh Kyle's name upon it. Thinking that it could do with a good buffing, Flora opened the gate and went up the sloping path to the front door.

She rang the bell, but as soon as she heard the mournful tinkle from the back of the house she knew that there was

478

nobody in. The pie, after her climb up the hill, was beginning to become very heavy. She rang again for politeness' sake, and then reached up as Mrs. Watty had bid her, to feel for the front door key. It was a large one, easily found, and Flora inserted it into the keyhole, turned it, and opened the door.

Inside was a tiled hall, a staircase rising into gloom, and a smell like that of old antique shops, rather musty but quite pleasant. She went in, leaving the door open behind her. She saw the old-fashioned hatstand with a place for umbrellas, the pretty little inlaid table, the white painted wrought-iron banister. Everything was very dusty. There was a clock, but it had stopped. She wondered if it was broken or if nobody had remembered to wind it—or had the time to wind it.

There was a door on her right which she opened to find the most unlived-in-looking living room she'd ever seen, with nothing out of place, not a flower to be seen, and the blinds half-drawn. She closed that door and opened the one opposite to reveal a ponderous Victorian dining room. The table was mahogany and massive, and there was a sideboard of matching proportions ranged with decanters and silver wine-slides. All the chairs had been placed around the room against the wall, and here again the blinds were half-drawn. It had, thought Flora, all the cheer of a funeral parlor. Quietly, not wanting to disturb any ghosts, she closed that door and went down the hall toward the back regions of the house in search of the kitchen.

Here the deathly order ceased abruptly. It was not a large kitchen. In fact, for the size of the house it was quite small, but even so every available horizontal space had collected a formidable amount of clutter. Saucepans, frying pans, casseroles were all piled on the draining board; the sink was stacked with dirty dishes, and the table in the middle of the room bore witness to a snatched meal—not a very appetizing one at that, unless one happened to enjoy cornflakes, fried eggs, and fruitcake all at the same time. The final touch was the half-empty bottle of whisky which stood in the middle of the table. For some reason it loaded the sad disorder of the scene with potential disaster.

479

The refrigerator was in a corner by the cooker. Flora started towards it, tripped over the torn corner of a rug, and almost fell flat on her face. Inspecting the rug, she saw that the floor was dirty. It didn't look as though it had been swept for a week, let alone scrubbed.

She opened the fridge and quickly stowed away the pie before more horrors should offend her eye. Shutting the door, she turned and leaned against it, surveying the shambles as a number of thoughts ran through her mind. The most obvious was that Jessie McKenzie was a dirty slut and the sooner Hugh got rid of her the better. No man, however, feckless, could have got a kitchen into such a mess in a matter of days.

She looked at it hopelessly and her heart ached for him, and at the same time she knew that he would be mortified beyond words if he found out that Flora had seen it all. With this in mind, her instinct was to tiptoe tactfully away and let him think it was Watty who had delivered the pie.

Besides, she had to fetch Jason from school. Flora looked at her watch and discovered that it was only a quarter to three. She had an hour before she was due at the school. What could she do with the time? Walk around the harbor? Have a cup of coffee in Sandy's Snack Bar? But of course she would do none of these things, because even while she was considering them, she pulled off her gloves, unbuttoned her coat, hung it on the peg behind the door, and rolled up her sleeves. *You fool,* she told herself and searched for an apron. She found one slung by the sink, a blue butcher's apron, designed for a man and much too large for her. She tied it twice about her waist, found a dishcloth and turned on the hot tap. The water was boiling, and she told herself that this was the one good thing that happened since she walked into this benighted house.

In a cupboard below the sink she found, somewhat unexpectedly, a sturdy scrubbing brush, quantities of soap powder and a packet of steel wool. (It seemed that Jessie McKenzie had good intentions, even if she didn't carry them through.) These she made lavish use of. When it came to putting things away, Flora simply piled the clean dishes out of sight, hung cups and

480

jugs on hooks, then turned her attention to the pile of saucepans. By the time she had finished they were not only clean but also shining, and when she had placed them nearly ordered as to size, on the shelf over the cooker, they looked not only businesslike but attractive. Once she had achieved a clean and empty sink, the transformation of Hugh Kyle's kitchen took a surprisingly short time. She cleared the table, threw away the stale fruit cake, placed the whisky bottle tactfully out of sight, and shook the crumbs from the tablecloth. She wiped the table and various counters with a damp cloth. Everything shone. There is nothing in life so satisfying as rendering a very dirty room totally clean. Flora by now was enjoying herself. There remained only the floor. She checked the time and as it was only twenty past three, she took up the torn rug, bundled it out of the back door, and searched for a broom. That and a dustpan came to light in a dank cupboard which smelled of boot polish and mice. She swept the floor free of what appeared to be months of dirt, filled a bucket with boiling water and suds, and got down to work.

Three buckets and half a packet of soap powder later, she had just about finished. The linoleum shone wet, smelt clean, and revealed a pattern of brown and blue tiles, unexpectedly fresh and pretty. Only a dark cavern beneath the draining board remained, and into this Flora plunged head-first, by now so enthusiastic that she didn't even quail at the thought of mousedroppings or cobwebs or possible scuttling spiders. As her scrubbing brush scraped and banged against the wainscoting, the small enclosed space grew thick with steam. At last she laid down the brush, wrung out the cloth, and wiped away the last of the suds.

It was finished. Flora backed out from under the draining board and was just about to get to her feet when she noticed, through the legs of the kitchen table, planted fair and square in the middle of her clean floor, another pair of feet; brown leather shoes with rubber soles; the bottoms of tweed trousers. Sitting back on her heels, her gaze traveled slowly upward until it finally came to rest on Hugh Kyle's astonished face.

481

It was hard to say which of them was the more surprised. Then abruptly, Flora said, "Oh, damn."

"What's that for?"

"I hoped you wouldn't come back."

He did not comment on this, simply stared about him, completely bewildered. "What the hell are you doing?"

She was annoyed at being found out, not because of the lowly nature of her task, but because Hugh would be stupidly offended by her interference, and doubtless turn stuffy and dour. "What do you think I'm doing? I'm scrubbing the floor."

"But you shouldn't be doing that."

"Why not? It was dirty."

He looked about him, taking in the sparkling shelves and counters, the shining sink, the squared-off order of saucepans and crockery. His eyes came back to her face. He still looked bewildered. He put up a hand to rub the back of his neck, the very picture of a man at a loss for words.

"I must say, that's extraordinarily kind of you, Rose. Thank you very much."

She did not want him to feel too grateful. She said, lightly, "It's a pleasure."

"But I still don't understand. Why are you here?"

"Mrs. Watty cooked a pie for you and she asked me to deliver it. It's in the fridge." A thought occurred to her. "I never heard you come in."

"The front door was open."

"Oh, heavens, I forgot to shut it."

Her hair had fallen across her face. She pushed it back with her wrist and stood up. The huge apron drooped damply around her legs. She picked up the bucket, emptied it down the drain, wrung out the cloth, and slung the lot into the cupboard beneath the sink. She shut the door and turned to face him, rolling down her sleeves.

"You have a useless housekeeper," she told him, bluntly. "You should get someone else to look after you."

"Jessie does her best. It's just that she's been away. She had to go to Portree to see her mother."

482

"When is she coming back?"

"I don't know. Tomorrow or maybe the next day."

"Well, you should give her notice and find somebody else." She felt brutal, but she was annoyed with him, because no man had the right to look so tired. "It's ridiculous. You're the doctor in this town. There must be somebody who'd help you. What about your nurse, the one who works in the surgery?"

"She's a married woman with three children to look after. She has more than enough to do."

"But wouldn't she know somebody who could come and work for you?"

Hugh shook his head. "I don't know," he said.

She had seen that he was tired, but now she realized that at this moment he not only didn't know, he didn't care, whether anybody could find him a new housekeeper or not. She began to regret having attacked him, nagging at him like some discontented wife.

She said, more gently, "You know, you surprised me just as much as I must have surprised you. Where did you suddenly appear from?"

He looked around for something to sit on, saw the chairs which Flora had piled in a corner, and went to pick one up and set it by the side of the table.

"Lochgarry," he told her, settling back with his legs crossed and his hands in his pockets. "I've been to the hospital. I've been to see Angus McKay."

"Is that the old man you told me about who lived up Loch Fhada? The one who fell down the stairs?"

Hugh nodded.

"He finally agreed to go to the hospital then?"

"Yes. He finally agreed. Or should I say, he was finally persuaded."

"By you?"

"Yes. By me. The ambulance went out to Boturich and collected him this morning. I went over to see him this afternoon. He's in a ward with five other old men, all staring at the opposite wall and waiting for death, and he doesn't even know

483

what's hit him. I dispensed the usual dose of hearty good cheer, but he just lay there and looked at me. Like an old dog. I felt like a murderer."

"But you mustn't feel like that. It's not your fault. You said yourself that his daughter-in-law was at the end of her tether having to take care of him. And so far out in the country and everything. And he might have fallen downstairs again, or had some even worse accident. Anything could have happened."

He let her say all this without interrupting. When she finished speaking, he was silent for a little, watching her from beneath his heavy brows. Then he said, "He's old, Rose. He's frail and confused and now we've uprooted him. That's a monstrous thing to do to any man. He was born at Boturich, his father farmed Boturich before him, and his grandfather. Angus brought his wife back to Boturich, and his children were born there. And now, at the end of the day, when we have no more use for him, we cart him off and stow him away, out of sight and out of mind, and leave him to be cared for by strangers."

Flora was astonished that he, a doctor, should allow himself to become so emotionally involved. "But that's the way things are. You can't change things like that. You can't stop people's growing old."

"But you see, Angus isn't people. Angus is part of me, part of my growing up. My father was a busy doctor, and he didn't manage to find much time to spend with a small boy, so on fine Saturdays I used to bicycle fifteen miles each way up Loch Fhada to Boturich to see Angus McKay. He was a tall, rangy man, strong as an ox, and I thought he knew everything. He did too, about birds and foxes and hares, and where to find the fattest trout, and how to tie a fly that not the wiliest salmon could resist. I thought he was the wisest being in the world. All powerful. Like God. And we'd go fishing together, or up the hill with a spyglass, and he'd show me where the golden eagles were nesting."

Flora smiled, liking the picture of the old man and the boy together. "How old were you then?"

484

"About ten. A little bit older than Jason."

Jason. Flora had forgotten Jason. She looked at her watch, and then, in a panic, began to untie the strings of the apron. "I must fly. I'm meant to be fetching Jason from school. He'll think he's been forgotten."

"I was rather hoping you'd make me a cup of tea."

"I haven't got time. I'm meant to be there at a quarter to four and it's twenty to now."

"Supposing I call the headmaster and tell him to hang on to Jason for a bit."

Such a reaction on his part was unexpected. *Why,* thought Flora, *he's really trying to be nice to me.* She laid down the apron. "Won't Jason mind?"

"He won't mind." Hugh got to his feet. "They've a train set up at the school and if the boys are good, they're allowed to play with it. He'll jump at the chance of getting it to himself." He went out into the hall, leaving the door open. Flora stood where she was, staring after him. She had discovered that it is disconcerting when someone whom you think you have neatly pigeonholed starts acting out of character. She heard him dialing the school. She turned to fill the kettle, and put it on to boil. Hugh's voice came down the hall.

"Hello, Mr. Fraser? Dr. Kyle speaking. Have you got young Jason Armstrong there? Would you be so kind as to hold on to him for another fifteen minutes or so. Antony's young lady's on her way to fetch him and take him back to Fernrigg, but she's going to be held up. Well, if you want the truth, she's just about to make me a cup of tea. Yes, she's here. Well, that would be very civil of you. Thank you. We'll be here when he comes. Tell him not to bother to ring the bell, but just walk in. We'll be in the kitchen. Very well. I'm obliged to you. Goodbye, Mr. Fraser."

She heard him put down the receiver, and the next moment he appeared back in the kitchen.

"That's all settled. One of the junior masters is going to bring Jason down in his car and drop him off at the gate."

"Does that mean he won't get to play with the train set?"

485

Hugh went to fetch a second chair from the corner. "I wouldn't know."

Flora had found a teapot with a broken spout, a jug of milk in the fridge, and a couple of old, pretty Wedgwood mugs.

"I don't know where the sugar is, or the tea."

He delved into some cupboard and produced them. The tea was kept in a very old tin with a picture of George V on the side. It was bent and most of the paint had gone. Flora said, "This looks as if it's been around for some time."

"Yes, like everything in this house. Including me."

"Have you lived here all your life?"

"Most of it. My father lived here for forty years, and it would be an understatement to say that he didn't believe in change for its own sake. When I came back to take over from him it was like stepping back into the past. At first I thought I'd make all sorts of alterations and bring the whole place up-to-date, but before long the famous West Coast rot had set in, and it took me all my time and effort just to get the surgery built. Once that was up, I forgot about the house. Or perhaps I just forgot to notice it."

Flora felt relieved. At least he hadn't gone out and chosen the dining room furniture for himself. The kettle boiled. She filled the teapot and put it on the table. She said, politely, "It's a good solid house," and it sounded like telling a proud mother that her baby looks healthy when you can't think of another thing to say about the wretched infant.

"Tuppy thinks it's dreadful," said Hugh placidly. "A mausoleum she calls it. And I'm prepared to believe her."

"There's nothing wrong with it." She met his skeptical eye. "I mean," she floundered on, "it has possibilities." She sat down at the table and poured the tea. The atmosphere had become pleasantly domestic. Encouraged by this, she went on. "There's no house that can't be made very nice if you give it a little thought. All it needs is . . ." She searched for inspiration. "A coat of paint."

He looked amazed. "Is that all it needs?"

486

"Well, it would be a start. A coat of paint can do wonders."

"I'll have to try it." He helped himself to milk and a generous amount of sugar, stirring the lot into a real workman's brew. He drank it, apparently without scalding his throat, and at once poured a second cup. "A coat of paint." He set down the teapot. "And perhaps the blinds pulled up to let some sunshine in. And the smell of new polish. And flowers. And books and music. And a fire burning in the grate when you come back from work at the end of a long winter's day."

Without thinking, Flora said, "You don't need a new housekeeper, you need a new wife," and was instantly on the receiving end of a glance so sharp that she wished she had not spoken at all. "I'm sorry," she said quickly.

But he did not seem to be offended. He put more milk and sugar into his tea and stirred it. He said, "You know I've been married." It was a statement of fact, not an accusation.

"Yes. Tuppy told me."

"What else did she tell you?"

"That your wife was killed in a car accident."

"Nothing else?"

"No." She felt impelled to stand up for Tuppy. "She only told me because she's so fond of you. She doesn't like to think of you living on your own."

"After I got engaged to Diana I brought her back to Tarbole. The visit wasn't what you'd call a success. Did Tuppy say anything about that?"

"Not really." Flora was beginning to feel uncomfortable.

"I can tell by your face that she did. Tuppy didn't take to Diana. Like everybody else, she thought I was making a terrible mistake."

"And was it a mistake?"

"Yes. Right from the very beginning, but I was so blinded by my feelings I wouldn't admit it even to myself. I met her in London. I was at St. Thomas's working for my F.R.C.S. I had a friend there, John Rushmoore—I'd know him at Edinburgh University. We used to play rugger together. Then he got a job

487

in the City, and I met up with him again when I went south. It was through him that I first met Diana. She and John belonged to a world that I had never known, and like any country bumpkin, I was bedazzled by it. And by her. When I wanted to marry her, everybody told me that I was mad. Her father had no opinion of me at all. From the beginning he had me pegged as a hairy-heeled Scotsman after his daughter's money. My professor was equally unenthusiastic. I had another two years to go before I had a hope of getting my F.R.C.S., and he believed that I should put my career before my matrimonial aspirations. And of course my father agreed with him.

"It may sound strange to you, but my father's good opinion was the one that mattered most to me. I felt that if I had that, then the rest of them could go to hell. So I brought Diana home to meet him, and to show her off. It took some persuading to get her here. She'd only been to Scotland once before, on some grouse-shooting houseparty or other, and she didn't relish the idea of Tarbole. But I finally talked her into it, naïvely, imagining that my father and the friends I'd known all my life would be as besotted by her as I was.

"But it didn't work out. In fact, it was a disaster. It rained the entire time, Diana hated Tarbole, she hated this house, and she hated the country. All right, she was spoiled. And like so many spoiled women, she could be wholly charming and engaging, but only with people who amused or stimulated her. There wasn't anybody here who fitted that bill. She rendered my father speechless, and he wasn't what you'd call a talkative man at the best of times. He was immensely courteous and she was a guest in his house, but by the end of the third day we'd all had enough. My father brought it all to a head. He topped himself up with whisky, took me into his surgery, and told me he thought I'd gone out of my mind. He told me a lot of other things as well, but most of them are unrepeatable. And then I lost my temper and I said a lot of unrepeatable things. And by the time that session was over, there was nothing for me to do but bundle Diana back into my car and drive back to London.

We were married a week later. You could say because of parental opposition rather than in spite of it."

"Did it work?"

"No. At first it was all right. We were infatuated with each other. I suppose, if you were romantically minded, you'd say we were much in love. But our two worlds were too far apart and we had nothing in common with which to build any sort of a bridge. When we first met, I think Diana imagined herself as the social wife of a brilliant surgeon, but instead she found herself married to a struggling student who spent most of his waking hours at the hospital. It wasn't much of a marriage, but the fault was just as much mine as hers."

Flora wrapped her hands, for warmth, around her mug of tea. She said, "Perhaps if circumstances had been different . . ."

"But they weren't different. We had to make the best of what we had."

"When was she killed?"

"Nearly two years after we married. By then we were hardly ever together, and I thought nothing of it when Diana told me that she was going away for the weekend to stay with an old schoolfriend who lived in Wales. But when she was killed, she was in John Rushmoore's car, and he was driving. And they weren't going to Wales, they were going to Yorkshire."

Flora stared at him. "You don't mean . . . your friend?"

"Yes. My friend. They'd been having an affair for months and I'd never even suspected. Afterward, when it was all over, it all came out. Everyone had known, it seemed, but no one had had the heart to enlighten me. It's a shattering thing to lose your wife and your friend in one fell swoop. It's even more shattering when you lose your pride as well."

"Was John Rushmoore killed too?"

"No." Hugh was casual. "He's still around."

"Is that why you threw over your F.R.C.S. and came back to Tarbole?"

"I came because my father was ill."

489

"You never thought of going back to London?"

"No."

"Couldn't you still become a surgeon?"

"No. It's too late. I belong here now. Perhaps this is where I've always belonged. I'm not sure if I could have lived my life in a city, away from clean air and the smell of the sea."

"You're just like . . ." Flora began, and then stopped herself just in time. She had been about to say *You're just like my father.* Listening to Hugh, she had forgotten that she was meant to be Rose. Now she found herself consumed by an entirely natural compulsion to exchange confidence for confidence, memory for memory. Hugh had opened a door, which had previously been shut and barred in her face, and she wanted very much to go through it.

But she couldn't because, as Rose, she had nothing to offer him in return. As Rose, she could share no memories, offer no comfort. The frustration of this was suddenly more than she could bear, and for a moment she actually considered spilling out the truth. In his present mood, she knew that he would understand. She had given her promise to Antony, but Hugh was, after all, a doctor. Wasn't telling a doctor a secret rather like confessing to a priest? Did it really count?

From the very beginning, all Flora's finer instincts had reacted against the lie that she and Antony had embarked upon, simply because it was bound to affect and involve other and innocent people. But now it seemed that the lie had turned, and Flora herself was caught up in its tangled coils—bound hand and foot, shackled by it, and unable to move.

Hugh waited for her to finish her sentence. When she did not, he prompted her. "Who am I like?"

"Oh . . ." *I promise,* she had said to Antony, only yesterday on the beach. ". . . Nobody. Just someone I once knew who felt the way you do."

The moment was over. The temptation past. She was still Rose, and she did not know whether she was glad or sorry. The kitchen was warm and quiet. The only sounds came from outside. A lorry changed gears, grinding up the hill past the gate.

490

A dog barked; a woman, climbing up from the ships with her laden basket, called across the road to her friend. The sky was filled with the scream of gulls.

The peace was terminated abruptly by the arrival of Jason. The front door opened and slammed shut with a force that shook the house. It took them by surprise, and Flora jumped and looked at Hugh and saw her own blank expression mirrored on his face. They had forgotten about Jason. Jason's high voice pierced the air.

"Rose!"

"She's here!" Hugh called back. "In the kitchen."

Footsteps raced down the passage, the door was flung wide, and Jason burst in.

"Hello. Mr. Thomson brought me in his car and there's a great big boat in the harbor and he says it's come from Germany. Hello, Hugh."

"Hello, old boy."

"Hello, Rose." He came around to her side of the table and put his arms around her neck to give her an absent-minded kiss. "Hugh, I've drawn a special picture for Tuppy. I did it this afternoon."

"Let's see it."

Jason struggled with the buckle of his satchel and hauled out the drawing. "Oh, bother, it's all crumpled."

"That's all right," said Hugh. "Bring it here."

Jason did so, leaning against Hugh's knee. Hugh took the drawing and unfolded it carefully, smoothing out the creases on the top of the kitchen table. Once before, Flora had noticed his hands. Now, for some reason watching them deal so deftly with Jason's smudged and garish painting did something peculiar to the pit of her stomach. She heard him say, "That's a fine picture. What is it?"

"Oh, Hugh, you are stupid."

"Elucidate."

"I don't know what that means."

"Explain it to me."

"Well, look. It's an airplane and a man in a parachute.

491

And then there's this man, and he's landed already, and he's waiting for the other man, and he's sitting under a tree."

"I see. It's very good. Tuppy will like it. No, don't fold it again. Leave it flat. Rose will carry it for you and then it won't get creased again. Won't you, Rose?"

She was taken unawares. "What?" She looked up from the table and met the startling blue of his eyes.

"I said you'd look after the picture."

"Yes, of course I will."

"Are you having tea?" asked Jason. "Is there anything to eat?" He looked about him hopefully.

Flora remembered the ditched fruitcake. "I don't know. We just had a cup of tea."

Hugh said, "If you look in that red tin on the dresser there might be a biscuit."

Jason fetched the tin, put it on the table and wrestled it open. He produced from it a large chocolate biscuit, wrapped in silver paper.

"Can I have this?"

"If you want to risk it. I've no idea how long it's been there."

Jason removed the paper and took an experimental mouthful. "It's all right. A bit soggy, but it's all right." Munching, he stared from High's face to Flora's. "Why didn't you come for me, Rose?"

"I was making Hugh a cup of tea. You didn't mind, did you?"

"No, I didn't mind." He came to lean against her. She put her arm around him and pressed her chin against the top of his head. "I played with the train set," he told her in a voice of the deepest satisfaction. Flora began to laugh. She glanced across at Hugh, expecting to have him share her amusement, but he did not seem to have heard Jason. His expression was abstracted and withdrawn, and he was watching the two of them with the total absorption of a man on the verge of making some marvelous discovery.

492

* * *

Jason was in bed, Tuppy safely tucked away upstairs, and
Rose had departed—looking very charming—to be given dinner by Brian Stoddart. Isobel sat alone by the fire, doing her
knitting and listening to Mozart. To be on her own was for her
a rare pleasure; to listen to Mozart instead of the nine o'clock
news on television, an even rarer one. It caused Isobel a slight
pang of guilt, because Tuppy always listened to the nine o'clock
news, and the reason Isobel didn't have to was because Tuppy
was ill. But the guilt was not enough to be troublesome. And
she had had a busy day. After all that telephoning, she felt
exhausted. Squelching her conscience, Isobel knitted on, revel-
ing in the novelty of self-indulgence.

The telephone rang. She sighed, glanced at the clock,
drove her needles through the ball of wool, and went out into
the hall to answer it. It was Hugh Kyle. "Yes, Hugh."

"Isobel, I'm sorry to disturb you, but is Rose there?"

"No, I'm sorry, she's not."

"Oh. Well, never mind."

"Can I give her a message?"

"It's just that . . . she was here this afternoon delivering
a splendid pie Mrs. Watty made, and she's left her gloves behind. At least, I think they must be hers. And I didn't want her
to think she'd lost them."

"I'll tell her. I won't see her again this evening, but I'll tell
her in the morning."

"Has she gone out?"

"Yes." Isobel smiled, because it was so pleasant for Rose,
bereft of Antony's company, to be having some fun. "Brian
Stoddart's taken her out for dinner."

There was a long silence, and then Hugh said, faintly,
"What?"

"Brian Stoddart's taken her out for dinner. Anna's away
so they're keeping each other company."

"Where have they gone?"

"I think to Lochgarry. Brian said something about the
Fishers' Arms. He had a drink here before they went."

"I see."

"I'll tell Rose about the gloves."

"What?" He sounded as though he had forgotten about the gloves. "Oh, yes. Any time. It doesn't matter. Goodnight, Isobel."

Even for Hugh, that was fairly abrupt. "Goodnight," said Isobel. She put down the receiver and stood for a moment, wondering if something was wrong. But nothing occurred to her. Just her imagination. She turned off the light and went back to the music.

Lochgarry lay some fifteen miles to the south of Fernrigg, at the head of a sea loch and on the junction of the main roads from Fort William, from Tarbole, and from Morven and Ardnamuchan to the south. Long ago, it had been simply a small community of fisherfolk, with a modest inn to serve the needs of infrequent travelers. But then the railways had come, bringing in their wake wealthy sportsmen from England, and after that nothing was the same again. The Lochgarry Castle Hotel was built to accommodate not only the sportsmen, but their retinues of families, friends, and servants, and in August and September the surrounding hills echoed to the crack of guns.

After the Second World War, things changed again. Industry arrived, in the shape of a huge sawmill and lumberyards. More houses went up, as did a new school to take the place of the old single-room schoolhouse, and a little cottage hospital. The roads were widened and improved, and summer traffic swelled over the years to a flood. The seafields which sloped down to the water were transformed into caravan sites, and an area of rough pasture banked with clumps of whin and gorse had been landscaped into a nine-hole golf course.

The Fishers' Arms, the little inn which had stood facing out over the loch for as long as anybody could remember, bore witness to all that change. Over the years it had been many times enlarged, improved with bow windows, decorated with porches, painted white and trellised with creepers. Inside, up

494

crooked stairs and down sloping passages, were not only bed-rooms, but bathrooms as well. One owner built a bar. Another built a restaurant. A third bulldozed the garden into a car park. By the time Flora set eyes on it, its original modest form was lost forever.

The car park, when they reached it, seemed full. Brian parked his car and they stepped out into the blowy dusk. The air smelt of seaweed, and random lights of cottages were re-flected in the dark waters of the loch. From inside the inn came sounds of clashing crockery, the smell of good food cooking.

"It seems to be very popular," Flora observed.

"It is. But don't worry, I booked a table." He tucked his hand beneath her arm, and they crossed the car park and went up the steps and through the main door. Inside were bright lights and tartan carpeting and plastic flower arrangements. A notice pointed up the stairs to the ladies', and Flora detached herself gently from Brian, and said that she would go upstairs and shed her coat.

"You do that. You'll find me in the bar."

A white-coated waiter appeared. "Good evening, Mr. Stoddart. It's a long time since we've seen you."

"Hello, John. I hope you've got a good dinner for us to-night."

In the meantime, Flora made her way upstairs and found a ladies' that was a marvel of floral wallpaper and mauve flounc-ing. She took off her coat, hung it up, and went to the mirror to comb her hair. For the occasion she had put on her turquoise wool skirt (inevitable, as she had no other) and a long-sleeved black sweater. But she had dressed without enthusiasm, not really wanting to keep this date with Brian, but knowing that she had no excuse for getting out of it. Because of that, she had taken little trouble with her appearance, yet it seemed to be one of those times when everything looked right. Her hair shone like a fall of silk, her skin bloomed, her dark eyes were bright.

"You look so pretty," Isobel had said.

"You're glittering like something off a Christmas tree," Brian had told her as he packed her into his car, a shining

495

maroon 3.5-liter Mercedes. Flora had found time to wonder whether Brian had paid for it, or his wife. The drive from Fernrigg had been immensely fast, though otherwise without incident, and they had talked of trivialities. Whether this had been Brian's intention or Flora's own, she was not entirely sure.

She went downstairs. The bar was crowded, but Brian had somehow managed to get the best table by the fire. When she appeared through the door he stood up and waited for her to join him. She was aware of being watched. Eyes followed her across the room as though the sight of a woman who was unfamiliar, young, and attractive, was something not to be missed.

He smiled, as much for the audience as for her.

"Come and sit by the fire. I've ordered you a drink." They sat down, and he reached in his pocket and took out a gold cigarette case and held it out to her. When she shook her head, he took one for himself and lit it with a gold lighter that had his initials engraved upon it. He already had a tumbler of whisky on the table before him, but now Flora's drink came, borne on a silver tray.

The glass was frosted with ice. "What is it?"

"It's a martini, of course. What else would it be?" Flora was about to tell him that she never drank martinis, but he went on, "And I ordered it specially dry, the way you like them."

As he had apparently gone to so much trouble, it seemed churlish to refuse the drink. Flora took it from the tray and the cold burned her fingers. Brian raised his whisky to her, and his eyes watched her across the rim of the tumbler.

"Slaintheva," he said.

"I don't speak the language."

"It means 'good health.' It's Gaelic. The only word of Gaelic I've learned since I've lived here."

"I'm sure it's a very useful word. I'm sure it gets you out of all sorts of awkward situations."

He smiled, and she took a mouthful of the martini and almost choked. It was like drinking cold fire, and took her

496

breath away. Gasping, she set down the glass and he laughed at her. "What's wrong?"

"It's so strong."

"Rubbish, you ought to be used to them. You never used to drink anything else."

"I haven't had one . . . lately."

"Rose, you're not reforming, are you?" He sounded genuinely concerned. "I couldn't bear it. You used to drink martinis without batting an eyelid, and chain-smoke to boot."

"I did?"

"Yes, you did. Gauloises. You see, I haven't forgotten a single detail."

She tried easing out of this. "I do smoke still, but not very often."

"It must be the influence of a good man."

"I suppose you mean Antony?"

"Who else would I mean? I can't believe there have been that number of good men in your life."

"All right, so it's Antony."

Brian shook his head, a man bewildered. "What on earth induced you to get engaged to him?"

Having the conversation steered into such intimacy, so early in the evening, was a little like finding oneself skating on the thinnest possible ice. Flora became wary. "I should have thought there was every reason in the world."

"Give me one."

"I might, if it was your business."

"Of course it's my business. Everything you do is my business. But somehow it's wrong. You and Antony don't match. You're not a couple. When Anna told me you were going to marry him, I could scarcely believe it. Still can't, for that matter."

"Don't you like Antony?"

"Everybody likes Antony. That's his trouble. He's too damn nice."

"There's the reason you were asking for. He's nice."

"Oh, come off it, Rose." He set his drink down on the

497

table, and leaned toward her, his hands loosely clasped between his knees. He wore, this evening, a smoothly cut blazer, a pair of dark gray trousers very slightly flared, and Gucci slippers with the red and green trademark. His hair was very black, crinkling back from his forehead; his pale eyes, beneath the dark brows, were bright and watchful. In the closeness of the car she had been aware of the expensive smell of his aftershave. Now, she saw the gold gleam of his wristwatch, his cufflinks, his signet ring. It seemed that not one single detail had been neglected.

His scrutiny, and her reaction to it, were dangerous. She searched for some safer topic. "Did Anna tell you about Tuppy's dance?"

For an instant, annoyance clouded his bright gaze, and then was gone. He leaned back in his chair, reaching for his whisky as he did so.

"Yes, she told me something, just before she went off."

"You've been invited."

"Doubtless."

"Are you going to come?"

"I expect so."

"You don't sound very enthusiastic."

"I know Tuppy Armstrong's parties of old. All the same people, wearing the same clothes, saying the same things. But then, as I told you the other night, there are many penalties attached to living out here, in the back of beyond."

He did not look a man who suffered too many penalties.

"That's not a very gracious reaction to an invitation."

He smiled, once more all charm. "No, it isn't, is it, and if you're going to be there, looking as seductive as you always do, then wild horses wouldn't keep me away."

Despite herself, Flora laughed. "I won't be looking particularly seductive. In fact, I shall probably look singularly odd."

"Odd? Why odd?"

She told him that morning's drama of the dress, making it as good a story as she could. When she had finished, Brian was

498

incredulous. "Rose, you can't. You can't go to any sort of a party in some old rag out of the Fernrigg attic." '

"What else can I do?"

"I'll drive you to Glasgow and you can buy a dress there. I'll drive you to Edinburgh. Or London. Better still, I'll fly you to Paris. We'll stay for the weekend and go shopping at Dior."

"What pretty ideas you have."

"I'm glad you think they're pretty. I think they're irresistible. Come on, when shall we go? Tomorrow. You used to enjoy living dangerously."

"I am not going shopping with you," Flora told him firmly. "Absolutely, flatly, no."

"Well, don't blame me if everybody laughs his head off when you appear in something out of the dressing-up box. But one thing's for sure, if anybody can get away with it, then you can. Come on, drink up, John's semaphoring from the other side of the room, and that means our table's ready."

The dining room was very warm and dim with candlelight, with soft piped music. Most of the tables were already occupied, but theirs waited for them in the curve of the bow window, made snug by the drawn curtains. It looked very intimate. They sat down. Another round of drinks appeared. Flora, who was just beginning to feel the impact of the first martini, looked in some dismay at the second.

"I really don't want another drink."

"For heaven's sake Rose, stop being so boring. This is a night out. Enjoy it. You're not driving."

She looked at his dark whisky. "No, but you are."

"Not to worry. I know the road like the back of my hand. And I know the police force too, such as it is." He opened a menu as big as a newspaper. "Now what are we going to eat?"

There was scampi on the menu but also oysters. Flora loved scampi, but she loved oysters even more, and she hadn't had them for ages. Brian was complaisant. "All right, you can have oysters, but I'm going to have scampi. And then shall we share a steak? And perhaps a green salad? What else? Mushrooms? Tomatoes?"

499

Painstakingly, their meal was finally ordered. The waiter produced the wine list, but Brian waved it aside and asked him to bring a bottle of Chateau Margaux 1964. The waiter looked respectful, gathered up the menus, and went away.

"Unless," said Brian, "you'd rather have champagne?"

"Why should I want champagne?"

"Isn't champagne the suitable drink for romantic celebrations, for reunions?"

"Is that what this is?"

"It's certainly a reunion. And one that I wouldn't have missed for the world. As for the other, well, I suppose that's up to you, Rose. Or is it too early in the evening to expect you to make such a world-shattering decision?"

She knew a sensation of panic. The thin ice was beginning to crack and the conversation, unless Flora was very careful, was going to slip out of her control. She eyed him across the starched white tablecloth, the red candles, the wine glasses shining like soap bubbles. He was waiting for her to reply, and to give herself time to think she took a mouthful of the second martini. It tasted, if possible, even stronger than the first, but all at once everything became immensely clear and perfectly simple. All she had to do was to be very careful.

She said, "Yes. Just a little early."

He began to laugh. "Rose."

"What's so funny?"

"You. You're funny. Pretending to be so cool and prissy and hard-to-get. O.K., so you're engaged to that upstanding young man Antony Armstrong, but you're still Rose. And you don't have to pretend with me."

"Don't I, Brian?"

"Do you?"

"Perhaps I've changed."

"You haven't changed."

He said it with such assurance that she was prepared to believe him. Up to this evening everything that she had gleaned of Rose's character had been based on conjecture and guesswork. Now, unexpectedly faced with a man who obviously

500

knew the truth, Flora found herself reluctant to be told it. Illusions were perhaps childish but they could be comforting too, and Rose was, after all, her sister. For an instant something like family loyalty battled with curiosity, but only for an instant. Flora's finer feelings were not as strong as her curiosity, and stimulated by the punch of the drinks she had already consumed, she became reckless.

She put her arms on the table, and leaned across it, towards Brian. "How do you know I haven't changed?" she asked him.

"Oh, Rose . . ."

"Tell me how I was."

His face brightened. "Like you are at this moment. You've reverted to type already. You can't help it. You could never help it. You could never resist the smallest opportunity to talk about yourself."

"Tell me how I was."

"All right." His hands moved out to his tumbler of whisky and as he talked he turned it, but his excited eyes never left Flora's. "You were beautiful. Long-legged and marvelously young. Like a colt. You were sulky and you could be selfish. You were certainly self-centered. and you were sexy. God, you were sexy.and I found you utterly fascinating. Now. Is that what you wanted to hear?"

She could feel the heat of the candles, burning her face. The neck of her sweater was too tight, and she put up a finger to pull it loose. "All that," she said faintly, "at seventeen?"

"All that. It was a strange thing, Rose, but after you'd gone, I couldn't get you out of my mind. That had never happened to me before. I even went down to the Beach House once or twice, but it was shuttered and closed up and there was no trace of you anywhere. Like the tide, coming in and washing the sand clean."

"Perhaps that was just as well."

"You were special. There was never anyone quite like you."

"You speak from experience."

501

He grinned as though filled with modest pride. "The best thing about you was that I never had to pretend."

"You mean I always knew that I was just one of a long line."

"Exactly."

"And Anna?"

He took a drink from his glass before answering this one. "Anna," he said slowly, "is an ostrich. What she doesn't see doesn't worry her. And as far as her husband is concerned, she takes some pains to see nothing."

"You're very sure of her."

"Do you know what it's like to be loved to distraction? It's like being buried in a feather bed."

"Did you never love anyone to distraction?"

"No. Not even you. What I felt for you can only be described by one of those old-fashioned words that you find in the Bible. Lust. It's a wonderful word. You can really get your tongue around it."

With marvelous inappropriateness, their first course arrived. As disembodied hands set down plates and straightened knives and forks, Flora sat staring at the candle flames and trying to collect her scattered wits. Somebody took away her glass, and she realized that at some time she had finished her second drink. Now there was a glass of wine, shining like a great red jewel. The sweater she had put on had been a mistake. It was far too thick, the collar choked her, she was far too hot. Pulling again at the neck, she found herself looking down at a plateful of oysters. The waiter had gone. From across the table Brian asked her, "Don't you want them after all?"

"What?"

"You have an uncertain expression on your face. Don't they look good?"

She pulled herself together. "They look delicious." She took a slice of lemon and squeezed it. The juice was sticky on her fingers. Across the table, Brian was tucking into his scampi with the appetite of a man with a pristine conscience. Flora picked up her fork and then laid it down again. The question

502

stuck in her throat, but with an immense effort, she made herself ask it.

"Brian, did anybody ever find out . . . I mean, did anybody ever know about you and me?"

"No, of course they didn't. What do you think I am? An amateur?" She started to breathe a sigh of relief. "Only Hugh," he finished casually.

"Hugh?"

"Don't sound so horrified. Of course he knew. Oh, don't sit there gaping like a fool, Rose. He found us!" He grinned boyishly, as though recalling some youthful prank. "What a scene that was! He's never really forgiven me, but to be honest with you, I've always put that down to jealousy. I always suspected that he fancied you himself."

"That's not true!"

Her vehemence took him by surprise. He stared at her. "Why do you suddenly say that?"

"Because it isn't true." She cast about for some way to prove her point. "Antony said it wasn't true."

Brian seemed amused. "So you've already discussed it with Antony, have you. That's very interesting."

"Antony said he wasn't . . ."

"Antony would," Brian interrupted bluntly. "All his life Hugh's been a sort of father-figure to Antony. You know, the rugger-playing hero. Every boy should have one. Hugh pretends to be such a high-minded bastard, but his wife had been dead for three years by then, and at heart I suspect he's just as carnal as the rest of us."

She felt defeated. The possibility that Hugh had been in love with Rose had always been at the back of Flora's mind, ever since that first disconcerting encounter on the beach. It had bothered her a little, but it had not really mattered.

But now it did matter.

It was hard to know when it had started to matter. Perhaps that day when she and Hugh had stood at the foot of the stairs at Fernrigg and he had told her about Angus McKay, and the sun had come out and filled the house with a sudden,

503

golden light. Perhaps this afternoon, when he had taken Jason's picture and spread it out on the table to smooth out the folds. Perhaps when she had looked up, over Jason's head, and caught Hugh's look of wonderment.

She was hot no longer. Not cold. She was simply nothing. Numb. She wished passionately that she had never asked about Rose, had never found out about her; but now it was too late. The pieces of the jigsaw clicked relentlessly into place and the finished picture was repellent. Rose at seventeen, naked, tumbled on some bed, seducing—or being seduced by—Brian Stoddart.

But harder still to accept was the idea of Hugh ever having been in love with anyone as vile as Rose.

Somehow the nightmarish meal progressed. Brian, perhaps mellowed by whisky and wine, had stopped talking about himself and was describing at some length the new boat he was planning to build. He was well into this when John, the waiter, came across the room to tell him that he was wanted on the telephone.

Brian looked blank and unbelieving. "Are you sure?"

"Yes, sir, the girl on the exchange asked me to give you the message."

"Who is it?"

"I've no idea."

Brian turned to Flora. "I'm sorry. God knows who it is." He laid down his napkin. "Will you excuse me?"

"Yes, of course."

"I shan't be a moment."

He left her, weaving his way between the tables, and disappeared through a door at the back of the dining room. To be left alone was something of a reprieve. Flora pushed her plate away from her and tried to think intelligently, but the dining room was stuffy, her head ached, and she had drunk far too much. She stared at the candle flames, but they had started behaving strangely, and refused to stay in focus. She looked

504

around, caught the eye of a waiter, and asked for a jug of water. When it came she filled a tumbler and drank it in one long draft. She set down the glass and was aware that someone had come to stand across the table from her, his hands resting on the back of Brian's chair.

She recognized the hands. For the second time that day, she looked up and found herself face to face with Hugh Kyle.

Her first reaction on seeing him was a surge of pure pleasure: instinctive, so great that it took all words, all breath away.

He said, "Good evening."

He looked, if possible, larger and more overpowering than ever. He wore a bulky overcoat over his suit, and that caught Flora's attention, becuuse he did not look like a man come out to dinner.

"But what are you doing here?" The joy sounded in her voice and it didn't matter.

"I've come to take you home."

Flora looked around her. "But where's Brian?"

"Brian has already gone home."

"He's gone home?" She was being stupid. She knew she was being stupid. "But there was a telephone call."

"There was no telephone call. Or if you like, I was the telephone call. It was the only way I could think of to get Brian out of the place." His eyes were hard as blue glass. "And if you are thinking of going after him, he is now in his car and on his way back to Ardmore."

His voice was even, and very cold. Flora's pleasure was gone, dissolved to nothing, leaving a sinking sensation, like drowning, in her stomach. She realized that his coolness belied a scarcely suppressed inner rage, but she was too fuddled to try and discover what it was all about.

"He's gone without me?"

"Yes, without you. Come along, I'll take you home."

His high-handedness made Flora feel she should raise some objection. "I . . . I haven't finished my dinner."

505

"From the way you were behaving when I found you, it doesn't appear to be very appetizing."

His voice was cutting. She became angry, and afraid, too. She said, "I don't want to come with you."

"No? I suppose you intend walking. It's fifteen miles and a hard road."

"I could get a taxi."

"There are no taxis. Where's your coat?"

It took some remembering. "It's upstairs, in the ladies'. But I'm not coming with you."

He called one of the young waiters over and told him to go upstairs and find the coat. "It's navy blue. It has a tartan lining." The boy departed and he turned back to Flora. "Come along, now."

"Why did Brian go?"

"We'll talk about it in the car."

"Did you make him go?"

"Rose, people are beginning to be curious. Don't let's have a scene."

He was right. The hum of conversation in the rest of the room had dropped. From various tables, faces were turned towards them. The thought of any sort of a scene was anathema to Flora. Without another word, very carefully, she got to her feet. Her legs felt rubbery and peculiar. Concentrating, not looking at anybody, she walked out of the room.

The waiter had found her coat. Hugh tipped him and helped her into it. She began painstakingly to do up the buttons, but her fingers were so clumsy that she had only done up two before he lost patience, took her by the elbow and propelled her ahead of him across the hall and out of the door.

Outside it was dark and drizzling, with a chill wind blowing up out of the west across the water. After the heat of the restaurant, the wine, and the rich food, the piercing cold struck at Flora like a solid thing, and she felt she had been pole-axed. The darkness swung around her. She shut her eyes and put her hand to her head, but Hugh grasped her other wrist and jerked her forward across the puddled car park to where his car waited. She stumbled and would have fallen had he not been holding her, and one of her shoes came off. He waited impatiently while she retrieved it and struggled it on again, and then she dropped her bag. She heard him swear as he picked it up and stuffed it into the pocket of his overcoat.

The shape of the car loomed up. He opened the door and bundled her in and slammed the door behind her. He walked around the front of the car and got in behind the wheel. The second door slammed shut. She felt suffocated by the hugeness of his presence. Her coat was rumpled up around her, her feet were wet, her hair was tumbled and blown all over her face. She slumped down into the seat and jammed her hands into her pockets and told herself that if she started to cry, now, she would never forgive herself.

He turned toward her. "Do you want to talk, or are you too drunk to talk?"

"I'm not drunk."

He made no effort to turn on the car lights. She stared into the darkness and said, through teeth clenched tight with the effort of not crying, "Where's Brian?"

"I told you. He's gone back to Ardmore."

"How did you make him go?"

"That's no concern of yours."

"How did you know where I was?"

"Isobel told me. You left your gloves at my house and I rang Fernrigg to tell you. Isobel told me that Brian had taken you out for dinner."

"That's not a crime."

"In my book it is."

He always pretends to be such a high-minded bastard.

"Because of Antony? Or because of Brian?"

"Because of Anna."

"Anna knew all about it. Anna was in the room when Brian asked me out to dinner."

"That's not the point."

"Why isn't it the point?"

507

He said, wearily, "You know bloody well."

She turned to look at him. Her eyes, by now, had become accustomed to the darkness, and the pale shape of his face loomed before her.

His wife had been dead for three years, and at heart I suspect he's just as carnal as the rest of us.

Hugh had been in love with Rose. She had not wanted it to be true, but his sudden appearance, his resentment, made it true. In love with Rose. For this she felt she could have killed him.

"Yes I know," she told him coldly. "You're jealous." She did not know if it was Rose who spoke, or the wine she had drunk, or her own miserable disappointment. She only knew that she wanted to hurt him. "Brian has things that you don't have. A wife and a home. You can't bear that." It wasn't any good fighting the tears. They were brimming over, streaming down her face, and this was his fault too. And something else had happened, because she was no longer Flora. She was Rose, totally Rose. Rose thinking up the cruelest and most wounding thing she could say. Rose, saying it. "Your wife destroyed you by dying the way she did."

The last word hung in the silence between them. There was a short, considered pause, and then Hugh slapped her face.

It was not a very hard blow. If it had been, Hugh being the size he was, would probably have knocked her unconscious. But Flora had never been hit, by anybody, in all her life. Extraordinarily, it stopped her crying. Silenced by pain and humiliation, she simply sat there, her head ringing and her mouth slack with shock.

He reached out to switch on the lights of the car and she covered her face with her hands.

"Are you all right?" he asked.

Blindly, Flora nodded.

He took her wrists and pulled her hands away from her face. The effort of making herself look at him was almost beyond her, but she did it.

508

"Why do you want so much, Rose?" he asked. "Why do you want everything for yourself?"

I'm not Rose. I am not Rose.

Reaction set in. She had begun to shiver. "I want to go home," she told him.

9

FLORA

A thirst woke Flora in the night—a raging thirst as bad as some terrible form of torture. Her mouth felt dry and her head ached, and as soon as she woke, the horror of the previous evening broke over her, and she lay for a little in a welter of remorse, too overcome by misery even to be able to get up and fetch herself a glass of water.

Her eiderdown had slipped off the bed and she was cold. In the darkness she leaned down to pull it back into position again, and as she did this, she felt a stab of pain so intense that it took her breath away, and left her gasping and clammy with sweat. After a little the pain faded, but not entirely. She lay cautious, very still, eyeing the pain from a distance, waiting to see what it was going to do next. She was still thirsty. Carefully, she reached for the bedside light, but as she eased herself up into a sitting position, she was gripped by nausea, shot out of bed, and reached the bathroom in time to be violently sick.

510

* * *

By the time the gruesome session was over, Flora—racked by retching, and with her stomach emptied of everything except pain—was in a state of collapse. She found herself on the bathroom floor, dressed only in her thin nightdress, and with her thudding head supported by the mahogany rim of the tub. Sweating, she closed her eyes and waited for death.

After a little, when it had not arrived, she opened her eyes again. The bathroom, from that worm's-eye view, appeared enormous, distorted out of all proportion. Through the open door the passage stretched into infinity. The sanctuary of her bedroom seemed a world away. Presently, painfully, she pulled herself to her feet and, cautiously keeping close to the wall, made her way back to her bed. She fell across it exhausted and lay shuddering, without even the strength to curl herself up under the covers.

She thought, I am very ill. She was freezing cold. The window was open and the night air poured in over her and it was like being sluiced with buckets of icy water. She knew that if she hadn't died in the bathroom, she was going to die here, of pneumonia. With an enormous effort she slid under the blankets. Her hot-water bottle had gone cold and her teeth were chattering.

She did not sleep again, and the night seemed to last forever. Her pillows became hot and lumpy, her bedclothes tangled and soaked in sweat. She prayed for the morning—for a day that would bring people and comfort and clean sheets and something to stop her head aching. But there were still many hours to endure before the dawn slid palely into the sky, and by then she had fallen into a sleep of sheer exhaustion.

It was Isobel who finally rescued her. Isobel, concerned because Flora had not appeared at breakfast, came upstairs to investigate. ". . . You're probably just having a lie-in, but I thought I'd better . . ." She stopped when she saw the chaos of Flora's room: clothes from the previous night still littering the floor, left to lie where Flora had dropped them; the tumbled bed; the blankets askew; a sheet trailing on the carpet.

511

"Rose!" She crossed to the bed and found Flora white as a ghost and with a fringe of dark hair stuck damply to her forehead.

"I'm really all right," Flora told her in a desperate sort of a way. "I was sick in the night, that's all."

"My poor child. Why didn't you wake me?"

"I didn't want to disturb anybody."

Isobel laid a hand on her forehead. "You're raging hot."

"I had such a pain . . ."

". . . and you're all untidy and uncomfortable." Isobel twitched at the bedclothes in an effort to square them up, and then decided against it. "I'll go and get Nurse McLeod and we'll have you cozy in no time." She made for the door. "Now don't move, Rose. Don't even think of trying to get up."

When they came, bustling and busy, it was just the way she had dreamed. Concerned faces and gentle hands, clean linen, two hot-water bottles in woolen covers. A fresh nightdress, her face and hands sponged, the smell of eau de cologne, a bedjacket.

"Whose bedjacket is that?" asked Flora as they put it on her. She didn't have a bedjacket of her own.

"It's mine," said Isobel.

It was shell pink, very lacy, with wide, loose sleeves.

"It's pretty."

"Tuppy gave it to me."

Tuppy. Flora felt so guilty she could have wept. "Oh, Isobel, you've got Tuppy in bed and now me and the dance and everything." She did weep, the helpless tears gathering in her eyes and spilling down her cheeks. "I can't bear being such a nuisance."

"You're not a nuisance. Don't even think such silly things. And Nurse is here to take care of Tuppy and she'll help me take care of you too, won't you Nurse?"

Nurse was bundling up the dirty bedclothes. "Oh, we'll have her right as rain in no time. No nonsense about that." She went from the room, heavy-footed, headed for the washing machine.

512

Isobel wiped Flora's tears away with a tissue. "And when Hugh comes to see Tuppy," she went on, "we'll tell him . . ."

"No," said Flora, so loudly and clearly that Isobel looked quite put out.

"No?" she questioned gently.

"I don't want Hugh. I don't want to see a doctor." She took hold of Isobel's hand, meaning to hold her there until Isobel was persuaded. "There's nothing wrong with me. I've been sick, but I'll get better now. It's nothing." She was filled with panic. Isobel was gazing at her as though she had gone mad. "I don't like doctors," she improvised wildly. "I've always been like this, ever since I was little . . ."

Isobel, with the expression on her face of one pacifying a dangerous lunatic, said soothingly, "Well, we'll see. If that's how you feel . . ."

Flora slowly let go of her hand. "Promise, Isobel?"

Isobel withdrew out of reach and instantly became more firm. "Now, I never make promises unless I know I'm going to be able to keep them."

"Please."

Isobel had reached the safety of the door. "You have a little sleep and then you'll feel better."

She slept and was deviled by dreams. She was on a beach and the sand was black and full of spiders. Rose was there, too, in a bikini, walking along the edge of an oily sea with a long queue of men following her. But all at once the men saw Flora and Flora had no clothes on whatsoever. And Rose started laughing. Flora tried to run away, but her feet wouldn't move and the black sand had turned to mud. And there was a man behind her, he had caught her, he was hitting her face. He was going to kill her . . .

She awoke in a cold sweat to Nurse McLeod's gentle shaking. She looked up at Nurse's bespectacled, horsey face, Nurse's crisp white hair. "There now," said Nurse. "Time to wake up. Dr. Kyle's here to see you."

"But I'm not going to see him," Flora told her clearly. She was still trembling from the nightmare.

513

"That's too bad." Hugh loomed up at the end of the bed, a hulk of a man, scarcely focused. "Because he's going to see you."

The dream faded into oblivion. Flora blinked, and his image resolved into detail. She stared at him glumly, feeling betrayed.

"I *told* Isobel not to tell you."

"Like the rest of us, Isobel doesn't always do what she's told."

"But she promised . . ."

"Now, then," said Nurse, "you know Miss Armstrong never did anything of the sort. If you'll excuse me, Doctor, I'll leave you for a moment, and go back and see to Mrs. Armstrong."

"That's all right, Nurse."

Nurse left them, with a rustle of her starched apron. Hugh, gently, closed the door behind her, and came back to Flora's side. He sat, unprofessionally, on the edge of her bed.

"Isobel says you were sick."

"Yes."

"What time did it start?"

"In the middle of the night. I don't know what time. I didn't look at the time."

"Well, let's have a look at you." He pushed back her hair to feel her clammy forehead. His touch was cool and professional. She thought, *last night he slapped my face.* The memory was so impossible to believe that it could have belonged to another nightmare. She prayed that it did, and knew that it didn't.

"Did you have a lot of pain?"

"Yes."

"Where?"

"Everywhere. My tummy, I suppose."

"Show me exactly." She showed him. "How's your appendix?"

"I haven't got one. I had it out four years ago."

514

"Well, that's one possibility eliminated. Are you allergic to anything? Any food?"

"No."

"What have you been eating? What did you have for lunch yesterday?"

The effort of remembering was exhausting. "Cold lamb and baked potatoes."

"And dinner last night?"

She closed her eyes. "I had a steak. And some salad."

"And before that?"

"Oysters."

"Oysters," he repeated, as though approving her choice. And then, again, "Oysters?"

"I like oysters."

"I like them too, but they have to be fresh."

"You mean I ate a bad oyster?"

"It would appear so. Did you taste it? They're usually unmistakable."

"I . . . I can't remember."

"I've had trouble with the Fishers' Arms and their oysters before. I see I'll need to go and have a word with the proprietor before he kills off the entire population of Arisaig."

He stood up, produced from some pocket a silver case containing a thermometer. "It's funny," he mused. "I haven't had a call yet from Ardmore." He picked up her wrist to take her pulse.

"Brian had scampi."

"Pity," murmured Hugh, and stopped up her mouth with the thermometer.

She was, it seemed, trapped, prostrate, at the mercy of his cutting tongue. To escape from him Flora turned away her face and stared bleakly out of the window. Slow morning clouds rolled across the sky. A seagull was screaming. She waited for him to be finished, to take the thermometer out of her mouth, to go away and leave her to die.

But the moments passed, and he did none of these things. The room seemed to have been invaded by a curious stillness as

515

though everything it contained had been frozen or petrified. After a little, mildly curious, Flora turned back to look at him. He had not moved. He stood by her bed, holding her wrist, his eyes downcast and his expression thoughtful. The loose sleeve of Isobel's bedjacket had fallen back and from folds of shell pink wool, Flora's arm emerged looking, she thought, as thin as a stick. She wondered if she were suffering from some wasting disease, and he was trying to summon up the courage to tell her she was doomed.

She was rescued from this impasse by the arrival of Isobel, edging her head gingerly around the door before she entered, as though she were afraid that Flora might spring from the bed and start strangling her.

"How's the invalid?" she asked brightly.

Hugh dropped Flora's wrist and took the thermometer out of her mouth.

"We think she had food poisoning," he told Isobel. He put on his spectacles in order to read the thermometer.

"Food poisoning?"

"It's all right, don't sound so alarmed. You're not going to have an epidemic. She ate a bad oyster at the Fishers' Arms last night."

"Oh, Rose."

Isobel sounded so reproachful that Flora felt guilty all over again.

"I couldn't help it. And I like oysters."

"But what about the dance? You'll be in bed for the dance."

"Not necessarily," Hugh told her. "If she does what she's told, she should be up and about in good time for the dance. Just starve her for a couple of days and keep her in bed." He picked up his bag and stood, resting one hand on the brass knob at the foot of the bed. He said to Flora, "You'll probably feel very depressed and a bit weepy for the next day or so. It's one of the nastier symptoms of food poisoning. Try not to let it worry you too much." The moment he mentioned the word *weepy* Flora knew that she was going to cry again. Perhaps he

516

realized this, because at once, ushering Isobel firmly before him, he made for the door. As he went out, he looked back over his shoulder gave her one of his rare smiles, and said, "Goodbye, Rose."

Flora, bawling, reached for the box of face tissues.

He was right about the depression. Flora spent most of the first day sleeping, but on the next was overwhelmed by gloom. The weather outside did not help. It was gray, it rained, and there was nothing to be seen from the window save scudding black clouds and an occasional wet, wheeling gull. The tide was in. The waves breaking on the shingle beach below the house made a deeply melancholy sound, and the darkness invaded the house so early that lights had to be turned on at three o'clock.

Flora's thoughts, inward-turning, self-pitying, churned incessantly but, like someone treading a mill, got nowhere. Lying there in the strange bed in the strange house, she suffered once more from a dismaying loss of identity. And she could not believe that she had ever embarked on the mad charade with so much hopeful confidence, which, on hindsight, looked more like sheer stupidity.

"Identical twins are meant to be two halves of the same person, and separating them is like cutting that person in half."

Rose herself had said that in London, but at the time Flora had not thought it important. But now it was important because Rose was vile, without principles or morals. Did that mean that the seeds of the same vileness lay latent in Flora?

If their mother had taken Flora and their father had chosen Rose, would Flora have grown up into a person who, at seventeen, would cheerfully jump into bed with a married man? Would Flora have ditched Antony just when he most needed her, and flown to Spetsai with a rich young Greek? Would Flora have been sufficiently unscrupulous to use Rose as Rose had used Flora? At first all this had seemed beyond the bounds of possibility, but after that terrible scene with Hugh in his car, Flora was no longer so sure of herself. *Your wife destroyed you by dying the way she did.* Those were Rose's words. But it was

517

Flora who had spoken them. The dreadful sentence seared across her conscience. She shut her eyes and turned her face into the pillow, but that did no good, because she still couldn't get away from the inside of her own head.

And if this weren't enough, there were other anxieties, other uncertainties, which seemed to be heaped on top of her, like some deadening weight. How, when the time came, she was going to bear saying goodbye to the Armstrongs? And when she went, where would she go? She couldn't return to Cornwall. She had only just left, and Marcia and her father surely deserved a little time on their own. London then? It would have to be London with all its attendant problems. Where would she live? Where would she work? What would she do? She saw herself waiting for buses, queueing in the rain, shopping in the lunch hour, paying the rent, hoping to make new friends, trying to find old ones.

And finally, there was the specter of Hugh. But she couldn't let herself think about Hugh, because every time she did, she found herself once more dissolved into pointless floods of tears.

If you were Rose, you wouldn't care what the Armstrongs thought of you. You'd just say goodbye, and go and never look back.

I'm not Rose.

If you were Rose you wouldn't need to find a job and queue for buses. You could take taxis for the rest of your life.

But I'm not Rose.

If you were Rose, you would know how to make Hugh love you.

There didn't seem to be any answer to that one.

Everybody was extraordinarily kind. Isobel brought messages from Antony, whom she had telephoned in Edinburgh to let him know that Rose was ill. There was a clumsy bunch of flowers which Jason had picked, and a deep pink azalea from Anna Stoddart.

518

I am sorry you are under the weather, and hope you'll be up
and about by Friday. Brian and I send our love.

Anna

"It's out of the Ardmore greenhouse," Isobel told her.
"They have the most beautiful greenhouses over there, the envy
of my heart. Rose . . . Rose, you're crying again."

"I can't help it."

Isobel sighed, and patiently reached for the tissues.

There were also sessions with Nurse McLeod, who, once
she dropped her professional manner and stopped talking about
draw sheets, became quite cozy, bringing up her sewing to let
Flora see how her "ballgown," as it was now designated, was
getting along. "You see, I'm attaching the lining to the dress. It
gives it much more body, and I thought I'd make a wee belt.
Mrs. Watty has a pearl buckle in her button box that she can
spare."

There was a get-well card from Mrs. Watty, and from
Tuppy a bunch of the last of her precious roses, which she had
directed Watty to cut for her. Tuppy had arranged them herself,
standing the vase on her bedside table, and snipping the wet
stalks all over the eiderdown. Isobel had carried them down the
passage. "From one old crock to another," she told Flora, and
put them on Flora's dressing table.

"Does Hugh come every day to see Tuppy?" Flora asked
Isobel.

"Not every day. Not any more. He just drops in when he
happens to be passing. Why?" There was a smile in her voice.
"Did you want to see him?"

"No," said Flora.

Thursday morning dawned a beautiful day. Flora awoke
to a morning bright as a new coin. There was sunlight, blue
sky, and now the screaming of the gulls reminded her of summer.

"What a day!" Nurse McLeod crowed, bouncing in to
draw back the curtains, retrieve Flora's cold hot-water bottle,

519

and tidy the bed, which meant tucking in the sheets so tight that Flora could scarcely move her legs.

"I shall get up," said Flora, bored with her invalid existence.

"You'll do no such thing. Not until Dr. Kyle says you may."

Flora's spirits sank immediately. She wished that Nurse had not mentioned his name. Despite the cheerful weather, she was still miserable, although the miserableness now had nothing to do with being ill. It was just the usual routine stuff, and it was centered, pinpointed, on that unforgiveable thing she had said to Hugh. It hung over her like a great sword, and would continue to hang there, she knew, until somehow, she had made herself apologize to him.

The very idea made her feel ill all over again. She slid down under the covers, and Nurse cocked a professional eye at her. "Are you not feeling better yet?"

"Yes, I'm all right," Flora told her dully.

"How about something to eat? Are you hungry? I'll maybe ask Mrs. Watty to make a little semolina."

"If you bring me semolina," Flora told her coldly, "I shall throw it out of the window."

Nurse tut-tutted and went down to the kitchen with the news that one of her patients, at least, was well on the road to recovery.

Isobel appeared later on with a breakfast tray—not a very lavish one, to be sure, but there was toast on it, and some marmalade jelly and a pot of China tea. "And some mail for you," said Isobel. She took a postcard out of her cardigan pocket and laid it, picture side up, on the tray. Flora saw bright blue sky, bright green chestnut trees, and the Eiffel Tower. Paris?

Puzzled, she turned it over. It was addressed, in an untidy and unformed hand, to Miss Rose Schuster, Fernrigg House, Tarbole, Arisaig, Argyll, Écosse. Bewildered, Flora read the message, which had been written extremely small in order to accommodate it on the space allowed.

520

I said I'd be in touch. It was super finding you. Decided to stop off here for a couple of days on my way to Spetsai. Am sending this to you at Fernrigg, because I have a strong suspicion that by now you're there, in the bosom of the family and, who knows, perhaps married to Antony. Give him my love.

It was undated, unsigned.

"Is it from a friend?" Isobel asked.

"Yes. From a friend."

Cunning Rose. Isobel would never read another person's postcard, but even if she had, this one would have told her nothing. It felt, to Flora's fingers, dirty. She made a face and dropped it over the side of the bed into the wastepaper basket.

Isobel, watching her, was concerned. "You're not feeling ill again, are you?"

"No," Flora assured her. She smothered toast with marmalade and bit off a hungry mouthful.

When the meager breakfast had been consumed, Isobel departed bearing the tray, and Flora was alone once more. Despite herself, the message from Rose had both upset and angered her. As well, she was hating herself. She longed for the reassurance of a loving spirit. She needed a little fussing-over, a little caring. There was only one person who was capable of providing this, and Flora wanted her now. Deviantly, not waiting for anybody to say that she could, Flora got out of bed and went in search of clothes. She would go and talk to Tuppy.

Jessie McKenzie was back from Portree. Her old mother, who had taken to her bed after what was euphemistically known as "a turn," had decided, after all, that she wasn't going to die.

This sudden recovery had been brought about, not by the timely arrival of her dutiful daughter, but because a neighbor, calling to cheer the invalid, had left the news that Katy Meldrum, already the mother of a cross-eyed child called Gary, was once more in the family way. Katy was a shameless girl

521

and had always been so, impervious to both pointing fingers and the gentle remonstrances of her sorely tried priest. Now, with her belly swelling larger each day, she was walking the town scornful and amused, and speculation as to the identity of the father was rife. Most folk had their money on young Robby McCrae, the constable's brother, but there was talk of a deckhand off one of the boats from Kinlochbervie, and him a married man with a family of his own.

It was too good to miss. To die before the mystery was solved, thus missing all the fun, was unthinkable. The old lady heaved herself up on the pillows, walloped the wall with her stick and, when her startled daughter appeared at the door, demanded sustenance. In two days she was up and about again, gleaning gossip and adding her own opinion to those of others.

Jessie decided she might as well go home.

Home was one of the old fisher cottages, tucked down in the back streets of Tarbole, where she kept house for her brother, who worked as porter in one of the smokehouses. Early each morning Jessie climbed the hill to the doctor's house, where she answered the telephone, took messages, chatted to visiting tradesmen, gossiped with the neighbors, and drank tea. In between these diverting occupations, she banged cheerfully about the house, creating more dirt than she disposed of, did the doctor's laundry, and prepared his evening meal.

As often as not, since he was so busy, she was away home before he appeared to eat the fish pie, or the shepherd's pie, or the two fried chops (her culinary imagination was not extensive) which she would leave for him, hardening in the oven between two plates. Sometimes when she returned the next morning the dried-up meal would still be there, untouched. And Jessie would shake her head, scrape it all into the garbage can, and find someone to tell that if the doctor did not take more care of himself, he would be well on the way to a breakdown, or worse.

Being the doctor's housekeeper gave her a certain importance, a standing, in the town. What would he do without you?

522

folks asked. Jessie would shake her head, modest but proud. And what would they all do without her, she asked herself, answering the telephone the way she did, day in, day out, taking messages and leaving notes. She was indispensable. It was a rare sensation.

She therefore received something of a shock when she let herself into the kitchen that Thursday morning after her return from Portree. It was a beautiful day, and she had climbed the hill in the cold sunshine, filled with grim relish at the thought of the chaos she was bound to find. After all, she had been away for four days, and all the world knew that Dr. Kyle was a handless creature when it came to doing for himself.

Instead, she found sparkling order: a clean floor, a polished sink, saucepans neatly ranged above the cooker, and scarcely a dirty dish to be seen.

The shock was like a blow to her heart. Slowly, she realized what must have happened. He had found somebody else to take her place. He had let somebody else into Jessie's kitchen. Her mind made a quick catalogue of the Tarbole women as she tried to think who it could have been. Mrs. Murdoch? The very idea was chilling. If it had been Mrs. Murdoch, then the whole town would know by now that Jessie had been deposed. They would all be talking about her, probably laughing behind her back. She wondered if she was going to faint.

But her panic was calmed by familiar sounds from upstairs. The doctor was out of bed and getting dressed. She could hear him moving to and fro in his bedroom. She stood, gazing upwards. She thought, *Well, he's there and I'm here. And here I'm staying.* Possession was nine tenths of the law. (Or something. Jessie was vague on this point.) She only knew that if she was going to leave this house, she would have to be forcibly ejected. No high-stepping Tarbole female was going to take her place.

Thus emboldened, she took off her coat, hung it on the back of the door, and went to fill the kettle. By the time Dr. Kyle came downstairs, his breakfast was waiting. She had found a clean tablecloth. The bacon was done just the way he liked it, and the egg was well-cooked with none of those nasty jelly bits on the top.

He had stopped by the front door to pick up his mail. Now, as he came down the hall, he called out, "Jessie," and she replied, in a cheerful voice, "Good morning, Doctor!" and turned to greet him as he came through the door.

It was a little disappointing to see him looking so fit and pleased with himself, but at least he was not wearing the hangdog expression of a man about to sack his housekeeper.

"How are you, Jessie? How did everything go?"

"Oh, not so bad, Doctor."

"How's your mother?"

"She has great spirit, Doctor. She's made a miraculous recovery."

"Splendid. I am glad." He sat at the table and took up a knife to slit open the first letter. It was typewritten. A long white envelope with a Glasgow postmark. Jessie took time to notice this as she laid the bacon and eggs, with a little flourish, on the table in front of him.

She poured his tea, and set that down as well. The cup steamed invitingly. The toast was crisp. It was a lovely breakfast. She stepped back to eye him. He read to the bottom of the page, and then turned the letter over to finish it. She saw a flourishing signature.

She cleared her throat. "And how did you manage, Doctor?"

"Um?" He looked up, but he had not heard her. She decided that the letter must be of some importance.

"I said, How did you manage while I was away?"

He gave her one of his rare smiles. She had not seen him in such a good humor for years.

"I missed you, Jessie, as a son misses his mother."

"Get away."

"No, it's true. The place was a midden." He caught sight of the bacon and eggs. "Now, that looks good." He laid the letter aside and started to eat, it seemed to her, like a man who hasn't seen good food for a month.

524

"But . . . it doesna look like a midden now."

"No, I know. A good fairy came and cleaned it up for me, and since then Nurse has been keeping an eye on things."

Jessie didn't mind Nurse. Nurse ran the surgery. She was one of the family, as it were. Not an outsider. But the good fairy? If it was that interfering Murdoch woman . . . Once more Jessie felt faint, but she had to know.

"And who might the good fairy have been, if I'm allowed to ask?"

"Certainly you can ask. It was Antony Armstrong's young lady. She's staying at Fernrigg. She dropped by one afternoon and stayed to do the scrubbing."

Antony Armstrong's young lady. Relief swept through Jessie. It wasn't Mrs. Murdoch. So Jessie's reputation was safe, her standing in Tarbole unimpaired, her job secure.

Her job. What was she doing, standing here, wasting time, with all the house to be seen to? With an enthusiasm she hadn't shown in years, she collected dustpans, dusters, brushes, and brooms, and by the time Hugh departed for his morning rounds she was already halfway down the staircase, on her knees, noisily attacking dust and cobwebs. The air was rich with the smell of new polish, and Jessie was singing.

"We'll meet again, I don't know where, don't know when . . ."

At the front door he paused. "Jessie, if anybody calls, tell them I'll be in the surgery at ten. And if its urgent, they'll probably reach me at Fernrigg. I want to drop in and see Mrs. Armstrong." He opened the door, and then hesitated and turned back. "And Jessie, it's a marvelous morning. Pull all the blinds up and open the windows and let the sunshine in."

In normal circumstances, Jessie would have been hotly opposed to such outlandish ideas. But this morning she only said, "Righty ho." She did not even turn from her task as she said it, and his last sight of her was her round pinafored rump, a pair of straining nylons, and the legs of her apple green locknit bloomers.

525

He opened the door and said, "Good morning."

Tuppy was still eating her breakfast. She looked up at him over her spectacles because she had been reading her mail at the same time.

"Hugh."

He came in and shut the door. "And it's a perfect morning. You can see forever."

Tuppy did not comment on this. To be truthful, she was a little put out at being caught, even by Hugh, with her breakfast tray on her lap and her bed not yet straightened. She took off her spectacles and eyed him suspiciously, detecting a certain self-satisfaction in his manner.

"What are you doing here at this hour of the day?"

"I've got an early surgery this morning, so I thought I'd make a few calls first, and you're one of them."

"Well, you're far too early, and I don't know where Nurse is and I'm not ready for you."

"Nurse is on her way up. She'll be here in a moment or two."

"And you," she told him, "look like a cat that's been at the cream."

He came to his usual resting place, leaning on the rail at the foot of her bed. "Jessie McKenzie has returned from Portree. The air is full of song and the house is getting a good clean-through. Like cascara."

"That's very gratifying, but it doesn't explain your smug expression."

"No, not entirely. I have got something to tell you."

"Is it something I'm going to enjoy hearing?"

"I hope so." Characteristically, he came straight to the point. "I had a letter this morning from a young man called David Stephenson. He qualified from Edinburgh three years ago, and since then he's been working at the Victoria Hospital in Glasgow. He has excellent qualifications and he's been strongly recommended to me. He's about thirty, with a young

526

wife, who used to be a nurse, and two small children. They've had enough of city life, and they want to come to Tarbole."

"A partner?"

"A partner."

Tuppy found herself without words. She leaned back on her pillows, closed her eyes, counted ten, and then opened them again. He was waiting for her comment. "I wanted to tell you before anyone else," he said. "What do you think?"

"I think," she told him, "that you are without doubt one of the most infuriating men I've ever known."

"I know. Infuriating. Because I didn't tell you before."

"Here we've all been, trying to get you to take on a partner for months. And all you've done is evade the issue and procrastinate like an idiot."

He knew her very well. "But you're pleased?"

"Of course I'm pleased," she told him, crossly. "Nothing you could have told me could make me more pleased. But I wish I'd known you'd got this up your sleeve. Instead of going on at you all the time, I'd have saved my breath to cool my porridge."

"Tuppy, sometimes I think you forget I am no longer Jason's age."

"What you mean is, you are perfectly capable of engaging a partner for yourself without any interference from an old busybody like me."

"I never said that."

"No, but that was what you meant, just the same." But she could not go on being indignant and pretending to be cross. Her pleasure and satisfaction were very real. Now she allowed herself to smile. "You'll be able to ease up a little," she told him. "Have time to do some of the things you enjoy."

"It's not fixed up yet. He's coming to see me next Wednesday, to have a look at the place, get the feel of things."

Tuppy became practical. "Where will they live?"

"That's one of the problems. There isn't a house."

This was right up Tuppy's street. "We must all cast about and ask questions and see if we can find one."

527

"Well, don't start casting about until the deal's fixed. Until then it's still on the secret list."

"All right, I won't breathe a word. Dr. Stephenson." She said the name aloud and it sounded good and dependable. "Dr. Kyle's partner. Just think of that."

Having imparted his news. Hugh became practical. "How are you feeling this morning?"

"Better than I felt yesterday, but not as well as I'll feel tomorrow. I'm beginning to get restless, Hugh. I warn, you, I'm not going to sit here like an old crock for much longer."

"Perhaps next week you can get up for an hour or two."

"And Rose. How is poor little Rose?"

"I haven't seen poor little Rose yet."

"Well you must go and see her, make quite sure she's going to be all right. Really, that horrible oyster. People should be more careful. It would spoil tomorrow evening for all of us if she couldn't be there. The whole point of having the dance was for everybody to meet Rose."

As she spoke, he had wandered away from her bedside to the window, as though the lure of the radiant morning was more than he could resist. Watching him, wondering if he was listening to a word she was saying, Tuppy was visited by a strong sense of *déjà vu.*

She said, "You know, you were standing there, in the window, just where you are now, the day I felt so ill and I told you that I wanted to see Antony and Rose. And somehow you arranged it. You and dear Isobel, of course. I'm very grateful to you, Hugh. It's all turned out so well. I'm really a very lucky person."

She regarded his back view affectionately across the room, waiting for his reply. He turned from the window, but before he could say anything, there was a knock at Tuppy's door. Thinking it was Nurse come to fetch her breakfast tray, Tuppy called, "Come in."

The door opened and Rose came into the room. The first person she saw was Hugh, framed in the window. She paused for perhaps a fraction of a second, and then without a word did

528

a swift about turn and walked out again. Tuppy was left dum-
founded, with only a fleeting impression of Rose's long legs in
dark stockings and the swirl of a short pleated skirt like a
child's kilt.

Hugh recovered from the shock of this extraordinary per-
formance before Tuppy did.

"You come back here!" he called after Rose in, Tuppy
thought, a not very kind voice.

They waited. Slowly, Rose appeared again, hanging onto
the door knob as though poised for a second quick getaway.
She looked, thought Tuppy, about fifteen. Hugh was glowering
at her across the room in the most uncharitable way. It was
really a funny situation. In the normal way, Tuppy knew,
Rose's sense of humor would have got the better of her, and she
would have been overcome by giggles in which Tuppy was perfectly prepared to join her. But now Rose looked more like
crying than laughing. Tuppy hoped that she wasn't going to.

The outraged silence lengthened, and at last Hugh said,
"Who told you to get up?"

Rose looked more uncomfortable than ever. "Well, actually, nobody."

"Didn't Nurse tell you to stay in bed?"

"Yes, she did. It wasn't her fault."

"Why did you get up, then?"

"I thought I'd come and see Tuppy. I didn't realize you'd
be here."

"That's fairly obvious."

Tuppy could not bear any more. "Hugh, stop hectoring
Rose. She's not a baby. She can get out of bed if she wants to.
Rose, come and get this tray off my lap, and then I can have a
good look at you."

Rose, appearing grateful for an ally, closed the door and
came to remove the tray and put it down on the floor. Tuppy
took her hands and drew her down on the bed beside her.

"But you're so thin! Your wrists have gone like little twigs.
You must have had a horrid time." She began to have second
thoughts about Rose's getting up, for indeed, Rose did look

529

awful. "Perhaps you should still be in bed. And you must be all right for the party tomorrow. Just think of all the preparations wasted, if you aren't there." She was diverted by a happy thought. "One thing, you won't have to bother too much with the flowers, because Anna's coming over with all the pot plants out of her greenhouse. She's going to fill the Land Rover with them, the dear girl. And I thought perhaps a few big branches of beech leaves, they always look. . . ."

Her voice died away. Rose was not responding. She simply sat there, looking down, her face quite plain, all bones and without a scrap of makeup. Her hair had lost its luster and her usually sweet-natured mouth had a droop to it which caused Tuppy a definite pang of anxiety. And she remembered the young Rose of five years ago, and the sulks into which she had lapsed from time to time, apparently for no good reason at all. Then, Tuppy had ignored them, telling herself that all seventeen-year-olds were apt to be sulky. But she had never expected to catch that miserable expression on Rose's face again.

On Antony's account, she felt concerned. *Oh, dear, I do hope she's not going to be moody.* Moodiness was, in Tuppy's book, an unforgiveable sin, evidence of the worst sort of self-indulgence.

Her thoughts darted about, trying to imagine what could be at the root of this. Of course she had been ill, but . . . had she had a quarrel with Antony? But Antony wasn't here. Isobel, perhaps? Impossible. Isobel had never quarreled with anybody in her life.

"Rose." She became a little impatient. "Rose, my dear child, what's the matter?"

Before Rose could reply, could say anything, Hugh replied for her. "There's nothing wrong with the dear child except that she's had food poisoning and she's got out of bed too soon." He came back to Tuppy's bedside, taking professional charge of the situation, and at the sound of his voice Rose appeared to make some effort to pull herself together. Tuppy, as always, felt grateful to him.

"Now how are you feeling?" he asked Rose. "Truthfully."

"I'm all right. Just a bit wobbly about the legs."

"Did you eat some breakfast?"

"Yes."

"And you didn't feel sick again?"

Rose looked embarrassed. "No."

"In that case, the best thing you can do is to get out of doors for a little and get some fresh air." Rose appeared to be unenthusiastic. "Now. While the sun's shining."

Tuppy patted Rose's hand in an encouraging fashion. "There. Why not do that? It's such a lovely morning. It'll do you good."

"All right." Reluctantly, Rose got off the bed and made for the door, but as she did this, Tuppy's housekeeperly instincts rose to the surface. "Rose, dear, if you're going down, take my tray, and that'll save Nurse a trip. And if you see Nurse, tell her to come up. And," she added as Rose, burdened by the tray, made her way through the door, "if you are going out, have a word with Mrs. Watty before you do. She may want you to pick some beans."

As far as domestic arrangements were concerned, Tuppy seemed to have a sixth sense. Mrs. Watty, after exclaiming in surprise at Flora's appearance, agreed that, yes, she would like some beans, and produced a large basket which Flora was expected to fill.

"Does Nurse know you're up and about?"

"Yes. I've just seen her. She's got a face on."

"You'd better keep out of her way."

"I will."

Carrying the basket, she went back to the hall. She didn't want to pick beans. She didn't really want to go out at all. She had planned to cozy up on Tuppy's bed and be cherished, but those schemes had been thwarted by Hugh. How could Flora have possibly known that he would have already started his calls at nine o'clock in the morning?

She could not be bothered to go upstairs again for her coat, so she borrowed from the cloakroom one of the many

531

aged ones which hung there. It was a bulky tweed, lined in rabbit fur, and she was buttoning herself into it when Hugh appeared down the staircase, one hand in his pocket, and his bag bumping against the side of his leg.

"I've had a word with Nurse," he told her, "and she has accepted the inevitable. Are you just going out?"

"Yes. To pick beans," she added resignedly.

His eyes crinkled in amusement. He put out a hand to open the door and hold it for her. She went out in front of him. The dazzle of sunshine was blinding. Through the trees the blue waters of Fhada spread bright as sapphire silk, in all the extravagance of a flood tide. The air was like wine, the sky full of wheeling gulls.

Hugh looked up. "They're flying inland. That means stormy weather."

"Today?"

"Or tomorrow." They went down the steps side by side. "It's a good thing there's to be no marquee tomorrow night, or it would doubtless end up in the top of a tree."

They reached the gravel. Flora stopped. "Hugh."

He paused, looking down at her.

Now. Say it Now.

"I'm terribly sorry I said what I said the other night. I mean, about your wife. I had no right to say such a dreadful thing. It was unforgivable. I . . . I don't expect you to forget it, but I wanted you to know I was sorry."

It was said. It was done. The relief of having it over made Flora feel quite tearful again. But Hugh did not appear to be as impressed by Flora's self-abasement as she was.

"Perhaps I have an apology to make, too," he said. She waited. "But mine will doubtless keep."

She frowned, not understanding, but he did not choose to explain. "Don't worry about it. Take care of yourself. And don't pick too many beans." He started to walk away from her and then remembered something. "When is Antony coming?"

"Tomorrow afternoon."

"That's good. I'll see you tomorrow evening, then."

532

"You're coming to the party?"

"If I can. Don't you want me to come?"

"Yes, I do." She amended this by adding, "I only know about three people, and if you don't come I'll only know two."

He looked amused. "You'll be all right," he told her. And with that sparse comfort he got into his car and drove away, through the gates and out of sight. Flora watched him go, still miserable, only slightly comforted, and now very confused. *My apology will keep.* What was he going to apologize for? And why did it have to keep? She wrestled with those problems for a moment or two, and then, because any mental exertion was still beyond her, abandoned the struggle and headed for the vegetable garden.

It was Friday.

Isobel awoke, listening for the rain. It had rained all yesterday afternoon and most of the night. From time to time she had awakened, shaken out of sleep by gusts of wind or the rattle of a squall of raindrops, hard as flung pebbles against her windowpane. She was haunted by visions of wet footprints and mud being tracked through the house as Watty came in and out, the caterers unloaded their cases of china and glass, and people trod to and fro carrying trays of glasses, branches of beech leaves, and large, dripping peat-filled pots containing the Ardmore pelargoniums.

But at seven o'clock in the morning, it seemed to have stopped. Isobel got out of bed (when she got back into it again, it would all be over), went to her window, drew back the curtains, and saw a pearly grayness—mist lying on the face of the sea, a thread of watery pink reflected from the first ragged rays of the early sun. The islands were lost, and the still water scarcely moved against the rocks beyond the garden.

There was still rain about, but the wind had died. She stood there, reluctant to start a day which would probably not end for another twenty hours. After breakfast coffee, though, she knew that she would feel stronger. And this afternoon Antony would be arriving from Edinburgh. The thought of An-

533

tony arriving cheered her up. She went to run her morning bath.

Jason did not want to go to school. "I want to stay here and help. If I've got to come to the party, I don't see why I shouldn't stay here and help."

"You haven't got to come to the party," Aunt Isobel told him placidly. "Nobody's making you come to the party."

"You could write Mr. Fraser a note and say I'm needed at home. That's what the other mothers do."

"Yes, I could, but I'm not going to. Now, eat up your egg."

Jason lapsed into silence. He was uncertain about the dance because he was going to have to wear the kilt and the doublet that his grandfather had worn when he was Jason's age. The kilt was all right, but the doublet was velvet and Jason thought perhaps it was sissy. He was not going to tell his friend Doogie Miller about the velvet doublet. Doogie Miller was a year older than Jason and a good head taller. His father owned his own boat, and when he was old enough Doogie was going out with him as deckhand. Doogie's good opinion mattered a great deal to Jason.

He finished his egg and drank his milk. He looked at Aunt Isobel across the table, and decided to have a last try, for he was not a child to be easily diverted.

"I could carry things for you. I could help Watty."

Isobel reached across the table to rumple his hair. "Yes, I know you could, and you'd do it beautifully, but you have to go to school. And Antony's coming back this afternoon, so he'll be here to help Watty."

Jason had forgotten about Antony. "He's coming back this afternoon?" Aunt Isobel nodded. Jason said no more, but he sighed deeply, with satisfaction. His aunt smiled at him lovingly, not realizing that he was already deep into schemes to get Antony to put some feathers on the arrows he had made last weekend.

534

* * *

Later in the morning Anna Stoddart turned the Ardmore Land Rover in at the gates of Fernrigg, bumped along the potholed drive (when was somebody going to get those holes filled in?), and drew up on the gravel, alongside a blue van which she recognized as that belonging to Mr. Anderson of the Tarbole Station Hotel. The front door of the house stood open. Anna got out of the Land Rover and, with her hands in the pockets of her sheepskin coat, went up the steps.

Already the hall had been stripped of furniture and rugs, with those pieces of furniture too heavy to be moved pushed to the walls. Mrs. Watty, driving an old-fashioned polisher that made a sound like a jet engine, was engaged in buffing up the parquet. Isobel was coming downstairs with a pile of clean white tablecloths in her arms, and Watty was making his way down the kitchen passage with huge baskets of logs to be stacked by the open fireplaces. They all saw her, greeted her with smiles or nods, and continued on their way. Isobel did say, over the top of the pile of linen, "Anna, how lovely to see you," but she said it an absent sort of way, and when she reached the foot of the stairs did not stop but continued straight on, heading for the dining room. Anna, not knowing what else to do, followed her.

The big table had been drawn to one side of the room, and was already spread with red felt pads. Onto these Isobel now dumped her burden. "Heavens, they're heavy. Thank goodness we don't use them every day."

"But Isobel, you've done so much already. You must all have been so busy."

"Yes, I suppose we have . . ." Isobel took the top tablecloth and shook it out of its folds with an expert flick of her long narrow wrists. "Have you brought the pot plants?"

"Yes, the Land Rover's stacked with them, but I'll need someone to help me carry them."

"Watty can help you." Isobel smoothed out the folds of the tablecloth, and then abandoned it to go in search of Watty. Anna trailed behind her. "Watty! Mrs. Watty, where's Watty?"

535

"He's around somewhere." Mrs. Watty raised her voice over the sound of the polisher, but was obviously not going to switch it off, or do anything bout finding her husband.

"Watty! Oh, there you are. Can you help Mrs. Stoddart get some things out of the Land Rover? Oh, you're doing the logs. I forgot. Well, where's Rose? Mrs. Watty, where's Rose?"

"I've no idea." Mrs. Watty steered the polisher into a dark corner behind the curtains.

"Oh." Isobel pushed her hair out of her face. She was beginning to get flustered, and no wonder, thought Anna. "I'll find Rose," Anna told her. "Don't worry. You go back to your tablecloths."

"She's probably in the drawing room. Watty brought in some beech branches, and Rose said she'd arrange them, though she didn't sound very confident. Perhaps you could help her."

Mr. Anderson of the Tarbole Hotel, important in his new role of caterer, now appeared from the direction of the kitchen and asked Miss Armstrong if she could spare a minute. Isobel started back to her tablecloths, thought better of it, went after Mr. Anderson, then remembered Anna.

"I'm sorry, I must go. Can you manage?"

"Don't worry," said Anna. "I'll find Rose."

It was always like this. Anna remembered Fernrigg parties from childhood and they always followed the same pattern. Drinks and sitting out in the drawing room, supper in the dining room, dancing in the hall. Brian said that he found Tuppy's parties tedious. He complained of the same people, in the same clothes, making the same conversation. But Anna liked things that way. She didn't like things to change or be different.

Even the preparations, the apparent chaos, filled her with satisfaction, because she knew that by eight o'clock everything would be just the way it always was, ready and waiting for the guests to arrive, with nothing overlooked and no detail forgotten. Only this evening it would not be quite the same because Tuppy wouldn't be there. But still she *was* there, Anna told

536

herself, even if she wasn't able to stand at the foot of the stairs in her antique blue velvet and the inherited diamonds. She would be upstairs, listening to the music, perhaps drinking a little champagne, remembering . . .

Mrs. Watty said, "Do you mind moving, Mrs. Stoddart? I'm just about to polish that bit of floor." Anna apologized and got out of the way and went to look for Rose.

She found her in the drawing room, kneeling on the floor by the grand piano, trying to sort out the long twigs of beech which she had spread on an old sheet. There was a large pot beside her, patterned in roses, and some scraps of crumpled chicken wire. Rose's expression, as she looked up and saw Anna, was distraught.

"Hello," said Anna.

"Anna, thank heavens you've come. Everybody seems to take it for granted that I can do the most wonderful arrangements, and they won't believe me when I tell them that I can't even stick six daffodils into a jug without their collapsing."

Anna took off her coat, laid it on a chair, and went to help. "You have to cut the stems different lengths, otherwise they stick up like a broom head. Where are the secateurs? Look, like this. And then . . ."

Rose watched admiringly as the arrangement took shape. "You are clever. How can you be so clever? How do you know what to do? Did somebody teach you?"

It was marvelous to be told she was clever. Anna said no, nobody had taught her. It was just a thing she loved to do, so maybe that was why she was good at it. "Aren't there some chrysanthemums we can put with them? They could use a bit of color."

"Isobel asked Watty to bring some in, but she also asked him to do about a dozen other things as well and the poor man's nearly out of his mind."

"It's always like this," Anna told her. "It seems to be disorganized, but it's always all right in the end. And we can get some berries, or something, later. Where is this vase meant to be going?"

"Isobel thought on the piano."

Rose stooped to lift the bowl and put it in its place. Anna watched her with admiration. She saw the long, slender legs, the tiny waist, the shine of dark hair, artlessly casual. It was just the way Anna had always longed to look, and yet she was without envy. Was this one of the better symptoms of pregnancy, or was it because she liked Rose so much?

She had never thought she could like Rose. Before, when Rose was younger and Brian had brought her and her mother to the Yacht Club for a drink, Anna had been paralyzed by shyness of Rose, even a little afraid of her disparaging eyes and her thoughtlessly rude remarks. She had dreaded meeting her again.

But Rose had changed. Perhaps, thought Anna, that had something to do with Antony. She couldn't be sure of it; she only knew that Rose was a different person. Why, Anna hadn't even minded when Brian had asked her out for dinner. In fact, it made Anna feel pleasantly worldly to be going off on her shopping spree, knowing that her husband was to be so charmingly diverted while she was away. That was real sophistication —something that Anna had yearned for, all her married life.

Perhaps she was really growing up at last. Perhaps she was learning to accept things.

"What do you think of that?" Rose asked her, stepping back from the piano.

Anna, still kneeling on the floor, said, "That's just right. Rose, I want to tell you—Brian enjoyed his evening with you so much and he was so sorry about the oyster. He was really furious, and he rang up the Fishers' Arms and gave the manager the most terrible telling off."

"That wasn't his fault." Busy with broken branches and a few wet scraps of leaves, Rose knelt beside her. Her hair fell forward and Anna could not see her face. "And I've never thanked you for the azalea. You didn't need to send it."

"But of course I sent it. I felt responsible, in a way."

"How is Brian?"

538

"He's very well." Anna amended this. "Except, of course, for his eye."

"His eye?"

"Yes, poor man, he walked into a door. I don't know how, but he gave himself the most terrible bang and he got quite a black eye." She smiled, because Brian had looked funny, like a man in a farce. "But it's all right now, and fading fast."

Rose said, "How horrid for him." And then, "Do you think we should go and pick berries now, or bring in the pot plants?"

"We'll have to get Watty to help us do that." Anna felt a little shy. "The thing is . . . well, nobody knows yet, but I'm not allowed to carry heavy things. Hugh told me not to. You see, I'm having a baby."

"You *are*?"

Anna nodded. It was wonderful to have a confidante, another woman you could tell.

"Yes. In the spring."

"I am pleased. And the spring's the best time to have a baby. Like lambs and calves . . ." Rose became a little confused. "I mean, you've got all the summer in front of you."

"I wondered . . ." Anna hesitated. The idea had been in the back of her mind for some time, but now she was sure. "I wondered if you'd be a godmother. I haven't said anything to Brian yet, and of course I'd have to tell him, but I thought I'd ask you first. Anyway *I* want you to be a godmother. If you'd like to." Rose was looking uncertain. "If you would," she finished faintly.

"Yes, of course," said Rose. "I'd love to. I'm very flattered. The only thing is, well, I won't be here much, and . . ."

"It doesn't matter if you're here or not. You'll be somewhere. And one should always pick special friends for godparents." The emotion of the situation became too much for Anna. She shied away from it, reverting to a safer subject where she felt on firmer ground. "Now, if we had some dahlias we could do a sort of sunburst on top of the bureau. Tuppy's got lots of dahlias in her border. Let's go out and pick the lot. Poor Watty, it'll break his heart."

By the middle of the afternoon, everything had come to a full stop. Because there was nowhere else to sit everybody had gathered in Mrs. Watty's welcoming kitchen. Mrs. Watty, indefatigable, was making a batch of scones. Her husband, before getting into the fishmonger's van and driving to Tarbole to collect Jason from school, sat at the kitchen table with a face like an undertaker, and drank tea. (The massacre of the dahlias had been the final straw.) Nurse was ironing, and Isobel, visibly wilting on her long legs, pushed her hair out of her face and announced that she was going to her room to put up her toes. She waited for comments but nobody argued with her. Her eyes lighted on Flora.

"You too, Rose. You've been busy as a bee all day. Go and have a rest."

But Flora didn't want a rest. Instead she felt a deep need to be out of doors, away from the house, on her own.

"I thought I might take Plummer for a walk."

Isobel brightened. "Oh, could you bear to? He's been following me around all day with such reproachful eyes, and I haven't the energy to take him myself." Flora glanced at the clock. "When do you think Antony will be here?"

"Any moment now. He said he was leaving Edinburgh at lunchtime." Isobel stretched her lanky length. "I'm going to bed before I fall down."

She departed. Watty noisily sipped his tea. Flora went to get a coat.

She found Plummer in the hall, looking defeated by its unfamiliar appearance. He hated change the way he hated suitcases stacked by the front door. Ignored and forgotten, he had taken refuge in his basket, which had been hidden away beneath the stairs.

When Flora called him he gazed at her, hurt and dejected. When he finally realized that she was going to take him for a walk, his joy knew no bounds. He leapt from his basket, his paws skidding on the polished floor, his old tail wagging like a piston. Delighted noises came from the back of his throat. Outside, he dashed to find something to carry and came prancing back to Flora with a stick in his mouth so long that it trailed on the ground behind him. Thus burdened, Flora and Plummer set out.

It was cool, gray, very still. The sun had not broken through all day and the road was still wet from the previous day's rain. They went out of the gate and turned down the road which led to Tarbole. After a mile or so the road dipped and ran alongside the water for a hundred yards or so. A small beach lay revealed, which Plummer instantly went to investigate, but Flora, bundled in her coat against the chill, settled herself on the low sea-wall to wait for Antony.

There were few cars. As each one appeared over the top of the hill she looked up to see if it was Antony. She sat there for half an hour and was beginning to get cold before he finally appeared. She recognized his car at once, got off the wall, and stood in the middle of the road, windmilling frantically with her arms to make him stop. He saw her, slowed down, and pulled the car over to the side of the road.

"Flora." He was out of the car, and they met in the middle of the road and hugged. She could not remember when she had been so pleased or so relieved to see anybody.

"I've been waiting for you. I wanted to see you before anyone else did."

"How long have you been here?"

"It feels like ages, but I don't suppose it was very long."

"You look cold. Come on, get into the car."

She started to do so then remembered Plummer, who was finally sighted at the farthest end of the little beach, pursuing some apparently fascinating odor. Flora called, but he took no notice. Antony whistled and Plummer's ears pricked up. He turned, gazing expectantly in their direction. Antony whistled again and that did it. Plummer galloped back, scrambled handily up the rocks, leapt the wall like a puppy, and flung himself at Antony. It took some time to persuade him to get onto the

541

back seat of the car, along with a suitcase, a crate of beer, and a stack of gramophone records.

"What are the records for?" Flora asked as she settled herself beside Antony.

"They're for tonight, when the band goes off to eat buns and drink whisky. The party falls to bits if the music stops, and Tuppy's records are practically prewar, so I thought I'd bring a few of my own. But first things first. . . ." He turned toward her. "Are you all right?"

"Yes."

"You are a ninny. The minute I turn my back you start eating bad oysters. Isobel rang me up in a panic. I think she thought you were going to die on her. Were you having dinner with Brian?"

"Yes."

"I thought that's what she said." He seemed amused by this, but also unperturbed. "That'll teach you to go gallivanting with the Casanova of Arisaig. And what about the party to-night? Has Isobel collapsed yet?"

"Just about. I left her heading for her bed and a little nap. And Anna Stoddart and I cut all Tuppy's dahlias and Watty won't speak to us."

"It happens every time. And how's Tuppy?"

"Looking forward to seeing you. She says she's getting better every day. And she may be allowed up next week, just for an hour or two every day."

"Isn't that great?" Without warning he leaned forward and kissed her. "You feel thin. Your face is all bones."

"I'm all right."

"You've hated it, haven't you, Flora? The whole bloody business."

"No." She had to be truthful. "No, I haven't hated it. I've just hated myself. I feel mean and small and every day it's worse, because I get fonder and fonder of them all. One minute I'm Rose and I'm going to marry you and I'm not lying. And the next minute I'm Flora again, and I am. I don't know which

542

is worse. Antony, that promise I made—I've kept it. And you'll keep yours, won't you? You'll tell Tuppy the truth?"

He sat back, turning his profile to her, and stared dejectedly ahead, his hands on the driving wheel. He said at last, "Yes," and Flora felt sorry for him.

"It's awful, I know. In a way, I wish we could go back and you could tell her now and get it over, but with the party and everything . . ."

"I'll tell her tomorrow." That was final. He did not want to talk about it any more. "And now for God's sake, let's get home. I'm hungry and I want tea."

"Mrs. Watty's made scones."

"And let's put tomorrow out of our minds. Don't let's talk about it any more."

With that ostrich-like remark, he reached for the ignition key, but Flora stopped him.

"There is just one more thing." She put her hand into her pocket. "This."

"What's this?"

"It's a postcard."

"Pretty crummy-looking postcard."

"I know. I threw it in the wastepaper basket, and then I thought perhaps you'd better see it, so I took it out again. That's why it's all bent."

He took it from her cautiously. "Paris?" He turned it over, instantly recognized the writing, and read it through in silence. When he had finished there was a long silence. Then he said, "What a bitch."

"That's why I dropped it into the wastepaper basket."

He read it again, and his sense of humor got the better of him. "You know, in a way, Rose is quite a bright girl. She set this whole thing up, and you and I fell for it, like a couple of suckers. Or I did. The joke is definitely on me. And if one can remain detached, I suppose it's quite a good one. 'Decided to stop off for a couple of days.' Do you suppose she ever got to Spetsai?"

"Perhaps she met another man on the plane. Perhaps she's

543

in Gstaad or Monaco or . . ." Flora cast about for the most unlikely place she could think of and came up with, "Acapulco?"

"I wouldn't know." He gave Flora back the postcard. "Throw it in the fire when we get back to Fernrigg." He started up the car. "And that will be the end of Rose. Wherever she is, she's gone."

Flora did not reply. She knew that Rose hadn't gone. And she wouldn't go until Antony told Tuppy the truth.

10

HUGH

The band arrived just as Antony was on his way upstairs to change. They came in a small battered car belonging to and driven by Mr. Cooper, the postmistress's husband, and players and instruments were packed in so tightly that it took some time and thought to get them finally extricated.

That achieved, Antony led them into the house and showed them to their assigned space in a corner of the hall. There they established themselves—Mr. Cooper with his accordion; the fiddler (a retired roadman, some relation of Mrs. Cooper); and the drummer, a long-haired lad in high boots whom Antony recognized as a Tarbole boy, deckhand on his uncle's fishing boat. The three had decked themselves out in a sort of spurious uniform—blue shirts and tartan bow-ties—thus presenting a brave show.

Antony gave them all a nip of whisky, and at once they got down to business and started to warm up—the old man tuning

545

his fiddle and Mr. Cooper playing long, trilling arpeggios on the keyboard of the accordion.

Time was running short. Antony left them and ran upstairs to search out his evening clothes, which he was much relieved to find ready and waiting, laid out on his bed: shoes, stockings, garters, skean dhu; shirt, tie, waistcoat and doublet; kilt and sporran. The shoe buckles, silver buttons and skean dhu had all been polished, and his gold studs and cuff links arranged on the top of his chest of drawers. Somebody, probably Mrs. Watty, had been busy, and he blessed her heart, because as usual he had left everything to the last minute, and had resigned himself to a frantic search for the mislaid pieces of equipment.

Ten minutes later, the very picture of a well-dressed Highland gentleman, he was downstairs again. By now the caterers had arrived. Mr. Anderson, in a starched white jacket, was setting out smoked salmon on the buffet table, assisted by Mrs. Watty. Mrs. Anderson, a stately lady with a formidable reputation for good behavior, had taken up her position behind the bar and was engaged in giving the glasses a final polish, holding each one up to the light to check for possible smudges.

There did not seem to be anything more for Antony to do. He glanced at his watch, and decided there was time to pour himself a whisky and soda and take it upstairs to say goodnight to Tuppy. This he was just on the point of doing, when he was diverted by the sound of a car coming up the drive and grinding to a halt on the gravel outside the house.

"Who on earth can that be?"

"Whoever it is," said Mrs. Anderson, sedately plying her teacloth, "they're fifteen minutes early."

Antony frowned. This was the west of Scotland, and nobody was ever fifteen minutes early. More likely an hour and three quarters late. He waited apprehensively, with visions of himself spending the next half hour trying to make polite conversation into Mrs. Clanwilliam's hearing aid. A car door slammed, footsteps crunched on the gravel, and the next moment the front door opened and Hugh Kyle appeared. He wore

546

a dinner suit and looked, thought Antony, immensely distinguished.

"Hello, Antony."

Antony let out a sigh of relief. "Thank God it's only you. You're early."

"Yes, I know." Hugh shut the door behind him and came forward, his hands in his pockets, his eyes taking in the festive scene. "This is very splendid. Just like old times."

"I know. Everybody's been working like a beaver. You're just in time for a dram. I was going to pour myself one and then go up to see Tuppy, but as you're here . . ." He poured two whiskies, topped them up with water, handed one to Hugh. "Slaintheva, old friend."

He raised his glass. But Hugh did not appear to be in a health-drinking mood. He stood there holding the drink and watching Antony, and his blue eyes were somber. For some reason Antony was instantly apprehensive. He lowered his glass, without having tasted the whisky. He asked, "Is something wrong?"

"Yes," Hugh told him bluntly. "And I think we'd better talk about it. Is there somewhere we could go, where we wouldn't be disturbed?"

Flora sat at the dressing table, wrapped in the shabby blue bathrobe she had had since she was at school and applied mascara to her long, bristly lashes. Her reflection, the woman in the mirror who leaned toward her, seemed to have nothing to do with Flora Waring. The elaborate makeup, the carefully arranged fall of shining hair, were as formal and unfamiliar as a photograph in a magazine. Even the bedroom behind her was alien. She saw the glow of the electric fire, the drawn curtains, the ghost-like form of her dress hanging on the outside of the wardrobe door where Nurse McLeod, with some pride, had ceremoniously arranged it.

Her pride was justifiable, for it now bore no resemblance to the dim garment which Mrs. Watty had produced from the trunk in the attic. Bleached, starched, stitched, it waited for

547

Flora, crisp and cold as newly-fallen snow. The blue lining showed in bands between insets of lawn and lace, and a line of tiny pearl buttons ran from waist to throat.

Its presence was disturbing. Silent and reproachful, it seemed to be watching Flora and, like a disapproving onlooker, was quite unsettling. She knew that she did not want to put it on. All this time she had been putting off the moment when she had to come to terms with it, but now there seemed no further excuse to delay. She laid down the mascara brush and sprayed herself recklessly with the last of Marcia's scent. She stood up and reluctantly slipped out of the familiar comfort of the old blue dressing gown. For an instant her reflection stood before her: tall, slender, her body still brown from the summer's sun, the tan emphasized by the white lace bikini of bra and briefs. The room was warm, but she shivered. She turned from the mirror and went to take the dress from the hanger, step carefully into it, ease her arms into the long tight sleeves, and finally edge it up over her shoulders. It felt resistant and cold, like a dress made of paper.

She did up the tiny buttons. That took some time because the buttonholes were glued shut with starch and had to be worked open and each button coaxed into place. The high collar was agony—hard as cardboard, it cut into her neck below her jawline.

But finally, everything was done, the little belt buckled, the cuff buttons fastened. She moved cautiously to inspect herself and saw a girl stiff as a sugar bride on the top of a wedding cake. *I'm afraid,* she told herself, but the girl in the mirror offered no comfort. She simply stared back at Flora dispassionately, as though she didn't particularly like her. Flora sighed, stooped cautiously to turn off the electric fire, switched off the lights, and left her room. She went down the passage to show herself off and say goodnight to Tuppy as she had promised to do.

She heard the faint beat of jigging music. The house felt very warm (Watty had been bidden to turn up the heat) and smelt of log fires and chrysanthemums. Cheerful voices floated

548

up from the kitchen, creating an atmosphere of suppressed excitement—like the day before Christmas, or the moment of opening some mysterious tinsel-wrapped parcel.

Tuppy's door stood ajar. From within came the companionable murmur of voices. Flora tapped at the door and went in, and saw Tuppy plumped up against fresh pillows and wearing a white bedjacket tied with satin bows; and beside her, looking like a child out of an old portrait, her great-grandson, Jason.

"Rose!" Tuppy flung out her arms, a typical Tuppy gesture, gay, loving, rather dashing. "My dear child. Come and let us look at you. No, walk up and down so that we can really see." Rigid with starch, Flora obliged. "What a clever creature Nurse is! To think that dress has been in the attic all these years, and now it looks as though it's just been created. Come and give me a kiss. How good you smell. Now sit, just here, on the edge of the bed. Carefully, though, you mustn't crush the skirt."

Flora arranged herself cautiously. She said, "With this collar, I feel like a giraffe-necked woman."

"What's a giraffe-necked woman?" asked Jason.

"They come from Burma," Tuppy told him, "and they put gold rings on their necks and their necks go on forever."

"Was it really your tennis dress, Tuppy?" He gazed at Flora, scarcely recognizing her for the everyday person he had come to know, familiar in her jeans and sweaters. He felt rather shy of this new person.

"Yes, it really was. When I was a girl."

"How you played tennis in this, I can't imagine," Flora said.

Tuppy considered this problem. "Well, it wasn't very good tennis." They all laughed. She took Flora's hand and gave it one of her proprietary little pats. Her eyes were very bright, her color high, but whether it was due to excitement or to the brimming glass of champagne which stood on her bedside table, it was impossible to say. "I've been sitting here listening to the music, and my feet have been dancing away under the sheets, having a little party all to themselves. And then Jason came to see me, looking the image of his grandfather, and I've been telling him all about the party we had when his grandfather was twenty-one, when we lit the bonfire up on the hill behind the house, and all the country people came, and there was an ox roasting on a spit and barrels of beer. What a party that one was!"

"Tell Rose about my grandfather and his boat."

"Rose won't want to hear about that."

"Yes, I will. Tell me," Flora urged.

Tuppy did not need any more encouragement. "Well, Jason's grandfather was called Bruce, and what a wild boy he was! He spent all his days with the farm children, and at the end of the holidays I could scarcely cram his feet into shoes. But he was the child who always had a passion for the sea. He was never afraid of it, and he could swim really quite strongly by the time he was five. And when he was only a little older than Jason, he got his first dinghy. Tammy Todd—he works at Ardmore—well, it was his old father who built it for Bruce. And every year, in the summer, the Ardmore Yacht Club used to have a regatta, and there was a race for the children and . . . what was it called, Jason?"

"It was called the Tinker's Race, because all the sails were patched!"

Flora frowned. "Patched?"

"He means that all the sails were home-made," Tuppy explained, "all in marvelous colors, sewn together like patchwork. All the mothers worked for months, and the child with the gayest sails won the prize. And Bruce won it that first year, and I don't think any prize ever meant so much to him as that one did."

"But he won more races, didn't he, Tuppy?"

"Oh, yes. Lots and lots of races. And not just at Ardmore. He used to go down to the Clyde and sail with the Royal Northern, and then when he left school, he crewed for an ocean race, and went over to America. He always had a boat. It was the greatest pleasure in his life."

550

"And then the war came, and he joined the navy," Jason prompted, not wanting the story to end.

"Yes, he went to sea. And he was in a destroyer with the Atlantic convoys, and sometimes they'd come into the Gairloch or the Kyles of Lochalsh, and he'd get home for a weekend's leave, and as likely as not spend the whole time either working on his boat, or sailing one of the dinghys."

"And my grandmother was in the navy, too, wasn't she?"

Tuppy smiled indulgently at Jason's enthusiasm. "Yes, she was in the Wrens. They were married very soon after the beginning of the war. And what a funny wedding it was. It kept being put off because Bruce was always at sea, but finally they got married in London on a weekend leave, and Isobel and I had such a time getting there—all the trains full of soldiers and everybody sharing sandwiches and sitting on each other's knees. We did have fun."

"Tell us more stories," said Jason. But Tuppy threw up her hands.

"You didn't come here for stories. You came to say goodnight and then go down to the party. Just think, it's your very first dance. And you'll always remember wearing your grandfather's kilt and his velvet doublet."

Jason, reluctantly, got off the bed. He went towards the door. He said to Flora, "Will you dance with me? I can only do 'Strip the Willow' and an 'Eightsome Reel' if everybody else knows how to do it."

"I can't do either, but if you can teach me, I'd love to dance with you."

"I could probably teach you 'Strip the Willow.'" He opened the door. "Goodnight, Tuppy."

"Goodnight, my love."

He left them. The door closed behind him. Tuppy leaned back on her pillows, looking tired but peaceful.

"It's very strange," she said, and her voice, too, seemed tired, as though the day had been too long for her. "This evening I seem to have lost all track of the years. Hearing the music, and knowing just how everything is looking downstairs,

551

and all the fuss and the commotion; and then Jason coming in. And for a moment I really thought it was Bruce. Such a strange feeling. But a nice one, too. I think it has something to do with this house. This house and I know each other very well. You know, Rose, I've lived here all my life. I was born here. I wonder if you knew that?"

"No, I didn't know."

"Yes, I was born here and I grew up here. And so did my two little brothers."

"I didn't know you had brothers, either."

"Oh, dear me, yes. James and Robbie. They were much younger than I was, and my mother died when I was twelve, so in a way they were my children. And such dear, wicked little boys. I can't tell you how naughty they were, and the dreadful things they used to get up to. Once they built a raft and tried to launch it off the beach, but they got swept out to sea by the ebb tide, and the lifeboat had to go out after them. And another time they lit a campfire in the summer house and the whole place went up in smoke and they were lucky not to be roasted alive. It was the only time I ever remembered seeing my father really angry. And then they went away to school, and I missed them so much. And they grew into young men, so tall and handsome, but still as wicked as ever. I was married by then and living in Edinburgh, but oh, the stories I used to hear! The escapades and the parties! They were so attractive they must have broken the heart of every girl in Scotland, but so charming that no female had the heart to stay angry for long, and they were always forgiven."

"What happened to them?"

Tuppy's gay and valiant voice cracked a little. "They were killed. Both of them. In the First World War. First Robbie and then James. It was such a terrible war. All those fine young men. The carnage and the casualty lists. You know, even someone of Isobel's generation cannot begin to imagine the horror of those casualty lists. And then, so near the end of the war, my own husband was killed. And when that happened I felt that I had nothing left to live for." The blue eyes shone with sudden tears.

"Oh, Tuppy."

But Tuppy shook her head, denying sentiment and self-pity. "But you see, I had. I had my children, Isobel and Bruce. But I'm afraid I wasn't a very maternal person. I think I'd used up all my mothering on my little brothers, and by the time Bruce and Isobel turned up I wasn't nearly as pleased as I should have been. We were living in the south, and they were so pale and quiet, poor little souls, and somehow I couldn't make myself get enthusiastic about them, and that made me feel guilty and sorrier than ever for myself. It was a sort of vicious circle."

"What happened?"

"Well, my father wrote to me. The war was over at last, and he asked me to bring the children home to Fernrigg for Christmas. So we got into a train and we came, and he met us at Tarbole on a dark winter's morning. It was very cold and it was raining, and what a miserable little party we were, all dressed in inky black, gray in the face and sooty from the train. He had brought a wagonette and we got up behind the horses and drove back to Fernrigg just as the dawn was beginning to light the sky. And on the road we met an old farmer my father knew, and he stopped the horses and introduced the old man to the children. I remember them now, shaking hands so solemnly.

"I thought it was just for Christmas I'd come home. But we stayed over the New Year, and the weeks turned into months, and the next thing I knew, it was spring again. And I realized that the children were at home, they belonged to Fernrigg. And now they were rosy and noisy, and out of doors most of the time, just the way children should be. And I began to be interested in the garden. I made a rosebed and I planted shrubs and a fuchsia hedge, and gradually I began to realize that however tragic the past had been, there still had to be a future. This is a very comforting house, you know. It doesn't seem to change very much, and if things don't change, they can be very comforting."

She fell silent. From downstairs now came the sounds of cars arriving, the swell of gathering voices rising above the jig of the music. The party had started. Tuppy reached out for her glass of champagne and had a little drink. She laid down her glass and took Flora's hand again.

"Torquil and Antony were born here. Their mother had a difficult time when Torquil was born and the doctors told her that she really shouldn't have a second child, but she was determined to take the risk. Bruce was naturally very anxious about her, and so we arranged that she should come to Fernrigg for her pregnancy and to have the baby. And I think everything might have gone well, but Bruce's ship was torpedoed just a month before Antony was born, and after that I think she lost all will to live. There was no fight in her. And the worst bit of it was that I understood. I knew how she felt." She gave a wry smile. "So there we are, Isobel and I, right back where we'd started, with two more little boys to bring up. Always little boys at Fernrigg. The house is crawling with them. Sometimes I hear them running in from the garden, calling up the stairs, making such a racket. I think, because they died, that's why they've never grown old. And as long as I am here to remember them, then they are never really gone."

Once again, she fell silent. Flora said, at last, "I wish so much you'd told me this before. I wish I'd known."

"It's sometimes better not to talk about the past. It's an indulgence which should be kept for very old people."

"But Fernrigg is such a happy house. You feel it the moment you walk into it."

"I'm glad you felt that. I sometimes think it's like a tree, gnarled and old, the trunk twisted and deformed by the wind. Some of the branches have gone, torn away by the storms, and at times you think the tree is dying—it can't survive the elements any longer. And then the spring comes again, and the tree opens out into thousands of young, green leaves. Like a miracle. You're one of the little leaves, Rose. And Antony. And

554

Jason. It makes everything worthwhile to know that there are young people around again. To know you're here." Flora could think of nothing to say, and with a characteristic change of mood, Tuppy became brisk. "What am I doing, keeping you here, talking a lot of rubbish, when everybody is downstairs waiting to meet you! Are you feeling nervous?"

"A little."

"You mustn't be nervous. You're looking beautiful and everyone—not just Antony—will be in love with you. Now, give me a kiss and run along. And tomorrow you can come and tell me all about it. Every tiny detail, because I shall be waiting to hear."

Flora got off the bed. She bent and kissed Tuppy and went to the door. As she opened it Tuppy said, "Rose," and Flora looked back. "Have fun," Tuppy told her.

That was all. She went out of the room, and shut the door behind her.

It was no time to be emotional. It was simply childish to become sentimental, to get upset because an old lady had had a glass of champagne and started to remember. Flora was not a child. She had learned long ago to control her feelings. She had only to stand very still, and press her hands to her face and close her eyes, and in a moment the lump in her throat would stop growing like a great balloon and the foolish tears would recede and never be shed.

She had been a long time with Tuppy. From the hall the swelling sounds of the party, already well under way, rose to taunt her. She had to go down. She couldn't start crying now, because she had to go down, and meet everybody. And Antony was waiting, and she had promised him . . .

What had she promised him? What madness had impelled her to make that promise? And how could they ever have imagined that they would get away with their deception without destroying both themselves and everyone else involved?

The desperate questions had no answer. The dress she wore, starched and relentlessly uncomfortable, had become a

555

physical embodiment of her own shame and self-loathing. Wearing it was torture. Her arms were forced into sleeves that were too narrow; her throat constricted by the high, tight collar, until she felt she couldn't breathe.

Rose. Have fun.

But I'm not Rose. And I can't pretend to be Rose any longer.

She pressed her fist to her mouth, but it wasn't any good, because by now she was crying—for Tuppy, for the little boys, for herself. Blinding, salty tears filled her eyes and streamed down her cheeks. She imagined herself, blotchy and with her mascara running, but that was of no importance because she had come to the end of the charade. She could go to no party, face nobody. Instinctively, she had started back toward the sanctuary of her own room, and now she was running, like a person trying to escape—down the long passage, till she had reached her door and was inside, shut away. She was safe.

Now the music and the laughter were deadened to a faint murmur and there was only the ugly sound of her own weeping. The room felt icy. She began, clumsily, to undo all the tiny awkward buttons of the dress. The collar lay loose and she could breathe again. Then the bodice and the narrow cuffs. She wrenched the dress from her shoulders and it slid with a whisper to the floor, and she stepped out of it and left it there, like the discarded wrappings of some parcel. Shivering with cold, she snatched up her old familiar dressing gown, and without bothering to do up the buttons or tie the sash bundled herself into it, flung herself across the bed, and was abandoned, at last, to the inevitable storm of weeping.

Time was lost. Flora had no idea how long she had lain there before she heard the sound of her door open, and gently, close again. She was not even sure whether or not someone had actually come into the room until she felt the pressure on the edge of her bed as someone sat beside her. A warm presence, solid and comforting. She turned her head on the pillow, and a hand reached out and smoothed her hair back off her face. She

556

looked through swimming eyes, and the dark blur with the white shirt front gradually resolved itself into Hugh Kyle.

She had expected perhaps Isobel or Antony. Certainly not Hugh. She made an enormous effort to stop crying, and as the tears did recede a little, she wiped them away with the heel of her hand, and looked at him again. Hugh's image sharpened, and she saw a man she had never seen before—not simply because he was dressed differently, but because it was unusual for him to be so patient, sitting there as though he had all the time in the world, not saying anything and apparently prepared to let Flora cry herself to a standstill.

She made an effort to speak. To say something, even if it was only, "Go away." But Hugh—Hugh, of all people, opened his arms to her, and this she found impossible to resist. Without a second thought, Flora pulled herself up off her pillows, and cast herself into the waiting comfort of his massive embrace.

He seemed impervious to the damage she was probably wreaking on his crisp white shirt front. His arms were warm and strong about her shaking shoulders. He smelt of clean linen and aftershave. She felt his chin against the top of her head, and when, after a little, he said, gently, "What's wrong?" the words came, incoherent and disjointed, but still they came—a torrent of words, a flood.

"I've been with Tuppy . . . and she was telling me . . . the little boys . . . and I never knew. And I couldn't bear it. And she said . . . a leaf on the tree . . . and I couldn't bear it . . ." Telling him all this was not helped by the fact of her face being pressed so closely to his shirt front. "I . . . could hear everybody and the music, and I knew . . . I couldn't come down. . . ."

He let her cry. When she had calmed down a little, she heard him say, "Isobel wondered what had happened to you. She sent me to find out, and to bring you down."

Flora shook her head as vehemently as possible under the constricted circumstances. "I'm not coming."

557

"Of course you're coming. Everybody's waiting to meet you. You can't spoil it for them."

"I can't. I'm not going to. You'll have to say I'm sick again, or something . . . anything . . ."

His arms tightened. "Now come along, Flora, pull yourself together."

The room became very still. Out of the silence random sounds impinged on Flora's conscious mind: faint strains of music from the other end of the house, the wind rising, nudging the window, the distant murmur of the sea; and so close that it was felt rather than heard, the regular thud of Hugh's heartbeat.

Cautiously, she drew away from him. "What did you call me?"

"Flora. It's a good name. Much better than Rose."

Her face ached from crying. Undried tears still lay on her cheeks, and she tried to wipe them away with her fingers. Her nose was running and she could not find a handkerchief and had to sniff, enormously. He reached into his pocket and produced his own handkerchief. Not the beautiful silk one which showed from the top of his breast pocket, but a comfortable everyday one, the cotton soft from washing.

She accepted it gratefully. "I don't seem to be able to stop crying. I don't usually cry, ever." She blew her nose. "You won't believe that, but it's true. These last few days I don't seem to have done anything but cry."

"No, but you've been under a considerable strain."

"Yes." She looked down at the handkerchief and saw it covered with dark smudges. "My mascara's run."

"You look like a panda."

"I suppose I do." She took a deep breath. "How did you know? About me being Flora?"

"Antony told me. I mean, he told me your name was Flora, but I've known for some time that you weren't Rose."

"When did you know?"

"The day you were ill, I knew for sure." He added, "But I've had my suspicions for some time."

558

"But how did you know?"

"When Rose was here, that summer five years ago, she had an accident on the beach. She was sunbathing, or occupied in some other relatively harmless way, and she cut her arm on a broken bottle that some joker had buried in the sand. Just here." He reached out and took Flora's hand, pushed up the sleeve of her dressing gown, and drew with his finger a line perhaps two inches long on the outside of her forearm. "It wasn't very serious, but it had to be stitched up. I pride myself on being fairly adroit when it comes to sewing people up, but even I couldn't do a job that left no trace of a scar."

"I see. But why didn't you say anything?"

"I wanted to speak to Antony first."

"And have you?"

"Yes."

"Did he tell you everything? About me and Rose and our parents?"

"Yes, everything. It's quite a story."

"He . . . he's going to tell Tuppy tomorrow."

Hugh corrected her. "He's telling Tuppy now."

"You mean, this very moment?"

"This very moment."

"So . . ." She was almost afraid to say it. "So Tuppy knows I'm not Rose."

"By now she does." He watched her face. "Is that why you were crying?"

"Yes, I think so. I seemed to be crying for so many things."

"But an uneasy conscience was one of them."

Flora nodded—a miserable confession.

"You didn't like lying to Tuppy?"

"I felt like a murderer."

"Well, now you don't need to feel like a murderer any longer." He sounded, all at once, much more like his usual dry self. "So perhaps you'll get off that bed, and get into your dress and come downstairs."

"But my face is all dirty and swollen."

559

"You can wash it."

"And my dress is all crumpled."

He looked for the dress, spied it where she had abandoned it on the floor. "No wonder it's crumpled." He stood up and went to retrieve it, shaking it out of its creases and laying it across the foot of the bed. Flora wrapped her arms around her knees and watched him.

"Are you cold?" he asked her.

"A little." Without comment, he went to turn on the electric fire, pressing down the switch with the toe of his shoe, and then moved to the dressing table. Flora saw the green gleam of a champagne bottle and a couple of wineglasses.

"Did you bring those up with you?"

"Yes. I had an idea some sort of a stimulant might be useful." He commenced, neatly, to deal with the gold wire and the foil. "It seems I was right."

There was a pop as the cork flew out, an explosion of golden bubbles which he caught expertly, first in one glass and then the other. He set down the bottle and brought Flora over a brimming glass, and then he said, "Slaintheva," and they drank, and the wine was dry and nose-tickling and tasted of weddings and the best sort of celebrations.

The bars of the fire reddened. The room grew bright and warm. Flora took a second courage-bolstering mouthful, and said, abruptly, "I do know about Rose."

Hugh did not reply at once to this. Instead, he retrieved the champagne bottle and came to settle himself at the foot of the bed, his wide shoulders propped against the brass rail. He set the bottle handily on the floor at his side. He said, "What do you know about her?"

"I know that she had an affair with Brian Stoddart. But I didn't know that before he took me out for dinner. Otherwise, I promise you, I would never have gone."

"I imagine he reminisced in some detail."

"I couldn't stop him."

"Were you shocked, or were you surprised?"

She tried to remember. "I don't know. You see, I didn't

560

have time to get to know Rose. We just met in London for an evening, and then she flew off to Greece the next day. But she looked like me, and so I imagined that she *was* like me. Except that she was rich and she had all sorts of things that I could never hope to have. But that didn't seem to be basically important. I just thought of us as two halves of the same whole. We'd been separated all our lives, but basically we were still the one person. And then Rose went, and Antony arrived and told me what had happened, and that was the beginning of wondering about Rose. She knew Antony needed her, but she'd still gone off to Greece. That was one of the reasons I came to Fernrigg. I suppose to try and make up for what Rose had done." It was all too difficult and Flora gave up. "It doesn't make any sense at all, does it?"

"I think it makes a lot of sense."

"You see . . ."

But he interrupted her. "Flora, that first day I spoke to you on the sands by the Beach House, you must have thought I was some sort of a maniac."

"No."

"Out of interest, what did you think?"

"I . . . I thought you were perhaps a man who'd been hurt by Rose."

"You mean, that I'd been in love with her?"

"Yes, I suppose so."

"I never really knew Rose. She was certainly never concerned about me. And I don't think she even looked twice at Antony. But Brian was a different kettle of fish."

"Then you weren't in love with her?"

"Good God, no." Flora could not keep herself from smiling. "And what's that Cheshire Cat grin for?"

"I thought you must have been. And I couldn't bear it."

"Why not?"

"Because she was so vile. And I suppose," she added with the air of one determined to make a clean breast of the whole thing, "because I liked you so much."

"You liked *me*?"

"That was why I was so horrible to you that night you brought me home from Lochgarry."

"Are you always horrible to people you like?"

"Only when I think they're jealous."

"I wish I'd known. I thought you hated me. I also thought you were drunk."

"Perhaps I was, a little. But at least I didn't slap your face."

"Poor Flora." But he did not look particularly repentant.

"But if you weren't angry because of jealousy . . ." It took some working out. "Hugh. Why were you angry?"

"Because of Anna."

Anna. It was Anna. Flora sighed. "You'll have to explain. Otherwise I shall never understand."

He said, heavily, "Yes." He had finished his glass, and now reached down to where the bottle stood on the floor, and re-filled both their glasses. It was becoming as cozy, thought Flora, as a midnight feast.

He said, "I don't know how much you know about the Stoddarts."

"I know about them, because Tuppy told me."

"Good. That'll save a lot of time. Well, where shall we start? Five years ago, Rose and her mother came to stay at the Beach House, that you know. Looking back, I've never been able to work out why they came to Fernrigg at all. It was the most unlikely place for a couple of jet-setters like the Schusters, but perhaps they'd seen Tuppy's advertisement in the *Times,* or they thought it would be novel to get back to the simple life. Anyway, they came, and Tuppy is always very conscientious about her tenants. She feels responsible for them, as if they were houseguests. She invites them up to Fernrigg, introduces them to her friends, and I think that is how Rose and her mother met the Stoddarts.

"Anna was expecting a baby that summer. Her first. And Brian, perhaps frustrated by potential fatherhood, was amusing himself with the barmaid at the Yacht Club. She was a Glasgow

562

girl who'd come up to Ardmore for the summer just to do this job, and I think she and Brian probably suited each other down to the ground."

"Did everybody know about this?"

"Tarbole is a small community. Everybody knows everybody else's business, only in this case nobody ever talks about it, out of loyalty to Anna."

"And she ignores what Brian does?"

"She appears to. But Anna, beneath that diffident exterior, is a very passionate and high-strung woman. Very much in love, and possessive of her husband."

"Brian described her as an ostrich, only seeing what she wanted to."

"How charming of him. And of course, most of the time she is, but in some women pregnancy unleashes a number of very violent emotions."

"Like jealousy."

"Exactly. This time, Anna didn't bury her head. She suspected he was carrying on with this girl, and she worked herself up into a highly nervous state. What she didn't realize, and thank God she never did, was that Rose had now appeared on the scene. The only reason I found out was through Tammy Todd who works at the Ardmore Yacht Club. Tammy and I were at school together long ago when we were both small, and I think he felt that perhaps I ought to know what was going on.

"One morning I had a phone call from Anna, very early. She was incoherent with anxiety because Brian had been out all night. He'd never come home. I tried to reassure her, and then I went searching for him and I found him at the Yacht Club. He said there'd been a party, and rather than disturb Anna, he'd decided to sleep the night there. I told him to go home and he said that he would.

"But later in the day I got another message to ring Anna. By now I was away out in the country, a two-hour drive from Tarbole, visiting the young son of a sheep farmer. The mother suspected appendicitis, but mercifully, as it turned out, she was wrong. Anyway, Anna told me she was hemorrhaging. I told

563

her I'd get back as soon as I could, but that Brian was to call the hospital and get an ambulance. She told me that she was still alone. Brian had never come back. So I rang the ambulance myself and the hospital at Lochgarry, and I drove like the hammers of hell back to Tarbole, and when I got to the surgery I rang the hospital again, but it was too late. Sister told me that Anna had arrived, but she'd lost the child. She said that Anna was asking for her husband, but that nobody knew where to find him. I said that I would find him, and I put down the telephone and got into the car and went to the Beach House, and walked in and found Rose and Brian in bed together."

"But didn't her mother know what was going on?"

"I honestly don't know. She certainly wasn't in the house at the time. As far as I can remember, she'd gone over to Lochgarry for a round of golf."

"Hugh, what *did* you do?"

He put up a hand to rub his eyes. "Oh, the usual things. Lost my temper, flung my weight around. But of course it was too late to start being indignant, because Anna's baby was already dead."

"And now she's having another one." Hugh nodded. "And you weren't going to stand by and let it happen all over again."

"No."

"Were . . . were there any repercussions?"

"No. By the time Anna came out of hospital, Rose and her mother had gone."

"Tuppy never knew? Nor Isobel?"

"No."

"Nor Antony?"

"Antony was working in Edinburgh. He only met Rose fleetingly when he happened to be home for a weekend."

"What did you think when you heard Antony was going to marry Rose?"

"I was appalled. But I told myself that all this had happened five years ago. Rose had probably grown up. I prayed that she had."

564

"And Anna? Anna never found out?"

"Brian and I made a deal. The only one we're ever likely to make. The truth would have destroyed Anna. Thinking that Brian was running around with a little whore from Glasgow was one thing. Knowing that he was sleeping with Rose was another. It would have been disastrous, and inevitably it would have involved the Armstrongs."

"And what did Brian get out of the deal?"

"Brian, despite his tomcat tendencies, had a hard head. Materially, financially, Brian had more than anyone else to lose. He still has for that matter."

"You really hate him, don't you?"

"It's mutual. But this is a small place, a tight community. So when we have to, we endure each other's company."

"He couldn't have been very pleased to see you that evening at Lochgarry."

"No, I don't think he was."

"Anna says he's got a black eye."

Hugh looked amazed. "No? Really?"

"You didn't hit him, did you?"

"Only a little," said Hugh.

"What will happen to that marriage?"

"Nothing will happen to it. Brian will probably continue to sow his wild oats, if the words apply to a man of his age, and Anna will continue to ignore his peccadilloes. And the marriage will survive."

"Will the child help?"

"It'll help Anna."

"It seems very unfair."

"Life is unfair, Flora. Surely you've found that out by now."

"Yes." She sighed deeply. It was all very troubling. "I wish Rose had been nicer. I wish she hadn't become like that. Amoral and ruthless. Hurting everybody. She and I are identical twins. We were born under Gemini. Why is she like that?"

"Environment?"

"You mean, if I'd been brought up by my mother instead of my father, I'd have been like Rose?"

"No. I can't imagine that you would."

"Besides, I envied Rose her environment. I envied her mink coat and her flat in London, and the way she had so much money she could go anywhere and do anything she wanted. And now I'm only sorry for her. It's a horrible feeling." She rested her chin on her knees and looked thoughtfully at Hugh. "Now, I wouldn't want to be Rose."

"I wouldn't want you to be Rose, either. But for a bit you had me very confused. For years people have been telling me I work too hard, I must get a partner, I'm going to crack up. And I've simply laughed at them. But all at once I began to wonder if I was going out of my mind. First I found you cleaning my kitchen, which was so un-Rose-like and out of character that it was positively unnerving. And then I found myself telling you about Angus McKay, and the next thing I knew I was blurting out the story of my marriage. And that, if you can believe it, was even more out of character than Rose scrubbing the floor. I hadn't talked about Diana in years. I've certainly never told a living soul the things I told you."

"I'm glad you told me."

"And then just when I was beginning to think that perhaps Rose wasn't so bad after all, there she was, off on the razzle with Brian Stoddart again. And Dr. Kyle, the lumbering old fool, was left standing there with egg all over his face."

"No wonder you were so angry."

From far away came the strains of a waltz. One two three. One two three.

. . . carry the lad that's born to be king,
Over the sea to Skye.

He said, "If we don't go now, the party's going to be over by the time we get there."

"Do I have to go on being Rose?"

"I think you have to." He got off the bed, collected the

566

empty champagne bottle, and stood it, like an ornament, in front of Flora's mirror. "For one more evening. For Antony and for Isobel and to save about sixty people a lot of embarrassment." He went over to the basin, turned on the hot tap, and wrung Flora's washcloth out under the scalding water. "Now get out of bed," he told her, "and come and wash your face."

She was ready, creamed and combed and wearing a minimum of makeup. She had climbed back into the dress and done up most of the buttons, while Hugh had dealt with the tricky ones at the neck. It was still as uncomfortable as ever, but now, emboldened by champagne, Flora decided that it was nothing that could not be endured. *Pour être belle il faut souffrir.* She did up the belt and faced him.

"I don't look blotchy, do I?"

"No." That was all she expected, but he added, "You look quite enchanting."

"You look enchanting too. Successful and distinguished. Except that some reckless female has smudged mascara onto your shirt front and knocked your tie crooked into the bargain."

He glanced into the mirror to check this, and appeared to be astonished. "How long has my tie been like that?"

"For the last ten minutes."

"Why didn't you put it straight for me?"

"I don't know. It's so corny."

"Why should it be corny to straighten a man's tie?"

"Oh, you know, those old movies you see on television. The couple are all dressed up, and the woman in love with the man, but he hasn't realized it. And then she tells him that his tie is crooked, and she straightens it for him, and the whole thing becomes terribly meaningful and tender, and they gaze into each other's eyes."

"What happens then?" asked Hugh, sounding as though he really wanted to know.

"Well, then he usually kisses her, and a heavenly choir starts singing, 'I'll Be Seeing You,' or something, and they put their arms around each other, and walk away from the camera

567

with *The End* written on their backs." She ended inconsequently, "I told you it was corny."

He seemed to be considering the pros and cons of the situation. He said at last, "Well, one thing's certain. I can't go downstairs with my tie standing on its head."

Flora laughed, and carefully, meticulously, put it straight for him. Without fuss, he stooped and kissed her. It was the most satisfactory sensation. So satisfactory that when it was over, she put her arms up and around his neck, and pulled down his head and kissed him back.

But his response was baffling. She drew back and frowned up at him.

"Don't you like to be kissed?"

"Yes, very much. But perhaps I'm a little out of practice. It hasn't happened to me for such a long time."

"Oh, Hugh. You can't live without love. You can't go on living without loving somebody."

"I thought I could."

"You're not that sort of person. You're not meant to be lonely and self-sufficient. You should have a wife, and children running round that house of yours."

"You forget, I tried it once and made the most abysmal failure of it."

"That wasn't your fault. And there are such things as second chances."

"Flora, do you know how old I am? Thirty-six. I shall be thirty-seven in a couple of months. I'll never make a fortune. I'm a middle-aged country doctor with little ambition to be anything else. I'll probably spend the rest of my days in Tarbole, and end up as set in my ways as my old father. I never seem to have any time to myself, and if I do, then I go fishing. That's a dull future to ask any woman to share."

"It needn't be dull," said Flora, stubbornly. "It can never be dull to be needed and to be important to people."

"It's different for me. It's my life."

"If somebody loved you, it would be her life, too."

"You make it sound easy. Almost facile."

568

"I don't mean to."

He said abruptly, "What will you do when all this is over? I mean, this time with the Armstrongs."

"I'll go away." It was hard not to be hurt by his sudden change of subject.

"Where?"

Flora shrugged. "To London. To do what I was trying to do when I met Rose. Find a job. Find somewhere to live. Why?"

"I suppose I'm just beginning to realize what a void you're going to leave in all our lives. A darkness. Like a light going out." He smiled, perhaps at himself. Shying from sentiment, he became practical. "We must go." He reached out and opened the door. "We must go *now.*"

She saw the long passage stretching ahead; she heard once more the voices and the music. Her courage faltered.

"You won't abandon me?"

"Antony will be there."

"Will you dance with me?"

"Everyone will want to dance with you."

"But . . ." She could not bear to let go of this tenuous thread of friendship which at last lay between them.

"I'll tell you what. We'll have supper together. How would that be?"

"You promise?"

"I promise. Now let's go."

Afterward, when it was all over and a thing of the past, Flora's memory of Tuppy's party for Antony and Rose was reduced to a number of brief and totally unrelated incidents—blurred impression without order or priority.

It was coming down the stairs into the hall with Hugh beside her, like a couple of deep sea divers descending into a world of light and noise, with a multitude of upturned faces waiting to welcome her. Each way she turned there was someone waiting to introduce herself or himself, perhaps to kiss or

569

congratulate her, or shake her hand. But if she remembered a single name, she was quite incapable of fitting it to a face.

It was a number of large young men in kilts and small old men, similarly attired.

It was being ceremoniously led into the drawing room to be presented to Mrs. Clanwilliam. Mrs. Clanwilliam's hair was either a wig or a bird's net, crowned by a tiara of antique diamonds, and she sat by the fire with her stick by her side and a strong whisky in her hand. She was not in the best of tempers and had been in two minds about coming to Tuppy's party. There wasn't much point, she told Flora, in coming to a party if you couldn't dance, and had to sit by the fire like an old crock. The reason, she added in the hooting voice of a very deaf person, that she was unable to dance was because she had broken her hip falling off a stepladder while attempting to paint her bathroom ceiling. She was, she added as a casual afterthought, eighty-seven next birthday.

It was the Crowthers, dancing together in the middle on an "Eightsome Reel." Mr. Crowther uttering cries which sounded as if he were calling odds, and Mrs. Crowther whirling the skirts of her tartan silk dress, and disclosing shoes designed for highland dancing, with ties that came up over her ankles.

It was champagne. It was a very old man with a face the color of loganberries telling someone that Tuppy was a splendid little woman, and if he'd had any sense he'd have married her years ago.

It was dancing "Strip the Willow" with Jason, who swung and turned Flora down a long line of partners. The room spun like a top around her. Disembodied arms appeared from nowhere to catch her. Silver cuff buttons dug into her arms. She was held and turned again and delivered back to Jason.

It was Anna Stoddart in a surprisingly becoming dress, sitting on a sofa with Isobel, and looking as pretty as Flora had ever seen her.

It was turning from the bar and finding herself face to face with Brian Stoddart. She instantly searched for evidence of his black eye.

He frowned. "What's that piercing glance for?"

"Anna told me you'd walked into a door."

"Dr. Kyle should learn to keep his nose out of other people's business and his hands in his pockets."

"So it *was* Hugh."

"Don't put on that innocent face, Rose, you know bloody well it was. It's just the sort of thing he'd enjoy boasting about. Interfering sod." He looked about him morosely. "I'd ask you to come and dance, but jumping up and down isn't my idea of dancing and the band doesn't seem to be able to play anything else."

"I know," said Flora sympathetically. "It's tedious, isn't it? The same faces, and the same clothes, and the same conversation."

He gave her a wary glance. "Rose, do I detect a note of sarcasm in your voice?"

"Perhaps. Just a very small one."

"You used to be able to do much better than that. You're losing your touch."

"That's no bad thing."

"You sound like a girl who's been brainwashed."

"I'm not the same girl you knew, Brian. I never was."

"Unhappily, I was beginning to suspect that." He stubbed out his cigarette. "It breaks my heart, Rose, but I fear you've reformed."

"You could try it yourself."

He looked at her, his pale eyes hard and bright as a bird's. "Rose, spare me that."

"Don't you ever think of Anna?"

"Almost all the time."

"Then why don't you get a glass of champagne and go and sit beside her and tell her she's looking beautiful?"

"Because it wouldn't be true."

"You could make it true. And," she added sweetly, "it wouldn't cost you a single penny."

571

Antony had been nearby all evening, and she had danced with him, but there had been no opportunity to talk to him. She knew that before the evening was very much older, it was essential that she get him to herself. She found him at last in the dining room, standing at the buffet table, loading a plate with smoked salmon and potato salad.

"Who's that for?"

"Anna Stoddart. She's not going to stay till the end of the party, and Isobel insists that she has something to eat."

"I want to talk to you."

"I want to talk to you, too, but there hasn't been a chance."

"How about now?"

He looked around him. Nobody seemed at that moment to be either needing or demanding his attention. He said, "All right."

"Where can we go?"

"You know the old pantry, where Mrs. Watty and Isobel clean the silver?"

"Yes."

"Well, gather up some champagne and a couple of glasses, and try to look as if you're going to the kitchen on urgent business. I'll meet you there."

"Won't we be missed?"

"Not for ten minutes. And even if we are, everyone will think we're indulging in a little snogging and will politely look the other way. See you."

He left her, bearing Anna's supper in his hand. Flora collected two glasses and an opened bottle of wine. Looking casual, she headed down the kitchen passage. The pantry led off the passage before one actually reached the kitchen, so nobody saw Flora go in, or even knew she was there.

It was a narrow room, with a window at one end, and long cupboards down each wall. There was just room in the middle of the floor for a small oilclothed table, and it all smelt of polish and scrubbed wood, and the stuff Isobel used to get the tarnish off Tuppy's best forks.

She sat on the table and waited for Antony to join her. When he did, it was with the air of a conspirator. He shut the door gently behind him, and leaned against it, like a beleaguered heroine in a bad film. He grinned at her.

"Alone at last." They surveyed each other across the room and his grin became rueful. "I'm not sure if I've ever before endured an experience like this evening. I just pray I never have to go through it again."

"Well, perhaps it'll teach you a lesson. Not to get engaged to girls like Rose."

"Don't you be so sanctimonious. You're in this up to your neck, just like I am."

"Antony, I want to know what Tuppy said."

His smile died. He came forward, reached for the champagne bottle and filled the two glasses which Flora had brought. He picked one up and gave it to her.

"She was very angry."

"Really angry?"

"Really angry. Tuppy can be quite a formidable person." He hitched himself up onto the table beside her. "I've never had such a rollicking in my life. You know the sort of thing. Never lied to me in your life, and now just because you think I'm in the last stages of senility, et cetera, et cetera."

"Is she still angry?"

"No, of course not. Never let the sun go down on a quarrel. Kiss and make friends. I've been forgiven, but I'm still feeling about three inches high."

"Is she angry with me, too?"

"No, she's sorry for you. I told her the blame was entirely mine, which it was, and that you had simply been coerced into a situation which was right over the top of your head. You knew I'd told Tuppy?"

"Yes. Hugh said that he said you had to."

"He's known for some time that you weren't Rose."

573

"I didn't have a scar on my arm."

"It's like something out of the Arabian Nights. The lad with the starred scimitar on his left buttock is the rightful prince. How was I to know Rose had a scar on her arm, silly bitch." He took some champagne and sat gazing dolefully down into the glass. "Hugh arrived early this evening. I couldn't think what the hell he was doing until he fixed me with a cold eye and said that he wanted to talk to me. It was like being sent for by the headmaster. We came in here because there wasn't anywhere else to go, and I told him the whole long, complicated story. About you and Rose, and your parents separating, and about Rose going off to Greece, and you being in the flat when I came to London. And he said I had to tell Tuppy. Now. This evening. No more delay. He said that if I didn't, he would."

"If you hadn't told her, I couldn't have gone through with it tonight."

Antony frowned. "What do you mean?"

"I don't know. I suppose you can only lie for so long. At least, to somebody who trusts you. Somebody you love. And although I seem to have done nothing but lie for the past seven days, I'm not actually very good at it."

"I should never have asked you to come."

"I should never have said that I would."

"Well, having decided that, let's have some more champagne."

But Flora got off the table. "I have had quite enough." She smoothed down her dress, and Antony laid down his glass and reached out to take hold of her shoulders and pull her toward him. He said, "You know, Miss Flora Waring, you are looking quite exceptionally pretty tonight."

"It's Tuppy's tennis dress."

"It's nothing to do with Tuppy's tennis dress, charming though it is. It's you. All bright-eyed and radiant. Sensational."

"Champagne, perhaps."

574

"No. Not champagne. If I didn't know you better I'd say you were in love. Or loved."

"That's a pretty thought."

"I still haven't worked out why the hell it isn't me."

"We decided that ages ago. It's something to do with chemistry."

He pulled her into his arms and gave her a resounding kiss. "I shall have to go to night classes. Learn all about it."

"Yes, you do that."

They smiled. He said, "I've probably told you before, but you are the most super girl."

In love. Or loved.

Antony was no fool. All evening Flora had been aware of Hugh. He stood, head and shoulders above the rest of Tuppy's guests, his presence refusing to be either missed or ignored. But since they had made their entrance down the stairs together, they had neither looked nor spoken to each other, although his had been among the masculine arms which had swung her through the dance she had done with Jason.

It was as if they had an unspoken pact. As if he too had recognized that their relationship had become all at once so precious a thing, so delicate, that a clumsy word or a proprietary glance would be enough to snap it. The small, shared understanding was enough to fill Flora's heart with hope. Those reflections, which would have done credit to a daydreaming fifteen-year-old, surprised her. She was, after all, twenty-two, and her grownup past lay littered with friendships and affairs and half-hearted infatuations. She thought of London: coming out of a restaurant to satin-wet streets and the dazzle of neon signs with her hand in some man's hand, deep in his overcoat pocket. And that summer in Greece. She remembered a clifftop carpeted in wild anemones and her companion with his sun-browned body and thatch of sun-bleached hair. It was as though over the last few years she had given away small pieces of herself—had perhaps, broken a few hearts, and in return had her own heart chipped once or twice.

575

But it had never been love, just looking for love. Having been brought up by a single parent had made the search more confusing for Flora, because she had no example to follow, no idea of what she had really been looking for. But now, in the course of this incredible week, she had come upon it. Or rather, it had come upon Flora like some sudden explosion of light, taking her so unprepared that it had rendered her incapable of any sensible sort of reaction.

And it was different. Hugh was older. He had been married before. He was a hard-working doctor, tending to the needs of a remote, rural community. He would never be rich, and his future held no surprises. But with piercing certainty, Flora knew that he was the only man who could fill her life with the things that she really wanted: love, security, comfort, and laughter. She had found them all in his arms. And she wanted to be able to return to those arms whenever she felt the need. She wanted him beside her. She wanted to live with him —yes, in that terrible house—and stay in Tarbole for the rest of her days.

It had certainly never been like this before.

At midnight the members of the band, sweating with exhaustion after two encores of "The Duke of Perth," laid down their instruments, mopped their brows with large handkerchiefs, and filed out in the direction of the kitchen, where Mrs. Watty waited to serve them supper and large tankards of export. As soon as that happened Antony and Jason, well-versed in procedure, produced the Fernrigg record player and the pile of records which Antony had brought with him from Edinburgh on the back seat of his car.

Most of the guests, even more exhausted than the band after the energetic dance, gravitated towards the dining room in search of sustenance and cool drinks. But Flora found herself sitting on the stairs with a young man who had driven all the way to Fernrigg from the far reaches of Ardnamurchan, where he ran a small salmon fishery.

576

He was in the middle of describing this venture to her when he realized that nearly everyone else had gone to eat supper.

"I'm sorry. Would you like something to eat? Would you like it here? I'll fetch you something if you like."

"It's so kind of you, but in fact, I said I'd have supper with Hugh Kyle."

"Hugh?" The young man looked about him. "Where is he?"

"I've no idea, but he'll turn up."

"I'll go and look for him for you." The young man stood up, dusting down the pleats of his kilt. "He's probably stuck in some dark corner with an old fishing crony, exchanging unlikely yarns."

"Don't worry about me. Go and get some supper for yourself . . ."

"I'll do that at the same time. I'd better hurry or all the cold turkey will have gone."

He left her. The record player had started up. A different music filled the air and after the jig of the accordion and the scrape of the fiddle, it sounded strangely alien and sophisticated, and reminded Flora of a life that seemed to have finished a long time ago.

Dance in the old-fashioned way,
Won't you stay in my arms.

Antony was dancing with a girl in a blue dress; Brian Stoddart, with the most elegant woman in the room, all black crepe and dangling earrings.

Just melt against my skin
And let me feel your heart.

She knew that Hugh would come and find her because he had promised. But after a little she began to feel ridiculous

577

sitting on the stairs waiting to be claimed, and slightly anxious, like a young girl afraid of being stood up on her first date. The young man from Ardnamurchan did not return and Flora wondered if he had joined in the fishing discussion. Finally, unable to contain her impatience, she got up and went to search for Hugh herself. She went from one room to another, casually at first, and then less casually, and finally without shame, asking anybody she happened to find herself standing next to.

"Have you see Hugh Kyle? You haven't seen Hugh anywhere, have you?"

But nobody had seen him. She never found him. And it was not until later that she learned that there had been a telephone call, that a premature baby was on its way, and Hugh had already gone.

The storm blew up during the course of the evening, and by the early hours of the morning had reached full force. For Tuppy's guests, putting on cloaks and coats preparatory to departure, it came as something of a shock. They had arrived on a calm evening, and now they had to leave in this. The opening and shutting of the front door caused gusts of cold air to sweep into the house. Smoke billowed from the hall fire and the long curtains bellied in the draught. Outside, the garden shone with black rain, the gravel was puddled, and the air filled with flying leaves and small branches and twigs newly torn from trees.

At last, running down the streaming steps, hunched into coats and scarves, heads bent against the wind, the last couple left. Antony shut the front door and, with some ceremony, locked and bolted it. The household trailed exhaustedly up to bed.

But there was too much noise for sleep. The seaward side of the house took the brunt of the storm's fury. The squalls came in great gusts, shaking the very structure of the solid old walls, and the voice of the wind rose to something very like a scream. And beyond all this, distant but menacing, was the surging boom of long rollers driven inshore by the swell of the turbulent ocean to smash themselves into clouds of white spume on the margins of Fhada sands.

Flora curled up for comfort, wide-eyed, dry-eyed, and listened to it. She had finished the evening with a mug of black coffee, and the thud of her own heart was as disturbing as a clock which chimes through the dark hours of the night. Her head was filled with jigging music, with random images, with voices. She had never lain so wide awake.

The first gray rays of dawn were beginning to seep into the sky before she finally fell into a restless and dream-haunted sleep, peopled by strangers. When she awoke, it was day once more, still dark and gray to be sure, but the endless night was behind her. She opened her eyes, grateful for the cold light, and saw Antony standing by her bed.

He looked weary and unshaven and slightly bleary-eyed, his copper head tousled as though he had not taken the time to comb it. He wore a tweedy turtleneck sweater and an old pair of corduroys, and he carried two steaming nursery mugs and he said, "Good morning."

Flora dragged herself out of sleep. Automatically she reached for her watch, but, "It's half past ten," he told her. "I brought you some coffee. I thought you might need it."

"Oh, how kind." She stretched, tried to blink the sleep out of her eyes, pulled herself up on the pillows. He handed her the mug and she wrapped her hands around it and sat holding it, yawning.

He found her dressing gown and put it round her shoulders, turned on the electric fire, and came to sit beside her on the edge of the bed.

"How are you feeling?"

"Ghastly," she told him.

"Drink some coffee and you'll feel better."

She did so, and it was scalding and strong. After a little she asked, "Is everybody up?"

"They're gradually surfacing. Jason's still asleep, I shouldn't think he'll appear till lunchtime. Isobel's been up for

579

an hour, and I doubt whether Mrs. Watty and Watty went to bed at all. Anyway, they've been beavering away since eight o'clock this morning, and by the time you put in an appearance, I doubt if you'd realize that there's been a party at all."

"I should have got up and come to help."

"I'd have let you sleep, only this arrived by the morning post." He put his hand into his back trouser pocket and produced an envelope. "I thought perhaps you'd want to see it."

She took it from him. She saw her father's handwriting, the Cornwall postmark. It was addressed to Miss Rose Schuster.

Flora laid down the mug of coffee. She said, "It's from my father."

"I thought it might be. You wrote to him?"

"Yes. Last Sunday. After you'd gone back to Edinburgh." She looked at him in apology and went on feeling guilty, trying to explain. "I had to tell somebody, Antony, and you'd made me promise not to tell anyone here. But I figured my father didn't count. So I wrote to him."

"I hadn't realized the need to confess was so strong. Did you tell him everything?"

"Yes."

"I wouldn't think he'd be very impressed."

"No," Flora agreed miserably. She began to slit the envelope.

"Do you want me to go away and let you read it in peace?"

"No, I'd much rather you stayed." Cautiously, she unfolded the letter. She saw, "My dearest Flora."

"Well, I'm still his dearest Flora so perhaps he isn't too upset."

"Did you think he would be?"

"I don't know. I don't think I thought about it."

With the comforting presence of Antony beside her, she read the letter:

580

UNDER GEMINI

Seal Cottage
Lanyon
Lands End
Cornwall

My dearest Flora,

I have already addressed the envelope of this letter as instructed by you. It is on the desk beside me now, proof that a lie, however well-meant, can never be contained or controlled but spreads like a disease, inevitably involving more and more people.

I was glad that you wrote to me at such length. Your letter took some reading and as you seem anxious for some sort of response, I shall try to deal with your problems in a fairly abbreviated way.

Firstly, Rose. The coincidence of your meeting like that was something that I always hoped would never happen. But it did, and so I owe you an explanation.

Your mother and I decided to separate within a year of getting married. We would have parted then and there, only she was eight months pregnant, and all the arrangements for the baby's birth had been made locally, so we continued to live together for that last month. During that time, we agreed that she should have the custody of the child, and bring it up by herself. She was going back to make a home with her parents, and she seemed quite happy to do this.

But of course, it wasn't a baby, it was twins. When Pamela was told, she became quite hysterical, and by the time I was allowed to see her, had made up her mind that she could not possibly cope with two babies. She would take one. And I would take the other.

The prospect, I don't mind admitting, appalled me. But Pamela, with that announcement off her chest, dried her eyes, and the babies, in two bassinets, were trundled into the room.

It was the first time either of us had seen you. Rose

581

lay like a little flower, sleeping, with silky dark hair and seashell fists curled up under her chin. You, on the other hand, were bawling your head off and seemed to be covered with spots. Your mother was no fool. She reached out for Rose, Sister put the sleeping baby into her arms, and the choice had been made.

But I made a choice too. I couldn't bear you crying. You sounded heartbroken. I picked you up out of your crib, and held you up and you gave a great burp and stopped crying. You opened your eyes and we looked at each other. I'd never held a child before that was so tiny and so new, and I was completely unprepared for the effect it would have on me. I found myself filled with pride, fiercely possessive. You were my baby. Nothing and nobody was going to take you away from me.

So that is how it all came about. Should I have told you? I never knew the answer. Probably I should. But you were such a happy child, so complete and self-contained, it seemed insane to introduce unnecessary questions and possible insecurities into your young life. Pamela had gone, taking Rose with her. The divorce went through and I never saw either of them again.

Heredity and environment are puzzling factors. Rose sounds as though she were turning into a very passable replica of her mother. And yet I cannot allow myself to believe that under different circumstances, you would have turned into someone selfish, thoughtless, or dishonest.

Which is why your present situation leaves me so concerned. Not just for yourself and the young man, but for the Armstrongs. They sound the sort of people who deserve more than an empty deception. I advise you both to tell them the truth as soon as you can. The consequences may be unhappy, but you have no one to blame but yourselves.

When you have done this, I want you to come home. This—as I used to say when you were small—is not an asking, but a telling. There are many things we need to

582

talk about, and you can take a little time to lick your wounds and recover from what has obviously been a traumatic episode.

Marcia sends her love with mine. You are my own child, and I am your loving

Father

She came to the end and wondered if she was going to cry. Antony waited. Flora looked up into his sympathetic face.

She said, "I've got to go home."

"To Cornwall?"

"Yes."

"When?"

"Right away."

She handed him the letter to read. While he did this, she finished her coffee and got out of bed, pulling on her dressing gown and tying the cord. She went to the window and saw the low scud of black clouds. The tide had reached the flood, and cold gray water broke and streamed over the rocks beyond the garden. A few tattered gulls braved the weather, their wings banked to the wind. The lawn below the window was littered with leaves and the remains of broken slate which had blown from some roof.

Antony said, "That's a nice letter."

"He's a nice man."

"I feel I should come with you. Take the brunt of the storm."

Flora was touched. She turned from the window to reassure him. "There's no need. Besides, you have enough problems of your own to sort out. Right here."

"Do you want to go today?"

"Yes. Perhaps I can get a train from Tarbole."

"The London train leaves at one o'clock."

"Would you drive me to Tarbole?"

"I'd drive you to the ends of the earth if it would help."

"Tarbole will do very nicely. And now I must get dressed. I must go and see Tuppy."

583

"I'll leave you." He laid down the letter, picked up the two empty mugs, and made for the door.

"Antony," she said. He stopped and turned back. She took off the engagement ring. It was a little tight, and it took some effort to get it over her knuckle, but it was off at last. She went to lay it in his hand, and then reached up to kiss his cheek.

"You'd better put it somewhere safe. One day, you're going to need it again."

"I don't know. I can't help feeling that it's not very lucky."

Flora said encouragingly, "You're just a superstitious Highlander. Where's your thrifty streak? Just think how much it cost."

He grinned, and put it into his pocket. "I'll be downstairs when you want me," he told her.

She dressed and tidied her room, as though to leave it neat were the only thing that mattered. She picked up the letter from her father, and went out of the room and down the passage to where, she knew, Tuppy was waiting for her.

She knocked on the door. Tuppy called "Yes?" and Flora went in. Tuppy was reading the morning paper, but now she laid it down and took off her spectacles. Across the room, their eyes met, and she looked so grave that Flora's heart sank, and perhaps this showed in her face, for Tuppy smiled, and said lovingly, "Flora!" and the relief of not being called "Rose" any longer was so great that Flora simply shut the door and went across the room like a homing pigeon, straight into Tuppy's arms.

"I don't know what to say. I don't know how to say I'm sorry. I don't know how to ask you to forgive me."

"I don't want you to start apologizing. What you and Antony did was very naughty, but I've had the night to think it over, and I realize now that you did it with the best intentions in the world. But then, the road to hell is paved with good intentions, and I was so angry with Antony last night, I really could have slapped him."

584

"Yes, he told me."

"I suppose he thought I was on my last gasp, and ready to accept anything, even a lie. And as for Rose, thank goodness he's not going to marry her. Any girl who could treat Antony the way she did—running away with another man—without even having the good manners to explain. I think it was very thoughtless and cruel."

"That was one of the reasons I came to Fernrigg. Because I wanted to help Antony."

"I know. I understand. And I think it was very sweet of you. And how you've carried on all this week, being Rose, is beyond my comprehension. And being ill in the middle of it. You really have had a wretched time."

"But you forgive me?"

Tuppy kissed her soundly. "My dear, I could never do anything else. Flora, or Rose, you are yourself. You've brought us all so much pleasure, so much happiness. My only sadness is that you and Antony don't seem to want to fall in love and get married. That's much more disappointing than having you tell me all those dreadful lies. But then, I know, falling in love isn't anything you can manipulate. Thank heavens. How boring life would become if it were. And now don't let's talk about it any more. I want to hear all about last night, and . . ."

"Tuppy."

"Yes?" Tuppy's blue eyes were suddenly watchful.

"This morning I had a letter from my father. Antony may have told you, he's a schoolmaster, he lives in Cornwall. I wrote to him at the beginning of the week, because I felt I had to tell someone what was happening, and of course I couldn't tell any of you."

"And what does your father say?"

"I thought you'd better read it."

In silence, Tuppy put on her spectacles, and took the letter from Flora. She read it through, from beginning to end. When she had finished, "What an extraordinary story," she murmured. "But what a very nice man he must be."

"Yes, he is."

"Are you going to go home?"

"Yes, I have to. Today. There's a train at one. Antony says he'll drive me to Tarbole."

Tuppy's face became all at once drawn and old, her mouth bunched, her eyes shadowed. "I can't bear you to leave us."

"I don't want to go."

"But you'll come back. Promise me that you'll come back. Come back and see us all, whenever you want. Fernrigg will be waiting for you. You only have to say the word."

"You still want me?"

"We want you because we love you. It's as simple as that." Having made this clear, she reverted to her usual practical manner. "And your father's right. I think you must go home for a little."

"I always hate saying goodbye. And I feel so badly about Jason and Isobel and the Wattys and Nurse. They've been so kind, and I can't imagine how I'm going to tell them . . ."

"I don't see why you should have to tell them anything. Just say a letter has come for you, and you have to leave. And when Antony comes back from the station, he can explain it to them all. He got you into this situation and that, for certain, is the very least he can do."

"But all the people at the party last night?"

"The news will filter through the grapevine that the engagement is off. It will be a nine-day wonder, that's all."

"But they'll have to know, sooner or later, that I was never Rose. They'll have to know sometime."

"That bit of information will doubtless filter through too, and they'll wonder a little and then forget about it. After all, it isn't really that important. Nobody's been hurt. Nobody's heart has been broken."

"You make it sound so simple."

"The truth always simplifies everything. And we have Hugh to thank for that. If it hadn't been for Hugh, taking charge, goodness knows how long this stupid farce would have gone on. We owe him everything. We always seem to be in his debt, if not on one score, then another. He's very fond of you,

586

Flora. I wonder if you realize that? You probably don't because he's naturally shy of showing his emotions, but . . ."

The words died away. Flora sat intensely still, staring down at her own clasped hands. The knuckles showed white and her dark lashes made smudges against the sudden pallor of her face.

With a perception sharpened by years of dealing with young people, Tuppy caught her distress. It chilled the air, and stemmed from some emotion far deeper than a natural reluctance to say goodbye. Much concerned, Tuppy laid her own hand over Flora's and found it icy cold.

Flora did not look up. "It's all right," she said, sounding as if she were trying to reassure Tuppy about some unbearable pain she was suffering.

"My dear child, you must tell me. Has someone upset you? Is it Antony?"

"No, of course not . . ."

Tuppy cast her mind back, searching for clues. They had been talking about Hugh, and . . . Hugh. Hugh? As though Flora had spoken the name aloud, Tuppy knew.

"It's Hugh."

"Oh, Tuppy, don't talk about it."

"But of course we must talk about it. I can't bear you to be so unhappy. Are . . . are you in love with him?"

Flora looked up, her eyes dark as bruises. "I think I must be," she said, sounding completely uncertain.

Tuppy was astounded. Not because Flora had fallen in love with Hugh, which Tuppy found totally understandable. But because it had happened without Tuppy knowing all about it.

"But I can't imagine, when . . ."

"No," said Flora, suddenly blunt. "Neither can I. I can't imagine when it happened, or why, or how. I only know that it can't have any future."

"Why can it have no future?"

"Because Hugh's the man he is. He's been hurt once and he doesn't intend getting hurt again. He's made a life for himself, he doesn't want to share it, and he doesn't need another wife. He won't let himself need one. And even if he did, he doesn't seem to think he has enough to offer her . . . I mean material things."

"You appear to have talked it over in some detail."

"Not really. It was just last night, before the party. I'd been drinking champagne, and somehow that made it easier to talk."

"Does he realize how you feel?"

"Tuppy, I have a little pride left. Short of flinging myself at his head, I seem to have reached the end of the road."

"Did he talk about Diana?"

"Not last night, but he has told me about her."

"He would never have done that unless he felt very close to you."

"You can be close to a person, but that doesn't mean you're in love with them."

"Hugh is stubborn and very proud," Tuppy warned her.

"You don't have to tell me that." Flora smiled, but there wasn't much joy behind it. "Last night, we were going to have supper together. He said he wasn't going to dance with me because everybody else would want to dance with me, but we'd have supper together. So stupid to let it be so important . . . but it was important, Tuppy. And I thought perhaps it was important to him, too. But when the time came, he'd gone. There was a phone call, a baby coming. I don't know. But he'd simply gone."

"My dear, he's a doctor."

"Couldn't he have told me? Couldn't he have said good-bye?"

"Perhaps he couldn't find you. Perhaps he couldn't take time to find you."

"I shouldn't mind, should I? But it did matter, terribly."

"Will you be able to go away, and forget him?"

"I don't know. I don't seem to know the answer to anything. I must be out of my mind."

"On the contrary, I think you are exceptionally wise.

588

Hugh is a very special person, but he keeps his qualities well hidden beneath that manner, that sharply honed tongue of his. It takes a person of considerable perception to realize that the qualities are really there."

"What am I going to do?" Flora spoke quietly, but it sounded to Tuppy like a cry from the heart.

"What you were always going to do. Go home to your father. Pack your clothes and find Antony and say goodbye and drive to the station. It's as easy as that."

"Easy?"

"Life is so complicated that sometimes it's the only thing left to do. Now give me a kiss and run along. Forget everything that's happened. And when you come back to Fernrigg, we'll start all over again, with new beginnings."

"I can never thank you properly." They kissed. "I don't know the right sort of words."

"The best way to thank me is to come back. That's all I want."

They were disturbed by small sounds from the end of the bed. Sukey had decided to wake up. Her claws scratched the silk of the eiderdown as she made her way cautiously up the length of the bed, apparently with the sole intention of clambering onto Flora's knee and reaching up to lick her face.

"Sukey! That's the first time you've been nice to me." Flora gathered the little dog up into her arms and pressed a kiss on the top of Sukey's head. "Why is she suddenly being so nice?"

"Sukey takes notions," said Tuppy, as though that explained everything. "Perhaps she realizes that you're not Rose after all. Or perhaps she just wanted to say goodbye to you. Is that what you wanted, my darling?"

Sukey, thus addressed, forgot about Flora and went to curl up in the crook of Tuppy's arm.

Flora said, "I must go."

"Yes. You mustn't keep Antony waiting."

"Goodbye, Tuppy."

"It's not goodbye. It's au revoir."

589

For the last time, Flora got up off the bed, and went to the door. But as she opened it, Tuppy spoke again.

"Flora."

Flora looked back. "Yes?"

"I never thought of pride as a sin. To me it's always seemed rather an admirable quality. But two proud people, misunderstanding, can make for a tragedy."

"Yes," said Flora. There did not seem to be anything else to say. She went out of the room and shut the door.

It took so little time to pack, so little time to clear her room of all traces of her presence. When she had finished it appeared impersonal, stripped—ready and waiting for the next person who should come to Fernrigg to stay. She left the white dress that she had worn the night before hanging on the outside of the wardrobe door. It was creased now, molded to Flora's shape, grubby around the hem, and stained where someone had spilled champagne down the front of the skirt. She opened the cupboard and took out her coat. With this over her arm, and carrying her suitcase, she went downstairs.

Everything was back to normal. The hall looked as it always did, furniture back in place, the fire smoldering, Plummer sitting beside its warmth, waiting for someone to take him for a walk. From the drawing room came the sound of voices. Flora set down her case and her coat, and went in and found Isobel and Antony standing by the fire deep in conversation. This ceased instantly as Flora appeared, and they stood there, with their faces turned towards her.

Antony said, "I've told Aunt Isobel."

"I'm glad you know," said Flora, and meant it.

Isobel appeared to be stunned by confusion. It had taken her some time to understand what Antony had spent the last fifteen minutes trying to explain to her. She was tired and suffering from lack of sleep, and in no condition to listen to, let alone comprehend, the long and involved story.

But one fact was sadly clear. Rose—no, Flora—was leaving. Going. Today. Now. Just like that. Antony was going to drive her to Tarbole to catch the London train. It was all so

590

sudden and unexpected that Isobel felt quite faint. Now, seeing Flora so pale and composed, it began to be real.

"There's no need to go," Isobel told her, knowing it was hopeless but still wanting to try to persuade her to stay. "It doesn't matter *who* you are. We don't want you to go."

"That's very sweet of you. But I must."

"The letter from your father. Antony told me."

Flora said to Antony, "What about the others?"

"I've told them you're leaving, but I haven't told them you're not Rose. I thought that could wait till later. It might make things a little easier for you." She smiled her thanks. "And Mrs. Watty's packing you a box lunch. She has no faith in restaurant cars."

"I'm ready when you are."

"I'll tell them," said Antony. "They want to say goodbye." He went out of the room.

Flora went over to Isobel's side. "You'll come back, won't you?" said Isobel.

"Tuppy's invited me."

"I wish you were going to marry Antony."

"I wish I was too, just to belong to such a marvelous family. But it can't work out that way."

Isobel sighed. "Things never seem to work out the way you want them to. You think they're all beautifully arranged, and then in front of your eyes, they all fall to pieces."

Like my flower arrangements, thought Flora. She heard the voices of the others, coming down the passage from the kitchen. "Goodbye, Isobel." They kissed with great affection, Isobel still not quite clear how this unsatisfactory situation had come about.

"You will come back?"

"Of course I will"

Somehow, the last of the farewells were accomplished. They all stood in the hall with sad faces and said what a shame it was she had to leave, but of course, she would be back. Nobody seemed to notice that she was no longer wearing Antony's engagement ring, and if they did, they made no com-

591

ment. Flora found herself kissing Nurse, and then Mrs. Watty, who pressed a bag containing plum cake and apples into the pocket of Flora's coat. Finally Jason. She knelt to his height and they hugged, his arms so tight around her neck that she thought he would never let her go.

"I want to come to the station with you."

"No," said Antony.

"But I want . . ."

"I don't want you to come," Flora told him quickly. "I hate saying goodbye at stations, and I always cry and that would be dreadful for both of us. And thank you for teaching me how to do 'Strip the Willow.' It was the best dance of the whole evening."

"You won't forget how to do it?"

"I shall remember for the rest of my life."

Behind her, Antony opened the front door, and the cold wind flowed in like a sluice of icy water. Carrying her case he went down the steps to the car, and she ran down after him, her head bent against the rain. He flung her suitcase into the back of the car, and helped her in and slammed the door behind her.

Braving the weather, they had all come out into the open to see her off in style, with Plummer standing at the front of the little group, looking as though he expected to have his photograph taken. The wind tore at Nurse's apron, blew Isobel's hair into confusion, but still they stayed there, waving as the car came around in a circle and sped away from the house down the spine-jolting, potholed drive. Flora twisted around in her seat and waved through the back window until the car turned into the road and the house and its occupants were lost from sight.

It was over. Flora turned and slumped in her seat, her hands deep in her pockets. Her fingers closed over Mrs. Watty's "box lunch." She felt the shape of the slice of cake, the round firmness of an apple. She stared ahead, through the streaming windscreen.

But there was nothing to be seen. The rain closed in on them. Antony drove with the side lights on, and every now and

592

then a large wet sheep materialized out of the gloom, or they passed the side lights of another small car, going in the opposite direction. The wind was as strong as ever.

"What a horrible day to be leaving," said Antony.

She thought of the day they had climbed the hill; of the islands, looking magical, floating on the summer sea; of the crystal air and the snow-capped peaks of the Cuillins. She said, "I'd rather it was like this. It makes it easier to go."

They came down the hill into Tarbole and saw the harbor full of boats, stormbound by the weather.

"What time is it, Antony?"

"A quarter past twelve. We're far too early, but perhaps it doesn't matter. We can go and drink coffee with Sandy, just the way we did that first morning when we arrived from Edinburgh."

"It seems so long ago. A lifetime."

"Tuppy meant it when she asked you to come back."

"You'll take care of her, won't you, Antony? You won't let anything happen to her?"

"I'll keep her safe for you," he promised. "She can't forgive me, poor Tuppy, for not cutting my losses and marrying you, and bearing you back to Fernrigg as my bride."

"She knows it could never happen."

"Yes." He sighed. "She knows."

They were into the town now, running alongside the harbor. Waves broke over the low stone wall and the road was awash with salt water, the gutters choked with dirty foam. There was the familiar smell of fish and diesel oil, and the scream of air brakes tore the air as a huge lorry came grinding down the hill from Fort William.

They came to the crossroads, and then by the bank where Flora had once illicitly parked the van. The little station, gray stone, soot-stained, waited for them. The lines of the railway curved away beyond the platform, out of sight. Antony switched off the engine. They got out of the car and went into the ticket office, Antony carrying Flora's suitcase. Despite her protestations, he bought her a ticket back to Cornwall.

593

"But it's so expensive, and I can pay for it myself."

"Oh, don't talk balls," he said rudely, because he was feeling emotional and didn't want to show it.

Making out the ticket took some time. They stood and waited. A small fire burned, but the office smelt musty. Peeling posters exhorted them to go to Scottish resorts for their holidays; to take boat trips down the Clyde; to spend weeks at Glorious Rothsay. Neither of them spoke for the simple reason that there didn't seem to be anything left to say.

The ticket was at last ready. Antony took it and gave it to Flora. "To do the thing properly I should have bought a return, and then we'd be sure of your coming back."

"I'll come back." She put the ticket into her bag. "Antony, I don't want you to wait."

"But I must put you onto the train."

"I don't want to wait. I hate goodbyes and I hate railway stations. Like I said to Jason, I always make a fool of myself and cry. I'd hate to do that."

"But you've got forty minutes to wait till it leaves."

"I'll be all right. Please go now."

"All right." But he sounded unconvinced. "If that's what you want."

Leaving her case in the ticket office, they went out into the station yard. By his car, he said, "This is it, then?"

"Tuppy said au revoir."

"You'll write? You'll keep in touch?"

"Of course."

They kissed. "You know something?" said Antony.

She smiled. "Yes, I know. I'm a super woman."

He got into his car and drove away, very fast, and almost instantly seemed to have disappeared around the corner by the bank. Flora was alone. The rain was thin, but steady and very wetting. Above her, the wind banged about at chimney pots and television aerials.

There came a moment of hesitation.

Two proud people, misunderstanding, can make for tragedy.

594

She began to walk.

The hill, black with rain, seemed steep as the side of a roof.
The gutters ran like waterfalls. As she climbed up out of the
shelter of the town the force of the wind struck like a solid
thing, causing Flora to lose her breath and her balance. The air
was filled with blown spume and she could feel its salt on her
cheeks and taste it on her mouth. When she finally reached the
house at the top of the hill, she stopped at the gate to get her
breath. Looking back, she saw the gray and turbulent sea,
empty of boats. She saw the tall columns of spray rearing up
beyond the far harbor wall.

She opened the gate and closed it behind her and went up
the sloping path to the front door. Inside the porch, she rang
the bell and waited. Her shoes were sodden and the hem of her
coat dripped onto the tiled floor. She rang the bell again.

She heard someone call, "I'm just on my way . . ." and
the next instant the door was flung open and she was faced by a
woman of indeterminate age, spectacled and flustered. She
wore a flowered pinafore and bedroom slippers that looked like
dead rabbits, and with the certainty of someone who has just
been formally introduced, Flora knew that this was Jessie Mc-
Kenzie.

"Yes?"

"Is Dr. Kyle in?"

"He's still in surgery."

"Oh. When will he be finished?"

"I couldn't say for sure. We're all at sixes and sevens this
morning. Surgery's usually at ten o'clock, but this morning,
because of the accident, the doctor wasn't able to get started
'till half past eleven . . ."

"Accident?" said Flora faintly.

"Did you not hear?" Jessie was agog with the horrific
news. "Dr. Kyle had not even started on his breakfast when the
telephone rang, and it was the harbormaster, and seemingly,
there'd been an accident on one of the fishing boats; a derrick
cable snapped and a muckle load of fish boxes fell to the deck,

right on top of one of the young laddies working there. It crushed his leg. Seemingly, it was a mangled mess . . ."

She was unstoppable, settled down to a good gossip, with her arms folded across her pinafored breasts. Jessie was not fat, but her unsupported body appeared to be slipping in all directions. She was obviously a woman who put comfort before beauty and yet, Flora knew instinctively, should there be a whist drive or a church soiree in the offing, Jessie would be the first to lace herself into a formidable all-in-one, in the same way that some people only wear their teeth when company is expected.

". . . Dr. Kyle was there first thing, but they had to get the ambulance to take the poor laddie to Lochgarry . . . and Dr. Kyle went too . . . an operation, of course. He wasn't home till the back of eleven."

It became necessary to interrupt.

"Would it be possible to see him?"

"Well, I couldn't say for sure. Mind, I saw Nurse on her way home, so maybe surgery's finished. And the doctor's not had a bite to eat all morning. I've a pot of soup on the store, and I'm expecting him any moment . . ." She peered at Flora, her eyes, behind their round spectacles, bright with curiosity. "Are you a patient?" She probably thought Flora was pregnant. "Is it urgent?"

"Yes, it is urgent, but I'm not a patient. I have to catch a train." The moments were slipping by and Flora began to be desperate. "Perhaps I could go and see if he's still busy."

"Yes." Jessie thought this over. "Maybe you could."

"How do I get to the surgery?"

"Just follow the wee path round the house."

Flora began to back away. "Thank you. I . . ."

"It's a terrible morning," Jessie observed, conversationally.

"Yes. Terrible." And with this, she made her escape out into the rain.

The concrete path led around the side of the house and beneath a covered way to the surgery door. Flora went in and found it empty, but muddy footmarks all over the polished linoleum, chairs standing around the walls, and a few disarranged magazines on a table bore witness to the queues which had tramped through during the course of the morning. There was a smell of disinfectant and wet mackintoshes. At the far end of the room, a small office had been formed by means of glass partitions, and inside was a desk and filing cabinets and boxes of card indexes.

The door with his name on it stood at the far end of the long room, and Flora went toward it, her wet shoes leaving a fresh track of damp footprints behind her. She found it in her heart to be sorry for whomever had to clean the floor at the end of the day.

With a conscious gathering of courage, she knocked at the door. There did not seem to be any reply, so she knocked again, and from within his voice bellowed, "I said, *Come in!*" It was not a good start. Flora went in.

He did not even look up from his desk. She could only see the top of his head, and that he was busy writing something.

"Yes?"

Flora shut the door behind her with a small slam. He looked up. For a moment he appeared to be transfixed, and then he took off his spectacles and sat back in his chair the better to stare at her.

"What are you doing here?"

"I've come to say goodbye."

She was already wishing she had not come. His office was impersonal and unnerving. It offered neither encouragement nor comfort. His desk was enormous, the walls were the color of margarine, the linoleum brown. She caught sight of a case of sinister-looking instruments and hastily averted her glance.

"But where are you going?"

"I'm going back to Cornwall. To my father."

"When did you come to this decision?"

"I had a letter from him this morning. I . . . I wrote to him at the beginning of the week to tell him what was happening. Where I was. What I was doing."

597

"And what did he have to say to that?"

"He said I had to go home."

A glimmer of amusement crossed Hugh's face. "Are you in for a hiding?"

"No of course not. He's not angry. He's just being very kind. I told Tuppy, and she said that she thought I should go. And I've said goodbye to everybody at Fernrigg and Antony brought me to Tarbole in his car. I've got my ticket and my suitcase is at the station, but the train doesn't leave till one, so I thought I'd come and say goodbye to you."

In silence, Hugh laid down his pen, and stood up. All at once he seemed as enormous as his ponderous desk, in proportion to it. He came around to where Flora stood, and sat on the edge of the desk, bringing their eyes to the same level. She thought he looked very tired, but, unlike Antony, he had apparently found time to shave. She wondered if, between the premature baby and the young boy with the crushed leg, he had had any sleep at all.

He said, "I'm sorry about last night. Did you wonder what had happened to me?"

"I thought you'd forgotten about having supper with me. And then someone told me about the phone call."

"I did forget," Hugh confessed. "When the call came through, I forgot about everything else. I always do. It wasn't until I was halfway there that I remembered our date, and then, of course, it was too late."

She said, "It didn't matter," but it didn't sound, even to Flora, very convincing.

"Believe it or not, it mattered to me."

"Was the baby all right?"

"Yes, a little girl. Very small, but she'll make it."

"And the boy, this morning, on the fishing boat?"

"How did you know about that?"

"I've been talking to your housekeeper. She told me."

"Yes, she would," said Hugh dryly. "We won't know about the boy for a day or two."

"You mean, he may die?"

598

"No, he's not going to die. But he may lose his leg."

"I am sorry."

Hugh folded his arms. "How long are you going to stay with your father?"

"I don't know."

"What will you do then?"

"Like I told you last night, I suppose. Go back to London. Look for a job. Look for somewhere to live."

"Will you come back to Fernrigg?"

"Tuppy's asked me."

"But will you?"

"I don't know. It depends."

"On what?"

She looked him straight in the eye. "On you, I suppose," she told him.

"Oh, Flora . . ."

"Hugh, don't push me away. We've been so close. We can surely talk."

"How old are you?"

"Twenty-two. And don't say you're old enough to be my father, because you're not."

"I wasn't going to say that. But I am old enough to recognize the fact that you have everything in front of you, and I'm not going to be the man who takes it away from you. You're young and you're beautiful and very special. You may imagine that you're marvelously mature, but in truth, your life is only just beginning. Somewhere, some time, you'll find a young man waiting for you. Someone who hasn't been married before, and has more to offer you than second best—who one day will be able to afford to give you all the good things of life that you truly deserve."

"Perhaps I don't want them."

"Mine would be no sort of a life for you." He was trying to be very kind. "I tried to make you see that last night."

"And I told you that if somebody loved you, that would make it the right sort of life."

"I already made that mistake."

599

"But I'm not Diana. I'm me. And that terrible thing I once said to you was absolutely true. By dying the way she did, Diana destroyed you. She's destroyed your trust in people, and your confidence in yourself. And she's made you so that to stop yourself from being hurt, you're prepared to hurt other people. I think that's a horrible way to be."

"Flora, I don't want to hurt you. Can't you understand? Supposing I did love you? Supposing I loved you too much to let you destroy yourself?"

Bleakly Flora stared at him. It seemed an extraordinary time to start talking about love, right in the middle of a quarrel. For they were quarreling, momentously, their voices raised to a pitch where, if Jessie McKenzie were sufficiently curious to put an ear to the wall, she would be able to hear every word. For Hugh's sake, Flora hoped that that was not happening.

She said at last, "I don't destroy that easily. If I've survived this last week, I can survive anything."

"You said that Tuppy had asked you back to Fernrigg."

"Yes."

"Will you come?"

"I told you, it depends . . ."

"That was a ridiculous thing to say. Now, when you do come . . ."

Flora lost her temper. There seemed to be no way of breaking down his stubborn pride without actually going to the lengths of telling him that he was behaving like a fool. "Hugh, I'm either coming back to you, or I'm never coming back at all."

The silence that followed that outburst was fraught with the astonishment of both of them. Then Flora stumbled on, with the hopeless despair of one who knows that she has burnt her boats behind her. "Though why I should bother, I can't imagine. I don't think you even like me very much." She glared at him crossly. "And your tie's coming undone," she added, as if this were the last straw.

It was, too. Perhaps he had dressed quickly and carelessly. Perhaps, during the course of the morning, it had simply

600

slipped of its own accord, the way her father's so often did, and . . .

Her reflections came to a dead halt as she suddenly realized the significance of what she had so thoughtlessly said. She stared at the wretched tie, waiting for Hugh to pig-headedly straighten it for himself. She decided that if he did this, she would walk out of this room, and down the hill, and she would catch the train and go away, and never think about him again.

But he made no move to do anything about the offending necktie. His arms remained rigidly folded across his chest. He said at last, "Well, why don't you remedy the situation?"

Carefully, slowly, Flora did so. She pulled up the knot, set it neatly in place, dead in the center of his collar. It was done. She stood back. He still didn't move. It took more determination than she would have believed possible, just to look up and meet his eyes. She saw him, for the first time disarmed and defenseless as a very young man. He said her name and held out his arms, and the next instant, with a sound that was halfway between a sob and a shout of triumph, Flora was in them.

She said, "I love you."

"You impossible child."

"I love you."

"What am I going to do with you?"

"You could marry me. I'll make a marvelous doctor's wife. Just think of it."

"I've been thinking of nothing else for the past three days."

"I love you."

"I thought I could let you go, but I can't."

"You're going to have to let me go, because I've got a train to catch."

"But you'll come back?"

"To you."

"How soon?"

"Three days, four days."

"Too long."

601

"No longer."

"I shall ring you up every night at your father's house."

"He'll be impressed."

"And when you do come, I'll be on the station platform, with a bunch of roses and an engagement ring."

"Oh, Hugh, not an engagement ring. I'm sorry, but I've had enough of engagement rings. You couldn't make it a wedding ring?"

He began to laugh. "You're not only impossible, you're intolerable."

"Yes, I know. Isn't it awful?"

He said it at last. "I love you."

Jessie was anxious about the pot of soup. If the doctor delayed a moment longer, it was going to be boiled to nothing. She was already partaking of her own midday meal: leftover potatoes, a leg of cold chicken, and a tin of baked beans. Her favorite. For afters she was going to eat up the tinned plums and custard and then make a strong and restoring cup of tea.

She was about to pick up the chicken leg in her fingers (it didn't count, provided you were on your own) when she heard voices, and footsteps running up the path from the surgery. Before she had time to dispose of the chicken leg the back door was thrown open, and Dr. Kyle stood before her, holding by the hand the woman in the navy blue coat who had come asking for him.

The woman was smiling, her hair blown by the wind all over her face. And Dr. Kyle's face was a picture. Jessie was at a loss. By rights he should be exhausted, weighed down by troubles and hard work, treading heavily up from the surgery for his bowl of soup, the sustaining broth that she, Jessie, had concocted for him.

Instead, here he was, all smiles and bouncing good spirits and looking as though he were good for another forty-eight hours without a wink of sleep.

"Jessie!"

She dropped the chicken bone, but he didn't seem to have noticed, anyway.

602

"Jessie, I'm going down to the railway station, I'll be back in ten minutes."

"Righty ho, Dr. Kyle."

It was still raining but, although he wore no raincoat, it didn't seem to bother him. Out he went again with the woman still in tow, leaving the back door standing open and a wind like a knife pouring into Jessie's kitchen.

"How about your soup?" she called after him, but it was too late. He had gone. She got up to shut the door. Then she went through to the front of the house, and, cautiously, not wishing to be observed, opened the front door. She saw them going away from her down the path. They had their arms around each other and they were both laughing, oblivious of the wind and the rain. She watched them go through the gate and start down the hill towards the town. Their heads disappeared below the top of the wall, first the woman's and then Dr. Kyle's.

They were gone.

She closed the door. She thought, Well! But she knew that sooner or later, she would find someone to tell.

603